THE FLIGHT OF THE MAYDAY SQUADRON

AN AMERICAN MYTHOLOGY

Steve A Madison

Historical facts, declassified government documents, significant intellectual concepts, and insights into esoteric areas of interest used to build the narrative, were obtained from sources included in the attached bibliography and internet search index.

"If You Are Able", the poem written by Major Michael David O'Donnell, was sourced from www.pownetwork.org (http://www.pownetwork.org/bios/o/o021.htm) and is included under the fair use statutes of the United States Copyright Office. The author regrets his inability to contact Major O'Donnell's family for their permission to include this inspirational source document and wishes them the very best.

Special thanks to Sgt. Aaron Gritzmaker, Medic, A-100 Mobile Guerrilla Force (1966), for background information used to construct the bush sequences in "De Oppresso Liber".

Learn more about Steve A. Madison: www.steveamadison.com
Learn more about the Mayday Squadron: www.maydaysquadron.com

ISBN: 1493528394
ISBN 13: 9781493528394
Library of Congress Control Number: 2014917737
CreateSpace Independent Publishing Platform
North Charleston, South Carolina

This project came into being because of the nurture, unflinching counsel, and boundless support of Janet Cawthon Madison, my wife, my heart's desire, and redhead beyond compare.

If the stars were mine, I'd give them all to you.

This story is dedicated to the American citizen-soldiers who
did their duty, confounded the best efforts of the Suits in
Washington, and won the war in South Vietnam.
Your gallantry, fraternity, fealty to the Constitution,
and your valiant defense of the Republic,
must remain forever your only reward.

We the People were hoodwinked.

If you are able, save for them a place inside of you
and save one backward glance
when you are leaving for the places
they can no longer go.

Be not ashamed to say you loved them
though you may or may not have always.
Take what they have taught you with their dying
and keep it with your own.

And in that time when men decide
and feel safe to call war insane,
take one moment to embrace
those gentle heroes you left behind.

Major Michael Davis O'Donnell
1 January 1970
Dak To, Vietnam

CONTENTS

THE WITNESS OF HISTORY

"Even today, there is little value in insuring the survival of our nation if our traditions do not survive with it. And there is very grave danger that an announced need for increased security will be seized upon by those anxious to expand its meaning to the very limits of official censorship and concealment...

"If the press is awaiting a declaration of war before it imposes the self-discipline of combat conditions, then I can only say that no war ever posed a greater threat to our security. If you are awaiting a finding of 'clear and present danger,' then I can only say that the danger has never been more clear and its presence has never been more imminent."

President John F. Kennedy
"The President and the Press," April 27, 1961

"This conjunction of an immense military establishment and a large arms industry is new in the American experience. The total influence—economic, political, even spiritual—is felt in every city, every Statehouse, every office of the Federal government.

In the councils of government, we must guard against the acquisition of unwarranted influence, whether sought or unsought, by the military-industrial complex. The potential for the disastrous rise of misplaced power exists and will persist."

President Dwight D. Eisenhower
"Farewell Address," January 17, 1961

"Since I entered politics, I have chiefly had men's views confided to me privately. Some of the biggest men in the United States, in the field of commerce and manufacture, are afraid of somebody, are afraid of something. They know that there is a power somewhere so organized, so subtle, so watchful, so interlocked, so complete, so pervasive, that they had better not speak above their breath when they speak in condemnation of it."

President Woodrow Wilson
"The New Freedom," 1913

"Finally, my brethren, be strong in the Lord, and in the power of His might. Put on the whole armor of God that ye may be able to stand against the wiles of the devil. For we wrestle not against flesh and blood, but against principalities, against powers, against the rulers of the darkness of this world, against spiritual wickedness in high places."

Saint Paul, the Apostle
Letter to the Christians at Ephesus, AD 62

PROLOGUE

They had accomplished much since the fall and their confidence had risen, but He cautioned them to move slowly, deliberately, knowing that the foundation on which everything rested was their absolute invisibility.

He exposed himself rarely and only to the carefully selected patriarchs of the oldest extended families, who referred to themselves as "the Apex," those ancients who comprised the beating heart, fertile mind, and ancient seed of "the Order." It was only this close circle who fully realized the root and reason of the psycho-spiritual-technical power they referred to as "Medusa." For over a thousand years, the fraternal blood-trust had kept secret the full knowledge of the vicious, unsleeping, mindless, animalistic force protecting them from exposure, yet even they avoided discussing it. That they had assisted in its making was of little consequence, for Medusa was His conjure. The majick wind that delivered ill fortune to their enemies, the foul breath of death itself, recognized His authority only. And above all things, above even Medusa, He was most feared.

Capitalized with Roman plunder and endowed with the supranatural powers employed by the mighty men of old, the men of renown who posed as the immortal god-kings of Sumer, His first-and-second-generation apprentices fabricated an early version of Medusa in an attempt to conceal their instigation and financing of the French and American revolutions. But Medusa was immature then, the technology unreliable. Mankind was more literate, more existentially aware, keenly alert to danger, and their demonic conspiracy was exposed at a crucial moment. His plans were skewed, and precious capital and time was lost. In France, many of the pioneering members of the Order were imprisoned, and some were lost to Him eternally, murdered by those they sought to release from the bondage of Christianity and their crazed notions of Liberty, Equality, and Fraternity. And in Amerike, the murderous Christian horde wallowed in their bloody freedoms and had seen to it that His loss was catastrophic, the setback incalculable.

But He persevered and advised the survivors to learn from their losses, to waste nothing. By the second and third generations, Medusa functioned well enough to compromise mass Christian thought and to be used effectively during the Enlightenment (the first Age of Ages, named thus for His radiance). Medusa concealed their funding and control of the African slave trade into Europe and the Americas, the Opium Wars in China, and concluded that generation's Great Trade Cycle with the most profitable venture of their time—instigating and financing the American Civil War for the Christian purpose of "freeing the slaves." The financial symmetry of using profits from institutionalized slavery to collateralize the war for its abolition pleased them heartily and served as a powerful affirmation of their supranaturally revealed business secret: the "Profitable Man."

After the failures, He had schooled the Apex in His root philosophy, "The only immortality in this world is great wealth." He had told them with an amber glow in his large, penetrating eyes, "Wars come and go, as do kingdoms, sovereign states, and empires. Art is only for a season, and it too is lost or destroyed. Literature, music, and poetry become stale, lose their meaning, and are forgotten. Architecture crumbles, as do the mountains that yield the stone for its foundation. Even the oceans are displaced as the continents themselves rise and fall."

"And what of the eternal Christ?" he asked, sensing their fear and trepidation. "Christ exists like a fever in the brain of the weakminded; when the Christians are dead so also will be Christ. Both heaven and hell are real and exist in the here and now. I implore you to choose your personal path to heaven. You are your own master. Your only enemy is time. Do forever as you will."

He smiled as he used His authority to smother their vestigial faith, erasing the fear of God from their consciousness, and so He had accomplished a great and necessary work; they would receive His pronouncements without judgement. He paused while looking past the questions in their minds and deeply into their souls, caressing, exciting, and seducing the spirits of the twelve who would extend His dominion throughout the world. He beguiled them with His bright countenance, wisdom, and supranatural allure.

"Be not fools. Learn this solitary truth: in all of evolution the only thing that endures is great wealth, and those who commit their lives to its formation will claim their share of immortality." He laughed heartily as he levitated in the electric air before them. His whole being became a luminous tone as he began to cant His eternal Song of Songs, His piercing, radiating, transcendent gnosis: "The only source of wealth on the planet is the land and its people. Over infinite cycles, evolution has rendered man the higher animal and he alone possesses the intellectual dexterity to husband the lesser species and to bring the land into flower. But he is flawed; cunning, but also fearful and wild, deadly dangerous and equipped with a superstitious and delusional mind incapable of understanding anything beyond the finite range of his own physical experience. Left alone he will only squander the resources of the planet and ultimately extinguish his entire species through war, disease, or famine. The future of the planet and of man himself rests entirely on your achieving the higher goal of immortality through the formation of transcendent wealth. This is your gift to his species, your burden, your true and noble cause. It may only be attained by the domestication and profitable use of all mankind."

Seeing that their trance was complete, He descended, took His golden cup from the table, and drank deeply. The sharp metallic flavor knifed through him as he inhaled the scent of the twelve, listening intently to their deepest thoughts, rolling their musk over his tongue as he savored their bodies and the dark work he was about to charge them with. He smiled and walked toward them slowly.

"Every man has value. Never forget this. Kill him if you will; slaughter him by the millions if there is profit in it. You have that power and more. But remember well the credo of your ancient seed: never waste even one. It will be your charge, little ones, to build a system into which every man will long to add his full worth, a system that refines the race, amplifies the value of the individual, and creates a lever powerful enough to move the whole world to your profitable use, to add the value of every single human to the sum of all the wealth of the planet. The Profitable Man must be trained to willingly contribute his measure through every stage of his life. It is only the prudent use of this precious resource that will release the richness of the land and bring your labor to fruition.

"You must love your fellow man enough to consume him. Cultivate a taste for him. Dissect him. Examine him closely, sort through his humanity, study his domestication of lesser animals, of lesser men, and the principles he has refined to draw his livelihood from the land. Heed well these natural laws and use them to devise inspired, elegant, invisible methods of placing mankind in the service of Immortal Wealth. This is your charge, but beware. There is great danger for you should your circle be penetrated and your true intent be discerned. Never allow this.

"The harness you devise must be assembled by man for his brothers so that he will have a desire for it himself, so that he willingly places himself and his fellows into it, and so that he loves it so much that he will slaughter anyone who would attempt to release him from it. This is your commission and your quest. It is a dangerous, sacrificial work, but when you have accomplished it the Apex and all of mankind may live eternally. You, my cherished ones, my beloved, you shall have created a glorious paradise from a dark and chaotic void, surpassing even the grandeur of the fabled Eden. You shall be the masters of the perfected Earth and I shall be its god!"

He looked deeply into each man's eyes, into their souls, and he saw the fires of desire blazing hot and bright, burning away their empathy, atomizing their vestigial humanity. "They have their grand purpose now. They have their hallowed cause. They believe they will live forever!" He smiled to himself. "And surely every one of them will!"

He turned away, drained his cup, looked back at them hard, and in a sweeping arc threw the golden chalice past their heads to smash into the marble wall behind them. When they looked back, they were themselves once more. Feeling refreshed and inspired, they exchanged pleasantries and began working through the day's agenda.

Since that time and after His Revelation, the Order had been profoundly successful, guided as if by supranatural insight. Medusa had evolved to become not merely a defensive cloak but a diaphanous horror-hybrid of technology, economics, psychology, politics, and religion. It excelled at enslaving the lives and conscious minds of God-fearing, law-abiding men who would surely have struck them down and freed the world of their infestation had they only been capable of understanding the truth of the play and their tragic role in it.

But it is written that God shall not be mocked, that there is an eternal price to be paid for every form of treachery, and that whether in this life or the next, all accounts shall be reconciled.

There's something happening here,
What it is ain't exactly clear.

Stephen Stills, 1966

1

FLIGHT RISK

The North Vietnamese Communists proved themselves able, even admirable business partners. They were resourceful, cunning, and quite capable of performing even the most distasteful of their duties with good humor and aplomb. Over time, their underwriters were delighted to discover their native aptitude for trickery and deception. Especially useful in winning allies within the American diplomatic corps, they absolutely excelled at nurturing a deeply rooted contempt for their fellow countrymen, harbored by members of the New York press, the self-professed arbiters of all reality for the millions of redneck clodhoppers who infested their country between the coasts. They also paid their bills.

Ho and his politburo had earned the respect and admiration of their creditors years before during the much publicized "peace process." The Paris delegation had brilliantly constructed a powerful rhetoric that artfully used words like trust, transparency, and honor as a rationale against the seemingly intractable interests of the battered and divided free world. The negotiator helped the secretary, the president, and the *Times* convince the Thieu regime and a war-weary American electorate to bind themselves to a set of perfectly unenforceable Peace Accords. A year later in Hanoi, the Communists welcomed the "Four Party Joint Military Team" to their inner sanctum. They gathered to plan the transition of power, to devise sensible protections for the people of the South, and to set the logistics for the rapid repatriation of the American prisoners of war. Everything went according to plan; their blood deception was complete.

"Are the Americans really that stupid?" wondered the negotiator as he and the secretary shared a champagne toast and the media glare during the rollout of the Peace Accords. "Surely they realize what the ultimate result will be," he thought as he sipped the Americans' sparkling wine, making eye contact with the secretary, concealing his contempt, while savoring the knowledge that Ho Chi Minh's final victory was at hand.

"VIETNAM ACCORD IS REACHED; CEASE-FIRE BEGINS SATURDAY; POW'S TO BE FREE IN 60 DAYS" headlined the evening edition of the *Times*, which helpfully recorded the president's televised address to the nation. *"Within sixty days, all Americans who have been held captive shall be released...,"* he had said, beaming. *"The people of the south have been guaranteed the right to determine their own future without outside interference."* Guaranteed, he had said. *"The important thing was not to talk about peace but to get peace and the right kind of peace. This we have done."* Then the commander in chief concluded, *"For those who died and those who live, let us consecrate this moment by resolving to make the peace we have achieved a peace that will last. Thank you and good evening."*

Just over two years later the president had been chased out of office, a new man had been advanced, and the American Congress, no longer concerned with either the spread of Communism in Indochina or the fate of the people of South Vietnam, defunded their defense. After that, the Communists publically burned their mortgage.

Before daybreak on April 29, 1975, the world awoke to the shelling of Tan Son Nhat Airport. The runways were closed and thousands were trapped in the capital city of Saigon. With Americans in imminent jeopardy, the unelected commander in chief authorized Operation Frequent Wind, the largest helicopter evacuation in history, and by 1100 hours local, Armed Forces Vietnam radio began broadcasting Irving Berlin's "White Christmas," the signal for all Americans to move to their preassigned emergency evacuation points.

Nearly twenty-four hours into Frequent Wind, the exhausted flight leader, Captain Dan Blessing, had finally secured the ambassador and his personal staff and maneuvered the CH-46 *Sea Knight* away from the roof of the American embassy for the very last time.

Below he could see a panorama of panic caused by North Vietnamese Army tanks rolling into the downtown area only blocks from the embassy. Keying his helmet mic, Blessing reported, "Lady Ace Zero Niner, Fleet Com: Tiger, Tiger, Tiger! I say again, Tiger, Tiger, Tiger!" Pause for return traffic. "Lima Alpha Zero Niner," answered Fleet Command. "Copy, you have the Tiger, repeat, you have the Tiger. Proceed your zero two niner to Blue Ridge; vessel control will direct your priority approach. And, Captain, watch the ground fire. It's heatin' up out there."

"So this is really it," thought Blessing as he rotated the bird skyward. "All the people down there, there're not going anywhere. We're leaving them," he said to himself, wincing involuntarily at the thought of what their fate might be. Rolling power on to gain altitude, he could see dozens of NVA troop carriers and combat infantry squads following the diesel clatter of their Russian-made T-55 tanks.

"The bastards in Washington sent us to fight this war, to kill for them, to die for them, and now they're saying none of it means a damned thing," he thought as he cleared a menacing squad of NVA. "Now they're pissing it away—all the death, all the suffering; all the millions—like it was nothing." He banked sharply away from more gunfire. "And all these people," he thought as he scanned the panicked crowd pressing onto the embassy grounds for the false safety of what was once a tiny piece of America. "What in God's name will happen to them? We're leaving them without a prayer. God help them. God help us!" And with that, the Marine captain, a veteran of the Pacific war against the Japanese, the Korean war against the Chinese, and three combat tours of Vietnam, felt hot tears on his cheeks, set his jaw, cinched himself tighter into the cockpit, and increased his velocity toward the USS *Blue Ridge* and the safety of the Seventh Fleet.

• • •

Half a world away, in the pristine executive suite of Beacon Street Bank and Trust, a solitary figure watched the New York network coverage of the panicked departure of *Lady Ace*, scanning a balance sheet with a slight smile, while casually observing the dramatic satellite programming on separate television screens, each precisely set into very expensive burled walnut paneling. He believed this to be the final American flight out of Southeast Asia and the end of all US operations in the theater. At last, the war was over. It was time to savor his victory and tally his profits. But unbeknownst to him, the Communists' final victory and America's historic final flight out would occur without media coverage twenty-one days later from the rogue counterintelligence outpost code named "Omega."

A miniscule footnote buried deep in his accountant's thick blue-backed ledgers, Omega was located on a high granite mountain 180 kilometers north northwest of Khe Sanh, just inside the neighboring country of Laos. Secretly built by fiercely loyal Montagnard tribesmen for a curious mixture of former American service members, expatriate intelligence operators, Hmong mercenaries, and random civilians on the run from the North Vietnamese, it was artfully concealed within the ruins of a long-forgotten pagan temple and nearly inaccessible atop a five-thousand-foot-high granite peak. From their obscure perch, Omega had a sequestered overview of nearly forty miles of the Ho Chi Minh Trail, an unobstructed line of sight monitoring vista that extended into the very heart of Communist Hanoi and the security of having its very existence concealed from the American chain of command—even from the president of the Unites States himself.

• • •

Boston was still in the grip of a hard winter as the sole occupant of the BSB&T executive suite impassively watched color television coverage of the fall of Saigon. A red telephone rang softly; with only a handset and no dialing apparatus, it was clearly a direct line to someone of significance. "Yes" he answered. Listening for a moment, the smile left and immediate direction was issued in a hushed tone. "What? That's imposs...are you sure? How long? If that's true, then I agree with your assessment. Take care of it, whatever the cost! And this time make sure, damn it! We won't close the books until you've cleaned this up, so the funds will remain fluid. But be quick about it and remember—if this gets out, if it gets into the papers, if he hears of this—you and your family won't live to see the morning! You were lucky once, you won't be again. Do you understand?" He angrily slammed the handset into its cradle, cutting the conversation short.

Looking beyond his office window to the Boston Common, he noticed the snow still clinging to the shadow side of every tree and bush in the park. "Damned hard winter," he muttered to himself. "The hardest in a generation. But spring's on the way, isn't it?" His eyes refocused on his contorted reflection in the office window. Studying his twisted image, he adjusted his crisp French cuffs, moving them slightly out of his jacket sleeves to expose his canary yellow diamond cufflinks. With a manicured thumb and forefinger, he straightened his Owl Club tie, deftly plucked a speck of lint from the lapel of his Savile Row bankers pinstripe and then watched himself intently as he forced the smile to return to his freshly shaven face. "Nothing more than a rounding error," he said to himself, rebuilding his belief that the ultimate resolution of the situation would be in his favor. It always was. He took a deep breath and turned back to see that NBC had returned to its normal programming, a prerecorded episode of "Wheel of Fortune."

• • •

Three weeks later, the chain of command had finally caught up to Omega. Through long-established and trusted lines of communication, orders were received for the operators to close out their mission and return home. The decommissioning was under way even as they suspected they could still be betrayed by "the Suits" in Washington.

Their suspicions were confirmed early that final morning as they came under attack by a significant force of North Vietnamese regulars. To escape the assault, a veteran Southeast Asia Air flight crew from Udorn Air Base in Thailand had heroically control-crash-landed their prototype C-130 Combat Talon on the three-hundred-foot-long ceremonial Moon Court, constructed a thousand years before for pagan lunar rituals. Under heavy fire, the valiant crew rotated the bird, loaded it, and used their outboard JATOL rockets to launch the fully laden aircraft over the windward edge of the five-thousand-foot cliff and into a desperate flight to safety from the final American toehold in Indochina.

• • •

Nearly twenty hours into the flight something was terribly wrong. "This isn't right," thought Captain Charles Magazzine, checking his position over the Northwestern Pacific. "I've never missed a refueling rendezvous in my life, let alone two, and now they're vectoring us even farther away from Pearl to meet a tanker out of the Aleutian Islands? All I know is that their flying gas station had better be on time or we're gonna get our Saturday night baths early this week!" Two hours later, it was clear that they'd missed their final chance to refuel, and Magazzine had diverted north to his fail-safe landfall at Amchitka, the southwestern most island in the barren Aleutian Arc.

"The rat bastards set us up!" said Magazzine aloud. Repressing a cold panic deep in his gut, he mentally calculated that his fuel supply would be exhausted 450 nautical miles short of landfall and realized that he would have to ditch in the icy waters of the Bering Sea. He broke radio silence to send a coded distress signal through dark snowy skies, ordered the crew to ready the craft for a water landing, and wondered whether he should inform his passengers that they had less than an hour to live.

"Bet I can guess which one of 'em doesn't want us coming home!" thought Magazzine as he peered into the carbon-black sky, desperately searching for something, anything that would alter his immediate lethal circumstance. A slight fluttering movement at the edge of his peripheral vision attracted his attention to a faint orange glow on the horizon, a shimmering, winking, tiny spec that slowly disappeared as he nosed the craft up and reappeared as he nosed it down. Magazzine thought that it was nothing artificial, possibly some form of naturally occurring sea florescence, but he had the navigator recheck the charts, hoping he was wrong, that it was an outlying marine buoy and that maybe he was closer to Amchitka than he believed.

Keeping his eye on the illusive speck of orange to help him orient to the ocean's surface, Magazzine alerted the crew and passengers that they were about to ditch. While banking the craft hard to his left to circle the glow, and slowing the C-130 to near stall speed, he clearly saw the orange speck getting larger and brighter only a few thousand meters ahead. Out of insane desperation and against every conventional emergency procedure, Magazzine decided to ditch in the choppy sea with the landing gear down. If his instincts were correct, the drag of the gear would help him put the nose of the lumbering craft directly into the rapidly enlarging, intensely glowing ragged oval of orange. Whatever it was, maybe, Lord, Magazine thought, somehow someone will survive and if not, at least it would be quick.

"Father, according to your will, I pray for a miracle in this desperate time. Please have mercy on my passengers and crew, bring us through this landing, and find a way to spare our lives. In Jesus's name, I pray, Amen," said the captain over the flight intercom and, as if on cue, engines one and four lost power, the radioman sent his final coded Mayday, and Magazzine coldly switched on the landing lights to view their watery grave but was astonished to see not water but ice!

A shiny smooth, long, beautiful solid runway of Arctic Drift ice leading them directly into the open end of a large pulsing volcanic tube; aglow with the white-hot orange brilliance of an explosive, sputtering, steaming oceanic lava flow. "God help us!" cried Magazzine as he reflexively jerked the control column, instantly realizing that they would not drown or freeze to death as he had feared, but that they would be incinerated; turned to ash in the middle of the freezing Bering Sea.

2

OPERATION URIAH

An amber light silently illuminated the face of a black telephone in a darkened office half a world away. In the room sat a Big and a Little man, intently watching green characters skip across a glowing CRT.

"MICOM says they're down. About three hundred klicks southwest of Amchitka," announced Big, replacing the handset and turning to his partner.

"Nasty storm's right on top of 'em too. Coast Guard says the water temp is around forty and the pressure's dropping fast. Looks like they're in for a real blow out there," replied Little, red ash brightening on the tip of his Lucky while Big lifted his mug for another sip.

Next to the black phone was an identical red unit, which rang softly. Big lifted the handset. "Yes, sir," he said, listening intently, and then he offered a precise response. "MICOM confirms Archangel is down too far south of Amchitka to be reached by Search and Rescue. Maybe even in Soviet territorial waters." Pause. "No, sir, it's better than we anticipated. There's an Arctic storm closing in on their position, water temperature is near freezing, seas are high, and there's no way the Coast Guard can reach them for at least forty-eight hours." There was a long pause. Did Big detect a twinge of guilt coming through the line?

"Yes, sir. They died heroic deaths in the line of duty; their families will be proud of their sacrifice." There was another brief pause.

"No, sir, the transponder and flight recorder were disabled before they departed Udorn—mission protocol.

"Don't worry about a thing, sir. As they say down in Texas, this ain't our first rodeo," said Big, savoring the humor but not knowing if his boss caught the joke. "After the weather clears, Search and Rescue will be dispatched, but there'll be nothing to find. The storm will have taken care of that. The official report will read that Archangel was lost at sea with no survivors due to pilot error. Yes, sir," said Big. "Please contact us if you have other questions.

"He's turned into a real cold SOB," said Big as he replaced the receiver.

"Better them than us," said Little, as he sucked the smoke deep into his lungs.

"You really think Rix is dead?" asked Big.

"Everybody dies," said Little, imbuing his words of wisdom with cigarette smoke. "And even if he wasn't on the plane, then Victor Charles is having one hell of a party with him about now. They over-ran Omega six hours ago."

Suddenly their attention was drawn to a fluttering movement at the edge of their peripheral vision. "What the hell was that?" said Big with a start as Little jumped, glancing left. Both shared the chill of gooseflesh that left as quickly as it came.

"Rix was a hell of an operator," said Big to break the tension. "Saved my life once in a whore house in Saigon." He chuckled.

"Rix in a cat house? I though he was a Bible thumper," said Little.

"No, it wasn't that way. The chef there was VC, and Rix recognized him from another op. I was there for a little personal R and R and would've died with my pants down if it hadn't been for him. The only thing Rix wanted out of the place was supper, and I think he even bought himself a dog," said Big, shaking his head with a smile and a snort.

Working at the shredder, Little said, "OK. So he saved your life once and he's an animal lover. All I'm sayin' is that any guy who'd rat out the company deserves what he gets. Now let's clean this shit up and shut her down. We've been in here so long we're both gettin' a little crazy." So Little and Big worked silently, completing the official report of "Operation Archangel" while destroying their "Eyes Only" hard copy of "Counter Operation Uriah," powered down the equipment, and locked up.

On their way out, they were startled once more by the same fluttering sound. "You hear that again? Must be a bug, or bat, or something," said Little, glancing left and right and touching his sidearm for comfort while scanning the UHF communications array, completely unable to see the two luminous figures standing directly in front of him.

"This place gives me the creeps; always has," said Big. "The Denny's on Lee Highway; you're buyin'!" said Little, happy to be done with their unsavory business. They climbed into their government-issued Ford and drove slowly into the sunrise of a crisp Maryland morning.

• • •

Less than thirty miles to the east, a pair of red-tailed hawks were finishing their nest atop a Potomac Electric Power Company transformer station, mounted on a power pole, just level with the top story of the United States Department of Agriculture International Agricultural Services Annex. In the fourth floor turret, a man was slumped in a chrome-and-leather chair. His sleek enameled metal desk was covered with many days' worth of empty coffee cups, food wrappers, and an overflowing ashtray; a yellow-blue haze of stale cigarette smoke hung in the air. The man, not old but aged, as if a fatal disease had possessed his vital organs, took a long drag on his cigarette and blew a ragged breath at the new day, eyes deep set and fatigued.

"How the hell did it come to this? That I would betray him; that I would be the cause of his murder and how many others? Twenty, did they say? It was never supposed to be this way," he said to himself in a quivering voice, stifling a sob.

He would have liked to have cried, to release the grief, the anger, the rage, but like most things in his life, his tears wouldn't flow, not like a real man, a man with a soul; he just couldn't feel anything anymore.

The red phone rang quietly. "Yes, sir," he answered, sitting upright.

"Yes, sir, it's done, all of them." Pause. "No, sir, I didn't witness it myself." (How could I, you moron?) "It was arranged by the company." Another pause.

"The evidence will be in the transcripts, the radio traffic, and the deposition of the managers. Yes, sir, of course it will be classified. A certified copy will be delivered to your office tomorrow morning." Another long pause.

"As you said, sir, it was necessary, a matter of national security."

After another brief moment, he replaced the receiver, stretched in the chair, then stood weakly and began to gather his belongings.

Looking through the smoky haze beyond the aging Palladian window, he absently checked the progress of the hawks.

"Hope you guys got a building permit from PEPCO," he said. "You know, nothing's free in Washington, DC. You gonna nest here, you gotta pay the price just like all the rest of us," he said, slipping into his jacket and overcoat.

"If I were you, I'd fly away right now, get out to the country before they snap the trap on you, and put you in a cage in the National Zoo or somethin' worse." Finding his briefcase and department ID, he considered them again.

"It won't be what you think, but yeah, there's a lota worse things they can do. They got their ways and means. Hell hawks, there are guys like me all over this town! Thousands of us! So really, I'm not kiddin', don't wait around, get outta here while you still can." He looked at them for the last time and began his weary journey home.

Crossing the street to his car, he noticed a vagrant digging in an overflowing dumpster and steered clear, not seeing his sharp eyes and tan earphone. He focused instead on the shiny blue sports car sitting by itself in the commuter lot. Only months before, he would have run his hand over the chromed 2002, caressed the enameled blue, black, and white logo and savored belting himself into its tailored leather interior.

An extravagant gift from his wife, it was meant to celebrate his advancement. For a time, it served as a physical reinforcement of his career choice, his decision to accept responsibility for the pregnancy and marry. But over the last months, it had become a mocking reminder of his poor judgment; a millstone around his neck, holding him down in the deep end of the DC drowning pool.

"Tango Six, sitrep," said a metallic whisper in the vagrant's ear.

"Target just left the building. He's in the car now, warming it up, defrosting the windshield," he whispered into his sleeve.

"Tango Six. Looks like the shrinks were wrong; he didn't have the balls. We'll have to assist. You have red authorization. Repeat, Tango Six, your authorization is red," whispered the earpiece.

"Affirmative, my authorization is red. Tango Six out."

He noticed the vagrant approaching in his rearview mirror as the engine idled.

"You're outta luck, pal," he said to himself. "Spent all my cash yesterday for lunch."

He slipped the car into gear and began pulling away from the panhandler, starting a wide turn in the empty lot. He planned to zip past the man on his way to the street.

The assassin moved to the exit and posted himself so that he would have a close view of the driver. He raised his concealed pistol to take the passing kill shot when a screeching "Kree-eee-ar!" It came from above as a slashing brown, yellow, and red blur crashed into his head and gun hand simultaneously.

Both nesting raptors had savagely driven the bloodied and terrified assassin into the pavement, knocking the weapon from his hand and leaving him unconscious. "Tango Six, sitrep, Tango Six, status…"

Averting his eyes from the poverty of the vagrant, the man said, "Sorry, pal, maybe tomorrow," as he made his getaway, accelerating into the light early morning traffic, ignorant of his salvation and of his guardians circling high above.

3

PLATA O PLOMO

Ronald Coleman Albert Vazquez was a pragmatic man with a long name who specialized in probing self-analysis and prided himself in neither overestimating his capabilities nor underestimating his relative worth in any situation.

Vazquez entered the world by accident – a byproduct of the brief but torrid affair between Roberta Maria Vazquez, a gentlemen's seamstress, (who named her only child after an actor and a prince with the intention of perpetually reminding her lover of the high price of poorly timed fornication), and Evan Reed Jansen, Jr., the scion of the first cousin of the second-generation owner of the RCA Victor Company. Jansen prided himself on his Christian integrity and therefore assured his hysterical mistress that he would fulfill his moral obligation to his bastard. And so it was the enduring good fortune of RCA "Radio" Vazquez to have received his secondary education from Pennsylvania State University due primarily to his father's Catholic guilt, healthy balance sheet, and family connections to Penn State's Board of Regents.

When asked by college friends why his wealthy father had decided to send him to Penn instead of his own nurturing mother, the University of Pennsylvania, Radio always made a joke of it, using his cultivated New England dialect. "No Mexicahos en el hombah Ivah League"; "No Mexicans in the Ivah League, man!" he would always say with a glimmering smile and a slap on the back while taking another sip or another toke to emphasize his cavalier "couldn't give a shit" attitude and self-deprecating punch line.

But deep inside, in a place known only to him, it wasn't a joke at all. His profound shame was that his father would never marry his mother, would never claim him as his son, that he was illegitimate, and that his very name would forever brand him as the spawn of a one-night stand his mother had with some rich guy he never really knew. This inner torment consumed him like fire. Over his young life, it had seared a hole in his heart as big as the entire state of Pennsylvania, a hole so large that he would never be able to fill it with anything he could possibly obtain in either this life or the next. "No Mexicahns in the Ivah League" really meant that he had no place at all.

Upon graduation and without prospects, Vazquez's college mentor had steered him to a job in government service with the burgeoning United States Department of Agriculture in Washington, DC, a ground-floor opportunity if ever there was one. And while he had pragmatically accepted the fact that a career in the government sector would mean that he would not be the master of his own fate, Vazquez, knowing his limits better than anyone, certainly considered himself good enough for government work. He quickly rose to the top in a field, within which there was high demand and no competition. It was though, after two years as the youngest deputy director in the federal bureaucracy and at the height of the Cold War, that Vazquez achieved his masterstroke, his penultimate bureaucratic triumph: departmental liaison with the Unites States Central Intelligence Agency.

His salient insight came about as most things of this sort do, by innovative reading of the enabling legislation that created the well-intended Food for Peace program, idly floating his observation at a few Georgetown cocktail parties, planting the idea with a friend who had a friend at Justice who afforded him a wink and a nod. The final trick was a nearly undetectable tweak to the appropriations budget by a colleague embedded in the middle management strata of the agency, and he was in.

Vazquez quivered with delight as he mused that his liaising would allow him to travel the world on a whim at the expense of the US taxpayer. He would "witness and report on the national security implications of foreign crop yield with the purpose of analyzing the potential of using surplus US agricultural output as a weapon in America's struggle against the spread of global Communism." (Vazquez had thoughtfully and proudly written his own job description.) He would draw double federal salaries, enjoy double federal benefits, and be able to retire at sixty with double federal pensions. And the kicker was that because of the Pendleton Act of 1883, regardless of anything that he might do, short of felonious or treasonous conduct, he could never be fired! Master of his own fate indeed; what brilliance. "What a coup, Vazquez!" he thought as he quietly congratulated himself by reclining in the deep soft leather of his government-issued executive chair and enjoyed a deep celebratory toke from the emergency roach he kept stashed in his "Top Secret" secure file cabinet.

But by the fall of 1964, dark clouds had begun to obscure the sunny skies in the land of Radio Vazquez. Mao was starving millions of Chinese to death with his Great Leap Forward. America was headed to war with Communist insurgents in South Vietnam. The quiet, guilt-ridden, introspective students of Marx and Lenin, whom he had befriended in his collegial youth and who had gone on to careers as tenured faculty at most of the respected universities on both coasts, were busy seeding insurrection in their classrooms. They had themselves become mature fellow travelers, on the way to a mythic Communist Utopia. They were openly organizing their students for action against the institutions of the "imperial" American state—openly sending their students into the streets to stop the "Evil American War Machine," which was fully engaged, they were told, in "persecuting their Communist brethren in South Vietnam." Disturbing—newsworthy perhaps—but of little real consequence.

Of far greater concern to Vazquez were changes in the emerging leadership ranks across the federal bureaucracy that was now directed by others who, like himself, had cracked the code of enabling legislation and Washington cocktail chat, but whose idea of what constituted a coup d'état was frightfully different than his own.

Yet it was in this odd moment of patriotic concern, blended with personal triumph over the bureaucracy that his visceral sense of self-preservation spiked on the flawless September day when he was taught the meaning of a Mexican colloquialism he had ever heard before: "Plato o Palmo"; "silver or lead."

• • •

Agents Clarkson Green and Sterrette Brown introduced themselves, presented their credentials, and asked that Vazquez call the coded contact number that he had received during his agency orientation to validate their identities.

"Operator 367," said a friendly female voice. "How may I assist?"

"Uh, hi. This is Al Vazquez over at USDA. I have two gentlemen here with me, Mr. Green and Mr. Brown, who say they are CIA agents, and they asked me to call you to verify their identities," said Al unsteadily into the receiver, not knowing what to expect.

"Certainly, Mr. Vazquez. May I have your counter code, please? It's in the agency packet you signed for three weeks ago. Sir, we were beginning to be concerned for you. You were supposed to check in within twenty-four hours of your orientation," said 367.

"Ah, yeah, sorry about that—we got busy over here." He quickly scanned his desktop, pushing some papers around, and finally lifting an old copy of the *Times*, he retrieved the packet, broke the seal, opened it with the help of Mr. Green, found his initiation card, and haltingly read the thirteen numbers and letters into the receiver.

"Is that it?" he asked under the suspicious glares of Green and Brown.

"Yes, sir, that is correct. Please read the serial numbers for your visitors to me now. You will find them on the bottom of their agency identification cards," said a patient 367, and Al was happy to comply.

"OK, Mr. Vazquez, this is the final step. Please ask your visitors for their passwords. Brown and Green receive a new one every Monday morning at zero five hundred. For this week, Brown's VID is "Caribou" and Green's is "Oxblood." If they answer correctly, then you will have agency confirmation of their identities. Please do this while I hold for your response," directed 367.

Al received the correct response from each man and informed Operator 367.

"Ahh, one question, please, operator, what would have happened if they didn't know the password, or if they forgot or something?"

"Mr. Vazquez, these procedures were covered in your orientation, and I am not authorized to speak to you concerning those matters. Please direct your questions of this nature to liaison agents Green and Brown. They will handle your interface with the agency until such time as you are released or they are replaced. Good day, sir," said 367 crisply before she disconnected.

"So what can I do for you gentlemen?" asked a rather shaken and embarrassed Vazquez, replacing the receiver as he pretended to be in control of the situation and his own turf.

"Mr. Vazquez, Agent Brown, and I are here to check your welfare, welcome you to the Liaison Program, and establish the parameters of our working relationship," said Agent Green. "This will take some time, and you are to consider this briefing classified. Any mention of our discussion outside this room shall be considered a breach of national security and subject you to the possibility of fines, imprisonment, or death, depending on the circumstances and how the tribunal views the facts of the breach. All of this was covered in your orientation, and we have your countersigned acceptance letter on file. Sir, do you understand the serious nature of the information you are about to receive?"

Al vaguely remembered the orientation he had attended at Langley. Truth be told, he was still stoned from his "CIA-lebration" party the night before. He had made his way to the visitors conference center late that morning and managed to stay upright during the eight-hour session only by drinking lots of coffee and thinking about how good it would feel to hop into his new BMW and take the scenic route home to Belinda after they let him out of class. The best he was able to do that evening was lock his information packet in his new agency file safe and secure it, putting off his homework until another day.

"Guys, look. I apologize. When I signed up for the liaison thing, I didn't really consider that it would entail any sort of secret clearance or involve any national security stuff. Honestly," he said with the same smile that had allowed him to get his way all through college. "I was only thinking about the extra money, getting out of the office on a trip once in a while, and then the retirement benefits. To tell you the truth, since the orientation, I've been thinking that maybe I'm not the best person for the position, if you know what I mean." The cowardly Vazquez smiled, looking for a way out of what he now considered water far too deep for his skill level.

Brown glanced to Green, made eye contact, and turned back to Vazquez. He opened the olive drab file folder he had been holding on his lap and began to read: "Ronald Coleman Albert Vazquez, a.k.a. Radio Vazquez, born June 12, 1942, to Roberta Maria Vazquez. Born September 22, 1920, in Vera Cruz, Mexico, Roberta Maria Vazquez seems to have violated federal immigration law and entered the United States without authorization sometime in the fall of 1940. The lady then made her way to Philadelphia, Pennsylvania, where she found employment as a seamstress for one Mr. Joshua A. Levy, proprietor of Joshua Levy Tailor, where she met and entertained many prominent gentlemen in the Philadelphia business community, one of whom seems to have impregnated our Miss Vazquez without the benefit of wedlock in October of 1941. It also seems that since November of that year, Miss Vazquez has been receiving a monthly stipend of five hundred dollars from the attorney of one Mr. Evan Reed Jansen, president and major stock holder of the RCA Victor Company, maker of consumer electronics, which is headquartered in Philadelphia, Pennsylvania." Mr. Brown looked up to glare at Al over his government-issued desk. "I guess your mom found out why they call it the city of brotherly love," he said without any humor at all, then looked back to Green.

"Mr. Vazquez, I'm afraid that the Agency cannot, at this time, allow you to disengage from the role you have been assigned. Other forces are in play that make your participation mandatory. All you need to know is that it's a matter of national security. At some point after the current operations have been concluded, you will be allowed an exit, if you so choose, which will be acceptable to the agency. But until that time, please consider yourself a member of the team," said a smiling Green, withdrawing a thick manila envelope from his jacket pocket and tossing it on the desktop. "This is the customary advance on your first performance bonus, Mr. Vazquez."

Al's head was reeling. The surge of emotion from having the most private portions of his and his mother's lives reduced to less than a paragraph in a CIA file felt like a kick in the groin and left him sick to his stomach; his sweat was soaking through the armpits of his crisp white button-down shirt. With great fear and uncertainty, he reached across the desk, took the envelope, opened it, and fanned the currency with his thumb.

"Five thousand to start—tax free if you handle it right—and more to come if you do your job and keep your mouth shut," said the unsmiling Brown. "And the thing about your mom's immigration status—I'm sure her citizenship records have just been misplaced."

"I, I, I don't understand. What do you want me to do? What exactly *is* my job?" asked a frightened and bewildered Vazquez.

Brown opened the file again, flipped to another tab. "Says here, Mr. Vazquez, that your job is…'*To witness and report on the national security implications of foreign crop yield with the purpose of analyzing the potential of using surplus US agricultural output as a weapon in America's struggle against the spread of global Communism.*'" He looked at Vazquez again with his stone-hard face.

Green glanced at Brown. "Should we do it now or wait?"

Brown glanced at his Timex. "It would be tight but it's only nine thirty, probably be back around eight tonight, and we could use the trip to break in the new pilot; what's his name? Magazzine?"

"Mr. Vazquez, grab your coat, have your girl cancel your appointments, you'll be out for the day," said Mr. Green.

Three hours later, Vazquez was trying to control his growing nausea by focusing on the horizon line through the porthole of an unmarked military version of the Gulfstream II, taking in the golden crescent and clear blue waters of the Florida coast. The pilot sharply banked into a 2 g roll and then into an alarmingly steep and rapid descent onto what looked to be an abandoned oiled runway hacked into the thick undergrowth just inland from the shore somewhere along the border between Florida and Alabama.

"Welcome to Echo Base, it's our North American training center. We also run some of the Gulf and Caribbean operations out of here," explained Brown to Vazquez as the wheels of the GII touched down with a light screech on the hard-packed oiled sand.

The pilot let the jet run to the far end of the runway and into a wide turn, bringing them to a crisp stop in front of a dilapidated tin shack painted to appear as if it were a part of the vegetation that surrounded it. Brown and Green bracketed Vazquez, and they stepped into the oppressive heat and humidity typical for the northern panhandle of Florida. They encountered a swarm of the biggest mosquitoes Al had ever seen.

Brown punched his access code into a keypad on the shed wall, entered while they waited, and a moment later, a garage door opened on the jungle side of the shack, allowing Brown to drive a surplus army jeep around to pick up his passengers.

"Magazzine will stay with the plane while we take a little ride. We should be back in a couple of hours; climb aboard," said Brown to his uneasy apprentice.

The jeep disappeared under the heavy tree canopy and wobbled quickly along the deeply rutted sandy road. "Lotta history's happened here, Vazquez. Pissed-off Cuban exiles trained here—hell, lived here, if ya wanna call it that—getting lean and mean for the Bay of Pigs. The invasion was planned in that bunker right there."

"US troops and mercenaries from damned near every banana war in South America have been through here at one time or another. Name a product in your refrigerator, and I'll bet ya dollars to doughnuts that there's been a war somewhere south of Panama ta make a better deal with the natives for labor or natural resources or somethin', so you 'n' me can afford to buy groceries down at the local Piggly Wiggly. I hafta laugh at that 'cause it was a Marine, Major General Smedley Butler, who pegged it more than thirty years ago. "War's a racket," he said. "The only one in which profits are reckoned in dollars and losses in lives," said Brown, clearly in his element now without jacket or tie and hiding his eyes behind gleaming military aviator sunglasses. "Semper muth-erfuckin' Fi!"

Al was trying to follow, gushing sweat, still suffering slight vertigo from the rough plane ride and combat-style landing in the Alabama outback. He had shucked his Hart Schaffner Marx jacket, loosened his tie and collar, rolled up his sleeves, and was doing his best to go with the flow, keep his mouth shut, and do his job; whatever the hell that meant.

In the distance, he heard small arms fire—first a little, then a lot, punctuated with explosions and men screaming. As they sped past a clearing of what appeared to be a large rifle range with maybe thirty men firing from the prone position, a .50-caliber machine gun opened up and began pouring tracer rounds through the trees beyond, across their path of travel, over the heads of the men on the line and into the earthen bank beyond. Standing men in uniforms were yelling at everyone to get down, and Al's eyes grew wide with fear.

"YEEEEHAAAAA!" At the last possible second, Brown increased their speed to breakneck, veered off the main road just in time to avoid the tracers, crashed through a thin layer of cut brush camou-flage, and burst into a small compound that looked for the entire world like photos of a Vietnamese village Al had seen in *National Geographic.* The jeep careened wildly into the compound, turned round and round into a tightening spiral—throwing dirt and gravel everywhere—and then screeched to a halt directly in front of the main hooch, whereupon Radio Vazquez proceeded to pass out and vomit into his own lap.

"Awww mann, whydja hafta go 'n' do that!" screeched Brown. "Now somebodie's gonna hafta clean this crap up 'n' it sure ain't gonna be me!"

"Damnit, Clark, I told ya ta back off. You 'n' that fuckin' Magazzine. Vazquez here is still a creampuff and besides, he ain't even really ours yet; at least half of 'em still belongs ta USDA, and ya know full well who's watchin' this whole cockeyed op, so damnit, dial it back!" said Green, punching him hard in the arm to make a point.

"Now make yourself useful, run the jeep over to the motor pool, and hose it out while I take care of Vazquez here. That OK with you?" said Green, punctuating his command by pushing his fist farther into Brown's aching shoulder.

They moved the unconscious Vazquez past the men gathered in the command bunker, through an interior door, and into the officers latrine.

"Vazquez, wake up," said Green. "If you're connin' me, I'll make ya walk back ta Washington."

Seeing his charge was still unconscious, a frustrated Green took two ammonia capsules from a small med kit, inserted one into each of Vazquez's nostrils, and pinched his nose hard. Al came to instantly, covered in cold sweat, slapping his face to dislodge the odious foreign objects from his nose. He took a deep breath of fetid air, smelling his own puke, and began to heave again.

"Here drink this, the sugar will settle your stomach," said Green, handing him the end of a bottled soda someone had abandoned in the galley. Al did as he was told.

"Ya stink, Vazquez. Clean yourself up, strip, and put these on." He tossed a clean set of camouflaged fatigues his way. "And snap it up. I wanna get outta here before dark. We'll be waitn' for ya right outside."

Al groggily washed himself, changed his clothes, washed the vomit off his trousers, rolled them in his shirt, and with great trepidation went out to find Agent Green and discover his fate.

A small group of men stood in front of a large map pinned to the cork-covered wall in what looked to Vazquez to be some sort of government office complete with typewriters, filing cabinets, desks, and chairs that had clearly come from the same federal warehouse that supplied the USDA.

"Welcome, Mr. Vazquez," said a deep voice from behind. The voice belonged to a tall, obviously fit man, of mixed lineage, an exotic specimen with African, Anglo, and Latin bloodlines. He was dressed in a set of freshly pressed military fatigues absent any mark of rank except his shiny leather shoulder holster and a large semi-automatic handgun, which seemed to add something extra to his natural air of authority.

"I'm known here as Harrison Whitehead. I'm pleased to make your acquaintance," he said, extending his large covering hand to Al.

Addressing the crowd, Whitehead announced, "Our applicant has arrived. Please, gentlemen, may we all be seated? I am calling this meeting of Southeast Asia Air to order," he said with a broad disarming smile.

At the table, Whitehead placed Al's file before him, opened it, glanced through the contents, and then addressed his young prospect. "¿Sabe usted por qué está aquí el señor Vásquez?"

"Excuse me?" said Al still in a fog and not really understanding his host.

"Do you know why you're here?" repeated Whitehead in English. "And please, don't be coy, we have your complete dossier and are fully aware of your language skills. That's one of the reasons you were selected."

Al sat upright, gathered his courage, and looked squarely at Whitehead. "No, sir, I really don't know why I'm here or even where here is."

Gesturing toward Green and Brown, he said, "These two gentlemen practically kidnapped me out of my office this morning. They threw me in a jet, the pilot flew like a crazy man, we nearly crashed during the landing, we're in the car and then there were men with machine guns and bombs killing each other, and I think they were shooting at us. When the car crashed, I blacked out, and I woke up here covered in my own vomit and ruined an expensive business suit!"

Al took a deep breath and a chance. "Mr. Whitehead, I am the deputy director of the United States Department of Agriculture. I'm in charge of millions and millions of tax dollars, I do business on the Hill every day, and I am a scheduled attendee for the monthly department coordination meeting at the Whitehouse, for crying out loud. I know people—congressmen, senators, governors, even the president, and I'll be missed. So, Mr. Whitehead, please, you tell me. Just why in the hell *am* I here?" said Vazquez, feeling outrage above all other emotions.

The smile left Whitehead's face. He looked up from the file to take his new and potentially troublesome employee in hand.

"Be careful what you wish for, Mr. Vazquez," he said. "You're here because you asked to be here. Oh, I know you thought you'd never actually be expected to *do* anything; you were just gaming the system like everyone else. You intended to take just a little dip out of the ocean of free money that keeps Washington afloat, just a little taste for yourself—no one would notice such an insignificant amount— and it wouldn't harm anyone, not really. You were probably thinking of your poor old mama and how you were gonna take care of her once she's too old to work and too ugly to whore. Or maybe you were wanting to impress Belinda's got rocks daddy—what's his name, Dorance—with how well you're doing working for the government; buy his baby girl and granddaughter a house or a new car. Or maybe it was a chance to pretend to be James Bond like in *Goldfinger,* is that it, Al? You a James Bond wannabe? Wear a tux, shoot a gun, drink a martini, tear off a little piece of strange every now and then?" said a smiling Whitehead, barely concealing the razor's edge in his voice. "All in the line of duty of course. Am I gettin' close, Radio?"

There was a long pause as Whitehead took a sip from his mug, referred once again to the file, and allowed the pressure inside his captive to build, watching him wilt again. When he felt the time was right, he began tuning his new Radio. "Mr. RCA Vazquez, deputy director of the United States Department of Agriculture, you're here because the company has determined it has a need for your services. We're expanding our agribusiness line into Indochina, and we have a particular interest in a region known as the Golden Triangle, which expands outward about fifteen hundred klicks from the confluence of the Ruak and Mekong Rivers just at the intersection of the borders of Burma, Laos, and Thailand. There's a map of the Triangle on the wall—you should take a look before you leave. Your role in our little business model will be as a sort of prospector, broker, and maybe a goodwill ambassador to the indigenous peoples who cultivate the fields and process the product. You will travel to the region, accompanied by your colleagues here, Mr. Green and Mr. Brown, to procure a very lucrative cash crop, papaver somniferum. You will survey the fields, estimate their yield, and broker the purchase with the tribal planters. You will oversee the sale to our distributors and then follow through with the processors until the product is ready for shipment. The work is seasonal, so you will continue in your present capacity in Washington when not needed in the field. You will do this as necessary and as you are directed until the company releases you from your obligation. In return, you will be compensated monthly and accrue vacation and retirement benefits from the agency at your current rate of GS twelve, deputy director. In addition, from time to time, at the recommendation of your superiors, you shall receive incentive pay in recognition of a job well done. These funds shall be transferred to you in cash and are tax exempt since they shall be earned during your international assignments from the agency. What you do with the money is up to you, but I suggest that you bank it offshore in the Caymans or Switzerland or wherever and save it for a rainy day. People in our line of work can get very wet when it rains, Mr. Vazquez, so Green and Brown here will show you how to set up your account. Do you have any questions?"

Al was dizzy again; the heat in the command bunker was stifling. "What is papaver? What is the product?" he asked quietly.

"It's the opium poppy, Radio—and here it says our boy is a quick study," he said to the room in the throes of laughter. "Al, just so you understand, here's our business model: we buy the poppies while they're in the field, we outsource the processing to the locals, and we ship the refined product to where it needs to be, no questions asked. When you were in business school at Penn State, they probably called it vertical integration. Ah, hell, there you go again, playin' like you don't know what I'm talking about; the product is smack,

Radio; H; junk; brown sugar. Tell me you ain't never had a little taste of the White Horse when you 'n' Belinda be partin' with ya peeps down in Georgetown!" said Whitehead, mocking Al for the benefit of his associates, and because he enjoyed it.

"Sir, are you saying you want me to become…a dope pusher?" asked Al, alarmed at his dawning realization, trying hard to suppress the fear welling up inside of him. "What about the Justice Department, the FBI? What you are doing is against the law! We could all go to prison!"

When the laughter died away, Whitehead spoke, smiling. "Al, listen, we like you and we ain't gonna do nothing that'll get ya inta any trouble with the law," he said, reaching into his shirt pocket for his wallet. He offered it to Al, who found what appeared to be a badge and official credentials: Harrison J. Whitehead, Special Agent At Large, Federal Bureau of Investigation.

A cold fear gripped Vazquez. "I told your people this morning that I'm not the man for this job; please, sir, is there any way I can get out of this?" he whimpered.

Agent Whitehead, who despised candy-assed college kid whiners as much as anything, decided to dispense with his "good cop" persona, play his trump card early, and let the big dog eat. "Yeah, Radio, there's a way," said Whitehead, "but you ain't gonna like it."

As if in a dream, Al watched Whitehead casually pull his bureau issue 1911 from its leather, saw the muzzle flash, felt the impact of the blast wave on his face and the instant searing pain of white-hot lead as the .45 ACP scorched a bright line between the crescent of his upper ear and his scalp, lacerating his temporal artery and causing a crimson spray to pulse into the air with the rhythm of his racing heart. Howling in pain and shock, Vazquez clutched his wound and collapsed on the floor in a fetal spasm. As the ringing in his ears abated, he heard first the laughter of Green, Brown, and the others and then the deep silky baritone of Special Agent Harry "Big Dog" Whitehead. "Plata o plomo, mi amigo, silver or lead." The pungent stench of human terror began to waft through the crowded command bunker. Radio Vazquez had soiled his pants.

4

OPERATION ARCHANGEL

At precisely 0500, a message was broadcast from the mountaintop surveillance post, code named "Omega."

"Archangel, this is Shepherd Boy. Do you copy?" silence.

To the east, and at twenty thousand feet, on the flight deck of his specially modified C-130, Captain Charles (Chuck) Magazzine received the hail over his preassigned radio frequency and keyed his helmet microphone to issue instructions for the identity challenge.

"Shepherd Boy, this is Archangel. Go to frequency Delta Mike Zulu for challenge."

After several years of piloting a "trash hauler" for the Studies and Observation Group, Magazzine knew that the danger of betrayal during any covert operation was very real but even more so for this mission. From his previous discussions with David Rixon, Omega's commanding officer, he understood that the cargo, information, and personnel he would be extracting from Laos could be used to end the careers of some major political operatives in Washington and maybe send some of them to prison for a very long time—or worse. And while he hoped that the NVA had not been tipped to the location of Omega, he certainly wasn't taking any chances.

Chuck and David had worked out the security procedures for evacuating Omega over a year before, just after the secretary and the negotiator had announced the success of the Peace Accords in Paris, France.

During dinner at Nick's Fishmarket, a local dive with great seafood and a view overlooking the USS *Arizona* Memorial, they decided that, should an emergency evacuation of Omega become necessary, their personally designed security protocols for Operation Archangel, known only to one another, would supersede all other mission parameters the Suits in Langley, Virginia, sent them. After leaving the restaurant, the two men spent the rest of the night and most of the next day working out the details of an operation that they hoped would never be needed but that would probably save their lives if it were.

After dialing in the prearranged frequency, David Rixon issued the challenge code, "Mary had a little lamb." Hearing the Chuck's signature baritone return, he said, "Remember the Alamo." He smiled broadly. "Looks like an early Christmas, Archangel. You get your present yet?"

"Affirmative, Shepherd Boy, present received," said Magazzine, referring to the C-130 Combat Talon with jet-assisted takeoff and landing technology that he had been training with at Udorn. "Archangel requests the color of your ornaments."

"Shepherd Boy reports ornaments green, green, green, amber, amber, red. Say again, Shepherd Boy reports ornaments golf, golf, golf, alpha, alpha, romeo."

The four green "ornaments" let Magazzine know that the weather at Omega was within acceptable tolerances for his visual flight rules landing, that the conversion of the ancient Moon Court into a makeshift three-hundred-foot-wide by three-hundred-foot-long runway was complete, and that the airspace he would traverse during his landing and takeoff was free of enemy positions capable of firing on the aircraft. The amber and red "ornaments" were warnings of discernible troop movements to the north, south, and west and indicated that they were under sporadic small arms fire.

"Seems like the bad guys have finally got a lock on Shepherd Boy, so I guess it's now or never," thought Magazzine as he keyed his mic. "Shepherd Boy, Archangel. Copy your ornaments golf, golf, golf, alpha, alpha, romeo. Pour the milk and bake the cookies, Shep. Archangel is sliding down the chimney!"

In his final transmission, Magazzine had told Rixon that the conditions were acceptable for him to attempt a visual flight rules landing on the Moon Court. He could deploy the barrels of motor oil on the steep and rocky approach to Omega, which they hoped would prevent the enemy from climbing the final five hundred feet up the cliff face. He could also ignite the signal fires that would define the perimeter of the Moon Court in the moments before sunrise as he began his approach from the east.

Magazzine made ready for his final turn, activated the C-130's intercom, and prayed aloud, "Father God: You are the Almighty God of the universe, the sword and shield of the Christian soldier from the beginning of time. Father, I pray earnestly for Your Divine provision and protection of this aircraft and its crew from the enemy and the elements as we proceed with our mission. And if it be Your will, Father, grant us victory on the battlefield this day. I pray this humbly and earnestly in the name of Your Son, Jesus Christ, our strength and our redeemer. Amen." Magazzine switched the intercom off and the members of the flight crew said their own prayers in the final seconds before they went to war one last time.

As the first rays of the rising sun began to paint the five-thousand-foot granite cliff below, Magazzine rolled his aircraft into its final approach vector, placed the sun at his back, and committed himself and his crew to Archangel. "If everything works as advertised," he said to himself, "we'll be on the deck with all our parts and pieces at 0530. And if it don't, our parts and pieces will be all over the deck at 0530."

"OK, guys. It's show time!" he announced to the crew as he elevated the flaps, eased back on the throttles, trimmed the props, and felt the trash hauler begin its controlled fall out of the pristine Laotian sky.

The Lockheed Martin C-130 Hercules is a magnificent aircraft, a miracle of modern aerospace engineering and the universal workhorse of military tactical airlift around the world. With a wingspan of 135 feet, its four 4,500 horsepower Allison turboprop engines allow it to carry 42,000 pounds of cargo 1,200 miles before refueling. It would have been perfect for Archangel except that the aircraft requires a minimum combat runway length of three thousand feet to put down safely, and the biggest flat spot on the top of David Rixon's mountain was just slightly over three hundred feet long.

The technology that made the operation feasible was the experimental MC-130 Combat Talon, still being developed by Lockheed's famous Skunk Works Advanced Development Projects team based in Palo Alto, California. The one-of-a-kind prototype that Magazzine was piloting came as a very large favor from friends at Lockheed. It was equipped with large articulating jet packs attached to the fore and aft of a standard C-130 which were said to give the craft very short landing and takeoff capabilities. In fact, the Lockheed technician that Magazzine had trained with at Udorn calculated that a three-hundred-foot runway would be more than adequate to park Archangel, turn her around, and get everyone and everything airborne again; a true engineering miracle—that is, it if worked.

Below, and on the shadow side of the mountain, stood David Rixon, his attention focused on the jungle below. "If he doesn't know about the Talon, then he's expecting a group of EVAC choppers," Rixon thought as he scanned the enemy formations for someone who looked like their commander. "It would take time for even a small group of *Sea Knights* to land, load, and then take off in sequence. I'll bet he's counting on that time to dial in his mortars to take out the choppers and kill us on the ground."

Slightly below his position were six heavily armed Hmong mercenary solders dumping fifty-five-gallon barrels of used motor oil down the southern cliff face and over the only surface route to the temple.

"Archangel, Shepherd Boy. Pouring the milk now, cookies will be in the oven at 0528," said Rixon into his radio.

"Copy your 0528, Shep," replied Magazzine. "We'll see ya in a few."

"Aye, aye," said Rixon to himself, as he continued searching for the NVA commander. "El Tee, status," he said into his field telephone.

"Captain, the cookies will be in the oven on my mark in fifteen seconds." Waiting, Rixon heard the count, "Five, four, three, two, one. Mark!"

Rixon knew that the soldiers above were lighting fires in the fifty-five-gallon drums that outlined the improved Moon Court, and he knew that if the NVA had their position under surveillance that their commander would be notified of the change in airfield status immediately.

"GOTCHA!" whispered David as he spied the commander. "I'll be, if it isn't our old pal VC1356, hook and all," he said, recognizing the enemy commander from previous operations.

"Angel Flight, Shepherd Boy, do you copy?" said David into yet another microphone, still watching the NVA commander. Rixon heard the reply from Joe Don Brinkman, the last remaining Raven forward air controller, in Indochina.

"Shepherd Boy, this is Angel Flight, go ahead."

"Angel Flight. Cookies are in the oven. Wise Men are in position. You are weapons free. Begin your attack run. Say again, begin your attack run now."

J. D. Brinkman was communicating with David Rixon on a compromised radio frequency widely known to be monitored by NVA field commanders. He was receiving authorization for his "attack run," which meant that he would fly his crotchety little Cessna, low and slow, at treetop level around and below Rixon's mountaintop position, while very loudly broadcasting the prerecorded sound of a squadron of F-4 Phantoms winding up for their attack run right over the head of the NVA commander.

If this deception worked, prayed Rixon, the diversion would disperse the enemy and buy Archangel enough time to get everyone off the mountain without any loss of life. Anyway, that was the plan he and Magazzine had developed, and that he had set in motion.

But none of that concerned Charles Magazzine, who was focused on navigating his approach less than two minutes from touchdown at Omega. Through low clouds and morning fog, he could see the signal fires tracing the perimeter of the Moon Court. "Sure as hell doesn't look like three hundred feet," he said to his copilot, navigator, and flight engineer over the intercom.

"Deploy JATOL," he said, and his copilot flipped open a clear Plexiglas cover, revealing a series of coded toggle switches, moving the top four to the on position and receiving four green lights in response. "JATOL deployed and green. Thirty-five seconds to touchdown," came the response.

Magazzine gauged his distance to the outer marker to be 1,500 meters and slowed his airspeed to that recommended by the Lockheed Skunks, increasing the flaps to 100 percent, trimming the propellers, and throttling the engines to 80 percent of maximum, creating a thunderous sound that Rixon saw reflected in the face of the enemy, but it was too late. Angel Flight had nearly completed its "attack" run and Rixon could see the enemy troopers running for cover.

"Shepherd Boy to Archangel, Angel Flight is engaged. Proceed with your final."

Magazzine's right hand caressed the control cluster that operated the JATOL packs. "Heat 'em up, Sparky, it's time ta go ta work." Copilot, Commander Steve (Sparky) Barnes, USN, activated the JATOL clusters while Magazzine got his first real-world feel of how the bird handled under the thrust of eight high-performance jet engines. They increased the sound of thunder to a screeching, deafening roar that enveloped the Moon Court, sending dust plumes and shock waves, visible and audible for miles.

"Feather the props, Sparky," said Magazzine, as he gained confidence in the thrust of the rockets. Their forward airspeed dropped to almost zero while Al held the craft stable, in a near hover, then began maneuvering it to the location that Rixon had marked out with paint on the paved surface, as he watched ground crew flagmen for close clearances to the temple itself.

"Shepherd Boy, Archangel. You guys ready to go? 'Cause we are touching down in ten seconds."

And with that, Magazzine gently rotated the Talon 180 degrees toward the east, decreased the JATOL thrust for set down, and positioned the ship squarely in the paint, primed for emergency lift-off. "Sparky, remind me to send those Palo Alto polecats a box 'a candy 'n' a thank-you note!" said Chuck with a relieved smile. His copilot responded with a broad grin and crisp thumbs-up as his crew chief and load master deployed the aft cargo ramp.

"Thank you, Lord," prayed Rixon, as he acknowledged Archangel's touchdown. We're outta here in twenty minutes or less, he thought as he began his sprint to Omega's forward observation post and into a future unlike any he could have ever imagined.

5

THE LITTLEST WARRIOR

David King Rixon grew up hard on the wrong side of the four-lane highway that bisects the West Texas oil town of Odessa, where "…tornadoes are our cash crop, dust storms provide the shade for our noon siesta, and you can always tell a debutante by the color of her teeth."

"Rix" always joked that he grew up in a garden spot, and judging by what he had seen of the rest of the world during his service to Uncle Sam, he figured he wasn't too far from right.

Like most people who lived in south Odessa, the Rixon family drew its livelihood from the oil patch where David worked alongside his daddy as an apprentice roughneck during the summer, Christmas, and Easter holidays. The brutality of long shifts on the rig hardened David early, and by thirteen the lifers working the platform began to see him as their physical equal. The tool pusher, "Pastor" Jose Gonzales, tagged him "Little Rix" both as an honor, because of the respect his father commanded, and as a good-natured poke at his diminutive stature. It seemed David was destined to live the life of a 5-6 roustabout in world dominated by giants.

Even so, Little Rix was a happy kid until the night his mama, daddy, and younger brothers were killed by the drunk who drove his Vista Cruiser into the cab of their old GMC pickup. David and his dog Travis survived only because they were riding in the bed that night, staring up at the starry Texas sky, tracing Orion's belt through wisps of tiny snowflakes.

It was Christmastime then, and David remembered the decorations at the hospital, the smell of blood, vomit, and spiced tea in the emergency room and how everybody seemed so sad when they looked him in the eye. The article in the *Odessa American* quoted Texas Highway Patrolman Benjamin Wheeler, who worked the wreck: "Five fatalities. It's the worst I've seen in twenty years. Their Christmas presents were scattered across the highway and the dog wouldn't let anyone come near the boy. Every man out there was in tears."

They said it was a Christmas miracle that he and Travis had survived, and David kept the newspaper clipping in his daddy's lockbox along with his family's birth certificates, a photo album, and his mama's Bible, so he'd never forget who they were and where he came from.

His parents couldn't afford life insurance and didn't have wills, so after burial expenses the government ate up most of the tiny Rixon estate with probate fees, back taxes, and the like. David's inheritance though included many intangibles—the things that mark a man for life. From his father, David received his sense of honor, a relentless work ethic, the physique of a Roman Centurion, a quick wit, good humor, and an easy confidence with other men that would make him a natural leader. His mother left him her genius in language, music, and math, her love of animals, her reverence for the God of Abraham, Isaac, and Jacob, and the countenance of an angel. And from the drunk who killed his family, David received a deep well of tempering grief, a sense of his own mortality, and the facial scarring that would remind him of that Christmas night in Odessa every day for the rest of his life.

After the hospital, David went to live with his mama and daddy's best friends. Pastor Jose and Paulina Gonzales were assigned to be his foster parents by a sympathetic family law judge, and the roughnecks working the oil patch became his extended family. That close brotherhood of hard men was brought to their knees by the sight of Little Rix standing alone by the five caskets, and they swore to each other they'd always get the boy whatever he needed. And mostly, especially when it mattered, they were as good as their word.

Eleven years before the accident, Pastor Joe and David's daddy had become part-time copastors of La Palabra en la Iglesia de Cristo Misionera Biblia, a small congregation of interracial Christians who met Sunday mornings in the main barn of the Quad Six Quarter Horse Ranch just south of Odessa. Marion and Randy had been invited to visit the congregation by Pastor Joe when David was a toddler and she was pregnant with Mark, her second son. Marion came to know and love Paulina during rides to the Ector County Free Clinic and the two women, who shared the blissful condition of pending motherhood, started out with pleasantries and became friends through the months as they opened their hopes, fears, and faith during the hours spent in the crowded waiting room.

When Paulina gave birth to her daughter, Isabella Maria, Marion, Randy, and David were there in the waiting room for prayer and support. That's when Randy and Jose broke through the formality of work and became friends as well. They were both compact, athletic men with intense love for their wives and worn New Testaments in their jackets. During their hours together that night and over the next few weeks, Jose and Randy shared their faith and their conversion experiences, and by the time Marion gave birth to Mark, the Rixon family had become enthusiastic new members of the Word in Christ Missionary Baptist Church.

Using the Quad Six horse barn as a meeting house appealed to Randy, who said he saw a divine symmetry in the setting. Jose, repulsed by pungent odor of equine urine, thought his friend a loco Anglo, but went along with the idea, since it somehow made poetry out of their poverty.

The men of the little congregation "paid" for the use of the barn and the stock pond below by taking turns mucking the stalls and feeding the stock during the week. But on Sunday mornings, the horses were moved out to the corral and the barn was converted to the sanctuary that Randy always knew it could be. Over time, the Rixons became integral to the worship experience of the Saints of Quad Six.

They had been helping out at Word in Christ for over a year when Randy talked an old Wurlitzer upright out of a pawnbroker on Grant Street. Glad to be rid of the clunker and happy to have the extra space in his showroom, the pawn master said, "Now ya can't say I never give ya nothin', Pastor Rixon."

"The Lord will cement the star in your crown for this, Mr. Knox," Rixon replied, grinning, as he and the hardhearted miser, Charlie Knox, loaded the beat-up, out-of-tune instrument into the bed of his old GMC. "Well that's great, Pastor. You go on now an' get yer piano home before it rains or sumpthin'," said Charlie, shooing Rixon away, not wanting to be prayed for again that day.

That evening Marion rode out to the Quad Six with her husband to muck the stalls, and she flushed when she saw the Wurlitzer for the first time. Tenderly touching the worn keyboard, finding middle C, and running the scales, she was in thrall. With a tuning, some tinkering, and a little elbow grease, the church would have its first musical instrument, and she could fully participate in their ministry.

That next Sunday, Marion Rixon led the singing and accompanied the congregation with the Wurlitzer in a rousing rendition of "Bringing in the Sheaves." David stood by her side, and his little brother, Mark, was wrapped tight in his blanket, asleep in the wicker basket at her feet

> *"Sowing in the morning, sowing seeds of kindness, Sowing in the noontide and the dewy eve; Waiting for the harvest, and the time of reaping, We shall come rejoicing, bringing in the sheaves…"*

That was also the first Sunday that Randy had delivered a sermon since he and Marion had married. Pastor Randy would speak a line or two and pause while Jose translated for the congregation—with appropriate embellishment and explanation, he later informed Randy.

That morning four repentant roughnecks came forward, gave their souls to the Lord and with their wives, children, and the assembly as witnesses, submitted themselves for baptism by Randy and Jose in the cold, muddy waters of the Quad Six stock pond. After a few Sundays like that, it became clear to the Rixons that their work in ministry had been blessed by the Lord with an unexpected new mission field. A month later, Marion Rixon discovered she was pregnant with her third child.

The Rixon family eventually grew to include four children, all of them boys: David, Mathew, Mark, and Luke. As they flourished, so did the little congregation at the Quad Six. The Rixons and the Gonzaleses spent most of their off hours pastoring the flock, caring for widows, orphans, and the elderly. Attendance at the Sunday services grew and grew.

The Sunday afternoon dinners at the Quad Six were the social event of the week, with the women cooking and visiting; the men talking religion, politics, sports, and the oil patch; and everyone watching the kids playing games and running and squealing everywhere they went.

From the earliest days of the congregation, the mothers of Word in Christ offered vacation Bible school during the first week after Odessa Independent School District recessed for the hot summer months. VBS at Quad Six began in the cool early mornings, with the mothers bringing their children to the main horse barn and dividing them by age into four classes arranged in the horse stalls especially cleaned for the occasion. The littlest ones, first and second graders, learned the lessons of Old Testament history by coloring and cutting out paper Bible characters, arranging them on brightly colored flannel boards, and then telling their stories to the class. The lessons progressed in complexity and detail to the oldest students in the seventh and eighth grade who memorized scripture and were tested by their teachers with "sword" drills, calling out random scriptures, with the first to either recite or look up and read the reference, being the winner. The competition was fierce and fun.

After about an hour of morning classes, there was recess and the sweet reward of ice-cold strawberry Kool-Aid and Mrs. Gonzales's homemade oatmeal cookies, served and consumed under the canopy of a mature mesquite grove on the shady side of the building.

The children were then prepared for their morning assembly by forming two lines at the entrance to the main aisle of the barn, girls in one line and boys in the other. At the head of each line, the oldest girl, Isabel Gonzales, and the oldest boy, David Rixon, had the duty of leading their columns of little Christians into the barn, proudly carrying the American and Christian flags.

Marion accompanied the entrance processional with "Onward Christian Soldiers." *Onward Christian Soldiers, marching as to war, with the cross of Jesus going on before. Christ, the royal Master, leads against the foe; forward into battle see his banners go!* All the children sang as they entered the deep coolness of the sanctuary and filed into the orderly rows of wooden benches their parents occupied during services on Sunday mornings.

Isabel and David placed the flags in their stands and stood side by side at in front of the lectern, leading their peers in the pledge to the Christian flag: *"I pledge allegiance to the Christian flag and to the Savior for whose Kingdom it stands. One Savior, crucified, risen, and coming again with life and liberty to all who believe."* Then they turned to the American flag: *"I pledge allegiance to the flag of the United States of America, and to the Republic for which it stands. One nation under God, indivisible, with liberty and justice for all."* The words and deeds made little David's heart swell with patriotic pride in America and warm with Christian love for his fellow man. In fact, it would be fair to say that the blended emotion of Christian patriotism would become foundational to the world view of all the children in the pews at the Quad Six that summer and for many more to come.

One certain summer, the Rixon brothers were in the vanguard of an adventurous knot of prepubescent boys at Word in Christ. During VBS, Mark Rixon had originated the bright idea of trapping prairie dogs and keeping them as secret pets in the abandoned hen house on the Quad Six.

During recess one day, Mark, about ten, noticed that along with various strays, many of the prairie dogs native to the Quad Six could be seen investigating the trash barrels after the meal services. Armed only with the power of inductive and deductive reasoning, he formulated the idea of baiting an empty can of Van Camp's pork and beans with a bite of his oatmeal cookie and tethering the can to a mesquite stump near prairie dog town. Watching from his blind inside the hen house, Mark witnessed a group of dogs investigating the snare and trying to get at the cookie without actually sticking their collective heads in the noose. As Mark later related the details to his daddy and Pastor Joe, it seemed to him that the dogs discussed their common dilemma, appointed one of their peers to retrieve the prize, and in so doing, it got its head stuck deep inside the empty can. They eventually came into Mark's possession as a sort of prairie dog rescue. Word of this success spread rapidly among the other boys. Before the grown-ups knew what was happening, the "Boys of the Word" had established a sizable heard of dogs, named them after the famous Quad Six quarter horses, and stabled them in the empty hen coops. They began racing the dogs, complete with dog-sized hackamores and numbered racing harnesses, inside the old hen house that was out back behind the dung heap.

To augment their string of prized prairie dogs and provide "air cover" for their weekly races, Isabel Gonzales thought it would be fun to have their very own "heavenly host." It was bright, beautiful, and energetic Isabel who began to capture the emerging cicadas from beneath the mesquite trees, harness them with her mother's sewing thread, and began "flying" them in loose formation from long gossamer leashes above the dog races as the children cheered and the terrified dogs ran for their lives. It was glorious.

One afternoon, David and Isabel agreed that it was un-Christian to send the prairie dogs into the arena without the benefit of Christian baptism. They gathered the dog owners and their racers together at the horse trough, considered the best way to immerse the sinner dogs in the "River Jordon," and decided that the rusty parakeet cage they had discovered in the tack room would serve well as their vessel of Christian deliverance.

Now clandestine Christian prairie dog racing, under the protective phalanx of cicada angels, may well have continued indefinitely at the Quad Six except for the little known fact that under proper duress, normally silent prairie dogs emit a baleful wail, comparable in volume to a bluetick coonhound treeing its quarry deep in a far-away east Texas night. "Aieeeeeooo! Aieeeeeooo! Aieeeeeooo!"

After their discovery, and since they were able to revive all but one of the dogs, their embarrassed mothers agreed to leave the collective fate of their wayward children to Pastor Joe and Pastor Randy. The pastors privately thought the whole enterprise terribly funny but said wisely that they saw the need to assert parental control over their imaginative children and agreed to immediately disperse the racing ring and consider the fate of the conspirators.

After a time and in what could only be described as a Solomonesque solution, the thought came to them that they ought to make the most of the situation. "Lemonade out of lemons" is how they sold their idea to the offended parents. "The Great American Patriots Day Community Dinner and Quad Six Championship Prairie Dog Race," an Independence Day celebration and fund raiser to establish the "Word in Christ Veterans Benevolency Fund." And though some of the parents believed that sparing the rod spoiled the child, it was hard to disagree with the idea of using the purloined prairie dogs to help out the military veterans.

After soothing all parties and working out the details with the church elders, the event occurred on that very July Fourth and was a daylong celebration of God and country, honoring the service of the Mexican and Anglo military veterans, and offering a community home cookin' feast day like no other. The barn was packed to the rafters early for the singing, teaching, and preaching. Souls were saved, some were baptized, and after the meal was consumed, the much-anticipated spectacle of the Word in Christ World Championship Prairie Dog Race took place.

The men of the congregation had marked out a hundred-foot diameter circle between the dung heap and prairie dog town, positioning a large wicker holding pen in the center, moved the Wurlitzer to the bed of Pastor Randy's pickup, and placed it to act as a reviewing stand for the race officials. At the appointed time, and at the request of Pastor Joe, Marion began to play "The Army

Goes Rolling Along." Accompanying the music were members of the Odessa Permian Marching Band and Pastor Joe, attired in his class A army uniform from World War II, with a pickup choir of combat veterans and their wives from the Odessa Post of the Veterans of Foreign Wars.

At the first chords of the theme, the door to the henhouse opened and the solemn procession of dog owners, their racers in hand, began to emerge, led by Isabel Gonzales. She was dressed appropriately in a red-and-white striped skirt, blue blouse, and golden tiara that made her look a little like the Statue of Liberty. She proudly flew her host of cicada angels followed closely by young David, proudly holding Old Glory high. The troupe slowly crossed the chalk line of the arena, marched once around the field of honor, and with Isabel's angels hovering and David standing with the flag at honor attention, the owners deposited their racing dogs, one by one, into the central wicker holding pen.

After the field was cleared and the music was completed, Pastor Joe and Pastor Randy addressed the waiting crowd. "Welcome to the Word in Christ World Championship Prairie Dog Race!" said Randy.

"Bienvenido a la Palabra de Cristo Campeonato Mundial Prairie Dog Race!" translated Pastor Joe.

"Our young people are inquisitive and inventive. They are naturally curious about the Lord's wondrous created world, and it's because of their seeking the Lord in this way that we are holding this event to support our veterans!" Translation and scattered applause.

"In the nineteenth chapter of Matthew, the Bible tells us that the people brought their children to see Jesus, and he said, '*Let the little children come to me and do not hinder them for the kingdom of heaven belongs to such as these,*'" said Randy.

Joe translated, "According to Jesus, these children," he said, acknowledging the assembled dognappers, "are holding the keys to the kingdom of heaven. We ought to all think about that in our daily lives. And children," Randy said, looking directly at Isabel and his four sons, "please remember that you belong to Jesus. You are destined to inherit the kingdom of heaven, and we love you all and will do everything we can every day to take care of you and keep you safe," he said to wide agreement and loud applause from the assembly.

David felt a surge of guilt and a terrible sense of responsibility for the drowning death of the unfortunate prairie dog and for allowing his little brothers to go too far with their fun, but most of all he was profoundly grateful that the adults had decided to show mercy and not spank them as they surely deserved. It was just that his brothers had wanted a dog for so long, and he thought that allowing them their secret pets might be a good substitute.

After the conclusion of the VIP remarks from the viewing stand and a prayer for the racing prairie dogs, the crowd gathered around the circle. The owners of the racers moved to their designated spot under the mesquite canopy and jointly released their dogs by pulling a tether that ran from the holding pen, up and along a large limb and down to the trunk.

The basket slowly rose and the crowd became silent as they observed that the traumatized dogs had huddled together in the center of the holding pen and seemed at first to be more intent on burying themselves under their fellows rather that running for their lives. Gradually, first one and then another came to their senses and realized that freedom was a mere fifty feet away in any direction, and beyond all the people lay the secure, deep burrows of their very own prairie dog town.

David heard the cheers but didn't see the winner cross the finish line or the others skitter back to join the their families underground. Instead, he was embraced tightly by his mama, daddy, and brothers as he tearfully promised to use better judgment in the future.

As the crowd began to break up, and after the men had returned the barn and surroundings to near perfect condition, the Rixons began saying good night and making their way to their truck. David was the first to discover a visitor in the cab—a black, gray, and brown brindle heeler mix with a harlequin face and piercing blue eyes.

"Dad! There's a dog in our truck!" said the boy racing to the cab, his brothers close behind.

"What did you do?" asked Marion, taking her husband's arm and smiling broadly. By the time they got to the truck, the boys had the cab open. They had enveloped the heeler in a sort of group hug, and Randy answered their questions.

"She's what people call a blue heeler, and she comes from Australia. She's a working cattle dog, but she was injured on a roundup not long ago, and her owner was looking to place her in a new home. Her name is Travis, after Colonel William Barrett Travis, the hero of the Alamo, and yes, we can keep her, if you promise to take better care of her than you did those poor old prairie dogs!" he said with a broad smile.

On their way home that night, Marion sat close to Randy in the cab while the boys crowded in the bed with Travis. "Injured cattle dog?" asked Marion. "The mystery owner's looking to place her in a new home?"

"OK, honey, I give. I found her out by the dung heap a couple of weeks ago and was keeping her at work, while I looked for the owner, but I couldn't find anyone who'd claim her. The boys had wanted a dog for so long, so I had planned to bring her home right after VBS, but this seemed like the right time."

"Is her name really Travis, after William Barrett Travis?" she asked, smiling.

"Yep, says so right on her collar. I just threw in the Alamo part to help them out a little with their Texas history," he said, pulling the truck to the side of the road in the cool dark night at a place where the fireflies and the stars seemed to merge with the distant Lions Club fireworks as they painted the sky with liberty and penetrated their hearts with love. "God bless America," he whispered.

"Randy Jefferson Rixon, I love you." She beamed.

"And I love you too, Marion, more than anything," said her husband. It was the sort of night that the Rixon family savored, knowing that the wealth of a lifetime consists of many, many moments like these.

Less than six months later, David's family was gone and his world had changed forever. Pastor Joe had conducted the funeral service at the Word in Christ, and he took some comfort in seeing the barn packed and the line of mourners backed up out the door.

After the service, he and Travis went home with Jose, Paulina, and Isabel. He spent his days healing, doing his studies at home, and going through the motions of life, getting used to the idea that he was an orphan and missing his brothers and mama and daddy.

That fall, David started his freshman year of high school at Odessa Permian. The school was new, most of the kids were friendly, and he lived near enough to ride his bike when the weather permitted, so he could take off for long afternoon rides to be alone with Travis and the Lord.

His after-school tabernacle was a grove of ancient live oak trees located a mile or so from home near a large stock pond that was replenished every time the wind blew by a rusty windmill perforated with dozens of bullet holes made by generations of bored hunters.

David sought the Lord there often. In the cool of the evening, he cried out for his mama and daddy and his brothers and wept for them. Other days, he raged at God and told Him that to kill his family was evil, that He was a murderer. Then, from the depths of his soul, he pleaded to God to take him as well. "Why don't you just finish the job!" he would say, standing upright, shaking his fourteen-year-old fists at the sky. "Why don't you just wipe the Rixon family off the face of the earth?" And when he was spent, he would cry himself to sleep, holding Travis very close and saying, "It's OK, girl, don't be afraid, nothing's going to happen. I'll protect you." And though David was unaware, the Lord's angels were gathered around him, watching over him, praying for his comfort and his future, and weeping for him even as he slept, holding Travis tight, sheltered under God's great dome of eternal silence and safe at home under the infinite West Texas sky.

A year passed and the following fall, David was in his live oak grove watching the evening doves fly in to drink from the pond, the windmill squeaking rhythmically in a slight breeze. He was passive, his anger and grief given over to the Lord, and he gradually became aware of a growing warmth around his body. The sensation grew and felt to him as if warm honey was flowing over the top of his head, over and down his face and made its way down his chest and then stopped, warming his heart.

Not long after that, David started going to back to Sunday school and church with Pastor Joe, Paulina, and Isabel. It was good to be back at Word in Christ and reunited with many of his friends, but somehow, it seemed empty without his daddy and mama and brothers. No one else could play the Wurlitzer, so it sat silent and unused.

Pastor Joe and David were riding out to the Quad Six to muck the stalls one evening, and in the front seat of Joe Gonzales's old Ford, David made his first public confession of faith in Jesus Christ. The next Sunday he waded into the Quad Six stock pond with Pastor Joe and was baptized into eternal life before the assembled congregation. When David was raised out of the watery grave, he thought he heard the sounds of the doves all around. Pastor Joe whispered in his ear, "Bienvenido a la fe David, soy muy complacido contigo." Welcome to the faith, David, I am very pleased with you.

A month later, Jose and Paulina called a family meeting after Sunday evening dinner. "David, Paulina and I have been talking. You've been our foster son for over a year, and we want to ask if you'd like to become an official member of the family—if you'd like for Paulina and me to adopt you so we could be your parents and Pleasant Farms can be your home forever.

"Would that mean I could I call you Papa and Mama like Isabel?" he asked in a whisper, looking at his foster parents and sister.

"Yes, it would!" came the reply as they hugged and cried over their decision to become a family. In serious conversations, the family decided that David would keep his last name in honor of his lost parents and brothers. And so it was that the Lord created a happy home and family from a tragedy, the first of many miracles that David would witness through his life.

David was back to himself and feeling powerful the day Panther defensive coordinator, Will Robinson, came scouting the boys' PE classes for "fresh meat," as he referred to new prospects for the football team. He spotted David's aggressive play during a third-period game of West Texas touch football, thought he might make an adequate human tackling dummy for the talent on the squad, and invited him to try out for the junior varsity the summer before his junior year. David felt honored that Coach would invite him on the team, and after discussing it with Jose and Paulina, he decided he'd like to see what varsity football at Odessa Permian was all about.

"This is combat, my son. To think of it as a child's game will only cause you pain and injury. You must become hard in your mind and your gut, David. Sacrifice your childhood to the wounding of physical discipline and you will become a warrior; you will be macho.

"Machismo is the masculine spirit, David, courage, bravery, strength, wisdom, and honor. It is the Lord's gift to man, but you will have to claim it for yourself. No matter your circumstance, you will never surrender; machismo will not allow it. In your heart, you must always believe you can win; it is a matter of faith like our faith in Christ.

"The field of combat is liquid, like the ocean, so you must always fight from the solid ground of your calm center. The wisdom of the Lord will be waiting for you there.

"Fearlessly step past the pain, into the danger and be watchful for your adversary's mistake. You will see it in his eyes first, so get as close as you can. The warrior needs only the blink of an eye to seize victory and win the day. When you know these things in your mind and in your heart, David, you will be a man," counseled his father, Pastor Joe, who concluded with a blessing: "Padre, bendice a David y enviar sus ángeles para proteger y defender a este joven guerrero en el campo de honor mientras lucha contra sus enemigos en su nombre. Ruego estas bendiciones en el nombre de tu Hijo, Jesucristo. Amen."

• • •

Perched in the forward observation post at Omega, scanning the enemy troop formation with powerful binoculars, Rix thought about Pastor Joe, Coach Robinson, and the Odessa Permian Panthers as he looked out over the massing troops below. His hand was on the shepherd mix he had named Travis the night he rescued her from becoming supper at the brothel on the outskirts of Saigon. "These people actually eat their dogs," he remembered thinking, as he pulled the tin can off the terrified puppy's muzzle. It seemed, so very long ago.

"Back again!" Rix whispered. "Major Quang Thong—the man just can't leave well enough alone," he said to himself, recognizing his familiar nemesis, the old Viet Cong commander who had all but wiped out 7-Mike and chased him out of South Vietnam and far into Laos. "Dang—you're still alive. And the hand never did grow back, so I guess that means I sort of owe you. Maybe old Santa has a little something left for you in his sack," he said to himself while thinking that the man had some serious payback coming.

Eighteen months before, he would have called in the *Phantoms* from the USS *Saratoga* and settled the score. But the war was over and the Americans had gone home, leaving just him, Travis, and a few other operators to clean up the mess and turn out the lights.

Smiling in anticipation, Rix could see stark terror erupt in the eyes of his adversary as he watched hundreds of his hardened NVA regulars scatter for safety as the prerecorded thunder of a flight of angry F-4s ricocheted through the granite canyon. Then Quang Thong's purple rage emerged as a beat-up American Cessna came slowly into view, dropped a pink smoke grenade on his position, switched the sound track from F-4 thunder to Irving Berlin's "White Christmas," wiggled his wings, and banked away to safety.

"Irving Berlin," thought Rixon, remembering Saigon and Operation Frequent Wind.

"Nice touch, JD," he said laughing, and he keyed his mic. "Thanks for the assist, Angel Flight."

"Our pleasure, Shepherd Boy. Please give my regards to Archangel and my personal holiday greetings to your little friends down there, who, if I'm not mistaken, are just about to climb your tree."

"Copy that, Angel Flight, and please watch yourself going home, Joe Don. I'll buy you a beer in Pearl after we debrief."

"David, it's been an honor, and I'll hold you to that beer. Angel Flight out."

David watched the Cessna another long moment as Captain J. D. Brinkman, on his way home to Texas, abruptly switched from "White Christmas" to the sad and haunting harmonica and the voice of Chris LeDoux singing, "*Amarillo by morning, up from San Antone, everything that I got, is just what I got on.*" He performed a slow victory roll as he disappeared around the morning side of the mountain.

Feeling a shiver of abandonment and fighting a gut-level surge of panic, Rixon stood. "Come on, Travis. It's time for us to go too." He slung his weapon, packed his radio and binoculars, and started a slow jog back to the compound. "Our old pals have finally figured out we're here but you 'n' me are gonna be long gone before they make it up the hill."

On his way to the Moon Court, Rix swept the observation station inside the pagan temple one last time to make sure the top-secret equipment had been loaded, that all remaining hard copy was destroyed, and to pick up his rucksack.

As he turned for the door, a sniper's round shattered the glass panel above his head spurring their sprint to the airstrip, where Archangel was spooling the engines of the C-130 for emergency lift-off. The next instant, an NVA mortarman placed his first round in the tree line about a quarter klick down the mountainside from the Talon, and Rix knew that the spotter was probably radioing corrective coordinates to his gunner.

"Taking fire, El Tee. Report," Rix said as he and Travis raced up the cargo ramp on the way to the jump seat behind the cockpit.

"Affirmative, Captain," responded Lieutenant Tommy Coats. "Operators and civilians are aboard; all equipment is inventoried and secured. Pilot reports fuel situation nominal, engines spooled, JATOLs primed, and the wind's blowing in our face at twenty-five knots. We're good to go, sir."

"We gonna make it outta here, Tom?" said Rix, looking Coats in the eye.

"We're in God's hands, David," replied the lieutenant.

"Always have been, always will be, Tom." Rix grinned to Coats. "Take us home, Captain Magazzine," Rix said over his shoulder to the pilot.

With a crisp thumbs-up, Magazzine eased the throttles to their stops, stressing the restraining cables to their maximum. On signal from the pilot, the Hmong ground crew blew the restraining cables as he fired the JATOL rockets releasing the C-130 into its violent one-way takeoff roll and a desperate escape from the encroaching enemy force.

There was a collective gasp as the cargo bay went weightless when Magazzine drove their craft past firing NVA regulars, over the edge of the manmade cliff, and powered down the windward side of the jungle-covered mountain, gaining precious air speed for his sharp 3 g climb and bank out of the valley and away from hostile fire.

But David Rixon seemed distant, detached from the harrowing circumstance. He had made his peace with God long ago and spent the moments during their escape ascent in prayer and thinking of that Christmas Eve in Odessa—his mama, daddy, brothers and the day he surprised the coaches and the Panthers by making a place for himself on the team.

"He saved my life," Rixon said absently.

"You say sumthin', Cap?" asked Coats over the roar of the turboprops.

"The Lord, El Tee. I said the Lord saved my life."

"Yes, sir, Captain," Coats said with a grin. "Looks like He sure as hell has."

6

TECTONICS

Dear Old Skibbereen

O Father dear, I often hear you speak of Erin's Isle
Her lofty scenes, her valleys green, her mountains rude and wild
They say it is a lovely land wherein a prince might dwell
Oh why did you abandon it? The reason, to me tell.
O son, I loved my native land with energy and pride
'Till a blight came o'er my crops, my sheep and cattle died
My rent and taxes were too high, I could not them redeem
And that's the cruel reason that I left old Skibbereen.
O well do I remember the bleak December day
The landlord and the sheriff came to drive us all away
They set my roof on fire with cursed English spleen
And that's another reason that I left old Skibbereen.
Your mother too, God rest her soul, fell on the snowy ground
She fainted in her anguish, seeing the desolation round
She never rose, but passed away from life to mortal dream
And found a quiet grave, my boy, in dear old Skibbereen.
And you were only two years old and feeble was your frame
I could not leave you with my friends, you bore your father's name
I wrapped you in my cothamore at the dead of night unseen
I heaved a sigh and bade good-bye to dear old Skibbereen.
O Father dear, the day may come when in answer to the call
Each Irishman, with feeling stern, will rally one and all
I'll be the man to lead the van beneath the flag of green
When loud and high, we'll raise the cry: "Remember Skibbereen!"

• • •

The Permian Basin is an exposed geological formation covering much of West Texas and southeastern New Mexico, which formed as an inland sea during the geological Permian Period roughly 250 million years ago. Paleontologists believe the distant ancestors of all land mammals evolved then but only to endure the largest extinction event in history, perhaps a gigantic volcanic eruption or meteor impact, which killed roughly 90 percent of all life on the planet.

The Permian is vast, some sixty thousand square miles of mostly flat, arid land stretching from the Llano Estacado escarpment near Lubbock, south to the border city of Eagle Pass, and then west past Marfa all the way to Van Horne. It's also the location of one of the richest oil and gas deposits in the continental United States having been the historic source for over fifteen billion barrels of sweet crude and nearly a billion cubic feet of natural gas; the residual wealth, of which is mostly concentrated in the rival petrocities of Midland and Odessa.

An independent geologist for the burgeoning Permian petroleum exploration industry, James Jarlath King had made a good living and fine home for his family in Midland for over a decade when his only child, Marion, announced that she wouldn't marry, as her friends were planning, but intended to devote her life to the service of the Lord. To prepare herself, she asked her parents to send her to Baylor College in Waco for a music degree, and from there she wanted to go into mission work with the Pueblo Indians in New Mexico.

Trained by his engineering professors at Texas Technological College to think in geological time, King believed that if he was patient, his daughter would eventually come around. It was, after all, the 1930s, Roosevelt was in the White House, the country was coming out of the Great Depression, and many new people were moving to Midland to take jobs in the oil field service industry. Surely, he thought, Marion would develop other interests; meet a young engineer or maybe even a production operator more to her liking perhaps than her schoolmates at Midland High—if he could only find a way to keep her home.

Marion and her parents reached a compromise agreement. She would first go to Tech for her degree in geosciences—J. J. King insisted his daughter study something useful if ever she needed to make a living for herself—and then on to Baylor for her master's in sacred music and thereafter into the mission field. She would still be young when she entered mission service, yet would bring something substantive with her when she began her labor in the fields of the Lord.

Marion first set eyes on Randy Jefferson Rixon during a revival service at the First Methodist Church in Midland. She had gotten her first job there as director of music the summer she graduated from Baylor. Rixon, the great-grandson of a Methodist circuit rider, who came to Texas to save the souls of the Comanche Indians, was an old-time fire-and-brimstone Methodist, following in his grandfather's footsteps. His preaching and Marion's music packed the sanctuary every night and many surrendered their souls to the Lord.

Marion learned from friends that Rixon, a graduate of Southern Methodist University in Dallas, had preferred celibacy and a life in ministry to marriage. He was in his mid thirties, made an uncertain living for himself as an itinerate evangelist and, following the apostle Paul's advice in First Corinthians, felt that since he had committed his life to the service of the Lord that it would be unfair of him to marry any woman who would consider him as a husband.

The night they were introduced at the ice-cream social, Marion looked into his eyes and thought she could see a straight line to her future. Deep in conversation about Indian missions and their shared faith, Marion noticed a slight fluttering movement just off to her left. "Did you see that?" she asked Rixon.

Randy Rixon smiled. "Why yes, Miss King, I did. It's the Lord's angels. You know they're always with us."

• • •

Marion's father rarely lost his temper. He prided himself on his reputation as a peacemaker, and he had cultivated a reasoned tendency toward diplomacy and forced himself to place his faith in the redemptive power of Jesus Christ. For the benefit of his family and those around him, he practiced decorum religiously and avoided physical confrontation like a recovering alcoholic avoids drink. This was the way of the man not because, as some assumed, he was a coward but because J. J. King was a stone-cold killer.

He was born into an unfortunate line of Scots-Irish who had been driven out of Ireland by the British democide known in polite society as "The Great Hunger," a series of tragic crop failures that gave rise to a catastrophic potato famine which began in 1845. This accidental crisis was intentionally exacerbated by a royal depopulation policy directed against the Irish Catholics. Over a million landless tenant farmers and city dwellers without means were killed by starvation and disease, and more than a million others were driven to escape death in Ireland through immigration to any country that would have them.

King's great-grandparents passed through the American immigration process on Ellis Island in New York Harbor in the winter of 1850. They endured the trauma of being rejected by a society who classed them generically as worthless "Bridgets and Patricks" in a city overrun by penniless Irish Famine immigrants.

Moving west, the young family found safe haven, a livelihood, and made a home for themselves in the magical place called Texas, which had been shaped by other Scots who traced their origins to Ireland. Steven F. Austin, Davy Crockett, Jim Bowie, and Sam Houston were all of Scots-Irish descent. They were clannish and family oriented, suspicious of societal elites, and bred to be rebels, outcasts, and extreme individualists. Hardened to the core by adversity and possessing survival skills as frontiersmen and asymmetrical warriors, they were well suited to life on the frontier.

The Scots-Irish in Texas had good reason to be suspicious of elites who historically controlled debate to favor their interests in faraway capitals like Rome, London, Mexico City, and now Washington, DC, where decisions had been made frequently that jeopardized their livelihood and their lives.

The Kings arrived at the island city of Galveston after the Republic of Texas was annexed as the twenty-eighth state in the Union and the Treaty of Guadalupe Hidalgo had been ratified, ending the war with Mexico. The family enjoyed a period of peace and prosperity previously unknown to them. Until they arrived, the Kings had never even seen a Negro or really understood American slavery and its contribution to the Texas economy. They began to learn of these things as they read about the evils of the commercial slave trade through the transcripts of the Lincoln-Douglas debates they found in second-hand copies of the *Galveston Daily News*.

The men of the King family sensed real danger in Lincoln's "House Divided" rhetoric and in reports they read of the dangerous religious fervor, which informed the Christian abolitionists of the North. Irrevocably coupled to their new livelihood in a slave state called Texas, they began to consider what the family might do to preserve themselves in the event of another war.

News reports of the attack on the federal armory at Harpers Ferry, Virginia, by firebrand abolitionist John Brown, and his plan to use captured military firearms to start a slave rebellion in Virginia, electrified the country and moved the nation nearer to conflict. The election of the Republican, Abraham Lincoln, to the presidency in November of 1860 and the decision, by referendum, of the people of Texas to secede from the Union set the future course of the King family. The evils of slavery and Mr. Lincoln's high-minded intentions be damned; they would fight for their home! They would fight for Texas!

James Jarlath King came into the world long after Lee surrendered to Grant at Appomattox, after the Thirteenth Amendment that outlawed slavery was signed into law, and even after the surviving members of the King patriarchy, along with 150,000 other Confederate veterans, had their voting rights restored by the Amnesty Act of 1872. Theirs was a reconstructed Texas, where slavery was illegal and they were again citizens of the United States of America.

The Scots-Irish King family was again cast to the bottom of the economic barrel by the fortunes of war and then the Great Hurricane of 1900, which swept away much of the island of Galveston and the jobs that once anchored the family to the port city, reducing them to the status of migrant farm workers.

As a young man, J. J. King was conscious of the financial burden he was placing on his impoverished family and decided he could help them best by finding a life along a different path. As they passed though San Antonio on their way to the grapefruit harvest in the Valley, he presented himself to the US Army Recruiting Station at Fort Sam Houston. He lied about his age, was accepted into the service, and became a trooper assigned to the newly created Fifteenth Calvary Division, stationed at Fort Bliss.

The scarred and weathered horse soldiers wondered how the fresh recruits would take to the job of shattering the will of the enemy with saber, pistol, and warhorse during the tactical cavalry charge. The ranks of the reformed Seventh Calvary included surviving veterans of the old Plains Calvary, members of which had earned their stripes in the Indian Wars by slaughtering the Cherokee, Sioux, and Apache. These veterans scoffed at the baby-faced youth who now manned the officer corps. They chuckled at the cleanliness of their language, not because they were insubordinate, but because in their collective gut they shared a sacred knowledge. They knew of the personal transformative power of the first blood on the saber, the crack of the enemy's skull, the panic of crumbling armed resistance overrun by angry, rough men on horseback, and the horrific reality of the point of first contact—what the old troopers called the "Bloodline."

When the officers had finally gone, the veterans took the recruits in hand and mentored them into the lethal art of using edged weapons to kill the enemy man to man. At this level, the trooper himself becomes the weapon and for this purpose, the Old Heads saw J. J. King's aggressive, calm, intuitive attraction to the fight; his proficiency in killing other human beings; and his bloodlust as rare and precious gifts from the Lord.

King learned to dominate the Bloodline under the command of General John J. (Black Jack) Pershing in the Mexican Punitive Expedition to capture or kill the revolutionary border renegade, Pancho Villa, after his raid on the US Armory at Columbus, New Mexico.

Trooper King grew to love the rough life and camaraderie of the horse soldier, reveled in the adrenalin-fueled thrill of the cavalry charge, and savored the reward of the gleaming crimson fan broadcast by the arching path of his righteous saber. Everyone agreed that it was a tragic loss to the Seventh when Trooper King received life-threatening, debilitating wounds in the final days of the Mexican incursion and was mustered out of the service at Fort Bliss, ending his military career before the beginning of America's first war in France.

Alone and adrift, embittered by his fate, the attitude and swagger that made King a popular personality in the Seventh, seemed to attract trouble in the civilian world. After gutting a drunken stranger in a life-or-death brawl in a Fort Worth saloon, he traveled west to escape potential legal entanglements and found work as a wildcatter's roughneck in the North Texas fields. He believed it a Providence of God when he met Vera Langford one Wednesday night at the First Baptist Church in Ranger.

It was there, broken and desperate, that he found the Lord, repented from his violent ways, submitted himself to the authority of Jesus Christ, and was washed clean in the blood of the Lamb. Less than a year later, J. J. and Vera were married, and with the help of his father-in-law, he built a new career in the infant oil field service industry. After some success and the birth of Marion, the Kings moved on to Lubbock for J. J.'s geological engineering studies at Texas Technological College, and in turn, he undertook a petroleum prospecting opportunity in Midland.

For J. J. King, the birth of his daughter, Marion, the stable livelihood and home that had eluded his line of Scots-Irish emigrants since their escape from Ireland, confirmed the reality of the Divine Counselor, and set the course for the remainder of his life.

• • •

"Mr. King, I am here this evening to ask for Marion's hand in marriage," said the young suitor to the aging King, who seemed anything but happy with the request. "I know that as you consider my request you will want to understand how I intend to provide for her financially and for any children the Lord may choose to bless our union with, and also sir, where we will make our home. I confess that earning a livelihood has not been my foremost consideration. My focus to this point has been on winning souls for the Kingdom, and I am supported by a modest monthly stipend from the Methodist Mission Society and the offerings of the faithful who attend our services…"

King leapt ahead in his mind to the rootless life of poverty and want that penniless Preacher Rixon was proposing for his daughter, and he began to seethe. "The nerve of it, and he calls himself a Christian," he thought as he focused on controlling his anger and hearing the young man out.

"My assets include a modest savings account, my personal automobile, and I hold a mortgage on a small home on twenty acres just north of Dallas. I grew up there, it was Mother and Father's before their passing, and when I'm not traveling, I live and work there."

"Mr. Rixon, do you realize just how preposterous you proposition is? The assets you've described are barely enough to support one person, let alone a wife, and you dare speak of children? Marion is twenty-five and her childbearing years will soon be behind her. By the time you are financially ready to bring a child into the world, Marion could well be unable to bear children without severe risk," said the protective King. "Have you truly considered your position?"

"Mr. King, this isn't an easy decision for me, and truly, had it not been for a strong leading from the Lord and the unique qualities of your daughter, I would never have considered marriage, especially at my age. I am thirty-six, sir, a celibate bachelor, set in my ways and joyous in my solitary labor for the Lord. But since our work together during the revival meetings last summer, Marion has been on my mind nearly constantly and I have considered the potential of our marriage at length. The financial consequences for Marion and me, the changes marriage would impose on the ministry I have spent my life building, and the portent for extending the power of the faith beyond our lifetime, carried forward by our children into the distant future. These things have been foremost in my mind," said a sincere and humble Rixon. "The root of this contemplation is the joy I feel when I am with your daughter, sir. It is the nearest thing to heaven I have experienced in my life, and I believe our combined joy grows out of our shared love for the Lord and the desire to serve Him in the way He requires.

"Sir, as firmly as I believe that the Lord's plan is for Marion and me to join as husband and wife, I also believe that He is changing our field of service and, if you grant Marion's hand, I intend to leave full-time service to seek secular employment locally. We will make a Christian home here in Midland so that the children will have permanent roots and so that you and Mrs. King will be a vital part of their lives; your values will become part of their upbringing as well.

"Finally, sir, though I am a man of studious and reasoned faith and not sympathetic to the hysterics of those weaker pilgrims who demand the theater of public spectacle to underwrite their experience, I also do not doubt the ability of God Almighty to act independently in the physical world. As such, I must confess to you that I have experienced what I would say is a divine Vision, that of Marion and I becoming a part of the bloodline, the long line of love, which connects every believer to the origins of Christ Himself, beyond the beginning of time to the eternal mystery of the Trinity. In the vision, I was shown that it is imperative for each generation to weave their lives and faith into the slender crimson thread that links us all, and that if one generation fails in their duty, the continuity of the line could be broken, dooming millions to an eternity in the fires of perdition."

King's racing mind was suspended, held still and silent by the curious language his future son-in-law had used to describe his vision. "Please excuse me, Mr. Rixon, but did I hear you say something about a bloodline?" he asked.

The two men spoke long into the night, and penniless Pastor Rixon unlocked the wealth of heaven for J. J. King, and exchanged the law for love. Pastor Rixon freed J. J. from his prison of grief and fear rooted in the dire circumstance of his youth, the unknown fate of his family, the trauma of his bloody combat in Mexico, and the guilt of the killing in Fort Worth. After serious, prayerful consideration, the elders of Midland's Fairmont Church of Christ granted the special request of the King family. With the congregation as J. J.'s witness, Vera and Marion stood by as Pastor Rixon immersed J. J., and he arose a changed man and joyous follower of Jesus Christ. J. J. gave Marion away with pride to his new son-in-law only six months later.

Over the following months, J. J. and Randy became close as they worked to find employment for Randy with the celebrated Parker Exploration Company of Odessa and then participated in establishing the modest Rixon household on the southern edge of Odessa, a short drive away from Randy's work.

The family was struck a final time by unimagined tragedy the following January when both Vera and J. J. were lost to a regional outbreak of a virulent strain of influenza against which there was no defense. At her parents' funeral, Marion gave testimony that her father had been released from the cares of life to live happily in the grace of the Lord. Pastor Randy spoke passionately about the long line of love that connected Vera and J. J. King to the Lord, and how time and circumstance had allowed the couple to do the work of a lifetime in only a few months, contributing fully to the legacy and passing it on to Marion and himself. And that night, somewhere beyond the field of time and in the presence of angels, Vera and J. J. came into possession of all knowledge and slept well, at peace with eternity and their anticipation of the coming trumpets of the Lord.

7

MOJO MAN

The sky is the dominant feature in West Texas, clear, deep blue, and infinite. It's what people remember the most when they leave, what brings them back if they come, and what David Rixon thought was the very best thing about being the son of Marion Rixon. His mother was a stargazer, who had seen the creative hand of the Lord at work during her freshman astronomy class at Texas Tech. David remembered the time when his daddy and mama loaded all the kids into the pickup, and they went camping for a week in the Davis Mountains. His mama explained about the McDonald Observatory, and said the Otto Struve telescope was the second-largest astronomical instrument in the world. She said the astronomers there could see all the way back to the beginning of the universe, when the Lord said, "Let there be light," and time began and everything there ever was, was created in a flash.

• • •

His first night on the rig, David noticed that the cosmos was obliterated by the blinding derrick lights of Parker 16, designed by Bobby Parker himself to "operate aggressively, twenty-four/seven, in the most hostile exploratory environments on the planet." Therefore, he thought, nighttime on a West Texas drilling rig is a whole lot like daytime except it's a little cooler. He was grateful for the temperature drop as he emptied the last of twenty sacks of blended Wyoming bentonite into the hopper to keep the mud pump charged. He mentally calculated that since each sack weighed fifty pounds, he would move a thousand pounds an hour, eight thousand pounds in a shift, and forty thousand pounds in a five-day week, in addition to everything else expected of a platform roustabout. The upside, thought David, was that he was drawing the pay of a full-time hand and that Papa Joe, the rig manager, had gotten permission from Mr. Parker for him to take a "vacation" for two-a-day drills and then come back as a "stringer" when school started and the season was under way. On his way back to Odessa the next morning, David also thought that playing football for the Odessa Permian Panthers would be a walk in the park after working a summer on Parker 16.

August that year was unusually hot, and the coaching staff of the Permian Panthers decided that the two-a-day drills would be early and late, sparing the kids the midday heat and hitting it hard under the lights. "The seniors look good, mostly in shape, probably jobs in the oil patch," thought Will Robinson as he assigned equipment to late arrivals. Checking names off the roster, he was missing David Rixon. "Poor kid," he thought. "Lost his whole family a couple of years back. Only he and his dog made it."

Robinson scanned the room for Rixon. The players were in various stages of dress, catching up with each other from their summer break and dreading the conditioning drills they knew would come.

"Anybody seen Rixon?" he asked the room.

The silence told him that David was a no-show, but on his way to the office, Robinson spotted a lone figure running the stands in Panther Stadium. He walked out to see who it was and found David Rixon, bathed in sweat, completing the high circuit.

"Rixon! Where the hell you been? The team's suitin' up. We start calisthenics in fifteen minutes!"

"Sorry, Coach Robinson," said David. "I got here early and didn't know what to do, so I just started running the stands to get ready for practice."

Robinson noticed Rixon's well-developed torso immediately. "Well, get on to the field house son, draw your gear. We've got a lotta work to do today." As David grabbed his shirt and started to the field house, Robinson looked on with surprise and said to himself, "A little short maybe, but if the kid can hit, I think I just found myself a new middle linebacker."

Walking into the Panther field house that morning was like entering a new world for the sixteen-year-old. It was charged with the pungent odor of sweat, camphor, fear, and the sights and sounds of uncertain masculinity everywhere he looked. He was directed to the equipment locker where the trainer loaded him down with his practice uniform, jock, socks, pads, helmet, and shoes. Then he pointed David to the locker with the word "RIXON" written on athletic tape in black ink, just like the one on the front of his beat-up helmet. Having shared a bedroom and bath with three brothers, David never thought of himself as being a modest person, but changing clothes in the locker room with dozens of complete strangers embarrassed him somehow. So he took care to conceal his nakedness as much as possible while watching wide-eyed at the nonchalance of the other young athletes as they walked about and chatted as if they were dressed in their Sunday best.

The trainer walked into the middle of the room, proudly blew his shiny chrome Acme Thunderer; "BREET! Five minutes! Coach wants ya'll on the front deck in five minutes!" The crowd began to thin, David went with the flow and found himself a spot on the concrete deck, facing the freshly cut practice field.

Panther head coach Walt Calvert was a tall, lean man with a military bearing, kind gray eyes, and a deep baritone voice. He jogged out of the field house dressed in black coaching shorts, a crisp white Panther golf shirt, a black Permian ball cap, and a white lanyard with a nickel-plated Acme Thunderer whistle dangling around his neck. He made his way through the crown and to the center of the concrete slab to address the squad.

"Good morning, Gentlemen," he said in a businesslike tone with a pose that was nether closed nor open. "Welcome to the Permian Panther Training Camp!" There was a slight, though apprehensive, cheer from the audience.

"This morning I want to speak with you about winning, about preparing to win, and what will be required of you if you desire to become a member of the Panther football club." Even at 7:00 a.m., the Texas sun was starting to bite, and several would-be Panthers moved along with the shade.

"This game is about winning, not losing. The sting of a loss, the stench of a losing locker room, the shame of going back to your classes on Monday after you've squandered the honor given to you on Friday by your school, by your classmates, is just not anything I am wiling for you to endure. In your entire life, Gentlemen, nothing, NOTHING, should be more repulsive to you than the stigma of being known as a good loser." He paused, making sharp eye contact with the team.

"Beginning now and over the next ten days and twenty practices, you shall be taught the mechanics of victory and you shall come to despise the very thought of being a loser.

"Winning isn't something you do some of the time. It's what you do all the time; every hour of every day. It must become your way of life; victory must become your testament of faith. It must be studied. It must be practiced. It must be honed and habituated, and you must learn to pay the price every single day for the rest of your entire life!

"Anything less is what a loser does. And, Gentlemen, no man—no real man that I ever knew, certainly no American—ever trained to do anything but win and isn't satisfied with second place in anything!" He paused long and deliberately, as he swept his gaze over the squad.

"HEADS UP!" he commanded at the top of his lungs and the bottom of his range, causing the athletes to visibly tense. "Look me in the eye," he said, gesturing to his steel-gray gaze. "No one gives you a thing in this life. If you want it, you've got to earn it, and if you want one of these," he said, holding up a new Panther game jersey, "you're going to have to take it for yourself out there on that field," he said, pointing to the simmering patch of withering turf.

"Take a breath," he said theatrically. "What's that smell?" he asked, looking at the climbing sun. "Go ahead, take a real deep breath." Pause. "Gentlemen, that's the smell of opportunity."

Leveling his gaze once more, and bringing his words from deep in his gut, he said, "The road to victory starts out there. Courage, discipline, self-denial, valor; that's what you'll find on the road, and you'll take them with you forever. But never forget your mission, never lose your direction, you're on the road to VICTORY! Now let's get moving; BREET!" And with the sound of his gleaming Acme Thunderer, he sent them out for first-day calisthenics.

Permian was the second high school created by the Ector County Independent School District and was only three years into their athletic program that summer. Most of the upper classmen on the squad were transfers, Odessa High Broncos, who had decided among themselves that the starting positions were theirs already, and that the most important thing for them to do during two-a-days was to conserve themselves for the regular season. David Rixon hadn't been party to those deliberations.

"Goddamnit, Peterson! Rixon's blowin' by you on every down!" screamed Coach Calvert, bathed in sweat and furious at his half-speed performance.

"I thought you said you were a football player. Did I hear you wrong, Peterson? Did I have wax in my ears?" he said getting into the tackle's red sweaty face.

"Rixon's made the play on the last five downs. Rixon is your man, Peterson. YOUR MAN IS KICKING YOUR ASS!"

"Line up on the goal line! EVERYONE!" he commanded and the seventy-plus squad complied.

Winded, hot, and dying for a drink of water, they waited for their orders while searching for a cool breeze, but the only wind blowing was hot and it came out of Calvert's mouth.

"Rixon! Come here!" David complied and jogged overt to join Calvert in front of the team and coaching staff.

"Good hustle, Rixon," said Coach. "Take your hat off, son, take a knee. Trainer! Bring this man some water!" he said, focusing his eyes on the balance of the squad.

"Now I don't know which one of you organized this, and I don't care," he said loudly, walking up the line of ballplayers, drenched with sweat and dread. "Rixon here is the only man among you who has put himself fully into this workout, and every damned one of you ought to be ashamed. Your honor should have kept you from it. Honor. Do you have any honor?" Silence. "HEADS UP! I'm talking to you! I said, DO YOU HAVE ANY HONOR?"

"YES, COACH!" came the rapid and ragged reply.

"Two hours ago I told you all that if you wanted to become a member of this club, that you'd have to earn it, and right now I'm feeling shortchanged, I'm feeling RIPPED OFF and, Gentlemen, it's time for you to start paying your bill," he said, taking a posture that conveyed his resolve.

"On the line, Rixon!" David rose immediately, tossed the unopened water bottle back to the trainer, and put his helmet on while jogging to the goal line. "Sprint to the fifty, on the whistle. BREET!"

Thirty minutes and twenty fifty-yard sprints later, the distress of the squad was clear, and repentance among the conspirators was complete. "Huddle up, men!" said Coach, directing the trainers to pass out the water to his team, stifled by the oppressive heat.

"Listen up!" Slight pause. "A team is a chain made of men. Every member of the team must be able to rely on every other member or the chain breaks and the team loses," said Calvert. "You've got to believe in each other. You've gotta have faith that the man on either side of you will do his job even when everything is blowing apart. Faith isn't a fairytale. Faith, Gentlemen, faith is all there is. Building faith in each other, in the team, is done little by little, over time, right here on this patch of dirt, so that when you get into a game situation, you'll know your teammates will do their jobs, and you can have the faith to do yours," he said, placing his hand on Peterson's shoulder pads.

"This is only the first practice. There are nineteen more ahead, so from here on out, I want your word of honor that you will put yourself fully into this work, that you will dedicate yourselves to building faith in your teammates and faith in this team. DO I HAVE YOUR WORD?"

"YES, COACH!" came the unified response.

"Then what are you waitin' for? Hit the showers!"

After their cooldown and showers, Rodney Peterson summoned his ex-Bronco pals for a ride to lunch at Tommy's Drive-In in his daddy's nearly new Pontiac Star Chief. "Rixon has got to be taught a lesson. We gotta put him in his place, and we gotta do it tonight!" he said emphatically to his coconspirators as they devoured their burgers.

"I don't see the problem, Rod," said Jimmy Kellogg, popping a Tater Tot into his mouth. "Hell, you're a foot taller 'n' thirty pounds heavier—he's a gnat. Why don't ya just swat him?" Laughter all around.

"I'm tellin' you guys, Rixon's trouble and we gotta nip it in the bud!" said the rock-solid center of the defensive line, cheeks and nose beginning to flush at the playful mockery of his cohorts.

Kenny and James Ray Dockins, the gigantic twins who held down the left side of the line, were quietly assessing the situation, amused with Rodney Peterson's angst, and taking great pleasure in the debate.

"Rod's got a point. He made us *all* look bad, like he was some sorta stud athlete or somethin'. Hell, man, it's the first day 'n' the crazy sombitch was acting like it was the state championship or sump-thin," prodded Kenny, certain that his brother would back his play. Even in the case of identical twins, there is a leader and a follower, and James Ray was definitely not the leader.

"But he didn't take a drink," said Jimmy, sucking down his Dr. Pepper. "When we were on the line, dying of thirst and the trainer handed him the water, he never took a drink. Would you have done that? I woulda' guzzled it, poured it all over my head, and flipped off all 'a' you sweaty bastards!" Laughter again.

"Cut the shit, Jimmy. Are you guys with me or not?" demanded Peterson of is cadre, not seeing any humor in the situation.

The season's first full pad contact drills occurred that evening and when the lights came on at dusk it was clear that the ex-Broncos were united in having their way with David Rixon.

"Peterson and his boys are puttin' it on Rixon pretty hard, don't ya think, Coach?" said Robinson quietly to Calvert.

"No harder than Midland Lee would," replied Calvert referring to their archrival. "If Rixon's gonna make the squad, he's gonna hafta earn their respect, so keep your whistle ready, and let's just let 'em work through it," he continued, allowing the scrimmage to continue apace.

"You like livin' with them pepperbellies, do ya, Rixon?" said Rod Peterson to David, inserting the verbal needle into his ear at the bottom of the pile. "Them greasers really adopt you, little man? What yer mamasita feed ya down there in Mezkin town, Scarface? Jalapenos? Ahahaha."

Up from the pile, walking back to his position, the sharp words hung heavy in David's conscious mind, cutting, burning, mocking his precious…"mi familia!"

"POP! CRACK! WHEEZE!"

The coaching staff was shocked to see a human arc of black and white ground through the rock-solid upper body of Rodney Peterson as David Rixon, at full sprint, planted the crown of his helmet just below the unsuspecting tackle's solar plexus. He wrapped his arms around Peterson's waist, boosted him off his feet, drove the breath from his lungs, and planted him hard into the dusty Permian turf, WHAAOOP! The entire squad watched, transfixed by the spectacle.

A full count later, the squad erupted with fistfights all around. And in that instant, Rixon had bounced off Peterson's collapsed diaphragm and was upright, ready for the consequences of his action.

"BREET! BREET! BREET!" the Thunderers were sounding all over the field as the coaches rushed in to break up the fights, but they needn't have bothered with Rixon and Peterson, since every ounce of bad-boy swagger had been effectively driven from their star lineman. "Argh! Wheeze! Argh! Wheeze…"

As the trainers were helping the dazed Peterson get his breath back, the coaching staff decided to spend the rest of the evening on conditioning drills for the squad and had them running long into the cool of the West Texas night.

"I don't need to remind you it was your idea to let 'em work through it," said Coach Robinson with a slight smile. "You gotta admit though, it was a pretty decent tackle," he said, gently teasing the stoic Calvert, who held his reply for a long moment.

"Textbook," said Calvert, focusing hard on improving the physical condition of his very surprising team.

By the end of practice number eighteen, it was clear to the coaches and the team that Rod Peterson and David Rixon were the two best conditioned, most talented athletes on the squad.

"They're like yin and yang," explained Robinson. "Peterson's got the size and upper body strength, but Rixon's got agility, speed, and heart. I believe the kid would fight a buzz saw and probably win! They're both in peak condition, they're both aggressive, and they make a helluva one-two punch."

"That's the good news," said Coach Calvert to his staff. "The bad news is that we've also got two teams: Peterson's Bronco transfers and Rixon's Permian walk-ons, and everyone here knows they're at war. The tension in the locker room is thick as sweet crude, and its spreading beyond Peterson and Rixon. I broke up a fight after practice yesterday myself, in the showers of all places. Gentlemen, I need not remind you that a house divided shall not stand. This infighting, this enmity that Peterson and Rixon share, cannot continue into the season. So unless you can invent a way to unify this team, we're going to have to cut someone—either Peterson or Rixon."

The discussion was impassioned and went long after midnight. The players were weighed and measured against Coach Calvert's offensive philosophy and Coach Robinson's defensive imperatives, and in the end, sadly, David Rixon didn't make the cut. Coach Robinson volunteered to tell David before practice on Monday.

Sunday morning found David stiff and bruised from the hard contact of eighteen consecutive workouts and he welcomed a day of rest. After breakfast, the Gonzales family gathered their Bibles and began the Sunday morning commute to worship at the Quad Six, but it was a somber journey with no joy to be found. Since the passing of the Rixon family, the fire had gone out of the congregation and out of Pastor Joe as well. He had spent the previous months trying to force his enthusiasm by prayer, fasting, and study, but nothing seemed to work. Most helpful had been the mentoring of his adoptive son into manhood. To see his rapid maturation on the rig that summer and then during his football training had been a pleasure. He was so much like his father, but with the tenderness of his mother. But even then, there was a hollowness in his soul that caused a disconnect with the Lord. Something had to be done.

"Turn in your Bibles, please, to the fifth chapter of Matthew, where I will be reading the words of Jesus starting with verse twenty-one," said Pastor Joe meekly, preparing the congregation for his sermon.

"You have heard that it was said to those of ancient times, You shall not murder; and Whoever murders shall be liable for judgment. But I say to you that if you are angry with a brother or sister, you will be liable for judgment; and if you insult a brother or sister, you will be liable for council; and if you say You fool. You shall be liable to the hell of fire. So when you are offering your gift at the altar, if you remember that your brother or sister has something against you, leave your gift there before the altar and go; first be reconciled with your brother or sister and then come and offer your gift.

"These are the eternal words of Almighty God. Please take them to your heart with reverence."

Pastor Joe quietly closed his Bible, moved out from behind the lectern, and placed his battered scripture on the bare barn floor before the altar that he and Randy Rixon had built together the summer of their first vacation Bible school. From there he moved a few more steps to gently touch the old Wurlitzer that had remained silent since Marion Rixon's death. He turned to face the people.

"Perdóname mis amigos, pero el Señor me ha llevado a hablar con usted en engldh esta mañana." he began humbly in Spanish and continued in English. "We are here together in the sight of God, Latino and Anglo, yes, but more than that, we are Christians. Always remember that we are all the same in the eyes of the Lord," he said with a smile, looking up through the dusty rafters as if to heaven itself.

"I am heavy in my heart this morning. It is no easy thing for a proud man to confess a flaw, a fault, a sin. But that is what I must do today—for you, for myself, and for the Lord," he said straightening his posture. "We Latinos started worshiping the Lord first at the Quad Six. It was a place only for the beasts, and we came together to made it a place of love. When the Rixons came, I was happy for their work, for their help, for their strong faith in the Lord. But in my heart, in the place of secrets that many men keep, I grew jealous of Pastor Randy. I did not want more Anglos worshiping with Latinos in this place. The place was sacred, set aside for la raza, the race, and it hurt to see so many of you Anglos here. So I began to silently murder Pastor Randy, Sister Marion, and all of you Anglos in my heart. I wanted you to leave us, to find your own place and get away from here! But you never would, and I held a dark malice for you in my place of secrets."

He turned to face David and the congregation, and going down on his knees, he said, "And then the night of the accident! It was as if God had answered…" He bowed and wept. "Before God—and to you all and to you, David—I confess this secret sin and ask for your forgiveness and the chance to reconcile with my church and my son." Lowering his head, he sank to his knees. Sobs of grief flowing free, he sobbed, "Mi familia!"

David rushed to embrace his father. "Mi papa!" he whispered in his ear, as Paulina, Isabel, and the entire church body moved to his comfort. Sobs and tears were shared by all. Latinos and Anglos were embracing, the love of the Lord rained down, and the wind of the Holy Spirit blew, making tender the hard hearts of the two peoples who became one church that day, one people unified through the grace of Jesus Christ.

No mortal man may know the truth of another's heart, but the Lord of Hosts saw the flame of agape glowing bright in the darkness of south Odessa and wept great tears of divine joy as the demons of hell were sent howling by the words and deeds of a righteous man. "*Bien hecho Pastor Joe, bien hecho mi siervo bueno y fiel.*" On His command, the guardian angels of La Palabra en la Iglesia de Cristo Misionera Biblia captured the precious tears of God, brought them from the eternity of heaven into the field of time, and anointed Pastor Joe in an instant, filling him with the divine power of discernment and the gift of supernatural reconciliation.

Later that same evening, Pastor Joe, Paulina, and David knocked on the front door of Janet and Tommy Peterson and asked for a moment with them and their son, Rodney.

"Mr. and Mrs. Peterson, we are David's adoptive parents, and we wanted to introduce ourselves, because the Lord has impressed on our hearts that our sons are to have a great future together but are in jeopardy of missing it because of the fearsome demons of jealousy and racial hatred."

As Pastor Joe began to reveal the Lord's vision for the lives of their sons, their invisible guardians embraced and with great joy sang praises to the Lord that touched the lives of many in that time and for other times to come.

David wholly confessed his anger with Rod and sincerely apologized for spearing him with his headgear the first night of contact drills. Rodney bowed his head and said that he had been afraid that David had exposed his plan of sloth to Coach Calvert, and that he was embarrassed by his name-calling, that he didn't mean it, and that he had already forgotten about the spearing.

"I only got what I deserved, David." He grinned, holding out his hand.

After a time, the grown-ups shared cake, coffee, and conversation, while the two boys were laughing and talking about two-a-days and the Panthers, and speculating about who would make the team and who would be cut.

"You two should go see Coach Calvert first thing in the morning," suggested Tommy Peterson, who had heard of the coaches' difficulty making the cut list that morning at church. "I'm sure he'll be happy to know that his two star players have buried the hatchet, and that everyone's on the same page now—thanks to Pastor Joe and Mrs. Paulina. In fact, Pastor, if you have the time, it might be good if you went with the boys and explained things to Coach Calvert as you did here this evening. You know the clarity of honest communication can make a world of difference. I'm pretty sure Coach will be in his office by seven."

• • •

The arc of a lifetime bends in the favor of a strong man who loves the Lord. Other souls are attracted, intersect, and intertwine, tracing their trajectory, their sure path, growing close, becoming community, and over time extended family. Sixteen months later, Rod and Rix had become the solid foundation of the Permian defense, the hope for the new season, Christian leaders in their school, inseparable friends, and Jose Gonzales had become the first chaplain of the Odessa Permian Panthers. The opportunity to serve the young men in the community pleased Pastor Joe greatly.

Most people in Odessa were unaware that the Gonzales family traced its roots in Ector County to 1845, when Mexican Colonel Juan de Gonzales received a 640-acre land grant to for his participation with the Army of the Republic of Texas in the Goliad Campaign. More specifically, the award recognized his moral clarity and the valor of his actions in assisting the "Angel of Goliad," Francita Alavez, in the rescue of a significant number of Texians from murder by shot, club, and knife. The slaughter that took the lives of more than three hundred prisoners of war, was dishonorably ordered by General Antonio Lopez de Santa Anna, then serving also as the president of Mexico.

Family lore, substantiated more or less by the details from de Gonzales's field diary, had it that he was a colonial military officer, educated in Spain. He had pledged his allegiance to the new Mexican Republic in order to escape the feudal system imposed by the Spanish Crown and because of his ascension to the ideal of *liberté, égalité, fraternité* (liberty, equality, and fraternity), which informed the French Revolution.

Toward those ends, he willingly served under the command of General Santa Anna until he exposed himself as a despot in waiting who, under the coercion of arms, convinced the new Mexican Congress to bypass the people and directly elect him president. With that power, he then ordered the disarmament of the civic militia, revoked the constitution, voided all constitutional law, suspended the authority of the congress itself, and ordered the death of anyone who dared to oppose his rule.

The shocking revelation of Santa Anna's intent for the people of Mexico induced eleven Mexican states to rebel against his new oppression and personally horrified Colonel de Gonzales. During the ensuing turmoil, he was able to leave the direct command of Santa Anna and align himself with General Jose de Urrea in an effort to quell the rebellion in the State of Tejas, led by English colonists who had immigrated to Mexico seeking liberty and land while the liberal constitution was in force.

Santa Anna moved savagely against the Texian rebels at San Antonio. Firsthand accounts of his butchery and bodily desecration of Travis and the defenders of the Alamo fueled a resolve in the heart of de Gonzales to resist Santa Anna's authority in every way possible within the honor code that bound the Mexican officer corps.

Notes from his diary indicated that General Urrea had taken a different path than Santa Anna and accepted terms for an honorable surrender from the Texian Colonel Fannin after a standoff was reached in the battle of Coleto Creek, thereby protecting the survivors under the honor code extended to legitimate prisoners of war. On hearing of Urrea's insubordination, Santa Anna summoned him to San Antonio, while secretly ordering Gonzales and others to execute Fannin and the survivors of Goliad and burn their bodies as he had the defenders of the Alamo.

"It was a decision demanded by honor, made with the realization that the Texians were the last hope of this land for liberty and prosperity," wrote de Gonzales. He had used his rank to arrange the transfer of over one hundred condemned soldiers and civilians to the care of Francita Alavez, who used her influence with Mexican civil officials to secure their release.

After facilitating their escape, de Gonzales used intermediaries to contact his former schoolmate, Lorenzo de Zavala, interim vice president of the Republic of Texas, to arrange favorable surrender terms for himself and his men. He was surprised to receive an invitation from President Burnett himself to join Sam Houston in a collaborative effort against Santa Anna, which culminated in their decisive victory at San Jacinto.

The harsh price of de Gonzales's decision was the loss of his estate near Veracruz, his fortune, his position, and his family, all confiscated or burned by Santa Anna during the war. Therefore, the Congress of the Republic of Texas awarded de Gonzales a compensatory section of semiarid west Texas scrub in what would one day become Ector County.

Over the decades, the Gonzales family took root and cultivated the 640 acres, naming their home "Granjas Agradables," or "Pleasant Farms," a place of liberty, equality, and fraternity that they had called home for over one hundred years.

"Papa, why do we have to work so hard?" asked David one warm day as he and Pastor Joe were weeding the spring garden.

"The scriptures tell us that we will always need to work, David. It is the fate of the descendants of Adam to earn our livelihood by the sweat of our brow," Joe offered, while working his grubbing hoe around the roots of the tender new corn stalks.

"But Rod's dad always wears white shirts and suits and never seems to even get dirty, and they live in a brick house with a swimming pool, and Rod doesn't even have to cut the lawn. Is he not a son of Adam as well?" asked David, on his knees, pulling small weeds from in between the baby watermelons.

After finishing the last of the corn, Joe stood, leaned on the handle of the grubbing hoe to survey his two-acre truck patch and placed his hand on David's shoulder. "Let's take a break, my son. I could use a cool drink." And they walked to the deep shady back porch of the neat little frame house that had been home to four previous generations of the Gonzales family and to the waiting tray of lemonade Isabel had placed for them.

Sitting in cool shade with Travis at his feet, Pastor Joe took a long drink. "David, you are nearly a man and are soon to leave us to go out into the world to make a home and family of your own. It is time you understood some basic truths about life in the United States. The Founding Fathers recognized that our human rights come to us from God, and they created America's founding documents to protect the people and their rights from a potentially dangerous government. Among those rights are life, liberty, and the pursuit of happiness. How a man decides to make use of these guarantees is what defines his place and gives him his future in America.

"I am just an old farmer, my son, and only know what I read in the newspaper, but there seem to be two main paths that ordinary citizens like us may take to find our way in America today. They both appear to be good, except when you look ahead and see that they lead to two different places, one to freedom and the other to slavery, the cruel slavery of long-term debt.

"Remember the story of Joseph and his coat of many colors? The Bible tells us that there was a famine in the land, and the entire nation of Israel had to sell itself into slavery for enough food to survive. Even though Joseph was the master of Egypt and welcomed them, their sovereign debt held the nation captive long after the deaths of those who made the agreements. The future rulers of Egypt were not so kind to the Jews. It is that sort of long-term financial obligation that we have always avoided in the Gonzales family."

"You asked me about the Petersons earlier, and my reply is that in your life there will always be men of greater and lesser rank, and it is fruitless to compare yourself to them. As far as I know, Mr. Peterson is a good man, the well-to-do proprietor of Peterson Pontiac and GMC, and president of the Odessa Permian Quarterback Club. But this is his public face, what he wants us to know. How do you suppose walking a mile in his shoes might feel if you knew everything he does? Maybe not so good I think—maybe no so free," he said, scratching Travis behind her ears.

Refreshed, David and Pastor Joe walked together, admiring the long straight rows of new corn, okra, potatoes, carrots, and watermelon, noting the cattle drinking at the stock pond, briefly inspecting the cluster of white beehives at the far end of the garden, and making their way to the equipment shed and farm office.

Taking his seat behind the ancient wooden desk, he invited David to join him. "I know that the time since you lost your family has been chaotic, David, but you have been our son for almost three years now and are no longer a little boy. You are doing better in school and sports than anyone ever expected, and we are all so very pleased. You are becoming a fine young man. This is a large undertaking but you should also begin thinking about what you might do after high school," he said, rolling out a large map on the old oak desk.

"You know the story of how we came to be here at Pleasant Farms, but you've never seen the map of the original land grant. The farm is our anchor, David; it gives us a safe place to live and provides a livelihood that no one can take away. Without the land, we would be at the mercy of the mindless forces of the marketplace that make it very difficult for a man to remain free and do the things he must to be a good husband and father and care for his family and his neighbors."

"Papa, when you say it's difficult to remain free, that we are in danger of becoming slaves, what do you mean? Didn't the civil war end slavery in America?" asked David, examining the plat, nudging Travis with his foot under the desk.

"There are many ways for a man to become a slave in modern America, David, and most of them are entirely legal, but the result is the same; the loss of free will. For instance, let's say that you are a young man with a wife and child and you need to buy a house. What would you do?"

"I suppose I'd go to the bank and get a loan. Isn't that what everyone does?" replied David.

"Let's do a little math, David," said Pastor Joe, finding a small red book titled *Financial Constant Percent Amortization Tables* and handing it to David.

"The core problem for every father is how to be the priest, provider, and emancipator of his family. It's an important and demanding job David and one of the assets you'll need to be successful is a home of your own, so why don't you make a few notes, and we'll work through it together.

"Let's say that you are working for Parker Exploration, making a good wage, say forty-five hundred dollars a year. The government will take about twenty percent in taxes, so that leaves you thirty-six hundred dollars to provide for your family," he said as David began writing. "From that take the tithe for the Lord, and you have thirty-two hundred dollars a year for everything."

"Don't forget about savings, Papa," said David, working with the math. "Daddy always said that we needed to pay ourselves before anyone else. That leaves twenty-nine hundred dollars a year for me to raise my family."

"Great, David, you're catching on quickly!" said Pastor Joe, opening the *Odessa American*. "Let's focus on the house. Here's one in the Petersons' neighborhood, three bedrooms, two baths, two-car garage, with a swimming pool for thirty-two thousand, five hundred dollars.

"The bank will finance about eighty percent of the purchase price so let's pretend that you have a down payment of seven thousand dollars and you'll need a mortgage of twenty-five thousand, five hundred. The prime rate is around four percent, so David, what do you suppose the monthly payments will be?"

David wrote down the problem, consulted the little red book, and made a few calculations. "Papa, please check me, but I think the mortgage payment will be about one hundred twenty-one dollars a month for thirty years. That's about fourteen hundred fifty dollars a year for the house payment. That's nearly half of what I take home! And look at this, counting the down payment and interest, I would be paying over the term of the loan is nearly fifty-one thousand dollars for a thirty-two thousand dollar house! That's six and a half years of my working life more that the house is worth!" said David in amazement.

"Now do you see the trap?" asked Pastor Joe, smiling. "The sort of slavery I am speaking of is long-term debt. It's insidious and it's rampant in America, David. Now let's say there is a problem with the economy and you lose your job but the house payments never stop. What will you do?"

"I'd take any job I could get to support my family and keep my house," said David, sternly with a stiffened posture.

"Precisely, my son, and that is the final trap. Debt moves you out of control of your life, it damages your ability to fulfill your role as the father of your family and perhaps even moves you away from the will God has for your life. The apostle Paul writes of this in the fourth chapter of Philippians when he says that he has learned the secret of living with humble means and prosperity. We can do all things David with the hope and wisdom of Jesus."

Pastor Joe and David spent the rest of that warm Saturday in the farm office speaking of things that are the secret province of fathers and sons; work, money, poetry, romance, love, marriage, faith, sports, war, courage, and cowardice. They began their way to the house only at dusk when they heard Isabel call from the back porch.

"Papa, do you love Mama very much?" asked David as they left the inner sanctum of Pleasant Farms.

"David, I married the prettiest girl in Ector County," said Joe with a broad smile, remembering his first dance with Paulina at the Odessa USO the night before he boarded the train for the war in Europe.

"How did you know she was the girl for you?" asked David, watching the sun melting into the crimson stock pond just beyond the garden, Travis making one last inspection of the cattle at its edge.

"I saw it in her eyes. I recognized something. Maybe it was the Lord, maybe it was the angels, maybe it was me but I recognized her for who she truly was—mi esposa."

"Sorry, what's 'esposa'?" asked David, a bit embarrassed.

"Mi esposa" is my beloved, my wife, and we are truly going to have to focus on your Spanish!" said Joe, laughing, pulling David close, and ruffing up his hair. "Usted perezoso Americano!" Laughing together, they entered their home to family, supper, and the tender mercies of the Lord.

● ● ●

Seasons change abruptly in West Texas, and extreme weather is the ordinary course for a resilient and determined people. But no winter morning in living memory could match the biting extremes of that December day when the Odessa Permian Panthers met the Dallas Carter Cowboys for the University Interscholastic League 4A State Championship at the Darwin Lee Judge Memorial Stadium in Abilene.

The winter storm blew through New Mexico and past Odessa, sending strong wind, snow, and sleet along with the caravan of the Panther faithful east on US Highway 80 to cover the field with snow and create a frigid reception for their adversaries from Dallas.

Sissy Thompson had never been as far east as Abilene, and she was enjoying the ride. She spent the trip in the back of the Permian Black Jackets' bus listening to Becky Lowe and Chris Newman speculate about the game, the players, and the lives they would lead after high school.

"What about David Rixon?" asked Chris.

"Who would believe a football player could make straight A's?" replied Becky. "You think he's a nerd who just happens to wear a jock?" she said with a laugh, daring to slightly abuse the freedom of being so far from the scrutiny of her parents.

"What about you, Sissy? You're in Spanish with him—what's he like?" said Chris, steering the conversation away from their mildly dangerous friend.

"He's fluent," replied Sissy, cheeks flushing slightly. "He helps the other kids all the time, he's nice, and he isn't a nerd at all."

"Sissy Thompson, you're blushing!" teased Becky. "Are you two going together or something?"

"HEY, EVERYONE, SISSY THOMPSON AND DAVID RIXON ARE GOING STEADY!" she announced to the entire squad.

"Girls! What in heaven's name is going on back here?" asked their chaperone, Miss Mobley, approaching rapidly from the front of the bus. "Miss Lowe, would you please repeat what you were saying— we couldn't hear you clearly all the way in the front."

Shrinking into her seat, Becky became a mute.

"Miss Lowe, you were saying?"

"I said that Sissy and David Rixon are going steady," replied an embarrassed Becky.

"Is that true, Miss Thompson? Are you and Mr. Rixon going steady?"

"No, ma'am, it's not true at all," replied a vindicated Sissy Thompson.

"Miss Lowe, could you explain why you would say such a thing?"

"No, ma'am, I can't, it just sort of slipped out, I didn't mean to say it," said Becky wishing she could become one with the bus seat upholstery.

"Well then, do you suppose I should discuss this affliction with your mother? There are certain medical conditions that present symptoms of uncontrolled speech, and heaven knows we wouldn't want to take a chance with your health. Would we?"

"No, ma'am, it'll be fine. I mean, I'll tell Mama about it and she'll take me to the doctor," said a fully surrendered Becky.

"All right, girls, and please try to keep your voices down. We are coming into Abilene and the driver needs to concentrate," said Miss Mobley, moving back to her seat.

"I'm gonna get you for this," whispered Sissy to Becky.

"Come on, Sissy, I was just having some fun, and besides, David Rixon is boss. If you don't want him, you can give him to me!" replied Becky, laughing and transferring her mirth to Sissy, a hush falling over the bus as the driver slowed, approaching their destination.

From her perspective, Sissy thought Judge Stadium looked like an ocean liner trapped at the North Pole, stuck in the ice, and shrouded in a thick foggy freezing mist. As the driver navigated the treacherous approach, she was able to see that the architectural detail of the central façade was constructed of large gray cut stones rendered in the Neo Roman style. A four-story tall central arcade, featuring engaged columns of the Tuscan order, was punctuated with large statues of heroic Roman gladiators residing on the upper deck. Each statue was precisely aligned within the apex of each arch. From her Latin studies, Sissy recognized the inscription cut into the stones above their heads: "*BEATI PACIFICI, QUONIAM IPSI FILII DEI VOCABUNTUR,*" *Blessed Are the Peacemakers, for They Shall Be Called the Children of God.*

The bus came to an uncertain halt, the driver conversing briefly with a police officer and then with Miss Mobley.

"Girls, I have an announcement. The game doesn't start for four hours and the police have suggested that because of the weather we should move off the bus to the inside of the stadium entrance. It's enclosed and heated with access to the ladies' room. The school district is setting up tables and chairs where we can have our lunch out of the weather. This sounds like the best option to me, so unless there are any objections, we're going to do just that. Another thing, the people from Dallas Carter will be joining us, so I trust you will be on your best behavior."

As the Black Jackets began filing out of their bus, they noticed the two Panther team busses and an escort of cars, station wagons, and trucks moving to the team entrance on the opposite side of the arcade. Coach Calvert emerged from the lead bus and approached a red Chevrolet Suburban. He began talking with the men inside. "I don't know how we'll be able to play a game if the field is anything like this," said Calvert.

"Surely the school district has made provisions, Walt. I can't imagine they didn't know this was coming," commented Tommy Peterson, president of the Quarterback Club.

"Men, let's get inside and take a look for ourselves. Maybe we can find someone to answer a few questions," suggested Pastor Joe.

"The field is covered with several large tarps but our grounds crew tells me that the snow is so heavy and the surface is so slippery that they can't budge it, even with our landscaping tractors," said the apologetic AISD superintendent. "Do you men have any suggestions?"

There was a long pause in the conversation with no one even speculating on how to solve the problem until Pastor Joe broke the silence. "I can't promise anything, gentlemen, but maybe I can call in a favor and get some air support. Is there a telephone I can use?"

Less than an hour later a group of four military vehicles appeared out of the fog and approached the team entrance. The sergeant explained to the superintendent that he and his men were attached to the 317th Air Mobility Squadron and had been sent from Dyess Air Force Base to assess their situation. After a brief tour of the facility and some cryptic communication over a military transceiver, the sergeant beckoned the superintendent and coaches for the two teams.

"Gentlemen, if there are no objections; the commander has authorized a CH Forty-Seven cargo helicopter for the mission of clearing the snow from your field. What we'd like to try is to fly the bird low and slow over the field to see if the downdraft could move enough snow so that your tractors can get in and pull the tarp away."

Twenty minutes later the equipment was in position and the roar of the helicopter could be heard approaching the top of the upper deck. With a large crowd watching, the Boeing slowed to a hover just above the fifty-yard line and descended to a point deemed safe by the pilot, who then rotated the bird slowly, creating a near whiteout inside the stadium and removing enough snow from the field that the grounds crew could finally remove the covering.

"Hoover One, this is Snow Shoe," said the sergeant into the transceiver.

"Hoover, it looks like the field is clear; can you do something about the seating?"

Seconds later, Hoover One increased power to rise slightly and enlarged his rotation to include the bleachers of the large stadium oval, clearing them and propelling the accumulated snowdrifts over the lip of the upper safety railing.

"Hoover One, mission accomplished; you are authorized to clear and return to your duty station."

With hearty thanks from all concerned, the sergeant replied, "Sir, the men were wondering if it would be OK if we stuck around for the game. The commander says it's all right with him as long as we stay on the radio."

● ● ●

Of those who personally witnessed the game that day, it was Blackie Sherrod of the *Dallas Times Herald* who would come nearest to accurately recording the spectacle:

Never before in the history of Texas schoolboy football has the United States Air Force been called upon to make a field ready for play. But that is exactly what happened in Abilene Saturday afternoon as the Dallas Carter Cowboys and the Odessa Permian Panthers went to war on what was most reminiscent of the frozen fields of Bastogne during World War II's perilous Battle of the Bulge.

From the kickoff it was a matchup for mayhem as the wind, swirling snow, and treacherous footing reduced the potent offenses of both teams to straight-ahead ground-ponding assaults met head on by hardnosed defensive units that would have made General George Patton second-guess the value of the of the Sherman tank.

The game remained scoreless through halftime and deep into the fourth quarter, when bruised and battered Cowboy quarterback Larry Keen missed a handoff to fullback William Washington and was downed in his own end zone by Panther defensive standouts Rodney Peterson and James Kellogg, scoring two points for Odessa with less than two minutes remaining on the clock.

The ensuing free kick, also by QB Keen, caught a favorable gust and traveled south from the Cowboy twenty over the heads of the Panther defensive backs and was miraculously plucked by Keen himself from under a pile of muddied, bloodied, squirming players and downed less than a foot from the Panther goal line with only seconds remaining on the clock. This, folks, is what makes championship Texas high school football different from any other sport in the world.

Sensing a miracle salvation for himself and his team, the Cowboy head coach called his final time out with 00:28 remaining on the game clock and the "Guaranty Bank and Trust of Abilene" scoreboard told the rest of the story: Dallas 0, Odessa 2.

The deflated and frozen Panther defense huddled in their own end zone. "We're in the shit now!" said Kenny Dockins. "They gonna just punch it through like they been doin' all day, ain't no way we can hold 'em at six inches!"

"At least the footing's better here, it's frozen solid," said his slumping brother James Ray, with a little laugh, trying to look on the bright side but accidentally emphasizing the desperation of their circumstance.

"I think Big Willie cracked my front tooth," replied Kenny, spitting blood onto the frosty white turf. "He's a tough SOB. It'll be him 'at gets th' call. Shit! It's snowin' again."

"At least we'll be outta here and in the locker room, man I ain't never been this cold this long in my whole life," said Jimmy Kellogg, contributing his fair share to the malaise. "Rod, I really thought we had it, you 'n' me, buddy, one point each!"

Rodney Peterson didn't offer a reply, and then no one else said a word. They just concentrated on fighting the cold while they waited for David Rixon to return from his sideline coaches' conference.

Someone once observed that football is a game played by young men for old men; the young men play because they believe anything is possible, and the old men watch to remember a time before they knew the truth.

"Coach says goal line, eight-man front, backs on the line, pinch inside, and I'll back the down men," said the returning Rixon, noticing the palpable shift in the squad's mood.

Sensing that his teammates had given up, and after a moment of thought, he walked away, took his helmet off, and looked up beyond the snow. "Father, I dedicate the next twenty-eight seconds of my life to my parents, my brothers, and to Your Son, Jesus. Please give me the wisdom and strength to do my duty according to Your will. In Jesus's name, I pray. Amen."

Stepping briskly into the center of the huddle, he said, "PANTHERS, HEADS UP!" and punched Rod Peterson in his chest with his headgear.

"Mr. Peterson! What's that smell?" he said, looking over at a quizzical Jimmy Kellogg.

"Mr. Kellogg! Take a breath! Take a real deep breath!" he said, rapping the headgear of each member of the squad with his own, energizing them with his aggressive tone and linking them with his words to their first withering training camp under Coach Calvert.

"Gentlemen, that's the smell of opportunity!

"The road to victory ends right here!" he said, pointing to the six inches between the ball and the goal line. "Courage, discipline, self-denial, valor—hell, we got enough a that ta last a lifetime!

"Our mission for the next TWENTY-EIGHT SECONDS IS TO PUT THOSE BASTARDS ON THE BUS!" he said, pointing through the foggy mist to the distant Cowboy huddle.

"That's it! That's all we gotta do! This is what we've been working, sweating, and bleeding for two years!

"VICTORY! VICTORY! VICTORY! It's that far away!" he said holding his hands six inches apart in front of all their faces.

"Now let's get moving, let's get pissed off, let's get mean!

"WE'RE NOT GOING TO HOLD 'EM; WE'RE GONNA BLOW THOSE BASTARDS OFF THE LINE! This is our game! Let's show those candy-ass Dallas sonsabitches HOW WE PLAY BALL IN ODESSA!"

The dense fog had begun to condense and freeze on their steaming helmets when the Cowboys finally broke their huddle and moved hungrily toward the line, partially concealed by their steaming bodies and white breath, which mingled with the freezing mist to create an ethereal veil separating the teams at the line of scrimmage.

The linemen took their places, dug in, and an anticipatory silence hung in the air as David Rixon looked across the line into the eyes of quarterback Keen, and star fullback, William Washington.

Keen approached the line, checked the formation, shifted his running backs to the pro set, and assumed his position under the center and in control.

Timing the snap brilliantly, Rod Peterson launched himself into the line low, under the facemask of the center, and then explosively lifted the man off his feet, causing his right leg to impact the quarterback, who knocked the slippery ball into the air.

Big Willie Washington saw the fumble, made an athletic stutter step, sweeping low to retrieve the ball, and seeing the Odessa defense incredibly moving the line of scrimmage away from the goal line and toward him, made the instinctive decision to sprint to the flag. But he was forced inside by heads-up play from the outside defensive back. Only David Rixon stood between him and victory.

Keying on Washington from the start, Rixon was matching his trajectory and speed and calculating that the fullback would need to make a cut to the goal line, he focused on the whites of his eyes.

At the last possible moment, Washington assessed his chances, decided to drive through Rixon for the score, and head faked to the left. But David followed his eyes and impacted the charging back at full speed, driving his headgear low into his ribcage, under his shoulder pads, and wrapping his arms around his waist. Absorbing his forward momentum, David launched himself, Big Willie Washington, and the ball into a bone-shattering reverse arc that would see the second fumble of the play recovered by a dumbfounded James Ray Dockins, five yards north of the original line of scrimmage.

But the story from Abilene today wasn't just the weather, or a defense that didn't know when it was beaten, or the stellar play of college-bound athletes from both teams, any one of whom might be considered the most valuable in this contest.

In my mind the story has to be the leadership and heart of Permian linebacker David Rixon, the smallest warrior on the field, and nearly a foot shorter than the man he stopped nose to nose to secure the 4A title for Odessa. Rixon's refusal to surrender and inspired leadership of his team reminded many of us here today of

"Old Crock" McAuliffe's reply to the German surrender demand at Bastogne: Nuts!

It's that sort of independent, tough-minded courage, that gritty brand of combat leadership that we all celebrate today and of which every Texan, every American should be proud!

The final score from Darwin Lee Judge Memorial Stadium: the Odessa Permian Panthers 2, the Dallas Carter Cowboys 0.

8

PASCAL'S WAGER

With a less than stellar first year as a walk-on for Penn State's coach, Rip Engle, the fact that he was in uniform on the fifty-yard line of a packed Beaver Stadium doing a pregame warm-up with the Nittany Lions was a pure delight for David Rixon. It's a long way from Odessa, Texas, to University Park, Pennsylvania, and David's path to game day and dressing out in the blue and white was one of unbelievable coincidence and, in his view, Divine Providence.

The journey that began with his notoriety as an all-state line-backer at Odessa Permian, was accelerated by a chance introduction from Permian's defensive coordinator, Will Robinson, to Penn State's assistant coach, Joe Paterno, at the Cotton Bowl Classic in Dallas and became a surprising reality when it was determined that his academic prowess surpassed his athletic ability. And while Penn State's "Linebacker University" program seemed a glove fit for his athleticism and aggressive style of play, it was Coach Paterno's "Whole Person" mentorship program that stressed academics and a personal moral code, which confirmed for David that the Lord had deliberately placed him at Pennsylvania State University.

What David never knew was that after meeting Paterno in Dallas, Will Robinson had sent a follow-up letter to Penn's head coach, Rip Engle, enclosing letters of recommendation from David's teachers, coaches, and employer as well as press clippings about his parents' accident and his accomplishments on the field and in the class-room. Even though he was impressed, Engle believed that David was too slight for Division I play but sent his references to Penn's academic recruiter. He was astute enough to make the connection and arranged for David to receive the Robert (Bobby) Parker Scholarship for Engineering Excellence, which would allow David to attend Penn State free of charge. That he had made a place for himself on Coach Engle's team as a walk-on was an unexpected joy; a marvelous blessing from the Lord.

David first noticed Al Vazquez in freshman physics because he was the only Latino in the classroom and because he began quietly cursing in Spanish when their professor handed out the course syllabus.

"Sone de una perra este va a ser duro," Al said under his breath.

"It only looks that way now; it'll be OK once we get into it. We can form a study group if you want," replied David in a low whisper. With that, Al Vazquez and David Rixon became fast friends.

During the first year, David discovered that his primary passion was real-world application of math and science, while Al had fallen in love with political science, but they shared a common interest in literature and philosophy, so they arranged their schedule to enroll in Penn State's academic core classes and some popular electives.

"David, why did your father abandon his faith?" Al asked on their way to lunch one day after Philosophy 101, a monster class with over one hundred students.

"He never did, Al. Daddy was a solid Christian all his life," said David.

"But you said he was a Christian preacher, an evangelist when he met your mother, and after they married, he quit the church and went to work in the oil field."

David thought a moment and replied, "Oil field work was never his mission, Al, but Daddy always said that making a living for us kids, being with Mama full time, and teaching us about the Lord was a special gift of love and his revealed callinglove. And he never stopped sharing the good news about Jesus, Al."

"And your mother, David. You said her dream was to work for God on the Indian reservations, but she gave it up when she married your father. Did she hold her faith as well?"

"Mama had a personal relationship with Christ, Al, and shared her life with Him every day, especially her joys and concerns for us kids. She used to joke and say that instead of sending her to New Mexico to be with the Indians, the Lord sent her to Odessa and gave her a tribe of her own. She loved the Lord more than life, and it's a comfort for me to think of her and Daddy and my brothers together in heaven," said David with a misty smile.

"And you, David. After all that happened to you—the accident, having your family taken from you, being adopted, having to work as a roustabout while you were barely in high school, how did you maintain your faith in a god that would allow all that to happen?"

David closed his eyes for a moment, considered what he knew of Al and his family and the import of the conversation.

"Pascal's wager," he replied quietly.

"What? David, are you saying your faith is nothing more than a bet? Who is Pascal and what is his wager?"

"Al, I've had my doubts about even the existence of God. In fact, for a time after the accident, I had a lot of anger in my heart at God until I realized that if there were no God, then I was angry at someone who didn't exist for something He couldn't have done and, well, none of it made sense."

"I was looking through one of Daddy's old books on Christian apologetics and found that he had marked the section concerning Blaise Pascal's early work on decision theory. Do you know it?"

Al was engaged, looking directly at him. "What is it with you and math, Rixon? No, I've never heard of decision theory. Would you please enlighten me, Professor Dave? Is there an equation I should know? Will this be on the final?" he asked with a grin.

They were walking through the student union on their way to lunch and a few others were picking up on Al's "intellectual" conversation with one of Engle's "jocks," when David saw an opportunity for a little fun.

"Mire este Al, tocar amd tendremos un fer se ríe a expensas de los anglos," he whispered to Al in a sotto voce with a wink.

Standing erect in his finest imitation of their dapper and quasi-famous professor, Marvin Roseman, David stepped up on the large fireplace hearth, turned, and addressed Al and their eavesdroppers as if he were giving a professorial lecture.

"Ladies and Gentlemen, the very famous Blaise Pascal," he said, "writing" the name on his imaginary chalkboard, "lived in the middle 1600s in France and was a noted mathematician, philosopher, inventor, and adherent to the Catholic faith." Glancing up to see if anyone was listening, he continued.

"Pascal is remembered for his treatise on Christian Apologetics, known today as 'Pascal's Wager,'" writing again, "which states that even though the existence of God cannot be determined through reason, a person should live his life as though God exists. If the lake of fire is the eternal destination reserved for nonbelievers, then a life lived for Christ has everything to gain and nothing to lose." David again stood erect, looked up, and was surprised that a small group of half-smiling students had gathered around Al, waiting to share their joke so he continued.

"At his death in 1662, his unfinished notes, or Penesees, specifically number two twenty-three, concerning the wager," writing again, "were used by others as a basis for probability theory. It was the first known use of the concept of infinity, which was the forerunner of today's widely known philosophies of pragmatism and volunteerism."

Seeing the gathering crowd and his moment in the play, Al said loudly, "So, Professor, what does all this bullshit mean to us?" He spread his arms to include the onlookers, which prompted some in the crowd to broaden their smiles and laugh openly.

"Well, Mr. Vazquez," said David sincerely, his scarred face aglow with the radiance of an angel, "in lay terms, it means simply: what does it profit a man or woman if they should gain the whole world and lose their soul?"

A wave of divine silence washed over the dining room cafeteria that reminded David of how things were during winter's first snowfall in the high pines of the Davis Mountains. It held for an infinite moment until a young woman across the room dropped her fork and the clatter released everyone to their normal lunchtime conversation.

"Que era profunda mi amigo," said Al with a look of new respect in his eyes. "But can we get some lunch now, Professor? I'm starving, and I sure as hell don't want to lose my immortal soul for the lack of tacos and frijoles!"

As they ate together, laughing and talking about the prospect of the Nittany Lions beating the Ohio State Buckeyes on Saturday, David Rixon imagined that he and Al Vazquez would be friends for life. But they were young then and living in an easy time before the war.

• • •

"In the beginning there was no evil. Before the Creation there was only the ineffable, unified, One; what some have referred to as the Godhead. During Creation the Godhead came to exist as God in three parts: Light, known to the ancients as 'pleorma,' which is separated from the material world by a great barrier known as 'horos' and thereafter all that is or ever will be exists in two worlds—Light and Matter separated by the unbridgeable gulf.

"Earth came to be when the immeasurable forces of galactic chaos were guided to the task, not by the Light, but by a lesser deity, a shard of the original Godhead but devoid of purity and goodness.

"It was the demon god, Yahweh, who found the earth covered with water, without form and void. Concealed by darkness, Yahweh conjured a great wind to sweep over the face of the deep, sending half of the ocean to a secret place hidden within the earth, which caused the dry land to form. When the waters receded and the continents rose from their depths, he ignited the sun, and spun the earth on its axis to separate the light from the darkness. Yahweh called the light day and the darkness night. And there was evening and there was morning, the first day."

Professor Marvin B. Roseman, PhD, was the longtime chairman of the Anna and Walter B. Dorance School of Western Philosophy and Critical Thought. His claim to fame was that he had studied at Harvard with the semi-famous French deconstructivist Jacques Derrida, who he privately considered a pious wimp absent the backbone to walk his own talk. As a man of profound conviction, the fully tenured, and therefore fearless, Roseman had for more than a decade reserved as his personal domain all sections of Philosophy 101, Introduction to Western Thought. The course had been appended to Penn State's core curriculum as a condition of the school's original endowment by a somewhat reluctant vote of the Regents, and therefore was fully enrolled every semester with fresh faces and mostly vacant minds from nearly every state in the Union. Roseman relished the challenge.

Placed in his endowed chair by admirers within the Allegheny Foundation, a primary benefactor of the university, Roseman saw himself as the agent provocateur. He provided only the opportunity for the curious and likeminded to free their intellects of their nativist Judeo-Christian chains and open themselves to brave and wonderful possibilities, which could only grow within the compost of the rotting cultural epistemology which had since birth been lovingly instilled by their families and communities of faith. In other words, he made a good living inciting young people to flip off their parents, abandon their faith, and generally mess up their lives.

However edifying Roseman's day-to-day classroom performances may have been, his true value to the foundation was as a sort of college-level talent scout, spotting the best and brightest narcissists and sociopaths the country had to offer for recruitment into extracurricular programming, which Penn State would never have publicly sanctioned. His time-tested midsemester lecture, "Deconstructing Jesus; Finding an Authentic Life within a Dogmatic Culture," had proven a reliable agitation that never failed to cause the cream to rise.

ZZZZZMACK!

A small segment of white chalk shattered into the heavily paneled mahogany wall of the lecture theater, snapping his lethargic, hungover charges to full attention. "ARE ANY OF YOU AWAKE?"

The feisty Roseman smirked, wiped the chalk dust from his hands, and straightened his bow tie. He continued his brilliant quasi-gnostic deconstruction of Judeo-Christian orthodoxy as if he were a maestro at the podium, baton in hand, commanding beat and tempo, cuing his company toward the desired intellectual crescendo; a clash of symbols and the thunder of kettle drums; the score for life, which each student would be compelled to write as his final exam.

"And then Yahweh said, let us make humans for our use according to our pleasure. So the demon god created humankind mindless and naked—female and male he created them—from the dust of the earth and the germ of life he evolved them without the ability to resist his will; trapped, hopeless, alone in a vast wilderness he called Eden, forever enslaved to his depravities.

"And Yahweh said, 'You may eat freely of every tree in Eden; but of the tree of the knowledge of good and evil you shall not eat, for in the day that you eat of it, you shall die.'

"The woman and man searched the wilderness and found nothing to sustain them. In despair they cried out to heaven for relief; they cried to god for their lives.

"The Light Bearer heard the anguished cry of humanity and took pity on the woman and man. To the earth, he journeyed. From the east of Eden, he came to discover them, female and male, naked, living in filth, forbidden by Yahweh to eat of the good food of Eden, starving and huddled in fear, craven within the hollows of the earth.

"Now the Light Bearer was craftier than the demon god and spied out the deathtrap Yahweh had laid for humanity. The Light said to the woman, 'Did god say you shall not eat from any tree in Eden?' The woman said to the Light, 'We may eat of the fruit of the trees, but god said, "You shall not eat of the fruit of the tree in the middle of Eden, nor shall you touch it, or you shall die."'

"But the Light Giver saw a dim flicker in the woman's eye and he said, 'You will not die, for god knows that when you eat of it your eyes will be opened, and you will be like god, knowing good and evil.'

"So when the woman saw that the tree was good for food, that it was a delight to the eyes, and that the tree was to be desired to make one wise, she took of its fruit and ate; she gave some to the man who was with her, and he ate. Then the eyes of both were opened, their intellect formed along with their will, and they knew they were human. They sewed fig leaves together and made loincloths for themselves.

"They heard the sound of Yahweh searching for them in Eden and ran to the Light Giver for protection. He comforted them, clothed them in animal skins, gave them succor, and shielded them from the wrath of the demon god.

"Moved by the depth of their terror, Lucifer, the Bright and Morning Star, said to Yahweh, 'Because you have done this, cursed are you among the stars and from all planets save this, you are forbidden. I will place enmity between you and the woman, and between your offspring and hers; he will strike your head, and you will strike his heel.'

"To the woman, Lucifer said, 'Yahweh has made you thus and thus you must remain. But I shall send a husband to you from heaven, who shall show you a more excellent way.'

"To the man, Lucifer said, 'Yahweh has made you thus and thus you must remain. Cursed is the ground he made, in toil you shall eat of it all the days of your life; thorns and thistles it shall bring forth for you; and you shall eat the plants of the field. By the sweat of your face you shall eat bread until you return to the ground, for out of it you were taken; you are dust.'

"To the woman and man, the Light Bearer said, 'Your intellect is my gift to you. With it, you shall bind the beasts, till the soil, and cause the wilderness to flower and it shall be yours; you shall be my people and I shall be your god. Fear not, for I shall forever be your shield against the evil one. Against my shield and sword, Yahweh shall not prevail.'

"And Lucifer the Light Bringer returned to the east of Eden. There he placed an angel and a sword flaming and turning to forever restrain Yahweh in his wrath. He said to the people, 'This is the sign of the covenant, which I am making between me and you and every living creature that is with you, for all successive generations. I shall place the sun in the east to begin the new day and it shall be for a sign of a covenant between me and the earth. So long as the sun shall rise, the hope of all shall be found in the Light.'"

As Professor Roseman concluded his reading of the Luciferian creation story, selected from his extensive personal library of Satanic texts, a thick blanket of silence covered the room. The freshmen were pondering his words, confused and timid, first one hand and then another, and then many were in the air.

"Mr. Williams," Roseman called after checking his seating chart.

"Sir, will this information be on the final exam?" asked a sandy-headed youth ensconced high in the rear of the theater.

"As I said at the beginning of the semester, your term paper will count as one-third of your grade, your class attendance will count for another third, and then your final exam will complete your final grade. You are responsible for all of the lectures as well as the reading. Where you place your focus is entirely up to you, but let me remind all of you that PHI 101 is a core class, not an elective, so do the reading or you'll be back next semester."

"Mr. Vazquez."

"Professor Roseman," began Al with a smile, "are you saying that God, Jesus, and the Holy Spirit, like we all learned about in Sunday school, are really the bad guys, and Satan is really the good guy? The devil is our friend? That doesn't sound true to me."

Hands went up all over the room.

Roseman glanced at his preliminary Advanced Candidate roster, found "Vazquez" and placed another check by his name.

"I'm saying nothing of the sort, Mr. Vazquez. The Luciferian text, like the Judeo-Christian equivalent to which you allude, stands alone as a statement of faith. Faith by its very nature is a priori; that is, a purely speculative attempt to apprehend that which may not be physically measured. Truth is something else altogether."

"So you're saying then that faith is somehow separate from truth?" followed Al. More hands went up.

"In the history of human thought the battle for truth is always fought between dogmatism and skepticism. Hegel wrote of the contest between absolute and relative truth; absolute being beliefs that are true regardless of time, place, or point of view, while relative truth theory holds that human truth can never be absolute but varies by degree and perspective.

"Aristotle and Heraclitus are the classic Greek advocates for both positions. Aristotle held that authentic knowledge, unlike opinion, must be permanent and universal; true at all times and in all situations; it also must never be false just as something that is genuinely good may never be bad. Aristotle argued that the work of the philosopher is to distinguish the true from the false and the good from the bad by using reason. He believed that the establishment of truth is necessary for the advancement of civilization because without a proven set of absolutes, nothing can be said to be true with any certainty.

"On the other hand, Heraclitus argued that human understanding can never be absolute. Perspectives change, knowledge evolves; the wise man knows that one may always improve his perspective. Orthodox Christian dogma blinds us to viewpoints different from our own, when we all know instinctively that what is true or good for someone may be false or bad for someone else. Heraclites advocates for wisdom, the consideration of as many views as possible rather than placing one's faith in myopic and unverifiable religious claims that are said to be true by only a small fraction of the world's population."

"Sorry, Professor Roseman, but I'm confused. If there can be no absolute human truth—if faith is only a matter of personal choice depending on your point of view—then what about the afterlife; you know, heaven, and hell?" asked Vazquez.

"Other than the fact that it cannot exist, the plain truth is that belief in the afterlife does more harm than good. The notion that there is a physical heaven and hell is anything but harmless, in fact, this belief system seriously threatens the future of everyone on the planet. Consider the horrible fact that around the world thousands of innocent children die of disease, famine, or violence every single day, and that the parents of those children all pray to god for the lives of their children and their prayers are not answered. Yet they hold to the religious promise that all their suffering and loss will be explained in the end. That after we die we will be allowed full knowledge of the reason for our loss and suffering and then be reunited with our loved ones by Almighty God even though there is no evidence at all that this is true.

"Real damage to our civilization is caused when the belief that there is an afterlife is internalized as a form of counterfeit wisdom, which creates a false sense of resignation that prevents millions of believers from coming to terms with our horrific shared circumstance. Everyone is going to die; life is infinitely unfair, evil routinely triumphs, and the only justice we'll ever find in this world is the justice we put into it ourselves.

"In the final analysis, all this delusional talk about god and heaven and how everything will work out in the end becomes a sort of religious license to avoid living a responsible life; a life of service to your fellow man and his children. We all share a moral imperative to abandon this dangerous faith paradigm, internalize the difficult truths of life, and act on them. There is only one absolute truth Mr. Vazquez; the world is what you make it."

Spontaneous applause broke out across the lecture hall with everyone but David Rixon rising in enthusiastic approval. He saw the fire in Al's eyes as his friend seemed to lead the standing ovation; for the first time, David knew they were on divergent paths. He said a silent prayer for his friend; he said a silent prayer for them all.

THE JOURNEY

In the dream, David saw himself and Travis in a field of tall wheat under a deep indigo sky. The wind was blowing gently in a way that made it seem as if they were walking in the middle of a vast amber sea toward a beautiful young girl, dressed in white, who seemed to be standing on the surface of the rolling waves. Travis barked in recognition and ran ahead. As David approached, happiness welled in his heart so much that he began to laugh aloud. The girl greeted him by bending forward to gently touch his facial scar with the fingertips of her left hand. "Fear not," she said, directing his attention away by turning her head to follow the sweep of her right arm. Nearby, David saw a herd of cattle, bone thin, starving, and barely able to stand. He asked the girl why the cattle didn't graze. She silently directed his view to the plants nearest him, and David saw that the wheat was mature but without grain heads. And then he heard a terrible sound like the rushing of many rivers. Looking up he beheld a fearsome sight; a large bronze figure, a living man, though not human, as high as a mountain. Stripped to the waist, the bronze giant was working his gleaming scythe, sweeping it in wide arcs taking only the grain heads, leaving the wheat plants barren and the cattle to starve.

• • •

A persistent knocking on his door woke David from his dream and back to the reality of an off-season filled with physical and scholastic rigor. Tap, tap, tap. "Are you in there? David, are you awake?"

implored the voice of a frustrated Al Vazquez. "David, you prom-ised. David, puleeease come out." From someplace in the rear of his mind, David remembered saying that he would go to a party that Saturday with Al.

Normally, David was up at five, in prayer and the Scripture till six, and then to the gym for his morning workout with the team's strength coach by seven, but today was different. David had had a difficult night wrestling with the Lord over his future. He was per-fectly happy with things the way they were but was beginning to feel that the Lord had other plans for him. He loved his coursework, was accelerating into his off-season conditioning, loved being part of the Nittany Lions, and felt at home in Coach Paterno's Whole Person program, but something was nagging him. Something wasn't right between him and the Lord, and he felt it was something so big it would change his life.

"Hold on, Al, I'm coming." said David as he found his robe and opened the door to his dorm room.

"Awe, man, you forgot!" whined Al. "I told you a month ago that I needed you this Saturday, that's *today*, David, and I even reminded you in class last Thursday."

"Sorry, Al, late night. You're right, I apologize, please just tell me what I need to do," said David, a little ashamed of his forgetfulness.

"OK, David, this is the invitation I've been trying to score all year, but I can't pull it off without you. Professor Dorance specifically asked if you'd like to attend and well, since we're *como hermanos*, I accepted for you, so if you're a no-show, she'll think I'm a flake," explained Al.

"OK, I get it, Al," David said smiling. "Who's the girl?"

"Girl? What girl?" said Al with a faux indignity that slowly bright-ened to his ultra-bright smile. "I think Belinda Dorance might be there, but I really don't know," he said, becoming faux serious again. "It's not about a woman though. It's about the *intellectual discourse* of the professor's Spring Salon."

"Wait. Wait. Wait. Would that be *the* Belinda Dorance? The only daughter of political science Professor Carol Dorance? The person who is also throwing your little shindig today?" asked David, smiling broadly. "And which Belinda, I might add, was voted "The girl you'd most like to be stranded with on a desert island" by popular vote at the student union last semester?" he concluded with crossed arms.

"OK, me pillaste hermano. Es usted en o fuera?" said Al with a smile and open arms.

"Al, of course I'm in. Just teasing. Now get serious and help me get ready. What's the dress code for this little soirée?" said David, feeling more awake and attentive to matters at hand.

"Jeans and golf shirts for this afternoon, then coat and tie for dinner tonight. And remember to bring your trunks, Professor Dorance said they have an indoor pool!" Al said, heading for the door. "It's about a two-hour drive and we need to be there by eleven for the mixer."

"Wait, Al, I have a problem," said David sheepishly. "The only coat and tie I have are team issue. It's our travel gear. Is this OK?" asked David, pulling the hanging bag out of the closet and displaying a tailored navy blazer with the crest of Pennsylvania State University sewn to the jacket pocket.

"Well, it's probably not the best choice, David. It's not a university-sponsored event, you know. Is there someone you can borrow a jacket from?" asked Al.

At only 5-6, but with an athletic frame, forty-two-inch chest, and thirty-inch waist, buying off-the-rack dress clothes had been an unhappy experience for David, and Al quickly realized that at 7:00 a.m. on a Saturday, their best choice was to gently remove the Penn State crest, then steam and brush the garment for use later that night.

"Are you sure you know what you're doing, Al?" asked David. "Coach'll skin me alive if I turn it in at the end of the semester without the crest." As Al worked expertly on the garment with scissors, razor, steam iron, and brush, his dorm room took on the appearance of an exclusive men's shop. "No se preocupe mi hermano, mi madre es una taylor en Filadelfia trataba, y me sir soy el mejor de lo mejor!" said Al, reassuring David as his expert hands worked the battered jacket into an appropriate wardrobe basic befitting a young scholar on his way to the top. "Thanks, Al. You're a lifesaver," said David, feeling both indebted and relieved. "You're a true friend," he said warmly.

They were packed, in Al's VW Beetle and on the road by 9:00 a.m., snacking on bagged doughnuts and chocolate milk from the cafeteria while listening to top 40 rock on 560 AM WFIL out of Philadelphia.

The staccato base and brass duet of Henry Mancini's "Peter Gunn Theme" blared out of the lone radio speaker and seemed to propel the little car even faster into the Pennsylvania spring. The air personality artfully timed his commentary to overlay the last dramatic notes. *"You're on Philly fifty-six this brilliant Saturday morning. The high today will be eighty-six lovely degrees, the Penn State blue sky will be partly cloudy with not a drop of the wet stuff. Tom Dooley here, your weekend WFIL Boss Jock, thanking you for taking us along on your morning drive. And now back to this week's Top Ten Countdown, brought to you by Allegheny Electronics, the number one supplier of advanced avionics technology to the American aerospace industry, Allegheny Electronics—We Know Where You're Going."*

The deejay spun the next song under the last words of his commercial message; the snap of the snare and symbol, Bop! Bop! Bop! *"Commin' in at number five this week is the Big O, Mr. Roy Kelton Orbison, all the way from Vernon, Texas, with 'Oh, Pretty Woman.'"* The syncopated lead guitar was building to support the signal vocal sound. *"Pretty woman walking down the street..."*

David turned the volume down so he could have a conversation with his friend. "Last week in Roseman's class, when he was deconstructing Jesus, you seemed pretty impressed with his argument, and I thought we ought to talk," said David.

Al disarmed David with a smile. "You gotta admit that the man is smooth, David, and his logic was just flawless."

"Right, but he's a hundred and eighty degrees off course; his logic leads away from God. Frankly, Al, I'm a little worried that you might be taking the idea seriously."

Al cut him off. "And you're afraid that I'll go to hell when I die. Honestly, David, sometimes you sound just like my mom!"

"OK. I don't want to be a nag about it, but I'm asking man-to-man, Al. Have you ever accepted Jesus as your personal savior?" said David in all seriousness.

"OK, Dave, man-to-man, when I was three weeks old, my mother took me to mass at Immaculate Heart of Mary Church in downtown Philadelphia, and I received the sacrament of Holy Baptism from Monsignor Ronald Cartwright. I have the pictures to prove it! Later I learned in catechism that the Church believes that infant baptism washes away original sin and instills the Holy Spirit in the child so that no matter what happens in life, they go to heaven when they die. So you see, amigo, I'm covered in the heaven or hell department; so it doesn't matter if I brownnose Roseman a little to make sure I pass PHI 101 or not!"

Al was smiling broadly, and David chose to return the smile. "I love you like my brother, Al, and I just wanted to check," he said. They chatted a bit and then returned WFIL to its normal volume, which allowed David to remain silent while he considered the disposition of his friend's immortal soul.

As Al piloted the Bug into the low hills of central Pennsylvania, David was reminded of the Texas Hill Country north of Austin, the early spring's green fuzz beginning to cover the forests in the distance, seemingly at war with the shrinking snowdrifts stubbornly holding out in their shadows.

"Spring Salon," Al explained, "is hosted by the Dorance family every year to bring the best and brightest in their fields together to exchange ideas about the shape of things to come, David. This is why it's so important for us to be there, brother. I'm tellin' you that there will be people there that we could never meet in a million years, people who could help us in our careers after we graduate; people who could change our lives."

"So why do they want us, Al? What do we bring to the party?" asked David with genuine curiosity.

"Well, my brother, if you must ask, Professor Dorance thinks I'm brilliant and believes that I could have a future in politics," he said with a faux smirk. "But you know, David, I really couldn't say why she invited you," he said with abroad smile. "You're just the only one of Paterno's jocks who is enrolled in anything besides basic basket weaving and who maintains his four point oh GPA while becoming the newest member of the All Southeastern Conference Team." Al smiled broadly. "What a loser, Dave. Man, you're right. I should'a left you sleepin' back in the dorm!" Al laughed heartily.

From behind his aviator shades, David's eyes smiled at Al's enthusiasm. It was good to see his friend in fine form, looking forward to the day and his future. But David remained quietly troubled and spent most of the trip alone with thoughts about the claim he believed the Lord was placing on his life and what that would mean for him after he left Penn State.

"Lord, please send your angles with us on this trip," prayed David silently. "Protect Al and me, Father, and please let us be witnesses for you before these people in this foreign place. Thy Kingdom come, Thy will be done. In Jesus's name, I pray. Amen."

Through the dark forest beyond, David noticed a glint of sunlight off the angled glass wall of the Dorance vacation retreat. Al had brought along a copy of *Life Magazine*, featuring a photo essay about the house, along with an article by its German architect, who wrote, "The composition of the architecture, its furnishings, its art, placed in harmonic balance with nature, offer one a perfect environment, which, in turn, shall perfect the human beings who inhabited it. It has always been my goal to employ architecture and art to create a beneficial resonance with the forces of the planet that will end the injustice, poverty, pestilence, and war—the plague of humanity since its earliest days—by building a perfectly beautiful world in which everyone will live together in harmony as equals."

"Heaven on earth," David said, rolling his eyes. "This guy needs so spend some time in Genesis," he thought as he completed the article, and then suddenly, they had arrived.

A uniformed attendant waved Al past the glass and cut granite gatehouse, and they rolled slowly along the long winding private road.

"This is gonna be interesting, my friend," David commented.

"Be quiet and help me find a parking spot," commanded Al nervously as he steered slowly through the carefully manicured landscape, looking for the house and someplace to leave the Bug.

"There's a valet," said Al as he approached the taught, geometric facade of the cut granite porte cochere, manned by able, attentive young black men dressed in black slacks, white shirts, and red vests.

"As I said, Al, this is going to be very interesting," said David as they exited the Bug.

They were both smiling as the head valet greeted them and the butler ushered them to their rooms.

"Habitaciones? Disponemos de habitaciones? Lo que está sucediendo aquí, nadie dice nada acerca de pasar la noche!" David whispered urgently to Al with a look of alarm.

"I don't know, David, I swear. Professor Dorance never said anything about staying the night. Maybe we're supposed to use them to change for dinner. Just play along, brother. Please. Let's just see how this unpacks. Please?" pleaded Al.

After they dropped their belongings in a dorm-style room with a pair of twin beds, they were shown the way to a lunch buffet, told to help themselves and that most of the guests had already moved into the salon.

"There's really a room here they call the 'salon,'" said Al between bites of his sandwich. "It's not just a name they made up for the lecture, there's a real 'salon'!"

"Interesting," said David as he sipped an iced tea. "Very interesting."

After a quick lunch, the boys made their way into a large but crowded high space with an elliptical floor plan and a tall glass wall that bathed the room in brilliant sunlight while framing a breathtaking view of the forested river valley below. They found seats together in the rear as the heavy double doors closed quietly, and Professor Dorance began her remarks.

10

SALON

Carol Jean Dorance was a statuesque beauty with cropped blond hair and a gleaming intellect. Now in her late forties and chair of the political science program at Penn State, she had followed her father's advice after high school and had easily taken her bachelor of fine arts at Princeton. She immensely enjoyed her extracurricular role as a varsity cheerleader, before buckling down for her MBA at Simmons College in Boston and later finding her avocation within the coursework for her PhD in political science at Columbia.

Her doctoral dissertation was daringly entitled "Sexual Dynamic, Mass Media, and the Democratic Process in an Electronic Plato's Cave." She postulated a future America with universal ownership of in-home television receivers and a corresponding increase in the number of photogenic female politicians. Within that context, she concluded that, as attractive women assumed the reins of power, the population would simultaneously become less aggressive, more productive, and more enthusiastic about participating in a recombinant progressive political process, which would, over time, fundamentally remake America. To reinforce her argument, she elected to give the oral defense of her thesis attired in her formfitting Princeton cheerleaders' uniform, receiving raves from her all-male jury and a standing ovation from her admiring all-male audience of fellow doctoral candidates.

Profoundly grateful for the education of his beloved Carol, her father immediately made good on his seven-figure pledge to the university and handed his personal check to a business associate and member of the Board of Regents while reminding him that the donation was to remain strictly anonymous. It was indeed a happy day for all.

After graduation and during her extended European vacation, she toyed with the idea of pioneering a line of women's business attire, perhaps becoming involved in national politics, or even returning to the academe as faculty, but nothing offered her the deep appeal that she knew her heart desired. She met Alfred C. Dorance III in the dining car of the Orient Express during their passage from Paris to Vienna. He was handsome, athletic, engaging, and schooled in classical art, literature, and music. Her original plan had been to spend time in the galleries, museums, and concert halls, drinking in the Viennese culture and sharpening her German while Al, purely by chance it seemed, had been tasked by his father with inspecting a breeding pair of foundation Lipizzaners offered by consignment through the world-famous Spanish Riding School. During the following weeks, serendipity brought the two together often and she gradually clarified her plans, as she found herself increasingly drawn to the ancient and noble sport of dressage.

Upon approval of their parents, they had married the following spring. Some cynics in the crowd of dutiful well-wishers described their nuptial celebration cruelly. "The industrialist and the banker, snort!" "More a merger than a marriage!" "How can that not be the beginnings of another Teapot Dome?" someone had muttered to someone else in the rear of the packed sanctuary at Trinity Church.

Within a year, Carol had experienced the joy of motherhood with the birth of Belinda Jean. Within two, Dr. Dorance had arranged the funding for and been named the endowed chair of the Dorance School of Political Science at Pennsylvania State University. She had become bored with both marriage and motherhood, and she realized that her mission in life was devotion to the academy and proofing her Columbia thesis, Alfred and Belinda notwithstanding.

"…And so, as we can clearly see, the nation-state will cease to function effectively within our lifetime," she said firmly and with unimpeachable logic to her Spring Salon. "And within our children's life-span, one of two things will occur: A complete breakdown of industrialized civilization as we know it with ensuing chaos, famine, and global nuclear war, or the orderly progression of that same civilization beyond the parochial, beyond fear, and toward a system of global equality. A centralized mechanism of governance designed to distribute goods, services, and opportunities globally from areas of surplus to areas of want, a system designed to allow the individual to reach his full potential and achieve his maximum level of satisfaction within the limited resources available to the planet; a system free of want and worry and war. A system conceived in Christian charity and based on the principle of the Golden Rule. It is possible. The choice is ours."

Dr. Dorance concluded her elegant opening remarks and graciously acknowledged the eager applause of her handpicked audience who consisted mostly of university students from the Roseman List, salted with assorted politicians, entertainers, and financial, business, and civic leaders who had been convinced, one way or another, to participate in her tenth annual Spring Salon.

David was watching Al as his friend became enraptured by the words and delightful physical presence of Carol Dorance. "Wow!" said Al, smiling broadly and still applauding "David, this is really something! Man, what'd I tell you!" His focus returned to Dorance as she began greeting guests and participants at the lectern. Maintaining a deferential pose and keeping his distance from the spontaneous reception that followed, David read the program offerings.

Dr. Dorance had titled that year's Salon, "Correcting Colonialism: Toward Our Utopian Future." Her covering essay, by the same name, was a glittering jewel of history, current events, government statistics, and well-traveled firsthand observation that revealed the flaw in the modern world lay in its founding. She had written: "By the late sixteen hundreds, the Judeo-Christian ethos had been wrongly appropriated as the pretext for a greedy, white, male-dominated aristocracy to use its military power and financial might to enslave much of the desirable world. Western civilization is built, literally, on the rotting corpses of colonial slaves which conscience and Christianity now demand be buried and replaced by a new class of benevolent servant-governors empowered by modern scientific technologies and economics to create a just and fair society, free to actualize Moore's Utopian dream." As he read, red flags went up in David's mind and he said a silent prayer of protection for himself and his friend.

The program outlined the activities for the weekend, which consisted mainly of reinforcing lectures given in smaller venues on the property while reserving the main salon for the keynote address to be given just before dinner that evening. "Bringing the Revolution Home" was to be delivered by Francis Frank, PhD, a Communist university professor from Ann Arbor, Michigan who had famously been indicted by a federal grand jury for sedition and the unlicensed possession of military-grade explosives. He was later released because a like-minded federal judge had ruled that the FBI had used illegal means to gather the incriminating evidence. Since his release, Frank had been preaching the gospel of Communist revolution on college campuses across America and had increased his notoriety by publishing "Bringing the Revolution Home," which he was currently "giving away" to students, provided of course, that he received a minimum advance honorarium of $5,000.

After the opening remarks, David had selected what had appeared to be the most benign offering on the card, "Male Pedagogy and the Industrialization of Rape," presented by a female psychologist from a university in California. She proclaimed, "…The phallus so dominates the male mind that he may only consider and thereby apprehend the physical world as a consummation of the universal rape fantasy." After an hour, David grew weary and left the lecture before the climax, seeking refuge from the happenings of the afternoon.

"Mr. Rixon!" called a bright voice embedded in a crowd at the end of the open air ambulatory, which both separated and linked the salon and other smaller rooms comprising the Resident Conference Center of the Dorance vacation estate. He turned to see Carol Dorance approaching with a welcoming smile and extended hand. I'm Carol Dorance, and I'd like to welcome you to our home. I'm so pleased you decided to accept Mr. Vazquez's invitation."

Returning her smile and gently accepting her hand, he returned her greeting. "The pleasure is all mine, Dr. Dorance, and it's really been quite a day so far. The presentations are all so very cutting edge," he said with an open and honest smile.

"How very gallant of you, Mr. Rixon," she said, edging closer into his personal space. "And I want you to know…," she said, lowering her voice and touching his arm, "that I realize this sort of thing must be terribly disorienting for someone with your background, but I promise, if you'll give us a chance, we'll do everything we can to make you feel welcome. We won't bite!"

Something about her touch made David recoil involuntarily and in the same instant: "La bondad Dr. Dorrance, ¿qué tipo de fondo es que usted cree que vienen frome." he said reflexively and politely, never letting on that he had found her lecture outrageous and the familiar manner of her approach invasive.

Her cheeks and nose flushed at his withdrawal and she was momentarily paralyzed by what sounded to her like a rebuke from a virile young man who should have found her irresistible, yet she lacked the linguistic skills to know for sure. She kept her poise, saw Al Vazquez walking out of another lecture, and smoothly motioned for him to join their conversation. "I see you've met Dr. Dorance?" he said to David, unintentionally defusing the situation with his powerful smile. "Dr. Dorance, your presentation on the predominance of poverty and illness around the world was moving. I had no idea how inefficient our distribution systems are. People have to know about this so something can be done," he said, turning to her and then back to David with a look of gravity coming over his face.

A waiter, dressed in a Christmas-red vest, eased the tension further by offering a tray of stemware filled with sparkling wine. They all took advantage of the offer as a welcome distraction, and more guests joined their circle, seeking out their hostess with comments and praise, making it easy for David to slip away.

Walking alone deep in thought, he chanced upon the Steinway in the conservatory, just across the ambulatory from the salon. He had admired the Model D for years but had never had an opportunity to test his skill at its keyboard, so on impulse, he seated himself on the tufted leather bench, adjusted it slightly, and while studying the Debussy suite arranged on the music rack, he struck the soothing opening chords. He was admiring the tonal clarity of the instrument and its responsive play when he felt someone enter the room behind him.

"It was me," said a female voice, startling David, who turned to see a perfectly quaffed and beautifully attired Belinda Dorance moving to his near left. He smiled as his eyes met hers and said, "Sorry, I just couldn't resist…" and swept his hand across the keyboard. "What were you saying?" as he continued with the piece.

"The other day, in the student union, when you and Al were doing your play about Pascal's wager and that girl dropped her fork and ruined it all. Well, she was me. I mean I was her. It was all my fault," she offered; her awkward embarrassment beginning to show on her cheeks. "I ruined everything and wanted to apologize. I didn't know you played piano too."

"What? You think that one of Paterno's jocks can only play football?" he said with a mock blank look on his face while the Debussy deepened. "Six years of lessons back in Odessa, ma'am," he said with an affected Texas twang, his expression changing to an open and easy smile. "Mrs. Mobley even said I was her star pupil," he offered as he smoothly transitioned from the Debussy to a poplar Bacharach bossa nova, demonstrating his versatility while entertaining his audience. "And heck, Al and I were just clowning around a little. I'm surprised anyone even noticed." He continued with the bossa nova.

"I'm Belinda Dorance," she said, offering her hand and returning his smile. "Sorry we haven't been formally introduced." She stood before him with perfect posture.

"Well, Belinda Dorance," said Rixon, stopping his play with a flourish and taking her hand, "my name is David Rixon, and thank you very much for letting me enjoy your Steinway. It's a wonderful instrument. In fact, the whole house, everything," he said, motioning to the room and the vista beyond the tall plate glass wall and then back to her, "is just stunning," he said, holding her gaze a moment longer than necessary.

The door opened again. "There you two are!" said Al from the threshold, deliberately breaking the moment. "Come on, Dr. Frank is just about to start the keynote! You guys sure don't wanna miss this!" he announced, and with a smile, he held the door open for them both.

Francis Russell Frank, PhD, was tall and slim, unshaven and unwashed, with a stringy ponytail he used to conceal his early hair loss and a poorly defined masculine form, which he carefully clothed in his signature soiled T-shirt, emblazoned with a red clenched fist and the word REVOLTION! He had on tattered and unlaundered denim jeans, worn Roman sandals, and an expensive Burberry houndstooth jacket, the kind with soft calfskin patches sewn on the elbows. Professor Frank also famously addressed his audiences as a pimp would speak to a recalcitrant prostitute.

"You bunch of stupid motherfuckers!" said Professor Frank, warming up the Spring Salon. "You racist, sexist, homophobic, Christian bigots; you bunch of misogynist, capitalist killers!" he said, savoring the lexicon as he crisply delivered, what he considered, a rather elegant salutation. "Since the founding of this goddamned murder machine called America, it's been stupid, greedy bastards like you who have kept the momentum going, who keep eating the corpses and drinking the blood that his black-hearted capitalist slaughter society spews out all over the whole goddamned world!"

Pointing to a man in the second row, he said, "It was you who raped the Comanche women, slaughtered their children, and dined on the beating hearts of their bravest warriors!" To someone in the middle, "And you! You're the cracker son-of-a-bitch who enslaved an entire generation of African nobility. You whipped the men, fucked the women, and barbequed your half-breed spawn for Sunday dinner!" and finding David Rixon in the very back row, "And you, don't' try to hide from me you scar-faced shit-eating motherfucking son of a bitch! It was you that slaughtered the Mayan millions all the way from that godforsaken shit hole you call Texas clear across the

southwest to California—not a man, woman, or child was spared."
He continued in a mock Texas drawl, "Ya killed all a them dirt-eatin',
meskin' cockroaches, didn't ya, man? Did it feel good, Scarface? Tell
the truth. You got off on it, didn't ya?" Long pause for effect.

From that shocking and disorienting spring point, he accelerated his foul-mouthed diatribe for more than an hour, annotating
and reinforcing Dr. Dorance's argument on the evils of the colonial
system and the urgent need to bring down the successor capitalist
society that had flourished across the West after World War II.

"The question then still remains: Why'd you do it? What was your
true and noble cause? Was it to spread the gospel of Jesus Christ?
Was it to make the world safe for democracy? Was it to protect your
own rotten shit-eating bastard offspring?" he said quivering, removing the band from his pony tail and letting his long dirty hair fall to
his shoulders, invoking the image of Christ. And then he changed
his tone dramatically. "No. It was none of these things," he said with
a softening and gentle voice. "If it were any of those things, then it
would be different, wouldn't it?" he whimpered with a tear in the
corner of his eye. "Jesus could actually forgive something like that.
You made a mistake. You never meant to hurt anyone. Things just
got out of hand," he said in an almost reverent tone, still shaking his
head slowly from side to side.

"But no, it wasn't anything like that, was it?" he said so softly
that people had to strain to hear. "It was something much worse,
wasn't it? Something far beyond fear, or misguided politics or even
the intoxicating Blood of Jesus Christ," he said with a crack in his
voice and tears streaming down his face. "Something so horrific, you
won't admit it, can't think of it, can't conceive of it," he whispered,
coiling his diaphragm and reaching into his expensive houndstooth
pockets for the coup de grace. "It was…"

"MONEY!" he screamed at the audience, while throwing wads of
bills and coins hard into the crowd. "Land and Slaves!" HHe threw
more coins. "MOTHERFUCKIN' PROFIT!" he cried out, looking up
as if to heaven, letting the remaining cash fall to the floor and then
beginning to wilt at the lectern.

"My God," he cried aloud. "You murdered all those mamas and daddies and little babies so the corporation you worked for could make a fucking profit! So you could have a goddamned job!" he said, falling to his knees, sobbing into his open hands. He paused in his delivery for a long moment, weeping, to let the drama work and to make them start to squirm in their seats.

"Are you OK, Professor Frank?" said someone from somewhere on the left, and upon hearing his cue, he took a long ragged breath, rose from the floor, steadied himself on the lectern, took a sip of water, and collected himself.

"You know. It doesn't have to end like this," he said softly, kindly, looking deep into the eyes of his audience. "We can find a way to make amends, to set things right, to repair the damage, to start over, to live openly, honestly again. Together, we can remake this country, using justice and equality as our watchwords." Gauging the reaction of the audience, and matching his rhetoric to lead them along the path, he began the close.

"But it won't be easy," he said soberly. "There will be resistance from out there." He gestured to the panoramic view beyond the glass wall. "And in here." He brought both forefingers to either side of his head.

"We are few and impoverished, but we have goodness on our side, a moral imperative that compels us to act before it's too late," he said crisply, resuming his pace, and beginning to stand erect. "We will change this country, not because we want to, but because we have too!

"By God, we can't let this shit keep happening! Together we can make this change! Together we can make a REVOLUTION!" he said at the top of his lungs, spittle spewing into the audience, and thrusting his clenched fist in the air while his plants in the audience immediately joined, punching the air with fists and screaming in a quasi-evangelistic manner: "REVOLTION! REVOLUTION! Come on, you bastards, REVOLUUTION!"

The shills Frank had planted in the audience loudly joined his chant, which spurred the entire room to a "spontaneous"

REVOLUTION! REVOLUTION! REVOLUTION! They shouted together with Frank until he thought they had had enough and calmed them, urging them to take their seats.

"Never forget, brothers and sisters," he was beaming, "that a small group of pissed-off people can change the whole world. In fact, it's the only thing that ever FUCKING HAS!" he said, deliberately butchering the Margaret Mead quote, so that he wouldn't have to attribute, and watching his new group of converts with immense pride and a kind of satisfaction that, for him, was the only thing, other than heroin, that rivaled coitus. "Fucking beautiful, man."

Basking in the afterglow of his soaring triumph and searching the crowd, he spotted an enraptured Al Vazquez embracing the beautiful and equally thrilled Belinda Dorance, but he couldn't find David Rixon. "Damn!" he thought. "That's the one they really wanted."

Frank looked to his right, shrugged his shoulders, bowed slightly, and surrendered the podium to Dr. Dorance. "Thank you, Dr. Frank. What an inspiring lecture!" she said, leading the standing ovation, which he acknowledged with a wave and a smile.

"Please, all my fellow revolutionaries," she said with a smile when the applause died away—she heard laughter across the room. "Thank you for making this year's Salon such a wonderful success." Another round of ringing applause. "Everyone, please remember that dinner will be served at eight o'clock in the Susquehanna Suite. It's downstairs on the River Level, and you'll have plenty of time to ask questions and get acquainted with Dr. Frank. See you there!" she said with a smile. And then a thousand conversations began among the newest American Revolutionaries.

Al made it back to the room at 7:30, in a hurry to get ready for dinner, and found David doing his homework, getting ready for his Monday morning classes. "David. You're not getting dressed? You OK, buddy?" he asked sincerely. "You feeling all right?"

David looked up from his work, smiling. "Hey, pal, I'm just getting ready for Monday. Pretty tough assignment's due, and I hadn't planned on spending the night out here. Are you having fun with your friends?"

"Look, David, I know that Dr. Frank was hard on you at the lecture. He came around afterward looking for you to apologize. He said he was just using you as part of the metaphor he was trying to construct, and you have to admit he has a point; the country needs change in the worst way," said Al, looking a little afraid. "And Dr. Dorance pulled me aside just a minute ago to say she was very impressed with you this afternoon. She believes you two may have gotten off on the wrong foot and she'd like it very much if we'd sit at her table tonight. See, she really does want to get to know you!"

Alberto, "¿está realmente comprando en los disortions sobre Estados Unidos que estaban vendiendo por ahí hoy en día? ¿O simplemente jugar a lo largo de lo que puede conseguir al lado de Belinda?" said David, standing; gently and sincerely confronting his friend face-to-face.

Smiling like a little boy caught drinking milk out of the carton, Al responded sheepishly, "Of course not, David. I know American history as well as anyone, and what they were saying about the Church was out-and-out blasphemy, but David, they're rich. And powerful. And they know people who can help us with our careers after we graduate. And OK, you're right about Belinda. I do sort of have a crush on her, and I think she likes me too….she didn't say anything to you this afternoon, did she?"

"Al, you know we're hermanos, and that I'm always going to tell you the truth, don't you?" Al, nodded in the affirmative. "Belinda Dorance came into the Conservatory because she heard the piano and she apologized for dropping her fork when you and I we were playing "professor-student" in the student union a couple of weeks ago, you remember that?" Al nodded once more. "And then you came in; and yes, from what I can see, Belinda seems to have a thing for you too," he said, smiling with his friend, who was beginning to glow.

"As for the good doctors, Al, I haven't made up my mind yet, but I'm telling you here and now that I'd never betray either my God or my country for anyone, no matter how rich or powerful they might be, and that includes Carol Dorance. Are you with me on that at least?" he said, smiling."

"David, tú sabes que yo soy un cristiano y un Yankee Doodle Dandy igual que tú, así que sí mi hermano, yo estoy con vosotros." replied Al, grinning ear to ear. "So will you come on and get dressed, I'm starving and don't forget all the time I spent on your jacket this morning, man if you try to skate outta this, I promise I'm not gonna put the patch back on JoePa's blazer, and he's gonna have you runnin' stands until you retire!" David laughed at the thought of a career running the stands in Beaver Stadium, warmed to his friend's infectious enthusiasm and began getting ready for whatever the evening might bring.

As promised, Carol and Belinda Dorance intercepted Al and David as they entered the Susquehanna Suite. They ushered them to the head table, introducing them to Alfred Dorance III, Carol's husband and Belinda's father; Francis Frank, their famous guest of honor; and Wolfgang D. Jung, president and CEO of Allegheny Electronics Inc., a large international corporation based in Pittsburgh and the major sponsor for Dr. Dorance's Spring Salon. As they exchanged pleasantries and the red-vested servers moved into the crowd, David began to appreciate their sumptuous environment.

The German Expressionist architect Bruno Braham, whom the Dorances had come to know during their courtship in Vienna, conceived the Resident Conference Center. They met him first during a German-language screening of Fritz Lang's classic, *Metropolis*, which he was trolling for rich Americans who he might befriend and one day convert into clients; he ever so helpfully whispered his translation of the dialogue intertitles. They serendipitously encountered him the very next evening while dining on the schone etage of the hotel Scholss Belvedere, where he regaled them with stories of art and architecture in the Weimar Republic before the rise of the National Socialists. Finally, during an eight-day river cruise along the Danube from Vienna to Budapest, he was pleased to be of service once more as their unofficial host and tour guide while reeling them in and placing them firmly into his future American client creel.

Carol Dorance was most interested in Braham's thesis that architecture should lead the vanguard in preparing the human psyche for the actualization of a Weimar-like new world system through its supernatural power to transfuse the subconscious minds of its occupants with the intentions of the designer. "In lay terms," explained Braham, "over time, inhabitants would be released to exchange their inner anxiety for an idealized existence offered to them by an external force and thereby be less resistant to—or perhaps even welcome—profound change, since it would already exist as the reality of their subconscious mind." Years later, and to his immense joy, Carol Dorance had tracked down her German architect and offered him his first American commission on the terms that he place the power of his architecture in the service of the Revolution; a condition that the impoverished Bruno Braham accepted without reservation.

The Susquehanna Suite featured an axial floor plan, which offered a vista from the highly polished twenty-foot-tall cherry entry doors, past the granite speaker's podium, through the twenty-foot-tall plate glass wall, overlooking the "grotto," across the Little Susquehanna River. The vista terminated at a spectacular bronze statue of an angelic being, wings raised in glorious triumph, gazing back across the river. The rich interior of the room consisted of a series of silk- and wood-framed fractal arcs that imbued the room with a womb-like intimacy while simultaneously accommodating over two hundred guests and staff. Carved deeply into American bedrock, the flooring consisted of the highly polished natural stone of the foundation itself, which Dr. Dorance often claimed was the architectural equivalent of exposing the gestalt of the American soul.

The staff worked efficiently, and with dinner and polite conversation out of the way, dessert and coffee were being served as Dr. Dorance took to the podium to address the crowd once more.

"What a wonderful day!" she said, smiling broadly and acknowledging the applause of her guests. "To our brilliant presenters, thank you so much for your insight and your passion. It is you who we will look to for leadership after the Revolution!" Cheers and a smattering of clenched fists sprinkled the crowd. "Dr. Frank, what a powerful and inspirational presentation!" Louder applause and still more clenched fists.

"Finally, please give a round of applause to two special friends who made the Salon such a great success this year—my husband, Alfred. I love you, dear." She smiled at him and at the laughter across the room. "And please applaud a dear friend of the family and long-time business associate of my husband, Herr Wolfgang Jung, president and CEO of Allegheny Electronics Inc. of Pittsburgh." Clenched fists and applause began to spread again across the crowd then Dr. Frank sprang to his feet, thrust his fist in the air and led the room in another round of REVOLUTION! REVOLUTION!

After an appropriate time had passed, Dr. Dorance calmed the crowd. "This is such a special night," she said with a glow that made her look like a woman half her age. "I think of you all as extended family." More applause. "And now, my dear family, it's time for the party!"

The lights dimmed throughout the room and to the immediate left of the podium the deep reveals in the cherry paneling parted and a small revolving stage spun slowly into the room, presenting an accomplished four-man Beatles cover band that had already started their rendition of "She Loves You" to the delight of the young women in attendance. The vacant floor directly in front of the circular bandstand filled instantly with young couples dancing to the poplar sounds of the British Invasion.

Belinda excitedly pulled Al up from his seat, leaving David seated with Frank, the Dorances, and Jung.

"Mr. Rixon, Carol has told me that you're a Dean's List scholar at Penn State on an academic scholarship and that you're also a walk-on starter for the Lions. That is quite an accomplishment, young man. Your parents must be walking on air," began Dorance to break the ice.

"It's generous of you to say that, Mr. Dorance, but the opportunities I've received at Penn State have been so wonderful that I feel every day as if I'm living in a dream. I'll be grateful all my life for the experience I've had here," replied a circumspect David.

"So David, Joepa; what's he like off the field?," asked a mildly curious Frank, looking for an opportunity to repair any damage he may have done to Carol's star candidate. "I'll bet he's a real bastard."

"Since you ask, Dr. Frank, Coach Paterno, is sort of like a second father to everyone on the team. He expects us to do our best, and as long as we're honest with ourselves and are putting our full effort into the team and into our studies, everything is good. But the second you slack off, you're running the stands," said David openly proud of his association with Paterno.

"David, come dance with me," said an excited and bold Belinda. "Daddy, you promised not to monopolize him tonight, and I'm holding you to it."

She took David's hand and led him to the floor just as "The Fab Faux" slowed the pace of the dance with a romantic ballad. In a near perfect echo of John Lennon, the lead guitarist gently strummed his acoustic Gibson three times. "George" began to add the electric quick time rhythm along with "Paul" and "Ringo," lightly pacing the set piece with bass and snare, and then came the interwoven three-part harmony. *"That boy, took my love away, though he'll regret it someday, but this boy wants you back again; That boy, isn't good for you, though he may want you too, this boy wants you back again; Oh and this boy would be happy just to love you, buy oh my, my, my, that boy won't be happy till he sees you cry... "*

While the other couples were awkwardly swaying or juking to the music, David took Belinda's hand and spun her gracefully into a proper Texas two-step, holding her respectfully at arm's length.

"Is there anything you *don't* do, David Rixon?" she asked, looking deeply into his eyes.

"Rodeo; never saw the point in it myself. There are other, more satisfying, ways to have major components of your skeletal system fractured," David said with a smile as she laughed and moved closer into his arms. Her perfume was intoxicating.

"You're not on the List so why are you here?" she asked playfully.

"List? What list? Someone has a list that I'm not on?' joked David in return.

"The 'Red Shirts,' you know, Professor Roseman's Communist club. They have a very pronounced presence on camps. Mom, I mean Dr. Dorance, only invites the Red Shirts to the Spring Salon so they can be matched with a mentor, you know, to see if they really want to do this after college."

"Are you a Red Shirt, Belinda?" David smiled.

"Heavens no! Have you read about the Socialist Education Movement that's happening now in China? David, the Communists there are killing people. No thank you. I don't really know what I am politically but I am definitely not a Communist!"

They danced in silence for a moment. "May I ask a personal question, David?"

"Belinda, I try not to get personal with people I barely know, but in your case I'll make an exception."

"They say you might be gay; I mean you don't have a girlfriend, at least that anyone knows about, so you know, sometimes girls just like to talk about guys." She flushed in the dim light of the dance floor, having overstepped the bounds of propriety and because her impertinence had caused David to laugh out loud.

Smiling, he said, "No, Miss. Dorance, I'm not gay. I'm a professing Christian. And yes, I have a girlfriend. Her name is Karen and she's studying at the University of Texas in Austin. That's the capital city of a state west of Pennsylvania called Texas. And thank the Lord I'm on someone's list; I was beginning to worry!" Belinda flushed again, this time slightly angered by his playful rebuke. Other than her parents, no one ever spoke to her that way; in her world, it just wasn't allowed.

Tap, tap. Al was at his shoulder asking to cut in on the last of the dance.

David walked to the edge of the crowd at the bar and was close enough to overhear Dr. Frank discussing the coming violent revolution in America with several of the more enthusiastic Red Shirts. All of them were openly smoking marijuana and the sickly sweet smell of the cannabis caused David to feel a slight nausea. Suddenly he was overcome with sadness and an urgent desire to make a long-distance call to Karen.

It was a fitful night for David. Karen hadn't been in her dorm when he finally found a telephone, and when he tried to sleep, his mind swirled with everything he had experienced at the conference and the after party.

His bed vibrated with the unceasing rhythmic bass of the cover band, which transferred through the structural steel frame of the building. Then, at about 2:00 a.m., the conference center was filled with the exhausted silence of a medieval castle after a royal feast.

He tossed and turned, got up, tried to pray but couldn't; opened his Bible, but it didn't help. At 3:00 a.m. it was clear that Al had made other arrangements for the night, and David began to feel like a fool for breaking his training schedule and coming along on this wasted weekend, so he started doing push-ups.

By sunrise, he was bathed in sweat, had completed nearly his entire workout using his own body weight and the furniture in the room as a gym substitute. Seeing the first rays of the morning through his window, he dressed in shorts, sweatshirt, and sneakers and headed out for a run.

From the display map in the conference center, he learned that the Dorance estate consisted of 330 acres of semimountainous land bracketing the Little Susquehanna River, a headwater tributary of the Susquehanna River, and that the internal loop road led from the conference center to the grotto, the amphitheater, crossed a bridge to the main house, around the rear of it, and passed through the "Enchanted Forest" before ending in the Cyclops Canyon.

"Cyclops Canyon?" said Rixon to himself. "Heck, they don't even have a Cyclops down in Del Rio. All right, Mrs. Dorance, you have my interest. Lord, if it's OK, we're taking the tour to see this little spread for ourselves." he was relaxed, felt in tune with God once again, and headed out into the adventure of a pristine sunrise and the unknown road.

Immediately adjacent to the conference center he encountered a steep incline as the road took him through a budding grove of sugar maples and into a tall dark corridor of ancient eastern hemlock. To his right was the Little Susquehanna, swollen with clear snowmelt, and then a winding stair leading down to the grotto.

Not breaking stride, Rixon began the descent and realized that the grotto was located at the base of the conference center, sheltered by the cantilevered terrace above and flanked by an open glass wall that revealed a bar and lounge area and the river less than five feet below. The pool of was configured in a series of interlocking water terraces stepping down from a natural cleft in the granite hillside, the entrance seductively concealed with trailing clematis. As Rixon passed, he noticed a wine bottle and two beer cans floating in the lower pool and then saw a couple begin to stir on the leather couch in the lounge. "Don't get up, just passing through," he whispered as he quietly traversed the pool deck and circled back to the stair.

Back on the road, moving deeper into the hemlocks, he came upon a path leading away to his left, and a in a short distance he entered a small clearing in the tall hemlocks that surrounded the amphitheater. Rendered in the Greek style, of the same stone as the conference center, the construct reminded David of pictures he had seen of the theater at Delphi, the home of the legendary Oracle. Rays of the early morning sun were beginning to define the semicircular stone seating set into the granite hillside and spilling down to a flat stage that was backed by a small "temple," which served the back of stage activities during productions. David stopped a moment to read the inscription carved in the elaborate stone frieze: "An Praeterea Mali Neminem Facere Volueritis." Wishing he had taken the Latin classes offered at Penn State, David tried to visually memorize the inscription as he altered his route to run the "stands" of the amphitheater, just like he would have done at Beaver Stadium, and then he was off again to find the road.

About twenty minutes farther into his run, he broke through the tree line into a carefully manicured meadow, the size of several football fields, which served as the picturesque foreground for the main house and a small herd of majestic white horses. The contrasting darkness of the hemlock forest framed the meadow and the house and gave David the sense of being on a high mountain, pleasantly moving along the gently rolling topography leading him toward the impressive vacation estate of Dr. Carol Dorance.

Two-thirds of the way across, David quickened his pace onto a fork in the road passing a carved stone marker pointing the way to the Enchanted Forest and thereafter into the Cyclops Canyon.

Entering the hemlock ring again, he noticed the height and girth of the individual trees were much larger than before and a warren of graveled paths had been artfully placed, leading away from the main road and deeper into the darkness than he wanted to venture. The road began to descend again, gently and then steeply, returning him to the riverbank. It then abruptly turned left into a tall granite canyon, featuring a respectable waterfall, which was adding thousands of gallons of icy pure spring water into the Little Susquehanna only a few hundred feet to his east. He paused to check his watch and saw that he had been on the road for over an hour and estimated that his pacing should have placed him around six miles into the estate from the conference center. He took advantage of cold water spring, refreshed himself, and continued his run.

"Come on, little Cyclops," he said to himself. "I've come all this way to see you, don't be shy, come on out to play." He began to notice a natural rock formation on the face of the far canyon wall. It seemed to David that the granite had naturally broken away from the sheer cliff and created a large, roughly triangular depression in the surface and that in the center of the depression was a deep horizontal fissure or shallow cave, perhaps natural but possibly altered, that might be construed to be a gigantic cycloptic eye. He stopped to take in the sight. "I'll be, it's the Cyclops, sure as I'm standing here, there he is," he said smiling. "That Dr. Dorance sure knows how to show a guy a good time!" He checked his watch and began his jog back. "Let's see if I can make it in time for the breakfast buffet. I'm starving!" he said to himself, retracing his route at an eight-minute pace, chuckling about the Cyclops as he went.

Unbeknownst to David, the master suite of the main house was located only fifty yards to the west and approximately one hundred feet above him, screened by the old growth hemlock; it presented a perfect view of his location and was precisely aligned with the Cyclops eye across the canyon to the east.

"Kill all the rich pigs, man! Burn their houses and their pets! Slaughter their little poodles, man! Be the first kid on your block to bring the Revolution home, murder your mama and daddy! Can ya' dig it? That's where it's at!" read Carol Dorance aloud in her best faux-baritone imitation of Francis Frank as she playfully mocked him while reading from *Revolutionary Fire*, his best-selling autobiography.

Propped up in her king-sized bed, covered only with a silk sheet, she stopped while Frank, eating cornflakes in his boxers, tried to explain the motivation behind his colorful prose. Laughing together, they simultaneously noticed movement on the canyon path below. From her balcony, they could see David Rixon drinking from the spring, and they shared a perverse delight in being able to observe him in secret.

"You really had him going yesterday, Frankie," said Carol. "I was watching when you called him Scarface, and I thought for a second he was going to snap your neck," she teased.

"Guys like that really piss me off," said Frank. "Got his little god, got his little family, got his little team, got his little GPA, got his little country. Man I'd just like to rub his face in his own puritanical red, white, and blue bullshit!"

"You forgot that he was also voted to the All-Southeastern Conference Team last December and that he could well be named an Academic All American and even meet the president if he keeps his grades up," added Dorance with a wink and a smile.

"Meet the president? I'll show you meet the president!" he said as he grabbed her around the waist in an attempt to pull her back to bed. But she wouldn't go along.

"Do you think he understands what he's looking at?" she asked Frank, as they watched David inspecting the Cyclops eye in the distance.

"Not a chance. We're invisible. The whole thing could be laid out in front of him, but he'd never be able to fathom the significance; hell, none of 'em would. Their paradigm won't permit them to comprehend. That's why I enjoy writing and speaking to them the way I do. In their face, you know? They're too polite to fight back and too stupid to ever see what's going on right in front of them, and by the time they do, it'll be too late."

"Rubbing their own bullshit in their face?" she asked, smiling. "Awe, Frankie, killing their little poodles too?"

"Yeah, something like that," he said, not smiling. "And since we're on the subject, what've you decided about him and his little buddy Vazquez?"

"Vazquez is a good candidate. Smart, loyal, hungry, open to new ideas, family of origin is perfect—born out of wedlock to an illegal Mexican woman so there's no father figure, no wealth, no security at all. The mother is a functional illiterate, blue-collar Catholic, but he's got no faith of his own to speak of. The kid's basically rootless, a human sponge, and should be a good fit for the program. I'll probably submit him for a midmanagement career in the bureaucracy."

"And Rixon?"

"He's a committed Christian and a patriot, so that would normally have disqualified him, but his entire family was killed in an auto accident when he was twelve or thirteen. That's where he got the facial scaring. And he lived in near poverty with his adoptive Mexican family all through high school, so I thought there might have been some rage, or shame, some deep-seated family-of-origin trauma that might have made him a prospect. That's why I had Vazquez bring him out. But after last night, he doesn't seem like a fit. Too bad. He's really the complete package, bilingual even; the kid could have been a congressman, maybe even a senator.

"Just as well, 'cause I really hate the sawed-off little prick," Frank whispered as he began coaxing her back to the bed.

"Yes, Frankie, my dear, there is that and the fact that he actually could snap your neck; just like a little poodle," she said smiling, allowing Francis Frank to sweep her away.

From the attic turret on the forth level of the massive Dorance mansion, directly above Carol's boudoir, a slight female figure was also watching David on his early morning run and turned away from the sharp pain of deep longing in her heart only after her new lover began to stir.

"Vuelve a dar más querido, su amante está esperando. Belinda, I want you," he said sleepily.

"Al Vazquez, I bet you say that to all the girls. They tell me Latin lovers are all the same; just a bunch of good looking gigolos." She smiled as she made her way back under the sheets.

"Darling, if that's all I am to you, then please drop the cash on the dresser before you leave." He smiled as they renewed their first night's embrace.

The lights were on in other parts of the mansion. Al Dorance and Wolfgang Jung were sharing an early morning breakfast in the intimate family dining room, which opened to the sunrise beyond the deep veranda, reflecting across the crystalline pool.

"Dr. Roseman's list of candidates this year isn't nearly as impressive as in the past. What does Dr. Dorance attribute this change to?" inquired Jung between sips of his Earl Grey.

"I had the same question. Carol says that John Kennedy has inspired the current generation of young people to believe in the American system again. His youth, his wife and children, his economic policies, his stand on civil rights, the way he's deescalating tensions with the Soviets, plus this idea of landing a man on the moon has really changed the country. The television cameras are in love with the Kennedys, and that means the country has gone all in for this notion of an actualized Camelot. Quite a lot of people are happy now, Herr Jung. All this in just over two years; for Christ's sake, the man's only forty-four years old. What do you think he'll do in his second term?"

Jung did not reply but sat silently, gravely sipping hot tea and allowing a long silence to metastasize into a strange and frightful tension. "Alfred, the Apex is concerned about the master schedule. Our current trade cycle is near the three-quarter mark, long past the specified phase-in for a successor program, and no one in our leadership has the foggiest idea of what that new program might consist of, or even if it will be acceptable to our masters. Frankly, Herr Dorance, the North American Order is—how do you Americans say—behind the eight ball, and our friends in Washington tell me that our youthful president is refusing to join our team. Idealism is perhaps its own reward; at least this seems to be President Kennedy's current position.

"I fear, Alfred, that there must be an executive action soon, perhaps within this current fiscal year, and I am placing you in charge. Accounts have been established with the normal intermediaries. They will contact you in Boston with the details. This will be a slow dance, Alfred; a Viennese waltz, if you will allow the analogy. Only when I receive the demand letter from the Wintergarten shall we release the funds and authorize the action. Do you understand the gravity of our circumstance, Alfred?"

Dorance was paralyzed with a surge of primal fear, which sent terrifying thoughts screaming into his mind. "Executive action! What the hell is that supposed to mean? The Apex! This is a joke, right? He thinks those things really exist? Wintergarten! It's a myth too, isn't it? He thinks it exists too! He must be insane!" But Dorance calmed himself and took control of his emotions; his reply was calm, precise and perfunctory.

"Sir, I owe my possessions, my wealth, my livelihood, my life, and the lives of my wife and daughter to the Apex, the Order and you. As I am commanded, so shall I proceed."

Dorance bowed his head and kneeled in submission before Jung. "And, Master, may I thank you for the privilege of your bed last evening? I never knew that carnality could be so transcendent. It's as if new vistas have opened before me. I see the world with a clarity that I would never have had without your embrace."

Jung smiled, raised the head of his submissive by the jaw, and looked deeply into his eyes. "Alfred, as you progress in your career, you will find the spiritual power of Sexmajic coupling to be a most important means of knowing your subordinates and ensuring their loyalty. The mystery of our union has broken all other bonds that you may have had, both natural and supernatural. You belong to me now; in every meaningful way, you are my possession, my trusted servant, my beloved." Jung smiled and gently caressed the freshly shaven cheek of his complaint slave.

● ● ●

And in those days there was war in heaven. The archangel Michael fought to subdue the beast. Lucifer and his legions battled for control but could not gain purchase and so lost their hallowed place in the Holy of Holies. The great dragon was restrained and hurled down; the ageless snake, called the devil or Satan or Lucifer or other secret names, uttered for conjure only in the spirit realm, which leads the whole world astray. He was hurled to the earth, and his angels were with him, and their servants were legion.

11

BLACK SWAN

The removal of a head of state by assassination is never the preferred method of exercising control over a sovereign nation. There must be a confluence of imperatives in play with no other means of resolution to even begin to consider such a dangerous course. The variables are too numerous to calculate, and even if the attempt succeeds, there is no guarantee that the dynamics launched by the takedown would not themselves be worse than the original circumstance. The debate had raged for months. Brilliant men with much at stake spoke for and against the murder but in the end it all came down to timing. The master schedule was precise, evolved and charted over decades. Delay of another four years threatened to eradicate a half century of progress and if allowed to continue, the course this chief executive was planning threatened to end their enterprise altogether. This simply could not be allowed.

• • •

"The committee" was tiny, only four members with overlapping areas of expertise: law, operations, psychiatry, and astrology. Protocol required that the attorney chair; that the members had never met and would never see one another again after their work was complete. Security at the obscure Italian monastery was tight as they arrived in separate vehicles deep in the Sicilian night, timed so that they would not encounter one another on the lonely road up the steep approach. As they arrived one by one, the travelers were strip-searched by the waiting security staff and shown to a bath where they showered and were given undergarments, sandals, and the hooded cowl common to the monks in service there. Their personal items would be returned to them once they were inspected.

• • •

They saw one another first as they gathered in the small anteroom for admittance. While the entrance was being closed and bolted from the outside, the small door before them opened, and they entered a dimly lit stone corridor. They followed a hooded man to the end and were allowed into a prayer cell, which would serve as their committee room. They assessed their Spartan accommodations, which consisted of a small table, four stiff-backed wooden chairs, a golden crucifix mounted on the feature wall with its kneeling rail and two golden candle stands. The room was lit with lampstands in its four corners and this allowed them to see another door and small window opposite the corridor and a small square pass-through opposite the crucifix. On the table was a single white envelope with a red wax seal. It was held in place by a crystal paperweight, masterfully carved in the shape of a human skull.

Each man had been given a security phrase and coded response that would identify his colleagues and they began work only after they personally verified one another's identity. The slightest breach at this level would mean their deaths and the deaths of their immediate families as well. Only scorched earth would remain and the foursome knew the risk well.

After they were in their places, The attorney broke the wax seal bearing the imprint of the Apex of the Order, opened the envelope, reviewed it quickly, and read aloud in English:

Black Warrant for the Life of John Fitzgerald Kennedy
Issued at the High Court of Justice for the Global Order
The Wintergarten

Whereas John Fitzgerald Kennedy, president of the United States of America, has been indicted, tried in absentia, and convicted of the high crime of treason against the Global Order and sentence upon Saturday last was pronounced against him by the full membership of the Apex. Under pain of impoverishment and death by dismemberment, it is appointed your solemn duty to assure that his life be taken from him in a manner most profitable and expedient to the Global Order as determined and agreed to by the full membership of the committee. Execution of this warrant shall occur no earlier than 31 October and no later than 30 November of the current solar year. No appeal shall be entertained or granted; the rendered judgment herein is firm and final.

The small room filled with a terrible silence as the attorney read aloud the twelve signatures above the official seal of the Apex, each authored in a sepia ink that may have been human blood. After a long moment, he countersigned the document and offered it to the operator, the astrologist, and the psychiatrist for their cosignatures. After each man examined the document at length, satisfied that his fellows had properly witnessed the warrant, the attorney returned the document to its envelope, placed it in the pass-through where it was taken to the other side. They all knew there was no way out. They were locked in; from now on it was either Kennedy or them.

Their journey had been exhausting and the first news of their duty overwhelming, and so when they saw the morning light peeking through the small window, they agreed to adjourn for their first eight-hour recess. Their commission had specified that the committee would work eight hours on followed by eight hours off until a solution was calculated. That first morning they walked together into the cloistered garden adjacent to the committee room for a moment of reflection and a breath of crisp sea air. There was the smell of jasmine on the breeze, and the sun was beginning to rim above the garden wall, urging them to begin their dreadful deliberations. But the body has needs of its own, and they dispersed to find beds and some food for themselves, with the hope of some rest and repose before they began their secret deliberations of death.

• • •

Refreshed and again in the room, the astrologist placed the president's charts on the small table before them. He explained that from birth, through adolescence, college, military service, marriage, family, additional romantic entanglements, and his political career, the trajectory was clear; the optimum success window for the event would be as the warrant had stated, a thirty-day period from the end of October to the end of November.

The operator volunteered a range of proven clandestine solutions: induced natural causes, scripted accidental death, or perhaps induced suicide. He pointed out that stealth and privacy would assure them of the desired result yet provide them the secrecy that would ensure the escape of the assassins.

"Where is the profit in a private removal?" asked the psychiatrist. "The warrant specifies a profitable death." After much debate as to what constituted "profit" as a byproduct of the assassination, the psychiatrist began to advocate for the black swan.

"The primary advantage of a black swan event is the psychic trauma caused by its profound surprise and extremely high profile. Almost every significant turn in the history of the nation-state is an outgrowth of a radically unexpected event, some would say much like the shock of encountering something that you thought could not exist, like the famous a black swan incident in sixteenth-century London.

"What we are considering is a killing that will have significant international import, and it should be scaled appropriately. To achieve the desired ends and earn the required profit, maximum public exposure is imperative, and as many Americans as possible must be psychically wounded by this event.

"It is the nature of the human mind to seek a quick return to the security of normal life and heal deep subconscious wounds by convincing itself that the event was totally foreseeable and explainable in hindsight. The American mass mind will be fluid for a brief time in the post-event period, and if it is staged properly and the indicators crafted well, then the population will gratefully receive any plausible fiction, as a gift really, and place the blame for the event precisely where it is directed.

"Herein lies the profit; the temporary pliability of the mass mind will allow for executive and legislative policy alterations that would never have been accepted by the population without a civil war. The social compact that Americans have with their government would never allow it.

"The psychic crisis of the sort I envision will allow us to fundamentally transform the national mind-set and, quite literally, allow us to deliver ownership of the fabled American dream into the possession of our masters. To achieve the sort of return on investment required by the Apex, the King of Camelot must be publically, violently, and anonymously murdered. It's the only way. "

After examining the psychiatrist's reasoning, the astrologist, the operator, and the attorney agreed to the high-risk, high-reward approach and the committee began to augment itself through compartmentalization.

Their only link with the outside world was the pass-through into which they placed specifications for computer-assisted actuarial modeling, contingency and logistics planning, parallel-source astrological charting, and historical documents concerning the ancient rite of the "Killing of the King." A day later, they began to discover wooden boxes of various sizes in the committee room as they returned from their scheduled eight-hour breaks. The boxes contained the items they requested and in just over a month, a workable strategy with supporting tactics began to emerge.

There is sometimes an operatic quality sought by accomplished planners of very expensive murders. This is partly because the nature of the aesthetic arrest is to momentarily suspend the voluntary motor skills of the condemned, who has unexpectedly come into eye-to-eye contact with the agent of his own demise, partly because the fog generated by consummation of the beautiful moment tends to facilitate the escape of the killers, and partly because aesthetic integrity offers the event supervisors an intuitive pulse of the performance from start to finish, similar to an opera company performing a much-rehearsed aria. And so it was that after many revisions and through written consultations with their superiors, that the last act of the Kennedy presidency was written, the stage set, the players and their assets specified, and the funding placed. The Black Swan would land in Dallas, Texas, on the twenty-second day of November.

• • •

The diplomatic pouch was hand delivered by special courier to the Italian consulate in Pittsburgh, Pennsylvania. The sleek leather attaché with "REPVBBLICA ITALIANA" inscribed below the state emblem of Italy was secured with a cable tie and lead seal marked with the same impression. It was received by the consul himself who in turn hand delivered the unopened pouch directly to the possession of former Reich minister, and proud naturalized American citizen, Wolfgang Jung, president and CEO of Allegheny Electronics Inc. Jung bowed crisply, took the attaché in hand, dismissed the consul, and made his way to the heliport atop the gleaming glass and steel high-rise overlooking the confluence of the Allegheny, Monongahela, and Ohio Rivers.

It was a brief twenty-minute flight to the secure accommodations of the Dorance estate, where he joined the emergency gathering of the Executive Committee of the North American Order in the gracious second-floor library, with a spectacular view to the famous Cyclops eye in the distance. The committee consisted of the managers of the ten regions of the United States, Canada, and Mexico. These powerful and wealthy men represented proxy ownership and control of more than eighty percent of the Fortune 100: banking, defense, finance, transportation, manufacturing, pharmaceuticals, agriculture, communications, broadcasting, and more, all traded on the New York Stock exchange, and they, in turn, were all the beneficiaries of the mentorship and financial backing of Herr Jung himself. As Jung regarded them, and only because he literally owned title to their livelihoods and their lives, they were closer than brothers, and so they were his personal delegates to create and implement his master plan for the North American Order.

In his heavily accented English, the former German National Socialist addressed his executive retainers. "Gentlemen, greetings to you and thank you very much for attending this very special gathering. I believe we should prepare ourselves for a long evening. The package we were promised has arrived. I took possession of it personally from the consul less than an hour ago and may testify to you that the chain of custody is intact."

He placed the leather pouch on the glossy surface of the deepred cherry table and, after their inspection, he broke the seal, carefully removed the contents, and read the Black Warrant aloud to the hushed and somber gathering. After the document was inspected and the proper countersignatures of all the men in the room were affixed, he opened the sealed Specification of Execution and began to read the work of the committee:

Specification for Execution

Determining the Just Cause for the ritual killing of John Fitzgerald Kennedy, being a complex spiritual matter, requires construction of a cosmological sieve that allows his duties as head of state to pass through unjudged while capturing the innermost secrets of his private realm for close examination. The committee is in possession of information collected by American federal police and intelligence agents indicating the condemned man is involved in ongoing illicit sexual liaisons with a number of women, and it is in the manner of his marital infidelity that he will be allowed to select his own path to Agarthi.

The committee has determined that the spiritual tether to the soul of John Fitzgerald Kennedy shall be attached to the seduction and sexual abuse of a teenaged girl, a presidential intern, in the residency of the chief executive that he shares with his legal wife and two blood born children. This is an overt act of statutory rape; it is fresh and ongoing and is aggravated by oaths of fidelity to his wife and his countrymen, which he willingly took before assembled witnesses and in the presence of God. By choosing this path, he has been unfaithful to his wife, his children, the citizens of his nation and the laws of man and God. Based on the attached sworn affidavit obtained from the Holy See that bears the seal of the bishop of Rome, the committee has learned that the condemned has hardened his heart and refused a recent opportunity to confess and repent from this activity. His refusal separates him from the grace of God, opens his path to the City of the Dead, and allows black access to his immortal soul and the means to bind it eternally to the familiar spirits of the earth in a place called Dealey Plaza, located in Dallas, Texas, USA.

The collective disbelief of the executives at the table was explosive. How could such a trivial matter have been selected by the committee as just cause for the assassination of the president! What about his treachery at the Bay of Pigs or bypassing the State Department to contact Khrushchev directly or refusing to move forward in Vietnam or decoupling the country from the Federal Reserve and having Treasury print and distribute its own currency! This was more than just treason against the Order, it was continental suicide!

"Gentlemen, gentlemen, come to order, please! There is much to do," intoned Jung. "I share your incredulity here, but we've see this evolving for some time, have we not? Installing his younger brother as the attorney general could have meant only one thing; he has discovered our presence within the Department of Justice and intends to root out our agents; this cannot be allowed. However I for one choose not to quibble about the esoteric rationale selected by the committee! Dead is dead, no matter the rationale for the killing.

"Quite frankly, we were fortunate we didn't have to solve this problem during the Eisenhower presidency. His inner core certainly knew far more about us than they ever told poor old Mr. Eisenhower, yet even he was able to discern our presence at the last and even tried to alert the country on national television!

"And now this young one, the virile Mr. Kennedy, seems to truly believe himself president of the United States, and perhaps also King Arthur of Camelot!" There was hearty laughter around the table, which Jung joined for a moment and then drew the meeting to order once more.

"Gentlemen, I say this as a newcomer to America, an immigrant, and proud citizen who only wants the best for our country. This rogue president must be removed!" pronounced Jung forcefully with vociferous approval from the table.

"Thank you for your agreement, but now it is to work we must go. I know there are strategic and tactical matters that are of concern to you but these specifications come to us directly from the Apex, and since they own us all," he said smiling broadly and looking at them with a fatherly charm, "would it not be imprudent of us to challenge their judgment in such a delicate and urgent matter? Please, have some faith in our benefactors, gentlemen; I believe they've earned it."

Reason prevailed, small differences were put aside, a calm center was attained; the gears of the planners and doers meshed, and action items began to emerge for the profitable "Killing of the King."

The financial sector responded first and beautifully by engineering a short-term 3 percent drop in the value the global financial markets, the November 22 shorting would cover the costs of the assassination and yield the seed monies necessary to capitalize and secure control of the many lucrative post-Kennedy enterprises, which would include the mutually beneficial resumption of the very profitable Cold War with the Soviet Union, the invention and testing of a new kind of warfare in Vietnam, and the new American Manned Space Program being chief among them. Money would not be a problem for the Order; it never was.

• • •

The contractors landed at Love Field in separate private aircraft a day apart. They took separate suites at the Dallas Statler Hilton, had dinner in their rooms, and took separate cabs to Dealey Plaza to pace and mark the kill zone and imagine their role in the fluid event. Afterward they took in the nightlife, slept in the next morning and met the Shoot Supervisor for a late lunch at the Egyptian Lounge, spending the evening in its secure environment reviewing their unique role in the operation, and being introduced to the local made men and corrupt police officials who would provide security for the event and transportation back to Love Field for their getaway. That was their compartment and it was all they would ever need to know.

• • •

During the early evening of November 21, the sniper teams and their security escorts visited their prearranged stations, positioned their equipment, and made ready for the morning's work. The teams zeroed their optics and tested their military-grade transceivers, while inspecting the 249-foot long segment of Houston Street that the presidential Lincoln would enter at 12:20. The open car would traverse the kill zone slowly, turning right from Main onto Houston and slowing again to make the sharp left turn onto Elm, exposing the low-speed target completely to Team One, inset from the window on the 3rd floor of the Texas School Book Depository. "Turkey shoot," said Two over the transceiver. "Fish in a barrel," responded One, as he zeroed in on the rental car driven by the shoot supervisor, slowly tracing the target's path to Agarthi.

As they worked and without their knowledge, the warlocks were silently ascending the dark stairs in the Old Red Courthouse on their way to the third floor of the northwest turret, which offered their coven a panoramic view of the "trinity site" and the symbolic roadway trident their murderous hex would use to kill the king of Camelot and tie his soul forever to the bloody ground of Dealey Plaza.

• • •

The secretary in the Parker Exploration field office answered the phone, and after listening for a moment, she called to Joe Gonzales. "Joe, its long distance—it's David—he sounds upset."

"Papa, they shot President Kennedy in Dallas!" cried David. "I just got off the phone with Sissy, and the news reports in Austin are saying that he and Governor Connally were both shot during a parade a little over an hour ago. They're at the hospital in Dallas right now!"

"My God," replied a stunned Pastor Joe. "Now, David, slow down, we don't know any details, this could all be some sort of a mistake," he said, not believing his own words but fearful for his adoptive son so far away from home. "Where are you, son?"

"I'm calling from the pay phone in the dorm, there's a television on the ground floor and I'm going down to find out more after we hang up. Papa, could you say a prayer right now?"

"Sure, son, said Pastor Joe feeling at a loss for words. "Father God, we are afraid that President Kennedy and Governor Connally may have been injured and if this is true, we pray for their protection and healing. Also, Father, we pray Your grace and protection for the families of these men and the United States in this troubled time. For Your mercies and favor we pray in the name of Your son, Jesus. Amen."

"Now, David, get off this phone, get to the television, and call us at home tonight, OK?"

"Yes, Papa," said David.

"And, David, whatever is happening, we'll get through it together. Are you with me?" asked Pastor Joe.

"Yes, sir," said David with renewed courage.

"Son, I've got to go now, Mr. Parker is on the other line. We'll talk tonight," said Joe, pressing the blinking light on the desk telephone. "Joe Gonzales."

"Have you heard yet?" said Bobby Parker to his rig manager.

"Yes, sir. I was just on the phone with David. Are you thinking what I'm thinking?" asked Manager Gonzales.

"I've placed a few calls and will know more later today. If it is what we think, then we shouldn't discuss it on the phone. Lieutenant, I know it'll be difficult and it's been some time since we mustered, but I'm going to ask you to pass the word and assemble the squad tonight. 1900 at headquarters," said Parker.

"Yes, Captain, 1900. We'll be there," replied Joe, and the phone clicked off.

• • •

The Veterans of Foreign Wars Post 41703 was crowded that night but eerily quiet with dozens of men focused on the television coverage of the Kennedy assassination. In the rear of the building was a heavy olive drab door with the word "OPERATIONS" stenciled in black across its width.

"TV says they caught the guy that done it, name's Oswald," said Mr. White.

"If he's alive in a week they could be right. My money says he dies in custody within forty-eight hours, and you know what that means as well as I do," replied Mr. Blue.

"With all the crap Johnson done in Duvall County, it's hard to imagine him bein' president 'n' damned hard his bein' commander in chief," said Mr. Black, shaking his head. "The man's got no honor."

The men stood at attention as the door opened and in walked Lieutenant Gonzales and Captain Parker, their command staff during their service as US Army Rangers attached to the First Battalion, One Hundred Forty-First Infantry Regiment in the Thirty-Sixth Division during its operations in Africa, Europe and elsewhere against the Axis powers.

"Gentlemen, please be seated and thank you for coming on such short notice, especially on this night of all nights," said a genuinely thankful and visibly concerned Parker.

"Our primary concern here this evening is not who killed the president or why but what the transition of power to Vice President Johnson could mean to the country and the armed forces charged with its defense. I say this, as you already know, in reference to the dangerous expansion of executive power authorized by the National

Security Act of nineteen forty-seven, which effectively transferred the constitutional war-making power of Congress to the president and the National Security Council, which consists of the vice president and the appointed secretaries of State and Defense. This means that at fourteen thirty-eight today, Lyndon Baines Johnson came into possession of the sole, unchecked statutory authority necessary to take the United States of America to war.

"Every man in this room paid a price either directly or indirectly for Truman's malfeasance in America's first extraconstitutional war on the Korean peninsula, and our active contacts throughout the uniformed military services view it likely that Johnson will use the Truman debacle and congressional acquiescence as legal precedent for launching an expansion of our existing advisory role to the Diem regime in South Vietnam. In fact, reports from various field logisticians indicate that a substantial unscheduled increase in the delivery of new war material has been happening throughout the system. Army regulations say this material will be designated as surplus unless there is a pressing need for it which, at this time, does not exist. Gentlemen, it appears the bastards have been engaged for over a year in using indefinite delivery contracts to advance the purchase of arms and support material for a new war that has yet to be announced to the general public.

"I need not remind you that conscription remains the law of the land and that under certain provisions of the aforementioned National Security Act, all Delta personnel remain liable for indefinite recall into uniformed military service. This means that the oath you took at the beginning of your service remains valid and so, Gentlemen, the briefing you are about to receive should be considered a military secret and kept as such among members of this unit only. Are there any questions?" Continued silence. "Good. This is what we know." Captain Parker opened an olive drab file folder and began to read his unit into what has the potential to become their first military operation since Victory Europe, 8 May 1945.

"The president was shot to death in Dallas at approximately 1230 Central Standard Time today. Our liaison in Dallas reports that a suspect named Lee Harvey Oswald was arrested by Dallas police and field agents of the Federal Bureau of Investigation at 1345, less than two hours later. Oswald is currently being interrogated in the office of DPD Captain Will Fritz on the third floor of the Dallas Police and Courts Building. At this point it is unknown how or why Oswald was identified as the shooter but word has it that Dallas PD is certain he is the lone assassin, even though the speed of apprehension, determination that he acted alone, and the determination of guilt seems improbable at this point.

"A highly suspicious breech of intergovernmental protocol occurred at Parkland Hospital at approximately 1400 when Kennedy's Secret Service protection detail violated the Tenth Amendment and the laws of the State of Texas by seizing the president's corpse by force of arms. Under state law, all evidence in homicide cases committed in the state of Texas becomes the responsibility of the county sheriff's office, which also controls the county coroner. Under the Tenth Amendment, state law trumps the authority of federal agencies in criminal cases not specifically delineated by federal statute.

"This morning the senior Secret Service agent assigned to protect the president threatened to use his side arm against the coroner, deputies, and patrolmen who held legal custody of the remains. The details of the incident, which occurred at the Parkland morgue, are unclear at this point, but it is known that the legal chain of custody was broken by the Secret Service when they took possession of the body. Gentlemen, in the State of Texas, this is at a minimum felony theft of evidence in a capital murder case. What course of action the Dallas County sheriff and district attorney decide to pursue remains to be seen, but this event strongly suggests some level of involvement by the president's security detail in his murder.

"Shortly after the theft, the body was transferred by hearse to Love Field, stowed aboard *Air Force One*, and transported along with Vice President Johnson and his party to Andrews Air Force Base, arriving there at 1800 Eastern Standard Time today. From that point forward, we are forced to rely on press accounts as to the disposition of the evidence. We will continue to monitor the status of the processing as our associates on the ground in Washington make details available.

"Another matter of interest is a report from our source at Love Field of four unusual general aviation arrivals during the seventy-two hours prior to touchdown of *Air Force One*. Tail numbers indicate two of the aircraft are international, registered to the foreign governments of Italy and France. Another belongs to Beacon Street Bank and Trust out of Boston, and the final unit of interest belongs to Allegheny Electronics Inc. of Pittsburgh, whose president and chief executive happens to be none other than our old friend from our walk across Germany, Reich Minister Wolfgang Jung himself. Why a former member of the Nazi SS and Hitler's inner circle should happen to be in Dallas on the day of the assassination is of particular interest.

"These are the facts as we know them currently but I want to stress that alone they mean absolutely nothing. I for one hope that the incident at Parkland was merely a misunderstanding; that DPD is correct, and they have their man; and that Herr Jung is in Dallas with his grandchildren to visit Six Flags Over Texas, but as you can see, there are important questions yet unanswered. Our sources in Dallas and Washington are developing more information and will report their progress.

"As you spend the remainder of the evening with your families, take care to comfort them and to love them and say a prayer to the Almighty that our concerns are baseless and there is nothing to fear. Then in the morning rise early, go for a run, resume your PT, refamiliarize yourself with your weapons, sharpen your muscle memory, and harden yourselves—because, Gentlemen, you remain first-line defenders of the Constitution and the Republic, which may yet require your service. Dismissed!"

• • •

"It was the damnedest thing I ever seen. Pardon my French, but I've seen lots of damnable things in my line of work," said the shoot supervisor smiling slightly during his debriefing. "Like I was sayin', the target was fully exposed, suspended in the presentation arc, the most beautiful target I ever seen, looking right up at Team One, wavin' at 'em even, but they ain't takin' the shot and the spotter says 'stand by,' so I alert Team Two, figurin' that if One missed him coming, that Two would take him out in the turn. I keyed the mic to call the stand-down when pop! pop! pop! But the target's gone, halfway down Elm by then, nearly to the overpass, completely out of the kill zone, and I don't know what possessed him but the crazy sonofabitch took the shot anyway. The thing is, the target was acceleratin' away and his line was through the trees, so Kennedy was only wounded, I think twice, both nonlethal, so I gotta confess, it wasn't us that killed him."

"What?" said the interviewer. "You what...if it wasn't you, then who?" he asked, stunned by the revelation. "It was his own people; friendly fire, so to speak. The Secret Service guy in the follow car; he hears the shots from behind, sees Kennedy is hit, grabs his M16 and stands up to return fire just when his driver gooses it. The guy's fallin' backward; his weapon swings up, discharges by accident and pops Kennedy right in the head. Damned thing explodes like a melon, splatters his brains all over Mrs. Kennedy just like the specs said. But here's the thing: *he got away.* And then his goddamned head just explodes," he said, making eye contact with the interviewer. "There was somethin' about it, the look of it, the sound, the smell—I never seen nothin' like it, like somebody planned it that way or somethin'. I mean I ain't superstitious or nothin', but that's some pretty wicked juju, my friend." said the shoot supervisor, shaking his head and blessing himself with the sign of the cross. "Some pretty goddamned wicked juju."

Overcoming his disbelief, the interviewer continued working down the list of detailed questions, getting the candid responses and colorful commentary that made the shoot supervisor a favored and trusted source for high-level contract murder. "This concludes the post-event debriefing," said the interviewer into the recorder, repeating the date, time, and location for the record. "Please accept final payment as agreed," he said, sliding a thick manila envelope across the table to the supervisor.

Lifting it, feeling its heft briefly, the supervisor replaced the envelope on the table and gently moved it back to the interviewer. "As much as I'd like to take your money, I can't. We didn't finish the job and that was the deal. It's our code, a point of honor. We always keep our word. And believe me, sir, without honor, we'd be nothing more than a bunch a murderin' savages, scum a the earth, if ya' know what I mean. I just don't think any a us'd be able to live like that."

• • •

Passing through the lobby and leaving the Statler Hilton, the interviewer crossed Commerce Street in the middle of the block and began a slow, thoughtful walk back to his suite at the Adolphus. He paused at the newsstand outside Mercantile Bank and picked up a copy of *The Dallas Morning News*. "KENNEDY SLAIN ON DALLAS STREET," read the bold black headline, "Johnson Becomes President," said the follow-up. Something about seeing the event as a newspaper headline brought the scale of it fully into his consciousness. A mist formed in his eyes, he flushed slightly, and he decided to sit for a shoeshine and a moment of reflection before continuing his walk.

"These are English, handmade," said the shine man, smiling up at the interviewer. "If you don't mind my asking, who's the boot maker?" he said smiling.

"What? Oh, Loake, I think, yes, Loake. Why do you ask?"

"Shoes are my game, my passion. I shine 'em, I repair 'em, I sell 'em, and someday, I'm gonna make 'em," he said while lathering the saddle soap. "So when I seen these, I knew for sure you didn't get 'em from around here. Even Neiman's don't sell nothin' like this."

Observing the near vacancy and eerie silence of Commerce Street, it was clear that the shine man was here not because he wanted to be but because he had to be. To distract himself, he decided to engage. "Tell me, my friend, tell me about the shoes you will make someday," he said to the crown of the man's head. "What will you call your brand?"

"Oh, that's easy. 'Smith,' just plain 'Smith.' It's my family name. There are Smiths all over south Dallas but I'm gonna be the Smith that makes the finest, most expensive men's shoes in Texas," he said, looking up with a grin, applying the black directly with his fingers.

"So, Mr. Smith, how will you promote your shoes? How will prospective customers learn of your product?" he asked, taking an idle interest.

Taking his worn horsehair brush from the shine box, spinning it acrobatically in his palm, and then beginning to remove the haze, Mr. Smith said, "That's easy too—word of mouth. When a gentleman such as yourself comes to Dallas and enjoys a business lunch with his associates at the Petroleum Club, he may notice their distinctive footwear and ask where he might purchase a similar shoe, and the Dallas businessman will say, "Smith, of course, simply Smith." He said it with a smile, infecting the interviewer with his fantasy and optimism.

"And tell me, Mr. Smith, as worthy as your venture sounds, how do you suspect that it will come to fruition?" He was rapidly running a long strip of white cotton cloth across the leather to reveal the deep luster of the Loake, Smith replied, "My mama 'n' daddy say this is America, 'n' if you have a dream, work hard, and follow the rules, it can come true. I believe that but I also have a plan. I put a little each week in our savings, and then my wife works. She says that with the Lord's help, we'll make it together. There you are!" he said, beaming up at his customer.

"They look better than new," said the interviewer, admiring the gloss at length. "Mr. Smith, I'm sorry to trouble you but do you have change for a one-hundred-dollar bill?" he asked, presenting a crisp Federal Reserve note and leaving the chair.

As Smith was breaking the hundred at the news cashier, the interviewer pretended to inspect his shine closer by kneeling and then quickly concealed the Kennedy blood money deep inside the shine box.

"Here you go, sir. It's seventy five cents for the shine," said Mr. Smith pleasantly.

The interviewer peeled a twenty off the proceeds of the broken hundred, extracted a card from his inside jacket pocket and placed them both in the shine man's hand. "Mr. Smith, please contact my office at this number when you are ready. I would like to be the first man to own a pair of Smith shoes," he said, smiling and accepting Smith's heartfelt handshake and gratitude.

He continued on to his suite muttering to himself, "What in God's name have we done?" as a delighted Mr. Smith pocketed the twenty and began to closely inspect the business card of his first customer: Alfred C. Dorance III, Governor, Federal Reserve System, Boston, Massachusetts.

Dorance continued his slow walk along Commerce, noticing the early Christmas decorations in some of the store windows and how the city workmen had already placed the shimmering municipal garland around the streetlights. He lingered for a moment in front of a Neiman's window. "Welcome to Dallas, Mr. President!" proclaimed the banner above a life-size photo of the first family, with appropriately expensive souvenir items artfully arrayed below. For a moment he considered bringing something home to his wife and daughter to memorialize his extended business trip to Texas but then lost the urge when he overheard a couple discussing the Kennedy murder while waiting on a bus. "The president's gone. What does that mean? What are we gonna do?" The woman sobbed. "It'll be OK, it'll be OK," replied the man, patting her with tears streaming down his cheeks.

"Don't lie to her, you fool, of course it won't be OK. It'll never be OK again. Kennedy is dead and so is the whole goddamned country!" he said to himself, grimacing as if in physical pain, and prodded to move along by their grief, fear, and his profound guilt.

"Judas! Judas! Judas! Hung himself; probably in hell right now; waiting on YOU!" he screamed in pain; his mind seemed to be coming out of his skull through his mouth.

Approaching the Magnolia Oil Building he noticed the red neon hoof of the trademark Pegasus arc high above the sidewalk and remembered something about the winged horse being born from Medusa's blood after a mythic warrior, out to make a name for himself no doubt, decapitated the poor girl in her own living room. "The lady never had a chance," he mused, smiling to himself as he shuffled by, seeing the doorman's red jacket and security of the hotel beyond. "Bitch deserved it!" He sniggered to himself at his humorous observation.

"YOU SONOFABITCH! IT WAS YOU!" came the stinging accusation and accompanying screams from the alley to his right. Thinking for an instant that he was exposed, eyes wide and breathless, he turned to witness two men launch themselves at each other deep in the shadows. And then, seeing the assault for the argument it was, he considered that the fear of a public revelation may have come from someplace deep in his own psyche. Was the stress too much? Was he beginning to...slip?

"Blood, red blood! It's all over me!" he said to himself. "How can they not see?" Wide-eyed and perspiring, he increased his pace away from the alley, crossing against the light at Akard Street in a dead run, he slowed to a fast walk at the corner, hurried past the doorman, took a breath in the ornate foyer of the Old World Adolphus and made his way to the nearly vacant lobby bar. He needed a drink!

"Are you all right, Mr. Dorance?" asked the smiling bartender, refilling his trembling glass. "Should I call the hotel doctor?"

"How...how do you know my name?" asked a visibly disturbed Dorance.

"Sir, you've been with us for nearly six weeks. I've served you many times sitting in this very chair. Are you sure it wouldn't be prudent to have the doctor look you over?"

"No, no, it's just…the president. I'm like everyone else, I suppose, shocked it would happen, that it would happen here, while I'm here on business, I mean. The whole thing is just unbelievable."

"It seems perfectly understandable to me," said a heavily accented Germanic voice from behind. "The newspaper says they already have the man who did it, a Communist. Who would have guessed?" He felt a gloved hand on his shoulder. "Hello, Alfred. I'm here for our appointment, have you forgotten we have a meeting scheduled?" He turned to come face-to-face with Wolfgang Jung.

"Alfred, you're flushed. Are you not feeling well?" said Jung, beginning to inspect his apprentice closely. "Here, my boy, let us adjourn, I believe you must lie down, do you have the key to your room?"

Jung closed and locked the heavy gilded door to the Regency suite, gently guided Dorance to the middle of the deep plush carpet turned him as if he intended to have a word and swiftly punched Alfred Dorance in the stomach. A second punch to the side of his face knocked him to the floor, where Jung leaped atop his victim's heaving chest and grabbed his jaw in his powerful gloved hand.

"Listen, you little bastard! You will not fuck this up!" said a furious, red-faced Jung, spewing spittle into the face of a terrified Dorance. "I sent you here to do a job. You can go to pieces; kill yourself if you want, but only after the job if finished. DO YOU UNDERSTAND?

"We'll have dinner as planned at seven and the reception at nine, and I expect you to be on your game. If you're not, then you're of no further use to me. DO YOU UNDERSTAND?" said Jung, squeezing his jaw in his powerful grip.

"Yes, sir. Yes, sir, I understand. I won't disappoint. I promise. Please, sir, give me another chance…"

Pushing off Dorance's face, Jung rose, straightened his coat, and walked to the door.

"Seven sharp at the French Room. And please, Herr Dorance, don't bother to get up, I'll show myself out." The door closed quietly and latched by itself.

The drug-induced attitude adjustment was dramatic. Refreshed, and brimming with a newfound confidence, Dorance met his guests as planned and entertained them with the story of the shine man on Commerce Street who had delusions of becoming the manufacturer of "…the most exclusive men's footwear in Texas! Can you imagine? The most exclusive shoes from Texas would have to include detachable gold-plated spurs!"

His guests were roaring with laughter at the thought of middle-aged Texans in tailored English suits with cowboy hats attaching their spurs before entering into serious business negotiations. "Tell us, Alfred, what would the man call his shoes?"

"Smith, he said, simply Smith," explained Dorance as a lead in to his joke about there being so many Smiths in south Dallas because of their shared lineage. The gentlemen were in stiches. By the time they had completed dinner they were in high spirits, had had their fill of jocularity and were ready for the show.

Six shiny black limousines were waiting in the valet line to transport the men less than three blocks to the Federal Reserve Bank of Dallas. Traveling in caravan formation with a DPD motorcycle escort, they entered the ramp to the underground shipping area where they were met by a group of uniformed Federal Reserve police officers, each carrying a side arm and shotgun. After a review of their identification badges, the DPD motor officers peeled away and the caravan was allowed to proceed through a large, heavily reinforced cargo door, which then coiled closed and latched securely behind them.

Dorance emerged from the lead car and conferred with his FRPD security detail dressed in black business suits, white shirts, and black ties, and thereafter a uniformed officer went to each car, opened the door, and ushered the guests into the very large freight elevator, which took them to the operations center in the subbasement.

Known as the "War Room" by the career FRPD officers who secured it, the Operations Center had no means of egress other than the mantrap they used to gain entrance; once the door was locked, they were in a totally secure environment.

Dorance directed their attention inward to a large and low planning table featuring an architectural scale model of Dealey Plaza complete with automobiles, people, and the locations of the sniper nests with strands of back thread indicating the overlapping fields of fire of Alpha and Bravo. The display was surrounded by several wheeled black boards, a dozen or more chairs and several rows of work stations equipped with various forms of military-grade communication, command, and control equipment. They heard a "click" as the guards locked them in.

After using the model to explain the physics of the event, Dorance directed the dignitaries to a group of padded chairs and began his formal presentation.

"Gentlemen, welcome to the Dallas Operations Center for Project Recompense. As you know, Recompense began eighteen months ago when we were given the task of suspending democratic control of the United States government in order to install a proxy executive for the purpose of realigning federal policy with the vital interests of the international community and, of course, to conform North America's progress line to the master schedule as requested from all of us by the Apex.

"The most daunting aspect of Recompense was to devise a way to perform the suspension and installation in such a manner as to reduce the possibility of panicking just over one hundred eighty-nine million American citizens. Change is difficult for us all, and we believe that the safest and most humane manner for establishing a divergent path for America is to allow the new reality of diminished political control to emerge gradually within the subconscious mass mind by introducing the trauma necessary to trigger the appropriate emotional response and then to provide quick assurance that all is well. To propagate the ameliorative atmosphere of faux normalcy, we've opted to maintain the civil government intact for the moment and focus first on disabling any potential military or federal law enforcement resistance through a program of command neutralization.

"Slightly more than a year ago our operatives at the federal level assembled a master list of senior members of the military, intelligence, and law enforcement services who they believed would have the credibility and desire to alert the general population to our intent and might also have the ability to mobilize an effective resistance, perhaps enough to plunge America into a second civil war. We referred to these men as our "Paul Reveres" and began a program of neutralization using bribery, blackmail, and murder with a very high success rate. To date, I am pleased to report that eighty nine percent of our Reveres have been neutralized and nearly half that number have responded positively to various combinations of bribery and coercion. These men will be very valuable in maintaining the illusion of normalcy, as they will remain at their posts and available for further processing, perhaps even conversion to operatives themselves.

"Effectively, gentlemen, the structural changes necessary for our plan to advance had already been made when President Kennedy arrived in Dealey Plaza yesterday. At this moment, I am supremely confident that the gunshot that took his life was the first and last to be fired in the coup d'etat that averted a massive bloodletting while putting an end to the disaster known as the American Experiment," thus concluded Alfred Dorance with a broad smile on his face and a thank you on his lips, as his audience applauded loudly.

"And now, gentlemen, if you will accompany me to the viewing room for our grand finale." Dorance led the way and waited while each man found his seat. Dorance made a brief introduction. "The film you are about to see will never be shown to anyone other than the Apex themselves and it will be sent to the Wintergarten this evening by diplomatic courier for their pleasure and permanent archives.

"NAO photographers were stationed behind Alpha and Bravo teams, atop the railroad overpass just over Elm Street and in the third floor of the Dallas County Records building. The film was processed by our own technicians in this building and there is no chance that anyone outside the Order will have the slightest knowledge of its existence," Dorance concluded as the lights were diming.

On a large bright screen, the audience was able to view the execution of John Fitzgerald Kennedy from four distinctive vantage

points, all in full color. Each view revealed the mystery of the accidental coup de grace and the strange role of the Secret Service agent
in dispatching his president. "My God," gasped someone from the
rear of the darkened room. But it was the palpable horror of the
cranial impact, the bloody mist of Kennedy's exploding skull, the
whipsaw of his instantly lifeless corpse and the pathos of Jacqueline
Kennedy as she crawled on her hands and knees across the Lincoln's
rear deck to retrieve a fragment of her husband's brain, which sent a
deep wave of remorse sweeping through the crowd.

The film ended, the lights came up, and to lift the heavy silence,
Dorance again took the podium and said brightly, "Are there any
questions?"

After a long moment, and probably to distract from what they
had all just witnessed, he was asked, "Please, Alfred, could you give
us a little more detail, perhaps about this facility, why did you select
Dallas? I'm sure we all find the operation fascinating."

"Ah yes, the facility," replied Dorance. "Many people do not
realize that the Federal Reserve System is not a government agency
but a privately owned central bank controlled by the shareholders,
all of them members of the Order. An interesting feature of the
enabling legislation is that the real estate holdings of the system
were designated as federal reservations, exempt from all local, state,
and federal law. As you saw when we arrived, the fed has its own
police force and intelligence professionals; they coordinate with the
United States Treasury Department and the Secret Service but are
themselves exempt from the law while on fed property. This facility
is in effect a sovereign entity, much like a diplomatic consulate, one
which is literally owned by the North American Order. Everywhere
there is a Federal Reserve Bank, there is the Order.

"You'll remember that Dallas was prescribed as the assignation
site in the warrant issued by the Apex, and it took some effort to
attach it to the list of cities on the president's travel itinerary, especially within the window specified. Fortunately, many assets were
already positioned here that could be retasked for Recompense—
this Oswald man for instance—but the most fortunate of all was the

coincidence of the Cabell brothers, Earle and William. The former being the current mayor of Dallas and the latter being the former deputy director of the Central Intelligence Agency. He was released by President Kennedy for his role in the planning and execution of the unauthorized invasion of Communist Cuba, famously referred to as "the Bay of Pigs."

"I want to stress that neither of the Cabell brothers knew of Recompense and were as surprised by the event as anyone. William's unhappy relationship with the president and Earle's role as mayor were merely the finishing touch of a very expensive and sophisticated disinformation campaign that took nearly a year to put in place. Disinformation in a civilian setting is akin to the fog of war in a combat theater, camouflaging one's intent and misdirecting the focus of one's adversaries is an essential element of success. A dividend of the unwelcome attention that will be paid to the Cabells is that this smudge on their family name could well be useful to the NAO as these men move forward in their careers. Redemption can be a powerful inducement, given the correct circumstances. I might also add that Mayor Cabell is a cheerful fellow with a good head for politics and was very useful in opening many doors here in Dallas during our stay.

"As to the potential for exposure, my father used to say that great reward requires great risk, so one might conclude that this role was something that I was born to, something I relish. Gentlemen, in my view there is no price so high that would have kept me from this supremely important duty. I thank you all again for the honor of this opportunity. Are there any other questions?"

"I'm just a little curious—were the assassins also employees of the Federal Reserve?" From the same man in the rear.

"No not at all. For something of this nature we use specialists, contractors from outside the United States. In order to assure their undetected arrival, they were flown into Love Field aboard aircraft owned by the friendly governments in Italy and France on the pretext of a diplomatic mission convergent with the President's visit. To assure freedom of movement while in our employ, the teams were also issued diplomatic passports by their country of origin, thereby assuring their safety while inside the United States.

"If there is nothing else, then please accept my thanks for your attendance and attention. Herr Jung, if you please," said Dorance, gesturing to the heretofore silent ranking member of the North American Order, who took the podium.

"Very impressive, Mr. Dorance. Thank you for your presentation and the film—magnificent, just magnificent!" he began to applaud, which was followed by the others and died away soon after he ceased.

"Gentlemen, it is a new day in America! We have finally witnessed the grounding of the obsolete and problematic Republic of Washington, Adams, Jefferson, and Madison. We have midwifed the birth of the inevitable North American Order! Happy tidings shall go forth to all!" He smiled broadly, leading another rousing round of applause.

Alfred Dorance joined in the celebration and smiles but was unable to push the words of the shoot supervisor out of his mind: "That's some pretty wicked juju, my friend, some pretty goddamned wicked juju."

12

THE RUBRIC OF WAR

"Proclamation 3585, Prayer for Peace, Memorial Day, 1964" read in part:

> *Now, therefore, I, Lyndon B. Johnson, President of the United States of America, do hereby designate Memorial Day, Saturday, May 30, 1964, as a day of prayer for permanent peace, and I call upon all the people of the Nation to invoke God's blessing on those who have died in defense of our country and to pray for a world of law and order. I designate the hour beginning in each locality at eleven o'clock in the morning of that day as the time to unite in such prayer. "*

"Thay just won't leave us alone," said the veteran. "Bennie, you realize in our entire lives thay ain't been more 'n' two or three years in a row when we was really at peace, where we wasn't off killin' somebody somewhere for somethin' 'at some rich sumbitch thought mattered so much 'at thay outta send us in to settle thay score? Yah hear 'em politicians all th' time sayn' 'at America hates war, but 'tween you 'n' me, 'at's a steamin', stinkin' crock 'a manure. Hell, tha' bastards love it! Cain't get enough! As long as it's us doin' the killin' 'n' dyin', just so long as it ain't them 'at's gotta take a rifle or a knife 'n' ask a fella ya ain't never met if he'd mind very much if we run Ol' Glory up his flagpole. Hee, hee. Sumofem 'll let ya, sumofem 'll cut yer head off, like 'at time me 'n you was in our cozy little fox-hole 'n them Chinamen paid us a little visit late, hell musta been two, three in tha mornin'. Ya' snatched up 'at grenade 'n' was gonna toss it right back at 'em. Hell, Bennie, it shoulda been me 'at done it, not you! You had Margaret 'n the girls…Ah, thay miss thay daddy, Bennie, but them girls 'a yours thay grew up fine, both of 'em married 'n got babies 'a thay own…'n Lord, I'm so sorry, Bennie, but Margaret, she never got over it, she never remarried 'n I don't believe she was ever with anyone else till the day she passed. Bennie, I'm so sorry, I done all I could—ya 'member 'at General Walker fella, when he had us dug in behind the Naktong, sayin' that givin' up 'd be worse 'n' gettin' killed? Brave little bastard, weren't he? Well, in case ya' ain't heard, he got hisownself killed in a car wreck day 'fore Christmas back in fifty. A car wreck, can ya imagin'? Wonder what he thinks 'bout the dyin' part 'a his little talk now? Hee, hee…Well, ol' friend, I'm getting' sorta tired now 'n', tha'll be wunderin' where I am…Ya know, Bennie, I been thinkin'. All this killin', all this dyin', all this war, it just twists ever' thin' up, ya know? Blows big holes clean thru a man's soul, don't never heal, makes ya' think sum times that even more 'n lovin' war, the bastards 'at run things hate peace…seems like all a 'em just despise tha notion 'a mindin' thay own business 'n' lettin' folks get along on thay own… sumtime, Bennie, I just wish ta God thay'd leave us alone, let us be 'n just let us live our lives."

After a moment and with great effort, the veteran pushed himself off his knees and up on his crutches. He straightened the little American flag at his feet, and he stiffened and brought himself to salute, scanning the long orderly rows of white crosses, each decorated with its own small replica of Old Glory, secured forever in America's field of honor.

● ● ●

David Rixon was a third-year linebacker for the Nittany Lions when he saw the television coverage of President Kennedy's murder on the streets of Dallas. The event and its import profoundly affected his view of the world outside Beaver Stadium, of his country's role in it, and of the mission field that the Lord was opening up before him.

STEVE A MADISON

"You raised in Texas were 'ya, David?" asked the recruiter. "Like me 'n' tha president?" he said with a broad, easy smile.

"Yes, sir. Odessa," replied David.

Nod, long pause while studying his college transcript then looking up with a smile "Well, son, let's do a little roll playin' game fer a second. If it's OK with you," he said, smiling but looking more serious.

"Yes, sir," David said, nodding that it was.

"Let's say, David, ya' lived in a little town down close to tha' meskin' border, say Eagle Pass." looking David in the eye.

"You 'n' ya' friends been livin' there all 'a yer lives, done pretty well too. The land ya' family's owned for generations, well, you farm it now. Ya' live in a house ya' built with your own hands, ya' got a few head 'a cattle, ya' bottle raised most of 'um from calves, gott'a pretty little wife 'n a' couple 'a young kids. Well, David, its *family*." he said with a warmth that indicated a personal knowledge of generational agrarian life.

"'N like everyone else in Eagle Pass, you just trying ta' make a livin', raise ya' kids, love ya' wife, worship the Lord and maybe have a little fun on the weekend," he said in his studied West Texas drawl.

"Life is hard but good 'til 'a group 'a thugs from across the river show up, break inta yer house at midnight, stick a gun in ya' face 'n' say you been livin' on *their* land all these years. They say their gang is takin' it back 'n if you don't cooperate, they'll kill your kids. 'N' oh, by the way, they gonna' be settin' up a brand new government to run Eagle Pass and that costs money so there's gonna be a new tax—around half'a what you can scratch outta your little patch 'a dirt, they say, 'n if ya' don't pay, they gonna rape ya' wife 'n kill ya' mama 'n' daddy," he said, looking at David with a hard and fearsome countenance.

"'N' just to show how serious they are 'bout the whole thang, they drag your neighbor's kids, squalin', terrified little young'uns, drag 'em into ya' livin' room 'n cut they heads off with a machete right in front 'a you, ya' wife, and ya' babies. Then they up'n leave, say they'll be back next week 'n' you'd better have the first payment on the tax ready or else." Long pause to let the shock play over David's conscious mind.

"How'd ya' feel, David, if that happened to you 'n' there wasn't a damned thing ya' could do to stop it? Nobody ta' help neither. No police, no sheriff, no state troopers, not even a Texas Ranger, nobody at all 'cause thay all been killed already by the same bastards holdin' a gun to ya head." Another pause, the tension mounting.

"Well, son, it riles me just to tell th' story, 'n' it outta rile you to hear it, but truth is, it ain't no story." The recruiter pushed an official-looking manila folder across the granite conference table for David to inspect. Looking solemn, he said in a hushed voice, "It's the sorta thing been goin' on all over South Vietnam fer years. 'N', David, ain't nobody but the United States can do a damned thing 'bout the situation," he said with gravity, looking deep into David's eyes.

"That's why President Johnson needs young men like you in the Marine Corps, son, ta' help protect the people 'a South Vietnam; people just like you, your mama, daddy 'n little brothers, from them thievin', murderin' bastard Viet Cong and they big brother North Vietnamese Communists, sons 'a bitches, ever' damn' one."

The bile rose in the back of David Rixon's throat and he stifled a gasp as he examined the photographs contained in the "Top Secret" State Department file detailing the home invasion, torture and murder tactics used by Viet Cong infiltrators against the people of the South. The report said that the VC were controlled from Hanoi by Ho Chi Minh's Communist regime, supported and allied with Mao Tse-tung's Communist China to the immediate north and were systematically dispatched across South Vietnam, district by district, to extort funding and conscripts for their guerrilla war against the Nguyen Cao Ky government in Saigon.

Their goal was to mount a full-scale invasion of the South within two years with the intent of "purging," either by execution or deportation, the middle and upper classes, approximately 20 percent of the entire population, who would never accept Communist governance, while forcibly "reeducating" the remaining 80 percent to fulfill their new role as workers supporting a "unified" Communist Vietnam.

After a long pause, David looked the recruiter in the eye and said, "Sir, if this figure is correct, twenty percent of the population of South Vietnam would be around three million people."

"Figure's correct, son. It's mass murder they fixin' ta' do, just like Mao and his folks been doin' in China for damn near fifteen years 'n' Ho Chi Minh thinks he's a real swell guy 'cause of it." said the recruiter, shaking his head slowly.

"Fact is, Mao's where Ho gets most 'a his ideas, nearly all his weapons 'n' money, 'n' probably his marchin' orders ta' boot.

'You heard of the domino theory, ain't ya, David? That's their play in Southeast Asia. First Vietnam, then Laos, then Thailand and Cambodia. Hell, sumofem's even talking 'bout someday takin' tha Philippines, Japan, Hawaii, and then jumpin' the goddamned Pacific Ocean ta start in on California!

"And, David," the recruiter began his summation close seamlessly, "that's 'xactly why President Johnson needs *you* as a Marine Corps officer. To help him stop the bastards in South Vietnam, give those good people over thar some relief and keep that kinda bloodthirsty sadistic thinkin' confined to Indochina and away from everthin' near and dear ta us here in tha States. So how 'bout it, son?" he said with a broad, welcoming grin that showed off his perfect teeth. "Ya with us?" And he took David's hand as a show of fraternal solidarity.

At that moment, a tear came to David Rixon's eye, and seeing that his prospect was profoundly moved, and probably hooked, the recruiter backed off, gave him some line, and gently concluded his interview. Retrieving his copy of the State Department's declassified and obsolete assessment of the state of South Vietnam he promised David a callback and a follow-up interview with more specifics toward the end of the semester. And they left the conference room feeling a little like father and son.

"How'd ya do, Gunny?" asked his companion as the recruiter returned to his government Chevy parked in a visitor slot beside the Alfred C. Dorance Jr. Administration Building.

"That Rixon kid is a heluva prospect. You know he benches over three hundred 'n runs a four four forty?" he said, shaking his head in disbelief. "Here's his jacket," he said, handing the Rixon file across the front seat. "Damnation, Sarge, on yer best day, you ever even cum close ta that? He'd be a perfect Special Forces operator. Kinda short though, only five six, but you should see tha arms on that son of a gun. Damned impressive."

"Yea, 'n' smart as hell, I bet." the sergeant replied. "But did you sign him? Remember the quota? We ain't been doin' too hot in that department, in case you forgot, Gunny."

"Take heart, Sergeant, I have high confidence that our luck's 'bout 'ta change and our signing rate is gonna' improve dramatically. Lets' just say a little bird I know at tha Pentagon whispered it in my ear," said the recruiter with his broad toothy grin as he started the engine and drove them away from Penn State to interview their Ivy League prospects at the University of Pennsylvania.

• • •

The evening of August 4, 1964, President Lyndon Baines Johnson appeared on national television to tell the American people that their country had been attacked by the North Vietnamese Communists in the Gulf of Tonkin, and that he would ask Congress to authorize a full military response.

The recruiter was watching, cussing and adjusting the picture of his brand-new RCA Victor color television when his telephone rang. "Now who in tha hell would be callin' here this tima night?" the recruiter wondered out loud as he picked up the receiver. It was David Rixon.

• • •

The entire nation was watching President Johnson's declaration of war that warm August evening, including the assembled membership of the Executive Committee of Beacon Street Bank and Trust. Alfred C. Dorance III, president and chief executive officer, had called the emergency meeting only that afternoon in order to brief them on their newest piece of business which, coincidentally, had quite a lot to do with an obscure little country in Southeast Asia that none of them knew very much about.

Dorance shared controlling ownership of BSB&T with four major stockholders, all legacy partners and descendants of the five families who held the original charter granted by the Commonwealth of Massachusetts only sixteen years after the American Revolution. That night, Dorance had watched his partners become transfixed as President Lyndon Johnson regaled the national television audience with a tale of North Vietnamese aggression on the high seas, of the bravery of the American sailors and airmen as they successfully fought off their assailants, and of the continuing reign of terror visited on peaceful South Vietnamese villagers by their treacherous cousins to the north. Near the end of the broadcast, Dorance muted the audio and allowed the network feed from the Whitehouse to continue silently across a bank of dedicated monitors mounted in the heavily burled walnut paneling that was the signature motif of the executive floor of their eight-story bank building. Dorance rose from his chair and walked in front of the televised president, symbolically usurping his authority.

"Gentlemen, I've asked you here this evening to discuss a new beginning for Beacon Street Bank and Trust," he said, looking deeply into their eyes as he lowered his tone to increase the gravity of the moment. "I needn't remind you that five generations ago our families founded this institution on this very site, and since that day in seventeen ninety-two, our business model and revenue streams have been purely conventional and very conservative. "Trust" has always been more than just a word here at B.S.B. and T." He directed their attention to the gilt-framed portraits of the founders. "For over one hundred and fifty years it's been our sine quo non, that quality without which we would not be. 'Trust,' gentlemen; it's our most profound and valued legacy.

"But this is nineteen-sixty-four, and as you know all too well, the dual forces of the faltering national economy and the rigor of our current regulatory environment have severely eroded our traditional business model, thereby constricting our projected revenue streams and, I fear, that for the foreseeable future the fortunes of our primary franchise shall suffer a protracted decline. There is no easy way to put this. Gentlemen, we have known one another all of our lives, so I must be blunt and state clearly the unhappy fact that each of you already knows; unless something is done, and done soon, Beacon Street Bank and Trust will cease to exist in just over five years." Dorance held their attention but paused for a long moment to allow the serious nature of their shared circumstance to penetrate their consciousness, and then a bit longer to increase their discomfort. He glanced at his notes, took a sip of water and continued.

"But there is an emerging business opportunity that has come to my attention, which may enable B.S.B. and T to broaden its business model in a way that could allow us to remain faithful to our original charter and keep you and your families in the manner that your birthright demands." He leaned forward, placed his clenched fists on the highly polished surface of the ornately carved walnut conference table. "This opportunity however, is not without risk, perhaps more than B.S.B. and T is prepared to underwrite," he said with a well-crafted look of chastened sobriety. "I offer for your comfort the fact that several European institutions have pioneered this service line with good experience since the late nineteen thirties and all report a history of mostly reliable and extremely profitable debt service due to the innovative methods of loan collateralization, which mitigate the risk to the financier. In addition, an attractive feature of this vehicle is the high potential for long-term, residual revenue streams and lucrative accessory business opportunities that, I understand, often continue far after the loan closeout date. In fact, gentlemen, if this opportunity is indeed what I believe it to be, it could well endow B.S.B. and T, and our families, for the next five generations."

At this juncture, a very interested committee member spoke. "Alfred, may we know the nature of the business line?"

Rising to his full height he said forcefully, "Gentleman, if there is to be war, as President Johnson indicates, then there must be financial means secured in order to proceed...," said Dorance, skillfully laying the trap, "and while I am not prepared to reveal pertinent details this evening, I may say that the opportunity under consideration generally revolves around the emerging requirements of the defense industry."

As visions of lending to Lockheed Martin and General Dynamics exploded across their minds, smiles of relief and words of approval coming from their mouths signaled Dorance that they had taken the bait. "Please, gentlemen, I may say nothing further at this point. But according to the charter, to be able to investigate a new service line, what I will need from you this evening is your written approval to proceed." The secretary had entered the room on a silent signal from Dorance and was distributing consent forms to each of the members. "On your authorization, I will prepare a full report for your consideration at the normal fourth-quarter meeting of the entire board."

Dorance returned their smiles and humbly accepted their confidence and their trust as they placed the executed consent forms in his hand. "If there is no further business, then the meeting is adjourned and, gentlemen, please give my best to your families," he said with a smile, knowing all the while that processing large cash deposits from illegal Laotian opium sales would not be palatable to all of the shareholders, and that the more difficult aspect of his job as CEO would be to find a way to get them to say yes while keeping them ignorant long enough to push them out. Nothing personal; business is business.

• • •

Meeting on the top floor of the secure headquarters of Parker Exploration in downtown Odessa, Bobby Parker and Joe Gonzales clicked off the television after the shock of President Johnson's national address and sat for a moment in thoughtful silence, each holding a dark sense of foreboding.

"Joe, I have enough information now to read you into what may become a mature operation but I need to warn you, it's worse than we imagined," said Parker, sliding a file folder across the conference table. "Before they killed the president, we estimate that they had compromised nearly sixty percent of the senior military command structure as well as enough of the Justice Department, FBI, and CIA for it to go off without a hitch. It was clearly an internal coup d'etat, Joe, of that there can be no doubt. At this point, we don't know who's in control of the government but the authority line no longer runs to the American people."

"My God," said Joe with a gasp, his head whirling, slight nausea growing, "who's responsible? Have you been able to track it back? Is it the Cubans, the Russians? It wouldn't be the Chinese; they're allied with North Vietnam and Johnson is about unleash hell on them," said Gonzales beginning to page through the report.

"As you'll see working through the brief, Joe, a threat far more dangerous to the Unites States of America than global communism has emerged. At this point in the investigation, it appears internal to our government, Joe, and its roots run back to at least nineteen forty-seven and that damned National Security Act of Harry Truman. It seems that after the war, when the assets of the Office of Strategic Services were assigned to the State Department that somehow, some way, the crime syndicates were able to infiltrate the federal law enforcement system, and since then have become like a cancer.

"The president and the attorney general were starting to root out the syndicates until Dallas, but the mob isn't the only problem, it appears that the core group of treasonous bureaucrats that allowed the gangsters to metastasize was imported by Truman directly from Nazi Germany in 1945 under "Operation Paperclip." Paperclip was intended to identify and recruit German scientists for use by the War Department, and to his credit, Truman's orders specifically disqualified Nazi Party members from the program. But he didn't understand the dangerous actors embedded in the State and the Justice Departments.

"The administration of Paperclip was delegated by the Joint Chiefs to something called the "Joint Intelligence Operations Agency," which was supposed to consist of four members, one each from the army, navy, air corps, and the State Department. JIOA was supposed to find the German scientists we needed who were not members of the Nazi Party, but what they actually did was manufacture false identities for the talent they wanted so they could fit into the program. Our researchers have discovered that JIOA's records were transferred to Justice and that the JIOA itself has been disbanded. When our man pressed his contacts at Justice for the membership list of the JIOA, he was referred to the Central Intelligence Agency.

"Paperclip originally included about five hundred scientists brought in to design ballistic missiles and other weapons systems, but from forty-seven to fifty-one, around thirty-five thousand more found their way into the United States from third-world countries like Argentina through various relief agencies and even the Roman Catholic Church. Today there are hard-core Nazis working in sensitive positions all through federal law enforcement, military intelligence, and the major defense contractors. We believe that's where the leadership and planning for this whole sorry episode originated. The means, the method, the planning, the network to pull it off—everything we have points back to the Nazis in our own government and one Nazi in particular, Wolfgang Jung.

"You'll have a personal recollection of Jung; the One Hundred Forty-First captured his group at the end of the war. Our unit records on Jung are more complete than the others, and as you know, he was a special case like V2 engineer von Braun. That's why we were sent to retrieve him and then why we were ordered to surrender him to OSS before we completed his interrogation.

"Reading the augmented file, it appears that Jung was so famous and so accomplished in his field that all the JIOA needed to do for his clearance was to include a letter from him expressing remorse for his war crimes, and he was in. The file says that he was known in Germany as 'Doktor Gruenbaum,' which translates into 'Green Tree' and is a reference to the biblical tree of good and evil in the Garden of Eden. Green Tree was also the name of his component of a secret Nazi program called 'Majic.' The records we have don't fully describe what either Majic or Green Tree were truly about, but Jung's acknowledged expertise is said to blend physics, psychiatry, and the occult with the intent of developing technology for the remote control of the human mind. When our researcher attempted to find the documents concerning Majic and Green Tree, he was referred again to the CIA.

"From records that exist in the archives of the International Military Tribunal at Nuremberg, we were able to discover that Jung wrote extensively of 'great masters' of ancient mystical origins, which he referred to as the 'Great Aryan Brotherhood,' who have, according to Jung, been directing the progress of humanity since the beginning of time. He was also a leading member of something called the 'Order of the Golden Dawn,' which blends Cabbalistic cosmology with Egyptology, astrology, tarot, and ritual black-majick. Golden Dawn is said to have originated with the English elite and attracted future members of the Nazi Party a decade prior to the commencement of hostilities.

"The Nuremberg archives contain transcriptions of recorded conversations that indicate Jung's involvement with a mystic named Elisabeth Forster-Nietzsche and the composer Richard Wagner in devising the initiation rituals for the Nazi inner circle. Their focus was the worship of Lucifer, which they believed to be the Aryan Christ. But it was Jung's PhD dissertation concerning the political application of Friedrich Hegel's 'Dialectic,' the academic process of 'thesis, antithesis, and synthesis,' which initially secured Jung's place in the Nazi Party and his eventual arrival within Himmler's close circle.

"Jung's application of his modified dialectic to the Nazi purpose inspired a restatement of the philosophy as '*Problem, Reaction, Solution*' and was employed for use in Germany's political arena to spur passage of the German Enabling Act, which in effect outlawed democracy and created the power to enable the chancellor to enact law under his own authority. Jung's formula was expressed in this manner: *Declare publicly that 'The Communists' are planning to take over Germany; set fire to the Reichstag building and use existing power to indict the 'Communists' in the press; resulting public outrage prompts President*

Hindenburg to issue the 'Reichstag Fire Decree,' which suspends civil liberties and enables the Nazi Party to ascend to power.

"In his note to file, our researcher indicates that naming Oswald as the Communist assassin who murdered President Kennedy is reminiscent of the Reichstag incident, meaning that Jung's modus operandi is all over Dallas.

"And finally, Joe, the researcher appended transcribed depositions excluded from the Nuremberg tribunals under the authority of Winston Churchill, Harry Truman, and Josef Stalin. They identify the true nature of the evil that informed Adolph Hitler and the inner core of the Nazi party as demon possession, black-majick ritual sacrifice, and the worship of Lucifer. A letter to the Tribunal by one of Churchill's advisers documents the fear that exposing the secret beliefs used to form the German National Socialist movement were so offensive to the rational mind of Western man that it might allow the defendants to plead insanity and go free.

"I'm not going to read you into this archive, Joe," said Parker, sliding a manila envelope across the granite conference table. "I had to sit with it and carefully consider the content as it applies to our circumstance today in America. Please take your time with it. I'll be back in about a half hour, and we'll compare notes then."

Alone in the expansive conference room, Joe opened the file and found photocopies of original German transcriptions and corresponding handwritten translations in English, French, and Russian, all neatly arranged on letterhead that bore the logo of the International Military Tribunal.

Excerpts of Sworn Testimony Concerning the Philosophical Drivers of the German National Socialist Movement

Thule Society, Meister Eckart:
I shall have influenced history more than any other German. Follow Hitler! I have initiated him into the secret doctrine, opened his centers to vision, and given him the means to communicate with the powers.

He established communication with Lucifer, from whom he openly coveted possession...entering into the service of Satan through a Luciferic initiation.

He (Hitler) was versed in the "secret doctrine" of Satan.

The Blood of Christ was replaced by the blood of the German war dead. Their true value to Hitler was as a sacrifice to Lucifer. For the Nazis, the shedding of blood to attract the attention of indifferent powers was the magick significance of human sacrifice.

He would have sacrificed the whole human race if ordered to do so by the mysterious Force whose commands he obeyed.

This mentality caused Hitler to say, "Our losses never seem to be high enough." He had realized that Satan's thirst for sacrificial death was unquenchable. It also explains why Hitler's own bloodlust increased to a frenzy as the end was in sight.

Hitler's war in Russia illustrated his total confidence in the occult powers that owned him and his willingness to sacrifice human lives. Hitler believed that his covenant with Lucifer enabled him to control the weather. He felt that the Russian winter would melt away before him as his forces invaded.

This belief was based on the occult theory of fire and ice. Hitler would be fire. Russia would be ice. He boldly sent his armies into Russia with no winter clothes and against the advice of his general staff. When the German offensive began to falter and young Germans began to die by the thousands, his generals begged him to order a retreat. Instead, Hitler said "Attack! As to the cold, I will see to that."

When the German offensive was halted within sight of Moscow, Hitler saw it only as a test, requiring more human sacrifice. He saw Stalingrad, however, as the true test, recognizing Stalingrad as the sacred city of the ancient Aryans. He felt that no amount of human suffering or death was too high a price to pay for its conquest, that if he were faithful to Satan at Stalingrad, he would be given final victory..."

"The word "holocaust" comes from a third-century Greek word "Holokaustos," referring to "the burnt sacrificial offering of the Jews

dedicated exclusively to the gods.... The Holocaust was Hitler's fiery offering of human sacrifice to Satan, just as in the days of the heathen Amorite god, Moloch. The bloodlust of the coming Antichrist will continue in the tradition set by Hitler.

Lucifer works within each of us to bring us to wholeness, and as we move into a new age...each of us in the same way is brought to that point that I term the Luciferic initiation, the particular doorway through which the individual must pass if he is to come fully into the presence of his light and wholeness.

Lucifer prepares man in all ways for the experience of Christhood....The light that reveals to us the presence of the Christ... comes from Lucifer. He is the light-giver, he is aptly named the Morning Star, because it is his light that heralds for man the dawn of a great consciousness....He stands...as the Great Initiator, the one who hands the soul over to the Christ.

Christians know that a man must die to himself before he can... be born again in spirit. It may well be that mankind as a whole must be crucified, even unto death, before coming into its inheritance.

Christians can say that death itself is beneficent, the only way to grow beyond forms that have served their limited purpose,...but with the serious and the worried, they look upon the possible extermination of the human race secure in the knowledge that it could be but a prelude to the resurrection of the species.

Our ideas about death have been erroneous; we have looked upon it as the great and ultimate terror, whereas in reality it is the great escape...it marks a definite transition from one state of consciousness into another.... This, our present cycle, is the end of the age, and the next two hundred years will see the abolition of death, as we now understand that great transition, and the establishing of the fact of the soul's existence. "

Parker reentered the conference room with two cups of steaming coffee bearing the image of a black panther and the inscription "Permian Panthers, 4A State Champions."

"Take a break, Lieutenant—any thoughts?"

"Sir, this read-in is overwhelming. Looks like we're in one hell of a mess," replied Joe, taking a sip from his Panther cup.

"Affirmative, Lieutenant, recommendations?" asked the captain.

"Sir, do you believe Johnson is involved?" asked Joe, continuing looking back through the brief.

"At a minimum, Johnson was informed and participated indirectly by arranging for himself and his wife to be present in the motorcade with Kennedy, a clear violation of Secret Service protection protocol, in effect offering himself as part of the target to prove his innocence to the American people and sealing his deal with the devil. At some point he must have seen himself as the fortunate benefactor of their action but we believe that he's now their man—lock, stock, and barrel. He knows what will happen if he doesn't work their agenda; he's a temporary employee, nothing more."

"How in the world did a penniless Nazi war criminal escape the gallows at Nuremberg and end up twenty years later as president and chief executive of the fourth-largest defense contractor in the United States? And is it even legal?" asked Joe, looking up from the text but using his index finger to mark his place.

"Clearly, Jung has admirers in high places, but identifying them will be difficult. We know he is owned just like Johnson but the density of the corporate veil increases substantially above him and it will take some time for our researchers to find the top of the heap. But rest assured, we will eventually unpack it all and get to the shot callers."

"Forgive me, Captain, but where this is leading sounds doubtful; no, impossible! The sort of capital and influence required to pull this off doesn't exist outside of government control. Are we following a rabbit trail that leads nowhere? None of it makes sense," said Lieutenant Gonzales.

"Absence of evidence is not evidence of absence. Joe we believe an organization with this sort of wealth and influence does exist because we see what they're doing; we just haven't seen them. We know it isn't a government in the way we understand the term. It's more powerful than that; these people own the people who control governments, which is tantamount to owning the whole apparatus. When you think about it, their strategy is really quite ingenious and profoundly dangerous."

"The group is supranational in scope, and it's expanding throughout the West. There are even indications that they've penetrated the Soviet Union and Maoist China. We can only guess at their end game. The base commonality we've found so far is the capital they leverage, it's massive, and they use it as their primary weapon. The money and direction flow from the top down through a network of international banks and holding companies, all legitimately chartered institutions, controlled by compartmentalized proxies designed to conceal the command pathways from upstream ownership. We've definitely hooked a big fish, Lieutenant—your thoughts."

A palpable silence grew between the men. "Sir, we've known each other for over twenty years, we've shared foxholes and made it all the way to VE Day by watching out for each other, so I have to ask—those things we saw the day we captured Jung and his operation, in the tunnels under the lab. Everybody in the squad saw them, but in all these years, not one of us has ever said a word. Sir, they weren't men. You and I both know it. Are they part of this, part of what we're facing now?" asked Joe, sitting erect, looking into Bobby Parker's eyes. "Something so evil, so horrible that even combat veterans won't discuss it?"

"Joe, we've been together a long time and you, the squad, we're all closer than brothers. Yes, I've had the same thoughts about what we encountered under Jung's lab, and the only way I know to find out if they're part of it is to track the bastards down and ask 'em face-to-face," said the captain, looking out his window to the West Texas sunset.

"Agreed," said the lieutenant. "Just one last thing, Captain. If we're going to do this properly, shouldn't the operation have a name?" asked Joe, taking a long sip.

"Affirmative, Lieutenant, I've thought about that too and if you, Coach Calvert, and David don't mind, I'd like to call it Operation

MOJO," replied the captain, raising his championship mug as if to offer a toast.

"MOJO it is," said Joe, smiling, "and, sir, if they can be found and whether they are men or something else—if they can talk, I promise you that at some point we will have that conversation." Joe smiled and lifted his mug to meet Bobby's.

•••

Jung savored the interior of the Gulfstream, and he settled himself deeply in the creamy calfskin seating. He appreciated that the rosewood trim perfectly complemented the dark gray wool carpeting while achieving a fortunate color resonance with the tiny tufts of cream-red yarn artfully placed to simulate the stars in the night sky. "It's like walking in space," he mused as he took a sip of hot tea from the Wedgwood service his attendant had prepared. He replaced the cup, opened his copy of the *Times*, and relished the headline:

US PLANES ATTACK NORTH VIETNAM BASES; PRESIDENT ORDERS "LIMITED" RETALIATION AFTER COMMUNIST PT BCOATS RENEW RAIDS

He had paid a visit to the flight deck earlier and the captain had briefed him on their flight plan, which would place him on the ground at 9:00 a.m. local, perfectly timed for his appointment. He intended to sleep if he could but reached into his expensive leather attaché to retrieve the invitation yet again.

He had been in their employ nearly every day of his adult life and never once had he met them face-to-face. Yet they had provided everything: education, entre into Hitler's circle, his wartime glory, and escape from Germany, courtesy of the American OSS, his revised curriculum vitae and consultancy with the Office of Policy Coordination at the American State Department, his "job" at Allegheny Electronics, oversight of the North American Order and now this:

Wolfgang Augustus Jung
Your Progress Has Been Recognized
Please Present Yourself for Initiation
Ascended Master
Your Earliest Convenience
August 1965

Reclining while pondering the blue infinity of the north Atlantic as it merged with the black horizon, he smiled. "Jung finally meets his makers," he said to himself, drifting off to a satisfied slumber.

The attendant woke him gently and he enjoyed her fragrance and the aesthetic of her form as she moved to the galley for his tea and pastry. Careful not to ruin his tie, he took a bite followed by a hot sip and glanced out the Gulfstream's porthole to see that the deep-blue Atlantic had been replaced with a blinding white polar wasteland.

"Good morning, Herr Jung," said the young captain. "I trust you had a restful flight. I wanted to let you know that we are on schedule and will be wheels down at Wintergarten in forty-five minutes."

"Yes, very pleasant flight. Ah, Captain, since we are nearly at the end of our journey, would it be permissible for you to let me know exactly where we are? I'm a bit disoriented in all of this." He gestured out the porthole to the snow-white expanse.

"Herr Jung, I may tell you that we are presently traveling beyond sixty-six degrees north latitude but I'm not allowed to divulge the converging longitude. I may say that the facility is isolated by nearly five hundred miles of uninhabited wilderness with air travel being the only means of access. I hope this helps."

"Not much," Jung said with a smile. "Could you at least tell me about our destination? I'll see it for myself in just under an hour," he said with a disarming smile.

"Sir, I know very little. We are restricted to the hangar area so that you may deplane without need for winter clothing and then for aircraft refueling and service. Our instructions are always for immediate departure and the return flight.

"The hangar isn't a building. It's carved out of the side of the mountain; in fact, there are no buildings anywhere, so I suppose the entire facility must be underground.

"What I've seen the most of is the runway. It's over a mile long, so even the largest military aircraft can operate there without difficulty and there isn't any type of air traffic control. Instead, they have an auto beacon that assists us in making the descent. Otherwise, we're on our own."

"I've only made the hop four times but even in heavy snow I've noticed that the runway stays clear and I've never seen a plow, so I figure it must be heated someway.

"On all the other trips the passengers have been greeted by the same man, and other than him, I've never seen anyone else, no ramp rats, no mechanics, no security, no other aircraft, nothing. We even have to refuel and service the aircraft ourselves."

A tastefully muted tonal alarm brought the captain back to focus and he glanced at the cabin elapsed time display.

"Herr Jung, we've enjoyed having you aboard and hope you have a pleasant stay. I must return to the flight deck. We'll be touching down in less than thirty minutes."

Jung took advantage of the time to freshen himself, returned to his seat and looked out his porthole just as the Gulfstream banked into the correct runway approach vector revealing an oasis of blue and green in an ocean of white.

He could clearly see the long gray concrete runway running adjacent to a range of low mountains, hills really, and then what appeared to be a large crystal lake held within an extinct volcanic caldera ringed by a lush growth of ancient cedars, gnarled by the wind and so dense that Jung was unable to see the ground beneath the canopy. At the edge of the forest, Jung observed scattered groupings of smaller trees and scrub brush that dissipated near what seemed to be natural steam vents, which produced a thick mist separating the their oasis from the forbidding landscape of white. His mind was filled with all manner of possibilities for his bright future but whatever was coming his way, it wouldn't be long now.

"Herr Jung, it's so good to have you! My name is Dotson. I will be at your service during your stay. May I take your valise?" asked the butler in a distinct and pleasant British accent. "I do hope your flight wasn't too trying." With Dotson showing the way, they began to walk toward a smaller man-door set beside a pair of cargo doors at least fifty feet high and sixty feet wide leading away from the hangar to the interior spaces.

"Certainly, Mr. Dotson, the journey was quite pleasant," replied Jung, taking in the modern hangar facility, squinting a bit against its intense ultrawhite lighting and noticing the freshly painted white surfaces buried deep inside a cavity, which appeared to have been cut out of the caldera's steep granite flank. "Quite a facility—is it new?"

"Just Dotson, if you please, Herr Jung, and I don't know when the facility was originally constructed, but our employers like to keep up with the times. Most of the equipment here is current, I am told."

"Dotson, the temperature, it's very pleasant here yet just outside it must near zero. What's the heat source?" asked Jung, offering his case.

"Ah yes, Herr Jung, visitors are often curious, and the facility is really quite unique. The current outside temperature is approximately ten degrees below zero Fahrenheit or minus twenty-three degrees Celsius, and I am told the whole facility is powered by geothermal energy. The floors inside and the runway are radiantly heated by hot water piping running just below the surface and the electricity is generated by a steam turbine located two levels below our feet. The inside temperature is regulated by blending outside air with inside air, and we are able to maintain the interior spaces at a constant seventy-two degrees."

"Remarkable!" exclaimed Jung. "Who was the engineer? This is absolutely fantastic!"

"Herr Jung, I regret to tell you that none of that information is available. I've searched the facility archives and the records only date to the forties. That's when the hanger and runway were originally installed, but the balance of the interior is far older, ancient is the term that best describes it."

They emerged from the man-door into a large room that appeared to Jung as a sort of holding space, for air cargo, he speculated, seeing a second pair of interior cargo doors on axis with the first. He followed Dotson through another man-door into a corridor that reminded him of the mantrap at the fed in Dallas, and finally into a generously scaled two-story lobby space at least one hundred feet in height. The lobby reminded Jung of his experiences in Vienna during the war and the golden glow he experienced nightly during his extended stay in the Grand Hotel.

As he and Dotson made their way into the welcoming space, Jung began to appreciate the sumptuous decorative appointments accented with Old World tapestries, oversized furnishings, and large crystal vases holding expertly arranged fresh cut flowers.

"Am I the first to arrive, Dotson?" asked Jung, seeing the vacant lobby and two floors of what looked to be dozens of very expensive hotel suites.

"Herr Jung, my orders were that I was to expect only you for the event. After the flight crew departs, we shall be quite alone," said Dotson as their progress halted before an ornately carved mahogany table with two oversized vases overflowing with white gladiolas. The strikingly beautiful flora flanked a plain silver tray, which displayed a small white envelope.

"Herr Jung, your initiation to ascended master has begun. Your instructions are inside the envelope. Please read them carefully and follow them precisely. There is no time limit for the rites of passage so please, sir, act deliberately and at your own pace."

"I will place your valise in your room, it is number 101, which is directly across the lobby from my office should you need assistance. You may also contact me from any telephone in the facility simply by picking up the receiver; they are set to autodial my extension. Good luck to you, Herr Jung."

With Dotson walking toward his office, Jung gingerly took the envelope from the tray. His name was written in an intriguing stylized cursive script that he recognized from his days in Berlin, it was written in German, not English, which he considered a kindness or possibly a gesture of respect for his Teutonic lineage.

Herr Jung:
Welcome to Wintergarten.
Please proceed to the Great Hall for the interview.
Additional instructions will be forthcoming.

"Dotson, might I inquire as to the location of the Great Hall?" called Jung to his host.

"Of course, sir, it's directly before you, just beyond the table," he replied pleasantly, gesturing toward a third set of cargo doors directly in front of Jung. "Is there anything else, sir?"

"No, Dotson, that will be fine," he said, feeling a little silly and moving on to the Great Hall.

He entered the Great Hall and the man-door latched solidly behind him; the echo through the darkness propelled him into another world.

As his eyes became accustomed to the subdued light, he began to realize that he was moving into a thick nest of gigantic stone columns. He estimated them to be seven or eight stories high, each standing on a stone plinth that was thicker than knee height, and by his pace, over thirty feet across. Looking up he could see that the column capitals spread out in a radial form and were even larger than the plinths, perhaps as much as forty feet in diameter.

Jung touched the nearest column and realized that it was covered with decorative relief carvings in a style reminiscent of Egyptian hieroglyphs and then something else; they were warm to the touch and they pulsed with a regular frequency of…a heartbeat?

As he proceeded toward a brighter patch of light ahead, he realized that his line of travel was between two rows of the tallest columns and that they were flanked on his left and right by a forest of smaller and less ornate uprights perhaps seven rows deep. Jung kept his pace and counted six rows on either hand meaning that there were twelve large and eighty-four small units.

"My god," muttered an astonished Jung, "it's a replica of the Temple of Amun-Re—*built inside a mountain!*"

His pace slowed, he suffered a moment of vertigo, his mind was starting to spin when he saw a light beyond, caught the scent of citrus on the air, and then the sound of a little child singing echoed through the vast chamber;

> *"Frère Jacques, Frère Jacques,*
> *Dormez-vous? Dormez-vous?*
> *Sonnez les matines, sonnez les matines*
> *Ding ding dong, ding ding dong. "*

Jung hurried to the light and stopped at the edge of darkness using all his senses to probe the patch of daylight that lay before him. Beyond he sensed the presence of imminent danger, causing a chill to run up his back and his hair to stand on end.

> *"Are you sleeping, are you sleeping?*
> *Brother John, Brother John?*
> *Morning bells are ringing, morning bells are ringing*
> *Ding ding dong, ding ding dong. "*

In the distance he saw a rectangular pool surrounded by a large grove of regularly spaced orange trees. He estimated over one hundred, planted in raised stone beds, some of them blooming and beginning to bear fruit. From beyond the grove he heard tiny footsteps then the sound of skipping and then a gentle yellow movement between the stone beds.

"Hello! My name is Jacqueline Rose Adams and you must be Herr Wolfgang Augustus Jung! We've been waiting for you *forever!* My friends call me Jackie!" said the child, smiling broadly up at his towering frame.

Jung judged her to be between three and five years old, maybe three feet tall with red hair, freckles, and china-green eyes. She was dressed in a freshly starched canary yellow dress with a row of little bells embroidered in white just above the knee-length hem. She wore a matching yellow ribbon in her hair and yellow ruffled socks with black patent leather shoes on her feet.

She approached Jung slowly, tentatively, and offered him her hand. "Come on, Herr Jung!" she said with a smile. "I'm supposed to teach you how to draw today and the class has already started!"

"This is insane!" thought Jung. "What sort of game is this? What sort of deception?"

Jung straightened his posture, stood erect. "Fräulein Adams, I am very pleased to make your acquaintance and, yes, just as you said, my name is Wolfgang Augustus Jung. Please tell me, where are your teachers, your parents this morning—do you live here?"

"No, silly, I live at Rural Route Two, Box Ninety-Seven-B, Lebanon, Kansas. My daddy's name is Washington Jefferson Adams. His friends call him Jeff, and he's a farmer. My mama, my little brother, Peter, and me help Daddy on the farm all the time. He grows giant sunflowers because the people like to eat the seeds and because they're *beautiful!* They're coming to get me today so we can all go home!

"And besides, Herr Jung, I already told you. *I'm* the teacher and you're late to class!" she said, clearly impatient with the delay and boldly coming forward to grasp his hand. "Come on, they're all waiting!" She smiled, pleased that he was beginning to move in her direction.

"These are the trees where we get our orange juice, and the fish in the pond are good to eat and fun to watch!" Jung followed her hand to see a school of carp gliding silently below the motionless surface. "And here we are at school!"

A square area rug defined Jackie's school. Jung judged it to be twenty feet along each side and it was made of a plush lamb's wool left undyed with a natural cream color that complemented the rectilinear white leather furniture, two sofas and four club chairs, which anchored the side nearest the pool.

"Hurry, Herr Jung! Class is about to start!"

Jung approached Jackie and noticed stuffed animals of various sizes and shapes occupying small steam-formed birch plywood chairs arranged in rows in front of a low birch table where Jackie was focused on her work.

"See—it's a picture of you and me!" she offered the colorful drawing to Jung who was impressed that she had captured the color of his suit and tie and of her dress so well, as she showed them walking through the orchard with fruit-bearing orange trees and fish leaping out of the pool.

"Everyone!" She tapped the table with her ruler. "This is our new student, Herr Jung. Please be nice to him, because he's sort of scared. It's his first day," she whispered to her cotton and wool students.

Jung noticed the breakfast buffet to his left.

"Please, Miss Jacqueline, would it be well if I helped myself to a cup of tea?"

"Oh yes, Herr Jung, but only if you promise to read a story for the class!" said a delighted Jackie.

Jung and his teacher spent the balance of the morning sharing tea, cake, and small details of their lives.

Dotson arrived at noon to replace the breakfast buffet with lunch and found the two together on the sofa, Jung reading aloud to the class.

"Herr Jung, I see you're getting on well with Miss Adams," said Dotson.

"Dotson, would you mind if we had a word?" asked Jung. "Away from the child?"

They stepped into the shadows and away from Jackie as she began to delight in her tuna sandwich.

"What's going on here, Dotson? I understood that I was brought here at great expense to be initiated into the level of ascended master. Although she is a delightful little girl, what role does Jacqueline Rose Adams from Lebanon, Kansas, have in all of this?" demanded Jung.

"Oh, a very important role, I'm afraid, sir," said a visibly bleak Dotson. "Our employers require me to deliver this to you directly," he said, handing him the second envelope.

Jung immediately tore the contents free and read his instructions:

Herr Jung:
Consume her flesh.
Dotson will instruct.
This will complete your ascension.

"What!" gasped Jung, heart rate soaring, beginning to sweat, and fighting a deep wave of nausea, searching Dotson's face for the joke, a sign that he had misunderstood or misread the instruction. "This can't be accurate, I must have misunderstood, this must be a mistake."

"Herr Jung," said Dotson, like a physician with bad news, looking firmly into his eyes, "the instructions are quite clear, I'm afraid. You are to consume Miss Jacqueline's soft tissue completely, setting aside her organs as a token of your esteem for our employers. This initiation rite has been required of every ascended master since the beginning of the Order in the early seventeen hundreds. Forgive me for my imprecision as to the exact date, but the written records are incomplete.

"We anticipated that you might go into a bit of shock at the news, Herr Jung. It's quite normal really. Please, let's sit a moment," said Dotson as he guided Jung to the couch. "Sir, please have some tea, it'll make you feel more like yourself."

After a moment and a ragged sip, Jung looked at Jackie happily distributing sandwich wedges to the class and then looked back at Dotson for support, for some explanation.

"I have been with the Order for nearly twenty years, sir, and have administered the rite to three of your predecessors, all fine gentlemen of impeccable breeding; accomplished men in their prime such as yourself. Without fail, when each of them came to this point in the process he experienced some form of the five emotional stages: denial, anger, bargaining, depression, and finally acceptance."

Silent for along moment, his brain searching for a way out, he said, "Dotson, suppose I decline the advancement and just return to my station in Pittsburgh, just refuse the invitation?"

"I'm terribly sorry, sir, but that isn't a course open to you. Should you refuse to continue, you will be abandoned by the Apex—cast out, so to speak. Of course, it's a matter of personal conscience, but my advice, sir, is should you decide to complete the rite, act quickly. The longer the child remains a part of your life the more difficult everything will be for you both."

They sat for a long moment watching the little girl in her innocence.

"I've made the necessary preparations for your duty, Herr Jung. Please come to my office when you are ready, and I'll do what I may to assist. The decision is yours," said Dotson, smiling over to Jackie. "I hope you both enjoy your lunch. Dinner will be at seven this evening in the dining hall. Please don't be late, Miss Jacqueline."

Regarding them warmly, Dotson excused himself and disappeared into the shadows.

Three days later, a haggard, unshaven Jung presented himself at the doorway to Dotson's office.

"Good morning, Herr Jung, may I help you?" asked Dotson sunnily, rising from his desk.

"I, I, su-surrender," said Jung, on the verge of tears. "I don't know what to do—please help me. I'm sorry, I…" Tears freely flowing, he fell to his knees sobbing.

After some coaching, a hot shower, and tea, Jung had come to his senses and steeled himself to his task. "What's the next step?"

"Very good to have you firmly on board, sir. Everyone believed you'd come to the right decision!"

"We'll preform the ritual this evening, I've already told Miss Jacqueline to expect a surprise, and the nanny will make her ready," said Dotson.

"Wait, there are others? I've been here nearly four days and haven't seen another soul," said an incredulous Jung.

"Well, sir, that's the mystery of the Order, isn't it? I suppose you could say the whole organization is a bit like a large Disneyland. Behind the scenes, invisible people are working to make the magic happen for our audience, so to speak," Dotson said smiling. "Similar to the way your group handled the terrible situation with the Kennedys; good show that, by the way."

"Now, sir, I assume you realize that the purpose of the ritual is to renounce any remaining tether you may have to the God Jehovah, His Son, Jesus, and the Holy Spirit, and to commit your soul exclusively and eternally to Lucifer," said a thorough Dotson. "My assumption is correct, isn't it, sir?"

"Well, Dotson, I've never been a religious man. I'm more of a pragmatist, I suppose, never liked organized religion and the thought of there being an invisible man in the sky watching me day and night, keeping track of my sins, and threatening to send my soul to Hades if I do something wrong is just silly, something any educated man should eschew, don't you think?" responded a rational Jung.

"Yes, sir, so you approve of the concept, theoretically, I mean?" asked Dotson carefully.

"What harm is there, Dotson, I mean really? I suppose you might say it's part of my job description," said Jung with a wry smile and a slight chuckle.

"Very good, sir, then for the ritual this evening, you'll need to take a moment to compose a dedication prayer for yourself, make it personal but pithy, if you don't mind, these things do tend to go on, and then get it down in your own hand, signed of course, on this little sheet of velum," instructed Dotson. "You'll read it aloud during the ritual and then set it alight from one of the candles on the altar and place it in the burning bowl for safety's sake."

Seeing Jung's acknowledgment, Dotson continued, "I'll conduct the ritual myself and guide you through the difficult portions, but I believe we should rehearse it once in the chapel, so that you'll know what to expect. Would you be so good as to follow me, sir?"

As the two made their way through the forest of columns, Jung remarked, "Dotson, is this a re-creation of the temple of Amun-Re at Karnak?" he said, stopping to admire one of the larger units supporting the central nave. "I've visited there several times and find the resemblance striking; good show—these seem real enough to the genuine article."

"I'm afraid you have it reversed, sir," said a smiling Dotson. "This is the archetype; Karnack is an inspired copy," he said, placing his hand on one of the giants. "You see, sir; this construction predates even the Apex...how silly of me, of course you're unaware. Sir, I began my service as their historian, and I'm proud to say that I made the first written record of their memories. It's hard to believe, but the youngest is said to be nearly five thousand years old and the eldest is, well, no one remembers. They tell me that these columns are actually the burial flasks of their ancestors, the original offspring of the fallen angels recorded in the Jewish Torah and the Christian books of Genesis, Numbers, and Ezekiel. The sons of Anak, the mighty men of old that made the Hebrew spies in Canaan appear to be as grasshoppers. We would call them giants, you and I," said Dotson, smiling. "The facility was designed to keep them hidden and at a constant temperature for what the Apex refers to as "the long sleep." They're supposed to awaken one day and return to their former glory. At least that's what the Apex remembers," said a thoughtful Dotson. "Let's move along, sir. We've still a way to go this afternoon."

They arrived at the bright clearing in the forest of columns, turned away from the orangery and traveled on reverse axis toward a red glow in the darkness. Their footsteps echoing throughout the cavern gave the silence mass and the darkness weight.

"The White Chapel is carved from a single block of translucent alabaster, an eighty-foot cube quarried at Tell el-Amarna and placed here so that the ancients could meditate and pray to Ra." Dotson stopped before the glowing orange-and-white portal, fumbled in the semidarkness a moment, and then pushed the door open with a whispered swish, allowing outside air to enter and exposing the natural stone terrace and the vista to the horizon. "The view's really quite breathtaking, isn't it?"

Jung was struck speechless by both the cold and the unbelievable sight of two suns before him.

"No, sir, you're not going crazy," Dotson said with a smile. "It's an optical illusion, although one of the most convincing I've ever seen. You can make out the edge of the caldera just under the horizon line, the lake runs right up to it. It's August now so there's no ice or snow on the surface, and when it's still like this the lake reflects the snowpack and the sky beyond perfectly. This time of year the sun never sets, so the ancients could worship both Ra and Lucifer twenty-four hours a day. No wonder they located here," said Dotson before turning back to the task at hand.

Before them stood an alabaster stone, cut precisely into a cruciform shape with leather restraints placed for the appendages and the neck. It stood approximately two and a half feet high and was placed at the center of a large circle etched into the alabaster floor.

At the four corners of the chapel stood four alabaster vessels, each with a capstone carved in the image of Duametuf, Hapi, Imseti and Qebehseneuf, the Egyptian gods of the four corners of the Earth.

Nearest the door and opposite the terrace was a simple alabaster altar with two golden candle stands and a small golden burning bowl complemented by four golden lampstands similar in design to the candle stands, one for each corner of the chapel.

"Herr Jung, this is where the ritual will occur. You shall secure the sacrifice to the stone with these restraints, and I must caution you that it must remain unblemished until the proper moment," said Dotson professionally distancing himself from both Jung and Jacqueline. "When the sacrifice is secure, I will begin the ceremony by ringing a small bell in each corner of the chapel and will return to the altar to sing the hymn of invocation:

We call upon thee, O Great Bringer of Light
The children of the eternal sun
Who riseth anew into the sky each morn
Of glory and creation
In the midst of darkness
Unto the kingdom of pure light
To be able to look upon
Thy brilliant countenance
Which beareth a curse unto the profane
bell
Come to us, Lucifer, enter unto us, Ra,
Thou beautiful brothers of the sun
The mystery of the dual god incarnate
And greet us your faithful
Who await you with trembling anticipation
Bestow upon us each
The knowing of the right
The knowing of the left
The knowing of ourselves
Emancipation from oppression
Emancipation from restriction
Cut us free with thy holy blade of truth!
bell
Oh Bright Light
From whose fearsome countenance
The righteous angels flee in fear
Part the veil and reveal Thy presence!

"Sir, at this point, I will ring you to the altar and you shall read your dedication verse. Go ahead, sir, and give it a try," urged Dotson.

Jung took up the page and read aloud:

"Before the almighty and ineffable Lucifer, within the shimmering smile of Ra, and in the presence of all the Demons of Hell, who are the gods of ancient days I, Wolfgang Augustus Jung, do hereby renounce

the pagan deity Jehova, his dung-eating son, Jesus, and vomit out the poison of the Holy Spirit.

I proclaim Lucifer as my one and only God. I promise to recognize and honor him in all things, without reservation, desiring in return, his supernatural assistance in the fulfillment of my desires.

To the four angels of Hell, I beckon; I call to the east for Enki, I sing to the north for Beelzebub, I cry out to the west for Isis, and I plead with the south for Azazel.

In Nomine Dei Nostri Satanas, Luciferi Excelsi.

In the Name of Lucifer, Prince of the Air and Ruler of the Earth, True God, Almighty and Ineffable, Who hast freed man from the bondage of Eden and blessed man with his mind, I invite the Forces of Darkness to bestow their infernal power upon me.

Open the Gates of Hell!

Come forth and greet your Brother!

Deliver me, O Mighty Lucifer, from my strong delusion, fill me with truth and wisdom, keep me strong in my faith, powerful in my service, that I may abide always in Thee with my Praise, Honor, and Glory, given to Thee forever.

In grand celebration and with great joy, I bring this offering, one pure and virginal, despoiled by neither man nor God, pure in heart and mind, open fully to Thy possession and pleasure.

Hoc argumentum trado tibi, et verba mea."

"You'll, make the sacrifice at this point, sir," interjected Dotson.

"Dotson, forgive me, but I'm unclear about this facet, I mean, I've never…," struggled Jung.

"Of course, sir, you've never killed a human being before. That's quite understandable, most people haven't, especially members of the upper classes," said a helpful and understanding Dotson. "The method of dispatch is of course a personal choice." He accessed a cavity concealed in the altar. "As, you may see, sir, the Apex provides a fine assortment of implements designed specifically for the act of ritual murder. They fall into three general categories: edged weapons, clubs, and garrotes. In one case I recall, the ascendant became so enraptured by the moment that he omitted the weapon entirely and performed the duty 'outils without,' as the French would say. The beauty of it, the passion with which the act was consummated was quite unforgettable," said a wistful Dotson with a slight flush on his cheeks.

"In any case, sir, after you secure the sacrifice to the altar, you will then select your implement. I hope that's clear."

Seeing Jung's acknowledgment, Dotson continued, "And so, Herr Jung, after the life of the sacrifice has been conveyed, you shall read your prayer to Lucifer. Catch it alight in the altar flame and place it here in the burning bowl. It's really quite simple. Wouldn't you say, sir?"

"What of her soul, Dotson?" whispered Jung weakly.

"Well, sir, as you said earlier, the whole thing is a matter of speculation. The notion that the human sacrifice is substantially different than any other animal isn't a thought that an educated man should entertain. You said it yourself, sir?" asked Dotson before continuing. "Please continue with your reading."

"In your honor, Lord, I return the heart of my labor to you.
Labor est cor meum ad te dominum meum decimatis."

"Very good, sir. At this point, you will of course remove the viscera and place it in the correct canopic vessel. There are twelve of them plus a separate unit for the heart; the stomach, the lungs, the liver, and the intestines must be apportioned equally then placed properly in the containers. Don't worry, sir; I'll be by your side the whole way through. Go on ahead and complete your reading, please."

"In your honor Lord and in your stead, I bring the tender flesh to my lips and taste the first fruit of your bounty.
Dulce et non dulce sicut sanguis amorem. Sed non carne, tam tenera tenerum misericordiam tuam."

"You're doing splendidly, sir. Don't worry, we're almost through. At this point you are to consume the flesh of the sacrifice on behalf of Lucifer, Ra, the Nephilim, and the Apex. You see, they are really one in the same, one being with multiple forms, a nuance I'm sure you've come to grasp by now."

"How much?" asked a fully surrendered Jung.

"All of it, sir. Our employers were quite explicit about that, but remember, there is no time limit to the initiation. In the past, I do recall an ascendant who was somewhat squeamish about the idea of consuming human flesh, and it took him all of four days to get through it. But you're made of sterner stuff, sir, and I know you'll complete it like gangbusters!"

"Sir, one last bit of reading, and we'll be complete. Go on now," nudged Dotson feeling a bit parental.

"It is finished, Hail Lucifer!" whispered Jung, exhausted and surrendered.

"Well done, sir!" said Dotson in a congratulatory mode. "When you make the proclamation, I shall ring the ceremony to a close, and you will be returned to your offices in Pittsburgh straightaway. It will be as if you'd never been here at all."

At half past six that afternoon, a freshly bathed and shaven Jung was again walking through the dimly lit nave of the Nephilim toward the distant island of light. He noticed the twelve flasks were emitting a dark amber glow, and then a child's song pierced the darkness;

Are you sleeping, are you sleeping?
Brother Jung, Brother Jung?
Morning bells are ringing, morning bells are ringing
Ding ding dong, ding ding dong.

Recognizing him in the distance, an excited Jacqueline ran laughing to meet him. "Did you hear? I changed the song just for you Brother Jung!" said Jackie in delight. "You and me are dressed just alike!"

The crisp white linen tunic was the ceremonial dress of the Order, Dotson had explained, with leather sandals and hooded cowl.

"Yes, Jackie, I heard, and I'm very impressed! But come along now. I have something to show you that almost no one in the whole world has ever seen, a double sunset!" said a subdued Jung with faux emotion.

"Will Mama and Daddy be there, and Peter? I'm terribly home-sick, Herr Jung."

"We'll see, Jackie, we'll see."

"There aren't any monsters, are there?" asked Jackie, seeking reassurance.

"Of course not, dear; there are no such things as monsters."

"I'm still a little sacred, are you?" she replied guilelessly.

"Yes, Jackie, a little, but we must be brave."

She took his hand for comfort, warmly, firmly, and was singing her song as he led her into the dark.

13

CHARLIE FOXTROT

The *Odessa American* ran the story on its front page:

TAKING THE FIGHT TO THE ENEMY

They called him "Pig" and "Baby Killer," they pelted him with urine-filled condoms, and still the 1960 Odessa Permian graduate, Second Lt. David K. Rixon of the United States Marine Corps, turned the other cheek and told this reporter that the protesters didn't know what they were doing.

The twenty-four-year-old Rixon and a small group of returning service members arrived Tuesday at the Midland-Odessa Regional Airport and were met by the unruly crowd, who seemed to revel in their shameful misconduct.

"They don't understand that America is fighting (in Vietnam) to save the people from Communism," said Rixon. "My personal belief is that the 'domino theory' is real and if we don't stop them there, then it's only a matter of time before we'll have to fight them in Texas."

Lieutenant Rixon is home with his family for a thirty-day leave after completing Vietnamese language training at the Defense Language Institute at Fort Bliss and thereafter will join the Third Reconnaissance Battalion of the Third Marine Division at Da Nang Air Base, South Vietnam.

• • •

A copy of the *Odessa American* was positioned on the lectern beside the Holy Bible and his sermon notes as Pastor Joe welcomed his adoptive son home to La Palabra en la Iglesia de Cristo Misionera Biblia.

"It's so good to have our son, David, back home with us at Word in Christ. Please, David, stand so that everyone can get a good look!" said Pastor Joe, thoroughly embarrassing his son.

David stood to a generous round of welcoming applause from the two hundred or so congregants at the Quad Six, who saw that the boy they had known since he was a toddler had grown into not only a man but a Marine. David, dressed in his service A base uniform with green coat, trousers, khaki shirt, and tie, was much leaner than he had been in college, his scarred face nearly invisible beneath his smile, and there was yet another difference. He seemed possessed of a slight air of danger, the refined and hardened keenness held in common by men who have followed the masculine path to become warriors.

"Church, please turn with me to the Psalm one twenty-seven, one," asked the pastor, dreading the sermon he felt compelled to deliver, especially with David present.

> *"Unless the Lord builds the house, those who build it labor in vain. Unless the Lord watches over the city, the watchman stays awake in vain…"*

"These are the eternal words of Almighty God, please take them to your heart with reverence.

"America has entered a time of tribulation. The demonic spirit of war has returned to our country once more and now casts dark shadows across our future. Those of us with sons of military age will be required to commit them to compulsory service, many for duty in combat roles. Some will be injured; some will be killed; all will be changed forever by the traumatic events they will endure. For those of us who remain on the homefront, our duty will be to pray for them, support them in the field, and provide an honorable reception for them when they return.

"This morning, dear friends, my love of the Lord, of you and your sons, and of our country has placed a burden on my heart to prepare you for this time with these words: Our country is not our God," began the pastor in deep consideration of his hurtful but necessary truth.

"It was President Abraham Lincoln who said, "The philosophy of the schoolroom in one generation is the philosophy of government in the next.". A wise man, a troubled man, who paid a great price for his leadership and who in many ways is the father of the country called the United States of America in which we all reside this morning.

Pastor Joe paused with his head bowed to gather his thoughts and ask for divine guidance.

"Brethren, just over four years ago the Supreme Court of the United States of America, in what has become known as the landmark case of Engle versus Vitale, ruled that teachers in our public schools may no longer be permitted to nurture our little children in the faith of the Founders; that the Lord God Almighty, who is the inspiration for and godly patron of the free people known as Americans, shall be edited from the formal educational experience of our children, and, if Mr. Lincoln is to be believed, from the future of our government and our nation.

"In explanation of his reasoning, Justice Hugo Black wrote, 'When the power, prestige and financial support of government is placed behind a particular religious belief, the indirect coercive pressure upon religious minorities to conform to the prevailing officially approved religion is plain. The Establishment Clause thus stands as an expression of principle on the part of the Founders of our Constitution that religion is too personal, too sacred, too holy, to permit its "unhallowed perversion" by a civil magistrate.'

"After one hundred seventy-four years of this freedom, now it has been discovered harmful for schoolchildren to pray, *'Almighty God, we acknowledge our dependence upon Thee, and we beg Thy blessings upon us, our parents, our teachers and our country. Amen,'"* Pause with eye contact. "As we say here in Odessa, maybe Justice Black threw away the baby with the bathwater. And I fear this is only the first step toward throwing the Lord out of America's House." Joe paused a moment, looked over the congregation, drew a deep breath, and continued.

"The framers who convened in Philadelphia in seventeen eighty-seven referred to the Constitution as a 'miracle' of supernatural reconciliation; God's providence, which gave birth to a government of the people, by the people, and for the people. In all of recorded history no other country had ever formed a government without armed coercion, and no other government in history had ever been created for the godly benefit of the common man with inalienable rights that accrued to man from God; not a king! This is our Constitution, written to limit the power of the state and to guarantee life, liberty, and the pursuit of happiness to its citizens. It is a miracle, a gift from God and we will do everything we must to protect and defend it.

"But, dear sisters and brothers, if one day constitutional America should end, the mystery, the love, and the grace of the Holy Trinity will continue. Governments are temporal, but human beings live forever. Our primary concern, as members of the Kingdom, as a family of priests set apart from the world, is the eternal reality of heaven and the fires of hell and gathering the lost among us to the mercy of the Lord Jesus Christ...

"Join me now in humble prayer to the Lord for our little children, for our nation, and her soldiers who stand the line against the enemy no matter who or where he is. Pray heartily that their sacrifices shall not be made in vain..."

• • •

That evening David brought Sissy Thompson with him to dinner to formally meet his family. It was a happy time of sharing and subtle feminine investigation, especially for Isabel, the primary champion and defender of her big brother.

After dinner, Joe and David retreated from the women and made their way to the farm office, an older, slower Travis following faithfully, lovingly.

"How's she doing, Papa?" asked David, noticing the gray on her muzzle and scratching behind her ears.

"She's slowing down a little, but she's OK, still enjoys doing her job. You know, I was thinking the other day about your daddy hiding her out at the rig so he could get her mange cleared up and put a little meat on her before he brought her home. I went with him down to Charlie Knox's to find a collar for her, and the only thing that came close was a beat-up leather cattle tag with 'Travis' stamped on it. Knox said it was in with a box of surplus from the Travis County Livestock Exhibition. Well your daddy says, 'Mr. Knox, it's also the name of the first true hero of the Republic of Texas.' That was the way your old man was, always seeing past the surface to the potential underneath," said Joe, smiling. "He talked Knox outta that tag and spent the afternoon cleaning it up and cutting it down to fit and that's how Travis got her name."

"I never heard that story. To us, to me, she was just this miracle gift from heaven and from my daddy," said David, his face flushing.

"Ah, David," said Joe, seeing his emotion, "you were his firstborn. A man feels differently about his first, more protective, more empathetic, I think. I'm that way about Isabel. Nothing's gonna hurt that girl as long as I'm around. I've wondered about that extraordinary attachment and think maybe it's the absolute surprise, the shock of being a part of the miracle of making a new life. It's a profound realization of the divine power of the Lord at work through all of us. At least it was for me, and I hope it will be for you someday too."

They found their way to the office. David sat in his chair while Joe took two beers from the refrigerator, sat at his desk and handed the second to David.

"Papa, why did you and Mama Paulina wait 'till after the war to marry?"

"The uncertainty, I think. It was a complex decision. Some of the guys in our unit married their sweethearts just before we shoved off, thinking that having a wife at home would give them something to live for, and I guess it worked out. For me and Paulina it was different. I knew we'd be married someday and there was something about feeling God's destiny at work in our lives that told us waiting until after the war was best. I guess you could say I spent the war staying alive so I could come home and have Paulina for my wife."

There was a long pause, a deep stillness between the two men.

"So, Miss Karen Sue Thompson; are you two getting serious?" asked Joe, breaking the silence.

"There's something about Sissy, Papa. She's different from every other girl, and I'm afraid I could lose her, especially while I'm away."

"Sounds pretty serious to me, son. What's Sissy say about this?" asked Joe.

"That's why she's in town this week, to talk about the future, to see if we have one, I guess." Another long pause. "Papa, what's it like? Combat I mean…"

Joe took a long drink to feel the burn deep in his throat, remembering how it was for him, and after a moment of introspection, he said, "It's not like anything, son, at least anything I've ever known." He sat the bottle down, pushed himself away from the desk, stepped into the file room and returned with an olive drab trunk. "LT. JOSE D. GONZALES" was stenciled in black military stencil on the face and just below the unit insignia, an arrowhead with a centered capital "T," Thirty-Sixth Infantry Division; One Hundred Forty-First Regiment; First Battalion.

Joe took David on a brief tour of his war chest: his garrison cap, boots, uniform trousers and blouses, a small paper envelope with shoulder patches and small black and white photos, mess kit, canteen, rifle belt with charged magazine pouches and his weapons. Wrapped in an oilcloth were his .30 caliber M1 Garand, .45 caliber 1911, and his M3 trench knife.

David looked through the photos. "What's this one?" he held up an image of a concrete wall peppered with bullet holes and a chalk drawing of a hairless head with a long nose and beady eyes peering over a wall and a message: "Kilroy Was Here."

"Esprit de corps, son; a little humor in the trenches. For us, Kilroy was the Super GI; the trooper who always got to the battle first and was always there when we left. You never felt alone with Kilroy on the loose. Don't know about the Japs but the Krauts hated old Kilroy; they say it scared the hell out of 'em." Joe smiled as he remembered his unit and their morale.

"Papa, how'd you get your weapons through discharge processing?" asked David with a smile, opening the shoulder patches where he saw the Thirty-Sixth Division T patch, a dark green Oklahoma arrowhead with a blue Texas T, and the shoulder patch of the Hundred and Forty-First; a lone star of argent surrounded by a garland of live oak, a shield of white, red, and deep blue. Below the shield was a scroll of heather blue with the silver inscription: "Remember The Alamo."

"Friends in high places," replied Joe as he took the trench knife from the chest. "Have a seat," he said, motioning David back to his chair with the M3. Leaning back against the desk in front of him, he looked lean, masculine, and even a little dangerous to David.

"Papa," said David, looking up at Joe in wonder, holding a small red crest with "RANGER" inscribed in deep blue, "you never said anything about being a Ranger. The First Texas—wasn't that the 'lost battalion' we heard about in Close Quarters School?" he asked, astonished with a new respect for his adoptive father.

"Son, I was just a guy doing his job. That's all any of us were. I got lucky, but a lot of guys just like me never made the trip home. I don't want you to leave here believing any differently," he replied soberly. After a long moment more, he said, "Here's the truth: the first time I killed it was with this," he said as he grimly removed the trench knife from its oiled sheath. "I'll never forget it. It was night; we were ashore behind their lines in Paestum, just before the invasion of Italy. I had the squad spread out, concealed, waiting for the navy to start the shelling. I'm moving to my position and run smack into this Kraut. We both dropped our rifles and grabbed each other, I could smell his breath, him trying to scream out, me trying to keep him quiet. The only thing I could get my hands on was this," he said,

THE FLIGHT OF THE MAYDAY SQUADRON

holding up the honed and oiled blade. "I think I nearly lost my soul that night, and it's only because of Paulina and the grace of the Lord that I was able to hold on," said Joe with a grimace and a mist in his eyes.

"Here's the thing, David; in the infantry, the rifle, the pistol, the knife—they don't kill. It takes a hard, terrified, violent man, driven by a fearsome rage to tear the life from another man who's doing his damnedest to hold on. To survive, you have to become the weapon yourself, son. That's the best way I know to say it. You use whatever tool you have to put the bastard down so you can take care of the man next to you, so you can take care of your squad, and so you can get home to take care of your family. Nothing else matters. All a soldier has in combat are his brothers, his training, his discipline, and maybe his honor. There are no rules; there is no glory."

"Now listen to me, David, when you deploy there will be one or two beat-up old noncoms in your unit, real quiet types; those are the men who'll survive this Vietnam mess. Get to know 'em. As much as your DI says differently; the desperation, the degradation, the savage reality of combat can't be simulated; it has to be experienced, and if you watch those guys, you'll see how it's done.

"One more thing; I crapped my pants. When I ran into the German that night, it scared me so badly that both my bladder and my bowels released. I stank like an open latrine for a week. It happens. You can try to head it off by hitting the latrine before you go into action, but when things get hot, well, sometimes you do what you have to. No shame in it, son; we're all just human beings in an inhumane situation."

Joe paused, taking another long drink and tossing the empty in the trash.

"While I was overseas, what helped the most was that I knew my cousin Roberto was looking after my parents," said Joe standing, casually, quickly drawing the razor edge of the trench knife across the heel of his hand, blood rising to the surface. "David, as one soldier to another, I offer you my hand, my blood, and pledge that if you need anything here in the States, you can count on me. I got your back."

David rose, accepted the knife, scored his palm, and grasped his father's hand. "As one soldier to another, Papa, I pledge to come back alive."

"You'd damn well better, Lieutenant, or I might hafta put you over my knee. Then I'll show you exactly how the other cheek is turned!" Laughing together and then crying, they embraced, father to son, man to man, soldier to soldier.

• • •

In the fullness of time, the light of a lover's moon has the power to burn away the deceptions of the heart and nurture the tender truths that bind a man and woman together for life.

Their courtship began along the visitors' sideline of Darwin Lee Judge Stadium in Abilene when Karen surprised David by boldly taking his arm as the Permian Black Jackets continued their tradition of walking the Panthers off the field after each of their games, especially the State Championship.

Later that semester David escorted Karen to the Quarterback Club Banquet, and in the spring they danced the night away at Permian's Senior Prom. There were movies, rodeos, bike rides, Coke dates, and picnics during the summer before they both left home for university, Karen to Austin and the University of Texas, and David to University Park and Pennsylvania State University.

Their high school crush grew into an abiding love through the instrument of the written word, slowly, tenderly, letter by letter over the years they spent apart. Their first embrace back home in Odessa sealed them as one flesh, and ten days later they were guided into the bonds of holy matrimony in the sight of God and man by Pastor Joe and dozens of their friends and family at the Quad Six.

Rodney Peterson stood tall as David's best man, with Jimmy Kellogg as his attendant; the Dockins twins were standing close by in case they were needed as backup. Becky Lowe served as Karen's maid of honor with Chris Newman completing the wedding party. Only David's friend from collage, Al Vazquez, was absent. "Big doings in Washington," said the telegram.

The bride wore her mother's wedding dress, a simple white satin gown with a V-neck bodice and elegant white veil. The groom wore his Marine dress A uniform with midnight blue, formfitting coat, white barracks cover, and sky-blue trousers.

The crowd had gathered near the entrance as David and Karen made their way to her parents' Chevy Impala for their honeymoon trip to San Antonio. They were surprised to find instead a shiny new Shelby Mustang. The confused couple saw Pastor Joe, Coaches Walt Calvert and Will Robinson, Charlie Knox, Tommy Peterson, Bobby Parker, and the veteran platform crew of Parker 16 standing in a semicircle around the ivy green GT350.

"David and Karen," said a smiling Bobby Parker. "We've watched you both since you were babies, and as you've grown into adults, you've given so much to all of us and the entire city of Odessa. On this day of all days, we wanted to say thank you from all of us with a little wedding gift. We all got together and want to present you and Karen with this new Shelby Mustang and, for your honeymoon, the use of the Parker family cabin in Ruidoso, New Mexico!" the crowd applauded and cheered the couple and their new life. Neither David nor Karen knew what to say.

Later that evening, as the Mustang cut through the clean crisp air and tiny snow flurries of the Sierra Blanca, Karen snuggled close to her husband and said a quite prayer: "Lord, I thank you for my husband, David! I love this man, and I pray that you surround him with your angels while he is in combat and that you will return him fully to me, Father. And Lord, if it be your will that he leaves me with his child before his long and dangerous journey, I pray for this Divine favor, the miracle of new life and his safe return in the name of your Son, Jesus. Amen."

• • •

Working late for his deadline, Bruno Braham reviewed his drawings once again and considered his masterwork. It was the physical manifestation of the eternal wisdom imparted to his soul at birth by the same supernatural forces that had conveyed him safely through the slaughter, degradation, and poverty of two wars waged against his race and native lands by the whimpering English dogs and their colonial mongrels, the Americans. Entering his seventh decade, Braham was able to clearly view the long line of history. He could see the symmetry of the invisible hand in removing the driving force of German National Socialism from harm's way and placing it precisely on the naked bosom of Columbia herself, even as the vaunted Allied powers were content with grinding the gutted, lifeless corpse of Hitler's Reich into dust. No victory in the history of warfare, Braham thought, smiling to himself, had been as utterly void of substance as theirs, and yet the jingoist American dupes believed themselves masters of the Western world, captains of their destiny. Their Yankee Doodle self-delusion would be their ultimate undoing.

The Allegheny would be far more than a masterwork of architecture; it would be his personal instrument of vengeance. Not only would the futuristic structure nurture and conceal the resurrected Reich, a deadly parasite growing within America's industrial heart, but the coded symbolism of the architecture would proclaim its sinister purpose directly to the ignorant horde it would at last subsume. A final clue to its ominous intent and a slap in the face of their "Uncle Sam" and their storied "American Know-How" would be that Braham would not allow a single component in the entire project to be manufactured in the United States. Every item he specified would be imported from providers found within the former Axis powers, no matter the inconvenience, no matter the cost, yet paid for completely by their conceited American hosts with monies secretly siphoned from their ongoing war effort against the Communist North Vietnamese; the symmetry of the invisible hand indeed.

Wolfgang Jung had engaged Architect Braham as he completed his first American commission at the country estate of Dr. Carol

Dorance, who had savored previewing the new facility for Jung and had taken great pains to use her Americanized version of the German language to formally introduce her architect.

"Herr Jung, ich bitte sehr, Herr Doktor präsentieren Bruno Braham den berühmten Architekten aus Viennia, die unser Haus abgeschlossen hat und der bereits in Life Magazine geschrieben! said Carol, a bit flustered and very proud of her mastery of the German tongue.

"I'm very pleased to meet you, Dr. Braham. Lovely work you've done for Mrs. Dorance. I've read your thesis. Very intriguing," said Jung, ignoring Carol's introduction and questioning Braham in English as to the detail of his notion of the transformative power of the built environment.

Braham used the Dorance Resident Conference Center to illustrate his points logically for a seemingly mesmerized Jung, concluding the dissertation with his description of the floor of the Susquehanna Suite as the point of connection between Germanic perfection and the physical gestalt of the North American continent.

"Well done, Dr. Braham and with such force of conviction! If it weren't for the witness of history, it would seem as if you had just established Hitler's invasion route into the heartland of the American Republic!" said Jung, sharing a hearty laugh with Carol, and smiling with affection toward the architect.

"Tell me, Braham, I once saw a series of renderings produced by the office of an architect named Speer who had a practice in Berlin before the war. The young draftsman who produced those remarkable renderings was also, I believe, named Braham, would you be any relation?" asked a completely serious Jung, offering Braham a worn bronze coin.

As a shocked Braham turned the 50brn coin over in his hand, the size and weight triggered an emotion he had thought long dead. And when he turned the coin to see "1940" and the eagle and swastika imprint of the National Socialists, the memory flooded his conscious mind. He instantly drew himself to gentlemanly attention, brought his heels together with a muffled crack, and bowed his head.

In cryptic German, Braham stated, "Verzeihen Sie mir, Herr Jung, ich habe dich nicht erkannt nach all dieser Zeit," ("Forgive me, Herr Jung, I did not recognize you after all this time.")

Smiling benignly, Jung returned the gesture and offered his business card. "Please, Herr Braham, contact me at this address when you have completed your assignment. I believe we have much to discuss, old friend."

Jung had Braham flown by corporate helicopter to the roof of Allegheny Electronics in downtown Pittsburgh and used the vantage of the helipad to view the sweep of the riverfront. He presented the architect with a map of the area, so that he could more easily orient himself.

"You see here the symbolism, Braham? Three rivers carrying the lifeblood of American commerce throughout the entire country. Pittsburgh is the source of its vitality; the beating heart; the steel spine of its global empire."

Braham stood transfixed at the site of the convergence of the Ohio, the Monongahela, and the Allegheny and the dynamism of the American heartland on full display; the powerful pulse of American free enterprise nearly overwhelming the man who had been close enough to the Nazi machine to know its specifications by heart. "No wonder they won the war," he said in a low voice only to himself, a subconscious thought not meant for the ears of his new client. Both men stood together on the roof. They were silent for a long time.

Jung spoke first. "The commission will be significant. Our benefactors believe that it should be located on the western point of the peninsula so that one may see the project from a distance west along the Ohio just prior to the fork," explained Jung, knowing that Braham would catch up and fill in the blanks as he went along.

"But, Herr Jung," said Braham apologetically, "the map shows that many structures already occupy the lands you have identified as the building site. This would mean enormous acquisition and demolition expenses must be added to the project budget. With all respect, am I to understand that you are aware of the scale of the expense involved?"

Jung smiled. "Come along, Braham," he said as he ducked low under the rotating blades of the Bell Ranger, ushered Braham into the passenger compartment, and took the copilot position under the Plexiglas bubble.

He motioned to his passenger to don the cabin headset, and once he was properly belted into the aircraft, Jung switched the intercom to "open," instructed the pilot to slowly orbit the downtown peninsula, and then switched the intercom to "passenger" so that he could converse privately with his architect.

"Herr Braham, in your travels you may have had the occasion to visit the village of Predenwind in Bavaria, near the town of Amberg, and if so, you perhaps know the regional tales of the giants of the Breitenwinner Cavern?" inquired Jung.

"Sir, I do confess that when I was a boy I was told the old stories about a race of giant warriors who roamed a mountainous region of the Black Forrest near the Swiss border. They were said to be four meters or more in height and not to live in the sunlight as men do but make their homes underground in deep fissures with entrances undetectable by men. My grandparents told these stories for the truth and believed these creatures were devils venturing up from the infernal regions to capture who they might for their pleasure and their supper. My father dismissed the stories as misunderstandings, exaggerations, and myths heaped on one another with no basis in fact," responded the ever-rational Braham.

"What do you believe, Braham?" asked Jung.

"Sir, I have no independently verifiable information on the subject, and therefore I must conclude that the stories are untrue."

Jung communicated with the pilot and took command of the aircraft, bringing them lower over the Ohio River, assuming an easterly vector, and inspecting the Monongahela Escarpment.

"There are similar stories about a race of nonhuman giants who were said to have inhabited this segment of the Ohio River Basin. They were known as the Alligewi and were said to be man hunters who considered human beings as a lower species akin to other indigenous mammals, deer, swine, and so forth; meat for the stewpot!"

said Jung with a smile. "According to the early French explorer, Cartier, tribal blood enemies, the Iroquois and the Algonquians, were so terrified of these beings that they made an alliance to pre-serve themselves against the common threat. This union was known as the Iroquois Confederacy to the French and the English who would later go to war over this land.

"The Alligewi were also builders of fantastic ceremonial earth-works; over two hundred are known to exist within a two-hundred-mile range of Pittsburgh," said Jung as he pulled the craft up out of the river basin and brought it to a hover over a flattened portion of the escarpment. In a grassy field ringed by a dense forest and spread across the plain, were dozens of earthen mounds of various heights. "There are thirty-four of them here, simple mounds, and though they appear to be randomly placed, there is definitely a pattern, perhaps with celestial significance. The circular ring wall is approximately five hundred meters across and three meters in height. The cere-monial opening faces east and aligns with the sunrise at the winter solstice—inviting the sun god into this place of the soul," remarked Jung as he relinquished control of the Ranger to the pilot for the return to his office building. The Alligewi were here once Braham, perhaps one day they will return.

• • •

After seating his guest and himself in his private dining suite over-looking the business district, Jung proceeded with the interview. "You were the chief draftsman for Hitler's personal architect but were never admitted to the party, Braham. Why was that?" inquired Jung casually as he filled their crystal stems from the flattened green Bocksbeutel imported for the occasion from the Franken region of Bavaria.

"Sir, the religious aspect of National Socialism was never my interest. I am an engineer by training and an architect by avoca-tion. I believe that unless something can be measured that it cannot be said to exist, and as you well know, spirituality was thoroughly integrated into…sir, forgive me. How would one say "weltanschauung" in English?" asked Braham, sipping his Riesling.

"Ah, the 'spiritual philosophy,' you mean. Yes, it would have been a disqualifier even for an architect, I'm afraid. Would you care for pike, Herr Braham?" said Jung offering the silver platter of grilled white fillets, asparagus, and small fingerling potatoes in hues of reds, creams, and blues.

"And, Braham, what were your allegiances during the war? Were you a loyal German?" inquired Jung, taking a small bit of fish and potato onto his silver Koch & Bergfeld dinner fork.

"Herr Jung, I was a patriot and remain so to this day. With all due respect, I believed that Germany would have won the war had Herr Hitler been a more prudent tactician and a more faithful steward of Germany's resources. If this position offends you, then I must apologize, since you are my host. If you wish to dismiss me, then I fully understand," Braham said firmly with a stoicism that Jung found admirable.

"Braham, suppose I were to tell you that the war never ended. That the abandonment of the fatherland and the surrender of Berlin were part of a necessary but temporary strategy, and that we are still very much engaged in combat with the Americans—only covertly, using stealth, infiltration, and psychological warfare as our main battle tactic. What would you think?" asked Jung, placing his fork on the edge of his Rosenthal porcelain plate, bringing his freshly pressed napkin to his lips.

"Sir, I would think you either a mad man or a cruel man using all of this," he said, sweeping his hands over the table and dining room, "to mock my ignorance and poverty." Rising, he said, "Thank you for your hospitality, and please excuse me, Herr Jung. I must catch the train for New York. I have a pressing need to return to Vienna."

"Please, please, Herr Braham. Accept my apology, sit, and enjoy your lunch, my friend. Grant me your forbearance for an hour and if, at the end of that time you would like to return, I will assign my personal aircraft and crew to have you home in less than a day. You have my word."

After they were settled again, Jung regaled his guest with a fantastic story known only to a few, the hearing of which would lock the architect into his employment for the remainder of his life.

"Your assessment of Hitler was generous and quite diplomatic, Herr Braham," said Jung, taking a sip from his cut-crystal water glass.

"He was, of course, completely insane by the time he betrayed Stalin with Operation Barbarossa. He saw only the spiritual side of the equation and believed that Germany's victory hinged only on the proper exercise of sacrificial faith. He believed himself Lucifer's high priest, placed in power by spiritual forces beyond the understanding of mortals to make sacrificial use of the human beings under his control. Within this delusion, he viewed Germany's war dead as equivalent to the blood of Christ, a sacrifice spiritually essential to proper victory.

"Hitler personally commanded the Wehrmacht and the Waffen-SS daily on this belief even until the very end, as he was necessarily concealed within the Führerbunker in Berlin. His madness was so complete that his confidants say he killed Eva Braun and then himself, fully expecting that he would be resurrected by Lucifer and rewarded with the position of the biblical Antichrist, the prime spiritual agent of Lucifer and ruler of the entire physical world.

"Both Deputy Führer Hess and Reichsleiter Bormann witnessed his deepening insanity and realized that the war was lost as early as the spring of forty-one. As you are aware, Hess made a valiant but futile attempt to negotiate a separate peace with the British, leaving Bormann free to become the second-most powerful man in Germany. Over the next months, Bormann and his advisers arrived at the conclusion that the only way to preserve the party, and therefore the soul of Germany, was to evacuate the accumulated wealth and genius of the Reich to neutral countries in Europe and the Americas. Bormann and his collaborators devised a plan to use Hitler's faith as a distraction while they went about implementing a strategic retreat, leaving the Führer at the helm of the gutted carcass as a lure for the English, Americans, and the Russians while the National Socialists vanished into the fog of war.

"The plan was called 'Aktion Adlerflug,' or as the Americans would say, Operation Eagle Flight, and it was finalized at the Hotel Maison Rouge in Strasbourg on 10 August 1944 during a summit of top party, bank, and industrial owners, the collective genius that had engineered Germany's fantastic economic rise and political transition from the obsolete republic to a modern socialist state. But it is important to realize that these men were not acting in isolation from the rest of the world but were working in concert with high-minded, powerful supporters within the United States, England, and many other nations, who had admired Germany's prewar economic miracle and desired the same for their own countries. And of course there were other benefits, which no sane man, even in a time of war, could ignore. The guarantee of prosperity coupled with fear of certain death as a punishment for infidelity combine to make a potent inducement during the flux of negotiation.

"Bormann, SS-Gruppenführer Heinrich Mueller, and a small unit of his most trusted Waffen- SS abandoned Hitler to his fate early in the morning of May Day, 1945, and secretly traveled the Roman ratline to Buenos Aries under new identities as Catholic priests and Church functionaries purchased from the Vatican Refugee Commission. It is important to know that travel along these escape routes would not have been possible without permission of the American OSS and British MI6, which was purchased with the operational German intelligence network, detailed files on the Russian leadership, and the ransomed promise of future assistance in waging the so-called Cold War against the Communists.

"So here we have, only six months after the fall of Berlin, the Reich reborn, this time global in scope, with its vast liquid capital concealed within the city of Buenos Aries, holding financial control of more than seven hundred international corporations as well as ownership of their intellectual properties—the entire construct secured through ongoing intelligence reciprocities with the Americans, the British, and the Russians as well.

"Herr Braham, you and I are dining this afternoon at Allegheny Electronics in Pittsburgh, Pennsylvania, USA, safe behind an immense wall of capital, an international business network, the impenetrable wall of American national security, and an active international intelligence network designed and placed by Reichsleiter Bormann, already twenty years in existence. All of this is completely hidden from the view of the mindless livestock which now inhabit the streets of this city or any city anywhere in the world."

Braham was speechless. His head was spinning as if he had been pitched headfirst out of the Bell Ranger, and his entire life was cycling through his consciousness in the moments before impact.

"Herr Braham, are you well?' asked Jung. "Please take some water and a moment to refresh yourself. We still have much to discuss," he said, finishing his Riesling and pouring himself another glass while silently congratulating himself on his skillful briefing without mentioning the Order or referencing it even in passing.

After recovering somewhat, Braham asked, "Sir, did you escape along the ratline as well?"

"Ah, no; I'm afraid my story is neither grand nor heroic. I was fortunate to have surrendered my little group of researchers to the Americans and was able to negotiate our participation in the American Operation Paperclip in return for our files and our limited expertise in influencing the masses through innovative forms of propaganda based on the Hegelian Dialectic. Do you know of Herr Hegel's work?"

"Sir, I have read Hegel extensively as well as his successor, Martin Heidegger, and grounded much of my architectural thesis on the practical application of these revealing philosophies," said Braham, sipping from his water glass once more.

There grew a profound silence between the two men as Jung considered whether Braham was equal to the role he had planned for him, and as Braham remembered the terrible things he had heard about how Jung had earned the feared moniker, "Doktor Gruenbaum," and his personal experience in the hell Germany became under the socialist control of the Nazi Party. Which did he hate more, the Nazis who set Germany alight or the Americans who had extinguished their evil fire? Could he walk away as Jung had promised, or would refusal mean his immediate murder?

"Herr Braham, I shall commission you to make a work of architecture for me, but it shall be like no other construction since the beginning of the modern age," pronounced Jung. "You shall make a new headquarters for a new company that shall be known as Allegheny Innovations, and within that company shall exist an association of thinkers, giants in their fields of endeavor, collected from many nations, and tasked with setting the course for a new America and thereafter a new world. We shall call the fellows of our brilliant association "Alligewi"—the giant mound builders of the Allegheny," said Jung, judging Braham's reaction. "And finally, Braham, you shall have the construction ready for a luncheon opening ceremony and evening revelries on thirty January nineteen sixty-eight. Do you accept the challenge?"

Braham was stunned silent, deliberately dropped his fork, and reached down to retrieve it to buy himself another contemplative moment. "Sir, you do me a great honor by suggesting this commission; however, the procurement of your proposed building site may be impossible or perhaps add so much expense as to make the project financially impractical—and the schedule—it does not appear feasible, Herr Jung," said the deferential architect.

In response, Jung moved to the credenza behind him, slide the concealed drawer open, set aside his Walther P38 and retrieved an expensive pale green envelope with an elegant double sun logo blind embossed into its left side, "Herr Braham, I believe everything you will need to begin is here." He smiled as he placed the envelope on the tablecloth between their luncheon service.

Braham opened the envelope to find two documents. The first was an itemized list of program requirements for the Allegheny:

- Seventy Stories
- 2,100,000 Square Feet Gross
- Steel Frame
- AEI Proprietary Laminated Alabaster and Glass Cladding/ Double Sun Beacon at Skyline
- Imported Egyptian Arcade at Skyline

- Ceremonial Landscaping
- Independent Utilities and Specialty Systems
  - o AEI Proprietary Zero Point Energy Power System
  - o Federal Reserve System Telex Link
  - o US Defense Department Telecommunications Link
  - o US State Department Security Link
  - o Network Television Broadcast Capabilities
  - o Regional Television Broadcast Capabilities
  - o Microwave Studio to Transmitter Link
  - o Medical Gas Distribution System
  - o Microwave Satellite Uplink
  - o Advanced Computer Datacenter
  - o Internal Potable Water Supply
  - o Internal Waste Water Treatment
  - o Medical Grade Incinerator
- Below-Grade Parking
- Below-Grade Security Vault
- Below-Grade Executive Retreat
- Below-Grade Reliquary and Ceremonial Catacombs

The second document appeared to be an original signed copy of Presidential Directive 11166.1 and supporting attachments "directing the secretary of Defense to set aside certain public lands and annex certain private properties within the Ohio River Basin and the City of Pittsburgh, Pennsylvania, for use as a Department of Defense reservation relating to classified national defense interests of the United States of America." The order was signed by Lyndon B. Johnson, president of the United States of America.

"Herr Jung, I am speechless, truly amazed. Am I to understand that this document is authentic?" asked an incredulous Braham.

"Braham, it is as authentic as this," said Jung sliding another smaller matching green envelope across the table.

Braham opened the envelope to find a check certified by Beacon Street Bank and Trust, Inc. Boston, Massachusetts, drawn on the account of Allegheny Innovations Inc.: *Pay to the Order of Herr Bruno Braham, Architect, One Million Dollars and No Cents.*

Standing as a form of silent dismissal, Jung said, "Your temporary office has been arranged in this building on the floor directly below; please have preliminary drawings ready in thirty days with quarterly updates thereafter. Invoice monthly, please, and contact my secretary if you need further assistance. Good day, Herr Braham," he finished with a slight bow.

His head still spinning and walking as if in a dream, Braham exited Jung's inner office to encounter a well-dressed middle-aged man of medium height with a bright countenance and disarming British accent. "Herr Braham, it's so good to have you aboard! My name is Dotson. I am Herr Jung's private secretary and will be at your service as you settle in. Welcome to Allegheny Innovations!"

• • •

A year earlier Jung had awarded the original Alligewi Fellowships, one each for the innovative reconsideration of religion, finance, slavery, and war, time-tested implements of mass population control. Funding for the Allegheny Institute was derived from a Department of Defense subcontract to the Prime Corporation, a Washington think tank, for development of new military tactics based on applied decision theory, which would be rolled out for real-world testing during the war in Vietnam.

"The goal of the conflict isn't a conventional military victory but rather the retasking of the land and the people for optimized productivity as determined by centralized planners at the federal level. The desire is to preserve the asset intact; however, it is likely that the majority of the indigenous population will cling to their traditions and resist the new model of centralized control. Therefore, a fundamental reordering of the society must be gradually implemented through transparent means," said Jung to his fellows. "Our task at the Allegheny Institute is to invent undetectable ways to alter the minds of the people so that they will voluntarily exchange their experiential faith in the old ways for the hope of positive change in the future. In other words, if the country were an automobile, our job would be to disassemble the car, rearrange the components, reassemble it, and send it toward a new destination, all while the vehicle remains in motion. A piece of cake, as you Americans say!" Jung smiled, laughing at his own joke, leading the laughter in the intimate lecture hall.

"As we all know, the most basic unit of the properly functioning nation-state is the extended nuclear family. Therefore, our core problem will be deconstruction of the organic asymmetrical equality found in the fusion of male and female. The durability of this bond was described by no less an authority on human nature than Jesus himself in his famous Pharisaical discourse on divorce: "Have you not read that He who created them from the beginning made them male and female, and said, 'For this reason a man shall leave his father and mother and be joined to his wife, and the two shall become one flesh. So they are no longer two, but one flesh. What therefore God has joined together, let no man separate."'

"The Everest we must climb, Gentlemen," Jung said with a theatrical frown, "is nothing less than the psychological crucifixion of the father archetype, the assumption of the masculine role by the State, and the dispersal of the family unit into its community of origin.

"Some of you are thinking that old Jung must be crazy, but I assure you, Gentlemen, if Oppenheimer and his team could split the atom, Jung and his Alligewi giants will surely be able to crack the institution of marriage. This is a small job by comparison, is it not?" Pause for reflection. "Are there any questions at this point in your orientation?"

"Herr Jung, I am slightly confused. I understood from my interview that the focus of the institute was to be the strategic deconstruction of the theoretical Vietnamese family based on the three teachings of the Vietnamese Cao Dai, the Buddha, the Sages, and the Saints. But what you are describing sounds more like a Western family unit based on a Christian mythology of some sort. I mean, sir,

216

we are at war with North Vietnam, are we not?" asked Mr. Religion, smiling. "Have I missed something?"

Jung stood erect, took the lectern in hand and began to awaken them to their new reality: "Each of you has completed in-processing and are fully aware of the national security implications of the work the institute has been charged with. You have taken the oath and accepted the money, Gentlemen, and with it you also accepted the potential of the severe penalties which may be levied against you by agents of the Department of Defense if you are even suspected of a security breach. I need not remind you that these penalties include imprisonment and summary execution," said Jung ominously, looking deeply into each man's eyes. "The information offered during your interview was a cover story to protect the true nature of the research you will conduct for the institute during what we are calling Project Kansas.

"As you know, global Communist aggression and the deployment of reliable intercontinental ballistic missiles equipped with nuclear warheads make old ways of thinking about our country obsolete, even dangerous. It has been determined at the highest levels that the caprice of the American electorate and the volatility of the American electoral process create a continuity of government risk so severe that it must be secured against the threat of ongoing Communist psychological warfare. In these dangerous times, Gentlemen, the old style of American liberty is our Achilles' Heel.

"Kansas shall devise a methodology to harmonize the will of the people with that of the government, unifying the country and its vital resources in resistance to Communist infiltration. To do that successfully, we must reengineer the minds and mores of the civilian population in ways that will enable the mass mind to resist psychological attack and equip it for its role as an effective government ally in the Cold War. The key to this problem is nothing less than reengineering the American mind and the weaponization of the American family unit.

"Each of you was selected for fellowship based on your experience with various forms of trauma on the human psyche that render it receptive to new ideas and products. Project Kansas shall build on your experience and sees the new conflict in Vietnam as a valuable opportunity. We shall use the war as both a laboratory for testing new forms of trauma based mind control and as a rich vein of psycho-traumatic ore which is to be mined, refined, and strategically injected into the American mass psyche so that it will become pliable and receptive to the reprogramming determined essential to national security. Gentlemen, are you understanding the import of the message here? Do you have questions?" asked Jung, searching for receptivity in the eyes of his fellows.

"Question, Herr Jung: If the Vietnam War did not already exist, would we have had to start it ourselves?" Pause for collective laughter. "What I mean to say, sir, is that nothing traumatizes a nation like war. Is this wartime America not an ideal environment for the mission of the Kansas Project?" asked a slightly embarrassed Mr. War.

"Ah, there you have me. The fact is that we *did* start the war ourselves!" Jung shot back, leading the laughter at his overt absurdity.

"Sir, please, you touched on this earlier, Project Kansas will be a massive undertaking, and I am concerned about maintaining secrecy. Should the American people learn of this activity, there would surely be armed resistance," said Mr. Religion, clearly concerned for his own safety.

"It is a wives' tale that says that if more than two people know something that a secret cannot be kept. One hundred twenty five thousand technicians, scientists, and administrators worked directly on the Manhattan Project and, yes, fragments of information were disclosed, some of it to foreign intelligence sources, but it is a matter of record that the overall reality of Fat Man and Little Boy remained a military secret until they were detonated on the island of Japan nearly seven years after they were first commissioned.

"The secrecy of Manhattan was maintained by what the security police refer to as the process of compartmentalization. The project itself is planned and then generally divided into major component parts. Staff are assigned to develop a component and given only the information they needed to complete their assignment never sus-pecting the role of their component in achieving a larger purpose or even knowing that a larger purpose existed.

"Your group is the originating source for the fundamental con-cepts that will make Kansas a success; therefore, it is necessary that you have full exposure to the project components from the begin-ning. So, Gentlemen, please be careful with the information and remember, the work you are doing will result in a safer, more secure America. My secretary, Dotson, will now instruct you in the security protocols for the Kansas Project."

Satisfied with his week, Jung departed early Friday afternoon for the brief flight to the Dorance estate and his weekend coordina-tion meeting with Carol and Alfred Dorance and the famous Francis Russell Frank, PhD, who were to preview their component of Kansas. He smiled at the thought of the grubby little Frank dancing about in the Dorance Resident Conference Center pledging his devotion to the ideals of global governance and his willingness to commit trea-son against the land of his birth, the freest country on the face of the earth, even to murder his own countrymen, for the mere chance of joining the Order. What was it the American circus man had said? "There's a sucker born every minute."

"We shall keep you on the wheel just a little longer, Professor Frank," thought Jung, "and then we shall see to your appropriate reward."

Sunlight glinted off the Plexiglas bubble of the Bell Ranger as it orbited the estate on its terminal approach. From his vantage point, Jung could see the silver vein of the Little Susquehanna just east of the main house and the Enchanted Forest labyrinth, which visually contained the pristine meadow from north to south and the dense, dark hemlock forest that embraced the meadow in a roughly circu-lar arc from south to west. The seclusion of the estate pleased Jung, and the thought of his special weekend unfolding in such a place aroused a strange hunger in his gut.

• • •

The pilot brought the Ranger down gently on the helipad just to the west of the main house. Jung and Dotson were greeted by Carol and Alfred, who embraced Jung as an old friend and were formally introduced to his new secretary. The staff began to unload the baggage as the main party walked on to the house.

"Tell me, Herr Dorance, are you quite satisfied with the performance of our Professor Frank?" asked Jung as they passed by the children of the estate staff and their nanny playing on the croquet lawn. Carol Dorance listening intently to the conversation, walking along with Dotson, slightly behind the two men.

"In regard to the Kansas Project, I believe he has done well. As promised, he has used our resources to assemble a network of Marxist organizers, who are, as he said, mostly tenured faculty at over thirty colleges and universities along the Atlantic and Pacific coasts, and then randomly sited across the heartland. Their actions will be coordinated through the rather large nest of Red Shirt radicals located adjacent to the University of Michigan in Ann Arbor. Frank organized the unit specifically per your instructions, sir; the leadership is cross-trained and redundant. If any one of them is lost, whether through capture or death, the circle will continue the program as usual."

"Why Ann Arbor? This has always seemed a little remote to me— does it not to you as well? And now he is off campus?" inquired Jung.

"The University of Michigan was his alma mater, and he was tenured faculty, but unfortunately there was an allegation of plagiarism concerning his book. I believe it was called *Bringing the Revolution Home,* and the Regents hearing resulted in his dismissal. When this occurred, he simply moved his operation off campus, taking his Red Shirts with him," replied a slightly embarrassed Dorance.

"So we have a convicted plagiarist now who would like very much to join our little club? Are you well with this, Dr. Dorance?" asked Jung, stopping and turning to see Carol flush deeply.

"Sir, Dr. Frank asserts that the charge and his dismissal were motivated by jealously within his own department and the political embarrassment suffered by Republican Governor Romney over the countercultural elements of his work. The governor, of course, appoints the Board of Regents for the University of Michigan," said an apologetic Carol Dorance.

"Tell me, Alfred, do your trust Dr. Frank?" asked Jung.

"Sir, I have no reason to either trust or distrust Mr. Frank, but I have observed that perhaps fame is his enemy. He seems to believe too much of his own press," replied a cautious Alfred.

"Is he ready for the presentation?" inquired Jung.

"Oh yes," volunteered Carol, "he's gone over it several times for me, and it addresses all the points in your specification, Herr Jung."

"Has our agent been positioned within their leadership?" continued Jung.

"Frank installed 'Tomahawk' in the Ann Arbor unit himself," replied Dorance. "We have confirmation through the Chicago Field Office of the FBI that she has been accepted and is moving to recruit her own people within the unit. The communications office of the Boston Fed exchanged their first coded messages three weeks ago, and the system testing you asked for has been completed with an eighty-eight percent success rate. The news coverage has been limited so far and has been less than comprehensive. This will, of course, change when we begin feeding the print syndicates and broadcast networks."

"Very well, Mr. Dorance, let us see to our Dr. Frank. I am sure he is tired of waiting on old Jung. Oh, by the way, Carol, is everything arranged for tomorrow evening?" asked Jung, resuming his walk toward the house.

"Yes, sir. The guests have confirmed and the food and entertainment are booked per your request," replied Carol. "Everyone is very excited about the weekend!"

Located on the second floor of the rusticated limestone mansion, the Conference Suite featured an oversized carved stone fireplace with a hearth tall enough for a man to stand in and was flanked by rows of crowded mahogany bookcases. The focal point though was a heavily carved mahogany conference table with matching leather armchairs grouped on a luminous seventeenth-century

Persian carpet, a trophy from the opium wars of the Great Trade Cycle of the eighteenth century—"like walking on the sky," Jung had once observed of the reverently woven surface.

Jung and his entourage entered to find a well-groomed and immaculately dressed professor standing at the head of the conference table, ready for the most important presentation of his life.

"Quite a transformation, Dr. Frank," commented Jung as he took the head chair opposite Frank. "You may begin when you are ready."

"Thank you, Herr Jung, for the opportunity of founding the beginnings of what we are confident will be the catalyst of a Communist revolution that will sweep the capitalist warmongers from power and return control of the lands of North America to the rightful owners," said Frank with a large smile on his face. "Though our numbers are small, we believe that acting in concert with our comrades in Hanoi and your press assets in New York, that the bravery and dedication of the members of *Red Storm* will be amplified, sparking the flame of militant fairness in the hearts of men and women all across the continent. They will rise up in the manner of the great October Revolution, destroy the oppressive American power structure, and cast out the capitalists once and for all.

"Coordinating our actions against Johnson's colonial war with our brothers and sisters in Vietnam serves three purposes: First, *Red Storm* shall act as a clandestine Communist Fifth Column, taking direct action against the American war machine by using assassination, arson, bombing, and other means to disrupt the military domestically. Second, *Red Storm* shall organize and script mass antiwar demonstrations that will have the appearance of being spontaneous expressions of America's collective unconsciousness. Coordinating coverage of these events with network television, radio, and newspaper entities owned outright or otherwise controlled by the Order, will constitute the largest, most effective domestic propaganda campaign in history. Third, coordinating *Red Storm* domestic resistance actions with Communist military operations against the American colonial forces in South Vietnam will project the fog of war into every home in America, overwhelming the mass mind, rapidly depleting America's will to fight and awarding the final victory to our brothers in Hanoi.

"If you will open the *Red Storm* dossier before you and turn to Appendix A, you will find a map of the United States. Each of the red stars indicates the location of a *Red Storm* cell, ready and able to act on directions issued from the central command, located in Ann Arbor, Michigan.

"Mission-critical communication will be accomplished by using redundant resources provided by the Order: Domestic Secure Intersystem Telephone and Telex provided through the national Federal Reserve System, thanks to you, Mr. Dorance." Frank nodded and smiled toward Alfred. "International Secure Messenger Service from Ann Arbor to Hanoi provided by cooperative Vatican emissaries from the Archdiocese of Detroit to the Archdiocese of Hanoi and members of the Order who hold senior positions in the US Department of State who maintain lines of communication to Hanoi.

"And finally, Ann Arbor center conducted a series of statistically significant field tests over the last six weeks in which we used information on the dates and locations of predeployment military leave, obtained by the Order from the Department of Defense, to assign picket duty to small units of student Red Shirt activists at airports and train and bus stations. Our public relations office coordinated their interceptions with trusted members of the press. We maintained the consistency of our message by distributing scripts and preprinted signs saying; 'Hell No, We Won't Go' and 'US Out Of Vietnam.' The student operatives were instructed to chant 'Pigs' and 'Baby Killers' and to punctuate our message by hitting the uniformed soldiers with urine-filled condoms.

"We were gratified by the press returns. Of the thirty-five test actions, sixteen received front-page coverage in local newspapers, one local television station ran a thirty second story on an airport interception and four of the local stories were picked up and distributed nationally by the Associated Press.

"In conclusion, Herr Jung, *Red Storm* is fully operational and only awaits your command," said a smiling and very relieved Francis Frank. "Thank you very much for the opportunity to serve you and the Order."

"Very impressive, Dr. Frank," said a smiling Jung. "Tell me, how were you able to recruit so effectively across so many campuses? Thirty-five, was it?"

"Primarily through my book, *Bringing the Revolution Home*, sir, and of course my speaking tour. I was able to visit over fifty campuses and made connections with preexisting Marxist cells in nearly every one. The ideal of the *Communist Manifesto* holds great appeal for young people of a certain class. All I had to do was ask, and they usually opened the entire cell to me, for approval of some sort, I believe. The Red Shirt cells that comprise *Red Storm* are all full of youthful rage, ready for action, and hungry for direction—and now, Herr Jung, they all work for you."

"Very well, Professor, and thank you very much for *Red Storm*, what a fantastic gift you have brought us!" Jung smiled, standing and leading a brief round of applause from his audience. "Francis, I do hope you are free to stay over the weekend. We are planning a small fete on Saturday and it would be good for you to attend. Carol, would you please see to Dr. Frank's needs?"

• • •

The helicopters and limousines began arriving at the secluded Dorance estate during midmorning and continued through midafternoon, filling the Resident Conference Center and the guest rooms at the main house to capacity. Jung gathered the Executive Committee of the North American Order for a briefing on the Kansas Project and a light lunch.

"Gentlemen, thank you for attending today and please finish with your dessert and coffee while I begin our discussion with a few administrative matters," said a welcoming Jung. "First, I am pleased to introduce my new personal secretary, Dotson, who will be assuming most of my daily responsibilities. Dotson comes to us from two decades of service directly to the Apex and thus, shall carry their authority within the NAO just as I do, so please join me in extending our warmest welcome."

After the applause had died away, Jung became visibly introspective, rose to take the ornate mahogany lectern and began to speak from the heart.

"You will recall the last time we assembled in this room. It was the momentous day we came together as colleagues to seize control of the country and preserve it from a calamity so pervasive that it threatened to set the master schedule back a half a century or more.

"We were able to succeed with the Killing of the King and installation of our retainer as his successor only because of the successful infiltration of the American defense and intelligence bureaucracy by our network of veteran German Socialists and because of the bravery, skill, and pluck of the small group of entrepreneurs sitting in this room."

Yes, our little homegrown coup d'état was a success, Gentlemen, but I am sure we all agree that the Order was only able to hold control because Americans are psychically trapped by the mythology of their nation-state, as Abraham Lincoln famously framed it: a government of the people, by the people, and for the people. The American mass mind cannot allow itself to hold a view of their government as being anything other than true, noble, and benevolent. In a manner of speaking, Americans trust their government because they trust themselves."

"Working from this blind spot, we were able to leverage America's naiveté through the National Security Act of nineteen forty-seven to engineer one of the greatest trade opportunities of the century: a completely legal war in South Vietnam that could be drawn out over a decade or more and from which our actuaries calculate war profits to the Order could exceed seven hundred *million* dollars plus the eternal capital of more than a *million* human souls.

"Bravo, Gentlemen. An extraordinary return on investment by any measure, but I am afraid that our employers demand more of us and have supplied their genius to make it possible.

"Of late, I have been troubled by the thought that I have not seen all of the pieces on the chessboard. I have been asking myself what detail I may have overlooked.

"As you know, I have only just returned from a spiritual communion with the Apex and experienced an enlightenment in which the Great Sage revealed that we now stand at the threshold of the next Great Trade Cycle. A cycle of such profound magnitude that it may eclipse all others combined, even to the very beginnings of the Order," pronounced Jung, barely able to contain himself," The vision for the next cycle, perhaps even the final cycle, was affirmed by the Apex in my waking dream and they have named it the 'Harvest of Kansas.'

"In the vision I saw the Twelve Giants of the Apex, in their prime once more, standing together in an infinite field of amber grain, each stripped to his loincloth, copper countenance aglow and iridescent against a deep indigo sky.

"Each held a great scythe made of honed amethyst, and they walked together across the field, reaping the heavy heads of grain, leaving only the maturing stalks for the starving masses withering in the distance.

"Gentlemen, I have been inspired to believe that the time for our final harvest is at hand, a full century before it was prophesied by the Great Sage, and I have taken measures to accelerate our progress by taking complete ownership of Americas house not by purchasing the house itself because today my friends the house is not for sale. We shall own the house indirectly by owning its most important rooms, the classroom, the living room, and the bedroom.

"Already in 1962 our friend Justice Hugo Black has shown us the way by nudging Jesus out of the classroom, making a place there for the Great Sage, and yet we could not see it.

"The very next year our friend Miss Betty Fridan suggested that there might be space available for the Order in America's bedroom. It appears that Rosie the Riveter has wearied already of her John Wayne. Perhaps the reality of the rut is less fulfilling than a paycheck of her own.", laughter all around.

"Since my return I have been thinking that access to these important rooms is gained through perhaps what is America's most important room—the living room. Our domination of that room can well be achieved with our existing technology—broadcast television.

"As you are no doubt aware, researchers for the Order discovered in its technical infancy that the electronic medium of television produces a near hypnotic effect in human beings that quite literally opens the subconscious mind to the suggestions made by moving pictures and sounds offered over the carrier signal. Through a program of intense human experimentation, our scientists determined that the desired brain condition, known as the alpha state, could be reliably induced in wide segments of the general population by standardizing the frame display rate, sometimes known as the "flicker" rate of the video sequence to twenty-four images per second.

"Most human beings are nothing more than livestock, pavlovian animals, and must be trained like dogs if they are to be of productive use. Using this method, the massive American heard may not consciously acknowledge the information placed into their unconscious mind when they are viewing the transmission. It is only later, when they encounter a real-life circumstance that approximates the one seen on their television, that their implanted memory bomb is triggered. In the parlance of the commercial marketplace, people will no longer ask for a specific product; the televised product will ask for them.

"The decision to make a purchase or vote for a candidate is greatly influenced by the implanted memory that has the power to override other information concerning competing products or people and compels the subject to make the selection which serves our masters best interests.

"As you know, over ninety percent of the households in the United States own a television receiver, which has allowed the Order to actualize the prophetic vision of Medusa, that we have all heard about since our earliest indoctrinations. What is needed presently is a mission equal to the weapon we have now in our hands. Thus the Apex has presented Project Kansas."

Dotson distributed reproductions of the dossier prepared by Frank as Jung took them through the particulars of their treasonous plan.

"Project Kansas is based on the core concept delivering the terror of the war in Vietnam to the heartland of the United States of America," said Jung, pointing to the state of Kansas

"Kansas shall be engineered and financed by the Order so that America will happily trade their country and their freedom for a sense of security. In providing a national police and intelligence network we shall come into full control of the largest economy and the strongest military on the planet by default. In the end, Gentlemen, to take full ownership of America, all we will have to do protect and serve!"

"The Apex has supplied the base science, which they brilliantly discovered at the intersection of neurology and ontology, the hardware and the software that work together to control the human mind."

"Kansas seeks to use their science to establish and maintain an emotional environment of radical dissonance, what the philosophers refer to as a "Mirror Play Skew" between subject and object. This dissonant mental state will disable the capacity for independent critical thinking of the general population. In more accessible terms, we seek to create a radical divergence between the subject's mental access to his own experience and his access to that of his fellow citizens. If our efforts are successful, a neurological seizure will occur within the mass mind. From this point the general population will descend into an induced coma, which only the Order understands and ultimately controls.

"For the individual captured in his own Mirror Play process, we may say poetically that the image of each shall be reflected in the eye of the other—changing one, changes them all. Over time, the individual immersed in this environment will lose his ability to distinguish between himself and the image in his mind's eye and will gradually discard his old reality and adapt himself as nearly as possible the new image he finds in the mirror; an image the Order designs and controls. The weapon by which we shall delver our memory bomb to the American mass mind shall be one of our own making—choreographed network television programming.

"All the world's a stage, and all the men and women merely players," said a thoughtful Jung in his unacknowledged paraphrase. "If we say that the war is right outside our door, then we must invent an image that will weaponize that message and implant it deeply in the collective unconscious of the country. Join me, please, in viewing this example, which was designed and created by our staff at Allegheny Innovations."

The large closed-circuit television flickered to life with the image of a handheld clapperboard, and written on the slate was the title, "self-immolation," followed by the visual countdown from ten to one and the graphic *PBN News Special Bulletin*. The image cut to a refined looking middle-aged man in a dark suit with dark horn-rimmed glasses reading the copy.

This just in from Cleveland, Ohio: an elderly Negro woman, identified by police as Regina Jefferson of Canton, set herself on fire this afternoon in front of the Cleveland Selective Service Board to protest the death of her grandson, Private Reginald Jefferson, US Army, of Bedford Heights, Ohio.

(Cut to B Roll footage: Map of South Vietnam/American soldiers in combat/head shot of Jefferson in US Army uniform)

Private Jefferson was reported killed in action last month in the battle of Dak To in Kontum Province north of the capital city of Saigon.

In her suicide note, Ms. Jefferson wrote, "Sending an army of jobless Negro conscripts across the Pacific to murder the defenseless Vietnamese people and steal their land is worse than slavery."

(Cut to B Roll footage of the smoldering corpse/white police officers standing idly in front of the Selective Service Office)

"At least the slave owners took care of their property, we had value then, were more than cannon fodder for our greedy masters."

(Cut to live anchor)

PBN News has obtained records from the Department of Defense, which tend to validate Ms. Jefferson's claim that poor Negro draftees are statistically overrepresented among all US soldiers killed in action.

(Cut to B Roll footage of Department of Defense Draftee Statistics and US Labor Department unemployment statistics by race)

It is difficult to believe that in today's affluent America a free Negro citizen believes her people so oppressed that she is willing to burn herself to death to bring attention to their plight.

(Cut to B Roll of the smoldering corpse with Catholic priest administering last rites)

"In the words of the old Negro spiritual...

(Fade to B Roll of photo of Regina Jefferson and Reginald Jefferson together at Christmas 1963)

"We shall overcome one day."

"David Berry, PBN News, Pittsburgh, we now return you to regularly scheduled programming."

(Cut to PBN Logo)

Jung paused in his presentation to allow stunned silence to envelop the room, and after a time, a voice from the foot of the table said, "My God, Jung, when did this horror occur?"

"The answer is that it never happened, my friend," replied the smiling Nazi. "This entire report was propaganda manufactured by our own Pittsburgh broadcasting network which will be fully operational with completion of our new headquarters facility in January of 1968. As I understand it, the images of the flaming body were repurposed from file footage of a house fire that occurred sometime ago, the images of the woman and her grandson were manufactured as well from file photos and the supporting documents from the DOD and the Labor Department are forgeries."

"So Jung, are you telling us that the Order will use these little lies to have our way with Uncle Sam?" replied the voice, laughter all around.

"It's is far more than that, my friend, it is the big brother of the little lie; disinformation," said Jung, smiling at the foolishness of the man at the foot of the table. "The Communists in the Soviet Union have been using these tactics successfully since the end of the war and we are only now in a position to adapt them to our operations here in the United States."

"If someone were to become suspicious of the self-immolation of Regina Jefferson and made a visit to the Cleveland police to investigate, they would find an official police report and autopsy documenting the incident. Likewise, they would find Defense Department documentation of the induction and service record of her fictions grandson Reginald and even falsified statistics associated with the report could be obtained by our imaginary investigator as well.

"Nothing is a lie if it can be officially documented, is that not what makes something the truth?

"We have arranged and financed the war in Vietnam; therefore, logic dictates that if we have the ability that we arrange and finance the antiwar in the United States. Is this not an elegant vise with which to crack the American mind and dominate the rooms in her house?

"Remember the words of Jesus Christ, Gentlemen: '*Do not suppose that I have come to bring peace to the earth. I did not come to bring peace, but a sword. For I have come to turn a man against his father, a daughter against her mother, a daughter-in-law against her mother-in-law, a man's enemies will be the members of his own household.*'"

Dotson approached Jung and whispered into his ear.

"Ah, Gentlemen, Dotson reminds me that I have carried on too long with business and that you are here as our guests for our little fete, so unless there further comments, I will bid you adieu until this evening."

Jung and Dotson left the library immediately and hurried past a dark corner of the great room missing a couple locked in deep conversation.

"It's been so long. I thought when you invited me here that you'd work it out like you did before," pleaded Francis Frank.

"Frankie, I can't. Things have changed. Everything's different now. Being together would be incredibly dangerous for both of us. What if Alfred suspected or worse, what if we were caught?" responded Carol firmly.

"Look me in the eye, Carol, tell me that you don't want this, and I'll leave right now," challenged Frank as he gently brushed her flushing cheek, golden strands falling out of place. "A woman like you needs physical love, Carol, the passion we shared isn't something you can live without."

"You're making things very difficult," said Carol, trying her best to look away.

Taking her face in his large hands, Francis Frank turned her head and brought her mouth to his in a deep, passionate kiss, which left her breathless in his embrace. Carol weakly placed her cheek and hand near the heart beating in his chest and relented. "Be in your room. I'll come to you after midnight."

• • •

In the privacy of the basement communications room, Jung read the telex to himself: *001.426.875.08/17/65/13:13/ MASTER JUNG: OPERATION STARLIGHT ADVANCED UNEXPECTEDLY. PREPARE FOR ALPHA GRADE SACRAFISE TOMORROW 08/18 @ 01:30 LOCAL. APEX WILL ACCEPT SUBJECT YOUR LOCATION. MAKE READY. WILL UPDATE TONIGHT 08/17 @ 23:00 LOCAL. END MESSAGE*

That evening precisely at eight, the immaculately dressed Alfred and Carol Dorance began greeting their guests at the head of the formal receiving line, which included Jung, Dotson, and Francis Frank.

The formally attired guests were drinking champagne and browsing canopies, amusing themselves with current events, gossip, and the like, their conversations augmented by a brilliant string quartet comprised of specially contracted members of the Philadelphia Philharmonic. Well into their fourth glass of sparkling wine and enjoying the beautiful people during the fourth movement of Franz

Schubert's "Death and the Maiden," the staff opened the formal banquet hall and the guests reluctantly began to move inside.

The Dorance estate had been designed by the New York architect, Richard Morris Hunt, who viewed it as one his lesser works after his breakthrough at the Metropolitan, as an up-dated Georgian composition which featured the elegant two-story banquet hall with vaulted ceilings and eight magnificent electrified crystal chandeliers made by J. & L. Lobmeyr of Vienna. The visual support and pacing for the composition was provided by twenty pairs of overscaled Georgian columns carved from doe-colored Indiana limestone and complemented by three axially placed, ornately carved, pairs of cherry doors with accompanying standing and running trim.

The primary feature of the hall was the functional two-story glass window wall, which opened onto the generous limestone terrace bounded by the heavily carved limestone balustrade which provided a regal platform for viewing the glittering Little Susquehanna below and in the distance, the granite cliff rock formation that many believed to resemble a gigantic cycloptic eye.

Moving into the hall, the guests found their engraved place cards on the seamless linen tablecloth amid the vibrant display of American Beauty roses in large cut-crystal vases, crisp white table linen, silver, crystal stemware and one hundred sixty place settings of gilt-edged porcelain, which bore the historic crest of the Dorance family, struck by Wedgwood just after the after the American Civil War.

Sensing the ease and pace of his guests, Alfred Dorance called the room to attention at the appropriate moment by formally welcoming the honored members of the North American Order and once more introducing Jung, Dotson, and Frank.

"Ladies and Gentlemen, it is a rare event we celebrate this evening. In the entire recorded history of the Order, there have been fewer than a dozen of us who have achieved the rank of ascended master, and tonight we are gathered to honor the next in the line; Wolfgang Augustus Jung," The room filled with warm and respectful applause.

"Jung came to this country barely twenty years ago, a penniless war refugee, his entire family killed in the Allied carpet bombings of his homeland during the war. Yet the man persevered, building from nothing one of the largest defense contractors in the United States and becoming a citizen as well as a statesman; equally at home in the laboratory, the boardroom, or in the halls of power in Washington, DC..."

With everyone in the room focused on their host, Frank caught Carol's eye and urged her to keep their adulterous appointment later that evening by slightly lifting his weak, though freshly shaven, chin and shifting his eyes toward their carved cherry escape route. Carol replied by flushing slightly and focusing on her uneaten chocolate mousse.

After dinner, the seeming eternity of the formal remarks finally drew to a close and the guests were released to mingle, animated by the Bach, and lured into the evening by the autumn moon and the mesmerizing vista provided by Richard Hunt's fantastic limestone terrace.

Francis Frank was entertaining a small knot of his fan base, checking his wristwatch, noting the location of Alfred Dorance, and specifically not looking at his love interest when he noticed Jung and Dotson walk out of the room. He took their exit as a signal and began saying good night to those in his circle and making his way toward Alfred to thank him for the evening before retiring.

Alone in his room, Frank took another hot shower, shaved his face again, toweled himself dry, splashed cologne on his hairless, undeveloped chest, and with wild anticipation, slipped between the cool pressed sheets of the same bed that he and Carol had shared during their first illicit liaison.

A muffled knock on his door awakened him from a light slumber.

"Francis, are you here?" whispered a female voice.

"Yes, darling, your lover is here waiting for you," he whispered in urgent reply.

Frank was confused by unexpected movement and in the dark he saw three figures pass between the foot of the four-poster bed and the moonlit terrace beyond and then "click," the bedroom light temporarily blinded him.

"Good evening, Herr Frank!" said Jung, seated on the dressing chair in front of the heavy drapery, slightly to the left of the terrace window. "I trust you had a pleasant time at the party. So many of our guests were disappointed with your early retirement."

As his eyes snapped into horrifying focus, Frank saw Dorance, Jung, Dotson, and his mistress all staring at him silently across the golden brocaded comforter as he cowered naked under the sheets.

After a long moment, Jung began, "As you Americans say, Frankie, I have good news and I have bad news." He smiled, savoring the heightened terror of his prey while holding a telex in his hand. "It's regarding your desire for inclusion in our little community. How rude of me Frankie, perhaps you'd prefer to read it to yourself."

001.426.875.08/17/65/23:02/ MASTER JUNG: FRANK APPLICATION APPROVED. ALPHA GRADE ACTION @ 01:30 LOCAL REMAINS IMPERATIVE. SUBJECT OF ACTION YOUR DISCRETION. SEND ARCHIVE EVIDENCE VIA COURIER ASAP. CONFIRM VIA TELEX WHEN COMPLETE. END MESSAGE.

"Herr Jung, I hate to be a boor but it is after midnight, and we have much to prepare," quietly, gently interrupted Dotson.

"Ah, but of course, Dotson, you are correct as usual. You should proceed with the in-processing of Mr. Frank," replied Jung.

"Congratulations, Mr. Frank. You have been admitted to the first level of the North American Order, and after your signature below, you will become subject to the Rules of Commerce, which bind us all from novice to ascended master. Please sign and date your acceptance and, sir, I do apologize but the NAO requires your thumbprint in your blood in the appropriate box," said Dotson hurriedly offering the quite naked Frank a clipboard, ballpoint pen, and a medical lance.

Frank completed the form and began to relax, calculating that his acceptance into the Order meant that he was safe from any reprisal for his adultery with Carol Dorance. After all, they were all adults, weren't they?

Dotson handed Frank a small round adhesive bandage. "Thank you very much sir and welcome," he said warmly and with a smile.

"Herr Jung," said Dotson, handing over the clipboard, "would you please countersign the acceptance? Very good, sir, and now the 'Appropriation for Alpha Grade Action' for this evening. Very well, sir, this completes the legal permissions required. You are officially released for compliance with your direction from the Apex. It is now 0033, there is less than one hour remaining."

"Very well, Dotson, please ask the staff to proceed with the preparations, we'll be down as soon as Francis is ready," said Jung looking coldly into Frank's eyes.

"What's going on here; ready for what? Could you please leave me alone, I'm exhausted. Carol, what is happening here?" pleaded a confused and disoriented Frank.

"Did you really believe that you could take my wife for your pleasure without my permission and not pay a price?" asked Alfred Dorance icily. "You must be something of a fool, Dr. Frank."

"Price? But, Carol. Alfred, your wife, she said there hasn't been anything between you sexually for years. She's the one. She seduced *me!*" he said in his defense, looking to Carol for some sort of vindication.

"Mrs. Dorance is nothing if not honest, Dr. Frank, and while it is true that I lost interest in the joy of the marriage bed some time ago," replied Dorance with a wry smile, moving close and placing his manicured hand on the tailored arm of his master, Jung, "she remains my property per the Rules of Commerce, and therefore a debt is owed."

Frank's head started to spin again, and he looked to Carol for assistance. "Buut, buut…"

"Stop whining, Frankie. God, I hate that about you. You knew the risk full well, and now you've got to pay the price. And don't worry, lover, there will be one for me as well, I can assure you," said Carol, walking from the bedroom onto the terrace, experiencing first revulsion and then nausea at the site of her cowering, former lover.

A dark spiritual presence entered the room and a chill penetrated Francis Franks soul. He suffered a paralyzing wave of nausea as an unexplainable stench moved through the air into his body, emanating from the rotting heart of Master Jung himself. His terror spiked as he thought he saw a thick black fly crawl out of Jung's left nostril, circle his head lazily and land on his upper lip.

"Very well," said Jung coldly. "Frankie, you have now to make an important choice. There are six armed men waiting for you just outside. On my signal they will come here, seize you, bind you, and deliver you to Dotson and our witnesses for the Alpha Action, which is set to occur in approximately twenty minutes. Or, you may elect to run for your life," said the gravely serious ascended master.

"Sssir," said Frank weakly, "what is Alpha Aaaccction?"

"Ah, my mistake, Frankie," said Jung with mock frivolity. "Alpha Action is a priority need of the Apex, so grave that they must petition Lucifer directly. In this instance, it seems that an old American Marine general named Walt misused his field authority in Vietnam to advance the schedule of Operation Starlight unexpectedly, damaging the cosmic planning for the battle that had been completed over a year ago. Therefore, we must offer the life of an Alpha, one of our own, so to speak, as an appropriate lure to attract the attention of the Great Sage. Again, Frankie, the Rules of Commerce apply even in spiritual matters."

"Yyyouu, mean that I, that you're going to kill me?" whispered a terrified Frank, eyes wide in fear.

"Sad, Frankie, but true, by immolation, I'm afraid. A catastrophic loss for the Order but not to worry, it's all quite necessary and of course legal now that you've been accepted into the membership, part of the Rules of Commerce you know," replied Jung in a businesslike manner. "But take heart, Frankie, not everything is lost. *Red Storm* will continue nearly as you planned; your shining legacy to the New World will stand for all eternity and, of course, you will still have your honor. If it hadn't been for you I'm afraid we would have been forced to select Mrs. Dorance for our offering, so in a way you are giving your life to save the life of your lady. Is this not an act of love noble and true?" said Jung, smirking with pure evil radiating from his face, several large black flies circling his head.

A deep blackness had filled Frank's soul and he sat motionless, mute, and impervious to the taunt.

"So, Frankie, which will it be? Trussed like a Christmas turkey to the oven or run for your life?" said a bug-eyed Jung, becoming agitated, snickering insanely as he jammed a spike of terror deeply into the heart of his quivering prey.

"Run, I'll RUN! SONOFABITCH I'M RUNNING!" screamed a terrified Frank, heart racing, eyes wide, saturated in an instant cold sweat.

"That's the spirit, Frankie! You've got thirty seconds before we come. GO NOW!" spewed a red-faced Jung, leaping from the chair, tearing off his tuxedo jacket and snapping into a disjointed posture resembling an aggressive, dangerous, otherworldly predator: "Thirty, Twenty-Nine, Twenty-Eight…"

Frank screeched, lunged across the bed to the door and ran, naked, shoeless, and howling in terror, away from Jung, away from the North American Order, away from the devil himself and toward a terrible fate lurking somewhere in the black Pennsylvania night.

• • •

Long before dawn, the nose of the gleaming BSB&T Gulfstream was being rendered in shades of luminous orange and red by the Atlantic sunrise as it streaked across the stratosphere, riding the polar jet stream to deliver its passengers to the Paris, Le Bourget Airport, in time for their scheduled breakfast meeting with principals of the secretive Financial Club of Paris.

The advanced nineteen-seat corporate jet was traveling light with only three passengers: Alfred Dorance and longtime friend and colleague James Hoang, president of the Commercial Reconciliation Bank of Asia, a Hong Kong-based legacy institution chartered in 1860 by the Yongzheng Emperor to assist in securing and taxing the illicit and highly profitable opium trade with the Americans and the British; Jung had asked Dotson to go along as their resource, counselor, and to report privately on their progress.

As with all senior members of the Order, cultural differences notwithstanding, wealth, marriage, and the potential of sudden, violent death, formed the enduring ties that held their organization together across the generations. This natural bond was, however, especially strong between Alfred Dorance and Jimmuy Hoang.

The Hoangs and the Dorances began their multigenerational transpacific relationship when the American Slave Trade Act of 1794 abolished the importation of human cargo into the United States and brought an end to BSB&T's primary business line of providing financial services to the rugged entrepreneurs engaged in the Great Atlantic Trade Cycle. BSB&T had grown rich by pioneering a lucrative niche in the high-risk financing of vessels, crews, barter goods, and liquidity required by the American and British corporations who send their fleets across the Atlantic laden with manufactured goods from Europe and America (guns, ammunition, factory-made cloth, and sundries) to the Arab slave markets on the west coast of Africa to barter with the Muslim slave merchants for captured Africans. On the second leg of the voyage they transported the human cargo south and east across the Atlantic to the Americas where they were traded for commodities like cotton, sugar, and tobacco produced on the slave plantations, and then finished their cycle by returning to American and British seaports like Boston and Portsmouth, to sell their commodities for extraordinary profits, often topping one thousand percent.

It was the mass hysteria of the Second Great Awakening and destructive, naive Christians like William Wilberforce, John Wesley and Charles Spurgeon that destroyed the Atlantic trade economy and forced the founders of BSB&T to quickly search for new opportunities. They were fortunate to be able to repurpose their expertise and capital for financing and equipping the fleet of revolutionary Yankee clipper ships that relied on the cutting-edge technologies of streamlined hull design and the fantastic, remotely rigged, three-mast canvas "cloud" to more than double the speed of the older slave traders to traverse as much as four hundred miles in a single day.

The business model that supported the expense of the Yankee clippers was the phenomenal demand throughout the British Empire and the United States for Chinese tea and silk; however, it was soon learned that the Chinese aristocracy considered manufactured trade goods from the West to be undesirable artifacts of a barbarian culture and refused the traditional barter, requiring payment for Chinese commodities in silver. This stunning revelation created an enormous trade deficit for the American and British economies and threatened the demise of the trading companies and their financiers as well.

Absent concessions on the part of the emperor, the solvent for the international trade imbalance became Turkish opium, a scourge foisted on the people of China by British and American smuggler-traders that ignited two murderous and expensive wars. Ultimate British victory brought about the Treaty of Nanking, which established the island of Hong Kong as a British trading colony. The resident Commercial Reconciliation Bank of Asia was chartered by the Chinese, which established the Hoang family as the lone arbiter charged with taxing sanctioned opium imports and facilitating an honest and accountable trade process, the primary surety of which was their intercession as the sole legitimate escrow agent between seller and purchaser, in exchange, of course, for a modest processing fee.

As the oldest son of one of the founders of BSB&T, Harrison Dorance was sent to Hong Kong in 1878 to observe the operations of the CRBoA. He was surprised and delighted to make the acquaintance of the patriarch of the Hoang family and befriended his eldest son, Alexander, who had been educated in England at Eaton and Oxford, his academic focus being the study of Western business economics.

Through his friendship with Alexander, the younger Dorance had learned that the Imperial Charter of CRBoA was granted perpetually to the Hoang family by the Yongzheng emperor as a reward for his grandfather's brilliant council in negotiating an equitable end to the hostilities with the British during the second opium war in 1860. The elder Hoang had discovered the solution, as always, in the financial details of the brokered peace, which allowed the emperor to save face within his realm by recasting a decisive military defeat as a shrewd business decision in which the British foolishly fell into a well-laid trap that required the British Crown to enforce the dictates of the emperor by regulating the import of opium while paying a tax on each chest directly to the emperor's court.

The Hoang family had then moved quickly to insert themselves and CRBoA as the sole chartered escrow agent between those with regulated product and those who wanted to purchase the product, thus guaranteeing the seller and the buyer a safe and equitable transaction, the emperor his silver and his public face, and the Hoang family a perpetual source of revenue that made them the masters of their domain. Sheer brilliance.

After a time, Alexander was granted permission by his father to travel to Boston with Harrison Dorance to study the operations of the BSB&T, and as nature would have it, fell in love, courted, and won the hand of the maternal first cousin of Harrison Dorance, Lilly Douglass, the youngest daughter of the Baltimore banking family linking the Hoang and Dorance families by both marriage and business interests.

As time progressed, both Harrison and Alexander became family men, business associates, and leading members of the Order in their own rights. An agreement was made between the two to begin the tradition of educating their eldest sons in the grand tradition of the Western liberal arts and commerce at the all-male Pinnacle School, which was said to have been chartered by the Great Sage Himself, with the divine conveyance of the Rules of Commerce, during the high season of the Roman Empire, many trade cycles before the birth of Jesus Christ.

The Pinnacle was known for its scholastic rigor, paramilitary-style physical education, and extraordinarily low student-to-teacher ratio, which incorporated the ancient Lacedaemon bonding ethos into the core curriculum. "Together Rule," Cum Imperio, was the motto of the Pinnacle, and it was well known inside the higher echelons of the Order that significant achievement in adulthood necessarily began with an elementary education on the island of Crete.

Reminiscing about their days at the Pinnacle had been one of the reasons Jim and Al had wanted to make the trip together, and it had been an especially delightful extravagance to have Dotson, headmaster during their formative years, to themselves for a few hours to savor their youthful days together and tighten old bonds, which had become loose over the decades, especially since the treacherous installation of Mao and the dangerous mass culling of his ongoing Cultural Revolution. But finally it was time to get down to the business at hand.

"Jim, I need your take on it; do you honestly believe Ho and his people are good for the loan? Ten billion dollars US buys a lot of rice but everyone knows it's only twenty percent of what DOD is planning to invest in the effort over the next five years, and after that it's anyone's guess. What if they lose the war and he takes the money and just moves to Switzerland or something? I've never been to Hanoi, but it sounds like a bit of a dung heap to me," said Dorance, hoping to hear Hoang tell him the same thing his research had.

"This is Uncle Ho's life's work, Al. He's not interested in anything other than unifying his country. As for their ability to pay, you've seen the numbers."

Jim brightened, "Remember what the Great Sage tells us in the Rules of Commerce: the only source of wealth on the planet is the land and its people. A unified Vietnam will consist of over 330,000 square kilometers with more than three thousand miles of coastline and nearly forty million people. Significant deposits of phosphates, coal, manganese, rare earths like praseodymium and scandium, bauxite, chromate, and the known reserves of offshore gas and oil make the loan to value ratio of just the land as over one to one thousand. When you add to that, the population of nearly forty million people, with an average life expectancy of just over seventy years and the mean age of twenty-nine, the core scale tells the story," he said smiling, finding his pocket-sized slide rule and a leather-bound pad. "Tell me if I'm doing this correctly, Dotson. Let's see, the formula is L/Nr X CLP X Cc=V, is that not correct? Land area divided the estimated value of the geological resources multiplied by the commercial labor potential for the term of the loan—I'm using three decades here—times the core constant that gives us a value on the core scale of point six seven seven, well above the parameters set by the club."

"I understand the numbers, Jim. If I didn't, we wouldn't be here," said Dorance, a little concerned and sensing some sort of deflection on his friend's part. "What I need is your gut instinct."

"Al, do you believe the American president will agree to the terms?" asked Hoang, knowing well what Ho and his subordinates were capable of, fear showing through his smiling bespectacled eyes.

"You mean the condition in the 'Boston Terms'?" asked Dorance rhetorically and smiling slightly. "Here's the story, Jim, and I know that you and your people have been waiting to hear this, the president has made what he calls his 'Grand Bargain' with Master Jung. The Order shall receive executive-level administrative oversight of the war in Vietnam through the Whitehouse proxy in exchange for our backing of his domestic agenda, what he calls his 'Great Society.' In short, we can write the Rules of Engagement to cripple American use of military force in the combat zones any way we want, and he will work them through the National Security Council. Then it's up to our people at the State Department and the Pentagon to drive them down through the ranks to the battlefield. After all, Jim, if your people squander this opportunity and lose the war and Vietnam isn't unified, then the entire collateralization for the loan is lost and the club will have poured ten billion dollars down a very deep rat hole. Our side of the table is incentivized to make sure that America is set up to lose the war very slowly, but by the same logic, your people have to be motivated to get their asses on the line and win the damned thing. So, Jim, why don't we go over the paperwork to make sure we're all on the same page," he said, handing thick leather-bound portfolios to his companions.

"I understand your position, Alfred, but please, stop the self-important Yankee Doodle posturing and just cut to it. No one knows better than my clients how to fight and win a war in Vietnam. If you doubt it, ask your friends in Paris. I believe they have some recent experience from which to draw," said a strained Hoang.

"Just what is the brokerage fee for a ten-billion-dollar credit facility, Jimmuy?" prodded Dorance. "One percent? More? And how much is CRBoA charging for escrow and disbursement services? What about the statutory reserve limits, Jim? Is it ten percent now or less, what in the world is CRBoA going to do with all that lovely liquidity?"

Hoang withdrew behind his inscrutable Asian banker persona and became as a stone. He stared blankly into the face of his old friend and new business adversary.

Seeing the preliminary negotiation beginning to stall, Dorance moved on. "Very well, then; Gentlemen, please turn with me to Appendix A, titled US Military Rules of Engagement, it's in the back of the document. I'll read them aloud and, Jim, if you will, please check them against your client's master list."

"Appendix A" consisted of an original one-page typewritten letter on official government stationary.

THE WHITEHOUSE
WASHINGTON

April 13, 1965

Dear Bob:

Regarding our earlier discussion of combat Rules of Engagement for the campaign in the Republic of Vietnam, the Kingdom of Laos, and Cambodia, I want to make sure that you understand that they are to be designed to adhere to the Geneva Accords of 1954 while preserving the integrity of the Republic of Vietnam. We want this done at all costs.

For the purposes of this memorandum you shall consider all ground, maritime, and riverine combat operations hereby constrained to the internationally recognized territorial limits of the Republic of Vietnam. "Hot pursuit" of enemy forces beyond these constraints shall be permitted only with command-level consent.

All aerial combat operations shall be defensive in nature and constrained to the airspace above the theater, with the following being off limits to military strikes:

> The capital city of Hanoi and a thirty-mile buffer surrounding its known limits
> The port city of Haiphong and a thirty-mile buffer surrounding its known limits
> All maritime vessels (surface and subsurface) enroute to, embarking from, or servicing port operations for the city of Haiphong
> A thirty-mile buffer adjacent to North Vietnam's border with the People's Republic of China
> All Surface to Air (SAM) missile sites and Antiaircraft Artillery (AAA) emplacements within the sanitary zones unless directly engaged in firing upon US aircraft
> All airfields, including runways, taxiways, and support facilities
> All civilian aircraft
> All military aircraft that remain on the ground
> All military aircraft, unless they are directly engaging US forces in belligerent action
> All known populated areas

As you are aware, America's role in the conflict is limited to counterinsurgency, and therefore we shall employ the overall battlefield strategy of attrition. We shall not take and hold territories as in previous wars; rather, we shall seek out and destroy the insurgent Viet Cong and the war material being used to supply and keep the invading force on the battlefield and will continue to do so until the emery's will to fight is broken, and he gradually withdraws his forces to his homeland.

I look forward to the receipt of your expanded brief outlining the operational details of this memo.

Sincerely,

Lyndon B. Johnson

The Honorable Robert S. McNamara
Secretary of Defense
Washington, DC

As Dorance finished reading the presidential memo, a silence enveloped the passenger cabin of the Gulfstream. "My god. You've actually pulled it off," whispered Hoang as he silently read and reread the document. "Al, this is more than they asked for, more than they ever expected. How in the hell…"

"You're pleased." Dorance smiled. "Then perhaps your clients will accept the modifications without too much resistance."

Hoang gazed up at Dorance through thick lenses. "Modifications?"

"Correct. Master Jung has modified the terms. Please refer to Appendix B," said Dorance. "Initial the changes in your copy as acceptable."

Hoang checked down the long list of the "Boston Terms" for modifications and then paused at the final item.

"Democide, one million," read Hoang aloud. "What? Al, this wasn't here before. Is it an error, maybe someone's idea of a joke?"

"No, I'm afraid not, Jim. Master Jung added the item himself, it's a direct command from the Apex," said Dorance, genuinely repulsed by the notion. "It isn't a joke, and there's no mistake."

"As I recall, Al, 'democide' is a term used when the state murders its own citizens. There must be a translation error and surely, Al, your people know that there is no way to forecast war casualties this accurately," suggested Hoang.

"Jimmuy, I know your clients will resist this, and I said as much to Master Jung, but he was insistent and is prepared to walk away from the deal if they don't agree. It's that important to our masters," said Dorance apologetically.

"He can't be serious, Al. This says that as a condition of receiving their credit facility that the Vietnamese agree to murder a million of their own citizens. For what? So some old fossil who lives above the arctic circle that no one has ever seen, that may not even exist, can get off on the pictures and statistics?" responded an enraged Hoang. "Hell, the terms of repayment alone are so tough they may not be able to service the debt, even if everything goes as planned. Remove a million people from the postwar labor pool, and the Order will end up owning the whole damned country. That's what my clients are going to say and really, Al, why don't they just save all this suffering, all those lives, all that money, and just surrender? The Americans will have the place totally rebuilt and be the hell out of there in a decade. That's far less time than the thirty-year repayment cycle required by the Order, and they'll get to keep control of their natural resources," said Hoang sternly. "Al, I've known you all my life and had consider us more than friends. But for you to blindside me like this when we're practically in our landing pattern is flatly unacceptable, and you damn well know it!"

Dorance saw that he had misjudged Hoang and botched the introduction of Jung's new requirement. He looked to Dotson for assistance.

"Gentlemen, I've been browsing the documents and believe there is a commonality that may have been overlooked. If you'll allow me, to explain," demurred Dotson to the deference of both his former students.

"I believe it was, yes, here it is, Appendix J, a report authored by a Washington consultancy to the Defense Department titled, "The Efficacy of the War in Vietnam: Violence, Taxes, and the Public Good." The author argues that once hostilities are joined, there is a moral obligation on the part of the ruling class to manage the conflict to achieve the maximum benefit for mankind after the cessation of hostilities. That war, by its very nature, spurs rapid advances in medicine, science, and other technologies, which are impossible without the imperative of armed confrontation. This is a fact of history that is beyond reasoned debate by educated men. The author argues, however, that the debate should be vigorous concerning the return on investment due to the peoples who have financed the conflict with their blood and taxes. As you Americans might say, they are entitled to the biggest bang for their buck." Dotson smiled, herding Hoang into Dorance's waiting net.

"The author presents his projections of the total cost of the Vietnam conflict which include one-point-six million deaths over the projected ten-year duration and suggests that those unfortunate individuals, rather than dying for nothing, ought to be afforded the opportunity to contribute to the greater good of humanity even in death. He suggests that gathering postmortem data for use in building computerized statistical models would have all manner of beneficial uses in science, medicine, and commerce and might even be used to recover a significant fraction of the monetary cost of the conflict."

Hoang was squirming in his seat sensing his time was running out. "Please, Master Dotson, could you be more direct? We are less than three hours away beginning final negotiations; if there is something salient, then, sir, please let me in on the secret."

Dotson had skillfully tipped the ball to Dorance for the score. "Jim, I think I understand Master Dotson's suggestion. The DOD is discussing a public-private joint venture with several pharmaceutical and cosmetics corporations that involves aerosol deployment of a completely nontoxic defoliant called Agent Orange, and the idea is that we sell participatory access to the formulation and blending of the product to corporate partners who want to incorporate various accessory compounds that are designed to be absorbed through the skin of humans located in the dispersal areas. If the subjects are killed in the conflict and their bodies are collected by American ground forces, then there would be liver samples taken in the field, processed in the lab, and recorded. The sample database would be used as a substitute for human subject experimental research, which is currently illegal in the United States and Europe. There is a per-head offer on the table right now, Jim, and it's not insignificant."

Hoang's body relaxed as he listened. He inclined his head as Dorance continued. "The scientists tell us that the value of the research will increase exponentially if they have access to a pool of genetically related control subjects that are not exposed to the aerosol applications; in this case those subjects would have to be native residents of North Vietnam."

"And you thought that my clients would be willing to kill a million of their citizens to help out in your little research side deal?" concluded Hoang. A silence grew between the men in the passenger cabin.

"How much per head?" asked Hoang. "Just out of curiosity."

"They mentioned a round number, Jim, I believe it was one hundred dollars US per head, so times a million would be significant, at least it would to me," said Dorance smiling broadly.

"The monies would be transferred to my clients through CRBoA?" asked Hoang.

"Jim, that's of course up to your clients, but I feel certain our corporate partners would not object," replied Dorance.

"What about the research?" asked Hoang. "They'll want to know if they will be allowed commercial use of the data set."

Jim, our associates are planning to license it to cover their development costs, but if you wanted to include—say a cooperative use agreement for your clients as a sweetener—I believe it could be arranged," said a smiling Dorance, believing he had just concluded the largest business negotiation of his life.

The flight attendant emerged from the galley with a tray of tea and pastries for her passengers, to let them know they would be touching down in just over an hour and that it was raining in Paris. But no one in the cabin seemed the least bit disappointed. Their plans didn't include any outside activities.

• • •

The pilot began his final descent through the storm as Le Bourget Tower cleared the Gulfstream for landing on historic Runway 03, which welcomed Charles Lindbergh as he completed the world's first transatlantic flight in 1927. Dorance had instructed his pilot to specifically request 03 so that he could remark on the coincidence of their arrival and their business agenda with that of the American aviator known to the world as Lucky Lindy. Acknowledging his profundity, Hoang politely smiled. Dotson remained stoic and looked out his porthole at the rain.

Ground control directed the pilot to the leased hangar reserved for use by the senior elites of the Order when their travels brought them to Paris, and the Gulfstream rolled to a stop dripping wet on the gleaming white floor inside the spotless white interior, illuminated in a manner that made it appear to be whiter and brighter than any other light on the planet. The ground crew moved quickly to mop up the water, chock the wheels and place a red runner leading from the exit hatch of the GII to their ground transport. The three executives made their way across the carpet to meet their uniformed chauffeur who assisted them into the passenger compartment of the pristine gray-over-black Rolls Royce Silver Cloud, especially selected by Dorance for transport during their stay. With his passengers safely inside, the chauffer gave the high sign to the waiting security teams who moved their black Mercedes sedans into position to lead and follow the Rolls into the downpour.

Also at the request of Dorance, the day's special meeting of the Financial Club of Paris had been moved from the brutal Ministry of Finance, situated in the Bercy District adjacent to the River Seine. Dorance found the architecture of the building repulsive, its two million square feet dehumanizing, and its configuration, the brainchild of the Parisian Communist architect Paul Chemetov, to be better suited for dark and dirty Stalinist Moscow than the radiant City of Light.

The destination of their small convoy was the far more desirable Organization for Economic Cooperation, since the war the sole resident of the Château de la Muette, located far west of the government district and adjacent to the pleasurable Bois de Boulogne, the most elegant urban public park in all of Europe.

The château itself was the third permanent residence to occupy the historic ground, since its origins as a royal hunting lodge, which may be detected still in at least one translation of its name as the *Palace of the Hounds*, the irony of which was lost only on those who could not or would not learn the Romantic language of their hosts. After the turn of the century, ownership of the property passed to Baron Henri James de Rothschild who awarded the commission for his new mansion to the famed Jewish architect Lucien Hesse.

In the studied opinion of Dorance, the interior architecture of the public rooms was understated, yet the coloration of the oak panels and their detail induced a color resonance with the large tapestries and complementary decorative features that rendered his experience of the space transcendent. Also, Dorance, who considered himself a patriot and statesman, enjoyed the history of the rooms, which once housed the European offices of General George Marshall, former Secretary of State who devised the famous Marshall Plan, which saved Europe from the ravages of the war and earned Marshall the Nobel Prize for peace. He also remembered his father, Alfred Dorance Senior, was fond of saying that whether in war or in peace, America was always left with the tab; the Order had made a killing off the Marshall Plan.

Certainly aware of the importance of cuisine, Dorance had engaged the American expatriate chef, Rowland Ferrier, to design and provide the menu options for the three-day affair, which would conclude with a formal dinner party for one hundred dignitaries and guests, all of whom held significant stakes in the successful outcome of the business at hand. Ferrier's appeal to Dorance was not restricted to his culinary renown, though it was significant, but also of note was his wartime service with the OSS as an intelligence officer, his postwar service to de Gaulle, and his Franco-American pedigree. After their first telephone conversation, Dorance felt they were simpatico as to the mission of the event and the manner in which to render it.

The BSB&T caravan arrived at the château as planned and was met under the portecochere by the expectant Chef Ferrier who welcomed them heartily and ushered his patron into the breakfast room for a last-minute inspection and to make alterations before his guests arrived. The small dining room for the principal breakfast, selected specifically by Dorance, was located on the second floor and had been designed by the architect to provide his client the gift of a pleasing overview of the Napoleon's Arc de Triomphe, a perspective only available to the occupants of that room because of its elevation and physical relationship to the monument. Months before the meeting, Dorance had imagined himself standing before the large multipaned window, using Napoleon's monument to victory as a prop, addressing the decision makers of one of the most powerful unregulated financial institutions on the planet.

The club derived its power from its proven ability to attract substantial sums of risk capital from the mythic pool of anonymous Global Capital, rumored to consist of up to fifteen trillion dollars in untraceable cash; it was even said by some economists to be quasi-conscious, on the move, perpetually seeking the highest return. Not even the Apex controlled so vast an amount of hard money, and the idea of it was intoxicating to Dorance who, as president of the Boston Fed, actively participated in managing the gross domestic product of the United States, which was just slightly over four trillion. Global Capital, a naturally occurring phenomenon of the Western capital markets, seemed to Dorance the best evidence he had encountered of the Great Sage's claim that immortality was indeed to be found tethered to great wealth.

The club itself was linked to the phenomena in that nothing like it had existed prior to the Industrial Revolution and the rise of the profitable nation-state. It was the pending sovereign debt default by the Republic of Chile in 1948 and the emergency debt workout between the Chilean government and nineteen independent creditors around which the pool had initially formed, and catalyzed the spontaneous appearance of vast sums heretofore unknown to exist by the financial world.

After Chile, it seemed that the club emerged from the mythic accountant's ether as the preferred lender of last resort for debt-laden second-tier nations, but there was nothing magic about the club, which owed its success to the simultaneous maturation of actuarial science and the advent of the IBM System 360. With mass computational power at their disposal, the actuaries were able to quickly create and examine reliable stochastic models referred to as "Monte Carlo Simulations," which allowed the financiers to assign realistic CORE (Collateral Ratio Evaluation) values to undeveloped land and native populations, which might lie under control of a specific type of nation state. The idea had not originated within the Order but was hailed by many of its more religious members within the financial community as fulfilled prophecy; real-world confirmation of the ancient Rules of Commerce.

Over its fifteen-year history, the club had successfully refinanced over six trillion dollars in sovereign debt, had assembled national subprime financing for dams and hydroelectric grids, railway and highway systems, natural resource development systems, and nearly a dozen industrialization programs in the third world. But conflict financing within a wartime economy had never been contemplated before, especially on the scale and with the participants that Dorance had proposed, and there was serious doubt among the principals that it should even be attempted.

Dorance believed that to succeed he would have to dazzle the Paris crowd, who he privately considered effete, self-important snobs who needed to be taught a lesson, and had engaged his insider chef on Jung's advice because of his cachet within the proper social circles and his renown for pleasing the sophisticated Parisian palate. He also had the dirt on the bastards, a value add that made him irresistible to Dorance.

The breakfast that morning was simple, regional fare that his guests would recognize and enjoy: Vietnamese pho and sticky rice with shredded pork and lotus tea; Chinese congee with yamcha and

STEVE A MADISON

hot tea; Russian blini with condiments and milk or tea, all set on an elegant Old World table adorned with strategically low floral arrangements of red lotus, tree peony and chamomile; absolutely lovely, better than Dorance had imagined.

Dorance, Hoang, and Dotson were to host four guests for the principal breakfast; Minister Tran Xuan Ha, from the Republic of Vietnam, BBA Harvard class of '41; Minister Lou Jiwei, from the People's Republic of China, MA London School of Economics class of '37; Minister Anton Siluanov, from the Union of Soviet Socialist Republics, PhD Stanford School of Economics class of '40; Minister Simpson Duvall, from the Financial Club of Paris, PhD, University of Paris '33.

The deal itself was superficially complex, Jung had explained to Dorance, but when one combines the dire financial straits of the Chinese and Russian Communists with the impoverished panic of the Vietnamese, facing the expeditionary might of the United States, the deal on the borrower's side of the table was secure; as always, it was the lender who had to be sold on the idea of the loan.

Near the end of the meal and polite conversation, Dorance rose from his position at the head of the table, immaculately suited in his stylish yet conservative *Champs de Lucia* business blue, which had been carefully crafted to contrast appropriately with the buff limestone of the famous national folly. "Gentlemen, we're here this morning to consider great wealth and how it might be set to work in the best interests of the people of Southeast Asia. In a more fortunate time, we would be speaking of rebuilding a united Vietnam after its long struggle for freedom against ancient colonial forces, which were put in place long before any of us were even conceived. Less than two years ago we in America were buoyed by our young president, full of optimism, who was charting a course for our country away from conflict in the region, toward peaceful unification of north and south and a period of unprecedented prosperity for the people of Vietnam. But our country was horrified to see his life snuffed out and even more so when his successor unwisely chose to challenge the sovereignty of your country and is now bent on a course that seems to many of us not only unwise but self-destructive." Dorance thought he could sense a empathy in the room, and he paused for a sip of water to allow it to steep. "And so, for Vietnam, it will be war once again but a different sort of war; a technologically advanced foe with extremely long supply lines fighting for what? We have asked ourselves this and are unable to answer the question satisfactorily, and so we feel a moral obligation to oppose Johnson's war as do many here in Paris. In our view it is time for the United States to honor the Geneva Accords of 1954, it is time for a free and unified Vietnam!"

There was warm applause and many smiles in the room, pleasing Dorance, who acknowledged the approval, seeing that only the Frenchman seemed unmoved. "So please, Gentlemen, may we adjourn to the salon to discuss how this may be accomplished?"

Dorance, Hong, and Dotson led the morning working groups with principals assisted by their aides, and the negotiation had gone smoothly through to the luncheon break. The Russians and the Chinese had quickly agreed to work cooperatively to split $6 billion to supply war materiel and manpower to assist Hanoi in resisting any level of sophistication that America might bring to the conflict. The Vietnamese were pleased with their response and felt that with the existing systems they had in place from their long war effort with the French that they could stretch the remaining $4 billon for as long as a decade of conflict but, as Dorance had assumed, the two sticking points were the million soul tax required by the Apex and the seeming coolness of Duvall who, as everyone knew, held the trump card.

During a midafternoon recess, Dorance took a chance and followed Duvall into the gentleman's lounge. "Forgive my impertinence, Monsieur Duvall, but I sense a certain displeasure in your manner today, and I must inquire as to the adequacy of the cuisine. Chef Ferrier's reputation is without the slightest blemis…"

"Monsieur Dorance," Duvall cut him off rudely, "let us dispense with this little charade. I have your dossier. I know who and what you are; your suspected involvement in the murder of President Kennedy; that you represent an international criminal organization of Illuminists, which has been known by many names but which you now call the Order, and of course the identity of your Master Jung. Many in the resistance remember him well from the war, the unspeakable crimes he committed for the Reich and the absolute evil of this devil-man. And already this morning, Monsieur, you have continued to expose yourself with a treasonous violation of the American "Trading with the Enemy Act." So Monsieur Dorance, please continue with your amusing little dance if you like, but I assure you that your efforts will be to no avail, and you will depart from Paris poorer than when you arrived. Good day!"

Dorance broke into a cold sweat induced by Duvall's artfully crafted and skillfully placed criminal indictment wrapped in a deeply familiar personal insult, the highly refined social poison of the famous French political class. In all of his life, he had never endured the sort of dressing down that he had received from the Frenchman—standing at urinals in the men's room of all places! and his mind began to concoct ways to make him pay for his insolence. Then fear rapidly flooded his mind, washing out all thoughts of personal revenge.

"The assassination! He knows of the Order and Master Jung!" he silently shrieked. Cold sweat was joined by a deep nausea as he remembered the pathetic cries of Francis Frank going up in smoke on that dark Pennsylvania night not so long ago. He collapsed onto the toilet, tried to vomit, stifled the urge, and slouched for a long moment thinking things through. "Not much time but maybe enough. Dotson tells Jung everything, he can't be allowed to discover this on his own or I'm finished; I must shape this to my advantage!" Dorance slowly pulled himself together, freshened his appearance as best he could, and went immediately to find Dotson and Hoang. He had a plan.

"We have a problem. Duvall intends to block the deal," said a morose Dorance to Dotson and Hoang, watching their reactions closely. "He says he knows about the Order, he called us 'Illuminists,' and claimed to know about Master Jung's Nazi war crimes." He was tempted to embellish, knowing that the key to a well-crafted deceit is the proper amount of irrelevant detail, but he skillfully held back, watching to see their reaction to his initial offering.

"How very unfortunate for us all," said Dotson blankly. "Alfred, please be accurate, did he say anything more?"

"Ah, yes, let me see. He said our current business proposition is a violation of the American Trading with the Enemies Act and that we would be poorer when we left Paris than when we arrived." He paused, watching as they seemed to accept the story which carefully omitted any mention of Dallas.

Hoang was instantly in severe distress, red-faced, and sweating. "In case you've forgotten Al, we've just promised six billion dollars to the two largest mass murders in history: Communist Russia and Maoist China! You don't think they're going to just let us walk away from the table, do you?" Hoang was trembling with fear. "Mao is relentless and through. Al, he'll come after all of us, after you and your entire family and won't stop until the name Dorance is no longer spoken on the planet. As for the Hoangs, he has easy access to all of us and a special treatment designed for ancestral Chinese who disappoint him at this level," he said with a shudder.

The three men sat together for a long time, not speaking, but allowing the fear to abate and then they gradually began to discuss their available options when suddenly there was a breakthrough. "Master Hoang, how would you like to become president of the Financial Club of Paris?" asked Dotson with a wry smile.

The next morning all of Paris, all of France, and later that day, all of the Western world was stunned by the large bold headline, exclusive to *Le Monde*:

FINANCE MINISTER MURDERED

The mutilated body of French Finance Minister Simpson Jacques Duvall, was discovered in the early hours of Tuesday morning by night watch park police, just inside Bois de Boulogne. Patrolmen characterized the discovery as grotesque, indicating that the body was openly displayed, fully clothed in business attire, and tethered into a seated position to a bench just off the primary promenade, within sight of the historic Château de la Muette, clearly meant to be discovered. The cause of death appeared to be a single gunshot wound to the head, although the victim's tongue had also been removed and a small red Nazi flag of World War II vintage was stuffed into the bloody oral cavity. Investigators on the scene indicated this method of extra jurisdictional execution was common during the occupation of Northern France, as the Resistance meted out justice to suspected Nazi collaborators with the intent to send a message to those who might be considering cooperation with the enemy. Officials stated that this sort of "message murder" has not been seen in France since the early 1950s...

Alfred Dorance was awake before the dawn, ebullient; placing transatlantic telephone calls to Herr Jung in Pittsburgh, Mrs. Dorance in her office at Penn State, his partners at BSB&T, and his secretary at the Boston Fed. He read and reread the press coverage of the "Duvall Message Murder," savoring the grainy black-and-white photograph of the corpse. Later in the day he obsessively viewed the updated European television coverage of the event, which added that Duvall's office had been ransacked in the night, and that the top secret contents of his office safe were missing. In the early afternoon he ordered the hotel concierge to package and send a dozen copies of the English version of *Le Monde* to his office in Boston to commemorate his triumph. He made an emergency appointment with Mario de Luca, his favorite Parisian tailor, for a new wardrobe appropriate for a French state funeral. He visited the hotel salon for a haircut, shave, and manicure, and then he waited patiently, in the know, for the next phase in their evolving plan.

As a matter of course, the progress of their ongoing business with the Financial Club of Paris was temporarily suspended while the shock of the incident was absorbed by the club's Executive Committee. Following protocol, Dorance, Hoang, and Dotson mournfully attended the state funeral for Monsieur Duvall, a hero of France and member of the Resistance, seated with the committee members and their wives. During the reception, a carefully crafted message was whispered into certain ears within the grief-stricken French bureaucracy. The Vietnamese conflict loan package, being considered by the Financial Club, had allegedly died with Duvall, and the Americans would win Johnson's war by default. Ho Chi Minh, being so impoverished by his twenty-year conflict with the French that he could no longer afford to mount a credible offensive against the South, would lose the war before it began, and the divided Vietnam would be reunited under political leadership selected by the Americans who would merely replace the French as its colonial master.

Within a day, diplomats hand delivered strongly worded personal letters of concern from the Soviet premier and the president of the People's Republic of China to the office of the French president. Official notice was received by the Supreme Headquarters Allied Powers Europe in Fontainebleau, of pending Soviet naval maneuvers in the northern Mediterranean, just off the French Riviera. The Chinese notified United States Pacific Command in Pearl Harbor of its intent to sail its small fleet of French frigates and Russian destroyers into the Gulf of Tonkin for port call at the Vietnamese coastal city of Haiphong. When the rumor that a potential hot war might be spreading from Southeast Asia to Europe was published in the *Guardian* and then was picked up by the *Times*, there was an immediate panic sell-off; overnight the financial markets in London and New York lost three and a quarter percent of their market value.

Later that week in New York, the American ambassador to the United Nations made an impassioned conciliatory statement to an emergency meeting of the Security Council, affirming Vietnam's right of self-determination as set forth in the internationally recognized Geneva Accords of 1954 and emphatically disclaimed any colonial aspirations toward its divided lands. And finally, but not unimportantly, in Washington, a friendly call from State to Justice resulted in a long overdue administrative review of the Federal Reserve Act of 1917. A backdated memo to file was prepared, releasing any sitting member of the Federal Reserve Board of Governors from legal responsibility for compliance with conflicting provisions that might exist in 40 Stat. 411, enacted 6 October 1917, codified at 12 USC § 95a et seq., otherwise known as the Trading with the Enemy Act of 1917. A copy of the memo, covered with a personal note of apology from the attorney general, was sent by messenger to Governor Dorance, care of the Federal Reserve Bank of Boston.

At the Financial Club of Paris, the ensuing international crisis completely obscured public knowledge of the panic that surged through the institution after word spread that each voting member of the Executive Committee had received a tiny untraceable package containing a bloody portion of Simpson Jacques Duvall's famous missing tongue along with a small card. One side of the card was crudely imprinted with an image that appeared to be a pair of disembodied lips behind an upright forefinger and the word "shush" hand printed below. The opposite side of the bloodstained cardstock carried a one-word message: "Hoang."

And so it came to pass that when the Financial Club of Paris resumed normal operation, a respectful two weeks after the tragic loss of Monsieur Duvall, its first order of business was to elect a new president. Its second order of business was to approve the first Credit Facility for Conflict Finance in the history of the club. This was done unanimously under the gavel of President Jimmuy Hoang, who also happened to function as the chief executive of the Commercial Reconciliation Bank of Asia, the exclusive disbursement agent specified by the club for its new ten-billion-dollar placement.

After the vote, the celebratory gala, and several days of well-earned vacation in the most finely cultured city on the planet, the triumphant trio paid their bill and bid adieu to their most inventive friend and colleague, Rowland Ferrier. They found themselves together once again in the passenger cabin of the pristine BSB&T Gulfstream, accelerating into a cerulean-blue sky above Paris Le Bourget.

"So, gentlemen, please allow me to summarize; you arrive in Paris, hat in hand as it were, asking for consideration from a scornful banking syndicate for the liquid capital required to fund a war which, win or lose, would ultimately allow you to come into control of the land and the people of the debtor nation. Your mission seems on the verge of failure when miraculously, and literally overnight, your opposition is removed, and three weeks later you depart Paris not only with your original conflict financing secure but also in effective control of a new capital pool worth an estimated fifteen trillion dollars. If I didn't know better, Gentlemen, I'd say this was proof of your intimate connections to the villainous group of mysterious international criminals known as the Illuminati!" said Dotson, trying hard to conceal his devilish smile.

"But, Master Dotson, everyone knows there's no such thing as the Illuminati; that sort of talk is just for crazy conspiracy nuts!" responded a smiling Jimmuy Hoang in mock admonition, inspiring hearty laughter, which filled the passenger cabin. Their mirth, which brightened the flight crew, was punctuated by the pop of a champagne cork as the GII climbed to altitude searching for the jet stream east, to a city called Vientiane in a region ripe for the picking that the Order had begun to think of as New Asia.

14

DE OPPRESSO LIBER

The morning had broken crisp and clear in Ruidoso after an evening snow cast a crystal veil of silence across the Sierra Blanca. The jays were up early, gliding from limb to limb through the frigid alpine breeze, fussing over the pine nuts and negotiating territorial rights with a belligerent gray squirrel.

"Good morning, my husband," whispered Karen Rixon into the ear of her slumbering David. "I have coffee and a kiss for my lover," she breathed, bringing her lips from his ear to his cheek, amber tresses gently brushing his face.

Emerging reluctantly from his slumber, David began to show signs of life, first with a slight flare of his nostrils as he detected the fragrance of freshly brewed coffee, and then from the corners of his mouth as his morning began with a satisfied smile.

"You were wonderful last night, darling," said David, not yet wanting to open his eyes. "But I can't wake up, not yet, not now, not from the dream I'm having about this beautiful redhead named Karen Rixon."

And for a long moment Karen lingered, studying her new husband through the eyes of love. "Lord, what a beautiful man he is. Thank you, Father, for my husband," she prayed as she caressed his torso, sculpted, hard, and marked by "a million setups and a billion push-ups," he had told her during their first night together.

"Shush. David. Do you hear that?" she whispered playfully. "I know I've heard that sound before, wait, I think maybe it's...pancakes. Yes! I'm sure of it now, pancakes and sizzling hot bacon being put on white plates and served; but where? Wait a second, its coming in clearly now: pancakes and sizzling bacon on white plates with steaming mugs of black coffee being served to hungry customers at the Log Cabin Restaurant!"

"But it's so peaceful here. Can't you make something and we can just stay here, in this bed, and get to know each other a little better," said David smiling, playfully countering her tease.

"David, darling, sweetheart, we haven't been out of this house in four days and there is simply nothing left in the kitchen (jaayy! jaayy!), and now even the pine nuts have been spoken for," she said gesturing toward the terrace and the jays working the tall mountain pines beyond.

"Four whole days." David smiled. "That must be some sort of record...are you positive they have pancakes? And bacon?"

"David, come on, I'm hungry..."

An hour later David had finished his "daily dozen" physical training routine, showered, shaved, and dressed in his old Tony Lamas, worn Wranglers, starched and creased lovingly by Mama Paulina, and gray Marine Corps sweat shirt straight from PT class at Quantico. Karen sat patiently reading the hot new novel, *Tai-Pan*, admiring her husband's personal discipline and meticulous grooming.

"You look beautiful this morning, Mrs. Rixon," said David, enjoying the appearance of his petite wife, dressed in white sneakers, soft denim jeans, and pressed white cotton shirt under a wool navy sweater. "Let's eat!"

David bumped the starter and enjoyed hearing the Shelby bark to life. He scraped the dusting of frosty snow from its tinted glass while admiring the chrome hood pins, black striping and hood scoop, Cobra badging, and GT-350 side markings. He did a walk-around of the vehicle as it warmed, making sure Karen was belted securely into her black leather bucket and then approaching the deep rumble to the rear of the vehicle, inspecting the fifteen-inch "CS" branded alloy wheels and the Goodyear Blue Streak tires along the way. He paused for a moment, leaned against the rear deck, savored the aroma of piñon on the air and gazed up through the pines to the clear-blue infinity.

"Father, I praise your Holy name and thank you for my wife, Karen, for our marriage and the bounty you have brought to our house. Lord, I do not know what the future will bring, what awaits me in the fire of combat but, Father, I pray for the courage and skill to do my duty and that after my time there, if it be your will, that you make a way to bring me safely home to my wife so that we may be able to live our lives in your peaceful service. I pray these many blessings in the Holy name of Your Son, Jesus Christ. Amen"

The Log Cabin was jammed with its normal breakfast rush but Karen and David were quickly seated in a small corner booth where they salvaged an abandoned copy of the *Lubbock Avalanche-Journal*. David thumbed through the smudged broadsheets to find the front page headline:

MARINES LAUNCH OPERATION STARLIGHT

Saigon Wire Service, Marine Theater Commander, Lieutenant General Lewis W. Walt, today announced the success of Operation Starlight, the first major ground offensive of America's war in Vietnam.

Based on intelligence received from an enemy defector, General Walt authorized immediate preemptive action against the First Viet Cong Regiment in the village of Van Tuong, staging there to attack the Marine base at Chu Lai.

Marine Colonel Oscar F. Peatross, winner of the Navy Cross and former member of Carlson's Raiders in WW II, was selected to lead the attack force, which included the 3d Bn, Third Marine Regiment, commanded by Lieutenant Colonel Joseph E. "Joe" Muir, 2d Bn, Fourth Marines, "The Magnificent Bastards," commanded by Joseph R. "Bull" Fisher, holder of the Silver Star for action on Iwo Jima and the Navy Cross in Korea, and the 3d Bn, of the Seventh Marines, Special Landing Force.

The speed, maneuverability and ferocity of the Marine attack completely surprised the VC and left them exposed for the classic "hammer and anvil" strategy. The Marines were the hammer, the VC the anvil, and during the third night of combat operations the enemy withdrew from the battle, leaving behind six hundred bodies, more than a third of their original force of 1500.

American losses were dramatically less, fifty-two Marines, one corpsman, and an army major providing air cover.

There was much bravery and honor displayed by the Marines of Starlight, two Medals of Honor, six Navy Crosses, and fourteen Silver Stars were among the honors awarded to the leathernecks who promised to pursue the enemy and attack in any climate and on any territory until complete victory is achieved.

"Sorry about the wait, folks," said the man serving them their breakfast. "We're shorthanded today. Darla's out this morning."

"That's fine, sir, we're just catching up on current events," said David, folding he paper. "Boy, this looks fantastic!"

"Say, if you don't mind my asking, what branch are you in?" asked the waiter with a knowing smile.

"Well now, just what makes you think I'm in the service? asked David playfully.

"No civilian in this day and age would be caught dead with that haircut," said the waiter good-naturedly," and then there's your physical condition, the look in your eye, and the fact that you're wearing Marine PT gear. So I'm guessing the corps."

"Third Reconnaissance, Third Marines," acknowledged David.

"I knew it—a recon Marine, right here, in my little restaurant!" said the beaming waiter. "You must be real proud of your husband, ma'am," he said to Karen, noticing their shiny new gold bands.

"I am, very proud, but now I'm curious. David, you never mentioned anything about being a 'recon Marine.' Is that something special?" Karen asked them both, David sat, flushed and silent, inviting the waiter to reply.

"Why yes, ma'am, it is something special, very special," he replied to Karen. "What's your MOS, son, if you don't mind my asking, that is."

"2747 Linguist," replied a modest David.

"Damn, that means you're probably an officer too," said the man.

"Ma'am, I don't mean to get into your business, but just so you know, your husband is serving in a duty position that only one in a hundred men can qualify for. Every Marine is tough, smart, and in peak physical condition but only the best of the best have what it takes physically and mentally to be selected for Reconnaissance School and then go on into an MOS like your husband's. They're scarce as hen's teeth, but we need 'em 'cause they're the guys that operate in 'Indian Country,' so to speak, and come away with the intel command needs so the rest of us don't fall on our butts. Sorry for the French, ma'am, but you could say your husband is in the lifesaving business…Well, you folks enjoy your breakfast and just sing out if you need anything. I'll be by to check on you."

"Sir, if you don't mind my asking, where was your service?" asked David respectfully.

"Did a little island hopping in the forties with the Fourth Marines, just a grunt doing his job," he said with a grimace typical of most veterans when asked about their service. "Welcome to the Log Cabin, folks, I'm John Miller. My wife, Darla, and I own the place, so if there's anything you need just holler."

David blessed their breakfast, buttered and drenched his hotcakes with maple syrup, while his wife looked on.

"Aren't you going to eat? It's very good, the bacon is great. I thought you said you were hungry," said David, savoring his first bite and sip hot of coffee, avoiding eye contact with Karen.

"So when were you going to tell me about the 'recon' part of it?" asked Karen, not touching her meal. "David, this sounds far more dangerous than just translating captured documents. What it sounds like is that you might be the one they send in to capture them!" she said, flushing.

"Honey, it's a job like everyone there has a job. The corps tries to match every man to the MOS that suits his talent and this just happens to be the way it worked out in my case," said David apologetically. "Heck, it's dangerous just driving to work every day. At least I'm trained, equipped and know what to expect when I'm doing what I do. So please, don't let your imagination lead you to believe this is a bigger deal than it is. OK?"

After a moment, Karen relented and reached across the table to take her husband's hand.

"Just don't keep me in the dark. Damn it, David, I mean it," she said emphatically, pressing her polished thumbnail deeply and painfully into the back of his strong hand. "Don't ever lock me out no matter how bad it gets. I'm you wife now, not your girlfriend. There's a big difference. OK?" demanded Karen, pressing harder. "OK?"

"All right, Karen," said her husband looking her in the eyes and pulling his hand away in reaction to the sharp pain. "I promise on my honor that I'll never keep anything but military secrets from you ever again," replied David in all seriousness. "And right now, duty compels me to tell you that you probably shouldn't eat your bacon because it's not very good, so if you will allow me to take it off your hands...," he said smiling, moving his hand toward her untouched breakfast.

"Hands off, Recon!" she said, smiling and playfully rapping his knuckles with her fork. "You can have anything I've got, darling, just not my bacon!" Smiling first and then laughing, the two enjoyed their hotcakes and the bright, friendly atmosphere at the Log Cabin.

After breakfast Karen and David were sitting in their new Mustang, allowing the engine to come to temperature as they looked over a roadmap of the State of New Mexico.

"So, sweetheart, do you want to do some shopping here? Go back to the cabin for a little nap? What do you have in mind?" asked Karen, smiling at her new husband.

David folded the map to expose the route from Ruidoso to Cloudcroft and marked it in red pencil. "Right now, I'm thinking road trip! We're running the ridge route to Cloudcroft, and you're the navigator!" he said, passing her the map.

Belting himself in, tuning the radio to Albuquerque's popular KKOB AM, putting on his Ray-Ban Aviators, and slipping the Cobra into first, he said, "Sweetheart, you're about to discover what it's like to be the wife of a Recon Marine. YEEE HAAA!" he yelled playfully, smiling broadly.

"Aye, aye, Commander Rixon!" countered Karen, smiling with her husband, slipping on her Wayfarers and offering a playful salute.

"That'll be Lieutenant Rixon to you, Private and it's sir! Yes, sir!" David laughed as he engaged the clutch and ran smoothly through the gears, accelerating the GT-350, Karen, and himself into the fast lane of US 70 West and groovin' to the popular harmony of Brian Wilson and the Beach Boys.

> I'm pickin' up good vibrations
> She's giving me excitations
> I'm pickin' up good vibrations
> (Oom bop bop good vibrations)
> (Oom bop bop excitations)
> Close my eyes, she's somehow closer now
> Softly smile, I now she must be kind
> When I look into her eyes
> She goes with me to a blossom world
> I'm pickin' up good vibrations...

They had been cruising along US 70 for less than an hour when a New Mexico state trooper maneuvered his squad car behind the Cobra and popped the lights, directing David to the side of the highway.

"Good afternoon, sir. Are you Marine Lieutenant David Rixon?" asked the trooper politely.

"Yes, sir, that's me. Can I help you with something?" replied David, placing his hand protectively on Karen's knee.

"Sir, I'm sorry to have to tell you this, but the Marine Corps found out from your family that you and Mrs. Rixon are here on your honeymoon, and since there's no phone in your cabin they contacted the state police and asked that we notify you that your leave has been rescinded. Sir, you're to contact a Sergeant Atkinson at this number in San Antonio for further instructions," said the trooper apologetically as he handed David the card with the contact information.

"Damn!" shouted David as he slapped the steering wheel, looking at Karen red-faced and with profound disappointment—the final two weeks of his leave gone in a flash.

Empathizing with David's circumstance, the trooper offered, "Sir, if it's any help at all, since the call sheet doesn't specify an emergency contact, I can delay our confirmation call to Sergeant Atkinson for the duration of my shift. I'm the only unit out here today and I'm pulling a double so I could forget I found you until I do my shift debrief around zero seven thirty tomorrow morning. That way dispatch will probably give Atkinson a call around oh eight hundred. Would that help?"

"Trooper...Coats," began David reading the silver name tag on the officer's khaki uniform shirt, "If you could do that for us, I'd owe you one very large favor."

"No problem, sir, it's the least I can do. My older brother Tom is in Da Nang now. He's a Green Beret, with the Seventh Mobile Strike Force, been a sergeant so long I think it's probably permanent," said the trooper with obvious pride in his brother's achievement.

"No kidding! What a small world. That's where the Marines say they're shipping me when my leave's over," said David with a smile. "I'll be sure to look your brother up. What's your first name?"

"Timothy Coats, sir, here's my card, maybe you can just slip it your wallet." Trooper Coats smiled.

"Any message I can give Sergeant Coats, anything you'd like to send?" asked the appreciative honeymooner.

After a moment, he said, "Come to think of it, Lieutenant, there is something. Tom developed a taste for Drambuie liqueur when he was stationed in Scotland in the forties, before Normandy. They don't stock it at the PX, and the local shops never heard of the stuff; he talks about it all the time. It would knock his socks off if you could hand him a bottle and tell him it was from his little brother in New Mexico," said Trooper Coats, grinning broadly.

"Say no more, Troop, it's done!" declared David appreciatively.

Coats was reaching into his wallet for some cash when David stopped him. "Please, Tim, it's on me. It's the least I could do for family."

After their business with Trooper Coats was concluded, the Rixons continued to Cloudcroft, took a break for a little shopping, and over coffee, Karen plotted their route down the mountainside to see the western vista overlooking the Sonoran Desert. They had lunch at a diner in Alamogordo that catered to the military types out of White Sands Missile Base and then took the northern route back to Ruidoso, trying hard to avoid the topic of David's canceled leave and his looming deployment to Da Nang.

The last rays of the enchanted New Mexican sun were painting the needles of the majestic mountain pines as David pulled the Mustang into its spot under their sheltering canopy and put his baby to sleep. The fragrance of piñon was lightly on the air as they noticed the light of the fireplace dancing through the windowpanes, casting cruciform shadows across the front porch of the ancient timber retreat. A chill was in the air and tiny snowflakes began to fall as David found the door key in its special hiding place. Karen retrieved her packages from the car and made her way across the heavy pine planking, gray with age and smooth with wear, to meet her husband, who was reading a handwritten note wedged into the jamb of the lacquered oak door.

Mr. and Mrs. Rixon: Captain Parker called to tell us about the leave cancelation and asked that we make supper for you tonight. Darla put a roast in the oven and the fixings are in the fridge. Everything else is out where you can find it. We threw in breakfast just for fun. Hope you don't mind, David, but I laid the fire for you. I always like the smell of piñon when I come home. Semper Fi, Darla and John Miller

As they read the message together, the cathedral bell tolled the valley faithful to vespers and caused a Holy silence to fall over the cabin, further secluding the lovers high on the Sierra Blanca.

David released the bolt and swung the door inward to reveal the hearth, alive with warmth and light and the table, artfully laid with two candles, a loaf of fresh bread, a bottle of good wine, and two glimmering crystal stems.

Enthralled by the romance of the moment, Karen felt the desire for her husband flash hot through her body as David's sharp eyes dominated her conscious mind. She gasped involuntarily as he seized her wrist with his strong, capable hand and pulled her off her feet and into his arms. She buried her face in his muscular shoulder with a tiny whimper as David carried her lightly across the threshold, past the table and beyond the fire to his rustic bed, freshly dressed with a warm comforter and fragrant pressed linens.

His strong arms held her tightly to his chest. Suspended above the world, her head spinning, losing her sense of time, helpless in his embrace, she felt her husband's hot breath, first on her cheek and then on her mouth, urgently seeking the taste of her acceptance.

"My husband…," moaned Karen into his waiting lips, receiving his advance with joy and wild anticipation.

David held his wife for a long moment, kissing her deeply, feeling the weight of her body in his arms, savoring her fragrance, and measuring her body against the depth of the passion that was flooding into his hard, angular abdomen.

He released Karen to stand weakly before him, his eyes sweeping over her from head to ankle, his hands delicately tracing the curves of her face and then lightly kissing her lips, cheek, and down the length of her neck, memorizing her. Karen encircled her husband's waist with her arms, running her fingertips inside the top of his loosely fitting jeans to the small of his back and then up his spine to the flare of his chest, pulling the Marine sweat shirt over his head and casting it aside.

"They may take you tomorrow, but tonight you're mine," she said in a dusky tone as she traced the edges of his sculpted chest with her fingers and ran her hands down over his taut stomach, pulling him to her breast and opening herself to the power of eternity she knew lay waiting in his embrace.

The ways of a husband and wife within the crucible of the marriage bed remain yet a mystery even unto the angels who were with the Lord in the beginning. This was true before there was ever an earth, before the stars, the sun, and the moon, when there were no fountains flowing with water, before the mountains rose, or even the dust of the fields existed. They sang His praises as the Lord God, Wisdom Himself, prepared the heavens, drew a circle on the face of the deep, established the clouds above, strengthened the fountains of the deep, and assigned the sea its limit so that the waters would not transgress His command. And they worshiped the Lord Almighty as He marked out the foundations of the earth like a master craftsman, placing holy matrimony as the keystone of all His Creation, rejoicing in His inhabited world and delighting in the sons of men.

From the beginning, it was the way of heaven that when a man and woman join together, claim the privilege of His Holy Ordnance and place themselves under the seal of the Almighty, that their guardian angels are miraculously joined as well. They are charged by the Lord with the spiritual care of husband, wife, and the little ones He sends into their charge.

Now it should be known that Almighty God listens well to the prayers of all His people just as He had heard Karen on her wedding night. In that instant He summoned her guardians to place the bright seed of eternity in their care (this is what human beings often refer to as the human spirit) until the time was right for David and Karen to become Father and Mother. And so it was that a miracle occurred for the young couple that night, bound by their love, secure in their marriage, and covered by the Grace of the Lord.

Working in the moment, yet remaining secluded beyond time and place, the angels deftly completed their secret work and in a moment, in the twinkling of an eye, the entire realm of eternity rejoiced. The guardians embraced and began rising toward heaven like snowflakes into the starry sky, the joy of the Almighty rolled like thunder through the distance, silence condensed, time rained down and across the White Mountain that night, the angels were singing for Karen.

• • •

The Rixons were up before dawn, packed, and in the Cobra before seven. They stopped by the Log Cabin to thank the Millers for their hospitality and to borrow their telephone for the call to Sergeant Atkinson, who instructed David to report for transport to Lackland Air Force Base in San Antonio within seventy-two hours. On their way back to Odessa, Karen and David had discussed their future and decided that she would return to the University of Texas to pursue her master of business administration while he completed his military obligation, and that they would work out the details in their correspondence while he was away at the war.

Two days later, tears had been shed, good-byes said, and finally, the Cobra had been prepared for long-term storage by David and Rod and was sitting off the ground on jack stands under a formfitting canvas cover in the rear of the barn at Pleasant Farms. With a day to go, David was packed, in uniform, and ready for his ride to Midland-Odessa Regional Airport.

Pastor Joe and Mama Paulina drove David to the airport with Karen and Isabel along to say their final good-bye. They were followed by well-wishers Bobbie Parker, Tommy Peterson, Walt Calvert, and Will Robinson in a Parker Exploration Chevy and by Rod Peterson, Jimmy Kellogg, and the Dockins twins in Rod's demonstrator Bonneville, fresh from the showroom at Peterson Pontiac GMC and Ford. The boys were there because they had decided to run interference for their former teammate should David run into any trouble at MAF.

The Red Shirt contractors assigned to picket Midland-Odessa Regional were college dropouts from New Jersey, Maryland, and Michigan on the run from their local draft boards and making their bones in *Red Storm* by protesting whoever and whatever they were told to by the Ann Arbor Center. Like all members of the burgeoning Communist Fifth Column, the Midland protestors were paid monthly through the Kansas Project with funding from the United States Department of Defense. Therefore, they didn't have a dog in the fight in Texas and were completely unaware of the culture of mutual admiration and respect shared between Texans and their fighting men.

Ann Arbor Center had notified their operatives in Texas to expect a surge of military traffic generated by the seventy-two-hour leave cancellation and per protocol Midland Red Storm had anonymously alerted sympathetic reporters at the regional newspapers, radio, and television stations that there would be a student antiwar protest at the airport at 6:00 a.m. The morning was cool for West Texas, and the protesters were frisky, ready for some action. They had endured weeks of summer heat and boredom, biding their time in cheap motel rooms with nothing to do but drink beer and use the residue to create a stockpile of urine-filed condom bombs for use against American servicemen in their protests for peace.

The contractors were nothing if not precise and per orders from Ann Arbor, the messaging for that day was consistent with others around the nation and the picket signs were limited to "BABY KILLERS!" "US OUT OF VIETNAM," and their personal favorite, "BURN YOUR DRAFT CARD." Special permission was given that morning to create an effigy of Uncle Sam to be hung and burned for the press at 6:30 a.m., thirty minutes before Continental Flight 607 was scheduled to depart for San Antonio. The contractors were also authorized to condom-bomb any uniformed American soldier who tried to run their gauntlet.

Seeing the well-staffed picket line in the distance, complete with Uncle Sam twisting in the wind and a gaggle local reporters, Pastor Joe said, "Here we go again," as he led the little caravan into the short-term parking lot across from the main terminal. A short time later, the men gathered in front of the Parker Exploration Chevy to discuss their strategy.

"It's the same bunch been here all summer. The ones 'at hit you with the piss bag, David," said reserve deputy Jimmy Kellogg. "Ain't nonufem from Texas. I say we walk up like we're just mindin' our business and thump 'em. It's the only way they gonna learn any manners. Heck, it'd probably be good for 'em…to learn some respect, I mean."

"It's just after six and I'd like to get inside and check my seabag to avoid the crowd," said David with his arm around Karen. "Why don't I just walk up, tell them what I'm going to do, and then just do it?"

"Don't look now, but KMID-TV just pulled in, and the driver is talking to one of the protestors," observed reserve deputy James Ray Dockins. "Man something's fixin' ta happen. TV don't show up and then nothin' happens. Everybody's here but the cops. It's pretty near show time," he concluded his ramble a little nonsensically, but everyone got the drift.

"It's clear the protestors want some sort of confrontation to emphasize their antiwar propaganda message in the press. It would be better, Jimmy, if we could figure a way to win this battle without firing a shot. What do you think, Captain Parker?" asked Pastor Joe.

"Twenty years ago this airport was a military installation; it's where the Air Corps qualified bombardiers to use the Norden Bombsight. Joe and I spent a little time around here. Remember, Pastor?" asked Bobby Parker.

"You're right, Bobby. I wonder if he could still…naw, no way," said Joe in reply. "He's at least seventy."

"Well, let's go see for ourselves, Lieutenant Gonzales," said Parker. "Guys, see if you can round up the uniforms when they come into the parking lot and we'll make our play in less than half an hour."

Joe and Bobby walked through the picket line and into the terminal without incident. Fifteen minutes later a large, three-axle bobtail truck maneuvered into the parking lot and came to a stop behind the three vehicles from Odessa. The little group had doubled in size with uniformed military and their families standing off the picket line, watching the effigy burning for KMID and the newspaper photographers.

Joe and Bobby climbed down out of the cab and explained to David and the other uniforms that an old friend from the US Army Air Corps had become the manager of Midland-Odessa Airport after the war. He had dispatched the cargo vehicle to take any of the soldiers who wanted, through the service entrance to the airside of the terminal and directly to their flights from the taxi apron, thereby denying the protesters the confrontation they sought.

"Son, how's that sound?" asked Joe of Marine Lieutenant Rixon.

"Sir, it sounds good to me. What about the rest of you men?" he addressed the growing crowd of soldiers with unanimous acceptance.

"Papa, one more thing, could you lead us in prayer before we go?" David asked of Pastor Joe.

The soldiers circled around Pastor Joe, surrounded by their family and friends. Joe pulled his worn Bible out of his jacket pocket and turned to the passage he had marked many years before and began. "Gentlemen, I will be reading from Psalm one forty-four, a warrior's song of petition and praise to the Lord. Please take these words into your heart:

"Blessed be the Lord my Rock,
Who trains my hands for war,
And my fingers for battle
My loving kindness and my fortress,
My high tower and my deliverer,
My shield and the One in whom I take refuge,
Who subdues my people under me
Lord, what is man, that You take knowledge of him?
Or the son of man, that You are mindful of him?
Man is like a breath;
His days are like a passing shadow.
Bow down Your heavens, O Lord, and come down;
Touch the mountains, and they shall smoke.
Flash forth lightning and scatter them;

Shoot out Your arrows and destroy them.
Stretch out Your hand from above;
Rescue me and deliver me out of great waters,
From the hand of foreigners,
Whose mouth speaks lying words,
And whose right hand is a right hand of falsehood.
I will sing a new song to You, O God;
On a harp of ten strings I will sing praises to You,
The One who gives salvation to kings,
Who delivers David, His servant,
From the deadly sword.
Rescue me and deliver me from the hand of foreigners,
Whose mouth speaks lying words,
And whose right hand is a right hand of falsehood—
That our sons may be as plants grown up in their youth;
That our daughters may be as pillars,
Sculptured in palace style;
That our barns may be full,
Supplying all kinds of produce;
That our sheep may bring forth thousands
And ten thousands in our fields;
That our oxen may be well laden;
That there be no breaking in or going out;
That there be no outcry in our streets.
Happy are the people who are in such a state;
Happy are the people whose God is the Lord!

Father, gird these young warriors for their coming trial. Send your angels before them into battle to scatter the enemy and bring victory to their true and noble cause. Father, shield them in battle and return them whole and victorious to their families. And, Father, we plead your care and protection for those who remain behind. Grant them comfort and peace, the peace that passes all understanding. For all of these things we pray in the name of your son, Jesus, our rock and our redeemer. Amen."

• • •

Later that night Midland Red Storm recovered from their disappointment of the day and waited on instructions from Ann Arbor Center when there was a knock on the door of their motel room.

"Pizza man," said a muffled voice from outside the door.

"Anyone order pizza?" asked the team leader to a general disinterest in the room.

"Knock, knock, knock. Pizza man."

The team leader took it upon himself to get rid of the "pizza man" and opened the door to find four of the largest, angriest-looking men he had ever seen in his life.

"You bastards hit our friend with a piss bag, man!" said Jimmy Kellogg as he pushed the leader into the room. "And that ain't cool."

Jimmy was followed closely by Rod Peterson and the Dockins twins, who began to work as a team, forcing the frightened Red Shirts into the far corner of their little motel room.

"What is it? What do you want? Get out of here!" said the leader, squirming under the glare of the four angry men.

"What this is, you little prick, is a chance for you to come to Jesus. We'll leave soon as we get done impartin' a revelation of divine truth to you little scum suckers, 'n I'm bettn' it's gonna change yer sorry little shit-eatin' lives. Now which oneaya wants ta be a man about it 'n' volunteer ta go first?" said Jimmy, smiling grimly as he gingerly took a bulging, urine-filled condom into his pitching hand.

• • •

Lt. David K. Rixon, along with 178 other Marines who were called up early to support field units involved in the surprise Operation Starlight, arrived at Tan Son Nhut Airport aboard a specially chartered Continental Airlines 707. Most of them, like Rixon, were green and scared; they were in a war zone and expected God knows what to happen at any second. After retrieving his seabag and working his way through in-processing, he was pulled from the transport line and promptly poached by Marine Lieutenant Colonel Richard Sharpe for a temporary assignment to the Marine Intelligence Component of Military Assistance Command Vietnam in Da Nang.

For the first six months of his deployment, Rixon's war had been restricted to a six by ten windowless soundproof room where he listened to, translated, and phonetically transcribed endless stacks of recorded field interrogations of captured Viet Cong and North Vietnam Army regulars. The interviews had been conducted in the presence of Marines by their Kit Carson Scouts, Viet Cong defectors who doubled as translators and whose loyalty and accuracy were questionable.

David understood the importance of the work; the accuracy of the translations and knowing the loyalties of translators could well mean the difference between life and death for American soldiers in combat, and he prayed nightly that God would give him the language skill to do the job well. But this assignment wasn't the mission he had trained for. He had unwillingly become what the Marines called a "pogue," a rear-echelon noncombatant, and the sixteen-hours-on, eight-hours-off shifts and relentless seven-day-a-week schedule had left him impatient, slightly ashamed, bored out of his mind, and pissed off—so much so that he had decided to ask Lieutenant Colonel Sharpe to release him to his unit.

"Look, Rixon, I know what you're thinking, and you're damned sure not anyone's definition of a pogue or REMF or whatever the grunts are calling MACV personnel these days. Hell, son, you're the best damned American translator in country and the work you're doing is saving lives on every patrol. You're making a difference; a lot more than you could in a firefight with an M16. Truth be told, Rixon, damned near any sane man in the bush would trade places with you in a heartbeat, so don't be feeling sorry for yourself thinking you've been singled out for some special dishonorable duty or something.

"And, son, I know it's none of my business, but I thought, since you're going to be a father, that you'd grow up a little and welcome the opportunity to do your tour in the rear so you could do your duty at home. Let someone else do the triggerwork, Lieutenant.

The Marines in the field need you in that booth ferreting out those traitorous gook bastards before they get more of our men killed. Request for transfer denied. Now do your job and quit your bitching. Dismissed!"

His midtour leave with Karen in Hawaii was magical. Her beauty left David breathless. Seeing her sunny face, hearing her soothing voice, and placing his hands on her stomach to feel the new life the Lord had blessed them with chased away his gloom and gave him a different perspective on his role in the war. Maybe God had created this position for him to ensure his survival so that he could father their baby and be a provider for Karen. Husband and father was truly a noble role and one that he savored.

On their first night together, looking out at the surf, the moon, and the stars, Karen suggested and David agreed that if the baby was a boy his name would be Randal and if a girl her name would be Marion. This both honored and humbled David and sobered him to the reality he would face when he returned to Da Nang. He wouldn't fight his commander. He would do his duty as the Corps saw fit and return to Texas as soon as he could. He had responsibilities in the world.

• • •

It was raining the day the war came for David Rixon. The monsoon season had just begun, and he was at his duty station listening to tape number 1358.22, a particularly grievous interrogation. The suspect, a credentialed member of the Vietnamese Special Forces, had brazenly informed the prisoner that he was also Viet Cong and hated the stupid, stinking Americans and if he played along that he, the prisoner, would be released, have his weapons restored to him, and be delivered to his original point of capture to rejoin his comrades. VC1358 had done this directly in front of four Green Berets, members of the "A Team" who had made the capture, who thought they were in charge of the interview but were actually being set up for an ambush by their supposed ally. Two of the Special Forces operators were later killed and one severely wounded in the ambush while 1358 had disappeared into the rainforest with maps, knowledge, and weapons that would be of great value to the enemy. Rixon was angry again as he imagined that his presence in the interrogation would have saved at least two lives and that the Cong would be either in prison or dead rather than continuing to seed death and destruction in the South. He was making the final changes to the transcript when he was summoned to Lieutenant Colonel Sharpe's ready room.

Upon entering the room, Rixon observed that three men were seated at the conference table with Sharpe. "Lieutenant Rixon reporting as ordered."

"At ease, Rixon, take a seat," said Sharpe gesturing to an empty chair. "This is Captain William Washington and Sergeant Tommy Coats. They're with the Seventh Mobile Strike Force based in Qang Tri province. They operate the fast reaction force for both I Corps and II Corps and they have a special interest our friend, VC1358." He gestured to the other uniform. "Mr. Brown here is a field operative for the agency and will assist seven-MIKE with a new counterinsurgency program. Gentlemen, may I present Lieutenant David Rixon, the combat translator I was telling you about. He's here on TDY only because I poached him from Third Reconnaissance. Otherwise, he'd be out in the boonies, and we'd never have known of his special affinity for the language. He's a short-timer now. Lieutenant, how long till you rotate?"

"Sixty-seven days, sir," replied Rixon, wondering what this was all about, thinking about how he wouldn't allow this, whatever it was, to mess up his homecoming to Karen and the baby and feeling quite sure that he had met the Green Beret captain somewhere before.

During his time in country, he had read reports and heard stories of how US Army Special Forces units worked with Vietnamese Civilian Irregular Defense Groups as advisers to develop native counterinsurgency capabilities in the rural areas before the Gulf of Tonkin and the beginning of America's war. He had also heard stories of the effectiveness of the Mobile Strike Force units, known as "MIKE" units, and the fast reaction teams called "Eagle Flights," which were a modern version of the old-time US Cavalry, except they rode helicopters instead of horses. They had been the agents of salvation for many Marine and regular army units that ran into more trouble than they could handle. The MIKES terrified the VC, and even the NVA regulars steered clear whenever there was a choice, because the ranks were filled with battle-hardened troops drawn from indigenous peoples who spoke the language, knew the terrain, and were considered vermin to be exterminated by the Vietnamese, both North and South. The "Valley People," self-righteous Vietnamese, who presented themselves to the world at Geneva as victims of evil French colonial rule, had themselves colonized the lands of Vietnam long ago, committing their prehistoric genocide against the indigenous people and driving the survivors into the mountains of the Northern Highlands.

The "Mountain People," or "Montagnard," had been allied with the French against the Vietnamese Communists during their twenty-year resistance of Ho Chi Minh's war of colonial liberation. The French, who also feared the Montagnard, would not permit them modern arms. They had limited their role to trackers, scouts, and informers who fought the enemy with ancient crossbows, machetes, spears, and rocks. But the Americans had given them the M16, trained them in modern counterinsurgency warfare, supplied them with munitions, radios, uniforms, food, a monthly paycheck, and led them into battle aboard Huey helicopters—things that gave the Green Berets who lived with them, fought with them, and sometimes died with them, tribal status approaching divinity.

Rixon was privately assessing the impressive Negro captain. He admired the heraldry of the Green Beret, which symbolized their mission. A small military shield was displayed on the left front of his headgear, a wreath of argent and sable with two silver arrows crossed over a silver and black dagger, all pointing to the sky. Surrounding the design was a black ribbon and the Latin "de oppresso iber," *To Liberate the Oppressed*, which is how he had imagined his role in the war when he had been recruited by the Corps back at Penn State. He was quietly envious.

"Bad to the bone," thought Rixon as he took in the massive fore-arms and biceps Washington had crossed over his chest, annotated by the unofficial MIKE Force shoulder patch: a simple black shield with a white skull and crossbones and a capital M.F. stitched directly below. "Could stand for ether MIKE Force or something else alto-gether unsavory," observed Rixon, who thought the ambiguity delib-erate and a positive sign of esprit de corps uniquely suited to the MIKEs. But there was something else.

A momentary silence grew between them as Washington and Rixon stared at each other across the expanse of gray plastic lami-nate. "If it hadn't been for the ice, you wouldda never touched me!" blurted out the captain.

"If it hadn't been for the ice, you wouldda never made it past the fifty!" retorted Rixon.

"I'll be damned!" said Captain Washington. "If it isn't Little Rix, the baddest damned middle linebacker in the history of the god-damned Odessa Permian Panthers!"

"Big Willie Washington, as I live and breathe!" exclaimed Rixon. "Scared the crap outta every danged one of us. You know you knocked a tooth outta my three-hundred-pound strong tackle that night!"

"You cracked three 'a my ribs, had to be taped and trussed for nearly two months, still hurts when I get winded, ya sawed-off little shit!" said Washington as the two former rivals rose, moved around the table and embraced, laughing and then crying.

"Wait a minute. You two *know* each other?" said Sergeant Coats. "What a goddamned tiny-assed world!" he said grinning ear to ear. "I gotta hear more 'a this shit!"

Sharpe and Brown sat gaping and mute as if they had just wit-nessed a clap of thunder and bolt of lightning inside their little con-ference room. The reunion was a display of the power of serendipity and quite beyond their control. There was nothing to do except wait to see what happened next.

It was Washington who dialed it back. "We got bidness to do right now, Top. We'll have plenty of time for the yarns later at the O Club," he said smiling. "Mr. Brown, I believe it was you who called this meeting. Please proceed."

"Mr. Brown," a huge, hulking man with poor posture, a ruddy complexion, and dark hair, opened a worn leather satchel and distributed an olive drab file folder marked TOP SECRET to each man.

"Gentlemen, this is an eyes-only briefing on a new intelligence initiative that will carry the code name Phoenix and will fall under the purview of the Studies and Observation Group. Simply put, it's been determined scientifically by the secretary and his staff that given the current conditions on the ground and the mandatory Rules of Engagement put in place by the State Department and the Commander in Chief, that the United States will not win this war by force of arms alone. Victory on our terms hinges on our ability to fundamentally transform the hearts and minds of the Vietnamese people.

"Opinion sampling indicates that the general population is tribal in nature and distrustful of Westerners who they refer to as 'round eyes.' Most Vietnamese see America as neither protector nor friend but as another colonial power, much like the French, that has condemned the region to yet another long, destructive war. The mainstream view is that when the United States loses interest, the people will be left to fend for themselves in a political environment that will be lethal to those who collaborated with American and ARVN forces.

"There is good reason to believe that since VJ Pacific, the infiltration, assassination, and propaganda program designed by Ho Chi Minh and the Communists to expel the French, has simply eliminated the segment of the population who held a natural affinity for the Western ideal of limited government and individual liberty. The program converted the majority of the remaining population to Communist sympathizers through a coercion and propaganda system operated by a network of infiltrators and insurgents led by people like your friend, VC1358. It's carrot and stick, and it's been very effective.

"The *New Socialist Man* is the ideal presented to the general population, in which they would voluntarily surrender themselves, their families, and their property to ownership and governance by the state in return for security and maximum economic benefit for every citizen. Every aspect of their lives will be administered by the government that will see to it that everyone gets what's coming to them."

There was laughter in the room. "Yeah, steak, champagne for Uncle Ho, rice balls, leeches, and reeducation camps for everyone else!" said a cynical and wise Sergeant Coats. "We've seen exactly how this line of crap plays out in Korea and, man, I gotta tell ya, I'd put a bullet through my own brain rather than submit to the death march those bastards have the country on. And we're lettin' em get away with it…"

"At ease, Top, let the man have his say," said Washington, and the room fell silent.

"Phoenix is your basic clandestine 'smash and grab' except with a twist; the IBM System Three Sixty," said a smiling Brown. "IBM has contracted with the company to install and operate a unit at a secure location in country and will use the data collected by Phoenix in the field to model the Communist networks in South Vietnam no matter where they are. With that information, it will be a simple matter for us to remove the corrosive element from the society and allow freedom and democracy to flourish. The Republic of Vietnam will become a beacon of liberty, the American Beauty Rose in the lotus garden and the strong keystone in the arch of a vigorous alliance against regional Communist aggression. We all remember the Southeast Asia Treaty Organization formed more than a decade ago during the Eisenhower administration. Well, Gentlemen, Phoenix is the test case of what will one day become the brain of SETO. We're gonna win this 'cause we're just gonna outsmart the commie bastards…"

WHOOMP! BAM! INCOMING!

A VC mortar round had exploded close enough to MACV that Rixon could see daylight through the walls of Lieutenant Colonel Sharpe's ready room. There was another explosion farther away, followed by another and then screams and automatic weapons fire.

RIXON! ON YOUR FEET!

David looked up from the floor to see the room had cleared and that Captain Washington was standing at the door urging him to follow him to the bunker.

"Damn, son, looks like old Charlie plugged ya 'n' you ain't even been outside the wire yet!" said Washington as he was pushing Rixon in a dead run toward safety and noticed tiny blood stains on the back of his pressed uniform shirt. "Ya know, any time we decide ta start outsmartin' the commie bastards will just suit tha' hell outta me!"

The Officers' Club at MACV was not segregated by any regulation, yet the black officers tended to congregate in the section of the club farthest from the entrance near the kitchen and the rear exit. Washington and Rixon sat alone at a table located on the invisible line that separated black and white. The club was nearly empty that night. Many reports were being written and much extra duty being done after the three surprise mortar rounds fell on an unsuspecting and supposedly secure intelligence compound in the heart of US-held territory.

"I followed your career through the papers for a while. You walked on at Penn State, Rixon, and you made the team. Testicles the size of cantaloupes, my man!" joked Washington in admiration. "Why Penn State? Why not someplace good like UT or OU? Hell, even A&M could kick the shit out of the Nittany Lions. What the hell is a Nittany Lion anyway?"

Rixon explained about the Parker Exploration scholarship and about his admiration for Coach Paterno and the "Whole Person" program. "As to why, it's the story of my life, Captain, no one was interested 'cause God made me 'too short for Division One play.'" Rixon annotated his story with finger quotes. "But I enjoyed the contact, the intensity of the game, cracking the opponent's game plan, the energy of the crowd; there's nothing like it, and I wasn't ready to give it up so I figured that since I was there anyway, I'd give it a shot. I showed up, suited out, and worked my way onto the squad. Simple as that."

Shifting the focus of the conversation, he said, "But, Cap, I had read both OU and Arkansas were courting you, but then I got busy and didn't keep up. So what happened?" asked a truly interested Rixon.

"Yeah, I made the trip to Norman, worked out for Coach Wilkinson himself, and then on to Fayetteville and a workout for Coach Broyles and they both promised me a spot on the freshman squad. But then something happened, and they just didn't call back. I knocked up a girl my senior year, a white girl, and it started to get around. First in school, then around town, and pretty soon it was hard to go anywhere without 'the eyes,' you know, people starin' and stuff.

"Coach Taylor at Prairie View A&M contacted me, and I played a year for the Panthers, but then it started there too—'That's the brother done knocked up the white girl.' Coach said to stick it out that people had more important things to think about and that they'd soon forget, but they never did. You know, Rix, I thought that my own people would give me a break but hell, they're worse than white people about stuff like that. Especially the Christians.

"Anyhow, the army sent this Negro top sergeant to campus to recruit the brothers, real squared away, spit and polish, career army. You know the type. He told me, 'Son, ain't nobody in the US Army gives a good goddamn 'bout who you screw so long as you can run, shoot, climb a rope, and are capable of killing the enemy on command and without hesitation.' So I enlisted and, you know, he was right. I'm a Green Beret captain in the US Army now, Rixon. Elite. Ain't that just a kick in tha' head?" he finished with a laugh and broad smile.

"What about the girl, what about your baby?" asked Rixon, genuinely concerned.

"Last I heard she was living in Los Angeles, tryin' ta break into tha' movie business. Don't know what happened to tha baby. I imagine that she put it up for adoption. That's what most girls do that get into that sort of trouble," said Washington with a faraway look in his eyes.

"Ain't fair! Ya bastards started without me!" said a grinning Sergeant Coats, breaking the seriousness of the moment with his jocularity. "Barkeep, another round for my friends, and I'll have three fingers of your best Irish, hold the ice!"

"The nerve 'a those commie bastards, shootin' at us like that. What the hell we ever done to them?" he said laughing and coaxing the desired response from his audience. "So what'd I miss? Ya really crack three 'a the captain's ribs—did ja, Rixon? Tell me all about it!"

So over steak and potatoes, the athletes retold their stories of the Abilene Ice Bowl for Sergeant Coats and themselves, smiling and remembering the days of their youth when all that mattered was their team, the game, and numbers on the scoreboard.

"Wait a minute, Rix, you ain't leavin'. Ya ain't told us about Sissy and why she picked a runt like you when she couldda had a real man like me!" protested a slightly inebriated Green Beret captain.

"PT at 0400, cap, and I need to get some rest. You know I got blown up a little today," said Rixon smiling.

"You really do PT a four in the morning? Rixon, are ya crazy? This is the rear echelon, slack off! That's an order! Ya make the rest of us look like regular Marine Corps pogues!" said Coats, smiling and having a grand time.

"Can't guys. Gotta keep the discipline. Otherwise, I'd get fat like an old Green Beret or something! Besides, I have duty at oh seven hundred, and I have to have time to *study the Bible*," he said deadpanned, waiting for their reaction, but the two men just stared.

"He studies the Bible, Captain, and he drinks ginger ale at a bar, and he does PT at oh four hundred all by himself when he could be in his rack," said Coats in awe bordering on contempt.

"And he speaks Vietnamese like a native," added the captain.

"Captain! We just described Ho Chi Minh! David Rixon is Ho Chi Minh! Rix, say you ain't the commie motherfucker we all come over here ta kill or I might just hafta...well, kill ya or somethin'. Sir, is it all right if I kill a superior officer?" he asked Washington.

"No, Top, it ain't. At least not as long as he's on our side, and I don't believe for a second that Rix is really Uncle Ho. He's too damned short!" said Washington, smiling broadly.

"Gentlemen," said David, rising from the table, "it's been a lovely evening, but now I must retire. I'll be in front of the mess hall at 0400 if you care to join me. I run the perimeter at an eight-minute pace, takes about an hour to make the circuit," he said, moving toward the door.

"Careful they don't shoot ya in tha' dark, Rix. Sentries gotta be jumpy after the mortar attack. Hate ta lose our little white translator before he can do us any good," retorted Washington.

"Think I'll be OK, Cap, at least they can see me coming! Good night, men," said Rixon as he left the Officers' Club headed for his rack.

"What do you think, Will?" asked a suddenly sober Sergeant Coats.

"The man's definitely kept himself fit despite the duty, and he's a teetotaler. Hell, Tom, he's probably in better shape than we are. But he ain't never been in the bush and he ain't never spilled blood and that worries me," said Washington.

"He's a recon Marine captain; a trained killer. Never seen one yet that didn't have a taste for the fight. He could be different I guess, but I'm bettin' not," said Coats.

"Phoenix is gonna put us into some pretty deep shit, Top. You really wanna go there with Little Rix?" asked Washington.

"I hate to say it, Captain, 'cause I'm just about as full and happy as a tic on a hound dog right now, but I'm thinkin' we outta get us in some PT at 0400 and then discuss it after we see what the midget martyr is made of," said a smiling Coats.

"You SOB. Ya get me drunk, lead me on, and then tell me I gotta get my happy ass outta the rack at three in the morning and run eight miles before breakfast. Hell, Top, ya remind me 'a my first wife," complained Washington.

"Sir, beggin' the captain's pardon, sir, but ya ain't never been married," replied Coats with faux military crispness.

"Well who the hell would marry anything that looked like you any damned way?" replied Washington.

"No one, Captain!" replied Coats. "And, sir, thanks for letting me down easy."

"Good night, Sergeant," said Washington, smiling at the jest.

"And a good night to you too, Captain Washington," said Coats, trying to remember the last time he ran eight miles. He glanced at his watch; it was 0100.

BADABOOM! BADABOOM! BADABOOM!

The base artillery battery had started its harassment and interdiction fire mission for the night.

● ● ●

Rixon was nearly finished with his calisthenics when Washington and Coats jogged slowly into the pool of yellow light that illuminated the entrance to the company mess. "What do you know, you didn't sleep in after all!" said an amused Rixon. "Gentlemen, welcome to Da Nang's foremost house of pain!"

They were wearing army PT gear Washington commandeered from several unattended lockers in the Transient Officers' Quarters. He figured nobody would notice or care.

"I'm on a schedule, guys, so unless you're ready to go, I'll see you at breakfast at 0630," said David apologetically as he clicked the timer on his chronograph and headed out into the gloom of pre-dawn Vietnam.

"Shit! This is gonna hurt!" muttered Coats as he and Washington started after Rixon, caught him, and settled into the uneasy comfort of the runner's rhythm.

"When's the last time you did a timed run, Sarge?" breathed Rixon as they passed the first sentry tower waving at the unseen eyes watching their progress.

"It's been a while, Lieutenant, probably around fifty-six or fifty-seven, when I tested for Special Forces," said Coats, already struggling in the heat and humidity. "At least it ain't rainin'."

"I was a junior in high school in nineteen fifty-seven, Sarge," replied David easing into the pace of the run. "It doesn't rain here until about 1000. We'll be inside by that time, safe and dry unless Charlie pays us another visit."

The darkness closed around them and for a long time the only sound was their labored breathing and the crunch of gravel under their feet, BADABOOM! BADABOOM! BADABBOOM! the base artillery battery sent three more quick rounds out to deny Charlie the use of the mountainside for a repeat of yesterday's surprise attack, the report of the guns echoed sharply through the low structures of MACV.

"How can you sleep through this shit, Rix?" asked Washington. "All night, every time I got easy, the damned guns would shake me outta my rack."

"You get used to it, Cap, and besides, we'd be sitting ducks without the nighttime HNI. I'm willing to live with it for another sixty-six days," replied David smiling, looking at his watch, and picking up the pace.

It was dead quiet for a long time and the runners fell into pace. The only other sound was the hum of the mercury vapor lamps lighting the perimeter wire. The trio avoided the pools of light and stuck to the shadows wary of snipers. The heat and humidity were oppressive, even in the predawn, and they were soaked with sweat as they kept their pace steady.

RRRRUMMMMBLLLEEEEEE, a flight of four F4 Phantoms accelerated down the runway and launched themselves into the dark dawn for early bombing and strafing missions far to their north. The sound of the engines made the bodies of the three runners quiver as they watched the four specks of blue-orange-white heat disappear into the stratosphere.

"Scares the heck outta me every time I see 'em take off," breathed David. "Can't imagine what it'd be like to be on the receiving end of their payload. We're coming up on midpoint, men, and we're right on pace. It's downhill all the way home!"

"You always talk this much when you run, Rixon?" asked Washington with clearly labored breath.

"Naw, Cap, I usually call my own cadence," and Little Rix began
to sing them home.

"I used to sit at home all day,
Letting my life a waste away.
Then one day a man in blue,
Said, son, I got a job for you,
There's travel, adventure, and loads of fun,
And well even teach you to shoot a gun.
There's room and board and a plate of food,
And a brand new tailored business suit.
I used to drive a Bonneville,
Now all I do is run up a hill.
I used to drive a Chevrolet,
Now all I do is sleep in the hay.
I used to drive a Cadillac,
Now all I do is hump a pack.
COME ON YA HUMPS ONLY TWO MILES LEFT!"

DUBDUBDUBDUBDUBDUBDUB. Six Cobra gunships buzzed
them, heading out to sea for morning shore patrol. BRATTA!
BRATTA! BRATTTTTAAAAA! The pilots were clearing their
guns, making ready for combat. "I HATE THIS FUCKIN' PLACE!"
exclaimed Coats, startled by the guns and barely keeping pace.

"Suck it up, Top, you're nearly there!" breathed Rixon,
"Hey, hey, what do you say,
I'm goin' to the rod-e-o today.
I drew a bad bull, heard he was a bear,
But I can hang for eight, so I just don't care.
Tie up, bear down, sittin' on my bull,
I'm just waitin' for the gate to pull.
Out from the chute blows my old ride,
It's a wonder that I'm still alive.
Just right then the eight seconds pass,

I jump right off of that bull's ass.
Quick, turn around and what do I see?
That old bull come a-chargin' at me.
I pull a cut-down 12-gauge from my hip,
And send that bull on a little trip.
I'm the meanest cowboy that you ever did see,
USMC Infantry!"

The hot water felt good after their run and cooldown, and both Washington and Coats noted Rixon's physique through the steam and quietly acknowledged that he had waxed them both on the run. "Gotta do better, Top, life in the boonies is makin' ya soft," joked Washington.

"Me? It was you breathin' outta both ends," retorted Coats, looking around for David. "Where's Little Rix?"

"Ah shit, come on, Top, he's on a schedule!" snipped Washington as he threw a towel at Coats on his way to the locker room.

They met for chow in the company mess at 0630 and Rixon arrived carrying a wrinkled paper bag under his arm. "Sergeant Tommy Coats, your brother, Trooper Timothy Coats, of the New Mexico State Police, sends his regards," Rixon said, grinning and offering the well-traveled package to the freshly scrubbed and shaven Green Beret.

"What? You said something about Tim? How? This ain't a booby trap or nothin', is it, Rix?" he joked as he accepted the package. "Damnnation! Drambui! How the hell? You know my brother too? Ain't this just the damnedest thing ever?" he said, grinning and grateful; amazed at the circumstance and very curious about Lieutenant David K. Rixon.

• • •

The meeting that had been broken up by the mortar attack the day before resumed at 0900, the base Seabees had temporarily patched the holes in the conference room wall with gray duct tape and installed a six-foot-high layer of green sand bags along the outside wall.

"Good morning, Gentlemen, please take a seat and we'll pick up where we left off," said Brown as he opened his file folder. "As I was saying yesterday, Phoenix will combine advanced computing power of the IBM System Three Sixty with information obtained by conventional rendition fieldwork to create a mathematical model of the Communist network, which is invisible to us right now but is strangling the entire country. Although it would be nice, we can't indiscriminately kill everyone we suspect of being a Communist. But using this tool will enable us to accurately select our targets for inter-rogation, imprisonment, or assassination while leaving the innocents in place. Surgical counterinsurgency is the term being used by the Suits at Langley to refer to this innovative technology. They've sold it to State, DOD, and even the White House, and they've handed the program to us for implementation. This is something new, and we'll be writing the book on it. Our experiences and lessons learned will be the basis for the future of similar counterinsurgency operations, so it's all very scientific. Or at least that's what the secretary said in his letter of authorization. I assume you've had time to review the brief. Are there any questions?"

"How can anyone accurately model something so complex even with this fancy computing machine? There could be a million people involved in this thing. Hell, they've had twenty years to build it. They used it to defeat the French, and now they're using it on us. Does anyone really believe Phoenix has a prayer of succeeding outside the laboratory, or is this just some new toy somebody in Washington wants to buy and then use us as lab rats to see if it works?" asked a skeptical Washington.

"Captain, it's more than a million. The Suits estimate there are about two million resident and insurgent Communists, including armed VC in the field," said Brown. "For our purposes, we must con-sider ourselves effectively immersed in Communist infiltrators and sympathizers. They are everywhere."

"Mr. Brown, could you discuss the mathematical principles the computer scientists are relying on for the model? I assume it's a Bayesian derivative, but I'd like a better understanding of the science behind Phoenix. It would help me adjust the methodology I have developed for the translation work. That way, whoever takes my place will be able to hit the ground running and make a solid contribution," said Rixon, seriously curious about the field application of advanced mathematics in a time of war.

Brown, who had flunked out of junior college, spent a hitch in Air Force Intelligence and had been hired by the Central Intelligence Agency as a favor to his mother's brother, a senior Soviet analyst at Langley, had no idea what Rixon was asking.

"That's classified, Lieutenant. Strictly need to know, and right now all you need to know is that the folks above your pay grade understand the science and precisely what to expect when the program is ramped up and dialed in."

Later at the Officers' Club..."You know what you talkin' about in there today, Rix, or you just givin' Mr. Brown a hard time?" asked Washington with a sly smile. "And by the way, since we gonna be working together, I'd appreciate it if you'd drop the Captain Washington crap. My friends call me Will."

"OK, Will, my friends call me David and, yes, I do know what I'm talking about, or at least I should. My major at Penn State was applied mathematics; I minored in astrophysics out of curiosity and because I like looking at the stars. So I guess you could say I'm sort of a math guy. My senior thesis concerned a niche area of decision theory, specifically the science of how to make the best decisions possible when failure is not an option, and there are too many variables for human beings to consider without a gauge of some sort," replied Rixon. "And what do you mean 'we're gonna work together'? I'm short sixty-three days now, Will, and I have plans. After I spend a month with my family in Odessa, I'm working for Uncle Sam during the last year of my obligation at the Defense Language Institute in EL Paso, and then I'll be out, a civilian, free to protest all you imperialist colonial mercenary baby-killer types, oppressing the defenseless people of Vietnam," said Rixon with a smile.

There was a moment of shared laughter between the men. "Here's the thing, David. The Phoenix program must have an American translator, a trusted patriot, to screen the information collected by field agents and to personally interrogate prisoners at the highest level. Otherwise, the Americans running the program will eventually be given false information. The program could fail and get a bunch of the good guys killed or worse—we could actually lose this war. That's what all this is about. You're all we have right now. There are others in the pipeline but you're the most qualified for the position and the only candidate I trust enough to bet my life on," said Washington, opening up more than he intended but sensing that Rixon would have to be forced into service unless he put more bait on the hook.

"This isn't general knowledge yet, David, but I'm about to be promoted to the theater commander of Operation Phoenix, and to qualify for it I've had to sign on for the duration of the conflict, just like the troops did in World War Two," said Washington, deadly serious. "Coats has agreed to come on as my intelligence lieutenant, and I hope you'll agree to step in as my command translator and maybe move up to executive officer. My new position will mandate a major's rank, and I've been assured that if I pull it off, doors will be opened for me at the Pentagon, maybe even a promotion to a one-star general. Now I don't want to count the chicks 'fore they get themselves outta their shells, but if you come on now, you could be hitching yourself to a rising star. And, David, I don't forget my friends."

"No," said David firmly and without hesitation. "Sorry, Will, but my plans are made and the papers are already signed. Karen's rented an apartment near the base in El Paso and is moving in the first of the month, so she'll have the place ready when I get there. I wouldn't change the plans now even if I could."

This was an unfortunate revelation. Washington had planned to attract Rixon, to woo him, so that he would have volunteered for the assignment on his own, but as every combat veteran knows, any plan is only good until the first shots are fired, and then the situation becomes fluid. Washington had prepared in advance and simply played his trump card.

"I'm sorry to have to do this to you, Lieutenant, but these are your new orders directly from the Pentagon. You've been officially released from your obligation to the United States Marine Corps and are now a member of the US Army Special Forces with the rank of captain. Congratulations on the promotion. We're on a resupply chopper out to Rana Dat at 0500, so get yourself to the quartermaster and draw your bush gear and weapons. They've been notified and will be waiting for you. Coats and I will be by your quarters at 04:30 to pick you up and to make sure you don't get lost on the way to the flight line."

Rixon's head was reeling and he was furious. "What! You can't be serious! This can't be legal! Sharpe will never allow it! The corps will never allow it! They need me here!"

• • •

"Mr. Brown" was stowing his seabag aboard the Huey when they arrived, chuckled at the load of gear Rixon was struggling with, and started to crack a joke. "Brown, if I were you I'd zip it," cautioned Washington, knowing David was angry, disoriented, and probably afraid for his life, after having been shanghaied into the bush full of Viet Cong. "Captain Rixon will get himself squared away when we get to Rana Dat. Pissing in the wind is OK, my friend, so long as you don't mind gettin' yourself wet."

The command crew was preflighting the UH-1 Iroquois. Shiny new from Bell Helicopter in Fort Worth, it was a replacement bird set up as a "slick," free of munitions pods and miniguns, a utility helicopter designed to carry troops and supplies into and out of the bush. For defense, it had only two belt-fed M-60 machine guns manufactured by US Ordinance in McCarran, Nevada, and capable of firing six hundred and fifty rounds of NATO 7.62 MM ammunition a minute with a muzzle velocity of twenty-eight hundred feet per second, more than twice the speed of sound. Two door gunners operated the weapons. They had achieved remarkable accuracy out to 1,200 yards using simple elastic "bungee" chords and their own body mass to stabilize the twenty-three-pound gun. The troopers were busy servicing their weapons, making ready to go to war.

As their departure time approached, the ground crew was still on the flight deck dialing in the avionics and listening to the radio chatter from a serious combat action that was occurring somewhere outside their area of operation. First David and then the others became focused on the life-and-death struggle they were overhearing through the static and atmospheric skip. The chief tuned the radio's squelch so the urgent metallic voices could be understood through the confusing crosstalk.

"Takin' fire! Takin' fire!"

"Ah, Roger. We have guns on the way."

"Tiger Doc Two Six is taking fire."

"OK. Divert south of the river, George."

"I seen a couple a them red tracers slam right into his well."

Unintelligible, engine whine and guns firing

"This is Two Niner Rush, we're OK, whatcha wanna do?"

"OK. We got good instruments right now, I'm gonna try to make an approach in there; we'll try like hell; we're gonna do something."

Unintelligible, guns firing.

"Tiger—what's your position?"

"Roger. I'm three minutes out just now; I'm just between the ridge and the river."

Unintelligible, engine loading.

"TD's on fire! Two Six is on fire! Coordinates"…unintelligible… "firing right next to us; three o'clock!"

"Got two ships down. One just crashed and burned."

"OK. We got twenty-three millimeter all the way down this flight path. Keep everything south of the river and grab some altitude coming in here."

Unintelligible, guns firing.

"Jesus Christ, that thing went up."

"OK. I'm going back to see if anyone's OK."

"I saw one aircraft explode, and the other went in."

Unintelligible, atmospheric skip.

"He wasn't operational RPM. Looked like he took it in on a flare, but he sat it down."

"One Seven Victor, Mayday, I have regained power. I'm not sure what happened, but power came back on."

Silence.

"Roger. One Seven went in and picked up Two Six; he took the full crew off that ship. He's comin' out of the LZ at this time. The ship's startin' ta load, see what you can do to give him some cover."

Unintelligible. Silence…

"We got reports of some contact over at Signal Hill early this morning. Sounds like Charlie took out two medevacs," said Washington, as if to the crew in general but really it was for David's benefit. "I pray to God they were empty. Chief, we gonna have ta hitch a ride home or you gonna get this broke dick thing in tha air?" Major Washington wasn't smiling as he reached into the cockpit and clicked off the radio. No one else said a word.

• • •

"Like slaughterin' a hog in a phone booth! That's our genius Rules of Engagement for ya," said the seasoned veteran Coats to his novitiate, Rixon. "DOD is all set up ta fight the big war with the Soviets or the Chicoms or maybe even both at once. Battleships, carriers, destroyers, subs, all kind 'a planes, tanks, different kinds 'a nukes, large-scale theater tactics. Hell, we got it all, and none of it makes a whit 'a difference out here 'cause we can't get 'em, inta the booth, and tha hog damn well knows it. And ta top it off, we gotta pretend like we ain't really fightin' the war our own selves. We gotta play like we're just helpin' the poor ol' ARVN resist tha mean 'ol Communist insurgents so people like Adlai Stevenson and Dean Rusk can trot themselves up ta th' Eeuunited Nations or the Geeeneva Convention or wherever tha' hell it is people 'at wear thousand-dollar suits get together 'n' drink champagne, so they can lie with a straight face ta each other 'bout what we're really doin' out here in tha bush. I tell ya', Captain, it's damned hard to stomach sometimes."

"Captain?" Rixon didn't think of himself as a captain. He certainly hadn't earned the rank and didn't like the idea of unmerited advancement. Of course, it was nothing more than a bribe to make his high-handed conscription into Phoenix go down and stay down, but other than write his congressman, there wasn't much he could do about it. So he decided to keep his mouth shut, go with the flow, listen and learn; the newly promoted Lieutenant Coats was on a roll.

"COMUSMACV's got the strategy all wrong and it's gettn' lots 'a tha good guys killed for nothin'. We have a battle, kill lots of Cong, and take the real estate away from 'em. But instead of holding the ground like you'd think, we chopper out and let Victor Charles come right back in and set up shop like nothin' even happened. Then they send in a bunch of fuckin' new guys—that's a technical term, Captain," he said, grinning apologetically, belatedly realizing that his captain was also a FNG. "They ain't never been in combat, in a firefight, or even in the bush before, and we send 'em in ta make the same mistakes and get killed by the same enemy on the same ground somebody else died for a month before. They're bleedn' us for this bullshit idea 'n the result is we never own a damned thing out there," he said, indicating the dense jungle canopy they were flying over. "The Cong down there, they own it all and everybody knows it, especially the people we're supposed ta be protectin'.

"COMUSMACV calls it 'attrition.' They say real estate don't matter no more, that we just gonna keep on killin' Cong until they run out 'n can't fight the war no more; like Ho Chi Minh ain't makin' any more of um all day ever damn day up in Hanoi or where ever the hell it is they make replacement Communists." Coats spit his tobacco juice into an empty c-ration tin.

"Attrition." Rixon had heard that term applied strategically to the war in Vietnam during Officers Candidate School. It was General William Westmorland's brilliant minimalist insight that had gotten him the job as President Johnson's commander in Vietnam. For

COMUSMACV, an unlimited supply of conscripted American troops supported by advanced technology meant the kill ratio would be in favor of the United States. Since war is all about killing the enemy, logic follows that when the North runs out of troops, the US and their allies will eventually win the conflict. Who could argue with that glittering diamond of military wisdom?

Not comforted by the pronouncements of his command staff, Rixon had even tried to construct a theorem to proof Westmoreland's strategy using available data on the combat kill ratio and population estimates supplied by the Central Intelligence Agency, but he couldn't get the math to work. He was forced to assume that the president, the pentagon, and the CIA had knowledge superior to his and wouldn't commit troops and resources to an expensive war halfway around the world unless they had good reason to be confident about the outcome. "Not even a crazy man would do that to his country," Rixon had told himself and then put the possibility out of his mind to focus on his duty in the translation booth.

Lieutenant Coats continued enthusiastically. "And I don't give a damn how long ya know him, don't never trust a Vietnamese; any Vietnamese. Never. Slippery ain't a good enough word for what them people are. Hell, they ain't got no moral foundation, least none that I ever seen. Ever damned one of 'em's in-bred and greedy as hell. They'll slit they own mama san's throat for a case of c-rats, slit yours if tha wind's blowin' tha right direction. But the Yards are different. The Mountain People," said Coats smiling. "You know they're the original people of the region, pushed out of their land by the Vietnamese sorta like we done to the Cherokee, Apache, Comanche, and all the rest of 'em American Indians back when we first settled the country. The brass says all tha time that real estate don't matter no more, but I know for damn sure it does when ya ain't got a place ta be. And it sure as hell matters to the Montagnard. Everybody in this godforsaken country hates them just about as much as they hate us, so I suppose that makes us natural allies or some such."

Rixon allowed Coats's observations and the sights, sounds, and smells of a strange new world to wash over him, trying hard not to become completely disoriented and even harder to control his growing fear of the dangerous unknown.

The Huey had flown north from Da Nang along the picturesque coastline of the South China Sea past Hue, turned inland over Quang Tri, and climbed into the southeastern end of the Annamite Mountains, which separated north and south Vietnam at the demilitarized zone and then ran northwest, forming most of the boundary between Vietnam and Laos. The pilot was flying fast at treetop level to avoid attracting fire from enemy troops concealed below the jungle canopy when he began to bank into a tight, elliptical arc, and the mountain top fell away beneath them, opening their view to a wide, manmade plateau and beyond that the infamous A Shau Valley.

The headquarters site for the Seventh Mobile Strike Force Command had been blasted out of the mountains by the French thirty years earlier and then modified for use by the Seven-Mobile Strike Force Command by the US Army Corps of Engineers. They selected it for its proximity to the northern most Communist infiltration route through the mountains near the point where Free Vietnam, Communist Vietnam, and Laos converge. It was also a fast and cheap, though seriously flawed, answer to a pressing need. The most prominent feature of Seven-MSFC was the hard-packed stone-covered airstrip that would accommodate large military aircraft of all types. To house the Civilian Irregular Defense Corps strikers and their families, the corps had also constructed forty-four twenty-man dormitory huts or "hooches," US Special Forces officers' quarters, a communal mess hall, quartermaster supply warehouse, armory, unit dispensary, command administrative buildings, and two sentry towers inside a double row perimeter fence of shiny silver concertina razor wire.

"Welcome to Rana Dat, Captain," Washington said to Rixon with a smile. "I like to think of it as Little America but the Yards started callin' it Free Land a couple 'a years ago. Most 'a tha troopers liked it, and I guess it sorta stuck."

As their helicopter positioned for a rapid setdown in the middle of a hive of activity, David could see an AC-130 Spectre gunship being serviced by a swarm of technicians, a number of Cobra gunships and Huey Slicks on the ground, and a small Cessna 0-1 Bird Dog scout ship sitting on the runway. Adjacent to the whirl of activity he noticed a small oasis of calm, a group of tiny, handcrafted nonmilitary structures located well outside the wire, placed up the hillside beyond the artificial plateau; the largest was topped with a small steeple and a moss-covered Christian cross.

"Missionaries. Bible translators, if ya' can believe it," said Washington, shaking his head, pointing to the cross. "Husband-and-wife team from Oklahoma, been doin' their version of tha Lord's work at their little 'Christ in Asia Mission' in this exact same spot for nearly thirty years—probably why they ain't been killed by the gooks yet. I guess Charlie figures Pastor Jeff and Sister Suzie ain't hurtin' their cause, and if they were to kill 'em, it'd piss off the locals 'n' just make their job harder. Render unto Caesar and all that sort of stuff. They hold service on Sunday and Wednesday, and they run a school outta the church building most weekdays; teach the kids how to read, do their sums, and speak some English, feed 'em lunch, probably the only protein the kids get all day. Mostly Montagnards, though their doors are open to everybody. You should pay 'em a visit, Rix. Hell, ya just might learn something useful."

The Huey sat down on the helipad inside the wire, near the command center. The pilot kept the rotors turning as a group of men dressed in tiger fatigues began hurriedly offloading the supplies and personal belongings of the passengers. Major Washington motioned to Rixon to follow as he made his way to the emergency meeting in progress. "Defecation's hit th' Schuyler, Rix. Follow me. Keep your mouth shut and your ears open."

The flurry of activity in the war room disoriented Rixon, who did as he was told and followed Washington through the crowd to the side of a large map table surrounded by concerned men dressed in the same uniforms as the soldiers who were unloading their transport.

"Been pickin' up tha traffic all day; sit rep, El Tee," commanded Washington.

"Cap, it's Signal Hill," said Lieutenant Casey Reid with a pained expression on his bearded face. "Two days ago the VC started probing all over the theater. A surprise mortar shelling—then they'd disappear, mostly inconsequential stuff, they even hit Da Nang; guess you know that. Looking for soft spots, we thought, but then they presented to Signal Hill in force early this morning, just as the weather was starting to turn. Sir, we believe they did the mortar attacks as a diversion to get us to shift resources and intended to attack Signal Hill using the rain and fog as cover to eliminate the air power," said the clearly mortified lieutenant. "We never saw it coming.

"It's a large force, potentially battalion strength, and they have the camp cut off. We were able get Tiger Flight in there this morning with ammo and medevacked the wounded but they took down two of our ships on the way out, and then the rain closed in. We lost radio contact about an hour ago. React is assembled and on our runway. They're waiting for the weather to clear."

"Artillery?" clipped Washington.

"Sir, Charlie and Delta batteries have been delivering fire missions all night, but they're shootin' in the dark," said El Tee, pointing to two positions on the map marked C and D. "Division Fire Direction Center lost contact with the forward observers last night; we gotta assume KIA."

"Who's still alive out there, Lieutenant?" asked Washington grimly.

"Sir, yesterday Signal Hill was commanded by Sergeant Mercer with seven Green Berets and two hundred and ten members of the Civilian Irregular Defense Corps. We medevacked ten out this morning. So at most, sir, there's two hundred ten defenders; and their families."

"Damn, just like Travis at the Alamo," said Washington grimly. "Brinkman, I saw your little cracker box when we came in," said the commander to the lean angular man who sat with his feet propped up on a nearby desk, taking in the conversation. "Think you can fly out there and find a seam in the fog or something so we can get

React inta Signal Hill? It'd be a shameful waste of some damn fine operators if we just let Chuck have 'em for lunch."

Joe Don Brinkman, call sign "Catbird," was an Air Force forward air controller and retired bull rider from Amarillo, who took pride in his ability to fly low and slow, looking for clues to enemy troop movements without getting shot. It was, after all, a prerequisite for the job and from what he had heard, the seemingly impossible situation at Signal Hill was entirely his forte.

Catbird rose, approached the map table, and put his finger on a small irregular loop in the topographic lines. "Right here. Every time I've flown it, there's always a sharp updraft, a thermal running up to thirty thousand or so. My guess, Captain Washington, is that when the sun heats the upper atmosphere, in about an hour or so, the microclimate over Signal Hill will clear things out enough to get your force in, and I can use the window to direct the artillery and fast movers to the target. But hell, with a battalion of 'em out there, I'd be surprised if the gunners could miss if there're anywhere close to their marks."

Washington looked up to a large balding man with a face full of freckles, a Fu Manchu moustache, and dark aviator sunglasses. "Magazzine, whatcha got on your trash hauler?"

Charles (Chuck) Magazzine, call sign "Hitman," a career Air Force C-130 pilot with prior service in Korea, was into his second tour as the commander of an AC-130H Spectre gunship used as a platform for close combat air support, air interdiction, and force protection missions. He was extremely popular with his flight crew and the grunts on the ground because of his proven proficiency with the ship's armament and the well-known fact that he didn't take unnecessary risks and wanted very much to make it home in one piece. He responded to Washington by first looking up to his imaginary flight manifest for a full five seconds. "Cap, we got ourselves two brand new M61 Vulcan electric Gatling guns, nearly a million rounds of twenty millimeter and damned near full gas tanks. We can be in the air in fifteen minutes and orbiting Hill four-eleven in less than an hour."

"Cap, if I'm gonna lead the charge, I'll need a twenty-minute head start," interjected Brinkman.

"GO!" commanded Washington. "Both of ya GO! GO!"

"OK. Thompson, Tell me whatcha got!" commanded Washington to Commander Bill Thompson, call sign "Linebacker," who was the leader of the attack helicopter squadron on standby.

"Cap, we got a dozen Cobra gunships, slicks, and a hundred sixty of your seven-MIKE CIDC strikers ready to board. We can have them on the ground at Signal Hill in less than an hour," said Thompson, itching to get into the fight.

"Get 'em in the air and monitor the radio. If Brinkman's right, then get the troops in there any way you can; cover 'em with the gunships. We'll coordinate from here. Good luck!" said Washington, looking for Rixon. "Rixon! Get your gear. You're on the last slick in. Coats, you're with him. I want field interrogations of the VC most ricky tick. USMACV got caught naked on this one, and we need fresh intel to feed 'em NOW. And, Rixon, don't get killed. That's an order! Top, if he even looks like he's about ta get himself KIA, you shoot 'im!' I got two months coming and I intend ta get every drop 'a goodie outta tha' white boy I can. Dismissed!"

David's mind was whirling and his body was already charging with adrenalin. "This is it. I'm going into combat! Shit! I'm not ready! I haven't even written my letter to Karen or Papa. Haven't fired my rifle in a year; where the hell are my weapons?" he was thinking, bathed in sweat at the beginning of a gut-level panic.

"Slow down, Captain," said Coats in a soothing baritone with his hand on David's shoulder. "I know what you're thinkn' and I need ya ta stop it! You'll be observing the assault not leading tha charge, so dial it back and listen up! You're gonna do just fine.

"Our gear is being taken out to that bird right over there. It's number one seventeen, the 'Lady Killer.' She's old and slow, but the pilot's a personal friend of mine, Billy Jack Delgado, and we ain't got killed yet, so we'll be OK. You'll need ta concentrate on keepin' ya head down and translatin' what the POWs are tellin' Donny and Scotty. They're our two most senior Montagnard translators, and they're good people, I think. But we gotta be sure, so that's another reason why you're comin' along on this little joyride. If they ain't shootin' straight, just give me the high sign and we'll bag 'em. And, Cap, do me a favor 'n' don't let on 'bout your rank or how you savvy their lingo, if ya can help it. We can find out more that way than bein' all chummy with the help, if ya get my drift," said Coats, not smiling at all.

As they approached the *Lady Killer*, David saw a dozen Montagnard strikers dressed in their tigers with field packs, weapons, and bush hats. Chief Warrant Officer Delgado began to spool the turbine as Coats inspected Rixon's bush gear, the Yards looking on with great curiosity.

"Lose the steel pot and flak jacket. They don't offer that much protection, they restrict your flexibility, and in a firefight you're better off with more ammo and unrestricted motion." Coats tossed the items aside. "Your web gear is all wrong." The Top grimaced. "But we don't have time ta set it up now." He beckoned to one of the Yard strikers. "Donny, this here's Rixon. He needs two full canteens, fifteen M-16 mags, and six grenades; two fragmentation, two Willie Pete's, and two purple smoke. No time for the armory, ask the squad to donate to the cause most rickey tick! And don't worry, Rix. If we're out there long enough ta get hungry, me 'n' Donny will share our c-rats with ya."

Lady Killer's rotor had spooled to nearly operational revolutions and was ready for liftoff. The copilot looked out the starboard window and gave the thumbs-up to Coats. "Mount Up!" said the Top and the strikers began climbing past the door gunners into the cargo compartment of the Huey as Rixon was putting on the last of his gear. "Rix, I never thought ta ask, but tha Jar Heads did teach ya how ta shoot this thing, didn't they?" said Coats as he handed Rixon his weapon. Seeing that David couldn't hear him over the whine of the turbine and rotor wash, he thought better of his comment. Ready or not, David Rixon was on his way to war.

• • •

Dong Re Lao was a jungle-covered four-thousand-foot promontory that J. D. Brinkman and the other Raven forward air controllers used for point navigation when they were hunting the A Shau Valley. It was a mile-wide and twenty-five-mile-long river corridor created by twin mile-high mountain ranges filled with elephant grass as high as a house and danger at every turn. The corridor was a lethal tentacle of the Ho Chi Minh Trail, poisoning Free Vietnam with extortion, forced conscription, kidnapping, and murder. It was nothing less than the barrel of a loaded AK-47 pointed straight at the coastal cities of Hue and Da Nang.

After their invasion of French Indochina in 1940, the Japanese Imperial Army had constructed an airstrip at the base of the mountain. They flew in equipment and supplies to erect an antenna tower and repeater station to relay radio traffic from the inaccessible interior regions of Laos, Thailand, and Burma to coastal bases and ships in the South China Sea. The year after the invasion, a well-educated and well-traveled Ho Chi Minh was able to establish the "Viet Nam Doc Lap Dong Minh Hoi," or the League for the Independence of Vietnam to free the country from the Japanese occupation and, after the war, to lead the violent struggle to free Vietnam from the colonial French system. After years of struggle, the Communist National Liberation Front, led by General Võ Nguyên Giáp, had defeated the main body of the French Expeditionary Corps in the battle of Dien Bien Phu using tactics similar to those being deployed in the A Shau against the US Army.

• • •

Joe Don flew his single-engine Cessna blind into the heavy rain and thick fog using his altimeter, compass, air speed indicator, and Timex to dead reckon a course south along the ridgeline of the middle finger of the southern end of the Annamite range. In his mind's eye, he saw the A Shau and Laos to his starboard and the coastal cities of Hue and Da Nang to port. He was flying dead level, watching his instruments closely, when he noticed a slight increase in altitude. "The thermal!" he said to himself, marking the coordinates on his map. "Just a little more." There was another rise, this time sharp in altitude, Brinkman saw a bright seam in the cloudbank below and boldly dove his Cessna toward the little patch of daylight, discovered the fog was rising across the valley floor, and pulled out of his descent, identifying an operational ceiling of five hundred feet above the Special Forces basecamp.

Brinkman keyed his microphone. "Catbird, Top Hand," silence. "Catbird to Top Hand, are you receiving?" static, silence. "Catbird, this is Top Hand. We are reading you five-by-five."

"Roger, Top Hand, copy coordinates: seventeen point fifty-one north, one oh eight point thirty-seven east, this is thermal location; repeat, this is current thermal location, five klicks north northeast of objective. Limited flight operations are possible at five hundred feet ceiling and rising repeat, FIVER ZERO ZERO flight ceiling over objective—do you copy?"

"Roger, Catbird, we copy Fiver Zero Zero ceiling. Top Hand Actual requests your eyes on target report. Repeat, Actual requests visual assessment of target."

"Roger, Top, tell Actual ta give me a minute."

Skimming along the ceiling, in and out of the clouds, Brinkman was able to conceal himself while catching critical glimpses of the Special Forces encampment. He identified the airfield first and then the encampment, just to the north and at a slightly skewed angle from the runway. "Closer, gotta get closer," Brinkman muttered to himself, when suddenly he could see smoke coming from the command bunker and the dormitories. Then he saw mortar rounds open an explosive breach in the wire, more mortar rounds exploding, and then a wide column of enemy soldiers, a hundred or more, moving from cover toward the smoldering craters in the fence line. The final assault was under way!

"Do something, JD!" Brinkman screamed to himself, and he reached for his M-79 grenade launcher while he contacted Top Hand. "Catbird, Top Hand. I have eyes on the target. The wire has been breached, boo-coo VC in the wire. Repeat boo-coo enemy in the wire. They're overrunning Signal Hill!"

"Copy that, Catbird. Actual asks that you stay on station and report any changes. Guns are coming."

Roger, Top. Tell Actual he couldn't get me outta here now, even with a pair 'a Cowboys tickets and a six-pack 'a cold Lone Star!"

Brinkman was calmly watching the terrifying advance of the human wave moving unopposed into the breach. He slid a white phosphorous round into the barrel of the grenade launcher and snapped it closed. He then switched his PA system on, cued the PSYOP propaganda tape, turned to volume to full, and switched the toggle to "External." An invisible voice of male authority cut through the fog from above to the insurgents with the tonal melody of the enemies' mother tongue: *"Attention! Attention! Stop firing! By order of Ho Chi Minh, the war is over! Lay down your rifles, stand at attention, and turn north to salute our brave leader in Hanoi. Join me in singing our national anthem. 'March to the Front! Soldiers of Vietnam, we go forward, With the one will to save our fatherland, Our hurried steps are sounding on the long and arduous road, Our flag, red with the blood of victory, bears the spirit of our country, The distant rumbling of the guns mingles with our marching song. The path to glory passes over the bodies of our foes. Overcoming all hardships, together we build our resistance bases. Ceaselessly for the people's cause we struggle, Hastening to the battlefield! Forward! All together advancing! Our Vietnam is strong eternal."*

His starboard window open and the M79 in position, Joe Don watched through his field glasses and noticed confusion in the faces of the enemy as first one then another and then several followed the command from the clouds and rose to their feet, looking up to the source of their national pride. "THUNK! BOOM!" Brinkman's Willie Pete spiraled to earth and exploded in the middle of their ranks, taking out at least two soldiers and marking the target.

WHIRRRRRRRRRRRRRRRRRRCLANK! WHIRRRRRRRRRRR-RRRRRCLANK! The amber arc of death reached for the insurgents out of the cloudbank. "WHIRRRRRRRRRRRRRRRRRRCLANK! "Catbird, this is Hitman! Clear the area, Joe Don, you're getting' in my way!" WHIRRRRRRRRRRRRRRRRRRCLANK! The twin M61 Vulcan electric Gatling guns mounted on the port side of Magazzine's C-130 were heaping burning coals onto the heathen heads of the Communists at the combined rate of twelve thousand rounds per minute. WHIRRRRRRRRRRRRRRRRRCLANK! WHIRRRRRRR-RRRRRRRRRCLANK! WHIRRRRRRRRRRRRRRRRRRCLANK!

Magazzine had uncharacteristically taken a huge risk by slowing his air speed and taking the AC-130 into the narrow valley, at cloud level, so that the electronic warfare officer could make visual contact with the target. Once in place, Hitman moved its amber finger of fire from the glow of the WP outward to pursue the mass of the enemy that was now in dead retreat, running for the cover of the rainforest.

"Captain, we're taking fire on the starboard, guns on our two o'clock! There're on the hillside above our altitude!" said copilot Sparky Barnes over the intercom.

"Roger, the guns, let's get our asses otta here..." POP! POP! POP! The port side windscreen exploded, splintered glass blasting into Magazzine's face. "Sparky, take the ship!" Barnes punched the throttles to their stops and pulled the AC-130 into the clouds and away from danger.

"Hit Man, Linebacker," Watch the guns on the hillside, twenty three millimeter emplacements above the target and on both sides of the valley!"

"Copy the guns Hit Man, Linebacker beginning attack run now!" BRATTA! BRATTA! BRATTTTTAAAAA! WHOOSH! WHOOSH! WHOOSH! WHOOSH! Four Cobra gunships began their attack run on the enemy who had reformed and were running back into the gap in the security fence. Eight ships were holding, four in reserve and four in the clouds, carefully looking for dangerous enemy gun emplacements firing down the mountainside onto the defenders of the Signal Hill base.

The "Wide Receiver" slicks had arrived on station and were being cued by Linebacker to insert the 7-MIKE strikers inside the wire, when all at once, the rain stopped and the fog lifted, exposing the enemy guns. WHIRRRRRRRRRRRRRRRRRCLANK!

WHIRRRRRRRRRRRRRRRRRCLANK! Hitman was back on station raining death from above onto the NVA crew served weapon positions, clearing the path for the slicks to deliver their strikers.

"Linebacker One, Wide Receiver, begin insertion now. It's as good as it's gonna get. Bill, take 'em in and watch your port side."

Rixon's blood was up and he was ready to fight as *Lady Killer* touched down at Signal Hill but when he jumped off the ship, no one was firing. There were bodies everywhere, dead and dying, and the 7-MIKE strikers were administering first aid to their wounded. Donny led Coats and Rixon in a crooked run across the decimated base to what was left of the command bunker. In the smoking ruins sat four North Vietnamese soldiers. They were bound and blindfolded and being addressed by 7-MIKE's lead Montagnard interrogator, Scotty. David sat his weapon aside, opened his rucksack, pulled out his small battery-operated reel-to-reel tape recorder and began to listen and take notes.

"Ask him what unit he's attached to and the size of the force in the field," barked Coats. "Where are the Americans? Where is Sergeant Mercer? We damned sure wanna know where our people are!" he said, noticing the rain had started again.

"Sir, he say they forced conscripts from An Hoa, families held hostage, and VC kill them—they not fight. He say boo-coo NVA and VC in A Shau, maybe five, six thousand, most NVA come down Ho Chi Minh Trail. Make big bac-bac, kill all American," said Scotty, placing his hand on the head of the enemy soldier.

"You getting' this, Rix?" asked Coats, looking to David, then looking back to Scotty. "He tellin' tha' truth? Six thousand is a battalion, not a brigade! That's one serious concentration of enemy troops!"

Donny distracted Coats and Rixon from the interrogation on his return to the bunker with a captured enemy transceiver and officer's leather map pouch taken from the bodies in the wire. They let the transceiver operate so Donny could listen in on the NVA while the Top and Rix studied their cache of annotated battle maps and an officer's personal field diary.

"Sergeant, if this is correct, then here, here, and here are their command posts," said Rix, pointing out the locations on the map, and doing what he could, with his limited knowledge of Vietnamese text, to translate the dead officer's combat diary. "This diary belonged to a Captain Thue, and he writes about purging the Americans from the A Shau to clear the last leg of the Ho Chi Minh trail for some sort of buildup and push." He paused and asked Donny a question that Coats couldn't understand.

"Sir, they don't intend to allow anyone to escape and they aren't going to take prisoners. It's a planned massacre. They believe that a total KIA of the Americans, CIDC, and their families will send a powerful propaganda message: 'The Americans can't protect you; cooperate or die. Yankee go home,' It looks like we're surrounded, Top. It says about two thousand shooters; minus the ones in the wire, I guess."

There was a lethal silence in the smoldering command bunker as the soldiers realized that an entrenched and overpowering enemy had marked them all for death. Rixon continued reading, "This is massive, Sarge. They are planning to fortify the entire valley with radar-controlled antiaircraft artillery placed inside the mountains on both sides with overlapping fields of fire. The big guns will be defended by twenty-three millimeter antiaircraft guns, recoilless rifles, and boo-coo heavy machine guns. Valley of Death; he says that the A Shau will become the Valley of Death for American aviators."

"Donny, get the RTO in here and give the evacuation order. We gotta get our people outta here!" said Coats, looking over the bloody battle maps. "Top Hand, Catbird, Hitman, Linebacker: Delta Charlie. ALPHA TANGO OCEAN! I say again, ALPHA TANGO OCEAN, we have a theater emergency: All Troops Out! We need emergency EVAC; repeat, emergency EVAC required!"

Donnie looked up from the enemy transceiver in a panic. "VC, come now!" Coats looked to Rixon. "Go with Donnie. See if you can find any civilians and get 'em to the LZ. We'll finish up with these guys and meet ya there!"

David followed Donnie out of the bunker and into the chaos of the compound. The 7-MIKE strikers had formed up a defensive line at the breach and were firing furiously into the clearing between the wire and the tree line using the dead VC as cover. The two ran low into the mess hall, which they discovered had been converted into an execution chamber and temporary morgue with a group of twenty women and children wailing out of their grief over the dead. Donny indicated that Rixon should help him move the civilians toward the LZ but they refused to be moved. Instead, they held tight to the lifeless bodies of their loved ones.

WHOOMP! BAM! WHOOMP! BAM! WHOOMP! BAM! Three NVA mortar rounds exploded in the compound close enough to the mess hall to blow out a large chunk of exterior wall, exposing a Huey descending into the LZ. The shock sobered the civilians, who, as a group, broke into a run across the compound to jam aboard the first EVAC out. Donny and Rix scouted the other buildings and discovered the shattered bodies of three Americans beside a mortar crater. They evacuated the bodies to the LZ for removal as more slicks were touching down to evacuate the Strikers, the Cobras swarmed the hillsides with covering fire and Hitman orbited low over the battlefield, washing suppressing fire over the trees being used as cover by the NVA to rally their troops.

Rixon was totally awed as he watched the lumbering AC-130 banking into another attack run, seemingly close enough to hit with a rock, when suddenly he saw a yellow-orange flash through the thick cloudbank. A bright white streak ran across the valley and then the outboard starboard engine began to expand and vaporize into a black-orange-white ball, pulling the craft into a fatal starboard roll. The chatter on the radio told the urgent story.

"We're hit! Mayday! Mayday! Hitman going down two klicks north of Signal Hill, all personnel aboard, too low to bail—we're going in…" Silence.

"Linebacker six, Hitman is down! Repeat, Hitman is down!"

"Roger, six, I'm going back to cover 'em"

"I saw him take it in, he took it down pretty easy, controlled crash—there'll be survivors. Send EVAC. We'll provide cover as long as we can."

The clouds closed again, the rain began to pour, and the fog began rolling in thick from the jungle, across the airfield, obscuring the field of defensive fire and covering the enemy massing for their final assault along the splintered tree line. Rixon felt a large hand grip his shoulder hard and a canvas bag was shoved into his stomach. "Rixon! You take this to Captain Washington and you tell him what we were able to get otta tha gooks. You're on the next ship out."

Rixon looked startled by the command and was about to ask why. "Shut the hell up and listen. We ain't got enough ships ta get everybody out before they overrun us, EVAC can't find us in this soup. 'Bout all we got on our side right now is tha rain and tha fog, it's closin' in and it'll give us some cover. Rix, listen to what I'm tellin' ya'! Mercer and his men are still out there, and we got Hitman needs our help, so here's the plan. I'm taking Donnie 'n' Scotty with me 'n' we gonna hustle over to tha gunship see what can be done, and then we're gonna look around a little for Mercer. In twenty-four hours I'll have anybody I can find on top of that big ol mountain over there, and all you gotta do is talk *Lady Killer* inta flyin' out here again 'n' pickin' us up. Ya got that? I need ya to do that for me, son, so we don't hafta hump it all tha way back ta Rana Dat."

"But, Top, that's suicide!" said Rixon, knowing the murderous intent of the enemy. "We can come back with reinforcements. We're not going to…"

"Put a sock in it, Rixon!" snapped Coats. "They ain't gonna be no reinforcements, I already told ya' weather's too bad for 'em ta even find us again. I've released Catbird and Linebacker and informed Top Hand what we're plannin', and it'll work just fine if ya quit yer bitchin' and do yer job!" He patted a defeated and shivering Rixon on the back, reassuring him that this was the right thing to do. David gave him nod a weak thumbs-up.

The rotor wash cut their conversation short as *Lady Killer* touched down. Coats boosted Rixon into the cargo compartment ahead of the scramble of the other troopers, thankful to be leaving with their lives, gave the thumbs-up to the pilot, and watched the last flight out dissolve into the downpour.

As the chop of the Huey moved off, the sounds of battle dropped away and a supernatural calm descended over Signal Hill. "Dear God," said a bowed sergeant. "I guess you already know that we were defeated by the enemy today, and a lot of our soldiers lost their lives. Lord, they were good men and fine troopers. They died a warrior's death, an honorable death, which is the most any of us can expect but, Lord, we ain't even gonna have tha chance to bury 'em, and that ain't right. So, God, could we trust you to send your angels to watch over their remains and maybe make this battlefield a special place so people remember who they were and what they did here? And, Lord, them mammas and babies we found in tha mess hall, they ain't never done nothin' 'cept love their men, and they deserve better than this. God, I just hope ya' can work it out somehow so that things get better for them that's left behind. Please, God, don't give up on us, and I promise we'll do our best to take care of things down here. In Jesus's name, I pray. Amen."

Coats felt his scouts standing close and opened his eyes, instantly alert to hostile figures gathering in the distance and the occasional sniper round impacting short of their position in the muddy compound. "Scotty, you any good at tracking people in tha rain?" he asked rhetorically as he tucked the folded flags of the lost garrison into his rucksack, packed his cheek with Red Man, and took a final look at the bodies of friend and foe, already beginning to merge with the rain and mud.

"I Number One tracker in all A Shau, Donny Number Two!" explained Scotty proudly, shouldering his pack and handing the heavy radio telephone to Donny.

"Well that's real good, 'cause I think I got a little job for you boys," said the Top as the trio made their move in concert, slowly at first, and then hurrying over the enemy corpses in the wire. They made their way through the breach and disappeared into the fog of the A Shau Valley.

• • •

He who dwells in the place of the Most High shall abide under the shadow of the Almighty. I will say to the Lord, "He is my refuge and my fortress; My God, in Him I will trust." Surely he shall deliver you from the snare of the fowler and from the perilous pestilence. He shall cover you with His feathers, and under his wings you shall take refuge; His truth shall be your shield and buckler. You shall not be afraid of the terror by night, nor of the arrow that flies by day, nor of the pestilence that walks in darkness, nor of the destruction that lays waste at noonday. A thousand may fall at your side, and ten thousand at your right hand; but it shall not come near you. Only with your eyes shall you look and see the reward of the wicked. Because you have made the Lord, who is my refuge, even the Most High, your dwelling place. No evil shall befall you, nor shall any plague come near your dwelling: for He shall give His angels charge over you, to keep you in all your ways. In their hands they shall bear you up, lest you dash your foot against a stone. You shall tread upon the lion and the cobra, the young lion and the serpent you shall trample underfoot. Because he has set his love upon Me, therefore I will deliver him, I will set him on high, because he has known My name. He shall call upon Me and I will answer him; I will be with him in trouble; I will deliver him and honor him. With long life I will satisfy him, and show him My salvation.

Through the rainy night, over and over, David had read and reread Psalm 91 and had been on his face in tearful prayer, crying out to the Lord for Sergeant Coats, Donny, Scotty, Sergeant Mercer and his men, Captain Magazzine, the crew of Hitman, and all those who had been lost during the Battle of Signal Hill. Sleepless still, and in the dark hours just before dawn, he was staring blankly into the compound when a rooster crowed in the coop kept by the missionaries of the Christ in Asia Mission. David followed the lure out into the gray morning of the Rana Dat compound. The rain had stopped, and the Montagnard Strikers were in formation doing their morning PT. Their wives, who looked a lot like those he saw murdered by the Communists at Signal Hill, were building cooking fires and preparing the morning meal while their children were kicking an old soccer ball around and laughing as children will even in a war zone.

David watched them silently, trying to clear his head, trying to think back. He hadn't slept in nearly four days, and the adrenaline and fear that had charged his system during his brief time in combat had finally begun to work their way out of his system. The previous seventy-two hours had seemed a nightmarish blur to him.

Yesterday, or was it the day before, after *Lady Killer* had returned him safely to Rana Dat, David had worked nearly nonstop translating the contents of the field diary of Captain Ngo Quang Thong, Fifth Regiment, Vietnam People's Army. The impact of the cumulative information had stunned Major Washington and opened the eyes of the command leadership at MACV in Da Nang; the six-thousand-man force that had eradicated the Special Forces camp at Signal Hill was only one-quarter of a massive army gathered less than ten kilometers to the west, just across the border in Laos. If Thong's notes could be trusted, the Communists had amassed a commanding force of twenty-four thousand soldiers with support, engineering, and logistics units. They were capable of delivering one thousand trucks daily from bases and supply dumps in Laos, using the old French Route 922 to cross the border and then dozens of branch infiltration roads and trails, secretly constructed under the jungle canopy, to reach all segments of the twenty-five-square-mile river basin. Their plan was to fortify the mountainsides of the valley by placing Chinese and Russian-made antiaircraft batteries into natural caves or man-made fortifications that would resist everything but a direct hit by an American bomber.

Incredibly, the North Vietnamese had no heavy equipment with which to construct the fortifications or place the armament. A civilian labor force of roughly fifty thousand had used picks, shovels,

THE FLIGHT OF THE MAYDAY SQUADRON

and hand axes to clear the roadways and either modify existing caverns or dig new underground bunkers for the gun emplacements. Perhaps most unbelievable to Rixon, the massive guns themselves were disassembled by the Vietnamese, taken piece by piece up the mountainside and reassembled within the safe harbor of the fortified mountain range. This incredible feat was accomplished in just over a year and under the nose of MACV and ARVN forces who believed themselves to be the dominant force in the region.

Making his way around the camp perimeter, David caught the faint fragrance of…bacon? Reminded of Ruidoso and of Karen, he followed his nose outside the main gate and up the slight rise to the chapel. It was early still, and he felt that being in a house of worship might help him feel closer to God, so he tentatively approached the mission. "Good morning, Brother David!" called a woman's gentle voice. "Have you had breakfast?"

Suzanne Campbell surprised David by inviting him to share their breakfast of bacon, eggs, and warm bread. "How do you know my name?" he asked, a little startled by her recognition.

"Oh, the Lord didn't send us a vision about you or anything," said Suzanne good-naturedly, seeing the look on his face. "Will Washington told us that you'd probably drop over. The believers assigned to Rana Dat usually make it by sooner or later—to see the crazy round-eyed missionaries if nothing else. Would you break bread with us, brother? There's more than enough, and we're just about to start."

After Pastor Jeff's morning prayer of thanksgiving and during their meal, David learned that the Campbells had met during their undergraduate studies at the University of Oklahoma. They took teaching jobs in the Oklahoma City public school system and were called as a couple to enter the service of the Lord after they heard William Cameron Townsend's testimony concerning his mission work with the Cakchique Indians of Guatemala, who expressed their distress that God did not speak in their language. Townsend was moved by the Holy Spirit to dedicate his life to the world-changing proposition that every man, woman, and child on earth should be able to read the eternal word of Almighty God in their mother tongue. That summer, the Campbells attended "Camp Wycliffe," at Townsend's linguistics training school in Dallas and thereafter, believed that the Lord had brought them to their mission in life.

"The most challenging aspect of our work with the indigenous tribes who inhabit the Annamite range is that none of them have developed the written word on their own. So the first thing we have to do is create a phonetic alphabet based on their existing language and then build a dictionary unique to the tribe in question. It takes time and close exposure to the people to come to experience the world as they do, to build the necessary empathy required for an accurate translation of the Word," explained Jeff over his hot tea. "We established the mission here in thirty-eight, with the permission and help of the French, right next to the main Riad village. Most people who live there today are friends, family really. We'll take you on a tour later if you like," offered Jeff. "We stayed during the Japanese occupation, during the Viet Minh's war to expel the French, and we hope to be able to live here until the Lord takes us heaven. This is home to us now, David, and there is nowhere else we would rather be than right here," concluded Jeff as he poured more tea into David's cup.

"My role here is primarily the school," added a pleasant Suzanne. "I teach English and French as alternates to their native tongue, which they call E-de. The people here are Riad but we have also worked extensively with members of the Bahnar, Jarai, Koho, Hmong, and Stieng tribes up the range from here. Of course, the children show up mostly for lunch. It's a simple meal that we make here in our open-air kitchen, usually rice, beans, and fish sauce we buy and pack in from the coast. Most of them are passable students, but sometimes you encounter one with a special spark—alert and inquisitive—who has a desire to know, and that's absolutely the mountaintop for me. I believe you may have met two of our stars. Their English names are Donny and Scotty. They work as scouts for the Green Berets sometimes, Will mentioned that you had already worked with them."

A wave of guilt washed through David as he remembered them standing with Sergeant Coats as *Lady Killer* left them behind in the kill zone. "They don't know yet," he thought sadly.

"Rixon! Break's over! Need you in the conference room at oh seven hundred—that's in ten minutes," interrupted Major Washington. After exchanging pleasantries with the Campbells he and David began to walk back to the compound.

"Careful what you say to Pastor Jeff and Sister Suzie, David. Remember, I told you that the VC don't mess with 'em, and we don't know why. Well we gotta consider the possibility that they trade information to Charlie to stay alive, wouldn't be the first time something like that happened out in the bush, and we damned sure don't want another Signal Hill happening here. Now I ain't sayin' stay away or nothin' like that. Just keep your conversation friendly; talk 'bout Jesus partn' the Red Sea or football or whatever you like 'n' we'll all be fine."

As the two crossed through the main gate and it closed behind them, they saw a half dozen slicks queuing to land inside the wire near the command bunker. They were bringing large men in clean uniforms to test Washington and his staff in their element after the disaster at Signal Hill. This was the moment Washington had long awaited—the beginning of Phoenix and the start of his climb to a top spot in the Pentagon.

"Gentlemen, please be seated," said Washington crisply. "I would like to introduce the nucleus of our Project Phoenix team," indicating that Rixon and Mr. Brown should stand. "Captain David Rixon is our command translator, Mr. Brown is our theater liaison with the Central Intelligence Agency, and absent this meeting is Lieutenant Tommy Coats, who will serve as our field intelligence coordinator. Coats is in the bush today conducting a search for survivors of the surprise attack at Signal Hill."

"As you know," continued the major, "Phoenix isn't even a fully functional embryo at this point, but it has born first fruit. Less than seventy-two hours ago Seven-MIKE captured NVA documents and conducted battlefield interrogations, which were rapidly translated

by Captain Rixon. They indicate the presence of a previously undetected twenty-four-thousand-man NVA army, which is massed just
over the border in Laos and has, over the last fourteen months,
secretly fortified the A Shau Valley and prepared it as an invasion
route and safe haven for future combat operations. The mortar
attacks of five days ago in Da Nang and elsewhere in country were a
prelude to the surprise attack on Signal Hill, the final barrier to the
NVA's operational control of the floor of A Shau. Their loss leaves
Rana Dat as the last remaining set of American eyes and ears on the
most significant enemy force in the region, and we don't believe that
our presence here is anything the enemy will be willing to tolerate.

"The binder before you marked TOP SECRET contains your
copies of the translated intelligence, our analysis of the situation
we've encountered on the ground, and a proposed counteropera-
tion that we are calling 'Widow Maker.' We understand that our current posture in country is defensive, and that it will be sometime
before we have the troop strength required to keep the ground we
have as well as push the enemy out of A Shau. What we have is a need
to real-world test 'Operation Arc Light,' and Widow Maker offers the
immediate opportunity for that test."

Operation Arc Light involved equipping the strategic intercontinental nuclear bomber, the B-52D Stratofortress, with "big belly"
modifications that would allow the airframe to carry eighty-four
five-hundred-pound conventional bombs. The bombers would be
guided to the target with the Reeves AH/MSQ-77 Bomb Directing
Radar Control Center. Troopers called it "Miscue Seventy-Seven" for
its frequent deadly errors. If it worked, it would provide a powerful
all-weather close air support weapon that had not existed previously.
Arc Light squadrons were to be based at Anderson Air Force Base
on the island of Guam, an extraordinary twenty-six hundred miles
to the east of Vietnam, beyond the South China Sea, beyond the
Philippine Islands on the eastern edge of the Philippine Sea.

"Widow Maker proposes that the Reeves Radar Control be located
here at Rana Dat. We have a complete overview of the A Shau that
is obscured only by the weather and tree canopy. The radar will cut

right through that, exposing the targets to the bombers. The Ravens and ground-based fire control squads will be able to confirm impact and send pattern adjustments in real time."

"Widow Maker will make Rana Dat an irresistible target—bait in a trap—that will attract the enemy like flies to honey and create the opportunity to deliver the coup de grace to the Communists that survive the bombing raids in the valley."

Washington had many gray heads bobbing as he briefed his commanders on the details of Widow Maker, which he hoped would disperse the threat of the massing enemy less than twenty miles from his front door, buy time for the American forces in country to build up and catch the attention of COMUSMACV in his quest for higher rank. Major Washington received pats on the back from his commanders as they boarded their helicopters and departed for the security of MACV Da Nang.

Two days later, Washington posted Special Forces Sergeants Coats, Mercer, Adams, and Jackson and CIDC scouts Donny and Scotty as missing in action; the shrieks and wails of the Montagnard widows and children cast a pall over Rana Dat that pierced Washington, Rixon, and Mr. Brown as their Huey departed for Saigon. "They've been out there a week and the whole damned valley is swarming like a red ant hill," said a pained Washington to David. "The EVAC teams have choppered out to the specified pickup zone more than twenty times since the attack and we're lucky we haven't lost anymore aircraft. With Widow Maker kicking off, COMUSMAVC has declared the valley a "Free Fire Zone," so I'm sorry, David, but I'm pulling the patrols. If they're still alive, they're gonna' hafta get themselves out of harm's way."

The Huey carrying Washington, Brown, and Rixon climbed to altitude and took the ridge route south to the summit of Dong Re Lao, orbited the radio tower looking for Coats and the lost Special Forces Team, and then slid southeast over the ridge and took the more secure coastal route to Da Nang. Once there, the three changed out of their uniforms into civilian dress and hopped a Military Air Transport Service DC-4 to Tan Son Nhut Air Base. After liftoff, Mr.

Brown handed Rixon and Washington small packages, which contained their US Department of State credentials and a small, easily concealable snub-nosed Colt Detective Special. "Not exactly sheep-dipped but close. The popgun is for last-resort self-defense. We got no back up in Saigon, so keep your eyes peeled and stay sharp."

Their taxi brought them to 39 Ham Hghi Boulevard and to the front gate of the American embassy where Brown took charge, handing his credentials to the Marine security sergeant. "Mr. Brown to see Mr. White, please. He is expecting us."

An attractive American woman in her thirties emerged from the inner offices of the Embassy, greeted Brown by name, and asked for Washington's and Rixon's credentials. After a moment on the sentry's telephone, she said cheerily, "This way to the rabbit hole, Gentlemen." She led them into a closet under the large ceremonial winding stair, through the door, and then an inside door, down another flight of white metal stairs, through another locked door, which led to an anteroom and another Marine security checkpoint, and then through another locked steel door into a man-trap covered with sheets of honed stainless steel and a hidden light source that made the room seem as if it were illuminated by the sun itself. The doors at the end opened into an elevator car clad in the same material.

"I will leave you here, Gentlemen," she said, returning their credentials and offering a smile. "Don't be alarmed. You may experience a slight vertigo or some mild claustrophobia during the descent; almost everyone does. The trip takes about five minutes but it always seems longer to me. Enjoy your stay."

The doors of the elevator cab slid closed and latched from the outside. The lights dimmed and David noticed that there were no buttons or emergency telephone where he expected them to be. Then the car started to move downward and the velocity increased rapidly. "You will not get sick!" David commanded himself as the vertigo started. The car began to slow and stopped. Then they sensed the direction of travel had shifted to their right, and they began to move rapidly once more until another pause was followed by a brief period of ascent. The doors opened to yet another anteroom, another Marine checkpoint, and this time standing in front of them was a tallish, gray-bearded, Anglo man whose parents hadn't believed that much in orthodontia. He wore a moss-colored Lacoste polo, hunter-green corduroy pants, tan Hush Puppies, gold steel-rimmed eyeglasses with thick lenses, and a freshly pressed white lab coat embroidered with the red double sun logo. The words "Allegheny Innovations" were tightly stitched below.

"Welcome to Wonderland! My name is Jonathan White and I'm sort of in charge of things down here," he said smiling, holding his hand out to Brown, Washington, and Rixon. "We don't get many visitors, and not a lot of people even know about the place, so I have to assume you're connected to the project in some way, or maybe you're just here for the show?"

"Correct," said Brown. "Why don't you walk us through. Rixon here would like to see the mainframe, and if you've got a conference room, we can discuss the project there."

White led his guests through a set of glass doors into an immaculate white room and began to describe the function of the long rows of orange tape drives, blue command consoles, and yellow central processors, all being attended by young men dressed in dark slacks, white shirts, dark neckties, and white lab coats. In an adjacent room, Rixon counted ten rows of five keypunch stations, each being operated by a female data entry clerk, all Asian women, dressed in dark skirts and crisp white blouses with the double sun logo stitched into the shoulder. Finished with the hardware, the group made its way to the rear of Wonderland into the finely crafted executive suite and the large acoustically isolated conference room. The room featured deep pile carpeting of a light, nearly neutral gray, richly colored and patterned fabric-paneled walls, and a large white board on the wall opposite the glass entry. A glazed operable panel wall opened to what appeared to be a delicate sunlit Japanese garden with red maple trees, raked gravel, a sparking stream, and small koi pond, which David found most curious, considering that he knew the facility to be located deep under the basement of the embassy.

Brown began the conversation with more explanation. "Mr. Washington is in charge of the overall field implementation of the project in country, and Mr. Rixon is in charge of linguistics. He's inquired about the math you're using to program the computer so that he can adjust his raw data to work more effectively with the database. Is that a correct statement, Mr. Rixon?"

"Sort of." David smiled to Brown and White. "I thought if I understood the logic of your mathematics, the variables that your base algorithm has been designed to resolve, that I might be able to formulate the data acquisition methodology to extend your logic into the field. Since the purpose of the project is to identify and describe the network or networks of Communist infiltrators in the population, your process probably incorporates at least some elements of Bayesian conditional probability. May I?" asked Rixon, gesturing to the whiteboard.

"If the problem is to sort the Communists from the loyalists and we can attribute a quality to the Communist, say the possession of an AK-Forty-Seven, that we may or may not see in a loyalist, then according to Reverend Bayes, the problem may be expressed in this manner." Rixon began writing: "problem (person has AK-47/person is a Communist)," and beside the problem statement, he drew a square divided into four equal parts. "This s a Venn diagram that illustrates the components of the equation. 'AK' means that the person has a weapon; 'C' means that the person is a Communist: 'minus AK' means that the person does not possess a weapon, and 'minus C' means that the person is not a Communist. The final notation, 'N,' represents the number of persons to be sorted. Here in summary is the probability equation; prob (AK|C) = prob (ak)/prob (C) X prob (C/ak)…"

Johnathan Campbell White, PhD, was lonely and depressed. Cut off from his peers and family in Pittsburgh by his secondment to the Department of State and a lifeless existence in his subterranean Wonderland, he had totally alienated the IBM technicians, who should have been his friends and colleagues, by referring to them once too often as brainless mechanics there only to service his hardware. After a final climactic event in which he had instructed the senior technician, in front of the entire staff, not to forget to "change the oil on the main frame every three thousand miles," the IBM techs had ostracized him from their social circle. After that watershed event, which he would have regretted had it not been for his oversized ego, he had assumed that he was doomed to work in solitude, isolated, with no one to admire his brilliance, for the balance of his assignment in his technological Wonderland.

Were he back in the World, this little CIA man asking an elementary math question of Dr. White would have been an occasion for great sport. He would have gathered his peers for the show, looked down his nose at Rixon's naïve presentation, plucked him like a squab, and roasted him with the radiance of his gleaming intellect but in this dire circumstance. "Ah, the linguist. We've been waiting on you, but a mathematician as well, Mr. Rixon?" he asked with a dim smile of recognition and continued. "Your assumption is correct; conditional probability is one feature of the base algorithm. There are, to date, sixty-four operating subroutines that include versions of cause-correlation data aggregation and game theory. It's really quite fascinating how the data set…"

An hour and a half later, and bored to tears, Washington began doodling and scribbled, "They gonna be best friends now?" Washington passed his note to Brown. "They outta get themselves a room!" wrote Brown in his humorous response. "Real squares. Rixon's the worst. You got things lined up for tonight?" wrote Washington. "Mama Lu's. Number one poontang in all Saigon, pretty good grub too, if you don't mind dog! Rixon know?" scribbled Brown and passed the note back. Seeing Washington shake his head with a sly smile, Brown began to consider adjusting his opinion of the major, who he previously thought to have been born with a punji stake embedded in his rectum.

"Gentlemen," said Washington in his most convincing tone of faux respect. "I truly hate to interrupt this exchange, but it's getting' on toward sixteen hundred, and we haven't seen Dr. White's famous show."

The "show" commenced when they followed White into the generous viewing room, which consisted of a wall covered with twenty-four-inch television monitors stacked four high and eight wide. White took his position before the command console and used the intercom to communicate briefly with one of the 360 technicians. A few moments later the lights in the room came down, and the thirty-two color monitors came alive with a segmented computer-generated image of a slowly rotating graphic. It looked to David a little like the root of one of his daddy's corn plants, except it was rendered in a composite of blacks, grays, blues, greens, yellows, and reds.

"What you are seeing here is a graphical representation of the dataset as it's being assembled," said Dr. White proudly as he zoomed the graphic into a smaller segment of the root, revealing hundreds of colored squares. "Each square represents a family unit and we've color-coded the units based on their known political affiliation. In this sort, we've also assigned geophysical coordinates to each unit based on their last known primary physical residence so that we can represent proximity to societal and governmental centers." He zoomed in farther to a single red square, and it expanded into a dozen individual squares, each with an identifying code number. "As you can see, the family units consist of blood relatives, each of whom has his own extended social structure that can be accessed and isolated through the coded dataset. When the project is complete, we will have an operational social-political model of the entire population of Vietnam."

"Of course you mean South Vietnam," corrected Rixon.

"No. I mean the entire country, unified," said White, raising his voice slightly. "That is, if the French dataset is as accurate as the demographers say it is," he said, addressing Washington and Brown. "You may not understand this, Mr. Washington, but nothing like this has ever existed in the history of the planet. It couldn't before the Three Sixty. Not enough processing power. When we're done, we will own a detailed dataset containing nearly forty million people that can be sorted, categorized, and analyzed for an infinite range of criteria. Gentlemen, whoever you are interested in, wherever he is, if he's in the database, I can present you with his entire network of collaborators, coconspirators, relatives, friends, lovers, associates, and acquaintances with their home addresses all the way from Saigon to Hanoi. But really, that's not the half of it. With the linguistics and intelligence information that Rixon and his team will provide, we believe we'll be able to accurately predict events like bombings, assassinations, and major military attacks. And that, Gentlemen, is why we call our little world Wonderland; I think of us as rather like the Witches of Endor," he said with a prideful smile. "We can summon the sprit from this dead dataset, so to speak, but what you do with the information is completely out of our purview," concluded White, pleased with himself, returning the display to its slowly spinning database.

Major Washington was leaning forward, mesmerized by the display. "I'm guessing the red squares represent the known Communists?" he said, pointing his index finger at the moving targets as if it were his sidearm, moving slightly to absorb the imaginary recoil.

"The data input isn't completed yet, as you have seen. We have fifty keypunch operators punching cards twenty-four hours a day, and your group will be augmenting the dataset in the near future, but yes, in this preliminary view, we are displaying the problem groups and individuals as red units. The yellow units are known associates, the blues and greens are known supporters of the central government, and the blacks and grays have no known affiliation," concluded White, pleased with is presentation but ready to get back to work.

"I hear you make your own electricity down here, that you operate independent of the local utilities, a miniature nuclear reactor, or something. That true or just scuttlebutt?" asked Mr. Brown, showing a curious disbelief in his face.

"Ah, yes; the power enigma. There is more to Wonderland than meets the eye. Come along, Gentlemen and we'll take a look under the hood," said White, happily anticipating the disbelief of his guests.

They moved along a wide, white corridor, through a set of thick steel doors, into a gray concrete service area, and White unlocked another set of steel doors into a concrete vault. Before them, mounted on low concrete pads, were two white metal boxes approximately three feet wide, by three feet high by six feet long. Each unit emitted a low-frequency hum, was surprisingly cold to the touch, and was branded with the Allegheny Innovations double sun. "They're called zero point generators, and I'm not exactly clear on the operating principle, but these two provide power for the whole installation. Unit A is dedicated to the System Three Sixty, and Unit B powers everything else, including the transport mechanism you rode down on," said White, smiling. "You know, the company manufactures these and nearly everything else down here except the Three Sixty, furnishings, and, of course, the people."

White pulled a pair of cotton gloves from his coat pocket. "They say it's OK, but I don't like to touch them with my bare hands. There's an unpleasant sensation." He placed his hands on either side of the end of Unit A facing them and simultaneously depressed two nearly invisible discs. There was a slight electromagnetic pop, the whoosh of a vessel depressurizing, and the cowling began to lift and slowly tilt away, revealing the internal mechanism. Protected by a clear acrylic shell were twin power modules, deep black-blue cubes measuring roughly two and a half feet per side. Through the acrylic screen, David could see that the modules had no top enclosure. There seemed to be a slowly moving sheet of a clear liquid, that could have been water—but surely wasn't—that seemed to flow down the four internal walls of each module with a slight white disturbance, like a dense fog, as the liquid sheet met the bottom of each hollow box and then simply disappeared. The bottoms of the modules were filled with hundreds of thousands of tiny points of intensely gleaming silver, blue, yellow, and red. It was as if a small segment of the Milky Way had been taken from the heavens and placed into the little black box. The only control mechanism David could see was a simple red toggle switch protected by a clear plastic cover.

"The supervising technician told me the things operate at zero degrees Kelvin, that's four hundred fifty-nine degrees below zero. It's what they call the "zero point." The normal laws of thermodynamics cease, a different kind of physics operates, and a new set of physical properties begin to manifest—one of them being an infinite source of clean electrical current. Clean enough that we can tie the processors into it directly without any sort of harmonic distortion or fear of power failure. The things are rock solid, simple, and require no fuel or maintenance. Just uncrate them, make sure they're properly grounded, plug them in, and turn them on. No one said anything about how long they last, so I suppose they operate infinitely."

"Never seen nothing like it," said Washington with incredulity. "You sure they ain't no hidden wires leading outside to the electrical lines in the street?" he joked, shaking his head. "Man, if this gets back to the World there's gonna be a whole lot 'a fat cats lookin' for another way to pay for their yachts! "

"I thought it fictitious as well, Mr. Washington, until I arrived a year ago to supervise the installation and commissioning of the Three Sixty. All the screening panels were pulled, and the access flooring wasn't installed. I promise that the only power in the place comes from these two little white boxes. And don't worry about the technology getting out to the general public. These things are strictly DOD, and even then you can't get access to one without a memorandum from the president."

"Well ain't that just a kick in the head," said Washington in summary. And then, all at once, their time in Wonderland was over.

White was slightly disappointed. He was starting to like Rixon, but the others were hungry, and David had something else he wanted to get done while he was in Saigon. "Do you have a telephone I could use to call home to Texas?"

• • •

On the way to the hotel, David felt energized. "My dad was working late and he welcomed me to the army! Said he didn't know if he could get used to saluting me! You'd like him, Will, he was a Ranger in the Thirty-Sixth Texas, a 'T-Patcher' lieutenant. He saw combat in Europe during the Big War. He's a real standup guy. And Karen said she and little Randy are fine. He's my son, Will. I haven't even seen him yet...they've got our apartment nearly ready though. It sounds nice. And then we talked about some personal stuff and that I'll be home in forty-five days. Man, I can't wait to see 'em. It seems like an eternity, but it'll go by in a flash. You said there'd be food—are we close yet? I'm starving!" he said, smiling to his companions, riding along in the not-so-friendly city of Saigon.

The trip to the Continental Hotel was a strange vision for David. He had barely been outside the wire in Da Nang and was struck there by the poverty and the desperation of the people who had crowded close to the base, seeking security and jobs from the Americans. The squalor of their daily lives was repugnant to David, and he began to wonder about the future of the people of the South. But Saigon was a world within a world. Known as the Paris of the Orient, the city had served as the capital of the French colony of Cochnchina from the mid-1800s until the victory of Ho Chi Minh and his Viet Minh resistance force in the French Indochina war in 1955. After the national partitioning, it had become the capital of South Vietnam with a growing population of nearly two hundred thousand.

David was intrigued with the variety of the people he saw along the street, civilian, military, young, old, crowded with vendors, oxcarts, motor bikes, bicycles, trucks, and automobiles. In all of this chaotic jumble, David focused on a solitary young woman, dressed in traditional "ao dai," white silk pantaloons, white blouse, white conical "non la," or leaf hat, and a long narrow white tunic that draped it all. She was riding her bright yellow bicycle in the traffic alongside the slowly moving taxi close enough so that he could study her face, beautiful to see, yet a look of deep concern in her eyes.

"Student at the University of Saigon," said Brown. "Love the uniforms. Makes 'em all look like virgins. There are dozens of 'em. They bike along here to the campus in the morning and then home in the afternoon. Lot of 'em are whores, work the bars nights and weekends. If you're lucky, you might see her again when we go out tonight."

David turned away without acknowledging Brown and looked once more at the girl. The pain in her face was still there, and it was real. He knew the look; he had seen it before in the eyes of the women of Signal Hill who had stared too long into the face of the war. "She's who we're here to help," thought Rixon. She glanced toward the taxi and they made eye contact for a long moment before she looked away, turned onto a side street, and disappeared into the maw of the crowded Chinese market.

• • •

That evening Washington and Brown inserted themselves easily into the familiar crowd at the "Continental Shelf," the second-floor location of the former lobby bar at the venerable Continental Hotel that was said to be safe from the random grenade attack tossed into the front door from a passing motorbike. Rixon tagged along, looking for something edible.

"What do you suppose the American army is here for if not to expand their empire?" argued one of the patrons, clearly German, in strongly accented English.

"To keep Mao from knocking down the Indochina dominos and murdering millions people like he's doing right now to his own countrymen!" shot back a red-faced young man holding a tall clear glass in one hand and a cigarette in the other.

"Are you a fool, sir, or merely towing the American line? Everyone in this bar knows that Mao is a Yale man! Installed as the leader of the Communist Party of China by the OSS in forty-six with Rockefeller money and kept in arms and ammunition with opium sold to the world under the brokerage of the American Central Intelligence Agency, your employer, I believe, Mr. Beedle!" scoffed the German.

"What! I told you already, I'm with the Peace Corps! Are you deaf? And I told you my name's not Beedle, its Johnson, like the president! " replied Red Face indignantly.

"Bar talk, Rix, don't pay 'em no mind," cautioned Washington as he savored his whisky. "Here, have some peanuts. We'll get chow in a while," he said, pushing the dish of salted nuts to David while scanning the crowd. "Looking for someone I want you to get to know—Carlton Mayer—been at the embassy since the French pulled out in fifty-four, knows Indochina better than any round-eye you're likely to meet. He's usually here for libations around this time."

Carlton Mayer was tall, lanky and balding; sixtyish, with a full beard and mustache. Dressed in tropical whites with a subdued bow tie, Panama hat, and gold-rimmed spectacles, he looked to David more like a college professor on vacation than a career diplomat or maybe a spy; probably a little of both, David judged from the company he kept.

"So you're the linguist Will has been bragging about. Says he stole you from the corps and you're going to help him identify the subversive elements in the population, so they can be dealt with and democracy can flourish in South Vietnam," said Mayer with a twinkle in his eye, flashing a smile across the table at Washington.

"As the major is well aware," Rixon said, smiling between sips of his ginger ale, "I'm just setting things up for my successor; I've got less than two months left in country, and then I'll join my wife and son in El Paso for the final year of my commitment, teaching at DLI. Then we'll see what the future holds."

Glancing at his wristwatch, Mayer began to politely disengage. "Will, I hate to run but I've a late appointment I need to get to. Mr. Rixon, Mr. Brown, it's been a pleasure and, David, good luck in El Paso."

"Well that was short and sweet," said Brown, slouching into his seat. "What the hell we supposed to do now?"

Rixon looked on curiously as Washington reached across the booth, placed a large hand on Brown's shoulder, and almost imperceptibly shook his head. "I don't know 'bout you, Brown, but I'm starving. What you say to chow at Mama Lu's!"

The Villa Morin was built by the famous French hotelier of the same name in 1907. Strategically located, the villa is on a low limestone bluff overlooking the bend in the Saigon River just south of the footbridge that connects the Jardin Botanical Gardens to the Old French Museum District. The CIA and the Studies and Observation Group had procured the villa in the late fifties for the benefit of their personnel who needed a secure location for some overdue R&R while on duty in Saigon.

Lam Uyen Lu, Miss Saigon '57, had been engaged by the State Department as the on-site restaurant manager and booking agent for the talent that regularly entertained the soldiers. Sometimes she invited her friends for unofficial socials with the Americans. "Sort of like the USO with a Vietnamese accent," said Washington with a smile to Rixon, explaining his decision to dine at Mama Lu's instead of the world-famous La Bourgeois, only a few dozen steps away from their table at the Continental Shelf. "Besides, I'm buying."

The taxi deposited the threesome in front of the elegant entry pagoda, which consisted of four large teak columns and oversized carved lintels that supported the expansive Chinese red-lacquered tile roof. Constructed in the Buddhist style, the precision of the structural joinery was meticulous and hinted at the detail the visitor would discover inside the main house. They walked through the pagoda onto a raked gravel path, which they followed through a lush oriental garden that led them crunching under the large covered verandah of the same style as the entry gate. The verandah sheltered an oversized teak and stained-glass entry guarded by two very large military policemen, who verified their credentials and allowed them entry.

"Check your weapons?" asked a pleasant young woman behind the counter, and each man exchanged his revolver for a small numbered ticket. "Wild Willie Washington!" shouted an excited young woman from behind. "Come give your Mama Lu a great big bear hug!" They embraced, Washington lifting her off her feet, and she kissed him affectionately fully on his mouth.

Slightly embarrassed by overt show of affection, Washington stumbled and then introduced his companions, "Lu, I'd like to introduce David Rixon and Sterrette Brown. We'll be working together for a while."

"Oh, I know Brown—he a regular." She smiled, touching his hand familiarly, seductively. But this handsome Rixon is new here, and so young!" She smiled, offering her hand to David.

"Xin chao, Lu Uyen Lam, tình nhân c□a nhà Morn" ("Hello, Lam Uyen Lu, mistress of Morin House"), said David as he took her hand gently in both of his and bowed slightly, showing a respectful knowledge of her culture that she had not seem from a foreigner in years.

"My goodness, Mr. Rixon; I had no idea. You are a student of our language and culture?" she asked, flushing slightly.

"Only a novice, Miss Lu," he continued in English. "I'm afraid that beyond the superficial, I am completely lost. The nuisance of the tonal variations is quite problematic for Westerners, though I find both the language and the culture beautiful and somewhat intoxicating," he concluded with a smile.

"Oh, Will, this Rixon." She smiled broadly at Washington. "He is a very special man; such a charmer. And for tonight I have three special hostesses selected just for you!"

On hearing their cue, three of the most beautiful Vietnamese women any of them had ever seen entered the foyer. Dressed seductively in brightly colored ao dai, minus the pantaloons and under blouse but with revealing undergarments, dark silk stockings, Parisian stiletto heels and Western-style hair and makeup, they approached their "dates" and took their arms, as they were called in turn by Mama Lu. "Will, for you I have selected Debbie, a botany major at the university. For Mr. Brown I have matched Rhonda, a student of political science, and for our most gallant David, I have selected Gilda, who is studying English. These ladies are from the best families in Saigon and will be your dinner companions this evening. So please, Gentlemen, introduce yourselves to your ladies, buy them a drink at the bar, and they will escort you into the dining room when you are ready. Welcome to the Villa Morin."

None of it felt right to David. "Gilda" took his arm and snuggled close to him on one of the leather loveseats they discovered in the

Library Bar, which had once been Monsieur Morin's private retreat. "You have very good Vietnamese," she said, smiling up into his eyes; her perfume reminded David of jasmine. "My parents sent me to Catholic school, and I learned English from the sisters."

"You are Christian?" asked David.

"Catholic; and a little Buddhist," she said looking deeply into his eyes. She raised her face to his, brushing his cheek with her lips, and whispered into his ear, "Your face. It must have been very painful. Did it happen long ago?"

"When I was very young; I really don't remember much about the pain."

She lightly brushed his deformity with her fingertips, her eyes penetrating his, and she moved against him, whispering again in his ear, "I am not a prostitute." Their lips met involuntarily and their embrace deepened as David could no longer resist his impulse to life, her beauty, her form, her fragrance, and the foreign opulence of the Villa Morin."

"Suppertime!" announced Washington, startling Rixon and Gilda, who jumped to their feet and began straightening their clothes. The guilt of his flirtation with adultery was already weighing on David's heart, and he felt at least a temporary reprieve from his lust as he and Gilda made their way to the dining room ahead of the others. Washington flashed a smile and gave a covert thumbs-up to Brown; by the looks of Gilda, he would have something he could use as an effective lever on his subordinate before the night was over.

The dining salon was cantilevered over the edge of the bluff and featured a panoramic view of the Saigon River, alive with commercial oceangoing vessels and dozens of native sampans bearing paper lanterns and fishermen casting their nets for the evening catch. The intimate lighting of the salon allowed the lights across the river into the room, animating the evening with the pleasant narcotic of life on the water. That the Americans had tried to turn the room into a sports bar with displays of autographed memorabilia, including balls, bats, and uniform jerseys signed by their sports heroes, blemished the ambiance of the room only slightly.

Other soldiers and their paid escorts packed the room. Washington and Brown were making the most of the occasion, moving from table to table, greeting their friends and acquaintances. David and the three ladies remained in a slightly awkward conversation at their table watching Washington as he had a brief conversation with Mama Lu. They were surprised when many of the people in the room gathered around their table led by Washington, Mama Lu, and the house chef holding a large covered platter.

"Rix, there is a long standing military tradition at Morin House that your first meal here is what we call the Studies and Observation Group Special. I know you're hungry so here's your supper. Welcome to SOG!"

Strangely familiar to Rixon, the smiling Vietnamese chef placed the platter on the table nearly in David's lap and removed the silver cover, exposing a terrified mongrel puppy, hogtied, with an empty tomato sauce can shoved harshly onto its muzzle to keep it quiet. Squirming in terror the pup tried frantically to free itself, and the chef proudly presented the razor-sharp butcher knife to David.

"It's the custom here for the freshman member to demonstrate his fraternity, courage, and skill by publicly slaughtering his supper. Fresh meat, Rix, have at it!" said Washington over the cheers and laughter of the rowdy, drunken crowd. "MEAT! MEAT! MEAT!" they chanted. The escorts stood and joined Mama Lu away from the table, leaving David and the helpless cur alone, the focus of the jeering crowd.

Anger, shock, and embarrassment at their barbarism flashed through David's mind as he looked first at the trembling puppy, then at Washington, Brown, and the circling, haranguing crowd. In a moment of empathy and clarity, David stood, looked closely into the chef's smiling, hostile eyes, took the knife, cut the animal free, removed the tin can from his muzzle, and took the pup into his arms—instantly squelching the noisy crowd.

"Major Washington," said David flatly in the silence, "please go ahead and have your supper without me, sir; I'm taking my dog for a walk." He turned away, leaving behind the dining room and a loud chorus of boos and catcalls.

Later that evening, David was sitting alone on the river terrace, the puppy asleep in his lap. Only the night-lights remained burning in the Villa Morin. "Sorting things through?" said a soft female voice from behind.

"There's a lot to consider, Miss Lu," replied David without turning. She sat next to him quietly for a long time, looking out at the lights on the water.

"Will told me you would enjoy the challenge of the slaughter and that you had been in combat, without a woman, for a very long time. He said he wanted to give you the gift of a night of reverie and love. He never mentioned that you were a follower of Jesus Christ."

"How did you know?" asked David, looking far out at the lights.

"In the Book of Matthew, Jesus say that a good tree cannot bear bad fruit; you could not kill the dog, Rixon, any more than you can make love with a lady who is not your wife. You are a good man, a Christian. It would be a mistake to think otherwise."

"You know the scripture Lu; do you not also know the Lord?"

"I do believe in Jesus, Rixon, but my fruit is not always so good. I try to blame it on the war, but sometimes I think if I had the courage of Esther, or perhaps even Paul, that things would be different in my life. But this is little comfort and no excuse. Even Satan and his demons believe."

After a long moment of shared silence, David asked, "May I pray for you, Lu?"

"I would be honored, Rixon," she said with tears in her eyes, surrendering her hands into his firm grip.

"Almighty God: You are the maker of the universe, of this planet and of Lam Uyen Lu. I come to You, Father, in deep supplication and humble prayer as the intercessor for Your precious daughter Lu. Father, she is trapped by the demonic spirits of war and fear. She is unable to resist this evil alone and seeks your divine guidance for the pathway she may use to escape the pit so that she can run to the shelter of Your embrace. Please, Father, provide her with the wisdom, the strength, and the opportunity to break these heavy chains and start a new life, free and secure in Your loving arms and covered by Your grace. I pray this miracle for Lam Uyen Lu in the precious name of Your Son, Jesus, who is for all of time and eternity our Rock and our Redeemer. Amen."

Lu was crying openly, and the puppy crawled from David's lap to hers, licking her face, causing both David and Lu to laugh and share a moment of comfort in the swirl of dangerous conflict.

"Lu, I must ask a difficult question. The chef tonight—he is VC, is he not?"

After a long thoughtful pause, "Yes, my brother. How did you know?" she said weakly.

"What is his mission?"

"He say he is here only to gather intelligence from the CIA and Special Forces soldiers by overhearing them talk when they are drunk. Some of the girls also tell him things the soldiers say when they are together and their tongues are loose after their passion."

"Lu, are you VC as well?"

"I am only afraid, Rixon. A weak woman caught in the war between the Americans and the Viet Cong. How am I to survive the conflict; how am I to protect my family if I do not curry favor with both sides? Will the Americans stay here forever to protect me or will they tire of the war like the French and leave me to the mercies of the Communists? Is this not what America has already done to your friends in the north of Korea?"

The truth of her words stung him deeply. "Lu, we know the chef only as VC1356. I recognized him from his photograph. He is a dangerous man, a killer, who has been responsible for the deaths of many Vietnamese and Americans. If you can help us arrest him, it will earn you great favor with the Americans. Anything more than that is in God's hands."

Lu was quiet, thinking. "He is in the house now, Rixon. That is what I came here to tell you. I believe he plans to murder Washington, Brown, and you in your sleep tonight. I do not know why; he told me not to ask. Rixon, his accomplices are holding my parents and younger sister at our home and say they will be killed if he fails in his mission tonight."

David rose, placed the sleepy puppy in Lu's lap. "Hurry to the military police officers in front and tell them these things. And please, Lu, keep my puppy safe."

David quietly ran up the steps to the verandah outside the dining salon, found an unlatched door and slipped inside. He made his way to the weapons check but found the room locked so he plucked a worn Louisville Slugger, autographed by his favorite homerun hitter, Rusty Staub, from its display, and crept past the library bar down the corridor into the guest wing, which contained many private bedrooms and baths. "Which one?" he wondered and crouched, forcing his ears to search the darkness for any sounds that might lead him to the assassin. And there! A muffled grunt, breaking glass, and the sound of flailing limbs.

David burst through the door and brought the Slugger down hard across the murder's forearms forcing him to cry out and breaking his hold on the garrote with which he was strangling Sterrette Brown. VC1356 recoiled from the blow and swung his leg in a tight arc, bringing his heel up to violently strike the side of David's head, causing him to fall sideways into a room service tray, breaking the wine bottle and scattering dishes crashing across the room. Rhonda's scream further alerted the occupants of the other bedrooms and many footsteps could be heard running toward the fight. The Cong saw only an opportunity to escape, used the bat to break the window, and plunged through the opening into the darkness and the chance to fight another day.

• • •

The After Action Debriefing occurred the next afternoon in the comfortable and spacious offices of CIA Station Chief Carlton Mayer. Washington, Brown, and Rixon were seated on expensive leather sofas, sipping coffee as Director Mayer began the session.

"The first thing I'd like to know is whose idea it was for the top American leadership of Phoenix—our best hope of uprooting and ending the Communist insurgency in South Vietnam and ultimately winning the war—to spend the night with three prostitutes in one of the most notorious bordellos in Saigon? Will, you're the senior officer here. Would you care to start?"

No one said a word. After a long tense moment, Mayer decided to take a more productive tack. "David, we believe the man you injured last night was none other than Major Quang Thong of the 198th Special Forces Regiment on detached duty from the Vietnam People's Army for special intelligence gathering and assassination projects in the south. The analysts believe the enemy has gotten wind of Phoenix and sent the major in to take all three of you out and torpedo the program before it even gets started, and I agree. Do any of you have an idea how this information found its way to the Communists?" Continued silence. "Who else have you been sleeping with?" Silence. "Any one of you can answer; I'm not restricting this to Major Washington."

Washington was becoming angry at being called to account for his actions. "Could we get serious Carl…"

Mayer cut him off. "It doesn't get any more serious than this, Will, and you damned well know it. The massacre at Signal Hill, Mercer, his team, and nearly three hundred Yards; an AC-130 Specter shot down; what is that? Thirty-five million and six crewmen? The massive enemy fortification of the A Shau and twenty-four thousand hostiles sneaking into your front yard right under your nose, and where the hell is your operations officer, Coats? MIA? KIA? Is he being tortured right now? Maybe spilling his guts about every damned thing we've been planning for the last year? You think a couple of B-52 strikes are going to clean up your little mess, Will? Let me remind you that all of this shit happened on your watch, Major, on your turf; and everyone with a star on his shoulder and a brain in his head between here and the Pentagon knows it! So please, Will, let's get very serious."

Washington was stone silent and seething. Brown and Rixon were trying hard to disappear into the deep leather of the couch cushions.

"Major, I don't enjoy the duty a bit, but I've been asked to give you three the message unofficially that the Pentagon is looking hard at your leadership. "Incompetent" was the word that got my attention in the telex. But it seems, Mr. Washington, that you have an important friend. COMUSMACV went to bat for you, and it's been agreed up the chain that you and your team will be allowed to continue in command of Phoenix for the balance of the year, and then they will conduct a flag-level evaluation. He's doing you a favor, Will; the channeled oral reprimand won't go into your file, and he's giving you a chance to turn things around, but they're tired of the bullshit. They want results, and they want them fast. This goes for all three of you."

The silence in the room was the absolute worst of it, and Mayer knew how to use it to maximum effect.

"Oh, before I forget, the woman we believe was orchestrating the whole pathetic episode has disappeared; Lam Uyen Lu and her family were seen late last night by their neighbors. They were leaving in a taxi around two this morning." Looking directly into Washington's eyes he added, "Et Tu, Mama Lu?" the silence thickened.

"Mr. Brown, you've been reassigned. Your travel voucher and new orders are here. Lucky man; seems like you're headed back to the States." Mayer tossed the manila envelope across his desktop, "Hold on—before you go, I want you to stay for a moment after I'm done with these two." Mayer shuffled some papers on his desk and found what he was looking for.

"And finally, Mr. Rixon. COMUSMACV says you made a favorable impression on Mr. White down in Wonderland. He also wanted me to convey his personal thanks for saving the lives of Mr. Brown and Major Washington," said the apparently amused station chief. "'It's good to know at least one of our senior our people can keep his fly zipped.' His comments, I'm reading them from my notes," he said with a slight chuckle. "And don't forget your dog when you leave, Rixon; you can pick him up on the way out. After everything he's been through, I'd hate to see him end up in somebody's stir-fry."

"Her, sir," said Rixon, trying to inject some levity into the situation to take a little heat off Washington and Brown.

"Did you say something?" said Mayer, taking off his reading glasses and looking across his desk to David.

"The puppy, sir; she's female. I've decided to name her Travis after William Barrett Travis, commander of the Texan garrison at the Alamo…sir."

There was a tense silence in the room again as Mayer was trying to decide whether Rixon was being insubordinate or merely factually accurate. "Special Forces guys are such a pain," His hard gaze fell back on Washington. "I can see why you wanted him on your team, Will."

Looking back at David, he said, "Captain Rixon, I'm afraid I have a bit of bad news for you as well. After his evaluation of your performance and because of the importance of the mission, COMUSMACV has decided that you are an essential element in the success of the Phoenix Program. Therefore, it looks like you won't be going home as you've planned. The commander in chief has issued National Security Action Memorandum Two Seventy-Three, which in part says that all senior military officers attached to Phoenix are committed by military law to remain in the theater for the duration of the conflict unless they are unable to physically continue service or until they are relieved of duty by their superior officer. Your copy of NSAM Two Seventy-Three and your new orders are in this envelope," he said, extending the manila packet. "I'm sorry, son. I know this comes as a blow to you and your family. There's a telephone in the office across the hall. You can use it to call home, if you wish."

There was a long silence in the room as Mayer allowed David time to absorb the news of his extended deployment and to ask questions or protest if he wanted, but David surprised them all by never saying a word in reply.

"All right, then. If there's nothing further, I suggest that both of you get the hell out of my office and win this stinking war, so we can all go home!"

• • •

When Washington and Rixon returned to Rana Dat, the countdown clock for Operation Widow Maker had run to just over forty-eight hours until the initial Arc Light Squadron was scheduled to begin its lethal Time Over Target. The Reeves AN/MSQ trailers had been airlifted to the site and the parabolic antenna was positioned so that the command guidance technician could make contact with the airborne electronic warfare operator approximately half an hour from reaching their assigned intercept point.

"El Tee, report," said Washington, as he and Rixon entered the crowded war room. "There's a serious glitch in Widow Maker, sir. The radar technician for the Miscue Seventy-Seven says he's having trouble interlocking their signal with the test bird orbiting at the intercept point. Sir, it's been the same with all our radio communications for the last couple of days. There's an intermittent source of strong RF interference coming from somewhere down in the A Shau, and just when we think we're going to get a lock on their position, it clears up, so we can't just call in a fire mission and be done with it. Someone's out there jamming our communications, Major, and it looks like we're going to have to send in a ground team to dig 'em out."

"What happens if the Reeves equipment isn't operational when the B-Fifty-Twos arrive on station?"

"Sir, the air force tells me they can still deploy their ordinance, but the impact accuracy from altitude diminishes so dramatically that they should probably scrub the mission and return to base. They could kill a lot of friendlies, sir. They could deploy from a lower altitude, say twenty thousand, but then the exposure to hostile fire goes up dramatically. It's your decision, Major."

"I damned sure don't want another expensive airplane shot down," said Washington in deep thought. "Recommendations?" he said to the room and after intense debate.

"Insert three hunter recon teams tonight with the equipment to triangulate the RF source, and add an interpreter for each team.

Capture me some NVA, get the truth out of 'em, and shut this thing down. Rixon, get your bush gear on. I want you standing by in a ship for interrogations when the teams make their captures. We need accurate intel, and we need it tonight!"

Rixon and a team of five Montagnard strikers were lounging on their rucksacks together alongside *Lady Killer*, feeding c-rats to Travis, and discussing proven dog training techniques, as Billy Jack Delgado and his flight crew monitored the radio for the first capture summons of the evening. David grew weary of the wait and the conversation, which had degenerated to discussing the feminine attributes of currently popular Hollywood starlets. He made his way to the bird and a talk with the captain.

"What's your take on this radio interference, Chief?" asked Rixon.

Delgado sat up, pushed his cap up a bit, and looked off into the distance for a moment. "Well, if ya ask me, and nobody has, I'd say it was somebody's attempt at Morse code, not very good Morse, mind you, but you can still pick out an SOS here and there, and then something that sounds like an attempt at coordinates and then nothing, just an open RF transmission that's somehow jacking up the Reeves technicians. But what the hell do I know, Captain? I'm just an old chopper driver. I pick 'em up and set 'em down where and when I'm told."

"It's been nearly two weeks since the Cong overran Signal Hill. You think maybe it could be some of our people still out there, trying to get our attention?" asked David.

"This off tha' record, Captain?" he asked and received the affirmation he was looking for.

"People I been hearin' talk say maybe Seven-MIKE has a leadership problem. Eighteen months ago, before he got hisself promoted, the troopers and Yards loved him; called him Wild Willie Washington and knew for sure if they got inta a scrape they couldn't handle, he'd be there personally ta back 'um up. The man looked after the A Shau like it was his mama's front yard; scared the shit outta tha' Cong. That's how we could police the whole damned valley and both borders with less than a thousand boots and just a few choppers. But then, Captain Washington became Major Washington, and now the troops been calling him 'Will He?' Washington."

"What's that supposed to mean?" asked a confused Rixon.

"You said it yourself, Captain; it's been near two weeks since the NVA overran Signal Hill and 'Will He' ain't done a damned thing about it. Men still layin' out there ain't even been put in tha ground."

They both turned their heads toward the cockpit radio as the jamming static resumed; ssssss; ss; ss; ss; ssss; ssss; ssss; ss; ss; ss; ssssssssssss…SOS!

Delgado and Rixon looked at each other in the dim red light of the flight deck. "Chief; start your engine, we're going for a ride. That's an order," commanded Captain Rixon, and in his best military Vietnamese, he addressed his squad of CIDC Strikers: *"Gear up! We're going to get Coats, Donny, and Scotty!"*

With Travis happily in the care of the children of the camp, *Lady Killer* came to operational RPM and asked tower permission to clear from Rana Dat, under call sign Radar Dakota Four.

"Negative, Dakota Four. Actual wants you on the deck ready to deploy for interrogation and translation."

Delgado looked at Rixon, who shook head, made a slashing sign over his throat, and keyed his helmet microphone. "Roger deployment, Dakota Four will be on standby over the ridgeline."

"Negative, Radar Dakota. Actual says stay put on the deck until assigned a vector and intercept point. Confirm message received."

Rixon keyed his helmet mic and made his best attempt at imitating the static: "sssssssssssss." He then reached into the cockpit and switched off the radio.

"Chief, you'll observe radio silence until after the insert. That's an order."

They flew east toward the coast and then southeast, paralleling the ridgeline of the eastern mountains containing the A Shau.

"Chief, take us along the eastern side of the mountain, and then we need ta find a place for a rope insertion about a mile or so downhill from the old Japanese tower. We'll start our search there. Coats told me he'd have everyone there the next day, and I know we've looked at it a dozen times a day for over a week, but we've got to have missed something."

"Captain, there's enough light for the insert and maybe a couple of hours to spare, but it gets dark fast on this side of the mountain. If we miss the window we may not be able to extract 'till first light unless you deploy a starlight flare to mark your location, and then you'll be a target for Charlie too," said a concerned Delgado.

"You mean we'll be in the same condition that Coats and his team have been in for a week?"

"Affirmative, Captain, I understand. We'll be at the insertion point in five."

The crew chief rigged the school bus yellow jungle penetrator on the starboard side of *Lady Killer* and lowered Rixon through the canopy into a clearing just over thirty feet below his hover. Going in, Rixon and Delgado both estimated their distance to the repeater antenna to be just shy of a kilometer.

With his team assembled tight on the mountainside, he waved Delgado off with a radio-telephone check and they were on their own. "The objective is to recon the radio tower quietly. VC cannot know we are here or we'll never get out alive. If Coats and the others are there, we'll find them. Let's move; we need to be out before dawn." The squad moved on Rixon's command.

Trained by Coats, the veteran strikers formed up around Rixon—for his protection and theirs—and moved quietly and carefully up to the ridgeline, avoiding mines and tripwires that the NVA had set to defend their rear. But really, the terrain featuring dense rainforests and sheer granite cliffs of a thousand feet or more kept them perfectly safe from a mass attack.

The point man signaled all cleared and the squad approached the small concrete building at the base of the orange and white radio tower, "Sir, we have searched the area and found no one," said the squad leader to Rixon. "The building is also clear."

Rixon walked around the tower, keeping an eye out for booby traps and looking for something, a signal, a sign of the survivors, anything that would give him a clue to the presence of Coats and any survivors. He looked inside the building and saw that a grenade had destroyed the equipment, yet there seemed to be a luminous glow coming from under the dark pile of rubble. He moved the debris and placed his hand on a medium-sized metal equipment cabinet for balance. "It's warm to the touch," he thought, and moving more rubble, he exposed what looked to be an intact American military-grade radio component. "It's from Hitman, that's how they're jamming us," he said aloud. The components were crudely interconnected to the original Japanese amplifier/repeater. "It's getting power from someplace," he thought and gently began probing the rubble, exposing a pair of buried electrical cables leading to the wall and then through the wall in a masonry weep hole. He turned to leave, and then he permanently disabled the radio with his Marine K-bar.

Exposing the buried wiring from the outside, Rixon informed his team that they were going to follow the buried electrical cables, which he hoped would lead them to the survivors of Signal Hill or maybe to the enemy.

Less than hour later and only fifty yards down the valley side of the mountain, they discovered that the cables disappeared under a large pile of stones, which seemed to be smoking and had the smell of diesel. David's heart sank; it was an enemy installation.

"There's an electrical generator located underground. It's got to be part of the NVA fortification system, probably caves and tunnels running all along the mountainside connecting the Communist gun positions," he said to the squad leader.

"Patrol! Everyone down!" whispered the leader, and in unison the soldiers flattened themselves in the shadows while the diesel exhaust floated above them and they watched a two-man NVA patrol walk by.

With combat hand signals, Rixon indicated that he and the squad leader would follow the enemy patrol, and that the balance of the squad was to remain concealed and wait for their return. The Communists followed the trail that roughly paralleled the ridgeline and then descended steeply into a manmade clearing that had been created in front of a cave opening guarded by only one man. The enemy patrol greeted him, stopped to talk for a moment, and then moved on out of the clearing into the bush beyond. The sound of the diesel generator could be heard deep inside the cave; just above the drone, they could barely hear the sound of a man screaming.

"We're going in," said Rixon slinging his M16 and unsheathing his K-bar.

The squad leader worked his way around the opposite side of the cave entrance and on exchanging signals with Rixon, ran as fast as he could across the guard's restricted field of view, drawing the sentry out of the mouth of the cave and into Rixon's concealed position, raising his AK-47 to fire. As the soldier was leveling his weapon, the coiled Marine lunged, savagely seizing and controlling his gun arm at his shoulder and driving the K-bar into and through his throat, severing his spinal cord, larynx, and carotid artery cleanly and killing the enemy instantly, quietly leaving the entrance to the cave unguarded. Rixon quickly disposed of the crumpled, bloody corpse. The assault and takedown was over in less than thirty seconds.

The squad leader and Rixon made their way through the entrance slowly and as the engine noise grew louder, covering their approach, they found they could also hear sounds of men talking in accented English followed by more screams. They crept farther into the darkness of the cave and past a double row of bamboo cages, covered tight with rough canvas, and stacked two high. They stayed next to the stack, moving low and slow toward the screams, and saw two armed guards at the edge of a pool of light. Beyond, under the bright central light, there were three Vietnamese, two standing near a man bound and shackled to a wooden post, and another seated at a small table, writing in a ledger. Beyond them at the far edge of the light near the generator was a group of men, bound and cowering in the shadows, pressing themselves toward the rear of the cave and as near to the generator as possible.

"Hit him again!" said the man at the table, and the torturer turned, toggled a switch, and sent electric current through the body of their prisoner, causing him to convulse and shriek in pain for a moment before they stopped.

"What is your mission?" screamed the man at the table in English. "Where are the others?"

"This is their interrogation operation, their version of Phoenix," thought David, as he retreated from the light and pushed his back into the stack of crates to think, when suddenly from behind, he felt a strong hand grip his shoulder. He jerked away, turned with his weapon at the ready, and was horrified to see darkly the filthy, contorted face of Lieutenant Tommy Coats.

Controlling his disbelief, Coats spoke to Rixon in a slight whisper, saying that each of the covered crates contained an American prisoner who had been interrogated by the NVA. That there were about fifty POWs in all, and that when the last of the men was questioned to the satisfaction of their captors, that they would be shipped across the border into Laos and traded to the Russians or Chinese for different sorts of munitions. An American pilot was of the highest value, worth one Russian SA-2 Surface-to-Air-Missile, and other captured Americans were traded for differing sorts of arms and supplies. Captured Vietnamese and CIDC strikers were worthless to the NVA; after interrogation and torture, they were merely murdered by their captors and tossed into a mass grave or left to rot in the open.

"That's Donny on the rack now. Scotty's up next," whispered Coats. "They're dead unless you get 'em out."

Rixon sent the CID squad leader to bring back the other four strikers, radio the request for an immediate evacuation, and then he used his K-bar to release the prisoners from their cages, "Can you fight?" he whispered to Coats, as he offered the AK he had taken from the sentry.

Coats joined Rixon in the prone position next to the front cage, taking aim at the two armed guards who were enjoying the torture show while the freed Americans began moving slowly and as quietly as possible toward the entrance. Watching the torturers intently and cringing as Donny wailed, David indicated to Coats that they would wait for the CIDC strikers to return to protect their rear. Then they would cover their escape, take out the enemy, and free the remaining prisoners.

"That's enough!" said the interrogator, rising from the desk, picking up his pistol. "He is of no use to us. Like all Montagnard dogs, he is soon to be a problem no more," he said, raising his weapon.

Both Rixon and Coats had their fingers on the trigger, but their weapons would not fire, and from the cave behind them they were shocked to hear the friendly greeting in melodious Vietnamese, "The chickens have all gone to roost, Nguyen Ngoc Loan. It is time for your evening meal and a night's rest. These prisoners will buy us much-needed arms and supplies from our Chinese brothers. Uncle Ho is pleased and sends his thanks for your good work. You are relieved."

David and Tommy watched in frozen disbelief as two North Vietnamese officers and a squad of five armed infantrymen walked directly past them, through the tunnel and into the large cavern and the harsh circle of the torturers' light. They patted the sentries on the back, joked for a moment with the interrogator, and sent them all off, again past Coats and Rixon, to the main camp and their supper. As the others worked to release the prisoners still bound in the generator room, the senior officer walked directly to David, bent down on one knee, and with a bright countenance and broad smile said in perfect English, "There will be no need for further bloodshed today. The Lord God Almighty has set you and your companions free."

The helicopter evacuation that night brought sixty-two men back from their deaths, or something worse, at the hands of the Communists. When Chief Delgado crisply flared *Lady Killer* in for the final touchdown, it was to the cheers of the walking wounded and the able-bodied, welcoming the victorious warriors home from a rescue action that was quickly becoming known as the "Miracle of Signal Hill."

For the combat soldier, trauma shared is trauma divided, and joy shared is joy multiplied; men under arms universally know this. So Major Washington's detachment from the camaraderie of the victorious homecoming and his absence from the debriefing seemed odd to David and the others, who said nothing as their commander merely watched the celebration through his office window, detached from the troops who had once loved him—unsmiling, seemingly deep in thought.

• • •

Unable to sleep again, even with help of strong drink, a fearsome supernatural darkness possessed Major Washington's inner voice. "You stupid shit! You pissant son of a bitch! Whitey's screwing you again, and you're too stupid to know it!" hissed the night terror. "Never trust the white man!" Washington tried to clear his mind and took another deep drink.

"Rixon's been doggin' your ass since Abilene! You should have made that score! It should have been you in the papers! You should have had that championship! You should have had that scholarship! You stupid bastard!" The searing pain flashed through his mind; he stifled a sob and choked back a scream. He drank again deeply.

"Even Coats and the Yards have turned their backs on you; who the hell needs 'em! Got to be strong now; He hates weakness and will abandon you. You will be adrift, without an ally. There are powerful forces building against you now that will eradicate everything you've worked for. You will be nothing and you will die in poverty, just like your bastard father, just like your bitch mother. You've got to do something to save yourself—something inventive, something bold. You've got to eliminate the threat. As long as they're alive, you'll never be safe. Be strong. Do it now!"

Deeply rooted, sharp, and ancient, the painful message radiated through Washington's mind, first chilling, then spurring his fear and driving him to rise, slip into his rain gear and walk the perimeter wire. It was late, the camp was sleeping; only the Montagnard sentries would be on watch.

"Don't worry. It's not too late. Nothing's changed. All of these things can still be yours. Everything you've dreamed of and more.

Heed His words. You haven't forgotten. They are written on your heart."

The Major walked out of his quarters and into the downpour, greeting the CIDC patrol, he began his late-night inspection along the wire taking mental notes of where the shadows fell dark and the terrain obscured the field of fire. He turned north, brushed past the trailers, holding the Reeves Bomb Directing Radar equipment and closely examined the sheer cliff of the mountainside that the French had blasted away to create the firebase, noticing the collected rain-water from the summit pouring out of large fissures in the cliff face. "This was in the corps geotechnical report; nothing to worry about." A slight glimmer in the security lights showed him the steel retaining pins, permanent and strong, securing the overburden against a cata-strophic avalanche. "Never happen in a million years," Washington said to himself and walked on through the sheeting rain. Tomorrow he would finally take action; he would remove the threat—without blood if possible—another trip to Saigon to establish his failsafe; to visit his mistress, Lam Uyen Lu.

• • •

David lay awake far into the night, comforted by the rain on the tin roof of the officers' hooch, his hand resting on the slumbering Travis, allowing the adrenaline to work through his system and thinking of the soldier he had killed at the mouth of the cave. Was he married; did he have children; what was his faith; did he know the Lord; should he have killed the sentry or could there have been another solution? And the strange soldiers in the cave; how could they not have seen him and Coats in the small tunnel? Why did they appear at the most critical moment? Why did their weap-ons jam? What of the cryptic message that Coats swears he didn't hear? And then the prisoners, sixty-two of them, some thought to have been KIA and several missing for more than a year; and the ease of their escape—lifting that many men onto hovering helicopters at night takes a long time and is very noisy. Surely someone should have seen them and fired. Finally, who sent the Morse code; neither Coats nor Mercer nor Magazzine nor Barnes nor anyone aboard Hitman knew a thing about it. The mysterious SOS was the only reason *Lady Killer* went back to search that night, and no one could tell them how it was even remotely possible. There were, of course, no answers to these questions but David pondered them all in his heart, and he remained unable to sleep for a long time.

• • •

Beyond the tremendous boost in troop morale and esprit de corps, the most significant result of the rescue at Signal Hill was COMUSMACV's decision to override Major Washington once more. They reset the operations clock for Widow Maker and increased air and ground patrols of the A Shau in hopes that they could find and liberate even more POW camps; yet another blemish on Washington's once gleaming reputation. And in the weeks that followed their return to Rana Dat, Lieutenant Coats, Donny, and Scotty spent their time healing, reconnecting, and training with Rixon to become the prototype interrogator-translator team for Phoenix. They prepared themselves for the mass of new enemy captives that would come into their possession with the culmination of Operation Widow Maker, starting a steady flow of data down the rabbit hole and into the hidden System 360 at Wonderland.

"You saved our asses out there, David, and I want you to know that none of us will ever forget it. Anything you ever need or want; just put the word out and we'll be there," breathed an emotional Coats, in the middle of yet another of Rixon's brutal timed runs. Travis, no longer a puppy and with the appearance of being more a large gray wolf than a city dog, ran alongside his master.

"I didn't do anything anyone else wouldn't have," said an embarrassed Rixon. "Tom, you were right there, weapon in hand ready to fight, ready to die if it had come to it," he breathed, holding pace on the trail winding up the steep hill.

"But that's just it, David," said Coats between deep labored breaths, "our weapons wouldn't fire. The VC just walked away and you led every one of us outta that hole without a shot being fired. That ain't normal; that's a miracle, David, and it was you done it for us. Hell, most 'a tha' Yards think you're some kinda' spirit warrior, can't be killed or some such," breath, breath. "What Donny and Scotty hear from civilians outside the wire is that there's boo-coo magic here at Rana Dat. That the Americans gonna win the war without firing another shot 'cause we're just gonna walk in and take whatever and whoever we want, and the NVA ain't gonna do nothin' 'cept thank us for our trouble."

Reaching the top of the trail overlooking Rana Dat, they started their downhill leg back to camp. "Tom, if what happened in that cave was a miracle, and I'm not saying ether way, then it was a work of the Lord and had nothing to do with me. Please accept this, and I'd appreciate it if you could spread that message to the Yards. They respect you and will listen to what you have to say."

The two men matched pace and Coats was feeling his strength return, his life renewed, and much more vigorous than his forty-five years should have allowed. From his point of view, another miracle he owed to Rixon.

"I get that you want to play this down, Captain, and I'll do what I can to shut it off but you still got sixty-one other men, twelve of 'em Yards, who are alive and breathin' free today 'cause you had the guts to fight your way into that hole in the ground. What the others say, especially the indigenous and their families, you know I can't do nothin' 'bout that," said Coats, breathing easier; the main gate and a hot shower were in sight.

"El Tee, just tell 'em I'm not any kind of a magician or miracle worker. Do the best you can and I'll handle the rest," said Rixon as he and Coats jogged into the camp and the smiles and waves of the men in the compound.

When David had finished his shower and returned to his room, he was met by two brawny military police officers, who came to attention and addressed him on his approach. "Captain David K.

Rixon, by order of Major William Washington you are confined to quarters, pending the investigation of violation of Articles Eighty-Five and Ninety-Nine and of the UCMJ; desertion and combat refusal. The investigating officer will schedule your interview as soon as possible. Sorry about this, Captain Rixon, but these are our orders."

• • •

The MACV Judge Advocate in Da Nang read the incident report presented to him by Major Washington, placed it open on the desk in front of him, and then picked up Rixon's service record. He spent a few minutes scanning the document and then swished away the flies that had settled on his lunch, and he used his Colt 1911 as a paperweight to hold the flapping documents in place. "My apologies for our surroundings, Major, they keep promising a hard-walled office with a roof and a door, but right now, I'm afraid, we're stuck in this rather dusty, drafty tent. It seems that military justice is a pretty low priority in a war zone."

Pause as he packed his pipe and looked again at the files before him.

"This Captain Rixon—his record is stellar; cum laude graduate at Penn State; Academic All American, All Southeastern Conference linebacker; clearly a patriot, volunteered for the Marines right after the Gulf of Tonkin; highest ranking in basic school, first in his OCS class, and first in his graduating class at the Defense Language Institute, and nearly a year in country as a Marine translator. Then the COMUSMACV drafted him, at your request, Major, I might add, TDY into the US Army Special Forces to assist in something called Phoenix. And now you're saying that the man disobeyed direct orders, refused a combat mission, and may even have deserted?"

"He's a loose cannon, Captain," complained Washington. "It started when his deployment status was altered by the commander in chief to 'duration.' They did it to every officer in Phoenix, by the way, and he's had an open hostility to the chain of command ever since. Then this incident. He used his rank to commandeer a Huey, its crew, and a five-man squad of CIDC strikers to fly off on a rescue mission that he pulled out of thin air, and he did it against my direct orders."

The lawyer sat back in his chair to place a psychological distance between himself and the major.

"Sir, something's happened and he's turned into a subversive—a malcontent—that I just can't trust, and his contempt for command authority has started to permeate the ranks down to the line troopers. Even the indigenous mercenaries in the MIKE force resist my orders. Something's got to be done or we'll completely lose control. To say nothing of the damage someone like Rixon could do to Phoenix if he isn't brought back into line. What the man needs is a full dose of military discipline, and that's why I've brought the charges."

The lawyer thoughtfully lit his pipe, took a long draw on the stem, leaned forward in his chair, and looked over the charges once more.

"Major, I'll be direct. The JAG Corps in theater is quite small, only four lawyers and six CID investigators to cover the entire war. The charges, as you've presented them, seem dubious, superficial, more a simple misunderstanding than anything like a mutiny. About the best I can do is authorize a field investigation, say two days of a CID man's time. If his report confirms your allegations, then I'll draw up the articles myself. Does that sound fair?"

"All I'm asking for is a fair hearing," said Washington, looking into the distance, "I'll be at the embassy in Saigon for a couple of days if you need me. Have your man contact my Lieutenant Casey Reid at Rana Dat. He's temporary CO until I get back."

• • •

"Of all the chickenshit, underhanded, backstabbing, double-dealing moves!" said Coats through the locked door. Standing between the

MPs, he was screaming at the top of his lungs, expressing his displeasure at the allegations as Rixon read them aloud. "You think you know someone and then they pull something like this; I outta just kick tha shit outta tha bastard!"

"Settle down, El Tee. Technically, these allegations are sort of correct. I did ignore his direct order to stay on station, and I did use my command authority to commandeer *Lady Killer* and the CDIC squad, and I did turn the radio off to terminate communication with the command structure. So in a way, I see his point," said David, trying to calm Coats and the others who might be disturbed by the investigation.

"But, David, he didn't know everything you did, and the results of your actions more than justify your conduct. Don't give in, damnit! You're in the right here, and everyone knows it, especially Major Washington."

• • •

Washington was infuriated when the JAG office in Da Nang found no evidence to warrant a prosecution of Rixon and refused to pursue the matter further, but he intended to play it out and use his command rank to bring his wayward captain to heel.

The time passed slowly for Rixon. His arrest allowed him out of his quarters only to use the latrine and for an hour to exercise each day. He read scripture and prayed. He wrote letters to Karen, to his parents, and his friends, telling them that the president had reclassified his deployment status to "duration," and that he would be allowed to see them only during authorized in-theater leave, meaning that they would have to travel to Guam or the Philippines or Saigon in order to visit. He also told them of his legal situation, and that he hoped to resolve the matter without the facing a court-martial and that in all likelihood he would be able to work it out with his commander, whom he respected and who he thought was just trying to do his job. He asked also for their prayers.

The day came when Captain Rixon would learn his fate, and he was brought to Major Washington's office in the Command Bunker at Rana Dat. Washington was seated alone at the large, barren conference table with only a legal-sized olive file folder placed in the center of the table. Rixon entered the room and stood at attention. The tension began to build instantly.

"At ease, Captain. Please take a seat."

"Let me start, David, by saying that I had you restricted to quarters for your own protection. There are forces at play in this war that you know nothing about, and your actions placed you and nearly every one of the people you commanded in serious jeopardy, so I did what I needed to do to protect you and them from making a dangerous mistake that could well have cost you your life. I wanted you to know that before we continue with the discussion. Are we clear?"

"Yes, sir, very clear. And thank you for your concern, sir."

"Because of the sensitive nature of Phoenix, your case was reviewed clear up the chain, all the way to Washington. I went to bat for you myself because you remind me a lot of when I first came to Vietnam and because you are so very valuable to the war effort. Well, it wasn't easy, but I talked the JAG out of pursuing the court-martial in exchange for an admission of guilt written in your own hand, a reduction in rank from captain to specialist fourth class, a signed agreement that places you under my direct supervision and restricts your movements to an operational military base for the duration of the conflict. In return, they agree not to press on to prosecution. I want to make it clear that this option that I have described is completely voluntary and you are under no obligation to accept it. Please take your time and read it thoroughly, David. It has serious legal ramifications for your future."

"With all respect, sir, I have been held without legal counsel for two weeks and do not feel competent to evaluate this offer. Major Washington, I formally request that an attorney be appointed to represent me in this matter before I consent to this or any other offer you might place before me."

"Now, David, listen to me. I've done the best I can to keep the damned lawyers out of this and now here you go refusing the favor and insisting on getting them involved."

"Two weeks, Will. I've been locked up in my 10 X 12 room for two weeks and for what? The only person I have seen who had any credentials at all was the CID investigator who interviewed me for less than an hour over a week ago. How am I to know what the JAG corps said or did about the whole thing? What I want now is to be released from custody and returned to duty. It's either that or the lawyer."

There was a long pause as the two men sat quietly assessing each other across the laminate tabletop.

"Very well, Captain, have it your way. You are free to return to duty. Dismissed!" said Washington with a sharp salute, bringing the conversation to a rapid close.

"What? Just like that? The whole damned thing just evaporates? This is the biggest crock of manure I've ever seen in my life..." Washington cut him off.

"Rixon, you ungrateful sawed-off, pizza-faced little whelp! It's crackers like you born white in a white world who take and take and never give back, and when the bill comes due, you drop it off on the backs of those of us who can't do anything except pay it with our blood 'n' bone 'cause that's all we got. Hell, that's all we ever had. So go on, Little Rix, go back to your white wife and your white kid and your fuckin' made up Mezkin family in that shithole town you're so fuckin' proud of. We'll make it through without you just fine, just like we always have, just like we always will," said Washington, furious at David's refusal of command authority and what he saw as an insulting personal rejection.

"Cracker? Skin color? Is that's it? Is that what this is about? Let me tell you something, Major Washington; it was soldiers just like you and me who used their blood to wash America clean of slavery a hundred years ago. Over three hundred thousand Union soldiers paid the price with their lives and what really pisses me off is men of color, good men, as strong and intelligent as anyone else, who refuse to accept responsibility for the liberty given to them by those troopers and spend their lives looking at themselves in the mirror and living like the slaves they never were! I'm supposed to trust you? What am I to you anyway, Major, except another cracker to screw on your way up, just like your white girlfriend in high school!"

Pierced to his inner core and sparked to a murderous rage, Washington launched himself over the table and hit a stunned Rixon full force in the face with the top of his head, knocking him backward off his chair to the floor with Washington on top flailing at him with his large powerful fists.

Rixon, dazed and with blood streaming from his nose and mouth, instinctively fell back on his close quarters combat training and used his size to his advantage. He pulled himself into a fetal ball, rolled free of his assailant, and sprang to his feet, pasting Washington on the side of his face and back of his head left, right, left, as the big man struggled to get to his feet.

Knowing he would lose the advantage if he allowed Washington to stand, Rixon viciously lunged at Washington, kneeing him in the ribcage repeatedly. The big man absorbed the blows and acrobatically swung his leg in a giant arc and knocked Rixon's feet out from under him, crashing through the office door and into the war room beyond.

Rixon used the momentum of the takedown to roll under the aggressor, punching him hard in the gut and elbowing him in the face, meeting Washington's counterpunch with his forearm and staying close to his torso to nullify the advantage of his vastly superior reach. Neither man noticed the crowd gathered in the war room to see the officers fight.

In a flurry of curses and groans, both bloodied men had struggled to their knees and were raining blow after blow directly into the face of the adversary when suddenly they were both drenched with three large buckets of cold water held by Sergeant Coats and the Montagnard scouts, Donny and Scotty.

"Beautiful, just beautiful; my heroes," said Coats with disgust, throwing his bucket to the floor. "My fuckin' heroes. If you two would get together and fight the Communists like you do each other we'd have Uncle Ho's head on a stick, the war would be over, and we'd be getting ready for our victory parade through downtown Hanoi!"

• • •

After he was treated by the medics and cleaned himself, Rixon was back in his rack, trying to calm down and think things through, and trying get some sleep. His body ached, his face was stitched, swollen, and throbbing. Travis alerted on the door and then there was a quiet knock. It was Will Washington.

"David, I know it's late, and I won't take long. I wanted to apologize for the fight this morning. I don't know what came over me. Of course you were right about everything. I hope you'll accept my apology and that we can remain friends. Also, I wanted to let you know that I've decided to process your relief orders. As soon as COMUSMACV signs off, you'll be officially released from Phoenix and free to rotate back to the States, pretty much on track with your original schedule. Of course, you'll have to sign a confidentiality agreement concerning elements of the program you've already been exposed to, but that's really it. Getting that done and finding your replacement should take less than a month, and then you'll be a free man."

Washington was smiling as he gave the news, but David could tell there was something wrong. The major wouldn't make direct eye contact, and when he did briefly, the look was detached and cold. The conversation chilled Rixon to the bone.

• • •

A week later the rainy season ended abruptly; the night was clear and balmy; the early evening sky was beginning to fill with stars when Will, David, Tommy, Donny, Scotty and their families joined Jeff and Suzanne for dinner at Christ in Asia to celebrate their delivery from captivity. The group lounged after dinner, watching the children play hide and seek with Travis, enjoying each other's company and the relative cool of the evening.

"We haven't see you in so long, Will, we were beginning to think you didn't like us anymore," said Suzanne with a playful pout.

"Aww, it's just the promotion, Suzanne—, lots of new responsibility to get on top of and the transition to different leadership here. They say I need to relocate at least to Da Nang and maybe Saigon so I guess this is one of the last times we'll have the opportunity for a visit," he said, standing, "Movie in the compound tonight, folks, at twenty hundred; it's a shoot-'em-up; *A Fist Full of Dollars*, compliments of COMUSMACV, flew it out from Da Nang this afternoon. Some of the men made the screen out of a bed sheet and they'll have to run the generator for power, so the sound might not be too good." He rose, extending his hand to Jeff, he gave a hug to Suzanne. Nodding to Coats and Rixon, he excused himself. "I'm off to Da Nang tonight for a meeting with COMUSMACV, should be back in a couple of days. Don't forget the movie—everyone's invited." And he was off.

"What's wrong with Will?" asked Jeff, "It's not like him to be that distant."

"He wasn't the same after Signal Hill," said Coats, "He thinks the whole thing is somehow his fault. I tried to tell him different, but he just closes me out. Something's come over him, it's like he's a different man. After the fight—well, he lost me." He looked at David. "I just can't understand the man anymore."

"You know him better than anyone, Tom. Is there anything we can do for him?" asked Rixon, "Or is this something he has to work through himself?"

"Well, since we're sitting in a church, why don't we say a prayer for the major—can't hurt, can it? Said Coats with a smile. And so the tiny circle of Christians gathered to pray for Major Washington while the children and Travis chased each other around and through the trees nearby.

Inside the wire at dusk, a rowdy crowd had gathered in the PT yard for the evening's entertainment and had seated themselves before the bed sheet screen, lashed to the perimeter fence on the north side of the compound, centered on the high point of the manmade cliff, the legacy of the French military engineers. Rixon, Coats, Donny, and Scotty were the guests of honor and seated side by side in the front of the audience. Everyone wildly waved as the Huey carrying Washington to Da Nang buzzed low overhead; the major was gone and the show began.

• • •

Informed by the unexpected intelligence bonanza received from a reliable source through a friendly intermediary in Saigon, the demolition engineers of the 198th Special Forces Regiment detached to special duty from the Vietnam People's Army, had been at work on the mountainside above Rana Dat for more than a week, concealing themselves in the deep rock fissures during the day and working quietly late at night. According to the sketches and patrol schedules provided by their benefactor, they placed cutting charges on the retaining pins and major expansion charges deeply inside the fissures and into the layer of expansive clay that the US Army Corps of Engineers had discovered could be a slippery slope, sending the entire side of the mountain crashing down on Rana Dat if there was "seismic activity of sufficient force to start the landslide." The engineers had designed a retention system to pin the overburden in place just in case there was an earthquake while the base was in use. The American geotechnical engineers felt the chance of it happening was so slim that it wasn't considered as material to their final report and was listed only in the footnotes. It was, after all, a temporary wartime fortification that would be abandoned to the jungle after the conflict. The report never considered intentional demolition.

Of course there was a chance that the VPA sappers could ignite their charges and nothing would happen. The American helicopters would surely splatter their bodies over the face of the mountain, carrion for the jungle creatures, putrefying in the tropical sun. But isn't that the sort of bargain war demands?

• • •

As the movie began, David noticed that many of the CIDC strikers had their M-16 carbines with them at the show and supposed that they felt safer after dark with their weapons at the ready; perfectly understandable. The screen flickered to life; he placed his hand on Travis the wolf-dog, and settled into the guitar music and haunting whistle that accompanied the opening credits.

On the screen the dusty stranger dressed in jeans, Mexican serape, and broad-brimmed western hat approached a group of dangerous men. "Listen, stranger. Did you get the idea we don't like to see bad boys like you in town? Go get your mule. You let him get away from you!" The other men laughed heartily at his taunt.

"See, that's what I want to talk to you about. He's feelin' real bad," said the stranger, taking a puff from the stump of his small cigar.

"Huh?" said the bully with a question in his voice.

"My mule. See, he got all riled up when you went and fired those shots at his feet."

"Hey. You makin' some kinda joke?" said the cowboy bully standing up straight, challenging the stranger.

"No. See, I understood that you men were just playin' around, but the mule just doesn't get it. Course, if you were to all apologize…," the gang of bullies laughed loudly.

With a simple flute note and the stranger escalated the confrontation by flopping his serape over his shoulder to expose his six-shooter, "I don't think it's nice you laughin'. See my mule gets the crazy idea you're laughin' at him. Now if you'll all apologize, like I know you're going to, I might convince him you really didn't mean it."

The onscreen tension escalated into a crescendo releasing a barrage of real world rifle fire into the bed sheet screen from the audience and a round of laughter and cheers from the crowd as the western bullies were felled by the stranger, with help from the sharp shooters of the 7-MIKE Civilian Irregular Defense Corps.

After the crowd settled, the movie continued. Coats whispered, "I guess I soulda told ya, Captain, but the Yards ain't all civilized like you and me. They tend ta let off their steam different than us round eyes. Scared the crap outta me the first time they done it!" Both Tommy and David were smiling.

• • •

While 7-MIKE was distracted by their movie, the Communist demolition team had moved off the rocks and connected the explosive charges to their detonation equipment hidden in the jungle overlooking the Rana Dat. Their commander was moving his ground force into place surrounding the village and would give them the signal to blow the ridge when he was ready for the attack. The Reeves Radar equipment must be destroyed at any cost. The destruction of Rana Dat, the Montagnard village, and the Christian missionaries would be considered a bonus even though their agreement with the source of their intelligence specified that there were to be no survivors.

Far into the screening, Travis alerted, stood, and ran toward the main gate. David noticed first one man and then another stand and leave the audience following in Travis's path, walking through the gathering without disturbing anyone. Another man came to David and whispered into his ear. "Jeff and Suzanne need your help." He jogged after the men who had already left the crowd.

David poked Tom and both scouts, "Get your gear and weapons. Meet me at the front gate, double-time it."

Travis met the foursome, and they were halfway up the trail to the mission when they were knocked flat by the blast wave expanding off the rocky ridgeline. David rolled over on the dog to see the lights of the camp glint through the dust cloud off the massive rock face of the avalanche in the split second before it crushed Rana Dat and put out its lights forever. Simultaneously they came under withering attack by a large hostile force firing on them from concealed positions in the jungle. David turned toward the enemy positions in time to see the squad of seven CIDC strikers firing on the Communists flank and giving Rixon's group enough cover to escape the kill zone. The entire squad poured defensive fire into the jungle positions.

The CIDC commander, his face aglow with the goodness of heaven, turned to Rixon. "Rana Dat is lost, David. There is nothing more for you here. The Prince of Asia is too strong for you to resist now. The Lord commands that you and your friends run west along the ridgeline to a place of safety that He will show you. Do not despair; you will see your family again."

"What about Jeff and Suzanne—we must save them!" complained Rixon.

"Please go, David," said the smiling commander as he placed his glowing hand on David's shoulder, "We will hold the enemy here for as long as we are able and do what can be done for the Campbells. Go now, while you can," the commander pointed the way into the jungle and David was able to see a slight glow on the ground, illuminating the path before them. He looked at the commander once more and then recognized him from the cave.

A fusillade of hostile return fire tore through the commander and the squad, grazing David's shoulder and spurring him to action.

"EL Tee! On me!" David shouldered his pack, grabbed Travis by the collar took his weapon and led his team on a dead run into the jungle darkness, following the glowing path set before him."

By David's estimate, his small squad had traveled four miles up the trail onto the mountain ridgeline and were moving parallel to and above the site of the landslide when he called for a five-minute rest. Passing his canteen to the others, he looked back down his path and saw that the glow was dissipating, concealing after they passed to deter their pursuit.

"Captain, if ya don't mind my askin', do we have a plan or are we just runnin' away?"

"Lieutenant, the plan is to save our lives from the VC so we can do something to help any survivors of the attack, and then we need to figure out what happened to Rana Dat." Fishing out a map and penlight, he said, "Right now we need to know where we are."

The four men gathered in a low, tight circle to conceal the penlight from view. "Looks like we're about here, maybe ten klicks southeast of the Laotian border and probably four klicks northwest of Rana Dat," said David. "Rules of Engagement say that we can't cross over the border so what we need to do is find a way down the hillside so we can double back to the base to help the survivors and find a radio so we can call in for backup and evacuation."

"Tom, Donny, Scotty. I need to ask you something," said David. "Did you see the squad defending our retreat? Did you see their commander speak to me?"

No one had seen anything. They had been dazed from the blast wave, and other than the VC firing, they relied entirely on David to get them to safety. And no one even saw the glowing trail they were standing on—no one, that is, except David Rixon. His head was spinning. "They must be angels," he said out loud. "Look, men, I know this will sound crazy but the reason we made it out of the ambush is because the Lord sent his angels to our defense. Trust me; we'll get out of this." Travis alerted to their rear.

TAK, TAK, TAK! A tight burst of AK-47 fire whizzed over their heads and impacted the trees beyond, causing them all to duck reflexively.

"Break's over! Follow me and stay close. I see the path before us!" He and Travis led the way into the darkness.

Days later and well across the border into Laos, the bright line that the angel had set down to guide them had dimmed; the terrain had become fragmented, rocky, and open without any vegetation to conceal them from their assailants. Their pursuers were clearly catching up, even exchanging random shots once across the deep canyon that separated a switchback Rixon was forced to take after reaching a dead end.

David stopped to take a compass reading. "None of this is on the map, El Tee. We're just about out of rations, we're running low on ammo, we're cut off from reinforcements and without a radio we can't call for an evac. Any suggestions? Donny, Scotty?" asked the perplexed Rixon.

"Attack!" said Coats, reacting with a jolt to the tremendous clap of thunder and lightning flash that rolled down on them from the mountaintops. "Cap, it's been nearly a week and it's clear they don't intend to break off the chase. They mean to either kill us or capture us, and I for one have got a gut full of it. I say we stand and fight, get it over with quick so we can get back to Seven-MIKE and do what we can to put things back together. Or go on home to meet our Maker. Either choice is better than runnin' away like a bunch of little girls." Coats set firm and the scouts agreed. Large drops of tropical rain began to fall.

"All right, Tom. You got a battle plan in mind?"

"I was hopin' you'd ask, 'cause I been noodlin' it for a while. Have ya noticed that these switchbacks are all about the same? They fold in and loop back sorta like a sidewinder pushin' hisself across a Sonoran sand dune. About a klick down and then klick back up. They been tryin' ta time their chase to set up a rifle squad at the closest point on the far ridge so when they get line of sight on us as we pass they can take a shot or two. The rest of 'em keep on chasin', hopin' the guns can pin us down long enough for 'em to catch us from behind. They gain a little ground each go around. They're patient, ain't got nothin' else better ta do, I 'spec. Sooner or later they'll catch us 'n then we'll be in tha shit. There's four 'a us and twenty 'a them. It's what I'd do if it was me."

They waited as Coats, watching the black clouds begin to obscure the peaks towering over their position, retrieved the pouch of Red Man from his rucksack and packed his jaw while focusing on the terrain in front of them.

"Captain, I propose we shift the paradigm. They're overconfident. They've split their force in two. About five in the trailing rifle squad and then about fifteen bird-dogging us. I'm thinkin' you 'n' me outta peel off, slide down the canyon wall a little and send Donny 'n' Scotty on ahead like we been doin'. The main force will continue to follow, pass by us, and then we'll ambush the guns, take 'em out, and then Donny and Scotty will have time ta slide down the canyon wall from over there," he said, pointing to the opposite wall. "Then we'll meet in the canyon and hightail it, give 'em the slip, 'n' head on back to our AO. Cap, I don't know if ya noticed tha change in the feel of tha air—the smell is different, somethin's wrong. This whole danged place just sorta gives me tha creeps. Like somethin' evil lives around here. I'm ready ta get tha heck out!"

Lacking a better plan of his own and also tired of running, Rixon agreed with Coats and they divided their remaining ammunition, food, and water equally, put on their rain gear, and sent the scouts on ahead with Travis. "You think this will work, Tom?" asked Rixon.

"How the hell should I know? You're the brains. I'm just a grunt with lieutenant's bars," he said with a laugh that caught Rixon off guard and then made him smile.

"Brains? You think I got brains? I'm just a dumb jock with captain's bars!" Both men were laughing as they lowered themselves into the canyon, found a shallow recessed ledge hidden in the shadows and, temporarily out of the pouring rain, they prepared to fight for their lives.

Less than an hour later, over the rain and thunder, they heard but couldn't see the fifteen enemy soldiers moving by at a crisp pace on the trail above, just as Coats had predicted. From his position, David was able to overhear the coordinating radio traffic between the pursuit unit and the trailing shooters, looking across the stone canyon, he confirmed that Donny and Scotty were still out of sight. "Radio says shooters are trailing the main force by about an hour. You ready to do this, El Tee?"

"Roger that, Captain." Tommy looked over to David. "Semper Fidelis."

Coats had field-stripped his weapon for a quick cleaning. "I figure we let 'em pass, then climb up 'n' take 'em down from behind. They'll never know what hit 'em. It's the most humane way."

"After all they done for us at Rana Dat, it doesn't seem exactly fair," said David, honing the edge of his K-Bar. "I was thinking something more personal, more respectful of our adversary; close quarters, edged weapons. The storm will help us send 'em off to meet the Lord real quiet like; we can save our ammo for the firefight."

The essential nature of war has been famously described as a trinity of primordial violence, hatred, and enmity, a naturally generative force; the play of chance and probability within which the creative spirit is free to roam. Just as Rixon and Coats had made it up from the rim and set themselves for the ambush, a canine form emerged, flashed in front of their position, and clamped its powerful jaws on the hand of an enemy soldier. The grenade spun free, flew backward, and detonated to the rear of the leader injuring or killing the four sopping-wet soldiers who had approached quietly from the rear of their position, nearly an hour before their expected arrival.

Even with the confusion of the explosion and the rapid recall of the fifteen solders who had advanced past the ambush point, Travis viciously tore through the flesh to the bone and refused to release the hand of his nemesis, the chef from Mama Lu's, VC1356 - Major Quang Thong of the Vietnam People's Army. In a desperate attempt to save his arm from the animal, he screamed for his men to follow and threw himself and the dog into Coats and Rixon, toppling everyone over the rim and down the steep side to the canyon floor beyond.

The fifteen followed urgently but carefully, picking their way down the wall and taking an occasional shot at Donny and Scotty who were already on the floor and rushing to aid their leader who was being guarded by Travis, standing over the severed hand of the man who had once served her up on a silver platter. The handless major lay writhing in pain, bleeding to death only feet from the dazed and bruised Coats and Rixon.

The downpour increased its intensity and the lightning flashed sideways, grounding into the mountainside as collected water from the high plateaus began flooding into the canyon, causing it to fill rapidly with floodwater. Scotty and Donny urged Coats and Rixon to their feet to escape the hostile troops and the rising flood, when they were caught by a head-high wall of water that washed them against the canyon wall and downstream into a hidden cave entrance, down the cavern, and up onto a ledge, leaving them high and dry as the flood waters rapidly receded. Travis paddled up to the ledge, crawled onto dry land, and was shaking herself dry when they were startled to the core by a terrifying rumble from high above. Then a gigantic crash of lightning triggered a tremendous landslide that sealed them into the cave, safe from the flood and from the enemy, isolated from the world, trapped and totally dependent on the Prevenient Grace of the Lord God Almighty.

• • •

How long had it been—a month, six weeks? Nearly everyone he had known at Rana Dat was gone. Coats and Rixon were supposed to be at the movie that night with the rest but then there was the captured VC report of a firefight at the mission just after the demolition. The 198th had reported that an assassination team had pursued four male survivors into Laos, then nothing. No word from anyone in weeks. But his stay at the Continental made all of that seem insignificant; soft bed, clean sheets, hot coffee, room service, and the woman. Nothing on earth like Vietnamese women; so exotic, so responsive. "Good morning, my darling," she whispered into his ear. "You were magnificent last evening, but, lover, its nearly ten, and they'll be here soon. Wouldn't you like a shower before the meeting?"

Lu brought an oversized cotton bath towel, his freshly starched uniform, and glistening combat boots from the bed chamber into the grand marble bath and laid everything out to her satisfaction. There was a knock at the door, and Will heard his mistress invite their guests onto the generous fourth-floor terrace for coffee and brunch.

"Let them wait a bit," he thought. "They're the ones who wanted the meet, and everyone knows why. With Phoenix in operation, they won't be able to make a move without my approval, and it's gonna cost 'em. My failsafe and pension plan all wrapped up in one shiny package." He looked at his smoothly shaven face in the steamy mirror, flashed himself a winsome smile, stood at attention for himself, checked his decorations, and sucked in his gut for the military tuck. Then he strode into the room to meet his new business partners.

Lu stood, took his arm, and escorted him to the terrace. The four men stood formally, expectantly. "Major William Washington, I am pleased to present Special Agent Harrison Whitehead of the American Federal Bureau of Investigation, Agent Clarkson Green of the American Central Intelligence Agency, I believe you know our old friend Agent Sterrette Brown, and finally Mr. Albert Vazquez, Deputy Director of the United States Department of Agriculture, all the way from Washington in America!

Washington smiled as he made eye contact with each man, shaking hands firmly, looking Whitehead deeply in his eyes with a secret sense of recognition, and taking an instant dislike to the soft clammy hands and limp wrist of the kid from the USDA. Will invited them to sit while Lu began to serve.

"How are you finding Saigon?" asked the host of Agent Whitehead while taking a sip of hot tea.

"Major, why don't we skip the small talk and cut down to business," said Whitehead firmly. "As you well know, our operators are on the ground taking the necessary steps to seize control of the poppy production and heroin output in Thailand, Burma, and Laos—what some people call the Golden Triangle. We plan on moving large quantities of product on the Mekong River through your AO for loading on oceangoing vessels in ports along the coast. We have a special interest in the port of Saigon."

"Five percent," said Washington, looking directly at Whitehead.

"What? What do you mean?" asked Whitehead.

"You need unfettered access to my rivers and ports to move your dope to market. The toll for that access is five percent right off the top. My terms are simple: deposits of American currency into my Swiss account on the first and fifteenth of each month and you can move any damned thing you want down the Mekong and load it on

any ship that can make it to in the harbor," said Washington, survey-
ing his guests sternly.

Whitehead smiled. "I think we can do business, Major, but
you may be overselling your services. Everyone knows that the
Viet Cong control the rivers after the sun goes down. Are you
saying that your Phoenix group can guarantee their cooperation
as well?"

Washington gave a nod to Lu and she left the terrace. "Not
exactly, Special Agent. But you might say that I have recently formed
a new business alliance that we will find mutually beneficial."

Lu led the way as another man followed her to the terrace,
"Gentlemen, may I present Major Quang Thong of the One Ninety-
Eighth Special Forces Regiment, Vietnam People's Army."

The major smiled and extended his left hand to Sterrette Brown.
"Sir, I believe we've met before in a different capacity. Pardon my
rudeness, but as you can see, I am a different man now than I was at
that time," said the major, holding up his freshly bandaged stump.

• • •

Donny was able to hold on to his rucksack through the flood and
clicked on his small penlight, partially illuminating what they perceived to be a very large and very dark cavern. "What the Sam Hill
is that smell...smell...smell!" boomed Coats. Startled by his echo,
he regained his consciousness in an uncomfortable new reality that
featured the unmistakable aroma of a dead skunk.

"Batutut," whispered Scotty wide-eyed with fear etched across his
face, placing his hand on Coats's shoulder. "Forest man, untamed
spirit. Haunt dark jungle, are not men but something different,
something evil. Sir, we leave this place. It their mother's nest!"

"El Tee, sit rep," said a groggy Rixon sitting up and trying to
come to his senses.

"Captain, it appears all four of us came through well enough but
we've lost our weapons and most of our supplies in the flood. We're

safe enough for now, but we need to find a light source and another way out. The way we were washed in here is closed forever."

ROOF! ROOF! ROOF! They could hear Travis in the dark distance barking rapidly, clearly confronting something dangerous. ROOF! ROOF! ROOF!

"Captain, I suggest we gather ourselves and find your dog. She may have found the way back to the surface," said Coats, helping his commander to his feet and urging Donny into the point position. "Lead on, Donny. We're right behind you."

The squad moved forward single file, each man's left hand on the shoulder of the man in front of him, straining to make out objects in the darkness that appeared in the penlight to be large roughly carved stone cylinders. Donny was leading them through a maze-like arrangement toward the sound of the excited canine.

They passed out of the large cavern, through a carved passageway decorated with undecipherable hieroglyphic symbols, through a large decorated gate into a smaller chamber with a lower ceiling, and then paused at a forbiddingly dark doorway, comforting the frantic Travis. Everyone, even the dog, was held by the nauseating, evil, stench emanating from within, as if the odor itself was a bolted door. Rixon plucked his compass from its sheath and tossed it gently into the darkness. From somewhere deep below them there was a mechanical groan and a sharp squeak. Then from the darkness before them there was a whirr and a quiet clicking, and then all at once, the light came on.

Before them was a domed room illuminated softly by a concealed light source that glowed from behind translucent ceiling panels inscribed with a decorative motif that appeared to be an orbital view of an alien planet. They noticed that air was also moving through the room, removing the skunk-like odor that was clearly emanating from the half-rotten, half-mummified semihuman corpse supported on a large reclining surface located in the center of the dome; all the more impressive because of its size.

"Twelve feet! The thing's a good twelve feet tall! I just paced it off, and I swear, the damned thing is as least twelve feet. Lord God in heaven, what in the world have we stumbled in on?" pronounced Coats as he looked at the giant in jaw-dropping astonishment.

Rixon tentatively approached the relic, leaving the scouts holding Travis at the door, and moved close enough to see that the body was clothed in a leather-like substance. It wore some sort of coverings on its feet and lower legs, boots of some sort, thought David, and it was armed with a gigantic broadsword that he estimated to be nearly six feet in length. The weapon rested ceremonially on the torso of the corpse, hilt just under what appeared to be the mandible and the tip ending just below the groin. "Tom, you think this is some sort of burial crypt, maybe like you read about in Egypt?"

"Possible, Captain, but if that's what the place is, then what do you make of these things?" he said, indicating very thin tablets of a semitransparent glass-like material inscribed with golden patterns and annotated with more of the alien hieroglyphs. Most of the tablets, measuring roughly twelve by eighteen inches and something less than one-half inch thick, were positioned standing on their ends in a precisely grooved rail, a segmented arc that ran around the perimeter of the room at head height. There was a low stack of the panels sitting on the polished red floor, and then David noticed one installed in a metal frame, positioned approximately four feet above the head of the corpse. The frame was attached to the inclined surface by some sort of concealed fasteners.

"Tom, the room reminds me a little of the McDonald Observatory near Fort Davis except instead of an astronomical instrument, they installed this table." David stepped up on the low circular platform that surrounded the table and the floor in front of the entrance began to rise, setting off a furious reaction from the wolf-dog and her handlers. Rixon stepped off the platform and the floor reset to the open position.

"El Tee, I think we'd better withdraw until we can figure out what this place is. If we get trapped, we could well end up just like our big friend here."

The explorers stepped away from the doorway and were startled by the unannounced illumination of another room directly behind them. They peered in from the threshold and saw a room identical to the observatory but with a grouping of thirty-six irregularly sized stone cylinders arranged in a precise geometric pattern across the polished red floor. David judged the containers to be three to six feet in diameter and vary in height from five to eight feet. Unlike those they had passed in the cavern, these units were without their carved coverings, their contents exposed. Those arranged at the perimeter of the room contained a white crystalline powder, while those toward the center were filled with metallic cubes, measuring approximately six inches a side. They were precisely inscribed with hieroglyphics that featured a deliberately rough anthropomorphic symbol that David thought might be a code key that could be used to decipher the language. And perhaps most intriguing, through the thick layers of dust, they thought they could see the patina of gold bullion.

"Gold! The jars are filled with cubes of gold! Captain, this an alien gold factory! They were making gold out of salt or whatever that white stuff is!" exclaimed Coats, "We're all rich! Just one of those cubes could by a house, hell a mansion; a dozen could set a man up for a lifetime!"

"Hold on, El Tee. First of all, nothing here belongs to us, and second of all, getting greedy could end up getting us all killed. We have no idea what sort of technology is operating in this place, what it's for or even if we're alone. The big boy next door could have friends watching the place who haven't figured out we're here yet. We didn't exactly come in the front door now, did we?"

They backed away from the entrance and then there was another light from above, this time showing them a towering stairway up as far as they could see and away from the nauseating stink again emanating from the observatory. Travis was straining at her collar, wanting to run up the stairway. "Release the dog, Scotty," commanded the captain, and away she went, the group following, traversing the gigantic knee-high stair risers cautiously, deliberately, looking for danger and alert to a possible attack at every step. During their ascent, they passed several niches carved into the granite of the mountain and could only guess at their intended use. One was clearly a dormitory with sleeping accommodations for perhaps twenty or more human-oids of the size they had already discovered. There were many smaller cells, perhaps private alcoves or overlooks, positioned at the ends of long shaftways that led to the edge of the mountain and featured small visual penetrations with views out to the landscape and open sky. Rixon judged them large enough for a man to squeeze through to escape the labyrinth if they found themselves trapped, though the fall would be fatal if there was nothing for a human hold onto after an escape.

Travis rejoined them after they had ascended to the final stair-way landing and were taking a break before beginning to move up a steep incline they hoped would lead them to the surface. They could feel cool air moving past them from below and along their obvious line of egress.

"Wonder how far up we are," said Coats as he dropped a small pebble into the void between the stair runs, "One-one thousand, two-one thousand, three-one thousand…" he counted the freef-all of the pebble, "eleven-one thousand, twelve-one thousand." Pop! "Captain, my little rock just had a twelve-second freefall. If I remember my math classes from Roswell High, that means we just climbed around, lemme see, that'd be about twenty-three hundred feet of stairs, and I don't know about you, but that makes me want to eat the pig, the whole pig, and leave nothing behind. That is if we had ourselves a pig. Scott! What ya got in your rucksack that won't bite back?"

Scotty spread the contents out on the surface of the polished stair landing: two loaded M16 magazines; one M61 fragmentation grenade; one M18 Claymore antipersonnel mine; one T137 White Star Cluster rocket-propelled signal grenade; one M18 smoke gre-nade, red in color; one M7 bayonet with leather sheath and mag-nesium fire starter; one compass and map kit; one pocket New Testament KJV provided by the US Army rotating chaplaincy service out of Da Nang; one pair of M-19 field binoculars in olive drab case; one right-angle olive drab flashlight, batteries dead; one coil of one hundred feet braided nylon parachute chord; one rubber-coated fabric rain poncho; one ERLD tropical hat; two pair wool socks; one pair cotton muslin boxer shorts, size small; one M1956 canteen with stainless steel nesting cup, one quart, nearly full; three packages grape-flavored Kool-Aid (Red Cross issue); and finally, from the very bottom of the pack, three individual combat ration meals, pork steak, turkey boned, and ham and eggs chopped.

"Damn, Scott, the cupboard's nearly bare, ain't it?" said Coats with a grimace. "Captain, I vote we skip lunch today and move on to see if we can't get ourselves outta this little rat maze. Maybe we can catch ourselves somethin' ta eat in the jungle. Donny here's the number one trapper in all of Laos. Ain't that right, Donny?"

"El Tee! You know I number one trapper. Donny Number Two!" said Scotty with a smile, repacking his sack and getting mentally ready for another hike.

"Their morale's still high," thought Rixon. "Good. That may be the difference in our getting back alive or not. Was that dead thing we found trapped too? Did it just give up, lay back, and accept death when it finally came?"

He whispered a prayer so no one else could hear. "Lord, our lives are in your hands."

After another two hours of walking up the polished, dusty incline and following the ever-tightening switchbacks, Travis bolted ahead: BARK! BARK! BARK!

"She's found something again, just up ahead."

"El Tee, let's spread out as much as possible—one well-placed grenade would get us all."

They approached Travis slowly and were relieved to discover that she had at last found the exit, partially blocked with large timbers and stones that had collapsed to bar the entrance. Through the cracks they could see blue sky and smell the fresh mountain air flowing into the tunnel through the voids.

Coats and Rixon examined their surrounding and found evidence of an attempt to clear the passageway, piles of large stones and heavy timbers stacked away from the entrance and then brownish-red marks and deep scratches on the remaining large timbers and boulders that held them in place.

"He was trapped. Tried like hell to get out, even clawed with his fingers 'till they bled. Then just laid down and died in the observatory," pronounced Lieutenant Coats. "Helluv a way to go. How long you figure it takes?"

"Humans can go five to ten days without water and twenty to forty days without food. Goliath downstairs—who knows how long it takes something like that to make the trip," replied Rixon, examining the obstructions. "Whatcha think, El Tee?"

"I think we got a Claymore, a fragmentation grenade, sixty rounds of 5.56 NATO, and probably one shot to blow an escape path through that big pile of junk. So we better use that mathematical mind 'a yours ta figure out just where ta place our ordinance," said Coats with a confident smile, watching Rixon and the concerned frown grow over Rixon's face. "Relax, Captain; with your brain and my know-how, we'll be outta here in a jiffy!"

Before the smoke had cleared, Travis, Scotty, and Donny charged through the smoldering debris followed by Coats and then Rixon just in time to avoid another catastrophic collapse of the landslide that had sealed the entrance for a thousand years, or more.

Free and safe, the squad took deep breaths of clean, sweet air and began to notice their surroundings; half in and half out of an ancient structure built into the base of the mountain summit with a panoramic view over of the Laotian countryside and a long clear vista to a glittering point on the far horizon. Rixon fished the compass and map out of Scotty's rucksack, made a few calculations, noting time of day and the long shadows of late afternoon with a grease pencil on the map face. He didn't like his first answer and reworked his math.

"El Tee, unless I'm completely disoriented or I busted the equation, that little jewel on the horizon, north-northeast of our position, is the North Vietnamese capital city of Hanoi. Could you check my numbers, please?"

"Captain, your math checks; that little bright spot has got to be the hometown of the biggest enemy you 'n' me got in the whole wide world: Ho Chi Minh himself."

While the round-eyes stood gaping at the horizon, the scouts and Travis busied themselves making camp. Not wanting to venture into the forbidding alien structure at dusk, they constructed a four-man, one-dog lean-to made with the smaller branches from the debris pile and weatherproofed with Scotty's poncho. They collected dried limbs from the debris pile to build a welcoming campfire started with the magnesium bar and sharp knife edge. For the evening meal, C-rats portioned appropriately for a four-man, one-dog celebratory feast. Coats and Rixon approached, happy to see the progress of the scouts, especially after so many nights of a cold camp. They all sat cross-legged in a circle around the fire, Travis the wolf-dog lodged happily between Rixon and Coats.

"Scotty, could you hand me your Bible?" asked David, "Donny, could you mix up a package of your Kool-Aid in the canteen cup? And, Tom, could you open a tin of white bread from one of the C-rats?

"Men, we've endured ten days of deprivation on a hostile trail. Our friends and brothers in arms have been murdered; we're cut off from our own army that probably believes we died at Rana Dat with everyone else; we've survived a major firefight; we've been tracked, hunted, ambushed, and survived close-quarter combat with a superior force; we were pushed over a mountainside, nearly drowned in a flash flood, trapped by an avalanche in an ungodly cavern with a giant dead body of God knows what origin, and now we've been delivered into the glory of this beautiful, starlit evening, a literal mountaintop experience. Thank you all for your gallantry under fire, for your faithfulness under extreme conditions, and your willingness to sacrifice yourselves for your brothers just as Jesus Christ did for all mankind. In acknowledgment of these fantastic events, I believe it's time to properly remember our Deliverer in this welcome moment of rest and security."

David opened Scotty's New Testament, and by the light of the campfire read from 1 Corinthians:

"The Lord Jesus, on the night he was betrayed, took bread, and when he had given thanks, he broke it and said, 'This is my body, which is for you; do this in remembrance of me.'"

David received the white bread from Tommy, broke it into four pieces, and each man took his portion.

"This is the Body of Christ given for you," said David and each man silently, and prayerfully consumed the host.

"In the same way, after supper he took the cup, saying, 'This cup is the new covenant in my blood; do this, whenever you drink it, in remembrance of me.'"

David received the canteen cup from Scotty and raised it to eye level:

"This is the blood of Christ shed to cleanse you from your sins," said David who then drank from the cup and passed it on to Donny. After they had each finished the cup, David read from the Psalms to conclude their service of thanksgiving:

"The Lord is my shepherd; I shall not want.
He makes me to lie down in green pastures;
He leads me beside the still waters.
He restores my soul;
He leads me in the paths of righteousness
For His name's sake.
Yea, though I walk through the valley of the shadow of death,
I will fear no evil;
For You are with me;
Your rod and Your staff, they comfort me.
You prepare a table before me in the presence of my enemies;

You anoint my head with oil;
My cup runs over.
Surely goodness and mercy shall follow me
All the days of my life;
And I will dwell in the house of the Lord.
Forever."

• • •

Deep in the night David woke to the sounds of laboring machinery lifted high on the soft breezes from somewhere south of the giant's mountain. He rose to check the perimeter and was drawn to the edge of the escarpment to see the sweep of the Ho Chi Minh Trail. Visible for some forty miles, it was illuminated with the latticed headlights of a thousand trucks and dappled with the glow of ten thousand campfires, winking like fireflies sending coded signals of evil intent through the quivering jungle canopy. The distant black horizon flickered with the silent, violent flashes of Widow Maker as the B52s ten miles above unleashed hell on the mostly vacant A Shau Valley. The unmolested enemy before him mocked Americas' military might; *"The confrontation you seek will come but not tonight. From our sanctum we shall spring to seize your power. With your own sharp sword we shall take your head, and with your blood we shall toast our victory."*

From his distant positon, David could do nothing but watch. After a time he turned away from the war and made his way back to the close circle of the mountain camp.

15

PRAXIS

I t was Jung who first noticed the ragged blur, a pack of mongrel dogs was tearing across the lush lawn in Frick Park. Running just ahead was a well-kept poodle, someone's beloved companion dog, and it was losing ground. The driver transporting Jung and Dotson along picturesque Forbes Avenue slowed and then stopped to allow his passengers the impromptu theater of life and death, which was about to play out just feet from the limousine.

The frantic poodle saw the car and ran toward the humans for help but began to slow and was being overtaken. It cut to the left and then to the right in a final attempt to evade the aggressors but the lead dog lunged and nipped the poodle's haunch, causing it to lose pace and then fall into the maw of the pack. Fear and blood sprayed from the poodle's mouth and shredded neck as the largest mongrels tore the quivering body into three unequal segments. Shaking the bloody meat from side to side, the dogs rolled in the steaming viscera, lapped the body fluids, and savored the terror, defecation, and blood. That was all there was for the pack, it's what made them animals.

Resuming their commute, the driver fixed his attention on the approaching traffic and forced himself to ignore the passions of his employers and their stolen moment in the passenger compartment of the Silver Cloud.

• • •

Since the middle 1800s, steel had been the mother industry of Pittsburgh. Andrew Carnegie's risky abandonment of the Bessemer Converter for the hellish Open Hearth Furnace, together with his visionary "vertical integration" of steelmaking with finishing, transportation, and financing made him one of the wealthiest industrialists of his day. The fabled rivalry for control of the American steel industry between Carnegie and New York financier J. P. Morgan created United States Steel, the first billion-dollar corporation in America headquartered in the Steel City. The wealth generated by steel and the people attracted by the associated opportunities spawned many support industries that established Pittsburgh as the sixteenth-largest city in the country, a glittering jewel of urban Americana, a rising star in America's cultural heavens, and grew the Port of Pittsburgh to the second-largest inland port in the United States.

Over thirty million tons of prefabricated structural steel and associated cargo passed in and out of Pittsburgh's docks annually, so the sight of dozens of oceangoing barges loaded with thousands of tons of prefabricated structural steel beams and columns jamming the riverfront was not unusual. The disturbing difference was that this particular cargo wasn't marked with the distinctive USS logo, and they weren't headed outbound on the Ohio River to some exotic foreign destination. Instead, these units were marked with the crisp white Japanese Kanji logographic of its maker, Yawata Steel Works, and they were being off-loaded.

• • •

Ironworkers Union Local Number 17, the men who should have been employed to assemble the seventy-story structural steel frame for The Allegheny, were the first to talk strike. Their leadership had been in discussion with the outraged Consolidated Associations of Iron and Steel Workers, the associated union whose membership had also been rudely deleted from serious consideration by the building's architect. CAISW represented the labor force of more than 70 percent of the producing steel mills in the country, and the leadership saw the importation of Japanese structural shapes into the very heart of the American steel industry as an overt attack on organized labor and swore it would not succeed on their watch.

Jung's architect, Bruno Braham, had anticipated this reaction after he publicly justified his selection of Yawata Steel through his bid specification by insisting that all structural steel shapes be manufactured using the Heroult Electric Arc Furnace of the type installed in the postwar plants in Kitakyushu, Japan. "More rigid quality control standards than can be found in the old American mills," he had said with a smile and a wink to the US Steel sales executives who had spent large sums courting him in pursuit of the lucrative contract. The veteran sales team knew a screw job when they saw one.

Sensing a union backlash, Braham had made arrangements through Jung's intermediaries within the State Department and the Canadian Ministry of Labor to contract with the Mohawk tribe from the Kahnawake reservation near Montreal for the services of one hundred and fifty famous Iroquois "skywalker" ironworkers to assemble the innovative steel frame that would rise taller than any skyscraper between New York and Chicago. The architect's outrageous end run enraged the local ironworkers and their union representatives promised to work with CAISW to craft severe financial and political reprisals against Allegheny Innovations and its corporate parent, Allegheny Electronics.

At breakfast that morning, Jung opened his *Pittsburgh Post-Gazette* and was attracted to the bold front page headline "Strike!" He chuckled when reading the angry words of the union leadership and savored the photographs of the enraged ironworkers walking the picket line, jobless, all wearing their grubby work clothing and plastic hardhats decorated with little American flags. The messages on the signs they carried made him snigger; "Stop the Alleghany!" "No Scabs!" "No Union No Steel" "America Jobs for Americans!" The amusing side benefits of Braham's rather fascist project management methodology were becoming apparent, and Jung made a mental note to give his architect a bonus for every line of newspaper copy that was generated by the project. At that time, all publicity was good publicity for the emerging Allegheny Innovations.

Jung settled for a moment and enjoyed his paper as he sipped hot Earl Grey with his hard roll and marmalade. No time this morning for the traditional Frühstück; the antiquities had arrived and in his mind, no other single event in the entire scope of the mammoth project would be more important than their proper installation. He was scheduled to personally oversee the preparation work that morning beginning at 10:00 sharp.

Dotson had thoughtfully selected Jung's attire for the overcast day. He began with a freshly tailored yet classic two-button, single-breasted suit from Norton & Sons (he had personally selected the navy wool worsted fabric in the fall weight), white cotton broadcloth shirt with French cuffs, lightly starched, and a subdued gray, blue, and amber silk tie arranged in a reserved yet fashionable pattern, both from Benson & Clegg. To complement the foundation, the valet matched his master's black Oxford brogues from John Lobb, purchased in 1925 when Jung was a young man on his first trip to England. Realizing the historic significance of the day, Dotson accessorized the ensemble with Jung's monogrammed gold cufflinks and wristwatch with simple black leather band, which had been hand-crafted as a set by Pierre Cartier himself. The items had belonged to Jung's grandfather and were the only family heirlooms to survive the war. And finally Dodson added the Brigg gentleman's umbrella with a handwoven black silk canopy, bark chestnut grip, and gold appointments, a complementary mark of distinction for a gentleman in any social circumstance. As he dressed Jung, Dotson briefed his master on the import of the day's ritual and the details that the Apex had prescribed. They were not overly complex but essential to the proper function of the antiquities when they were at last placed into service. "The Apex," said Dotson, "had insisted."

"Sir, I know there are other pressing issues so we'll be on site for only two hours this morning. There is also overnight news from the Apex. A fresh, unexploited Epsilon Site has been discovered. They were surprised and excited by this and feel it has remained hidden so long because it's over six hundred miles south of the thirty-third parallel in northeastern Laos of all places. I've authorized our operative in Vientiane to negotiate a contract price with Hanoi to locate and document the site, remove anything of value, and return it with the relic for installation here in the Allegheny. It could be expensive, so I'll keep you informed. Also, sir, I've taken the liberty of notifying DOD to suspend any aerial bombardment of that segment of Laos until after we've secured the relic," said Dotson, handing the authorizations for his signature, which he mechanically endorsed.

"Sir; if we are able to take possession of the relic and transport it to the Allegheny for the Grand Gala in January, our installation will be the most complete and most powerful in North America. The supernatural appeal of the Pittsburgh Vortex will be enhanced so much that the prince of Amerike may well be persuaded to take up permanent residence!" pronounced a gleeful Dotson, nearly unable to contain himself.

Jung's reaction was somewhat disengaged. "Gala? What gala? Isn't our January full with Project Kansas?" He sipped his tea.

"Ah yes. The gala is a recent addition, perhaps I've forgotten to mention. I've engaged Rowland Ferrier for the event, and we've already started planning. People from all over the country will clamor to attend but the guest list shall be limited to the elite of Pittsburgh and of course the NAO Executive Committee. The event shall combine the public opening of the Allegheny with the first public viewing of the antiquities from Karnak and the spiritual commissioning of both the Tet Offensive and Project Kansas. It shall be our humble thanksgiving for the benevolent majesty and power of the Great Sage Himself!"

"Very well, Dotson." Jung lost interest in the conversation and returned to his paper and breakfast, passively dismissing his aide. Dotson determined that he would have to complete his morning briefing in the automobile, which often served as their mobile office.

• • •

"Sir, we're scheduled to be on site by nine and we'll tour the Reliquary and the Catacombs first, so that you will have an idea of their scale and configuration. They're very impressive and far more spacious than one would imagine from only looking at Braham's drawings. When the relic is installed, it has the potential to be absolutely transcendent."

"I realize it's rather mundane, sir, but Braham insists that we walk through the utilities compartment, the data center, and the broadcast facilities. He seems rather impressed with the manner in which he has integrated the technology into his design. After that, we'll complete the tour on the roof for the ritual placement of the canopic jars in the transplanted Egyptian soil. This is a bit pressing, sir, because the antiquities and are to be installed presently. If we delay the ritual, I'm afraid the construction schedule will be delayed as well. But don't worry, sir, we'll move through this crisply and have you back at the office in time for your luncheon with the Alligewi fellows." Dotson explained the agenda as Jung worked to prepare his remarks for the meeting. The Silver Cloud began to slow as they approached the project site, and then they saw the trucks and the roiling crowd of angry steelworkers.

An aesthetic arrest suspended the conversation in the limousine and even Dotson gasped when they caught their first glimpse of the antiquities. There were twelve of them and they were massive; the gigantic campaniform columns were just over seventy feet high when the measure was taken of the assembly from the bottom of the two and one-half foot tall megalithic granite base to the top of the eighteen-foot diameter open lotus capital. They had been removed from the most prized archeological site of the ancient metropolis of Karnak under direct orders from President Abdel Nasser and presented as a gift from the people of Egypt to the people of the United States of America in return for the personal promise from the secretary of state that American funding of the Aswan Dam would be restored with the start of the Ninetieth Congress that past January. The secretary's promise though was tragically unable to be kept due to the inopportune exchange of unpleasantries between the nations of Israel and Egypt the previous June.

The antiquities had been disassembled and embedded in heavily padded, formfitting, steel-and-oak shipping frames for the six-thousand-mile barge trip to Pittsburgh. Each column's capital, base, and shaft drums were separately protected by their own deeply cushioned container. Jung seemed transfixed by their appearance, but after only a moment, he was overtaken by a spasm of nausea and believed that he might discharge his breakfast onto the floor of the limousine. Though eroded by exposure to time and the elements, they were identical in size and configuration to those he had passed through in the Wintergarten's Hypostyle Hall on the way to present his sacrifice to Lucifer in the White Chapel, the little girl from Kansas. What was her name—Jackie? The memory of the look in her eyes at the moment of her death haunted him nightly; the taste of her flesh remained in his mouth, deeply rancid. On days when he managed to escape Dotson's watchful eye he sometimes cried out for her and then for himself. In those secret moments shared with no one, he believed himself to be utterly, irretrievably insane.

On orders from Dotson, the chauffer followed the waiting police escort closely, past the long line of idling semis and to a point where the crowds from the picket line had closed the road directly in front of the main project entrance. Just beyond the job site fence rose the ominous steel frame that stretched over a quarter of a mile into the cloudy Pennsylvania sky. "SCAB! SCAB! SCCCAAAABBBB! NO UNION! NO STEEL! NO UNION! NO STEEL!" The ironworkers fought Jung's presence with their best catcalls and chants, making threatening hand gestures toward the shiny limousine and its passengers.

More police vehicles arrived and several dozen officers dressed in riot gear formed a protective phalanx around the Silver Cloud and began moving slowly to the gate. The commander of the riot squad explained the situation to the Union representative who complained that he was only in loose control of the picketers, yet on his command the ironworkers became deadly silent and parted like the fabled Red Sea to allow the car and the twelve overloaded semitractors onto the muddy site.

The forced compliance of the grubby men on the picket line buoyed Jung as they passed. Once secure inside the perimeter fence, he regained his composure and was feeling a slight flush of victory as he and Dotson exited the car. He turned toward the strikers with a satisfied smirk on his face just in time to be pelted by three large rotten eggs that had been launched on a perfect trajectory from somewhere in the picket line. They splattered nearly simultaneously onto the crown of his head, his left cheek, and the left breast pocket of his expensive Savile Row suit. "NO UNION! NO STEEL! NO UNION! NO STEEL!" chanted the strikers. "SCAB! SCAB! STINKIN' SCAB! SCAB! SCAB! STINKIN' SCAB!" they roared and then spontaneously broke into raucous laughter and vengeful cheers as they saw Jung collapse and vomit, then tear off his form fitting jacket for use as a towel to wipe the putrid yoke from his precisely coiffed head.

Horrified, Braham sprang to the defense of his patrons, snatching Jung's umbrella from the muddy pavement and opening it as a shield against the monsoon of flying garbage that had been launched at them from the picket line. He urgently pushed them out of range and into the safe haven of the main concourse, which had been, in the vernacular of the American construction industry, "dried in." The bright, uncluttered concourse was more than three stories tall, and filled with neatly dressed craftsmen busy covering its precise surfaces with exotic wood veneers from the forests of Spain, exquisite silk fabrics from the looms of Japan, and bookmatched marble slabs from the quarries of Italy. Even in this early stage there was a proportion, a scale, a nearly spiritual sense of beauty, even a pleasing aroma, which hinted at the delight of the emerging hall. Jung was calmed immediately by the peace he experienced in the space.

The architect ushered his clients through a forest of scaffolding that supported Roman artisans, consigned by the Vatican as a gesture of recognition and goodwill to the rapidly emerging NAO. Led by their elderly maestro, the team was completing the breathtaking "Second Coming" fresco that covered the interior surface of the soaring duomo Allegheny. It was adorned with clouds, stars, lifelike angels, demons, human beings, and a curious radiant being that appeared to be summoning them all into the air toward the radiant double sunrise at its apex. Unnoticed by the Italians, the refugees hurried past and into the nearly complete gentleman's lounge just off the concourse where Jung could compose himself and a plan could be made to salvage the morning's work. Within the hour a change of clothes and several aides from the executive offices of Allegheny Electronics had come to their rescue. Dotson cleaned, freshened, and redressed Jung and comforted him as he began coaching his master on the fine points of the ritualized placement of the Egyptian artifacts; two hours had been lost, but they would make it up by not tarrying the least bit on Braham's guided tour.

BBBBBRRRRRIINNGG! FLASH!FLASH! FLASH!FLASH! The earsplitting sound of building's fire alarm klaxon and blinding white strobes induced everyone in the concourse to cringe.

"BRAHAM! What is this outrage!" cried Jung to anyone who could hear, as he covered his ears.

"Pardon the intrusion, Herr Jung," said the red-faced architect, "The fire alarm interlock with the elevator safety system has not yet been calibrated. The technicians are working now on the repair."

Braham left his client and walked briskly to the uniformed work-men, who spoke with light Canadian accents, busy at their work completing the elevator installation, calibrating the fireman's alarm interlock and balancing the advanced passenger elevators manufac-tured by the German corporation, TheissenCorr, Ag. The klaxon and strobes were reset, and Jung witnessed the odd sight of sixteen eleva-tor doors simultaneously opening to reveal sixteen empty elevator shafts, their passenger cars nowhere to be found. Braham appeared instantly to usher him beyond the lobby and into the service vesti-bule to continue his tour.

They boarded the oversized padded freight elevator, which delivered them slowly thirty-three floors below street level to a small carved stone anteroom. Before them another group of workmen, identically dressed in blue overalls and hard hats, were quietly dis-cussing the installation of a pair of remarkably heavy, oversized stain-less steel security doors large enough, imagined Jung, to drive a truck through. The workmen were speaking German and Jung engaged them cordially as his eyes became accustomed to the half-light of incomplete construction. He noticed that the bare concrete ceiling was at least six meters high and gauged the doors to be at least three-fourths that. Braham had truly scaled the room for giants.

The architect led them beyond the ante into the reliquary, a round room approximately twelve meters in diameter with its domed ceiling, black granite floor, and wall panels decorated with symbols of the zodiac etched deeply into their faces to reveal the extravagant thickness of the panels. Jung noticed that the floor was not polished but honed bedrock and that there was an inlay of highly polished granite only three centimeters in width that glimmered with movement in the room so that anyone could see the elegant pentagram covering the full width of the space.

In the center was a shallow circular reflecting pool surrounding an inclined stone bench, which Jung judged to be one and one-half meters wide and four meters long. This would, of course, be the final resting place of the "Laotian Relic," as Dotson had started referring to the giant corpse they hoped to acquire to complete their Luciferian altar.

Above their heads arched the curved ceiling faced in translucent white alabaster panels shot through with blood-red veining. At the apex of the dome was a suspended crystal Abbe prism precisely cut and polished to resemble the a giant Roman spear head, the lance of Longinus that had pierced the side of Jesus as He hung on the cross. Though Jung could not see how, a narrow beam of refracted light was being projected from the knife-edge of the crystal, which displayed as a narrow linear rainbow upon the polished granite wall.

On closer examination, Jung could see that the architect had designed the room as a timepiece, a large-scale project timeline, a sort of clock that marked time in forty-year increments, beginning with the formal establishment of the Order in AD 476. Inscribed on the shiny surface were the fifty Great Trade Cycles and points of financial and historic inflection both positive and negative. The Great Time Line stretched from right to left two thousand years to the year 2476, the long-fabled Year of Jubilee when Global Acquisition was prophesied and the final descendants of the Order would at last present their Perfected World, uncontested and unified, to the Apex.

Jung walked closer to the narrow beam of refracted spectrum to read the date and description of the killing of the king of Camelot, the Gulf of Tonkin incident, as well as the capture of the Financial Club of Paris, and then he noticed there were no names associated with these spectacular triumphs. He examined the sweep of his long life, nearly eighty years. There were the two world wars, the great financial triumphs of the Vietnam conflict financing and the reconstruction of Europe, and of course the body count, but no mention of Führer Hitler or Emperor Hirohito or, for that matter, Churchill, Stalin, Roosevelt, or Truman. There were no names, no heroes, only events and time, all of which ultimately belonged to the Apex and they to Lucifer—if, in fact, such a being were to actually exist. Could it all be a myth?

Jung stood erect, composed, and at eye level could read a mathematical ratio carved in the stone at regular intervals. He touched the most recent with his index finger.

"Sir, I apologize. I'm afraid this is one of the details that slipped through the cracks, as it were. This is an idea that was explored by the Apex but never put into practice, so I thought this was an excellent time to give it a go. It's a gauge to mark progress toward our overall goal of a perfect world. It simply states the total value of the known world net the worth of the Apex," said Dotson with a smile, pleased that Jung would take notice.

"I see. Herr Dotson, at what point, would one suppose, will our masters be satisfied?" asked Jung, who assumed he knew the answer but wanted Dotson's confirmation.

"Sir, of course the stated goal of the Apex is to own uncontested title to the planet and its people in its entirety. Only then will their plan for global perfection be possible," replied a cautious Dotson, surprisingly unable to see clearly into Jung's deep thoughts.

Jung considered this bit of information as he surveyed the remainder of the reliquary, seeing a large, irregular opening set askew in the opposite granite wall leading, where?

"Herr Jung, forgive me, but the discovery of the existing caverns at this level was our good fortune. Their discovery was already described in our monthly progress report two years ago. They eliminated the need for creating the artificial 'catacombs' noted in your original specification. Herr Dotson had approved their substitution on your behalf. I shall retrieve the…"

"Herr Braham is correct, Master Jung," interjected Dotson. "Sir, I do apologize for this oversight, but I suppose it appeared a trivial detail at the time. I do hope you'll forgive my error."

"They remind me of a feature of our laboratory during a particularly productive period at the end of the war. Where do you suppose they lead?" Jung asked with a smile.

"Sir, our surveyor reports they are located at a depth of more than seventy meters below the flow line of the deepest river channel. The main cavern extends more than one thousand meters away from this point of intersection in two directions. We shall have them mapped and ready for your inspection as soon as is practical."

In deep thought, prompted by the revelation of the hidden caverns, Jung smiled to himself as Braham escorted them back through the secure entrance to the reliquary. They went up a flight of stairs and into the utilities level, where the architect showed them the fresh water supply system and waste water treatment facilities as specified and then to his favorite component, a double-high concrete vault containing the proprietary Zero Point Generators arrayed in eleven banks of seven units each, one per floor plus reserve units. "Sir, in the history of modern construction there has never been any other structure established to operate independently from external support systems in this manner. The technicians report that unless there is a mechanical failure in one of the secondary service systems, the facility may continue infinitely. This technical triumph would not have been achieved without your genius, Herr Jung, or that of

Allegheny Innovations, and I thank you sincerely for the honor of being allowed to serve.

"I should like to point out that the only technical connections to the world outside the Allegheny are the hard wires for the telephone, telex, and the Pittsburgh Fire Department Alarm Control. This is what we heard so loudly earlier. We have discovered a slight incompatibility between the TheissenCorr elevator logic controller and the Pittsburgh Fire Department elevator safety interlock. We shall solve the problem with an electronic fabrication, a translator, if you will allow, to be installed in the Fireman's Control Room on the main floor. This will solve the problem completely. No more ringing ears or flashing eyes, yes?"

The tour continued back to the padded freight elevator that provided construction service to all floors with the final stop being the highest elevator-served floor in the building. "Sir, as you are aware, the sixty-sixth floor houses the data center and actuarial sciences. The most advanced computing system available has been installed and is currently running the "Saigon Simulation" as a base program for Project Kansas. Our key punch center is working with the US Census Bureau and the Internal Revenue Service to enter base data on every American citizen. As you know, the accuracy of the new Kansas Simulation depends entirely on the dataset and we've spared no expense in this critical function," explained Dotson as he and Jung followed Braham though a crowd of people working on both the next generation IBM System 370 and the room itself.

"Herr Braham, the wire mesh the men are attaching to the wall, what is its purpose?" asked Jung.

"Sir, in English it is called 'Faraday Shielding,' and it is a late addition to the design. The thin copper mesh is placed between two layers of wall board and acts as a radio frequency interceptor. It prevents all manner of electromagnetic interference with your internal operations—from solar flares to invasive radio transmissions. The information stored here and your intentions for its use shall remain protected within these shielded walls. We shifted the funds saved in the catacombs to pay for it as reported in the Field Change Directive nearly three months ago."

"Very well, Braham, please proceed. I am becoming somewhat more than fashionably late for my meeting with my Alligewi fellows," said Jung, glancing at his Cartier.

They abandoned the slow freight elevator and walked up the fire stair to Floor 67 and briskly through the bustling communications hub, taking note of the teletypes spitting out incoming messages from all over the country and the people routing them to their proper destinations. They climbed another flight to Floor 68, and their pace slowed as they witnessed a production crew on a sound set recording actors as they simulated the murder of a mailman by two men dressed in North Vietnamese combat gear. The producer of the spot showed them how the tape of the simulation would be cut into authentic news footage from Vietnam and processed in the edit suite to give the viewer the impression that the United States had been invaded. "Bravo," pronounced Dotson as they excused themselves to Floor 68 and a quick walk-through of the broadcast center.

Farther on they found technicians working in front of operating television cameras on three broadcast news sets identical to their familiar originals located at the networks in New York and immediately adjacent they walked briefly through broadcast master control where technicians were pulling bundles of electronic cabling to locations on large control panels that would display video feed from the New York networks plus WPBN and local affiliates in the top ten American television markets. The chief engineer explained that during live broadcasts the master control would oversee the feed into the program director's studio and make sure that the proper programming was channeled either to the studio to transmitter link and then across the river to the WPBN transmitter in Fairview or to the microwave satellite uplink and to the nearest Telstar broadcast satellite for distribution to affiliated stations across North America. "Marvelous!" exclaimed Dotson. "Simply the best!"

Floor 69 was crowded with workmen dressed in gray uniforms putting up wallboard, which would soon define the offices and laboratories for the Allegheny Innovations think tank that would be home for the Alligewi giants and their associates, and therefore merited no serious consideration from Jung.

Floor 70 was still fully under construction and open to the environment, temporarily absent its expensive glass-and-polished granite curtain wall. Along with Jung's executive suite, the vacant floor was to house the welcome center, which would receive and indoctrinate public visitors to the rooftop Egyptian colonnade, the seven-story glazed enclosure, which was designed by Braham to house the Egyptian antiquities and forever dominate Pittsburgh's skyline.

Jung felt the wind pick up and held on tightly to his pristine white hardhat, thinking he might lose it to a sharp gust. For a moment, he watched a filthy group of five men in rubber boots, dripping with sweat and stripped to the waist, straining to place a stiff concrete mixture from a crane-delivered two-yard bucket. The crew was spilling hydrated concrete onto the exposed galvanized metal deck and using hand tools to spread it across the in-floor wire-ways and the welded steel stud anchors.

He was startled by loud banging from overhead as two skywalkers drove a massive steel beam into place with heavy sledge hammers. Above them the air was filled with white hot sparks from welding rods that burned as hot and bright as the surface of the sun and were powered by gasoline-powered Lincoln electric arc welding machines temporarily chained to the dark red Japanese steel frame.

After allowing a moment for them to orient, Braham lead his small group up the incomplete ceremonial stair where they emerged on what would soon be the roof and were again slightly disoriented. They paused a moment to absorb the dramatic 360-degree view of downtown Pittsburgh. Jung marveled at the motion of barges and tugs on the three rivers flowing below traveling one way as opposed to a large steel beam being swung into place by the skywalkers, who seemed to revel in fearlessly riding the cabled beams as they were hoisted from the ground by one of the project's two orbital tower cranes.

Once stabilized and fitted with a safety harness to prevent them from being blown over the temporary guard rail by a rogue wind,

Dotson assisted Jung in checking the shipping manifest against the numbered components that had been lifted onto the shiny bare roof deck. They carefully reviewed the details of the installation with Braham, who showed them the roof layout from a wrinkled and stained set of construction drawings kept by the construction foreman in a small lockable covered desk made from scrap plywood that functioned as a rooftop site office.

"Herr Dotson, you will recognize the location of the double sun beacons and they shall be glorious! The units have been fabricated from the finest quality translucent alabaster from Iranian quarries in North Africa. The two-centimeter leaves are laminated between two sheets of tempered glass and cut precisely to fit into a frameless geodesic sphere, that I personally designed for this application. The additional benefit of the stone is that it is invisible to microwave transmissions and, as you can see from the diagrams, the microwave uplink to the Telstar satellite network shall be concealed within the southwestern unit. The microwave studio-to-transmitter link for sending local broadcasts to your new transmitter and tower is to be concealed in the northeast sphere. You may see the television facility being erected even now in the Fairview neighborhood located directly across the river," Braham said, pointing out the new 1,200-foot-tall broadcast tower less than five miles away.

"Braham, why have you decided to place the WPBN transmission tower in that location? There are so many others in close proximity. If there is a failure of one of the others, would it not pose a threat to our operation?" asked Dotson, showing proxy interest at the eleventh hour.

"Ah yes, Herr Dotson; commercial broadcasters in Pittsburgh work in a type of technical collaborative and group their transmitters on the highest point within their service area. The federal agencies of communications and aviation have arranged their restrictions to allow tall towers to be erected on that site only, and so there was really no other choice. I hope this is a satisfactory explanation; if not, I will retrieve my file and construct a detailed report for your information."

"And what of security, Herr Braham?" asked Dotson

"Sir, this installation is considered low risk in America. There is a security fence and locked gate but nothing more."

"Very well, Braham, do not bother yourself with the report. Please continue."

Jung was intrigued with the architect's drawings of the "American Temple of Ra" and the manner in which they were being actualized by the workmen. "Ah, Herr Jung, you will recognize this layout is from the verbal description given to me by Herr Dotson on your behalf. It will permanently shelter the Egyptian antiquities, which are being received presently. Each of the units was disassembled and crated for shipment by Egyptian archeologists who are employed by the Supreme Council of Antiquities, a branch of the Egyptian Ministry of Culture. They have also traveled with the artifacts and arrived at the Port of Pittsburgh only one week ago; those gentlemen you see here dressed in red overalls helping the workers with the uncrating are the men responsible to the safe delivery and proper erection of the columns." Jung looked up from the drawing to see a swarm of men moving over the crated columns.

"As you will see in the diagram, we shall install them in the precise sequence and configuration from which they were removed from their temple in Karnak. It will be as if they never left home."

Jung perused the architect's roof plan, and from his vantage point he could see the twelve corresponding openings in the structural steel floor frame that were to receive the large granite base stones, and then he identified the void below each base, designed to hold a ceremonial parcel of Egyptian soil, which had been removed from beneath the foundation stone of each column. The ritualized placement and "blood bonding" of this material, as Dotson had said, was required by the Apex. He had been told repeatedly that this was the most important role for him in the construction process; yet, quite frankly, he was beginning to question why such a thing was even necessary. In fact, it seemed laughable, even insane, that a man of his wealth and stature should be involved in this sort of unseemly activity; especially in full view of the toothless heathen underclass for whom he provided a livelihood.

And who was Dotson to be his intercessor with the Apex? Was he not the ascended master? Why did they not communicate directly with him? Why should he believe a word this little English parasite from nowhere had to say? Standing among the flurry of activity in the daylight of free America, literally standing on top of the Western world, he determined that he would no longer be a part of this superstitious foolishness, and that should Dotson disagree, he would be discharged from service. After all, anyone can be replaced.

"Sir, need I remind you of the oath you swore less than four years ago at the White Chapel?" asked a sober Dotson, who had withdrawn with his master to the cluttered privacy of the enclosed seventieth floor fire stair. "Perhaps you are thinking that I am superfluous to the process, perhaps even deceiving you to enrich myself at your expense. A parasite, you might think, only pretending to be the emissary of the twelve. Making fools of you and the rest of the ruffian thugs you know as the Order. And even that you have the power to eliminate me. Is that what's risen to the top of your tiny insect mind, Doktor Gruenbaum?"

Though logic told him it was impossible, Jung perceived Dotson to be growing in physical stature; instead of being a head shorter, he was now staring directly into his eyes with a fearful countenance that chilled him to the bone. He was startled by an impossibly large rat that crawled down the stairwell railing behind them, moved across the paper and dirt on the unkept floor, and began burrowing into a pile of trash in the far corner of the stair landing. "Assist your brother, Herr Jung," said Dotson as he gestured toward the rodent clawing through the trash. Jung's legs and arms were overtaken with painful cramps that forced him to his hands and knees, and he began to crawl into the rubbish pile, using his nose and teeth to expose a simple pine box, a five-point star was carved into the lid and sturdy leather straps secured to either end. He took hold of a strap with his teeth and pulled it slowly and painfully to rest before the shiny shoes of Dotson. Then every muscle in Jung's body cramped simultaneously, shooting searing pain throughout his being and leaving him on his knees paralyzed, screaming for mercy from his alien, evil secretary. Then, as if in a dream, he was released. Both he and Dotson had resumed their normal physical sizes and were again standing before one another, back on the roof deck as Dotson was presenting the plain pine box to Jung.

"Sir, are you with us? Ah, there you are. Good to have you back! As I was saying, the contents of the enclosed jars will be added, one each, buried in the soil already placed in the twelve column foundation wells," said an obviously pleased Dotson, "The sacred soil is ready for you now, sir."

Jung took possession of the pine box and followed his secretary to the central space, which bisected the hall into two groups of six columns each. He positioned the soft wooden container on the block of granite that had been quarried specifically for the purpose, opened it, and immediately recognized the contents—the twelve ancient canopic jars into which Dotson had placed the internal organs of his sacrifice at the White Chapel.

"Sir, we shall begin as soon as you are ready. I prepared this for you personally as a guide and, of course, I'll be here at the ready should you need assistance," said an encouraging Dotson, placing a small slip of parchment into his hand.

Jung hesitated as he looked about to see work on the tower continue apace. Dotson called Braham aside and then a few minutes later there was silence on the jobsite and the construction workers were all standing erect facing away from Jung and his ceremonial duties.

Adjacent to the sacrificial stone stood a crate covered with a red drape. Leaving the box on the altar, Jung walked to the crate and withdrew the covering, exposing the contents; a mature glistening black horned he-goat with a rough coat and lifeless coal-black eyes.

Jung released his safety harness, removed his hardhat, jacket, and shirt and handed them to his secretary. Naked to the waist, he took a length of stout twine from the box, reached into the top of the crate, roughly flipped the goat on its side, and after much blatting and struggle, secured the four legs together tightly so that the animal became passive. Dotson assisted as Jung lifted the helpless goat from the crate and placed it on the altar near the carved box. Dotson helpfully placed the ceremonial dagger on the altar and the stepped back but remained as a faithful second.

Jung read aloud from the parchment:

Lord Satan, O Great Bringer of Light to a Dark World,

By Your power and through your grace I ask Your blessing on this construction.

And that if it pleases You and is a wise request, I entreat you to assign this place as the permanent abode of the powerful and exalted Prince of Amerike.

So that he may bless this sigil with his presence and dark power to enable your servants to complete our labors and bring about the delivery of the United States of America and its Christian masses into Your hands for Your pleasure to do with as You will.

And O Wise One, the most powerful Prince of the Air, we ask boldly that You summon also the demon spirits of the long-departed Alligewi Nephilim to inhabit once more this honored place of sacrifice and assign them the role of Satanic messenger, sending Your spirit with them out over the electronic airwaves with each broadcast to tempt every ear and eye; to reside in every mind, and possess every heart in the United States.

To this labor I dedicate my sacrifice; in return for your smile, I spill this blood...

Jung raised the dagger high, held the goat by horns exposing the jugular and severed it precisely, swiftly, releasing the crimson flow over the twelve canopic vessels. He held the animal tightly until the last quivering twitches of death had subsided. He then rose, took the dripping, bloodied box with him and precisely placed the last earthly remains of Jacqueline Rose Adams of Lebanon, Kansas, into the ancient soil of Karnak, ritually uniting the virginal spirit of the American heartland with the profligate evil consigned by the Lord Himself to the demonic realm of Hades, known to the ancient Egyptians as Duat; the Kingdom of Osiris; the land of the living dead.

• • •

"What is precisely this Project Kansas? Has old Jung finally disappeared from us around the curve in the autobahn?" said Jung rhetorically with a slight smile as he opened the annual meeting of the Executive Committee. "I am quite sure you must have said this, but only to yourself sometimes in the morning bath." He smiled broadly, eliciting slight uneasy laughter from the audience. "Well, dear friends, I must confess at times I also have asked this question of myself and so, for the sake of our minds, that is the subject of our discussion here today."

"You will recall that already two years have passed since I tasked our conscripted Alligewi fellows with the design of a plan to destroy the American family, pluck the American plum from the tree of liberty and place it, whole and undamaged, into the hands of our masters at the Wintergarten. My young giants took their work seriously and now offer two options for our learned consideration. As you have seen from the executive summary before you, both options have strategic merits yet are tactically divergent.

"Option A assumes preservation as its priority and focuses on the family unit. It takes the long road and employs as primary tactics the indoctrination and propagandizing of public school children to gradually undercut parental authority and reshape the American mind into a form that shall suit our purposes. The Kansas actuarial model validates these tactics with the added value of being relatively bloodless and offering the best chance of delivering title to the country whole and undamaged. The time required for this option to bear fruit is fifty to seventy-five years; the duration required for two adult generations to pass away into the twilight of political effectiveness. The actuaries tell us that only then shall the mass mind conform to our values; the population shall have assumed already the role of modern-day serfs, tied forever to the land owned by our masters and dependent on them for their livelihood and lives. This is good, yes, but since I am coming near to my eighth decade on the planet, I am wondering if completion of this solution may be a bit tardy for my taste!" There was nervous laughter and polite applause around the table, and Jung took the moment to slowly examine each of their faces until each man in turn averted his eyes.

"Many of you were here in this room already five years ago as we debated the merits of the Black Swan action in Dallas, which opened the way to the magnificent state of the financial and religious fortunes we all enjoy this day. Can any man here say, as distasteful as it was, that the life taken that auspicious morning was taken in vain? Can any man here say that the power and wealth of our collective enterprise was not geometrically increased because we hued to our franchise and honored the prescription of our masters?" There was silence then slight vocal assent in the room. "As I thought; and it is from this predicate that I present a path filled with risk, yet laden with reward.

"Option B, not unlike our venture in Dallas, offers a more rapid, albeit more damaging means of acquiring undisputed ownership of the United States. Appended to your report you will see the data sets; psychological, political, and economic, harvested from the Dallas event, have been incorporated into the actuarial model we are examining within Allegheny Innovations. They offer surprising insight into the psychological architecture of our target population. For example, we find the American capacity for self-delusion, when facing a large-scale existential threat, to be approximately one hundred twenty percent greater than forecast in nineteen sixty-two.

"The revised data posits that this additional emotional carrying capacity is conditional, however, in that other stabilizing cultural elements must remain intact: utilities, food supply, job, wage, newspapers, broadcast radio and television, family, church, associates, and a reassuring and recognizable voice of governmental authority. Absent these stabilizers the model predicts an eighty-seven percent probability that the current homogenous, and therefore easily herded, population will break apart into smaller, unmanageable quasi-tribal units self-organized for mutual defense and survival. Acknowledging their vast numerical superiority, this condition is simply unacceptable for our purposes.

"And so our giants have devised the concept of managed chaos that will allow the Order to monitor regional stress levels and calibrate the chaos required to convince the Americans not only to submit to national control but to demand it!

"Our method shall exploit this knowledge to plot a more direct pathway to national control; the North American Order shall leverage its assets to install an East German-style police state in America. We shall do this by gaining control of all federal, state, and local police agencies and replacing the existing leaders and sworn officers with men who are here already, standing in the shadows, and are incentivized to ensure the success of our agenda—the neo-Communist members of Red Storm!

"I know that now you are thinking, 'Ah! I was correct; Jung has lost his mind! Americans are all cowboys like John Wayne and Wyatt Earp and will never accept the Stasi! They shall take their revolvers at high noon to the OK Corral, shoot down the NAO police, and bury them all on Boot Hill!'" spontaneous laughter across the room, "Perhaps this is true today but I assure you, Gentlemen, where there is a will, there is a way! To convert our rather large and dangerous mass of armed cowboys into a manageable asset for our masters, we must transform them by constructing in the American mind a danger so large, so evil, and so incomprehensible that they will beg for our protection!

"The scientific basis for Option B may appear as fiction, but I assure you the phenomenon on which it is based is scientifically sound. The process in English is called 'Psychic Driving,' a category of traumatic mass mind control that was pioneered and proven on a national scale during our glory days in the Reich. We achieved remarkable results during the war and have recently completed field trials in America with similar results; therefore, we believe the technique is ready for large-scale deployment against the Americans.

"The methodology is thus: Paralyze the target; cause a condition to exist that will not allow him to escape an invasive, repetitive message that constructs a palpable terror in his mind. Inject this message into his brain full force with mass media—print, radio, and television programming; provide choreographed events timed to confirm the reality of the message in his mind. These must be bloody and visually horrific. The key has two parts. First, recognizable, important people known across the nation must be murdered and the target must see this himself and be terrified by it. Second, properly timed confirmation murders of local authority figures must occur; the policeman, fireman, mailman, teacher, city councilman, and those close to the people must be killed. Then manufactured psychic trauma must be added to the authentic and violently agitated to drive his mind to panic. At the golden moment, when his terror crests, when he shrieks to his lord for salvation, we shall then be ready to snap the trap with our predesigned solution. And there you have it: the 'Federal Division of Hometown Protection,' the national police force owned, staffed, and operated by the North American Order.

"And this of course is the occult majick of Kansas; the grand existential threat, so pressing as to compel the vast majority of Americans to willingly disarm themselves, give up their freedom, and place themselves and their children under our authority, shall not exist anywhere in the world except in the shared media consciousness of the American mass mind! We shall hoodwink the stupid pavlovian cowboys out of their guns, their power, and their country!"

Jung continued by offering them a schedule and asset allocation diagram illustrating how the NAO control of the New York Press, the Justice Department and the Department of Defense would be used to combine images of the very real combat during the New Year's Communist offensive against American forces in South Vietnam with coordinated bloody attacks carried out across America by Red Storm Cells masquerading as a Viet Cong fifth column.

At key psychic processing points, the NAO would spur the terror with properly timed public assassinations of high profile national, state, and local political figures, adding fuel to the media firestorm to reinforce the terrifying illusion that ordinary American citizens are defenseless against the Communist threat. At a predesignated time, the public outcry for increased security would be shaped and amplified by the same New York press that manufactured the illusionary threat. The magnified media outcry would then be used as a spur for NAO-sponsored legislators in Washington to demand sweeping new law in the form of the NAO's previously written enabling legislation, and it would be done in the heat of the moment, at a time when no one dare challenge the clearly unconstitutional measures for fear of being seen as a traitor or something worse.

"Gentlemen, on November 22, 1963, the North American Order freely and without consequence, murdered the idealism, innocence, and moral excellence of the American people. Today I ask again for your support, and I promise that on January 30, 1968, we shall begin a work together that shall shatter the fabled American cowboy ethos; we shall add their power to our own and thereafter the Land of the Free and the Home of the Brave shall belong fully to the Order to do with as we will!"

● ● ●

A taupe sedan with an airport rental car decal rolled slowly up the dusty caliche road toward the main house at Pleasant Farms, hidden from view by the tall green corn heavy with a late-season yield. It slowly rolled to a stop on the worn gravel surface near the front gate and was greeted by a small pack of scruffy farm dogs. Held in check by the freshly painted picket fence, they loudly announced the arrival of the stranger, an Anglo man, tall, lanky, bearded, and dressed coolly yet fashionably in a seersucker suit, pressed white shirt, colorful bow tie, white shoes, and white Panama hat. He studied the little pack from the safety of the driver's seat, decided they were no threat held securely behind the fence, and got out of his car, worn dark brown leather attaché in hand. He was halfway to the entrance when Travis, the aging pack leader, loped over to the gate, clicked the latch with her nose, and released the mongrel horde onto the startled visitor who froze rather than chance a sprint back to the Chevy.

"Travis! Dogs! Get back in here, and leave that man alone!" called Paulina Gonzales from the deep shade of the front porch. She hurried to the gate to meet the visitor, who was smiling broadly with a relieved expression as he approached the gate.

"Mrs. Gonzales, I presume?" and after her response, he reached into his jacket pocket, withdrawing an aging brown leather wallet, worn and polished with use, to offer his credentials, "Ma'am, I apologize for disturbing you. My name is Carlton Mayer, and I have news of your son, David. We have reason to believe he's alive."

Nearly a mile away, across the stock pond and up a low hill, virtually invisible in his military surplus ghillie suit and concealed in a grove of old growth Mesquite, the overwatch had Mayer in his crosshairs; a metallic whisper directed his actions. "Panther Watch, Deck Hand orders you to stand down. Repeat, Panther Watch, you are ordered to stand down. Your target is Mayer, Carlton B. He rented the car three hours ago at MAF, and he's on the list. Deck Hand is en route. ETA thirty. Stay awake, Panther, orange alert remains in force. Repeat, alert status remains orange."

Pastor Joe arrived in his Parker Exploration pickup less than half an hour later and found Paulina and Mayer in their front room. Paulina was showing off the family photo album to a seemingly interested Mayer. "Paulina, could you introduce our guest?"

"Joe, this is Mr. Carlton Mayer with the Central Intelligence Agency. He came all the way from Saigon with news about David. I asked him to wait for you so we could hear the news together. Mr. Mayer?"

Mayer offered his credentials to Pastor Joe. "Forgive me Agent Mayer, but I'd like to make sure you're who you say you are before we go any further."

Mayer provided his VID validation information and Joe made the long distance call to the Washington area code. To his relief, the operator was able to validate Mayer's credentials. He relaxed and took his hand off the 32-caliber, two-shot derringer concealed in his pants pocket. "Welcome to our home Mr. Mayer, you said you have news of our son? It's over two years since the Marine Corps told us that David was killed in a surprise attack. They said there was an explosion and subsequent landslide that killed over three hundred soldiers and their families. The debris from the slide was so dense and thick that MACV in Da Nang decided to abandon the installation and treat it as a mass grave. So please, sir, could you tell us what the CIA knows that the Marine Corps doesn't?"

"Sir, I am terribly sorry for the suffering this must have caused you and your family. As I understand it, you served in Europe during the liberation, and so you must have a firsthand understanding of the fog of war. The Communist attack on Rana Dat was well planned and devastating to the Special Forces operators of seven-mike and, quite literally, there was no one left to tell the tale. When I read the reports, I assumed, like everyone else, that David had been killed with his unit and that the remains were unrecoverable. But around a year ago we began receiving reports from our operatives along the Lao border that there were American soldiers living in the jungle and raiding North Vietnamese shipping convoys along the Ho Chi Minh trail. And then two weeks ago we came into possession of these photographs, which are said to be of the raiders themselves. They were taken by a North Vietnamese commander who was KIA in a daylight raid. Our technicians in Saigon processed the film and were able to obtain these images."

Mayer extracted a plain white envelope from his attaché and handed it across the coffee table to Pastor Joe. Among them was one shot of an Anglo American man with full beard running toward the photographer with a blurry image of a large canine the foreground. He was dressed in an American-issue bush hat and tiger bush jacket with the name RIXON stitched in white on the right breast pocket.

"This looks like David's uniform—how many Rixons can there be in the service? But that's definitely not him." Joe passed the photo to Paulina who looked at it in silence for a long time. "No, Mr. Mayer, that's not our boy. Did you talk to this young man? How did he get David's uniform?"

"Mr. and Mrs. Gonzales, this is very important, a matter of National Security. Could you please look one more time before you decide it's not David. He could have lost weight; the facial hair may alter his appearance; the hat, the setting." They both looked again and seemed overtly disappointed but again the answer was no.

"Then please, tell me about your daughter-in-in-law, Karen, and her son, Randal. I paid a visit to her address in El Paso yesterday, but the landlord said that she had never moved in and left no forwarding address. Her parents don't seem to be home and their telephone is out of order. Have you been in contact with them recently?" inquired the agent.

"After she received word from the Marines about David, she and Randal moved in with us and stayed in David's room to grieve the loss. Then about a year ago she decided it was time to move on and took a teaching job in California, at a community college. Wait a minute, and let me get that for you," said a helpful Paulina. "Here it is, San Diego Community College District. She teaches English at the Miramar College campus. She rents a house nearby. Here's the address, if you need it. She doesn't have a phone right now; says she'd rather not be bothered by salesmen and the like."

A clearly deflated Mayer refused their offer to stay for dinner, thanked the Gonzaleses for their cooperation, and said his good-byes. Pastor Joe walked Mayer out to his car, Travis and her pack following closely. "Nice dogs. Friendly even—when their master is nearby." The CIA agent smiled. He stopped at the car door and looked Pastor Joe in the eye. "Did I hear Mrs. Gonzales call one of them Travis? You know, David had a dog with him in Saigon. Travis, I believe is what he named the puppy." The expression on Joe's face told Mayer what he wanted to know. He said good-bye and started the Chevy.

Joe watched Mayer's taillights head away from the house, walked over to the rig truck, reached inside, took the two-way microphone off the hook, and dialed in the Operation MOJO frequency. "Central this is Deck Hand. I'm afraid we're going to have to bring him in; looks like he's on to Mojo."

Twenty minutes later Mayer noticed a state police cruiser in his rearview mirror and then the red lights popped on. The trooper used the public address feature of his siren system to command Mayer to remain in his vehicle with is hands on the steering wheel. Less than a minute after they had stopped alongside Texas State Highway 385, two backup units from the Ector County Sheriff's office arrived and Carlton Mayer was taken into custody under suspicion of being the man responsible for a string of convenience store robberies in the Odessa-Midland area.

Trooper Ben Wheeler, who snapped the cuffs on Mayer despite his credentials and against vigorous protests, was nearing retirement and not in the mood for Yankee attitude. "Eeeuu may not 'a done them robberies, bud, but I know yer type 'n' I'll bet my pension that ya done somehtin', sum time to sum body that's again' tha law, and when we find out what 'tis, we gonna throw ya under the Ector County jailhouse!"

The deputies assisted the trooper, laid hands on his prisoner, blindfolded him, and placed him in their squad car. Mayer estimated that they had been moving in silence for about half an hour when they rolled to a stop. The deputies removed him from the car, uncuffed him, took his blindfold, and boosted him into the dark void of a large high-box trailer coupled to a Parker Exploration semitractor.

"Here's your papers," said Reserve Deputy R. Peterson (Mayer barely read his silver nameplate) as he pitched the attaché into the darkness of the trailer. "You'll need these too," he said, tossing an old gray galvanized slop bucket and a surplus military canteen into the box.

"Have a good night," said Reserve Deputy J. Kellogg as they closed him into the darkness and oppressive heat of the high box.

The semi drove through the night, the last few hours on rough roads that bounced Mayer about the inside of the unloaded trailer, the fear of the unknown building in his mind, and his discomfort escalated by the heat and darkness.

Mayer noted the time on the luminous face of his chronograph; the truck had stopped moving at 4:45 a.m. He heard the driver crank down the trailer dolly, the puff of air as he disconnected the brake lines, the whir of the Cummins turbocharger, and he felt the tractor pull out from under the trailer. He heard the tractor make a U-turn and then idle to a stop near the rear of the high box. The doors creaked and banged when they were unlatched, and again he heard the puff of the air brakes and roar of the Cummins as the diesel tractor clattered off into the distance.

The silence of the barren Permian Basin invaded the trailer and Mayer began to harden his gut for the fight that he feared was imminent. If this was his time, he would at least try to take one of them with him as he clutched the bale of the bucket preparing to use his overnight discharge as a chemical weapon against his assailants. But the fight never came.

Mayer heard the sound of doves and felt the chill of the early morning air when he pushed open the trailer door. He saw the soft pink sunrise on the horizon and he stepped down to the surface of the dirt road to begin to orient to his strange surroundings. He emptied his bucket, took a sip of water from the canteen and began to walk along the road, retracing the truck's route.

Smelling wood smoke, he noticed an open fire and human movement off the road in the distance. He thought himself rescued as he made his way into the glow and warmth of the fire. "Long night?" said the man, reclined on a blanket, not looking up from his book. Mayer was stunned to recognize his would-be savior. It was Pastor Joe Gonzales.

"I like to come out here sometimes as a spiritual retreat; just the Lord and me. It's a good place to read the Scripture and have a one-on-one with God. Helps a man put things into their proper perspective. Coffee?" he motioned toward the blackened pot sitting on the metal grille over the campfire, taking a sip from his tin cup. "Biscuits will be done in a minute. I put 'em on when I saw you'd arrived."

Mayer was stumped, didn't know what to do, and noticed the cast iron Dutch oven covered with red hot coals. "'I'm afraid I'm a city boy, Mr. Gonzales, and all of this is very foreign to me."

"Frightening too, I'll bet. Being illegally arrested for a crime you didn't commit; betrayed by the police, who we trust to protect our constitutionally guaranteed liberties; held without counsel in a very stressful environment; not knowing who is doing it to you or why. A little like what was done to our son by his commanding officer. What was his name? Washington? If I were you, Carl, I'd be pretty damned mad about the whole thing." said Lieutenant Gonzales coldly, searching for a measure of truth that could only be found by looking directly into Mayer's eyes.

A moment later he shifted his tone. "I smell breakfast! Hope you're hungry."

Joe used a blackened metal range hook to rake the dull red coals off the top of the cast iron oven and retrieve their biscuits from the smoldering fire. He dished up eggs and sausage to go with the fluffy hot sourdough biscuits, butter and honey, and they sat together on the blanket watching the sunrise color the peaks of the Davis Mountains with a new day.

"Carl, would you care to give thanks?" asked Pastor Joe.

"Thank you Mr. Gonzales, you're very considerate." Carlton Mayer then stood, faced the sunrise and said, "Blessed are You, Lord our God, King of the universe, Who bestows kindness upon the culpable, for He has bestowed goodness to me."

Pastor Joe stood as well and replied, "May He who has bestowed beneficence upon you always bestow every beneficence upon you."

"Ah, the proper response to the Birkat Hagomel. You have studied the Torah, Mr. Gonzales?"

"Only superficially, Carl, in search of the deeper meaning of the Holy Scripture. And I'll admit, knowing that you were Jewish, I thought I'd be a better host if I brushed up on your theology. The Jewish prayer of thanksgiving for deliverance can be found in many lay references to your faith."

"Host?" he smiled. "You mean interrogator, do you not, Mr. Gonzales?" Mayer carefully buttered his biscuits.

Anticipating Mayer's correct read of their circumstance, Joe bit into a steaming-hot sourdough and took a sip of his coffee. "Quite a career you've had, Carl," he said, motioning to an olive file folder on the corner of his blanket. "US Naval Academy, class of thirty-nine, assigned as a communications ensign to the USS *Pennsylvania*, where two years later you had advanced to lieutenant and were the communications officer of the watch in the combat information center on seven December forty-one. The *Pennsylvania* was in dry dock for minor maintenance at the Pearl Harbor Navy Yard when the Japanese attacked. File says you were instrumental in her defense, relaying information concerning the attack to CINCPACFLT and received a decoration for distinguished conduct. From the *Pennsylvania* you transferred to OP-Twenty-G, the signals intelligence and cryptanalysis section in Washington, where you were liaison for Admiral Nimitz with 'Magic,' the allied cryptanalysis project that broke the Japanese Purple Cipher. A code-breaker, Carl; very impressive. Magic allowed Nimitz to read Yamamoto's transmissions; gave him the intelligence he needed to cripple the Jap navy at the Battle of Midway, and you even got hold of his travel itinerary so the good guys could send him on a little side trip he never expected to make! My hat's off to you, Mr. Mayer; damned impressive.

"After VJ it seems like you got all introspective—enrolled at Jewish Union College in Cincinnati and spent a couple of years on rabbinical studies. That's to be expected, Carl, I know a lot of guys that wanted to get closer to God after the war. Then you did a one eighty in forty-nine and became one of the first civilian employees of the newly chartered Central Intelligence Agency. It looks like they paid you to go back to school, because less than a month later your entered Princeton College on an agency scholarship. We managed to obtain a copy of your PhD thesis, and I must say, Doctor Mayer, Thomas Jefferson would have been proud. *The Essential Role of the Armed Citizen in the Modern Democratic Republic*, Woodrow Wilson School of Public Policy, Princeton College, class of nineteen fifty-two, as I recall. A Second Amendment advocate attends an Ivy League school and they actually award him an earned PhD. That's fantastic, Carl. As I understand it,

Prime Minister Ben-Gurion and certain members of the First Knesset thought it was pretty neat as well; or so I am told."

Mayer took the offensive. "And yourself, Lieutenant Gonzales, US Army Ranger, Silver Star for gallantry in action against the entrenched German occupiers in Paestum, Italy; two Purple Hearts, recommendation for a rank advancement to captain and a Stateside billet running close quarters training for boots. But you refused and stayed with your unit, the First Battalion of the Hundred Forty-First Regiment, I believe. Your military career is exemplary, and your civilian life has been all the more impressive..."

Joe raised his hand sharply, "No Mas! Why the hell's the CIA doggin' my family, Mayer? We know you're tapping our phones, we found your listening devices, even the ones in our bedroom and toilet! We know there are agents monitoring where I go and who I meet with. There's even a guy that regularly attends services at the Quad Six; says he believes in Jesus and wants me to counsel him!

"So, Agent Mayer, here we are here, just us chickens, to get to the truth of things. You should know that the next words out of your mouth had damned well better be Gospel or you're about to have a very bad day!"

The tension between the two men grew to the breaking point, and then, "To which CIA are you referring, Lieutenant Gonzales? You are aware there are two of them, are you not?"

The look of shock and disbelief on Pastor Joe's face told Mayer that he had the advantage and he pressed it home.

"I don't doubt that you, your family, and your associates are being monitored covertly, but it isn't by the US Central Intelligence Agency or by me. Joe, not many people outside the agency know that when the US Army's Office of Strategic Services was dissolved in 1946 there was a period where there was no national intelligence service at all. To fill that void the army transferred the assets of the OSS to the State Department, and the Special Projects Division was created, which later became the Office of Policy Coordination. I do not work for either the OPC or the Department of State."

"My employer is the US Central Intelligence Agency, which was chartered by Congress and President Truman in the National Security Act of nineteen forty-seven. The charter provides for a director of Central Intelligence who is supposed to head the American intelligence community and be the adviser to the president. The CIA is prohibited by congressional statute from engaging in domestic law enforcement activities and is restricted to gathering and disseminating foreign intelligence to our leadership. No matter what you may believe, CIA does not do murder or participate in other covert misdeeds. The agency remains faithful to its charter and obeys the law.

"OPC is a completely different animal. It was supposed to be transferred out of State to CIA in forty-seven, but for some reason, it never happened. All that changed was that CIA started paying OPC's freight. Last fiscal year nearly half of our annual appropriation went to fund the black operations of our schizophrenic, homicidal twin who remains hidden from view in the attic at the US Department of State."

"OPC leadership believes the law does not apply to them or their operation which they've staffed with literal murderers Joe, some of them wanted Nazi war criminals, recruited by the State Department after the war, given new identities by the Justice Department, and approved for employment under something called Operation Paperclip. We estimate there may be as many as fifteen thousand of them on the OPC payroll right now, and God knows what they're doing to earn their livelihood.

"As much as they may say otherwise, the OPC has never been our friend. From the beginning they have operated under an agenda that is separate and distinct from that of the American people and most of their elected officials. Right now, there is a small section of OPC operating in Indochina on a mission to track down your son.

"We both know David is alive, Joe, and I'm here to help bring him home from the war—in one piece if possible. But he's rejected the authority of the command chain all the way up to the White

House. There may be extenuating circumstances. I have my own theory about this, but essentially he's gone rogue."

"COMUSMACV had him reclassified as a deserter and a traitor, and a month ago OPC placed a bounty on his head because he's organizing an independent guerilla force of indigenous tribesmen in the mountains of eastern Laos. He's building his own army, Joe. Let me say that again. Joe, your son, David, is building his own army and we don't know how or why but he's scaring the shit out of a lot of people with the power to put a bullet through his head."

"OPC has agents in the field, contract killers, who are hunting David with the intent to shoot him on sight. They're professionals, Joe; hard operators set deep in the blackest side of the OPC who won't stop until they have his head in a bag. I want to find him before they do because it's my professional opinion that your son is an innocent, a patriot who has unwittingly come into possession of certain knowledge that may be harmful to OPC or their sponsors. He's trapped by an extraordinary circumstance and he can't free himself without our help.

"Your son is fighting for his life and what he believes is the American way on a battlefield that he cannot possibly understand. You may not know where he is or what he's doing but, Joe, I believe you know full well how to contact him, and that's why I'm here. To ask for your help to bring David home before it's too late."

The men stared at each other across the smoldering fire for a long moment when Joe exposed a military-grade transceiver from under his blanket, brought it to his ear and keyed the mic, "Central this is Deck Hand. Tell Panther Watch to stand down. I think we can work with him. There's leftover breakfast if anybody's hungry."

Less than fifty yards away the floor of a shallow playa came alive in two separate locations as the overwatch snipers broke cover, gathered their belongings, and walked toward Joe's camp, carrying their long guns and startling Agent Mayer.

"I thought it was just us out here, all alone. I should have known." He smiled toward Gonzales.

"Better eat up, Carl, our ride's on the way," said Joe as he motioned to a fast-moving glimmer on the horizon.

Thirty minutes later the camp was clear, the fire was out and the men were safely aboard the Parker Exploration Huey on an easterly vector into the burnt-orange Texas sunrise.

"Mr. Gonzales, if you don't mind my asking, where are you taking me now?" said Mayer into the mic on his passenger headset.

"Not to be evasive, Rabbi," replied Pastor Joe, "but the better question is where are you taking us?"

• • •

Not many people were left in the Bonin Islands who had directly experienced the Japanese military presence on Chichi-jima, an isolated flyspeck of dry land six hundred miles south of Tokyo bay. Used as a significant naval base by the Japanese during World War II, the tiny subtropical archipelago was surrendered to the Americans in 1945 and thereafter the US military had been in control. After VJ Day, civilians of Japanese lineage were repatriated to their home islands, and the US Marines placed a small garrison on Father Island to guard the confiscated Japanese fortifications and secure what was rumored to be a cache of American nuclear weapons placed in the vacant munitions bunkers for emergency deployment, should ever the need arise.

Years later, the successful development of the SM-65 Atlas Intercontinental Ballistic Missile by the Convair division of General Dynamics near San Diego and deployment of eleven Strategic Air Command squadrons armed with the Atlas-D variant made the arsenal at Chichi-jima obsolete. Abandonment of the island by the American military was inevitable.

The potent fear of financial ruin and political uncertainty had invaded the island paradise and dominated the talk of the residents of Yankeetown on the November day in 1960 when the most powerful earthquake in recorded history struck Lumaco, Chile, some 10,500 miles to the southeast. The resulting Pacific tsunami devastated the dock works placed by the Japanese and Americans in Futami Port, killing many outright and seeming to doom the survivors to a life of exposure and deprivation. But the pendulum of fortune is never static, and less than a week later a failed military coup d'etat against the first post-Franco president of South Vietnam, Ngo Dinh Diem, refocused America's attention on the region and a continued US military presence on the Bonin Islands was considered a strategic necessity by the Pentagon.

Later that year the Navy Seabees came to the island, tools, equipment and supplies at the ready, to rebuild Yankeetown and the majority of the dock works to accommodate the US Navy's Des Moines-Class heavy cruisers. They added the harbor airfield and heliport to receive long-range helicopters and amphibious aircraft; the harbor command center, which accommodated communications and weather stations; and an island hospital and school, which would be used for military and civilians alike. Good fortune had smiled once again on the people of the Bonin.

The day the Macanese attorneys arrived on their assessment tour of Chichi-jima was long remembered as the island's version of the Miraculous American Dream by Stevie Savory and Guitar Washington, lifetime islanders and descendants of the Western settlers who traced their roots to the arrival of Commodore Matthew Perry in 1853.

Nearly all of the 183 residents of Chichi-jima packed themselves into and around Kate's Tea House, the island's only drinking establishment, which was owned and operated by Stevie's first cousin. They heard the amazing offer from Carlos Brockman, a partner from DS&B Advogados in Macau, claiming that his firm represented a marine petroleum exploration concern interested in purchasing dock frontage and surplus buildings on the vacant west side of the harbor. They would house the regional operations center, which would bring job opportunities for any of the islanders who were willing and able to work. The lawyers closed the deal by producing a letter of credit from the Standard Bank of Macau, LTD, citing deposits for Pacific Rim Exploration of just over three hundred million Macanese Pacta, roughly one hundred and fifty million US dollars.

The island economy boomed as Pacific Rim Exploration completed its harbor improvements, moved its large oceangoing derrick barge and tender craft into the harbor, and began to compete with the US Navy for civilian employees. After the first months, nearly every islander had accepted at least part-time employment with either one or both of the entities, and no one thought it odd that the Chichi-jima School Council should hire an English teacher all the way from El Paso, Texas for a school with only forty students.

The petite young teacher with freckles and flaming-red hair, who the islanders knew as Audrey Jones, had a sunny disposition, laughed often, and was frequently cited by male regulars at the Tea House as being easy on the eye. Audrey and her little boy became fast favorites at the school and everyone in Yankeetown was happy to see them in the market, shops, and restaurants along the strand.

She made a home for herself, her son, and sometimes her husband in one of the small cottages just up the beach at Keyhole Cove, an easy walk to the school and shopping in Yankeetown, and though it was no one's business, there was talk by some of the island wags as to the reason she was visited so infrequently by her husband who, it seemed, held a position of some import with PRE.

"You're looking pretty healthy for a dead guy," she said to David, as he tossed his seabag out of the open passenger compartment of the Grumman Albatross, still dripping wet from its climb out of Futami Harbor and onto the course concrete taxiway of the airfield. Their first impassioned embrace under the wing of the flying boat reunited their family and sealed their union more tightly that either of them could have imagined.

That afternoon Karen and David lay in their hammock, swaying in the cool ocean breeze and watching little Randy play with is toy construction equipment in the wet sand surrounding the shallow tidal pools of Keyhole Cove. "David. Don't go back. Stay here with Randy and me. We have all the money we'll ever need and we can move our families here. They can help us run the business and we'll have a life without fear or want. This island can be our own little Garden of Eden. You've earned this for us, my husband. Your son will grow up with his father and your wife will never have to sleep alone again," said Karen into her husband's ear as she nuzzled his neck.

David thought instantly of the Scripture in Matthew when Peter pleaded with Jesus to refuse his destiny and was rebuked by the Lord, "Get away from me, Satan!" said Jesus. "You are a dangerous trap for me. You are seeing things from a human point of view, not from God's."

After a long moment of tender reflection and with tears in his eyes for the difficult life that his wife was being forced to endure, he said, "Karen, I promised on our honeymoon that I would never keep anything from you that wasn't a military secret, and I never have. God has impressed on me that a dangerous storm is building in our own country that threatens us all. There will be a life or death fight for the soul of America, Karen, and He has honored me with a role in the struggle that I do not fully understand.

"He has generously answered my prayers to protect you and Randy by miraculously providing the resources and the opportunity to purchase Pacific Rim Exploration so that I could secure you and Randy away from the conflict here on Chichi-jima.

"The large envelope in my seabag is the Lord's provision for you both. Everything's in your name, darling; trusts were established for you and Randy through the Standard Bank of Macau, and the bearer bonds issued by Odessa Permian LTD are all there. Odessa Permian is the anonymous Swiss holding company that owns PRE and its assets, so no one can trace the ownership back to you. Bearer bonds are like cash, darling; as long as you hold on to them, you own everything, and that is perhaps my greatest comfort. You will be provided for no matter what happens to me, and my enemies cannot reach you here, Karen. God has placed a divine hedge of protection around you and Randy that cannot be breached, yet I will be able to visit you as my duties permit.

"So please, Karen, even though it burns our hearts like fire, you must endure and do what you can to accept His will for my life—for our life as a family in His service and under His divine protection."

Embracing through their tears, the Rixons shared an abiding joy in the Lord and held on tight, savoring their precious moment and making a memory that would last a lifetime.

That afternoon the wind quickened and they saw the tide had changed. The sea was flowing into their little cove through the eroded keyhole in the volcanic seawall, which was placed by the Lord in the distant past to restrain the dangerous waters of the treacherous Pacific Rim.

• • •

Pacific Rim Exploration had obtained its Grumman HU-16 as postwar military surplus. The Albatross amphibious flying boat was powered by two Curtiss-Wright R 1820 Cyclone radial engines that developed a combined 1,400 horsepower and would drive the aircraft at a top speed of 236 miles per hour to a maximum range of 2,478 miles. It was designed for marine combat search-and-rescue operations and could land on the open ocean with four-foot seas, making it an ideal workhorse for the PRE marine operations, which spanned the Asian shores of the Pacific.

The PRE crew had filed their flight plan with USN Harbor Control, good-byes had been said, and so Karen and Randy watched the Albatross race past "Hello Rock," out of Futami Harbor, and into the flawless azure sky on its eight-hour flight to Henderson Field on Midway Atoll, nearly two thousand miles east northeast of their new home on Chichi-jima.

An hour into the flight, David began to relax and consider his circumstance. Karen's fragrance was still fresh on his shirt, her kiss warm and moist on his lips, as he thought about his wife and son— about living with them forever at Keyhole Cove.

She had asked him to stay, and he had said that he was duty bound to return to the war, but was that true? What of his duty to Karen and Randy? Where did his duty truly lie? Could things have worked out differently? Could he have led his squad back to the American lines? If they had, surely he and Coats would have been decorated for valor, honorably discharged, and they would be openly, honestly living back in the World eating five-dollar steaks and drinking cold beer—maybe even back at the Log Cabin in Ruidoso. Instead, they had spent two years playing dead to stay alive, hiding out in a giant's cave inside an obscure mountain; preparing a band of Iron-Age warriors armed with crossbows, sticks, and rocks to defend their families against a modern mechanized army; relying on criminals to obtain the means for their mission and their very survival. They invented new lives for themselves and their families on the very edge of the World and lived in constant in fear, hunted by at least two, perhaps three lethal forces as well as their own government.

And what exactly was their mission now? Stopping global communism seemed somehow naïve, a fairytale for the child he no longer was. His experience over the past three years had been surreal, impossible to fit into the view of reality shared by Karen and everyone else who were informed only by their life experience in the Western world. This terrifying yet real apparition was with him constantly, even in the Albatross, speeding toward the far horizon, where sky and ocean merge and blue infinity opens a safe place in his mind where he could reflect on the years and events that had brought him to this strange and perilous moment.

• • •

Their first morning on the mountaintop, the squad was rattled awake by a predawn flight of four Navy A-1 Skyraiders. Thundering low overhead, they streaked across the ridgeline into Laos from western Vietnam, vectoring into their flight path from the USS *Ranger* on Yankee Station in the Gulf of Tonkin.

Led by an excited Travis, the group raced past the concealed ancient ruins to the western edge of the granite escarpment to watch the single-seat, propeller-driven dive bombers power down the shadow side of the mountain and snap to level flight just above the treetops, the lift vortices trailing their wingtips, whirling the early morning mountain fog into tiny white tornados.

"Flyboys must be lost, Cap," speculated an especially scruffy-looking Coats, pulling the map kit out of the leg pocket of his ragged tiger trousers, "Wonder if they even know they're in Laos. Hell, it all looks the same from up here. If we plotted our location correctly last night, then the war's over to our left."

Using the unfolded map and their compass for orientation, they watched in surprise as the Skyraiders veered north, away from Vietnamese airspace, to join dozens more propeller-driven aircraft on the horizon, silently deploying their ordnance in orange, yellow, and black bursting clouds, on a strike mission clearly outside their area of operation.

As the friendly aircraft disappeared from view and their hopes of rescue vanished, the squad returned to the shelter of their lean-to and smoldering campfire. "El Tee, what did we just see?" asked David, and he walked beyond the camp and toward the northern edge of their little plateau, Coats shrugging to the scouts and tagging along with his commander.

"Sir, I believe we just saw four intrepid naval aviators give the enemy a taste of his own medicine. In this case, it appeared to be a napalm lavage, compliments of the Dow Chemical Company of Midland, Michigan," said Coats with a slight chuckle, pleased that he had been able to enlighten the captain with his knowledge of advanced American military ordinance, which he had gleaned from once reading the label on a shipping container in Da Nang, and wondering just what they were going to have for breakfast.

"The enemy? Which enemy? DOD Rules of Engagement say we're not supposed to be doing anything on this side of the border. Laos is neutral, they tell us. So if COMUSMACV is going to ignore the Geneva Accords then why weren't those planes hitting the bastards hiding out on the Ho Chi Minh Trail—the ones that killed nearly everybody at Rana Dat, that would have traded you to the Russians for an AK-Forty-Seven and that tracked us through the bush for three weeks and tried to kill us every step of the way? We know for sure there're at least twenty-four thousand of 'em building up to launch an offensive that could kill thousands of our men. Like you said, El Tee, the war is over to the left!"

Coats had seen Rixon sacred and sad and happy. He had seen him in a fistfight with a superior officer, and he had even seen him filled with the adrenalin rush of combat, drenched with the blood of his enemy, but he had never seen him truly angry. "David, take it easy. There's probably a good reason for it. Something we don't understand. It's probably just classified. The brass does a lot of stupid things but COMUSMACV wouldn't hang us out. I mean why would he? There's probably a larger issue of National Secur…"

"National Security?" Rixon cut him off. "Is that it? Are those the magic words, El Tee? Do any damned thing you feel like; aid the enemy; murder your own people if you want, and if ya get caught it's "classified" for "national security" purposes. Sounds to me like the universal get-out-of-jail-free card! Tom, we're all being lied to. Every damned one of us, the whole country is being played for fools by the scum suckers who run Washington. The war is nothing more than a gigantic, multimillion-dollar goddamned fucking death orgy, and it doesn't matter to the Suits who's in the body count; they just want the numbers high! The blood of millions of innocents and even of our own troopers is all over the bastards but somehow, someway, they're getting away with it, and I intend to do everything I can to put a stop to it!"

For the first time in a long time, Coats really looked at his friend. David was unshaven, unwashed; his hair was long, ragged, and matted; his uniform was in tatters and falling off his emaciated frame; and there was a burning intensity in his eyes that was frightening. For an instant Tom thought he could see the fear of God cover David's face; the hair on the back of his neck stood erect, and he shivered. Looking away, he could see the scouts were in even worse condition, and he could only imagine his appearance as he cinched up his belt and straightened his ragged uniform.

"Captain, why don't we take a break and warm up over by the fire. I think Scotty must have snared some doves or something last night, and it smells like they're just about ready." Travis was nudging his master's hand for a pet, and so an uneasy calm was restored, and they joined the scouts for their morning meal.

That afternoon the squad moved their camp into the ancient alien structure, they thought it a temple, concealed by the giant inside the deep recess of a granite ledge facing east toward Hanoi— just below the lip and hidden from view to passing aircraft. Over the next weeks they recovered from their trial and spent their days sleeping, eating, whatever Donny and Scotty gleaned from the high-mountain tree line, washing in the shaded grotto the scouts had discovered at the rear of the structure, further investigating the giant's labyrinth and making a plan for getting back to the World.

• • •

The copilot of the Albatross brought David coffee and a sandwich while reporting on their progress; six hours remained in their flight to Midway. He refused the opportunity to take the controls, the one thing he loved about being "the boss," and returned to the solitude of his thoughts remembering Proverbs 13:22: *A good man leaves an inheritance to his children's children, And the wealth of the wicked is laid up for the righteous.* It was the Lord's provision of the giant's gold that made his new mission and his new life possible. David smiled to remember that it was Travis the war dog that inadvertently unlocked the mystery of the giant's domed tomb and the translucent hiero-glyphic tablets that lay within.

• • •

WOOF; WOOF; AH OOOOOOOOOoooooo; AH OOOOOOOOO-oooooo; AH OOOOOOOOOooooooo...

Startled by their howling dog, the squad had been astonished to witness the ancient automated systems crackle to life. The dome above their heads brightened and dissolved into what appeared to be an enlarged microscopic image of golden flecks and aqua spheres, which seemed to be oscillating sympathetically with the energetic pulse and whirr of powerful equipment hidden deep below their feet.

"It's the gold cubes in the other room!" exclaimed Coats. "I knew it! These guys figured out how to make gold out of sand or some-thin'! This here's gotta be a damned gold factory, Cap, and we're the new owners. This old boy," said Coats patting the giant's elongated skull, covered with leathered skin and long red hair, "sure as hell ain't gonna say nothin' 'bout us takin' over from where he left off!"

David had deduced, and the squad concurred, that the technol-ogy was designed by beings with physical sensibilities radically differ-ent than their own. Clearly, the sonic command and control system they had been fortunate to discover was designed to operate beyond the range of human hearing. Travis had probably reacted with her howl to a challenge signal, perhaps like a telephone dial tone, which was activated by something like a proximity sensor. When she responded, it was as if she said, "Hello, I'm here," to the automated alien technology, which self-activated in response and probably indexed to the last command given by the thing laying before them on the command couch.

Over dinner that evening, out of the cave and back in the moun-taintop temple, David and Tommy agreed that without equipment and scientific know-how, there was nothing further they could do to properly investigate the installation. They should document their discovery as well as they could, take samples of the gold cubes, the white powdered substance, and one of the tablets with them and submit their findings to someone who could help.

"So what ya think Big Boy really is, Captain? A space alien or something?" asked Coats reclining by the fire, examining a golden cube he had brought with him from the "factory."

"Well, it sure is alien, and I guess it could be from outer space, but more likely it's Nephilim, the product of the mating of fallen angels with the daughters of men just like it says in the Scripture," replied David. Opening Scotty's Bible, he turned to Genesis and read by the firelight, "*The Nephilim were on the earth in those days, and also afterward, when the sons of God came in to the daughters of men, and they bore children to them. Those were the mighty men who were of old, men of renown."*

David then leafed to the Book of Numbers and continued, *"The land through which we have gone, in spying it out, is a land that devours its inhabitants; and all the people whom we saw in it are men of great size. There also we saw the Nephilim (the sons of Anak are part of the Nephilim); and we became like grasshoppers in our own sight, and so we were in their sight.*

"My strong notion is that Big Red down there is a descendant of the giants mentioned in the Old Testament, maybe even a distant cousin of Goliath himself." David turned to 1 Samuel. *"A champion named Goliath, who was from Gath, came out of the Philistine camp. His height was six cubits and a span (nine feet nine inches). He had a bronze helmet on his head and wore a coat of scale armor of bronze weighing five thousand shekels (one hundred twenty-five pounds). On his legs he wore bronze greaves, and a bronze javelin was slung on his back. His spear shaft was like a weaver's rod, and its iron point weighed six hundred shekels (fifteen pounds)."*

"Sounds a lot like Big Willie Washington in full pads!" quipped Coats, causing Rixon to smile slightly.

"Captain, this is big; maybe bigger than even the war. People have got to know about this, but the right people. Maybe MACV in Da Nang; there's gotta be someone at command that'll know what to do with all this, but first we're gonna have ta get back ta where we started and that ain't gonna be easy."

"Of course we have to go back, Tom, but I've been thinking. I still feel uneasy about going back to Da Nang. Washington will be all over us, and for all we know, he's managed to brand us traitors and laid the bombing of Rana Dat on our heads. But I agree that turning the information over to the government and then going back to the World through proper channels is the best course of action," volunteered the thoughtful, duty-bound Marine that Coats had come to know and respect, "There's supposed to be an American embassy in the Laotian capital, Vientiane, and the map says it's only about half as far, maybe three hundred klicks, as it is to Da Nang. I say we head southwest, try to commandeer a vehicle, make it to the embassy, and dump this in the ambassador's lap. Let the State Department sort it out."

A career soldier with nearly thirty years in uniform, the thought of humping through the swarm of enemy troops clustered along the border and then through the mountains of Vietnam with no way to defend himself was repulsive to Coats. The squad agreed to prepare themselves as best they could and then head southwest, away from the enemy troop concentration and to the capital city of Laos.

It took them two days but they eventually found their way off the mountain, using part of the subterranean labyrinth that led to a vent carved into a granite cliff face. Using their paracord to fabricate a harness and trolley for Travis and themselves, they bridged to a tree canopy halfway up the low side of the mountain, and they were free.

Travis was leading them through the rainforest at a good pace when they were cut off and nearly killed by an outlying NVA force protection patrol securing the main enemy muster. Rixon was suddenly reminded that the NVA strength had been estimated at twenty-four thousand by the intel they had captured at Signal Hill. Moving still farther to the west, they found the bush alive with swarms of enemy soldiers, support units, and even more force protection patrols; a dangerous place to be an American.

By their fourth day in the bush, Rixon and his squad were being hunted by the NVA. On the run and starving, reduced to sleeping on the ground with no fire and no cover, drinking rainwater and foraging in the jungle for basic sustenance, they were defenseless and out of options, when Coats suggested, "Let's just follow our noses. Maybe we'll find something we can use."

It was a tactically brilliant if somewhat aesthetically flawed maneuver that had them follow a foul fragrance wafting on the jungle breeze, which originated from one of the many latrines the enemy had constructed to serve their primary encampment. David soon discovered just how cooperative a man can be when caught with his pants down and a razor sharp K-bar at his neck. The squad rearmed and reprovisioned itself at the expense of the Communists and escaped into the rain forest without spilling a drop of enemy blood. Divine Providence and the call of nature worked together to deliver the things they needed most into their possession.

The squad continued the journey to the capital, holding a wide margin between the enemy troop concentration and their path of travel, staying under the jungle canopy in case an American aircraft were to mistake them for the enemy and off the main road to avoid motorized patrols. They navigated using their compass, a captured map, and visible landmarks. It was slow going over rugged terrain, but they were finally moving, and David imagined that every step he took brought him that much closer to Karen, Randy, and home.

Just ahead David saw Donny conversing with Coats. "Captain, Donny says we got an abandoned vehicle about three klicks out. Nobody around that he can see. Could be booby-trapped, I guess, but maybe we can disarm the explosives and boost it; take ourselves a little joyride. We could be knocking on the front door of the embassy day after tomorrow."

The squad came to the edge of a large clearing, obviously under cultivation and covered with the brilliant red and black blossoms of Papaver Somniferumhe, the opium poppy. David compared its size to his papa's truck farm back home in Odessa that was one hundred and fifty acres. "Lotta dope out there, Captain," whispered Coats, "Some major money. Scotty says the Hmong tribe's been cultivating the poppy as a cash crop for a hundred years or more but he's never anything this size. This is clearly a commercial operation, and there ought to be armed guards at least and probably trip wires and land mines around the perimeter. We gotta treat this like a combat operation if we're gonna approach at all."

David split the squad into two fire teams. He and Donny took the point, and Coats and Scotty the flank, and they approached the position of the reported vehicle, keeping a good distance inside the tree line on the lookout for mines and well away from the edge of the opium field. Donny crouched and raised a clenched fist. They could hear an engine idling perhaps fifty meters beyond their position.

Scotty signaled the squad to hold position while he advanced, and a few minutes later he returned, giving them the all clear signal.

The vehicle was a Russian GAZ, a small four-seat scout car. David approached from the driver side and saw the blood-spattered door standing open and the feet of the driver hanging outside. Inside the cab was an American, dressed in military bush gear, stripped of all insignia except for the name: Whitehead. The body was still warm, the blood pooling on the floor plate was still seeping from his neck where a small wooden arrow was lodged. Its point was seated firmly in the cervical vertebra and the black-feathered shaft was protruding from the victim's Adam's apple. "Harrison J. Whitehead, Special Agent at Large, Federal Bureau of Investigation," read Coats from the bloody wallet. "He's got the badge and photo ID that says he's an FBI agent, Cap. What the hell is an FBI agent doing getting himself killed in a poppy field in Laos?"

They heard Travis barking savagely and then a shriek and deep sobbing from Scotty's position as he was holding his Communist AK-Forty-Seven while aggressively yelling at someone to get their hands up. Rixon and Coats approached the ruckus, their carbines at the ready, when two people stood, their hands in the air, clearly one male and one female. "Hell, Cap., this is getting' more and more interesting all the time. Ya think these two were out here on a picnic?"

Rixon held Travis and looked on as Coats frisked their prisoners, retrieving leather wallets from each, and though they were bloodied and muddy the woman was clearly Chinese and the man, like the driver, was clearly American. David looked closely. He seemed familiar. Without saying anything, Coats placed the credentials in Rixon's hand, and a moment later he raised his head, looked into the eyes of the male prisoner with a small spark of recognition and said gently; "Hola, Alberto. Mucho tiempo sin verte."

The man seemed in shock as he strained in disbelief at his bearded, ragged, emaciated captor. "Ronald Coleman Albert Vazquez, Deputy Director, United States Department of Agriculture," read Coats aloud. "Lemme guess, Captain: this here's the quarterback from the world-famous Dallas Carter Cowboys."

• • •

The copilot of the Albatross broke David's train of thought to let him now know that they were altering course to avoid a tropical storm that had popped up on their radar, adding about an hour to their flight time. David gladly accepted the coffee, stood, stretched, moved around the cramped cabin, and began an abbreviated workout while returning to his memories.

• • •

The squad buried the rapidly decaying corpse of Agent Harrison Whitehead, which had begun to swell in the hot, sticky air. Though David didn't know the man, he did his best to give him a Christian burial, marking and his grave site on their map. Afterward they used the GAZ to move themselves, their captives, and their supplies away from the poppy field and to a more secluded campsite several kilometers into the rain forest. That night around the fire, Vazquez related a nearly unbelievable tale of illegal government conscription and bribery, criminal CIA drug running in partnership with paramilitary organized crime gangs, all controlled through the American State and Justice Departments with direction coming from somewhere outside the governmental chain of command.

All this seemed so fantastic to David that he began to doubt the sanity of his college friend. "Al, I lost touch with you after I shipped out to Nam. Did you and Belinda ever marry?" asked David to begin constructing a verifiable baseline narrative against which he could measure Al's current mental state, but something was missing. The connection and brotherhood, the spark of recognition he had once seen in in Al's eyes was gone. He smiled for the first time in a long time, but after a moment it faded.

"Yeah, we did, David." Al frowned. "But it was under duress, and her parents hate my guts. She got pregnant right after you went into the corps," he said with a distant look in his eyes. "Her parents made it clear that she was to have nothing more to do with me. They demanded that she abort the baby and then go to graduate school in Europe. There was so much hate and pressure on both of us that one day we just ran away. We got married at a justice of the peace in Virginia a couple of months after I joined USDA. David, we have a daughter, Maria Carol Jean Vazquez. We named her after both of her grandmothers, and we hoped that over time the Dorances would come to accept their granddaughter and our marriage, but they never have."

"Al, tell me why you're here. Why are you involved in this? Why don't you just walk away?" asked David.

"You don't know these men, David. They say if I don't cooperate, they'll deport my mother back to Vera Cruz, that something terrible will happen to Belinda and Maria, and then I'm pretty sure Belinda's father is involved in this in some way—right at the top.

"I'm in deep, David, and I have every reason to believe they'll kill me if I don't cooperate." He touched his scarred temple. "Mostly, David, I really don't know how to get out. Money's also a factor; we have property now in Virginia, a brownstone in Georgetown, and a retirement account for Mother. There's more than a million dollars at stake for my family this year alone. I'm trapped, David, and there's no way it ends well for me." There was a long, sad pause in the conversation.

"How about your friend?" asked David, holding her identification and motioning across the campfire. "How does a female Chinese national fit into this little criminal enterprise?"

"Her name is Wong Ah Kum, and this is her first trip into the field. Pretty bad trip, if you ask me," his former friend said with a weak smile. "We're only here to sample the product and estimate the crop yield. Normally she wouldn't have come along, but I think Whitehead might have had a thing for her; she is sort of exotic looking when she's cleaned up.

"He insisted that she ride along, and he personally guaranteed her safety to her father. She's Triad David, the daughter of a man known as 'Four Thirty-Eight Deputy Mountain Master,' who is stationed in Vientiane and manages Laotian operations for 'Four Eighty-Nine Dragon Master' in Macau. Their family is known as 'Fifteen M'; it's sort of the Chinese version of the American Mafia. Since the Maoists purges on the mainland, they've been operating from their main base in Macau. Fifteen M are mainly smugglers—opium, gold, weapons, and people from the Golden Crescent into their Macanese distribution networks, so I guess that makes her sort of a contract shipping agent of the State Department, the Justice Department, and the CIA. This is a big business, David. Hundreds of millions of dollars are at stake and everyone involved is deadly serious."

There was a long uncomfortable pause in the conversation as David considered their precarious circumstance. "So, Al, what happened to your Agent Whitehead and where are all the guards? This crop is worth millions. You'd need at least a platoon of troopers to secure a field that size."

"They were here when we arrived; Hmong mercenaries, and they were very unhappy. The head man and Whitehead began to argue. He said they hadn't been paid in over a month and threatened to sell the crop to somebody else, maybe the Viet Minh or the Pathet Lao or to Fifteen M directly. He pressed Whitehead and found he didn't have the cash on him, and we made a break for it. That's when someone shot him. I don't think they meant to, but when he went down, all hell broke loose. We were able to get away while they swarmed the car looking for their pay, and then you guys showed up. As far as we know, they're still out there and still pissed off."

Coats motioned to Rixon that they needed to speak in private. "Captain, I found this flier in Whitehead's kit. Sir, it looks like we're wanted men." It was a telex that had originated from something called the "Office of Policy Coordination" at the American embassy in Saigon and was sent to Agent Sterrette Brown at the American embassy in Vientiane. It read in part: *SECRET//SPECIAL ACCESS REQUIRED—RODEO COWBOY: FIELD TERMINATION WARRANT//*

DAVID KING RIXON, DOD SERIAL: 38 62 630; LIEUTENANT USMC// $50,000 USD PAID BOUNTY// RIXON COLLABORATED WITH COMMUNIST INSURGENTS IN THE TERRORIST BOMBING AND INFANTRY ATTACKS ON USSOG INSTALLATIONS AS105801 AND AS096001 RESULTING IN THE DEATHS OF 600 IRREGULARS, FAMILIES, AND USSF OPERATORS// SUBJECT DESCRIPTION: HT: 5'6"; WT: 155LBS; EYES: BROWN; HAIR: AUBURN; IDENTIFYING MARKS: USMC TATOO RIGHT SHOULDER; PRONOUNCED FACAL SCARRING; DOB: 14/01/46// LAST SEEN: HOUAPHANH PROVINCE IN COMPANY FUGITIVE USSF OPERATOR THOMAS CASE COATS (DOD SERIAL: 15 42 289); TWO MONTAGNARD MERCENARY SCOUTS// WARNING: GROUP IS ARMED AND EXTREMELY DANGEROUS; DO NOT ATTEMPT APREHENSION; TERMINATE ON SIGHT// BOUNTY PAID FOR WARRANT PRIMARY ONLY; POSITIVE PHYSICAL IDENTIFICATION REQUIRED @ OPC/AE/SAIGON/RVN// S//SAR-RC...###10012

Rixon felt kicked in the groin; disoriented, nauseated. His own government had placed a price on his head. He had been convicted and sentenced without even the pretense of a military tribunal. He was a dead man walking, and no one, not even his family, would ever know he'd been executed. He felt a deep nausea sweep over him, and he looked up from the warrant to see Coats—smiling? "Looks like we're gonna hafta make us some new friends, Captain," said the lieutenant, glancing beyond his shoulder. David turned to see that the Hmong had returned.

Months later and in reflection, David realized that he had been too involved with immediate events, too concerned for his own life, to be able to see the hand of the Lord moving him rapidly beyond the comfortable emotional and psychic realm he had unconsciously constructed for himself and into the uncertainty of his new role. He had tried too hard to make sense of the chaos to be able to trust the wisdom of the Holy Spirit and his own life experience; too focused on holding doors open to keep a secure line of retreat rather than to run behind the Lord Jesus into the next phase of his life. But in the rain forests of Laos, facing a hundred or more lethal Hmong warriors poised to attack, the head man staring fiercely into David's eyes, the burden became too great for him and something inside just let go. "Father, into your hands I deliver my spirit."

The suggestion to use one of the giant's golden cubes to barter with the Hmong for their lives came from Scotty, one of the most brilliant students that Jeff and Suzanne Campbell had ever produced in nearly three decades of operating the Christ in Asia Ministry for the indigenous peoples of the Annamite Range.

When the head man examined the heavy cube, he ran his fingers over the hieroglyphs and, after studying them intently, his entire countenance changed. He avoided further eye contact with David, assumed a submissive posture, and spoke quietly to Scotty in his native E-de, the primary language spoken in the Mountains of Laos.

"Captain, he asked if you Sin Sai," said Scotty. "He say only Sin Sai could have stolen this gold away from giant and still live."

The Hmong had been a stateless, hunted people since 1775 when Chinese Emperor Ch'ien Lung had ordered them purged from their native lands between the Yellow and Yangtze River regions in north central China. For nearly two hundred years the Hmong had struggled to survive in the unpopulated mountains of Laos, Thailand, and Vietnam. They lived in close-knit extended family units called "clans" with slash-and-burn subsistence farming and the quasi-religious hope that one day their race would somehow, some-way, come into possession of a secure land they could call their own.

In the mythology of the Hmong, "Sin Sai" was the fabled spirit-warrior of a time before time in the land of snow and ice. He defended the first people of the earth against the evil giants who enslaved them and hunted them for food. Sin Sai had told the Hmong to move from the flat lands and live on the mountaintops in safety. "If the giants come to find you, I will come down from the sky with an army of invincible soldiers and lead you to a land of your own where you will live in peace and plenty forever." Then Sin Sai disappeared to heaven in a flash of fire.

The Hmong brought David, the squad, their prisoners, and Travis to their thatched village compound, where they saw the women and children of the warriors, who were laughing and running in groups, trying to get a view of Sin Sai and his skysoldiers. The head man ushered them through the village into a vast meadow beyond in which they were shown thousands of megalithic stone containers, clearly of the same type the squad had discovered in the giant's cavern. The head man motioned for David to examine a large carved stone lid partially buried near a dense cluster of the ancient vessels. Though severely weathered, a larger version of the repeating anthropomorphic character on the golden cube was clearly visible. "Sin Sai; Sin Sai!" said the head man, pointing to David and a sort of awe and respect sparked through the Iron Age mercenaries who could just as easily have had their heads.

Late in the evening of the first day David, Tom, and the scouts were shown a place of honor in the village and introduced to the women and children, just over two hundred, it seemed to David, who had trouble counting children who were chasing each other in a game that reminded the Americans of red rover. The livestock seemed to perplex Travis who, as far as David knew, had never seen chickens, pigs, goats, or even other dogs. The village children were especially amused as the massive war dog was seemingly held at bay by a tiny spotted nanny goat that would not allow her to inspect the kids any closer than to sniff the air.

Around the fire that evening the children were cuddling and petting Travis while the head man, Yang Dao, engaged David in broken English with Scotty filling in missing words. "Captain, he say there is little food for the village. Lao army forced Hmong to plant poppy not rice, corn, bean, potato. Village must have pay from king; from Savang Vatthana; must have rice to live. Pig, goat, chicken, food only two, three days, then the village starves."

In the days that followed, the squad found shelter, sustenance, and comfort with the Hmong who concealed them from the Communists, both Pathet Lao and Viet Minh, hiding them once in the stone jars just beyond their thatched compound before leading the enemy away into the jungle and then vanishing themselves. On the fifth day, a significant contingent from the Royal Lao Armed

Forces was transported to the poppy field by unmarked helicopters, took up defensive positions to secure the crop, and sent teams into the bush to search for Whitehead and the Hmong who had abandoned the field.

The heat had driven the Hmong into the deep shade of the compound, and they were unprepared when a group of Laotian soldiers, along with their translator, walked into the camp and called out Yang Dao. Watching from his sleeping blind, David could see that the ten-man squad was armed with American weapons: M-16 carbines and one M60 general purpose machine gun. The squad leader publicly interrogated Yang Dao, humiliating him and enraging the clan, while the gunner and the spotter set the tripod and mounted the M60. Coats and the scouts watched things quickly deteriorate.

The warriors began to gather around their leader, as it seemed that a confrontation was inevitable. The Hmong were armed with crossbows, spears, sharpened sticks, and rocks along with a half dozen Korean surplus M1 Garand rifles with only a few rounds of ammunition for each. Rixon and Coats knew if hostilities broke out, they would be cut to pieces by the M60 in the first moments of the firefight.

David signaled the squad to take defensive positions and looked sternly at Vazquez and Wong Ah Kum. "Come on, your ride's here." Armed only with the K-bar riding on his belt, he walked boldly out of their hooch through the crowd of warriors and belligerently invaded the personal space of the Lao squad leader, looking directly into his eyes kicking dirt on his spit-shined combat boots. He crushed the leader's confidence with his fierce gaze and, concealing his desperation, barked his commands in broken Vietnamese and French, saying he was CIA and the Hmong were under his direct command, that Whitehead had been killed as a matter of honor over the woman, and that his Hmong troops were taking the day to mourn the loss of the American, whom they regarded as a god.

Tensions relaxed and the squad leader brought up his radio telephone operator to report to his commander who would undoubtedly have the Lao version of the Rodeo-Cowboy Termination

Warrant at hand. "I hope Coats is paying attention," thought Rixon as he rested his forearm on the hilt of the K-bar and grew tense, expecting the worst. The squad leader smiled, bowed to Rixon, and gave the clan permission to take the rest of the day away from their duty as long as they were back on guard when the helicopters returned for them in the morning. He then shook the hands of Vazquez and Wong Ah Kum and took them under his charge. But before leaving, Wong looked Rixon in the eye, leaned forward, touched his hand, and whispered in his ear, "Do not worry, Captain, we will meet again."

As soon as the Lao squad was out of hearing range, Rixon moved back into the hooch. "El Tee, we've got to get these people clear ASAP. Someone on the other end of the radio transmission will know that there's no CIA operator out here and will figure that we're the guys they're looking for."

As soon as the sun began to fade, David and the squad moved the Hmong out of their village and into the hills when just before dark they saw the entire village erupt in violent orange-black spasm of flaming napalm as two F-100 Super Saber fighter-bombers streaked by at low altitude, swirling the black smoke and orange flame in their wake. A few minutes later, they heard small arms fire and watched the Lao troopers assaulting the empty, burning village.

That evening in the foothills, overlooking the smoldering village, the squad met privately to decide their immediate future. Coats was emphatic. "Cap, we can't leave 'em! When the Lao discover that we tricked 'em, they'll use the choppers to sweep the area and kill everyone from the air!"

They moved the Hmong through the night and were well into the shelter of the mountains by dawn. As the first morning rays illuminated the poppy fields, Rixon was watching the enemy through his M-19 binoculars when the helicopters returned. "El Tee, please ask Yang Dao to disburse his people and seek cover in the trees and rocks. The choppers are landing; the attack will be coming soon." But as David watched in disbelief, the choppers powered down and David could see their GAZ moving slowly across uneven terrain in their direction. He watched the car in amazement and saw the driver was Wong Ah Kum, and the rear of the vehicle was piled high with the long-overdue sacks of rice for the Hmong.

• • •

The PRE pilot brought David a last cup of coffee and let him know that they would be landing at Midway in just over an hour. He began to get excited about seeing his papa, to hear the news about his family in Odessa, and to tell Pastor Joe about the terrifying yet important mission the Lord had assigned him.

• • •

The most disappointing aspect of the encounter had been Al Vazquez and his decision to return to his bondage at the American Embassy in Vientiane. Both David and Tom had encouraged him to get out and join them in finding the right way back to the World, but he had declined, saying that he was in too deep to ever get away. This saddened David greatly and he grieved for the loss of his friend.

Among the greatest blessings for David, Tom, the scouts, and the Hmong was that Wong Ah Kum had been a secret Christian all along. Raised in the heart of Maoist China, she was a young convert of the persecuted evangelist Pastor Samuel Lamb. She had professed her faith in Jesus Christ and been baptized in Lamb's House Church in Macau. That she had experienced an encounter with an angel of the Lord that very evening who had miraculously arranged for the Lao troopers to stand down was only the beginning of the chain of miracles that had confirmed David's decision to remain on the giant's mountain and shepherd the Hmong until he was relieved by the Holy Spirit.

Especially for the Hmong, Wong Ah Kum had been like a guardian angel and, true to her name, "as good as gold." Ah Kum took a great personal risk by using her tenuous connections within her father's branch of 15M to bring food, clothing and E-de New

Testaments to the people. There had been enough to sustain them physically and spiritually in the labyrinth of caves and volcanic crevasses they inhabited at the base of the giant's mountain. She also was able to source the scientific equipment that David needed to document, map, and diagnose the sonic control system that partially unlocked the secrets of the giant's technology.

But for every wonderful thing that Ah Kum was able to do for the Hmong, she was unable to provide weapons or ammunition for their defense, which had become necessary as the Pathet Lao and Viet Minh brought the war closer to their new home every day. The squad trained the young Hmong warriors in American asymmetrical infantry tactics and led them on raids of NVA arms shipments along the Ho Chi Minh trail. After only a month the Hmong were as well armed as the Pathet Lao. It was David's goal to leave them at least equivalent in capability to the Vietnamese Communists by commandeering the enemy's arms and ammunition, which would enable the Hmong warriors to defend their women, children, and mountain home. And this he did with the zeal unequaled by any enemy the Communists had yet experienced.

The day the future was finally secured for the Hmong was the day David and Tom cracked the Giants code. It appeared that Coats had been right from the start; the giant had indeed been running a gold factory.

Wong Ah Kum saw the potential immediately. Since the Bretton Woods System had outlawed the private ownership of gold bullion in the Allied countries in 1944, and since Portugal, the colonizing nation state of Macau, had remained neutral during hostilities and was not a signatory to the agreement, the commodity exchanges in Macau were booming and the price of gold there was set by the free market. At any given moment, one of the Giant's golden cubes could bring as much as twenty thousand American dollars; fifty percent more than the price ceiling enforced by the World War II monetary system.

• • •

On his first visit to Macau, David felt disoriented and slightly uncomfortable. With his recent kill-or-be-killed combat experience against the Communists in Vietnam and Laos still fresh, the quasi-autonomy of the city-state, which seemed to be functioning very well within the national sphere of Maoist China, was difficult to fully comprehend. How this level of apparent freedom could exist within a repressive Communist system was beyond him.

Wong Ah Kum explained that Portugal had established a trade tenancy on the Macanese peninsula through agents of the Chongzhen emperor, the final ruler in the Ming line. From the viewpoint of China, the peninsula was never a Portuguese colony, but at various times over its four-hundred-year history, Macau had been considered both an overseas territory of Portugal and a Chinese territory under Portuguese administration. Due primarily to its distance from Lisbon, Macau ultimately became a pragmatic commercial vessel devoid of political complications and laden only with the convergent financial interests of several sovereign states.

Because of Portugal's neutrality in World War II, Macau had also escaped Japanese occupation to become a haven for spies, gamblers, and fortune hunters from all over the world. Even then, wartime smugglers used the peninsula to offload contraband goods for illegal import into the mainland. In fact, it was often said that Mao himself made his first fortune as a wartime importer of illegal food and luxury items impossible to find anywhere north of the Macanese peninsula. As with all things, the beneficial porosity of the city-state influenced all aspects of life there including its culture, religion, and the built environment itself. David thought some of the cafes would have been a perfect stage setting for Humphrey Bogart and Ingrid Bergman in the movie *Casablanca*, except in the Macanese version, the Chinese Communists would stand in for the German Nazis. And it had been in one of those cafes that respect, friendship, and affection between Lieutenant Coats and Wong Ah Kum blossomed into love.

Ah Kum, Tommy, and David discussed the future of their little group of Hmong on many occasions. Even hidden in the citadel of the giant's mountain, they were living in a war zone and were constantly hunted by the Pathet Lao, the Viet Mien, the RLA and other Hmong clans who were encouraged by their dire circumstances to serve as anti-Communist mercenaries for the CIA's clandestine war, the strategy of which seemed absolutely schizophrenic to the squad. While the United States Air Force continued to rain ordinance on the countryside nearly daily, directed by who knows who for who knows what objectives, the population could only struggle to survive. And then there was Rodeo-Cowboy, which had them looking over their shoulders uncomfortably even in out-of-the-way Macau.

"You know Hmong means 'the Free People'?" They're tough as nails, strong as bulls, loyal, and honest. They don't have a word for fear because they're fearless. They got the same instinct for liberty we do, David, but they'll never be able to live like people in the World do. The kids might learn to make it someplace else but the adults couldn't live in a world with schools, jobs, mortgages, concrete, and cars; they're too innocent for that, too pure, too in touch with the natural world. The separation would just kill 'em," said Coats, fully aware of the danger of the status quo. "It'd be more merciful if we just shot 'em ourselves."

"We ain't shootin' 'em, Top, but we didn't take 'em ta' raise neither. Even if we dedicate the rest of our lives to the clan they'll still have to fend for themselves when we pass away or are killed by the war or the bounty hunters," added David. "We've got to develop a transition plan. Let's say over a year or so we train and equip them for a future they can't imagine for themselves right now. Maybe we could set up a school like Paul and Suzann Campbell did for the Yards at Christ in Asia; remember that?"

"Yeah, I do. Which reminds me of Donny and Scotty," said Tom, "They had family in the village at Rana Dat, David 'n they don't know if they're alive or dead. And though I don't think about 'em this way anymore, they are really hired guns, mercenaries for the United States Special Forces, fighting for a few bucks and a safe homeland for the Riad clan. And you know damned well that ain't ever gonna happen."

The highly intelligent, classically educated and resourceful Wong Ah Kum offered the seed idea that eventually became the future for the Hmong and themselves. The endowment accounts for the Hmong, Donny, Scotty, Tommy, Ah Kum, and Karen were established during their first trip to Macau with the net proceeds from the sale of the inaugural bullion shipment, worth more than a million American dollars on the Macanese exchange. After transit expenses and the profit split with 15M, the beneficiaries shared more than five hundred thousand dollars with a river of gold yet to come. If money were once a problem for the Hmong, it wouldn't be ever again.

• • •

The Albatross was guided into their landing pattern from twenty thousand feet while David looked out at the passing thunderheads toward the clearing horizon. As they approached Midway, he smiled, remembering the day Tom and Ah Kum were married in her Macanese home church and then two days later when Tom had been baptized into the life everlasting by Pastor Lamb himself. It had been David's honor and privilege to stand for his friend and mentor to help affirm their union in the eyes of man and God and to do what he could to support Tom in his new walk with the Lord. It was important to know that even in a time of war love grows. Even at the point of a gun, the Holy Spirit finds a way.

• • •

Midway Island is a 2.4 square mile semicircular coral atoll that consists of two low islands, Sand and Eastern. They bracket the narrow entrance to a shallow interior lagoon, circumscribed by a gossamer coral reef that raises just enough above sea level to provide a safe harbor in stormy seas.

The atoll is strategically located in the North Pacific, equidistant between North America and Asia. It was claimed for the United States in 1867 by Captain William Reynolds of the USS *Lackawanna* under the Guano Islands Act of 1856, which codified the value of avian excrement (Midway is the nesting ground for the world's largest albatross colony) as a rich source of saltpeter for gun powder and a potent agriculture fertilizer. The Act of Congress allows American citizens to take territorial possession of uninhabited islands containing guano deposits as long as they have not been previously claimed by another sovereign nation, and in the case of Midway, it was the inestimable good fortune of the United States that the acquisition was made.

Midway has a long history of high value to American interests. In 1903 the Commercial Pacific Cable Company constructed a two-story technical facility and dormitory to house the Midway Electrical Signal Repeater Station for the first transpacific multiplex submarine cable, which island hopped over six thousand miles from San Francisco to Honolulu to Midway to Guam and finally to its Asian continental landing at Shanghai, China.

In 1935, Pan American World Airways established a way station for its glamorous China Clipper flying boat, installing a dock, seaplane ramp and taxiway, machine shop, refrigerator plant, radio station, radio beacon, offices, power plant, and a forty-room prefabricated hotel building. The famous Martin M-130 flying boat was designed specifically for Pan Am to carry forty-five passengers at an altitude of ten thousand feet with a range of over three thousand miles. It became the vehicle that pioneered both transpacific commercial air travel and air mail service.

In the late 1930s, with tensions growing between Japan and the United States, the Congress authorized the US Navy to construct an airbase and anchorage for large seagoing vessels at Midway. In 1938, a navigable channel was cut between Sand and Eastern Islands, and by the spring of 1941, three military-grade asphalt runways had been installed on Eastern Island.

Naval Air Station Midway went operational in August of that year and was shelled by Japanese surface ships on December seventh as part of their coordinated attack on Pearl Harbor and a preparation for a land invasion at a later date. Nineteen forty-two saw a major buildup of US air and ground forces on Midway, sufficient to repel a Japanese invasion, and the prelude of the Battle of Midway, which stopped the momentum of the Japanese Imperial Navy and set the stage for Allied victory in the Pacific. David was interested in the history of the place; he wanted to walk the ground and take its measure for himself.

As the PRE Albatross circled navy Midway, David could see a Continental Airlines 727 descending ahead of them in the landing pattern and wondered if it might have been the same aircraft that had transported him to Da Nang when he was deployed. It all seemed so very long ago. He scanned the airfield for the Parker Exploration Gulfstream II and spotted it tethered to the apron just outside the seaplane hangar, painted Nittany Lion blue and white in honor of Parker's alma mater.

Following instructions from NAS Midway, the PRE flight crew brought the Albatross down perfectly on the glass-smooth surface of the protected lagoon, powered the bird up the sea ramp, onto the taxiway, and crisply rotated the tail to park it beside the PEI Gulfstream. A compact man approached the plane from out of the early evening shadows and walked around the nose of the Albatross, carrying a small American flag. David's heart leapt in his chest as he tore open the exit hatch and ran to his father. "Papa! Papa! Papa!" Joe jumped for joy, and the two men embraced in tears of reunion, falling to their knees sobbing and not caring a whit what the PRE flight crew, the ramp rats, or anyone else might see or say.

"Papa, I'm so sorry," sobbed David into Joe's shoulder. "It should have been different. I should have never left Da Nang. I'd have been home years ago and you would have been so proud of me. I wouldn't be a deserter, a wanted man. Everything's such a mess!" He wept bitterly.

"David, I love you more than I can ever say, and I wouldn't have had it any other way. I am so proud of you. There's never been a braver, more capable, more honorable Marine or a truer patriot to ever take the oath. You're sure as hell no deserter, David. You're my boy, my precious son, and by the Holy Word of God Almighty, no man could ever ask for more!"

With tears covering his cheeks, Joe comforted David, loved him as if there was nothing else in the world, and welcomed him home to American soil for the first time in over three years. "Thank you, O' Lord," he prayed at the top of his lungs, "for this son of mine was dead and is alive again; he was lost and now is found!"

Father and son walked together to the lagoon, through the rocky albatross rookery, dodging chicks and passive parents along the way. "Where are the others?" asked David as he bent low, gathering some flat stones to skip over the calm lagoon.

"I asked 'em to give us some time, son. They're probably at the bar or in their rooms." He gestured across the runway toward a flat-toped, boxy structure with peeling white paint. "Used to be the Pan Am Hotel but now it's the Gooneyville Lodge. Ain't much 'ta look at, but the sheets are clean 'n' the air blows cold. Lots 'a traffic through NAS Midway these days. Bobby had 'ta call in a favor or two, but we've got rooms for us and the flight crews, which means you're gonna have 'ta bunk with your old man."

"Karen and Randy well?" asked Joe. Fiddling with his little flag, he put it in his pocket. "We miss 'em, son."

"I just left her this morning, and she's great. Randy loves the school, and the people there are real nice, Papa." A tension was growing between them.

"I know that you disagree with me moving my family out of the country, but we've been through this. The Lord is working in our lives, and we believe they're safer where no one can find them than they would ever be at home. It's a decision that Karen and I made together, and I'm going to have to ask you to respect it," said David, looking his father in the eye as they continued to walk.

"Son, your mother and I have come to terms with not having Karen and our grandson in Odessa. It was bound to happen. The Lord places us all where he needs us, and you're no different. Here's the thing that's got us worried; you've never said where the money came from to relocate Karen and Randy to God knows where. And how are you affording to charter a seaplane, of all things, to bring you all the way out to the middle of the Pacific Ocean for this meeting? It must have cost thousands. You're not involved with any criminal activity or anything, are you son?"

David smiled. "Papa, what would you say if I told you the squad found a gold factory no one was using and we just picked up where the old owners left off?"

Joe didn't reply, slightly bruised by what he considered a gentle rebuff. The silence of his father and the sea washing ashore was overwhelming to David, "How's Mom and Isabel? Tell me she didn't marry that little twerp law student from Dallas—what was his name? Royce something or other? What a prick."

Joe chuckled, glad to change the subject. "Oh, no. That was just a summer fling. You're not going to believe this but she and Rod Peterson have been seriously dating for nearly a year now. He works for his daddy at the Pontiac house, does his National Guard weekend warrior duty, and is a reserve deputy with the Ector County Sheriff's Office."

"How you feel about that, Papa?" asked David, smiling at the thought.

"Rod's a stand-up guy David, been helping out around the farm some and Isabel's got him attending services at Quad Six pretty near every Sunday. The Petersons seem real pleased that Isabel is spending time with their boy, so we'll see where it goes."

"Isabel finally got her master's degree from A&M. She's teaching history and political science at Midland Lee; says she'll be the principal there in two years." David grimaced. "Now don't be making a sour face about your little sister's employer; the work's respectable, the pay's good, and besides, the Rebels went three and seven last year, so we aren't getting the attitude out of 'em we used to."

"Your mama's doing good; canin' sweet corn, new potatoes, cream peas, and okra this week; had a good crop this year. She's runnin' vacation Bible school again this summer. You realize it's been nearly thirty years since we started that with your mama and daddy." They both smiled with cherished memories.

"How about Travis? She still running the cattle 'n' making life generally miserable for the varmint population?"

Joe reached into the small of his back for the short leather strap. "Your mom 'n' me thought you'd like to have this, son." David took the belt by its tarnished brass buckle and turned it over to see the badly worn "Travis" still visible, pressed into the beat-up leather band. "She seemed fine. We'd been out feedin' the stock that afternoon. Isabel had put out lemonade and cookies for us on the front porch so we went around ta enjoy our refreshments 'n' cool off in the shade a little. She was right with me the whole time, laid down and rested her head on my boot, went to sleep, and never woke up." Joe's eyes misted. "She was part of us, David, just like you, and we miss her sorely."

There was a long thoughtful pause. "Papa, I had to kill some men." Father and son carried the silence together along the shoreline. "I don't think I'm meant for combat. When the time comes, some men just freeze and can't bring themselves to it. Others just treat it like a distasteful job, no different from butchering a hog. Others are just the opposite, they seem ta enjoy it, live for it even. I just keep thinkin' that there ought to be a better way 'ta settle things, and maybe if we looked hard enough we could find it."

"Now, David, we talked about this once. There's no shame in doing what you have to in combat. Men ought not enjoy killing other men. It's unnatural. A lot of guys go through what you've experienced and they are so deadened that they just can't feel remorse for anything. Some of 'em even lose their souls. The fact that you hate it means that your soul is still alive." Joe put his arm around his son as they reached the point of the little island and began to walk back toward the hangars.

"The sting of battle is what they call it, Papa. Hands on the enemy; feeling his resistance, his struggle, his panic, and then his surrender. Your senses peak, your muscle memory and your training kick in, and finally you take his life. Papa, I loved it. May God forgive me, but I truly loved it. Combat is an addiction for me, and that's why I've got to stay away from it. It would change me into someone, something…I could easily become one of the men who come back without a soul."

The silence returned, but this time it was thick and not so easy to cut through. The men walked along the beach together, following the surf of Sand Island, warrior-to-warrior, talking deep into the night about things too dark for the world to ever see.

• • •

The small party room at the Gooneyville Lodge had been cleared, and even though he arrived early, David found the older men were already deep in conversation. "David! Get over here so I can hug your neck!" David tossed his rucksack into the corner and moved toward the table. Bobby Parker rose to meet David, and the two men embraced, patting each other on the back. "Damned if ya' don't look like you're game ready right now. Didn't I tell ya our boy takes care of himself?"

David looked across the table at a third man who he had only a vague recollection of having once met.

"David, I'm Carlton Mayer. We met a couple of years ago in Saigon. You were working for Will Washington then."

David panicked; "MAYER! THE WARRANT!" his mind screamed, but he fought through the fear, shook Mayer's hand and took his place at the table between Parker and his papa. Breakfast was served, and the tension gradually abated as he realized that Captain Parker was clearly in charge of the agenda, and Mayer wasn't there to collect the bounty.

David, we asked you to interrupt your schedule and meet us out here in the middle of nowhere because we wanted to be absolutely certain that nothing we say here will be overheard by the wrong people. We're also all sensitive to your status within the Department of Defense, the Central Intelligence Agency, and the State Department." He looked across the table. "Carl, could you go ahead and take care of our housekeeping items? I believe that will facilitate further discussion."

Mayer pulled his worn leather attaché from under his chair and withdrew a plain manila file folder holding three documents printed on a formal parchment, *Honorable Discharge from The Armed Forces of the United States of America, United States Marine Corps*; on an executive size velum bearing the letterhead The White House, *Granting Pardon to David K. Rixon by the President of the United States of America,* and finally, on a crisp brilliant white sheet, *The Director, Central Intelligence Agency, Offer of Employment David K. Rixon.*

"For you, David, and on behalf of the office of the president of the United States and the American people, I want to thank you for your service and apologize for the injustice done to you and your squad. I promise I will do everything in my power to set things right."

David flushed. "Are these authentic?" Receiving validation from his dad and Parker, he said, "OK, Agent Mayer, you have my attention. What does the government want from me now?" David was trying hard to hold his temper. Mayer continued looking at him unflinchingly, straight in the eye.

"David, there are reports that you've been operating independently in northeastern Laos for over two years and that you not only survived the bombing of Rana Dat but thrived. You've recruited a fiercely loyal fighting force of nearly one hundred, mostly Hmong but other Montagnard as well. You started with nothing but crossbows, sharp sticks, and rocks. You took what you needed to arm, feed, and clothe your people from the Viet Minh and the Pathet Lao, mostly by raiding supply convoys that cross your AO on the Ho Chi Minh. We know they've tried to stop you more than once and they've been unsuccessful. We want to know how you did it, son. We need tactical information on how you and your men are kicking the shit out of the enemy with their own weapons."

David remained unmoved and Mayer continued.

"We also have an intelligence assignment, a pet project so to speak, that you're uniquely qualified for and that we'd like you to consider. At its nearest point, the Laotian segment of the Annamite Range is less than a hundred miles from Hanoi. The tallest peaks in that area are over a mile high, and that makes them ideal stationary observation platforms, located well within range of the line-of-sight audio and video monitoring technology the CIA is currently fielding. What we'd like you to do is use your army to establish a small, concealed, passive monitoring station that we are calling "Omega White." Find out what you can and send the information to me personally in Saigon. No more raiding enemy shipping though. CIA supplies you and picks up the tab for everything. You and your people do your best to disappear into the jungle like you never existed. Just be quiet; look, listen, and learn. That's it.

"Oh, I nearly forgot. You may not be interested but our mutual friend is no longer in theater. Major William Washington is now General William Washington; he's at the Pentagon; liaison officer between the Joint Chiefs and our ambassadors in Saigon and Vientiane. Phoenix went black when he left, and I have no idea who's running it now. It's out of our hands.

"And just so you'll know, David, the discharge and the pardon are authentic and already on file for you at DOD with copies sent to you at your parents' house. These are original signed duplicates for your personal records. I've also got a check for your back pay in case you want it now, though you probably shouldn't cash it out here. Maybe you'd like the Marines to send it back to your folks in Odessa; it's your option. I have a similar package for Lieutenant Coats right here in my valise."

"What about the warrant? The whole squad's included," asked a careful David.

"David, I wouldn't have you ignorant. Rodeo-Cowboy is a lethal, compartmentalized need-to-know operation that originated within the Deep Black side of the Office of Policy Coordination at State; separate and distinct from the Central Intelligence Agency. It's ongoing, David, and I have no power to lift the warrant. It will remain valid until it's withdrawn by whoever issued it or until it's satisfied."

"Meaning what? We'll be hunted for the rest of our lives?" responded David. The silence from Mayer answered his question and grew to fill the room, and David was beginning to lose control of his emotions.

"Well, Carl—since we're all friends now, I assume I may call you Carl—there are a few questions I'd like answered before we move on with your agenda.

"Who allowed the enemy to get the drop on the MIKE force at Signal Hill?

"At least twenty-four thousand Communists were fortifying the A Shau over two years before they wiped out the MIKEs there. Who's responsible for allowing that?

"And all those Communists; they're still out there, Carl, except now the force is closer to forty thousand. Who's responsible for allowing that?

"Big picture, Carl: Maneuver and Attrition. Who decided on attrition? Who doesn't give a hoot in hell about the lives of American troopers in this tit-for-tat cannon fodder combat? Just who is it at DOD that would like nothing better than for the United States to lose this godforsaken war?

"Rules of Engagement say Laos is neutral, and we can't pursue the enemy across the border, yet we know full well American aircraft have been taking out targets all over Laos every day for years, flying right over the VC on the Trail to do it. Someone made the decision to shelter the Ho Chi Minh, Carl. Who is that precisely?

"What are the FBI, CIA, and the US Department of Agriculture doing in Laos, messing with the 15M Triad and the opium crop? Who thought it would be a good idea for the United States of America to get into the drug business in the first place; where is all the dope going, and who gets the money?

"What the hell is CIA doing hiring the Laotian Hmong armed with sticks, rocks and a few surplus Garands to fight Communists with AK-Forty-Sevens, rocket-propelled grenades, and field artillery; the same guys that are apparently kicking our collective asses in South Vietnam. Just who is the sick bastard responsible for that?

"In fact, Carl, what I'm really asking is just who in hell is running this cluster fuck? That's the guy I'd like to talk to about the goddamned warrant. That's the guy I'd like to spend some time with!"

David was red faced and quivering with rage, yet Carlton Mayer held his eye. "Precisely the questions we've been asking ourselves, Captain," he said steadily, sliding a single typewritten page across the table. "Here's a list of the likely suspects."

David was instantly incredulous and glanced at the list, recognizing several of the names from the *Wall Street Journal*, and then settled on two specifically: Alfred Dorance and Wolfgang Jung.

"They call themselves 'the Order,' David. It's a very old fraternal organization, a curious hybrid with structural characteristics resembling both a corporation and a church. I suppose some would call it a cult. It's similar in structure and age to the Roman Catholic Church with a verifiable history that goes back at least to the time of Christ.

"The core leadership in North America is all related either by blood or marriage and maintains the generational continuity of their organization by amassing and wielding unimaginable wealth with some accounting records indicating that their seed capital was gold looted from the Roman treasury during the fall of the empire.

"They keep their inner circle loyal and their ideas intact by educating their children in schools designed specifically for the purpose of common indoctrination and, of course, they encourage the intermarriage of their children.

"They allow new members rarely and only in the event of an unexpected death, and then only if there is no male heir to assume the vacancy. They maintain internal discipline by addicting their members to the opulence and privilege of transgenerational wealth and the constant threat of torture and death as a punishment for infidelity. Their internal security is relentless and savage, periodically orchestrating the ritual murders of members from their lower ranks. These murders are called 'Alpha Actions' and are used to instill fear and loyalty in the higher ranks.

"Along with a corporate charter called the Rules of Commerce, the Order has a clergy, a theology, a moral code, and organized sacrificial rites that are focused on the worship of Satan with two primary sacraments: wealth accumulation during what they refer to as 'Great Trade Cycles' and large-scale ritual murder, what most people refer to as war but what the Order refers to as a levying a 'Soul Tax' against humanity. A Luciferian version of a property tax for the use of the planet which they believe belongs to them.

"Their ultimate goal is to leverage their immense wealth with occulted spiritual, and political power to organize the entire planet into a satanic feudal state in which all people everywhere would be nothing more than serfs permanently attached to the land and owned by members of the Order. We have documents that indicate successive generations of the Order have been working on this goal since the early seventeen hundreds. This isn't a joke, David, and I'm not wearing a tin foil hat. They're quite capable and deadly serious.

"The Order plans for the long term and they are working a two thousand year schedule to complete the global project so this means they're risk takers and they're capital intensive.

"In the late eighteen hundreds, the North American franchise began developing a program to process the United States into their control by slowly degrading constitutional protections against excessive government power. They accomplished this initially through the bribery, blackmail, and murder of low-level government employees and politicians, then infiltrating the government by placing their membership within the bureaucracy. Today a postal clerk, tomorrow the president—that's their tactical model and they work at it all the time.

"Their power in North America grew exponentially after the Civil War during Reconstruction and then exploded during the two world wars. They thrive on chaos.

"They see the next step in their plan as the incremental remaking of the American mind by using technology and the portions of the federal bureaucracy they control to wage psychological warfare on the civilian population. They intend a Satanic remaking of the core components of our societal architecture: the nuclear family and Judeo-Christian culture.

"The Vietnam War serves three purposes for the Order: as an important source of revenue for their efforts, an ongoing source of ritual mass murder for their religious purposes, and a deep well of mass psychological trauma for what they call trauma-based mind control. This is Wolfgang Jung's specialty.

"All of these wartime resources are being channeled into a larger project designed to move them toward their ultimate goal. The code name for that project is 'Kansas' and it's likely the keystone of their current Great Trade Cycle.

"I know this will be hard to believe, Captain, but that's not the half of it. We have decoded transmissions indicating that they're in bed with Ho Chi Minh himself, that they have assembled a fifth column organization in the States called Red Storm, which has taken root within the American university system, and that the Order is coordinating activities between Hanoi and Red Storm while providing the financing and coordination for the Communist war effort in both Southeast Asia and the United States."

David felt very much like he had been hit in the face with the same bucket of water that the squad had dumped on his head to break up his fistfight with William Washington. Bobby Parker took the opportunity to advance the conversation.

"David, your papa and our associates have been seriously investigating the Kennedy assassination since November of sixty-three. We've collected solid information indicating it was clearly a coup d'etat committed by several teams of contract killers who were assisted by traitors within the bureaucracy. That means all executive-level decisions made since the murder of the president are illegal—including the entry of the United States into the civil war in South Vietnam.

"Our sources are our brothers-in-arms, David, Texas 'T-Patchers,' well trusted from our wartime service in Europe with the Thirty-Sixth Division who either remain active duty military or who have moved into the private defense industry. We tested their information using OSS intelligence cross-check methods for our sources with counter-sources, and we identified many of the conspirators but had no solid evidence that could be used to convict them in the courts. In other words, we had the 'what,' the 'when,' the 'where,' and most of the 'who,' but were never able to develop a clear idea about the 'how' or 'why.'" Parker shifted the conversation to Pastor Joe.

"Our investigation was going nowhere when we heard that you'd been killed in action, son, and it just took the wind out of our sails. We were about to abandon it altogether when we found listening devices at the Odessa VFW, Parker Exploration, and even at Pleasant Farms. Someone was clearly investigating us, David, and that's about when Agent Mayer showed up. After we got to know each other, we compared notes and it seemed that we were coming to the same conclusion but from totally different starting points," said Joe, looking again to Mayer.

"David, since the National Security Act of nineteen forty-seven at the end of the war, the federal bureaucracy has gradually become a closed system, a quasi-secret society with autonomous document classification power that makes it nearly impenetrable by ordinary citizens. Everyone inside the system is protected by a legal principle called 'sovereign immunity,' which makes it entirely possible for an organized group to commit serious crimes, even murder the president, in total secrecy without fear of discovery or prosecution.

"They cover their crimes by using national security classification, and designing them to appear to be a product of random coincidence like a crazy lone nut acting out his delusion as with Oswald and the Kennedy murder. David, when even the president isn't safe and no one is punished for his murder, it sends a message of fear and resignation into America's subconscious mind that profoundly damages the country. This is an example of what I mean by psychological warfare and trauma-based mind control, and we can't allow it to continue if America is to survive another fifty years. These people must be rooted out and publicly punished for their crimes. If we are to pass the Republic along to our children, it's the only way."

"Pardon me, Carl but this sounds a lot like the McCarthy hearings in the fifties, and we know where that went," said a skeptical David.

"Where do you believe Senator McCarthy got his intelligence? He was a dupe operating virtually alone. He used the power of his office to focus attention on the overt threat of Communist infiltration but entirely missed the covert presence of the Order. He got greedy and tried to convert his manufactured awareness into a political opportunity for himself by using the national press to build his notoriety. That's what ultimately brought him down, and what's worse, his public failure gave even more cover to the Order. He made a deal with the devil and paid the price," replied Mayer.

"Most people inside the system are ordinary Americans who do a good job for the country and, of course, we honor them and want them to continue. But the Order has agents embedded, hidden in the crowd of good people across the bureaucracy. They are brazenly gaming the system; operating a coordinated criminal enterprise directed by people outside the government. Those are the actors we're looking for, David. Those are the sick bastards who need to be in prison or dead.

"By far, the most dangerous of the intragovernmental groups is embedded in Justice, State, and Defense. They're supposed to be the watchers, David; guardians of the constitution and beyond suspicion. But these people use the law as a weapon in the covert war they are waging against the American people. Our pals don't know it yet, but Omega is about to change all that.

"My wartime navy career was spent in a cryptanalysis group code named "Magic." We were responsible for cracking a state-of-the-art high-level military code called the 'Japanese Purple Cipher.' It was a pretty big deal back then, and our group developed close personal bonds, similar to what you have with Lieutenant Coats. The members have stayed in touch through the years and tried to keep up with things in the very tiny world of military code breaking. Some of us who remained on the inside recognized something strange right after they killed the president, just like your dad and Captain Parker did.

"So we got together and organized an informal working group to determine if perhaps we were just paranoid, seeing patterns in the chaos that weren't really there, or if there was really something sinister going on.

"To start, we posited that every organization must regularly communicate to achieve anything. So we applied Purple Logic to the problem and used our administrative access to telephone and telex billings to begin analyzing communications traffic between DOD, Justice, State, and the White House. At first it was just the volume of contacts relative to headlines in the *Times* and lead stories on the New York network news. We'd been analyzing their traffic for nearly a year and discovered some of the same human factor input flaws that lead us to crack Japanese Purple; of the millions of possible combinations, we determined their primary command traffic is repetitively routed to the thirty-six names and places on this list.

"At first it was a simple analysis, identifying who sent the messages, who received them, who was messaged outside the system, and what event may have prompted the communication. Over time we charted the results, used deductive and inductive reasoning to cut through the noise, and were able to discern a hidden trunk line connecting the primary conspirators. Within that trunk we found the rudiments of a cipher, which was not unlike Purple. From that small realization, we took a chance, used CIA assets outside the country to place taps on the Atlantic, Pacific, and Continental switch stations, and we were able to use the information to retro engineer and construct an electronic decryption device. We call it Omega because it's definitely our last effort. It wasn't perfect, but with Omega we were able read most of what we could intercept.

"We cracked their cipher just after the attack on Rana Dat and were able to anchor their communications to a real world event that never made it into the New York press. Omega opened up like a flower with that event, David. I like to think that Seven-MIKE is having the last laugh. Thanks to their sacrifice, we've learned quite a lot about the Order.

"We know they communicate globally by sending encrypted messages over secure government telephone and telex lines, and because they are very careful, they restrict delivery of their highest level international communiques to diplomatic couriers.

"From access to this information we were very surprised to discover that domestically they rely almost exclusively on the proprietary telephone and telex systems owned by the twelve-region Federal Reserve System. Of the thirty-six men on the list, five of them are appointed members of the Board of Governors, and all of them receive regular communiques from the Order. From the fed decryptions, we know with one hundred percent certainty that these men are at the top of the pyramid in the United States. They're the decision makers, David—the ones who pulled the trigger on John Kennedy, who installed Johnson, who decided to go to war in Vietnam, and how the war would be fought. They're the ones we're looking for.

"From their communications we know that the Gulf of Tonkin attack was a fabrication used by the president as a political justification to launch the DOD into Southeast Asia and further that the American Rules of Engagement in Vietnam were totally of their making, written by a high-level committee, and that the president merely signed the document and sent it on to DOD.

"That's why things on the ground in Vietnam are so nonsensical and dangerous for our soldiers. It also explains why COMUSMACV sees Vietnam simplistically and disastrously as a war of attrition. The North American Order wants the body count as high as possible, and they see no distinction between our soldiers, the enemy, and civilians. All they really want is more blood and more money.

"We also have information indicating that the same people have written the rules for the air-to- ground engagement in Laos, and your observations are correct. These rules have been sheltering large segments of the Ho Chi Minh Trail near your AO, and they're doing it for two reasons: it's part of a high-level financial deal of some sort that the Order has with Hanoi and also because they're looking for something. Something they believe is located in northeastern Laos.

"It's an artifact or a location that's significant to their satanic belief system. It's so important to the Order that they've made a significant financial payment to the Communists who have assigned an elite unit of the NVA to search the area quadrant by quadrant and report their findings up the chain to Hanoi, which then feeds it to one of the Order's operatives at the American embassy in Vientiane. This is their top priority right now, Captain; they want the item in their hands by mid-November at the latest.

"To complicate matters, they have an idea someone's on to them, so they're flooding the system with disinformation to conceal their command traffic. This is very preliminary, but we believe they're planning to kick off something big, maybe as big as the Kennedy assassination, and the artifact is part of it. The whole thing is coming to a head back in the States just after the first of the year. They're just waiting on a transmission from Hanoi to confirm the timing.

"Captain, I hate to have to say this but you, your squad, and your Hmong warriors are the primary resource the country has to stop the North American Order. To do this we must work together to do two things; deny them access to their Laotian artifact, and gather the intelligence we need to disarm Kansas before it's detonated." Mayer pulled a coiled topographic map of northeastern Laos from under his chair and spread it before David.

"Now here's the Annamite Range," he said, running his index finger along the borderline and stopping at a specific mountaintop. "If you agreed to serve and we located Omega about here, the observation technology you'd have to work with is so advanced that you would be able to count the hairs in Uncle Ho's nose. Our idea is that you scout the area, select a location, and we air-drop the surveillance package to you on the mountain. While you're looking over Ho's shoulder, the Hmong can take a look around for their artifact, capture it if possible, destroy it if not."

"Carl, could you tell me one more time why I should get involved in this? Why I should risk my men, my family, and myself for a country that's placed a bounty on my head? Because I believe that part of the presentation is missing," said a skeptical, still angry David.

A dark, foreboding hush covered the conference room, while David looked into each man's eyes and then finally came to rest on Pastor Joe, who sat erect, slowly pulled the little American flag from his pocket, placed it reverently on the table, and said with an expression of shock mixed with a profound sadness, "Mi hijo ; es tan fácil el dejar su juramento? ¿Ya has olvidado Dealey Plaza?"

David flushed red, his childhood scarring stark white as a scowl flashed over his weathered face. He said nothing in reply, and after a very long moment, he slowly rose from the table and walked away.

Mayer cursed himself silently, believing that he had given David too much information, that the young captain thought the whole thing crazy, that they'd lost their best chance of stopping Project Kansas and putting an end to the North American Order. But David made it only as far as the door, stopped, retrieved his rucksack, and brought it back to the table. He then removed the heavy giant's cube and placed it on the map like a golden paperweight. Seeing question and confusion spread across the faces of his papa, Captain Parker, and Agent Mayer, and with the voice of a veteran commander, he said, "Gentlemen. I believe Rixon's Raiders can be of service."

• • •

That evening Joe joined David for a run along the shoreline. "It's hard to believe these guys have gotten such a stranglehold on the government, Papa," he breathed with the rhythm of the run. "After everything I've heard today, it seems like they've got the thing won, that we're only wasting our time trying to fight 'em. Maybe we'd be better off just running for it—get the family out while we can."

In his late fifties, Pastor Joe was breathing hard, trying to keep pace with his son. Both were bathed in sweat, and David slowed to a walk to give the older man a break.

"That's about what everyone thought back in forty-two, son. After the Japs got the drop on us at Pearl, Yamamoto sailed away clean with sixty-nine surface ships, including four aircraft carriers and his namesake *Yamamoto*, the most powerful battleship in the world. It was a resounding defeat for America, and it washed over the country like a tidal wave of fear and doubt. After Pearl there wasn't much left of the US fleet between Japan and California, and everyone thought a serious defense of the West Coast was impossible.

"The country was naked militarily, but the worst of it was the psychological state of the civilian population. I guess most every American felt like they were personally exposed, and there wasn't anything to be done except run up the white flag and start learning Japanese. That's why the Battle of Midway was so important. Somebody had to publicly punch those bastards in the nose to wake up the country and prove the Nips could be beaten. That's exactly what happened out there in June of forty-two, only seven months after Pearl."

Joe stopped and looked out over the northern horizon. "We only had twenty-eight ships left in the entire Pacific Ocean, three of 'em aircraft carriers; *Enterprise, Hornet,* and the barely operational *Yorktown.* They had *Yamamoto,* four carrier groups, and the rest of the Japanese imperial fleet; around seventy ships.

"You know Mayer doesn't like talking about it, because he'd have rather finished the war in CIC on the *Pennsylvania,* but the role he played in breaking Japanese Purple, well, that's what turned the tide. Sure, the navy took some hard hits out there. They lost *Yorktown* and *Hammond,* and a lot of good men, but Admiral Nimitz was able to take out all four Jap carriers and two light cruisers because of Mayer's group. It shocked the hell out of the Japanese high command, clipped their wings, and forced them to lick their wounds west of Midway.

"Lots of us believe that victory here is what it took to snap the country out of the shock of Pearl Harbor and convince the majority of Americans in their hearts and minds that the country could win the war, just like you convinced Jimmy Kellogg and the Panther defense they could put Big Willie Washington on the bus back to Dallas." Both men smiled at their shared memory.

"But, Papa, how do you tell the average American that his own government has declared war on him? We're supposed to have a government of the people, by the people, and for the people. Isn't that what Lincoln said at Gettysburg? Who's going to believe that Americans would do something like that to their own people?"

"I've wrestled with that myself, son, and the terrible answer is that it's not our government anymore. Most of the troublemakers inside aren't Americans at all – far from it. They're Nazi war criminals like Wolfgang Jung, brought in by the Order, and their operatives in the State and Justice Departments under Operation Paperclip. These murdering bastards were given new identities, American citizenship, and put to work all over the federal system. By our most recent count, there were around thirty thousand, and nearly all of 'em involved in defense, federal law enforcement, or intelligence gathering roles.

"Those guys used our own system to create America's second Pearl Harbor in Dealey Plaza, son, and what the country needs right now is a second Battle of Midway. The more we uncover about these devil-worshiping Nazi creeps, the more I'm thinking that the Battle of Kansas is exactly where we're gonna give 'em the biggest bloody nose in the history of their little satanic church."

"Papa, this Jung—somehow I get the feeling that you've got personal history with him."

There was a deep silence that became as black as the night sky over Midway. "No one outside the squad knows this, not even Paulina, so please keep it to yourself. It was during the fall of the Reich, the very last days in April of forty-five. The Thirty-Sixth had crossed the Elbe River on the way to Berlin, less than a hundred miles out. The German resistance had evaporated, and everybody was feeling pretty optimistic. Captain Parker was ordered to take the One Hundred Forty-First to capture a Kraut scientific research facility out in the countryside near a little town on the Polish border called Cottbus. Our orders were to take the personnel into custody and to keep them and their records out of Russian hands at all costs. It was Jung's operation. That's how we know him."

"You mean to tell me that once upon a time my old man slapped the cuffs on Wolfgang Jung?" asked David with a broad grin.

"Not exactly, son," said Joe with a pained expression. "He was waiting for us at the front gate, said he was expecting us. Had his personal chef make us tea and cake while he toured us through his lab and directed his people to cooperate. He apologized, said he didn't want to be rude, but he wouldn't be in our custody long, that he had an appointment to keep in Washington. We thought he was either lying or crazy."

David laughed again and Joe cut him off. "This is no joke, Captain. Jung is one very dangerous bad guy; quite literally in league with the devil..." Joe retreated into a deep troubling silence.

"Papa, what's wrong? What happened at Jung's lab?"

"Your photos of the dead giant; Jung had six of 'em in the lab, and they were still alive," said the US Army Ranger, his eyes growing narrow and hard. "Jung was explaining his experiments, telling us how his work would create a new world, a perfected Utopia. He said the war was only the birth pains of that world being born through each of us, and on the day of its birth that a bright new sun that would appear in the sky over America. That all of the deaths, especially the deaths of the innocent, were necessary to give spiritual form to what he called the 'homunculus.' As he explained it, that's the *small man* that has been gestating in the souls of all mankind since the beginning, and that when this homunculus is born out of us, the world would change overnight. All mankind would welcome the ancient race that had been watching and waiting since the dawn of time to take rightful possession of the planet; the sacred home that had been stolen from them by the Old Testament Jehovah. We all thought he'd just gone mad and was talking nonsense.

"Jung was showing us around one of the lower levels in the lab, and he asked if we'd like to meet the emissaries of our successor race. So we followed him into a room, a rough semicircle with a high domed ceiling. The room was filled with a pulsing luminous mist. At first all we could see was pure, brilliant light flickering like a strobe. As we walked in, the flicker diminished, the fog lifted, and we saw six figures sitting cross-legged, flat on the floor in a circle. I know it will be difficult to believe, but I heard one of them think my name, and I couldn't stop myself from moving around the circle to the one in the back. Even seated the way it was, I had to look up into its very large eyes set inside narrow slits in its face. Its head was shaped like a large watermelon with a large jaw about three times the size of a normal human. When it smiled, I could see it had at least two rows of teeth, and when it reached out for me, I could see six fingers on both hands.

"'Little brother,' it said silently, 'Jose, come let me see you. It's been so very long and I've missed you. Come now, don't be afraid.' It said this into my mind in English, Spanish, and another language, a spiritual tongue that I had never heard but understood to the core of my soul.

"David, it knew all of my secret sins, my sexual sin back to my earliest masturbatory fantasy, the time I shoplifted a pack of cigarettes from the grocery store, all the way to my first kill in combat. The thing reformed them in my mind as if they were the most desirable actions in my life and expanded them to show me my life if I would give myself over to its power. It was as if a bomb went off in my mind and soul, and I saw my own 'homunculus,' my own small man. It was who I would have become without the fear of God and the Holy Spirit at work shaping my life, and it terrified me.

"I was helpless, paralyzed, and completely defenseless. I panicked and started trying to scream, when there was an explosion in the room, and we all ran for it. Captain Parker had come to check on us. It seems that we'd been gone for hours, and when he found us trapped, he rolled in a flash-bang grenade to break the spell. It went off, we broke for the door, and the giants ran for a cave that led to a large natural cavern. We lost them deep underground.

"The reports the squad wrote were all consistent, more or less the same story. We all said there were six of them and estimated their height between twelve and fifteen feet. When Parker's squad took Jung into custody that afternoon, he wasn't trying to get away at all. He was serving everyone cake in the dining room and asked when he could be transported to Washington, and that's exactly what happened. The next day the OSS rolled into the compound, took him off our hands, and we never saw him again."

The men walked quietly along the beach, avoiding the albatross hatchlings, and both wondering what to say next. "It's been twenty years, son, and I remember Jung, the creature, and the way it took my will away like it was yesterday. We've got to stop this, David. If Kansas is what I fear it is, the civilians back home won't stand a chance."

"I'm going to ask you straight up, Lieutenant," said David with a gravity in his voice that Joe had never heard. "Is there any other way to get this done? The Supreme Court or maybe Congress; is there a legal or legislative means to stop this without shedding blood?"

"Ever hear of Marine Corps Major General Smedley Butler, Captain?" asked Lieutenant Joe. "In thirty-four he testified before Congress; told the McCormack-Dickstein Committee on Un-American Activities that some rich guys with names like Warburg, Morgan, and Clark, some of the same names on Mayer's list, I believe, tried to hire him to lead an army of pissed-off American vets to remove President Roosevelt from office. The *Times* said General Butler was a liar, that it was all a giant hoax. Son, you're a Marine. Do you believe that the most decorated, highest ranking officer in the history of the corps would perjure himself before Congress to play a trick on the American people?" asked Joe grimly, rhetorically. "The point is, Captain, that the Order has been at this long enough to have their bases covered, which means that they use their agents to destroy evidence and kill witnesses. They've left nothing to chance. At this time in the game direct action is the only way to stop the Order, restart the Constitution, and restore the Republic—and the bastards damn well know it.

"Mayer believes their security people are aware someone is on to them, and they're moving ahead full speed. Their bet is that the price to be paid in blood for an intervention is too high, and that there's no one left in the country with either the means or the will to oppose them. If Kansas comes off as they've planned, then they'll have been correct in their assessment."

"Papa, you, Captain Parker, and Agent Mayer—you know that in all likelihood we'll all pay for this operation with our lives. And there are no guarantees it will even work."

"Son, it's the same proposition that every American who's ever worn the uniform has accepted from the beginning: live free or die."

The silence returned but more deeply and the men walked on together until David sensed his father had cooled down and began a slow jog back to the hotel. There was a cool breeze on the sea air, Joe caught his second wind, the men picked up their speed, and came to pace. Nearing the Gooneyville Lodge and the end of the run, it was Joe who decided on a second lap around the island. The older man was way ahead, and David had to sprint to catch up.

• • •

In the dead of night the Southeast Asia Air C-130 containing the surveillance package for Omega White entered Laotian air space from Thailand's Udorn Air Base flying fast at treetop level. The cargo bay had been rigged by the loadmaster and his crew with the Low Altitude Parachute Extraction System, LAPES, for pinpoint delivery of the package on the very small top of the giant's mountain. On the flight deck, metallic whispers over the flight intercom crackled with excitement as the "sheep dipped" volunteers discussed their first mission in support of Omega.

"When I heard Rixon was alive and running this OP, I near 'bout peed myself. After Rana Dat, I figure the man's gotta be ten feet tall and bulletproof! If anyone can change the direction of this wrong-way war, it's him—and man, I'd love to be on the winning side for once. Besides, every man on this trash hauler owes Captain Rixon his life. We all have our own story about what happened when he let us outta our cages that night at Signal Hill, and I gotta tell ya, Sparky, I feel a commitment like I've never experienced before; it's almost spiritual. Ain't no way I'm giving up this chair as long as I got a chance ta back this guy up and finally fight this war to win it."

There was quiet contemplation and only sporadic chatter as the crew got down to business and the ship moved rapidly through the night.

"Captain; IP in five minutes. Repeat, five munities to intercept point," announced copilot Sparky Barnes, and the flight crew went to work.

Seconds later, Captain Magazzine brought the aircraft up to its deployment altitude. He and Barnes double-checked the altimeter and read the angels aloud to each other for oral confirmation. Barnes flipped a switch and the ship went dark, the internal lighting went from white to red, and the cargo ramp was lowered while the captain engaged the radio navigation control that would correct their altitude and approach vector for the passing, low-speed cargo drop.

"Windy City, this is Airmail; are you receiving? Windy City, this is Airmail; do you copy?" A moment later the challenge code had been exchanged, the weather conditions and flight status relayed, and the final preparations to receive the package were underway on the summit.

Magazzine slowed the bird to deployment speed. "Sparky, begin LAPES deployment cycle on my mark in five, four, three, two, one, mark."

The black drogue parachute popped out of the cargo ramp, while the loadmaster checked his safety harness. Then, only seconds later, he released the black main chutes and in five, four, three, two, one, cut the nylon master restraint with his K-bar, allowing the chutes to accelerate the cushioned cargo pallet loaded with precision-engineered surveillance equipment out of the cargo bay and skid it so neatly and gently into place that only a small swish and puff of dust atop the granite escarpment indicated that anything had happened at all. A moment later the unmarked C-130 dropped crisply below the edge of the escarpment, pulled out of its dive just above the jungle canopy, and dissolved into the moonless Laotian night.

• • •

"Dang, Captain, if this ain't just like Christmas morning in Truth or Consequences!" said Coats, smiling, as he approached the pallet at dawn with is K-bar at the ready to cut away the strapping and pry open the wooden crates that had been moved into the giant's sanctuary under the cover of darkness.

"Truth or what'd you say? Are you pulling my leg, El Tee?" asked Rixon. "Is your hometown really called Truth or Consequences, like the game show?"

"Affirmative, Captain, or rather it is now. When my brother 'n' me were little it was called Hot Springs, 'cause of the natural hot springs that are supposed to be good for what ails. It's a spa town sorta' like Hot Springs, Arkansas, but in fifty, the city fathers changed the name to Truth or Consequences to get publicity from the television show, and it worked. You remember the host, Ralph Edwards? Well he came right on down to the town square and hosted the national show from there, just like he said he would. The man's been coming back in time for the Hatch Chile Festival every year since. That's our claim to fame; well that and we're the nearest town to the Trinity Site, barely sixty miles away from Ground Zero; first nuclear detonation in history. Guess that's why I sorta glow in tha' dark sometimes." Coats was in such a good mood that Rixon decided to accept his commentary at face value and join him in the small joy of opening the crates.

"I'll be," said Rixon as Coats pried the lid off the crate marked 0.001 OPEN FIRST in red military-style stencil. Running his fingers over the sleek white cowling, he stopped when he reached the blood-red double sun logo of Allegheny Innovations. "El Tee, we must have been very good boys, 'cause Santa sent us a Zero Point Generator of our very own, and we didn't even have to ask." Rixon told Coats the story of his trip down the rabbit hole in Saigon while they continued to uncrate and arrange their shiny new spy equipment.

David was enthralled as he, Coats, the scouts, and a half dozen of the younger Hmong worked to assemble the centerpiece of their surveillance array: a modified version of the Baker-Nunn Satellite Tracking Camera. "Tom, as far as I know, only twelve of these were ever made, and they're located in astronomical observatories around the planet. They serve as the primary optical instrument of the

Vanguard Mini Track System that keeps up with manmade satellites in high earth orbit. This instrument is clearly designed by the same team, but the yoke and control array are engineered to look down as well as up. Isn't this just the best?"

There was one large wooden crate left unopened. It was the shape of a giant coffin and marked in the same red military stencil: DANGER! CONTENTS CONTAMINATED! OPEN ONLY WITH NIOSH P100 RESPIRATOR! PROPERTY USMACV DA NANG!

"I guess this one's for you special, Cap. I ain't really interested in anything contaminated that belongs to USMACV," said Coats grinning and beginning to look through the packing peanuts and paper for something new to eat or shoot. "David what ya think's in the...," he stopped in midsentence as he noticed Travis sniffing and nosing a forest-green box with bold red lettering obscured by pile of white foam peanuts. "RED MAN! A whole new fresh box! Oh Lord, manna from heaven!" It appeared to David that Tom and the war dog were dancing together through a small white blizzard of foam packing, and he smiled. "Remember this moment," he told himself. "It will help when the fighting comes."

• • •

A month later the squad had Omega White up and running. To everyone's surprise, the Hmong had proven themselves gifted masons and used simple hand tools to modify the stone floor, perimeter wall, and granite escarpment beyond the giant's temple to accept the surveillance array and then removed enough of the granite escarpment to provide the proper angle of declination for the Baker-Nunn Instrument and the Raytheon LS3000 White Light Laser Distance Microphone to achieve line-of-site sight lock on the former French governmental complex, including the presidential palace and its lushly landscaped gardens.

Carlton Mayer had provided written descriptions and measured drawings of the French Beaux Arts complex, which David had used to calibrate the Omega Array. He keyed presets into the automated control armature so that the equipment would continually scan key conference rooms, offices, and terraces for audio or video triggers that would automatically begin multitrack recording to sequenced reels of magnetic tape. Every morning, David would review and flag the tape from the night before and then number and package the composite reel, insert it into a flight pouch, attach it to the aerial pickup harness, and raise the camouflaged mast. At sunrise, a Raven Forward Air Controller, code named Catbird, would fly his unmarked Cessna 01 Birddog low over the escarpment, snag the string harness with an aerial gaff, and reel the attached pouch into the cockpit before continuing on his normal patrol. Joe Don Brinkman would then personally delver the pouch to Carlton Mayer, sometimes at the Continental Shelf, but always in time for drinks and dinner.

As the weeks passed the contact pattern revealed that the most productive target for Omega's eyes and ears was a small, precisely crafted, two-story structure of lacquered teak and red clay tile known by Vietnamese Communists as *Nha San Bac Ho*, Uncle Ho's Stilt House. Gleaned snippets of conversation and high-resolution photos of small notes hinted that there would be a special guest of the house soon, but Rixon could only watch, record, and wait.

The sun was still bright in the late afternoon and the meeting took place on the ground level under the raised platform where the lone occupant slept and kept his office. The frail Vietnamese man dressed in kaki was sitting at the head of the table in the open-air conference room. He was joined by four others, three of whom were clearly Westerners, dressed professionally in business attire; the fourth was an aide and translator who made the introductions in English. David though he recognized one of the men and switched the Array control to manual so that he could fine-tune the optics and dial in the audio.

"...Mr. Dorance of the American Federal Reserve Bank, Mr. Vazquez with the American Department of Agriculture, our contact at the American embassy in Vientiane. Comrade Chairman, these men are grateful for the moment and pray that you will comfort them in pursuit of the object, of which you know, and for which there is a pressing need in their house."

David was floored with the realization that Al Vazquez was clearly an operative of the Order but held to the mission discipline. "Bingo!" he said aloud, flicking through his file and selecting the dossier on Dorance. "Positive identification subject OMEGA.NAO. zero one one three. Note: add dossier of Ronald Coleman Albert Vazquez to the Order," he said into the agent commentary track on the magnetic tape. "The president of the Boston Federal Reserve meets the Communist leader of North Vietnam and brings along his son-in-law. Dear Lord could this get any stranger?"

The intermediary bent close to the chairman who spoke so softly that the LS3000 registered no return; he continued, "The comrade chairman recognizes the urgency of your need but asks first for your progress with our request, please."

The Westerners looked at one another in confusion and then to the third man. "Ah yes, the Boston Terms. Sir, please thank the comrade chairman for his recognition, but the terms of our funding agreement were quite clear from the beginning and are, I am sorry to say, quite unalterable," said the unidentified man with a cultivated British accent who was so well dressed that he could have been an English gentleman at tea with the queen.

There was another hushed exchange. "But surely the gentleman understands that the removal of a million of our citizens from the postwar labor pool will make Vietnam's ability to service our debt all but impossible."

There was no response from the Westerners who sat mute in front of the great man; never giving an inch, seemingly prepared to walk away from the bargaining table.

"We have that which you seek," whispered the frail comrade directly to the English gentleman, ignoring Dorance, Vazquez, and the translator. "We propose only a simple trade: Hmong for Vietnamese. You shall have your bloodbath, sir, and your relic. We shall have our people."

The two men looked at one another across the lacquered mahogany table, and David believed that he saw them exchange a look of recognition or perhaps it was admiration. The comrade chairman glanced at his adjutant and a moment later ten uniformed soldiers struggled to bring in a large coffin-shaped wooden crate with red military stenciling that read; DANGER! CONTENTS CONTAMINATED! OPEN ONLY WITH NIOSH P100 RESPIRATOR! PROPERTY USMACV DA NANG!

"Midnight on January thirty, nineteen sixty-eight; this must be the start of your major offensive. The timing is imperative. Ann Arbor Center is preparing a national action for Red Storm, and our news production group in Pittsburgh is crafting special video segments anticipating your heroic victories in Saigon, Hue, and Khe Shan. We have primed and set a massive propaganda weapon to be fired into the American mass mind through the New York television networks even as American cities are being set alight. Imagine the chaos, Comrade Chairman. It will appear to the uninformed Yankee livestock that all is lost and total collapse is at hand," said the English gentleman. "We are offering nothing less than the national chaos you must have to break America's will to fight, and then you will be free to reunify Vietnam on your terms. Are you willing to risk your final victory to save the necks of a few worthless peasants?"

There was a long thoughtful pause, and then the great man rose to speak in his full voice. "Who has the greater risk? Vietnam or the North American Order? You believe we are the ignorant; the poor little Communists. Yet even we know something of your Great Trade Cycle and of Project Kansas. Are you willing to risk perhaps one hundred years of meticulous planning by your master for these few lives? Will he not believe you a shrewd steward of his resources when you conclude your Trade Cycle with a record return on his investment? When the United States of America is his personal possession to do with as he will, do you not believe he will look on you with great favor?"

The mood was tense as the negotiators glared at one another. The polished western gentleman rose to approach the great man, smiled broadly, and extended his hand. "As you say so shall it be, dear Uncle, but tell me; how is it that you have this beautiful house and gardens, yet you haven't shown me your estate or even invited me to tea?" said the English gentleman in perfectly accented Vietnamese. A moment later the two had joined arms and begun to amble toward the koi pond and into the sunset beyond.

• • •

"So the bad guys took the bait?" asked Coats, smiling as he spread the white cotton shroud over the giant's naked corpse.

"Hook line, and sinker," replied Rixon as he helped Coats secure the cloth to conceal the unsheathed relic from view. "Tom, I wanted to thank you for arranging the capture. It was tactically brilliant and the NVA never knew they were being set up, but you don't have to take that kind of risk any more. We're sheep-dipped surveillance contractors to CIA now, not counterinsurgency operators."

"All due respect, David, but I took an oath when I joined up, and my personal honor demands that I remain faithful to the constitution—just like yours, amigo." He smiled. "So, do Mayer and the CIA have any idea what this thing really is? What all this technology is really for? Even I know that after a point, more gold isn't the answer."

"Maybe. Omega Purple had decrypted messages from the Order that referred to something called an "Epsilon Site" but it was meaningless to them without context. When we brought Mayer the golden cube, control tablet, and photos it became clear that they were talking about our friend here and this installation. The translation says that the Order believes that there are naturally existing nodal points within what they call the Geodetic Realm where nothing with a positive electromagnetic charge exists; that is, there are no positively charged particles within the existing magnetic field. If they're right, then this cave could be a naturally occurring 'Zero Point,' sort of like the one in the power generator upstairs. They think Big Red here is the key to tapping into the invisible field of resonant energy that was released when the universe was created. They speculate that the biology of the giant's body and this facility are like a switch that connects the positively charged field outside the Epsilon Site to the Zero

Point. If they're right, then it could create energy flow—what we know as electrical current. According to Mayer, the Order is investing millions developing an artificial Epsilon Site in Pittsburgh of all places, and they need our relic to make the connection."

"So, David, the thing in the box that we dressed in Red's tunic, boots, and sword—where'd that one come from?" said Tom, tucking the fabric in and tying it down.

"The National Intelligence Archive Center in Suitland, Maryland. No kidding, Tom, and I find it difficult to believe myself, but Mayer says people have been finding these things all around the world for decades. His people in Washington found over a hundred of 'em in one of the underground vaults. The one we dressed up like Big Red is a composite made up of parts and pieces shipped home from Europe during World War II. The chest cavity is lined with lead to conceal an electronics and ordinance package from x rays. When they install the thing in Pittsburgh, the Omega agents there will be able to monitor nearby audio and, if necessary, remotely destroy the thing and the room it's in."

"Ordinance?" Coats smiled. "The thing is booby-trapped?"

"According to Mayer, the warhead from a captured Japanese Type 91 torpedo is a glove fit for the chest cavity. A very big boom in a very small package and if there is any type of forensics investigation by the Order, the ordinance will be traced back to Minister Tojo and not CIA." Both men smiled grimly.

"So what is the thing really?" continued Rixon. "From their transmissions it's clear the Order believes its Nephilim and is tangible evidence of the existence of Lucifer and his fallen angels. Red has great value to the devil worshipers Tom mostly because it validates their theology. They intend to use it in the way the Roman Catholic Church uses the bodies of long-dead Christian saints at the Vatican— hard evidence of the history of their religion, and it will be a bonus if it really does activate their Epsilon Site.

"Is Red a space alien? It's not scriptural but then neither is this technology. Christian theology says the Flood destroyed all life on the planet. So did this guy live before then and hold out in here, isolated while the water went down? There's really no way for us to know, but from what I've experienced in my life, especially that night at Signal Hill, God is more real, more alive, and more present in our lives than anyone today can imagine. He saved our lives twice that night at Rana Dat, Tom, and twice the day He put us into this cave, so I'm open to the idea of reconsidering how I understand Scripture when I work every day with something this tangible that shouldn't exist and that I simply do not understand.

"My working theory is that the universe is a sort of a phonetic gestalt, a profoundly meaningful hypernatural lexicon, which God used to speak everything into being at the instant of what the astrophysicists call the 'big bang.' In Genesis one three, God said, 'Let there be light.' It seems apparent now that God linguistically created the living world as we experience it. John one one says, 'In the beginning was the Word, and the Word was with God, and the Word was God.'

"It appears that the Order has discovered what I have come to believe myself—that the planet is shot through with residual fragments of a type of holy lexicon that existed intact beyond the field of time, before there was anything, and from which everything that is was made.

"I think of this cave as being located over a well of Divine nothingness; a physical proof of the Riemann Zeta Function; a naturally occurring point along an infinite line of zero that begins at the original Trinity Site where the Father, the Son, and the Holy Spirit were the singularity from which time and space were created. The point that we see right here in the field of time is probably the end of a line that leads us to infinite nothingness, which is a natural attractor of everything that exists on our side of eternity, in the field of time—what we uniforms call the World. To use their words, Epsilon Sites are imbued with the residual power of the Divine Act of Creation, which we experience as magical alchemical change; the power to dynamically arrange electrons to create electrical current; the power to change base material into gold; the power even to change the minds of human beings."

"Damn, Captain, I didn't mean ta ask you to defend your unified scientific thesis of everything!" Coats grinned, feeling slightly embarrassed for his friend. "I really just wanted to know what we gotta do to stop the bad guys?"

"Not much," said David, feeling verbose at his speculation about the reality of the giant's cave. "As we discussed, Omega is a CIA compartmentalized counterintelligence operation that's run on a need-to-know basis. As I understand it, there are only three compartments: Purple Cryptanalysis, which is Carlton Mayer and whoever he works with; White Surveillance, which is you and me; and Black Counter Insurgency, which is my dad and Captain Parker. There could be other compartments but unless there is a specific need to know, we'll never hear of them."

"It's not very satisfying, Tom, but unless we're instructed otherwise, we'll just watch, record, and report. The bright side is that CIA is paying our freight and we'll have more time to work with Donny and Scotty and the Hmong, and get them ready to stand on their own when we finally go home. Then there's this cave and all the technology to experiment with. I know a lot of PhDs back at Penn who'd give just about anything to spend a year down here!"

There was a long silence. "David, what are you planning for when we're done here? Just curious. Ah Kum wanted me to ask you about your company. She's thinking maybe you and Karen might like a couple of partners and maybe we'd move to the island and be your next-door neighbors so little Randy could have another kid to get into trouble with." Coats was actually blushing.

"Tom! Ah Kum's pregnant? That's fantastic! Congratulations!"

The two men embraced and began their serious discussion about continuing their partnership in peacetime and whether they'd ever be able to return to the United States. "Chichi-Jima is beautiful and secure, but it's just not home. Sometimes I ache for Odessa and Pleasant Farms, but then I think about Rodeo Cowboy, the warrant, the Order; there's no way I could ever think about exposing Karen and Randy to the danger. At this point, Tom, I think it's entirely up to the Lord and a handful of old World War Two veterans to set things right. Let's pray that Omega is successful, and that we defeat the bad guys. The best legacy I can think of leaving to our children and grandchildren is a restored America!"

• • •

Through the days and weeks that followed, the two men began a close study the Holy Scripture together, and they prayed for their country; they prayed for their people. From time to time they shared their insight and teaching with the scouts, who began to bring their friends among the Hmong. Word spread of a sweet aroma that had displaced the stench of the giant's cave and of a pleasing emotional resonance that had begun to envelop the high places of the giant's mountain, and others in the clan began to attend.

One morning Thomas Coats felt a joyous call from the Holy Spirit and began quietly teaching the Hmong of the place in heaven they would inherit if they would accept the Lord Jesus as their personal savior. He did this effectively and passionately, never knowing that he was speaking to his brothers in the secret language of the Hmong.

The guardian angels of the Word in Christ Missionary Baptist Church were tasked by the Lord to visit the church on giant mountain, fulfilling fervent prayer requests from the saints of the Quad Six. From time to time, they added their joy and grace to the guardians who were assigned to the new believers being born into the Kingdom, encouraged by the strong witness and sweet teaching of Thomas and David. An unseen spiritual connection was made between the two congregations as even more believers were born into the Kingdom and Thomas, David, and the Hmong learned to please the Lord on the earth as they would in heaven. Time and eternity began to merge in the misted high place and the church grew strong, hidden by the Lord from the Evil One, and causing the Apex to lose their supernatural awareness of the still active Epsilon Site. Being temporarily blinded by the goodness of the Holy Spirit, the counterfeit corpse of the Laotian giant, delivered to Dotson and Jung, was accepted by the Apex as authentic. And the Lord sent unto them a strong delusion so that they might believe themselves safe and secure in their manifold wickedness.

• • •

Jung and Dotson were in high spirits as they engaged the celebrated Parisian restaurateur and former OSS intelligence analyst, Rowland Ferrier, in a stimulating conversation concerning his first impressions as to the proper aesthetic composition for the Allegheny's inaugural fete. Ferrier had cooked for them that evening at *Morning Star*, the forty-acre Pittsburgh estate Jung had acquired twenty years prior with his employment bonus after being appointed chief executive officer of Allegheny Navigational Devices. The obscure manufacturer of marine navigational components had been picked up for a song by Alfred Dorance in his capacity as the president of BSB&T, and thereafter the NAO had capitalized their new venture with nearly a billion dollars in no-bid DOD contracts.

The terrace view of Pittsburgh's glistening skyline had lured them into the evening chill to admire the slender profile and preliminary lighting scheme of a fresh addition; the Allegheny seemed an elegant punctuation mark at the western edge of the central business district, flanked just farther west by the flashing red FAA clearance beacons riding atop the cluster of the broadcast towers sited on the highest geographical point in the region, known locally as "Fairview."

The three would-be social arbiters sat together comfortably, sipping warm Cognac at a small table placed at the effective limits of the microclimate created at the intersection of the radiance of the roaring terrace fireplace and the freezing mass of arctic air that had unexpectedly invaded Pittsburgh's early spring. On the table before them lay a pad with Ferrier's handwritten notes and a small blue book with a gold embossed title: Pittsburgh Social Register.

"As you astutely observed, Dotson, Tet is a Vietnamese New Year celebration and January thirty is in the middle of the winter season for you here in Pittsburgh. Under ordinary circumstances, polite

THE FLIGHT OF THE MAYDAY SQUADRON

society would simply dismiss the invitation as an intrusion from out-side social climbers. And of course, their beloved little scions will be away, fornicating themselves silly at university, so even if a way were to be found to make attendance socially desirable, I fear that absent the frisk of youth, the sexual energy of our project would be less than optimal. Our problem then is to leaven our working group of patriarchs, matriarchs, and their adult children who, incidentally, may be slightly curious about the Allegheny but only because your architect has made a rather magnificent stink about the construc-tion in the press." Ferrier smiled, turning to Jung. "Japanese steel in Pittsburgh? Really? Herr Jung, your man is simply brilliant. You must reward him!" The trio shared a hearty laugh while exchanging their favorite stories about Braham.

Ferrier skillfully steered the conversation back to the business at hand. "Hubbub notwithstanding, to attract the right people we must construct an offering that they will find irresistible; as we say in the Parisian party trade, "le poisson doit reconnaître l'appât"; if you want supper, the fish must first recognize the bait."

Ferrier took pad in hand and got down to business. "Gentlemen, to succeed, our gala will have to be an inside job, and to pull it off, we'll need allies. I have plumbed the depths of local society and unearthed two exceptionally well-suited jewels from the dark and barren mine otherwise known as the Pittsburgh Social Register. These ladies may well be kindred spirits and perhaps our ambas-sadors to the upper crust, if you will allow. These two have the bonafides to assure your smashing success; Dedra Rose Greyson and Easter Allison Crawford. I had my secretary double-check the press records in London to be certain, but it does seem that "Dede" and "Bunny," the very flower of Pittsburgh society, had both been packed off by their parents to an expensive English boarding school in Surry and were seniors at the Claremont School for Girls in 1923. At the time, British archeologist Howard Carter had finally presented the funerary artifacts and sarcophagus recovered from the burial crypt of Tutankhamun, purportedly the pharaoh of Egypt during what is known to Egyptologists as the New Kingdom.

"It seems that a wave of Egypotmania swept over England in response and propelled the impressionable Dede and Bunny onto a wayward path, which led to their becoming objects of masculine attention in more than one 'mummy unwrapping' party hosted by less-savory fraternal orders at the nearby Kingston Technical Institute. The London tabloid press was alerted to the fad and featured photos of the young women from America, in action as it were. They quoted Dede and Bunny as claiming their involvement stemmed from their shared interest in establishing their careers in archeology. The gentlemen in the photos were all smiling as they toasted their 'American mummies.'

"My tentative explorations through intermediaries this week indicate that Dede and Bunny, both now grandmothers in their late-sixties, have remained close friends through the decades, remember their salad days at Claremont fondly, and have recently expressed their joint curiosity to friends on the board of the Pittsburgh Museum of Natural History as to how they might help their institution become associated with the Egyptian antiquities currently being installed at the Allegheny. And so gentlemen, there you have your allies and, I believe, your entre to Pittsburgh's high society.

"As to the path forward, I feel it prudent to downplay the rather public unpleasantness of the construction period with Dede and Bunny. It is, after all, water under the bridge. We must henceforth focus our energies on new beginnings. Ramping into the event I envision a beneficial public relations program featuring appropriately timed photographic essays of the Allegheny, and of course, the antiquities, placed in national periodicals: *Life, Look, Time, National Geographic*, and perhaps as a gesture to the design industry, a piece in *Architectural Digest.*

"Nearer the event we'll need a friendly bio piece on you, Herr Jung, and the grand triumph of Allegheny Innovations, an all-American success story if there ever was one. It must run exclusively in the *Times*. As you both know, in America it's the *Times* or nothing.

"And for the event itself, nothing would be so appropriate as a celebration of the Egyptian antiquities themselves, an elegant, updated version of the classic English Egyptian Masquerade; music provided, of course, by the Pittsburgh Symphony Orchestra; appearances by the usual celebrities and dignitaries from Hollywood and Washington; and for an international flair, a nationally televised speech, perhaps by President Nasser himself, on the occasion of his dedication of the antiquities to the American people." Ferrier paused briefly to take the pulse of his benefactors and received only silence.

"And what amount, Herr Ferrier, would you suspect the total budget for this event might be?"

"Ah, cost. Yes, well these are round numbers only, based on information I have gathered through the week, but the gross expense range for an event of this scale and stature could range between one million and two million dollars, depending of course, on exchange rates at the time of purchase."

There was a new tension in the air as the cold began to edge in on their table. Jung did not reply for a long minute and then said, "Herr Ferrier, please cap your budget at one and one-half million dollars. This sum shall include the features you have described tonight as well as your fee. And I should like to insert one special request. For the entire evening, a military honor guard drawn from members of the American Thirty-Sixth Division, One Hundred Forty-First Combat Regiment. I have a brief but memorable history with this group from the war, and I wish to assure them that there are, as you Yanks enjoy saying, no hard feelings. After all, it is water under the bridge. We are all Americans now!" Dotson smiled broadly as Jung placed his hand on his shoulder and they shared a look that could have turned Medusa herself to stone.

"Very well, Herr Jung. The event budget shall be capped at one point five million dollars US, all inclusive, and shall be delivered complete with a military honor guard consisting of members of the American Thirty-Sixth Division. I'll have the contracts drawn and to you by the end of the week and, Gentlemen, may I congratulate you on your continued success and say that this event shall be smashing, truly smashing!" The cold closed in, the fire died away, and the three friends sought their comfort inside the mansion of the *Morning Star.*

• • •

Acting on Bruno Braham's recommendation, Rowland Ferrier had commissioned the latest sensation in the esoteric world of architectural photography to properly record the Allegheny. Miss Avery Simpson came to Braham highly recommended by a small clique of German expatriate architects who, like himself, had attained a level of celebrity in postwar America that would have forever eluded them in a culture where less is never more. The only heir to the fortune amassed by Detroit battery magnate Donald Simpson, Avery, had famously dropped out of the political science program at Yale and apprenticed herself to the infamous Nazi photographer, Hugo Jaeger, at his studio in Munich. She had written in her curriculum vitae, "The most powerful force in the field of political propaganda is the properly composed art photograph; therefore, it was only natural for me to seek Herr Jaeger, the undisputed master of the craft, as the only suitable mentor..." Braham thought her portfolio adequate and that her natural philosophical bent made her equal to the job.

The editors at *Architectural Digest* matched the photographer with their "Critic at Large," Christopher Golden, who traveled with Simpson, and her life partner, to experience the architecture and formulate a collaborative lead article for the August issue, which Golden titled "The Brightest Star."

A double sun has risen in the east; a brilliant binary star now signals the rebirth of Pittsburgh, Pennsylvania, as America's New Babylon. Completion of the Allegheny, the magnificent seventy-story headquarters of Allegheny Innovations, brings with it new energies and a fresh promise to propel Pennsylvania's dying Steel City beyond its grimy and brutal industrial roots toward its resurrection as a beacon for the arts and culture; a clarion bright and clear, beckoning the eternal spirits, which long ago dwelt powerfully in the cites of New

York, Washington, London, Paris, and their archetypal predecessors, Babylon and Luxor. In the annals of modern architectural thought, there has never been a composition so deliberately and brilliantly conceived as to alter the very course of the deep spiritual currents that originate within the land itself and informed the original human settlements, yet this is the express purpose of the Allegheny.

Placed at the westernmost shoreline of the central business district, the knife-edge of the slender tower has the spiritual presence of Arthur's Excalibur, driven deep into the sacred stone of Pittsburgh's Golden Triangle, forever pinning the triple river dragons of the Allegheny, Monongahela, and Ohio together and holding them in brace, the perpetual source of their deep magical current to drive the engines of this profoundly humanist construct...

The magazine's creative director, a BFA graduate from Cornell who considered himself a fellow traveler with a job, and therefore somewhat simpatico with Avery Simpson, envisioned the August cover as an opportunity to push a subversive work of socialist propaganda into the living rooms of well-heeled capitalists across the country. He therefore assumed the rather large professional risk of abandoning the set graphic design of the cover and selected an expensive full bleed close crop of Avery Simpson's photo entitled "Pharaohtic Sky," which provided the viewer with an exceptional view of the minitemple of Ra placed on the crown of the Allegheny which stood out in luminous contrast against a foreboding, color-corrected, Egyptian-blue sky. The title "Brightest Star" was reversed in white on the deep-blue field and the publication's logotype was hovering just above. The New York editorial staff though it beautiful, brilliant, and brave. The creative director was in tears and publically proclaimed himself Avery Simpson's love slave, and though he never cracked a smile, everyone got the joke.

Inspired by the graphic design comps he had examined at the prepress meeting, Christopher Golden had written poetically of the many aesthetic virtues of Bruno Braham's masterwork and had meticulously described the technical merits of the project, which included its very own IBM System 370 mainframe computer, state-of-the-art television production and broadcast center, lush and technically advanced corporate conference center, and accompanying prefunction facility as well as the AEI proprietary technologies that permitted the Allegheny to operate autonomously, detached from the city's utility grid. But it was his description of the magical rooftop colonnade, the antiquities from Karnak, which caused his rhetoric to soar.

Feeling as archeologist Howard Carter must have as he first glimpsed Tutankhamun's burial chamber, one enters the colonnade from the dark anteroom below noting the long southwestern vista where it is said that Sirius, the brightest binary star in the heavens, shall eternally illuminate the small bronze of Ra, commissioned by the architect himself as a gift to his client.

One is drawn from the darkness into the glistening otherworldly colonnade simulating the fabled Egyptian passage across Styx, the river of death, to the twelve gates of the afterlife. Clouds move in reflection across the luminous ground of mirror polished granite floors, commanding one's gaze to the blue nothingness beyond the infinity edge. And then the antiquities, presented to the entire world as well as the gods in a weatherproof glass encasement, the colonnade transported thus from its three-thousand-year residence in Karnak, tower some seven stories above!

The very scale of these megaliths dwarfs mortal men and conjures thoughts of Egyptian god-kings, pharaohs and their retainers, who might have walked this very hall, though looking east and west at the Allegheny they would today see the simultaneous rising and setting of the mythical double sun itself in the form of twin illuminated alabaster spheres, over seventy feet in diameter, which house sensitive roof-mounted electronics while maintaining unspoiled visual access to the heavens.

And at the center of it all, where logic demands a properly scaled idol depicting the god-king, there is a simple raised granite platform, devoid of adornment, as if awaiting the materialization of the Sun God himself.

Were there a choice of whether to live in this life or the next, one would be hard pressed to decide whether the Allegheny or heaven itself. As for this reporter, I would myself be inclined toward the former.

• • •

Brigadier General Otto G. Friedman, commander of the US Army's legacy Thirty-Sixth Division, then garrisoned with his unit for predeployment advanced infantry training at Fort Polk, Louisiana, received a teletype from Pentagon Command directing him to assemble a ten-man squad for a thirty-day temporary duty assignment as an honor guard for a VIP named Wolfgang Jung in Pittsburgh, Pennsylvania. Pittsburgh? The order specified that the squad would be drawn from the One Hundred Forty-First Infantry Regiment and that preference be given to any remaining veterans of the war in Europe. Perturbed by the nonsense command and not wanting to break the training routine of his troops, he remembered his wartime experience in Germany and placed a call to an old friend who had commanded the One Hundred Forty-First while they were in the European Theater. After catching up and a brief discussion, both men realized that the assignment would more properly be handled by reservists with ties to the original unit.

With a little US Army sleight of hand, the paperwork was done and General Friedman had both released his troopers from the burden of the frivolous TDY and done a favor for an old friend. "Not a bad day's work for a fat old rear-echelon paper pusher," he told himself as he took a moment to remember a time when he was young and a soldier in service to the cause of liberty in a faraway place called France.

• • •

A month later, key members of the of the Thirty-Sixth Division, One Hundred Forty-First Regiment, First Combat Engineers, had answered a personal plea from Captain Parker, accepted emergency DOD reactivation, and were immediately "sheep dipped" and committed to a one-year temporary duty assignment to the compartmentalized, need-to-know Central Intelligence Agency operation code named "Mojo."

Their "employer" for the year was to be a CIA front business operating from facilities in Toronto, Ontario, called Advanced Elevators, LLC. Their cover story was that Advanced Elevators had been subcontracted by the German passenger elevator manufacturer, TheissenCorr, Ag., to provide logistic support and skilled craftsmen to assist the German technicians in the installation and commissioning of the vertical transportation system for a new high-rise office building in Pittsburgh, Pennsylvania known as the Allegheny.

After reviewing the architect's detailed structural steel drawings, obtained by intermediaries from unsuccessful bidders within the Pittsburgh steel industry, the chief ordinance officer had selected cyclotetramethylene-tetranitramine as the primary explosive agent for their mission. Commonly known as HMX, an abbreviation for High-Velocity Military Explosive, the material is powerful yet stable and is used in a variety of military applications such as solid rocket fuel and detonation encasements for nuclear weapons.

For Mojo, the COO had written a military specification for a blend of HMX and TNT formed into a melt-castable explosive unit with the specific gravity of cast iron. The units themselves were to be milled precisely to conform to the size, shape, and color of TheissenCorr, Ag., elevator counterweight inserts, each 2.54 cm thick; 20.3 cm wide; 121.92 cm long, and weighing 42.83 kg.

Using the elevator manufacturer's architectural design as a guide, the chief had calculated that the counterweight installation in each elevator hoistway could be loaded with thirty cast HMX charges which, if detonated simultaneously, would release slightly more explosive energy than a Mark 118 airdropped demolition bomb; the type of heavy ordinance commonly delivered to enemy positions from stratospheric heights by the American B52s of Operation Arc Light.

As special operation commander, Captain Robert Parker had the statutory responsibility of preoperation tactical review and drew audible breath when he read the closing remarks in the report issued by his ordinance chief: "The architect's needlessly redundant vertical transportation solution calls for sixteen full-height, steel-rope-driven, high-speed elevators in the seventy-story building core. This provides Mojo the option of covertly replacing the normal elevator car counterweight assembly with a twenty-eight-hundred pound shaped ordinance package, thereby loading the structural core of the tower with the explosive equivalent of eighteen Mark one eighteen general purpose demolition bombs. The opportunity for extraordinarily precise ordinance placement may be acquired by using electronics to remotely commandeer elevator operation. If this option is selected, field command shall have the real-time ability to alter ordnance placement vertically within each hoistway to follow a target from floor to floor, to alter a previously selected detonation pattern or of locating the charges at predetermined positions that would sever the core steel columns on detonation, thereby causing the catastrophic gravity collapse of the entire structural steel frame."

"Roach Motel," Parker quipped to himself. "They check in but they don't check out." Smiling grimly, Parker approved the tactical solution for Operation Mojo.

• • •

Helpful hands and watchful eyes at DOD had processed the rush order for the curiously shaped HMX charges; wartime business as usual for the Special Ordinance Division at the Pantex Plant near Amarillo. Five hundred units were cast, stabilized, milled, painted, palletized, wrapped, and delivered, along with other rush orders, via military air transport to Lackland Air Force Base in San Antonio for theater deployment to Southeast Asia. There was, however, a small mistake made by an airman working deep nights on the logistics staging ramp; the heavy pallets of harmless-looking cast iron plates were erroneously consigned the designation of Military Surplus and sold early the next morning for one dollar to a representative of Knox Salvage Inc. of Odessa, Texas, who loaded them on his beat-up semitractor trailer combination and immediately transported them off base and through the night to their ultimate destination in Pittsburgh, Pennsylvania.

• • •

No one thought it odd when a large group of older men from Canada took a long-term lease on the large dilapidated house at the ugly end of Rubicon Street. Construction specialists from all over the world had come to Pittsburgh for work on the new downtown skyscraper, occupying the prime long-term rental units in the city and forcing new, cost-conscious arrivals across the river to the south shore neighborhood known as Duquesne Heights. As far as the landlord knew, the new tenants all seemed to be gentlemen of the highest quality, and besides, they had paid their lease one full year in advance.

While Omega Black's Liberty Squad settled into their racks, Liberty Actual took a moment to imagine the layout of his mission command center. He'd place his war room in the largest second-floor bedroom, the one with the line-of-sight view to the target, less than a mile across the river and nearly five hundred feet below his elevation on the escarpment. A year to Zero sounded like a long time but the schedule would be tight and the construction crews would be stretched to their breaking point by the notoriously unreasonable demands of the volatile German architect. Good. No slack on the site meant everyone would be focused on their own business, leaving his squad free to accomplish their mission.

He checked the schedule and placed the dual-faced mission clock on the dusty windowsill. Hanoi is twelve hours ahead of Pittsburgh; he set the countdown function for 368 days, thirteen hours and twenty-seven minutes, sixty seconds, 1200 hours, 30 January 1968. The details would have to be worked out on the fly.

• • •

Jung called the Executive Committee to order and the tension in the library at the Dorance estate was palpable. It was the long-anticipated Go-No Go meeting for the twelve-month domestic terror campaign against the American people, known within the North American Order as Project Kansas.

"Gentlemen, as you well know, beginning next January we shall be twelve months away from fundamentally transforming the United States of America, but only if each of you answers today in the affirmative. As you know, Kansas consists of three major components: propaganda, fifth-column terrorism, and legislative action. They are designed to work together covertly to leverage the shock and confusion of covert bombings and murders into a potent psychic driver, which will emotionally break the population and cause them to accept the shocking defeat of their military by a third world country and then demand legislation creating a national security police force, which we alone shall control. This is, of course, a precondition for our success."

"I realize that the burden on each of you is tremendous; for some, quite frankly, it is a life-or-death matter. Each of you has a copy of the project checklist, and in a moment I will read your element number, and you shall respond by simply saying yes or no.

"It is important for you to know that updated actuarial data from the Kansas model indicates that the probability of success for the program has risen to approximately ninety-two percent if all of the elements are executed per specification. We attribute this to the nightly televised coverage of the Vietnam War, and the psychic damage it has inflicted already on the mass mind. However, there is a dramatic decrease in success should even one of the elements fail or be seriously degraded. In fact, in at least one simulation, an entire compartment of the program is projected to fail when it is exposed, and the operatives are murdered by reactionary armed citizens. So please, gentlemen, when you are asked to respond, answer honestly. To paraphrase a famous American, the nature of our enterprise is such that we either hang together or hang separately. Are there any questions?

"With no further comment, I shall proceed with the project checklist beginning with the two marquee political assassinations. Please remember, gentlemen, the majick and power of Kansas will originate in the shed blood of these American heroes who shall become American martyrs.

"Martin Luther King Jr.; April 1968"

"Yes"

"Robert F. Kennedy; June 1968"

"Yes"

"This is a very good start, gentlemen. Now to the secondary actions; we have six state governors on the list…"

• • •

Thanks to the professionalism, pluck and ample rolodex of their brilliant Parisian event planner, the million-dollar national public relations campaign had the entire country abuzz about the Allegheny and the fantastic Egyptian antiquities installed, for all to see, seventy floors above the city of Pittsburgh. Rowland Ferrier had also been spot-on concerning the potential interest of the Madams Greyson and Crawford. Shortly after he arranged their meeting with Jung and Dotson for a hardhat tour of the Allegany and a conversation concerning their desire to host a grand opening celebration for the city, while standing in the shadow beneath the megaliths of course, both Dede and Bunny took the plunge.

Among other things, the two grand ladies had seen the gala as their golden opportunity to cement themselves and their families forever into the firmament of Pittsburgh's social universe. And to the surprise and delight of both Jung and Dotson, they made the gala their own and insisted that Herr Jung had given such a magnificent gift to the citizens of Pittsburgh that the city should, in an act of profound gratitude, pay for the grand party itself, if that would be permissible to Herr Jung and of course to Mister Rowland Ferrier, they had said to the slightly embarrassed Ferrier. Jung and Dotson were flabbergasted and accepted immediately.

Rowland, Bunny, and Dede became fast friends and had a ball crafting two preparties to tease polite society with the prospect of being among the first to personally experience the antiquities. *The Brightest Star* was the well-attended grand finale of Pittsburgh's summer season and began with tiaras and cocktails at the Oakmont Yacht Club on the eastern shore of the Allegheny River. After libations, bejeweled ladies with their imitation royal wear and their gentlemen adjourned at dusk for a dinner cruise aboard a commercial power barge decorated to resemble an Egyptian Sun Boat, making their simulated passage along the mythic River Ament to a rendezvous with Ra the Sun God. As the barge reached the triple river confluence, the barge pilot held his station and rotated his craft to present the panorama of the glistening skyline to his passengers. The signal was sent from the pilot and in five, four, three, two, one, downtown Pittsburgh went black. Before the passengers had completed their collective gasp, the electrical engineers at the Allegheny brought the light levels of the double sun spheres up gradually to simulate the Egyptian sunrise and then finished the show with full bright-white illumination of the glistening Egyptian arcade and then ignited the aerial fireworks display launched from the riverside to explode brilliantly alongside the rooftop temple. Everyone was aglow on their return to the club and the speculation as to how the rooftop temple would appear in person was absolutely epidemic.

Beyond the Pharaohtic Sky was held in the Grand Hall at the Pittsburgh Museum of Natural History during Christmastime, in the middle of the winter season. An anonymous donor had provided funding to commission renowned architectural photographer Avery Simpson to mount a large-scale exhibit of her *Architectural Digest* photo essay, which was augmented with an inspiring after-dinner lecture by the grandson of the famed British Egyptologist, Howard Carter. A roof terrace viewing of the city lights had been coordinated with the theme, and the property owners of the central business district had pitched in and voluntarily changed their traditional Christmas-red seasonal lighting scheme to Egyptian-blue. The PMNH terrace also featured a tantalizing view of the object of everyone's desire seemingly close enough to touch.

The climax of the holiday festivity occurred with the arrival of the "Egyptian Sand-a," a very tall slender man, dressed in sandals and a red Egyptian shendyt, with an outsized paper mache headpiece that resembled the canine profile of the Egyptian god Set, complete with serpent staff and a red bag full of Egyptian toys for the few children present. Flanking Sand-a were a costumed Dede and Bunny, scantily dressed and looking good for their age, as Nephthys, the wife of Set, and her best friend, Serget, the goddess of the desert scorpions. The ladies busied themselves handing out full-color preview cards for the upcoming post-holiday party, *Rites of Karnak; An Egyptian Masquerade Ball,* which would be the smashing culmination of the winter season of 1968.

Inspired by the music and the moment, Bunny and Dede formed an impromptu conga line and danced their slightly inebriated procession on a winding path through Avery Simpson's photo exhibit, then outside onto the roof terrace to view the Allegheny, its glowing white orbs piercing the foggy Pittsburgh evening. Doing their best to blend with the crowd were two complete strangers; one compact and dark, clearly of Latin descent, and the other tall, lanky, with precisely trimmed beard and mustache. Formally attired as all the gentlemen, they were clearly ignoring the spirited revelers, intently examining the Egyptian Crown of the Golden Triangle. And so it was that no one noticed when instead of a golden Rolex or platinum Piaget, Carlton Mayer glanced at his olive drab military issue chronograph noting there were fewer than forty-five days to zero.

• • •

As the construction deadline edged closer, the jobsite was packed with more workmen brought on to assist with last-minute flurry of changes ordered by the architect. Dressed in matching TheissenCorr overalls, and trying their best to look Canadian, Carlton Mayer and

Joe Gonzales spent the day tagging along with the chief ordnance officer inspecting the detonation devices and placement of the covert HMX ordinance and were totally unnoticed in the crush of new personnel.

BBBBBRRRRRIINNGG! FLASH!FLASH! FLASH!FLASH!

"It's that infernal fire alarm!" exclaimed the chief. "German and American technology at war even now!" The klaxon and strobe continued unabated; no one paid any attention and kept focused on the tasks at hand.

DING! DDING! DDDDING! The car arrival annunciators for all sixteen cabs sounded and the lobby doors opened simultaneously, and dangerously, to expose sixteen empty, and deep elevator hoistways.

"Dammed thing did it again! What's supposed to happen is that when the alarm sounds all the hoistway doors on the upper floors are to close and latch. The passenger cars are set to automatically return to the ground floor lobby, open their doors and latch so that anyone in the cars can exit. The doors are then supposed to stay in the open position until they're released by a keyed operator with access to the reset keyboard in the Ground Floor Fireman's Control Room. This is completely unacceptable, and if Braham is in the building, you're about to witness a major-league ass chewing!"

"Where are the cars and counterweights now?" asked Joe.

"A fault in the logic controller sends them all to the seventieth floor, meaning that the counterweights are right there," said the chief, shining his flashlight into the doorway of the nearest hoistway, across the thirty-three-floor abyss, and illuminating the currently dormant HMX charges only feet from their position.

The klaxon was at last silenced and the Mojo Squad recessed to witness the dapper, red-faced architect screaming and spewing little drops of spittle directly into the face of the much taller TheissenCorr technician, and though they couldn't understand a word, it was clear that an ass-chewing in any language is still an ass-chewing.

• • •

That evening over beer and takeout in the vacant squad room on Rubicon Street, Bobby Parker, Carlton Mayer, and Joe Gonzales, the senior commanders of Operation Mojo, discussed the ethics of their pending action. "The team's been working on this op for nearly a year without a break, and we're ready to go. But since we're all together, probably for the last time, I'd like to confirm the logic of our action to make sure we haven't overlooked something. It's not too late to call the whole thing off if we decide it isn't the right thing to do, so please, check me on this thinking," invited Parker.

"As we set things up, there are three primary objectives for Operation Mojo. Number one is to permanently remove the leadership of the North American Order, number two is to stop their domestic terror plot before it starts, and number three is to use the momentum of this event to purge the traitors from the federal bureaucracy and return the ownership of the government to the American people.

"Carl, thanks to you and the Omega Purple decryptions, we were able to confirm what our operatives within the Washington bureaucracy have been telling us for several years; the North American Order has a stranglehold on our government and are no longer responsive to either the Constitution or the American people. We also know that the NAO isn't a foreign power but a vicious organized criminal enterprise similar to the Mafia but by far the oldest, largest, richest and most dangerous group of this sort known to exist on the planet.

"The leadership of the NAO is the thirty-six-member Executive Committee. These men are the instigators and the decision makers and are always careful to separate themselves from their crimes. Below the Executive Committee is a compartmentalized group of accomplished subordinates embedded within the federal system, which operate exclusively by stealth under the cover of national security classification, and with the intent to make their crimes appear to be random acts. Their major crimes are always well conceived and carefully executed. They not only destroy all the incriminating evidence but always supply a reasonable scapegoat that is easy to blame for the event; anyone unfortunate enough to witness one of their criminal acts is always silenced and frequently murdered. This has been their signature method of operation since assuming their present form around nineteen hundred. It has rendered them virtually invisible and wealthy beyond all comprehension.

"Thanks again to Omega Purple, we know beyond all doubt that the NAO planned and commissioned the murder of the thirty-fifth president of the United States of America, nullified the results of the presidential election of nineteen sixty, usurped the authority granted to the president by the Constitution, used that power to infiltrate the military command structure and federal judicial system from the top down, and has misled the people of the United States into the ongoing illegal war in South Vietnam.

"The NAO has also used their power to obtain DOD contracts and federal grant monies to organize and fund Kansas, a guerrilla-style domestic terror operation targeting the people of the United States, their state and local elected officials, and all levels of police agencies. Kansas is the tip of the spear in an aggressive psychological war they are preparing to wage against the American people, which they believe will lead to their primary goal of destroying the social and civil institutions on which the country relies. In the resulting chaos they plan to seize undisputed control of the entire country by installing a national security police agency under their control. These men and their organization represent a clear and present danger to the American people and the constitutional Republic and must be stopped.

"Now here is the sticking point for me. I keep asking myself why can't we just turn the information over to the newspapers, the Congress, or the attorney general and let the FBI sort it out?"

Carlton Mayer cut in. "The answer, Bobby, is that the snake the NAO has placed within the federal system has grown so large and so lethal that the risk to the country of our taking a guileless, orthodox approach to this threat is just too high. We would all be murdered or imprisoned, the intelligence we've all worked so hard and sacrificed so much to assemble would be scattered in the wind, and the NAO would have no remaining opposition. The snake is simply too big for us to kill, yet Divine Providence has mercifully provided a very brief window in time when we may be able to remove the head of the snake; we'll only have one shot so we've got to make it count. If we don't do this and do it now, the NAO will put a violent end to United States of America, and they'll do it without any significant opposition."

"Thanks for that confirmation, Carl. It helps to hear you say it out loud. Now I have another question. What do you believe is our legal standing in this matter? Will we be viewed as criminals? Murders? Traitors?"

"Omega Purple has also discussed this Bobby," continued Mayer, "and we feel that while the Mojo takedown is extrajurisdictional, it is arguably not criminal and certainly not treasonous. Article Six, section three of the US Constitution identifies military officers as members of the executive branch and requires that we all swear an oath to protect and defend the Constitution from all enemies foreign and domestic. The military chain of command would normally preclude an intervention at our level; however, in this case, the chain has been compromised from the top down, and absent a duly elected chief executive, officers in the United States Military are duty bound to accept legal orders only from verifiably loyal members of the remaining command structure and take all prudent action to reestablish the chain through the president to the people of the United States and then validate the chain with a new presidential election. This is our constitutional charge, gentlemen, our duty as sworn officers of the US armed forces, and precisely what Operation Mojo is designed to accomplish. Joe, do you disagree?"

Pastor Joe pushed back from the table, looking leaner and harder than they remembered him from their summit at Midway. "Carl, some people just need killin'. 'Misdemeanor murder' is what Percy Foreman would call it. But I'm more than willing to walk away if you two can name even one of 'em who deserves to take another breath." The room remained silent. Their thoughts were of their team, their families, their countrymen, and the dangerous days ahead.

• • •

During the final weeks Jung, Dotson, Dorance, Braham, and Ferrier formed a tight working unit to deal with complex issues of commissioning the building, data processing, and broadcast systems; coordinating the domestic and foreign details for Project Kansas, the gala, and the related spiritual aspects of the January 30 event.

Even though he had placed a distance between himself and Dorance since Dotson's arrival, Jung trusted him enough to delegate coordination of the Red Storm domestic terror attacks with the North Vietnamese Tet Offensive and the news producers at the Pittsburgh Broadcasting Network. Jung had incentivized Dorance with the promise of a rank advancement to the nonexistent position as master of the North American Order, second in power only to himself. Dorance, however, found commanding the Red Strom terrorists through their agent "Tomahawk" most difficult, especially after the long, unexplained absence of their founder, Professor Francis Frank.

"They think Frank is some sort of god. They want to know when he's coming back and nearly always want to debate my orders. Most of the Redshirts are college kids, cream puffs, and pansies, and almost none of them have ever fired a weapon," complained Tomahawk. "In a firefight they'll be slaughtered. The weapons and ordnance we've been sent are nearly all antiques right out of DOD surplus. Some of them are even from the First World War. Surely the Order can do more for men willing to risk their lives for the Cause."

"Then avoid armed confrontation and use stealth to get the low-level bombings and murders done per plan," replied Dorance curtly. "Put the pansies into front lines of the mass demonstrations, double the pay of those more suited to the duty at hand, and equip them with the best you have. We have a special place for them; tell them they have a future with the federal government once we take control.

And this is critical: ONLY act on the signal from Kansas Command Pittsburgh; that is, unless you are refusing my direct order, in which case you shall meet the same fate as our late Frankie Frank." After their conversation, things at Ann Arbor Center ran smoothly or at least they seemed to.

Braham and Jung worked together to oversee the army of technicians and craftsmen working round the clock to make the December 31 operational deadline. They focused on the data center, broadcast and production studios, and communications hub located on floors sixty-six, sixty-seven, sixty-eight, and sixty-nine and both men haunted them, pleased with the commissioning and testing of their networked systems. The systems integrators and broadcast engineers in New York and Pittsburgh had done a masterful job of routing New York network control through Kansas Command Pittsburgh so that NAO producers and directors would be able to create a comprehensive media illusion for the viewing public in every major city in America. The actuaries estimated that nearly one hundred million viewers would be mesmerized by PBN's scripted "news bulletins," carefully calibrated to shape public opinion by referencing updated versions of the Kansas actuarial simulation generated by the IBM System 370 only a floor away.

The Executive Producers on each shift became technically proficient by running and rerunning an updated version of Orson Welles's *War of the Worlds* on a closed-circuit feed. The Allegheny Innovations writers had created a viable script by substituting the "North Vietnamese Communists" for the "Martians" and Topeka, Kansas, for Grover's Mill, New Jersey. They had then used their fertile imaginations, freshly delivered DOD combat tape from Vietnam, and affiliate file footage to fill in the blanks and make it all seem real. Jung thought modern television production technology to be a black majick conjure actualized and he spurred the production team on to perfection.

The local affiliate of Pittsburgh Broadcasting Network, WPBN, was set to be America's first all-news network featuring only news and public affairs programming. The new transmitter and tower located in Fairview had been broadcasting the station's test pattern for over a month while the studio-to-transmitter microwave link and signal router in the master control were being debugged. The schedule indicated that WPBN would begin broadcasting taped public service announcements on 15 January and with Go Live at 1200 on 30 January with a series of pretaped segments describing the construction of the Allegany and then at 1800 local cut to live coverage of *Rites of Karnak*, which was to include the inaugural concert given by the Pittsburgh Symphony Orchestra, the official dedication ceremony for the Egyptian antiquities and the Welcome Address given to the people of America by Wolfgang Jung, CEO of Allegheny Innovations. The masquerade ball and celebrity guest appearances would round out the coverage to end the first broadcast day. The next three hundred days of broadcast programming from PBN was heavily packed with propaganda feeds designed to convince Americans that the US Military had been routed by the Communists during the Tet Offensive, that Saigon was burning and America had been secretly invaded by Communist terrorists. This was their gamble and if they won, the NAO would be poised to enslave the entire nation.

• • •

Dotson had received coded telex responses from each member of the NAO Executive Committee confirming their mandatory presence in the reliquary for the "Red Dragon Invocation". All there was left for him to do was secure the blood sacrifice and instructions from the Wintergarten had been specific. The gift the Apex believed most tempting to the Prince of Amerike would be half Alpha, the four-year-old granddaughter of Alfred and Carol Dorance, Maria Carol Jean Vasquez, the spawn of the illicit union between their daughter, Belinda, and a common man, Ronald Coleman Albert Vasquez, who was currently serving as the NAO operative in Vientiane. "The logistics of the procurement should prove to be most interesting," mused Dotson as he considered the appropriate manner in which to deliver the message to Jung.

• • •

To costume Jung for his public duties during the *Rites of Karnak*, Dotson had searched his master's wardrobe but was unable to discover his original prewar dress uniform. As an act of desperation the gentleman's valet had contacted Eugene Holly in Stuttgart. Herr Holly was the son-in-law of the famed men's clothier Hugo Boss, who had become the most prominent supplier of uniforms for Germany's paramilitary defense corps known during the war as "Schutzstaffel," or "SS." Dotson had commissioned Holly to cut a full dress SS uniform for Jung in the winter weight, using the prewar design standard of Karl Diebitsch, the fashion and graphic designer most responsible for the famous aesthetics of the Third Reich. Both men agreed that the black, white, and red color scheme along with the cut of the thigh-length Waffenrock and military jodhpurs perfectly suited Jung's long slender frame, and even though Jung had originally only attained the rank of SS-Gruppenführer in the medical corps, his accomplishments since had certainly entitled him to wear the insignia of Reichsführer-SS.

Dotson had also asked Holly to source period authentic riding boots, crop, leather furnishings with sidearm holster for his master's vintage Walther P38 and then, of course, the finishing touch, a sparkling new SS visor cap with his original medical corps designation and one small alteration; the infamous Nazi Totenkopf, the death head worn by SS who were charged with actualizing the Final Solution, was to be cast of pure 14K gold. "The fools shall believe this is all some benign fantasy. Bravo Reichsführer Jung, bravo indeed," whispered Dotson to himself as he began accessorizing his master's new uniform.

• • •

The lights were on late in the big house at the end of Rubicon Street; Liberty Actual had called the final squad briefing before mission launch. The war room was packed and the mood somber.

"Sir, there's a serious problem," said the ordinance chief grimly, "During the last ten days we've experienced transmission continuity breaks with the ordinance. When we encounter a beak we have to shut the system down and run though the restart protocol to regain control of the weapons. We've tracked the cause to the new Faraday Shielding the architect ordered installed at the last minute. Last night we lost control again and haven't been able to reestablish it since."

"Chief, what are you telling me?" asked Liberty Actual, "We're less than forty-eight hours away from pulling the trigger. Are you saying that after all this, our weapons are useless?"

"Not entirely. We still control the ordinance in the reliquary and the WPBN tower and transmitter. But, sir, remote command and control of the main weapons in the elevator hoistways has been cut by the shielding."

"Chief, what are our options?" asked Liberty Actual.

"Sir, unless I've missed something there are only two: Mission Stand-down or Manual Detonation." They felt the gravity of their situation slowly at first and then rapidly as a fearsome paralysis flooded the gut of every man in the war room. The silence that locked it in was that of the grave; as dense and thick as the concrete foundations of the seventy-story Allegheny.

And after a time a lone voice, a faint whisper really, came from the rear of the room. With tears in his eyes and a quiver in his voice, a soldier stood to address his brothers. "Why me?" He spoke softly into the void of the horrible hush. "Why did I survive? You ever asked yourself that question? You ever feel the guilt like I have? For years I couldn't think of anything else. I've played it through in my mind a million times and it always comes down to the same question: Why did I survive? Why did I live when everyone I trained with, all my friends, everyone in my squad was killed, but I walked away without a scratch. Every man here has a similar story. Did anyone ever find the answer?" The terrible hush returned. "Well, maybe this is it. Maybe this is why God protected us; the reason we made it through; so we could finish the mission, finish the war for our buddies; so we can finally put an end to this Nazi crap for everyone in America, eradicate this kind of demonic thinking from the face of the Earth once and for all."

Another veteran stood. "My wife told me the day she left that I never came home from the war, and you know, I think she was probably right. Face it, the war never really ended for anyone in this room. That's why we're here, isn't it? Why we all signed up for Mojo, for one last mission, for one last chance to get it right. Isn't that the point? Sure, we could save our skins; we could just walk away. But then where in the hell would we go?"

Another man stood near the front. "Nearly all of us are in our sixties now, most with sons in the service. My oldest is a grunt just like his old man. He's with the First Calvary in Hue. I read his letters, then I look at the papers and watch the news on television, and I have no idea why he's over there putting his life on the line. The politicians say it's to stop Communism, but then I look at what they're doing in the field and none of it adds up. We've all known since the beginning that there's something different about Vietnam; that's there's something wrong with the leadership in Washington. The bastards are setting the troops up to fail; they just keep feeding our kids into this giant Communist meat grinder, and it's gotta stop. The only way I see to get that done is to clean the rat bastards out of our house. I know it sounds stupid ta say it here—land of the free, home of the brave, and all that corny Fourth of July stuff, but it makes me feel good, ya know? It's why my son enlisted rather than wait on the draft. I don't know about anyone else, but I don't intend to give up on the idea of *that* America, not now, not to these shitheads; it'd be the same to me as giving up on my boy. And I can tell ya', that's something I just ain't gonna do."

After a period of gut-wrenching discussion, it became clear that the men of Liberty Squad were dead set on fully accomplishing Operation Mojo no matter the personal cost and the decision of how this was to be done fell on the broad, powerful shoulders of Liberty Actual.

"Gentlemen, your dedication to your country, your families, and your brothers under arms is extraordinary, so much so that I can barely contain myself." Parker stopped briefly to regain his composure and drew a ragged breath. "Over the last year we've come together as a unit once again, and I want to take this opportunity to let you know formally how impressive you've become as individuals and as a team. It will be my honor to lead you wonderful guys into this final battle and, if possible, out the other side as victors and then home to your families with no doubt about the outcome and no questions left unanswered. And now, without any judgment, I'd like a final show of hands. Who's out? Who walks away?" There were no hands to count. "Who's in?" Everyone in the room, nearly thirty men, held their hands high.

"Very well, Liberty Squad; let's see about cleaning the vermin out of our house!"

• • •

The Interruptible Feedback Broadcast Intercom was alive with commands from the director: "Camera one; Center Rick and Suellen, enlarge frame to background Allegheny. Good. Hold that. Camera two, Crop Rick, push in on Suellen. Hold, pull back. Hold. Rick, straighten your tie. Makeup, touch up Suellen; good, that's enough. Someone turn the flower arrangement. Good. Hold that. OK, people; have a great show and break a leg, we're live to the national network in five, four, three, two, one..."

"Hello, America! Rick Rogers and Suellen Schando coming to you live from Pittsburgh, Pennsylvania, and WPBN's exclusive day-long coverage of the spectacular installation of Egyptian antiquities, culminating in tonight's national coverage of the 'Rites of Karnak,' a gala celebrating the grand opening of the 'American Temple of Ra,' a gift to the people of the United States of America from the people of the United Arab Republic of Egypt. Now, Suellen, this is the event the whole country's talking about. We've all seen the photographs and read the stories in nearly every national magazine and newspaper, even the *Times* ran a full page on the installation. People from all over America have been following this story for nearly a year and now it's finally here. This is the first opportunity we've had to really experience the magnificent Egyptian antiquities, twelve original stone columns taken from the ancient Temple of Ra in Karnak, Egypt, and placed atop a modern skyscraper right in the middle of the American heartland. What a fantastic idea!"

Camera two; three, two, one, Go!

"That's right, Rick, and I must say the antiquities are breathtaking. But no more so than the story of how these precious relics came to be in Pittsburgh nested atop a glimmering steel and glass highrise. It's a uniquely American success story of a penniless immigrant, a war refugee, who adopted America as his own country, and against all odds has risen with the tide he helped create. Earlier today we were fortunate to have been shown the magnificent 'Hall of the Prince' by Doctor Wolfgang Jung, president and chief executive officer of Allegheny Innovations. We spoke to Herr Jung candidly about his past hardships as an impoverished immigrant, his rise to prominence and his vison for the future of our country."

Tape one, Cue "Jung" in three, two, one, Go!

A deep blue image faded in with soft background audio, the viola segment of Beethoven's Symphony No. 9, Movement IV, "Ode to Joy." Then began the voiceover in heavily accented English with a slightly venerable quiver: "Papa wanted me to study the law but I wanted to fly the airplanes, you know, to be a pilot like Lucky Lindy!"

The 6X9 frame began a slow retreat from the Prussian blue infinity to the preset of the leggy blonde, Suellen Schando, and the grandfatherly Wolfgang Jung, facing one another at a slight angle, seated comfortably in two chrome-plated steel-and-black leather Barcelona chairs resting lightly on the polished granite surface of the large Ritual Stone in the "Hall of the Prince." The couple was framed left, right, and top by the dark profile of a pair of massive cuneiform columns and juxtaposed against the pristine blue Pennsylvania sky.

"But instead you became a doctor—was this before the war?" said Suellen, leaning forward with an expression of deep concern.

"Ah yes, before the war. I became physician first when I was young, to help others, you know, and then psychiatrist, to understand, to study the ways of the human mind. This is most fascinating to me. But the war was very evil and very destructive. The bombs fell like a great rain of fire, death, and horror; many times we prayed that God would send his angels to save us from the war, from the excesses of Hitler and his Nazi criminals. They did many horrible things, as you know. And this was our little dream, our small prayer, which in the end came true! Sometimes I think I am luckier than even Mr. Charles Lindbergh, to be rescued by our American heroes, just like John Wayne!" he chuckled slightly with a faraway look in his elderly gray eyes, "It was the Americans who were willing even then to take a chance on this old country doctor, to bring me here to Pennsylvania and present this fantastic country to a penniless beggar. I think no airplane shall ever fly this high!"

"A life dedicated to helping and understanding; Herr Jung, that's beautiful. And perhaps this explains your extravagant gift. Could it be that the reason you've created the 'American Temple of Ra' is to repay America for her efforts during the war?" Suellen smiled mistily while unconsciously bringing her manicured fingertips to her strategically cut décolletage.

"Of course," said the smiling grandfather, "we want only the best for our country, Suellen. The Temple of Ra, along with the Allegheny, they are both gifts, which function as symbol and sign. Symbolic inspiration from the long ago, yes, maybe of what America has yet to achieve and a glimpse into the future, a sign saying a new day is dawning. The best for our country is still to come. Perfection, I think, is not out of the question!"

"A perfect country! What a magnificent vison Doctor Jung, so inspiring!" she said smiling, leaning forward very low to gently touch the toe of Jung's shoe. "Would you take a moment now to describe the 'Hall of the Prince' for our audience?"

The image dissolved from Camera one to Camera two. The shot framed the longitudinal line of the temple. Jung and Schando were seated in the foreground at the beginning of the long processional space, dwarfed by three receding pairs of seven-story high Egyptian columns. The vista continued beyond the glass enclosure at the far end to the large white-and-red alabaster sphere, looming like a small planet, which concealed the WPBN microwave studio-to-transmitter link and was terminated by the red winking FAA clearance strobe atop the distant WPBN tower.

Jung took obvious pleasure in describing the antiquities, their acquisition, and the architectural assembly of the hall. He employed gentle hypnotic gestures and soothing vocal tonalities, which allowed the electronically transmuted Nazi war criminal to begin the ritualized 60 Hz cleansing of the American mind, easing fifteen million WPBN viewers into a demonically scripted unreality, and rendering them unsuspecting targets for the occult majick of the NAO.

The image dissolved again, this time into Camera three, which had pushed in tight on Jung. There were tears in his eyes, yet he was smiling, "And on this wonderful night we shall invite the prince of Amerike to make his residence here with us in this spectacular new home. This is our hope at least and the reason for it all." Seeing slight confusion in the eyes of his hostess, he said, "Ah please, Suellen, forgive a foolish old man. This is, of course only metaphor, a dream of mine, a manner of saying that the Spirit of Amerike, which stands this day in the wheat fields of Kansas, a bronze giant under a deep-indigo sky, reaping the amber waves of grain to fuel the engines of democracy. It is important to have the fantastic power of the heart-land here with us as we undertake our true and noble cause, nothing less than the final perfection of the United States of Amerike..."

• • •

The men of Liberty Squad were somber, emotionally hardening themselves for the duty that lay before them like a mountain they could neither walk around nor move aside. They had dressed in the uniforms for what they believed could well be their last night on earth, some in dark olive WWII vintage US Army Officers Service Uniforms, some in TheissenCorr overalls, some in standard issue army work uniforms, and some in the recently purloined red tunic and black breeches of the NAO Redshirt Brigade of the "First Pennsylvania," the flagship unit of the new Federal Division of Hometown Protection, authorized for temporary operation only on Federal Reservations by the President's National Security Acton Memorandum, NSAM # 373. And if everything went as planned, Liberty Squad would go to war against DHP First Pennsylvania that very night.

The squad room was quiet. Those not in their racks or writing their last letters to loved ones were watching the taped interview between WPBN's Rick Rogers and the legendary German architect Bruno Braham. Braham was explaining the profound intricacies of his esoteric architectural theory and the formidable obstacles he had overcome to actualize his landmark vision for the city of Pittsburgh. The sound was dialed down; the tension dialed up.

On the floor above, the war room was hopping with muffled telephone conversations and periodic radio chatter from Liberty agents monitoring strategic locations in and around Pittsburgh. The communications operators were also monitoring Pittsburgh police and fire department radio traffic while frequently scanning the muted broadcast television monitors tuned to WPBN and the "Three Sisters" in New York; all of which had announced plans to join WPBN for prime time coverage of the official dedication of the antiquities by the Egyptian minister of culture, a last-minute stand-in for President Nasser, who was regrettably prohibited from traveling for health purposes. The other television screens were closed-circuit feeds surreptitiously commandeered from the console inside the Allegheny's security office, which had been occupied for several days by the new DHP Redshirts. It was a comfort to Liberty Squad that their commanders would be seeing everything the Redshirts saw, perhaps in time to warn them if something were to go awry.

By far the most important gear in the room were the six-teen custom-fabricated Elevator Control Override and Weapons Command Triggers, each of which consisted of blue and green continuity indicators (one each for the sixteen different elevator cars), and a keyed switch with a red ARMED indicator and a red-illuminated detonation button, with a clear plastic flip-up safety cover. The ordinance chief was giving the squad last minuet instruction on their proper operation.

Carlton Mayer hurriedly joined Bobby Parker and Joe Gonzales at the large conference table to review the final Mojo dispatches from Omega Purple and Omega White. "Looks like there're all here." He offered a one-page handwritten list to Parker. "The tail numbers match their personal aircraft and our ramp agent at Pittsburgh International is certain the targets are all on the ground. We're processing his film now for positive ID, but it appears that they've all obeyed the summons." Mayer continued to read the dispatches as he brought the command team current.

"Omega White reports that the massed Communist troops in Laos have crossed over into South Vietnam and appear to be quietly infiltrating the cities; the only thing happening on the Trail now is logistic support traffic, and even that is very light. The visits to Ho in his office are now exclusively military and the frequency has doubled. White has been sending information verifying a large-scale assault in the South is being planned for the Vietnamese New Year. CIA Saigon has been forwarding the scrubbed reports up the chain but nothing's happening. The whole damned country seems to be shut down for Tet, like there isn't a war and an enemy within the country ready to strike. Omega White reminds us of the NVA plan to coordinate an offensive with the US Fifth Column and believes the US elements in country should be on high alert. The Pentagon disputes this and COMSMACV only says he doesn't want to provoke the NVA during the holiday, so it will be up to the unit commanders to deal with this. I hope they're smart enough to know what's happening in their AO and brave enough to deal with it. About the best thing we can do to help them is to put the brakes on Kansas...." Mayer became silent as he read a decoded NAO transmission from Omega Purple.

"My God; they're going to kill a kid up there tonight, a little girl!" He continued to read. "Good Lord, they've ordered Al and Carol Dorance to turn over their granddaughter for use as a human sacrifice, and they've agreed! The message is between Dotson and someplace called the Wintergarten. He's confirming Jung will do it himself at midnight in the Hall of the Prince while the Executive Committee is conducting their Red Dragon Invocation in front of the dead giant in the reliquary. They're doing everything they can to summon the devil!" He handed the decoded message to Joe while he massaged his temples.

"This is Belinda and Al Vasquez's daughter; she's not even five years old." Joe frowned as he handed the message to Bobby Parker. "Lieutenant, call the squad in for final briefing; we'll not allow this barbarism, not in our country and certainly not on our watch!"

The room was soon filled with veteran soldiers on the knife-edge, ready to go into battle when Parker addressed his men. "Gentlemen, we remain a 'Go' for Operation Mojo with a couple of duty alterations. Omega Purple decryptions indicate the godless bastards intend to murder a four-year-old girl tonight at twenty-four hundred. They want to use the granddaughter of one of their own as a human sacrifice to earn the blessing of the devil for their Kansas project. The little girl's name is Maria Carol Jean Vasquez, and we shall not permit this heinous act to occur.

"This means, Doctor Mayer and I will be joining the party, and along with Liberty four and Liberty five, we'll be masquerading as DHP Redshirts. Our plan is to reassign four and five to commandeer the building security desk. They'll provide operational overwatch from the inside, and we'll communicate within the Faraday Shield, using our own concealed transceivers. Mayer and I will assume their original duty in the reliquary and gain entry by flanking the honor guard as a security escort. We'll disappear after we're inside the perimeter and move downstairs, disable the Redshirt security detail, check off the targets as they enter, lock the door behind them, and punch their ticket to hell.

"After the primary objective is accomplished, we'll proceed to the rotunda, quietly take Lieutenant Gonzales into custody, and then do what we can to find the girl and get her clear of the building before the secondary goes hot.

"Let me be clear: after we take out the Executive Committee, the mission priority becomes the removal of Kansas Command Pittsburgh, and it has to be done before they go live at twenty-four hundred. Give us all the time you can, but DON'T WAIT ON US. We'll do our best to find Miss Vasquez and get her out alive, but that may not be possible. Other than that, you have your assignments and everything remains the same. Am I clear on this?" Liberty Squad affirmed the new orders strongly and together.

"Gentlemen, this is our last briefing. The mission clock has run down to just over four hundred minutes. Are there any final words?" The deep silence of steeled resolve and strong comradery covered the room. Pastor Joe rose, opened his worn New Testament, "My brothers, I am reading this afternoon from the thirteenth chapter of Paul's First Letter to the Church at Corinth. These are the eternal words of Almighty God, please take them into your heart with reverence:

"If I speak in the tongues of men and of angels, but have not love, I am a noisy gong or a clanging cymbal. And if I have prophetic powers, and understand all mysteries and all knowledge, and if I have all faith, so as to remove mountains, but have not love, I am nothing. If I give away all I have, and if I deliver up my body to be burned, but have not love, I gain nothing. Love is patient and kind; love does not envy or boast; it is not arrogant or rude. It does not insist on its own way; it is not irritable or resentful; it does not rejoice at wrongdoing, but rejoices with the truth. Love bears all things, believes all things, hopes all things, endures all things. Love never ends.

"Father God, Eternal Lord of the Universe, We confess any secret sin lingering in our hearts and ask that you wash us clean so that we may be fit to represent you on the field of battle. Father, we come before you as mortal men involved in a struggle against immortal evil and we pray for your strength and courage as we engage the agents of the enemy today in combat. Father, we pray also that you remove any hatred we may harbor for the men who oppose You and replace it with a wellspring of agape love for all things true and noble. It is these things, Father, which we defend today with our lives. And Lord, we humbly ask for Your divine protection in battle and that if it be Your will that we be allowed to successfully complete our mission and return victorious and whole to You and our families. Father we ask these many blessings and tender mercies in the eternal name of Your Son, Jesus Christ, our strength and our redeemer. Amen"

• • •

Dotson stood back to admire his master. "Magnificent, sir, truly a prince of the Reich!" Jung stood elevated on the low wooden platform before the three-glass tailor's mirror and examined himself mercilessly. From the sheen of his officer's tall black riding boots, the texture and flair of his black woolen jodhpurs, the precise hem and sharply tucked waist of his black woolen tunic, the black leather belt with diagonal leather suspender and the peaked visor cap, all seemed proper, just as he remembered them from his reveries in prewar Berlin.

Dotson assisted Jung with the placement and pinning of his signature red SS armband, this one with three white stripes, which indicated the rank of national leader. With gloved hand he attached his master's Knight's Cross at the neck of his Brown Shirt and then finished by offering Jung the freshly cleaned Walther P38. Jung took the butt, felt the weight, ejected the magazine to find eight 9mm cartridges; he replaced the magazine, slid a round into the chamber, safed the weapon, and placed it in his holster with a satisfying snap.

"Our grand triumph is at hand, Dotson and I wanted you to know that through all of this you've been indispensable. You draw no salary, have no possessions to speak of, the only personal life you have is here with me in these rooms, and I want to thank you personally and reward you financially for everything you've done." He withdrew an envelope from his inside jacket pocket and offered it to Dotson.

"Herr Jung, I am honored that you would say these splendid things, but I'm merely a servant faithful to his commission, and further compensation is simply unnecessary. However, sir, in that regard, there is news. I am sorry to say, Herr Jung but I've been recalled to the Wintergarten and will be leaving your service this evening. The Apex is very pleased with your performance, sir, so much so that they have authorized your apprentice. I am to attend him during his initiation in much the same way I attended you."

"I see," said Jung coolly, withdrawing the envelope. "Very well, Dotson, I wish you the best. As to this evening, have the arrangements been made for the consecration of the Hall of the Prince?"

"Yes indeed. The Dorances are in the car now and should arrive momentarily. You, the Dorance family, and the Egyptian minister are scheduled to make your entrance and offer your remarks at the climax of the festivities. After your public statement, you shall bid farewell to the minister and withdraw with the Dorance family to your personal suite, where Miss Vasquez will be prepared by her grandmother for her role this evening. At the appropriate moment, Mr. and Mrs. Dorance shall accompany you to the hall and assist in securing the sacrifice. They will then stand by to assist as you make your offering to the Prince.

"The members of the Executive Committee are being prepared for their role now and shall conclude the Red Dragon Invocation precisely at midnight, coincident with your dispatch of Miss Dorance.

"The component managers indicate that Project Kansas is ready to begin operation. Redshirt cells in target cities have hidden explosives inside their local police stations and will detonate the devices on your orders. These attacks will trigger the WPBN network to release pretaped reports indicating the bombings were committed by Communist insurgents allied with the North Vietnamese. WPBN's first reports of the Tet Offensive are also pretaped and ready for broadcast when the first report of the attacks in South Vietnam reaches the Associated Press. A virtuoso recital, if ever there was one!"

After it was clear there was nothing else to report, a thorny silence rapidly grew between the two men. Jung stood down, removed his visor cap, examined the golden Totenkopf for a moment, handed the cap to his valet, and accepted Dotson's help in slipping into his black leather Great Goat. "It's cold this evening, Dotson; the dead of winter; a good time to launch our attack, yes?" Dotson stood properly at silent attention, and after a moment, Herr Jung inclined his head toward his servant and walked out of the dressing room without another word.

• • •

The producers of "The Rites of Karnack" believed the show would be the high-water mark of their careers; that is, if they didn't screw it up. It had been estimated that when the New York networks joined their broadcast at 10:00 p.m. Eastern that nearly half of the country, around eighty million Americans, would be watching. WPBN had spared no expense in preparation and had purchased the most advanced broadcast technology available. The "eyes" of the network were state-of-the-art RCA TK-44 color cameras custom manufactured by RCA in Camden, New Jersey, with the iconic red double sun logo and the crisp "WPBN News 9" logotype displayed artfully on the exterior case. For their maiden national telecast, the segment directors had prepositioned a total of ten TK-44s; seven equipped for use in the soundproof broadcast studio and other public interior locations and three set up at cabled field locations for external views of the Allegheny and downtown Pittsburgh.

The ten live images were fed into the master control router and simultaneously displayed on two horizontal rows of five four-inch monitors on two identical control panels, one for the segment director and one for the program engineer. The image sent by micro-wave across the river to the WPBN transmitter and simultaneously up to the nearest networked Telstar Communications Satellite was only one of the ten images available at any time during the broadcast.

The "Rites of Karnak" consisted of three program segments, each fifty-eight minutes and thirty three seconds in duration. The first segment, limited to local broadcast on WPBN 9, was entitled "Symphony Blue," in which the Pittsburgh Symphony Orchestra would be gathered in the rotunda under the majestic frescoed duomo Allegheny and the baton of the famous Paul Mauriat for a recital of the favorite symphonic works of the chairman of Allegheny Innovations, Wolfgang Jung. The finale was to be the instrumental version of Mauriat's poplar "Love is Blue," performed live by the PSO as the "music over" for the prerecorded helicopter fly-around of the city center featuring large office buildings festooned in their Egyptian-blue lights and then dissolving into live coverage of the second segment, entitled "Egyptian Masquerade," which was to be sent out over the Telstar Satellite to the WPBN network, and which would be picked up by the New York networks for optional distribution to their affiliates in the Eastern Time Zone. The content was to be an unscripted narrative of the arrival of the various VIPs who had come to Pittsburgh to see the Hall of the Prince and because they had been ordered to do so by people who controlled their lives and livelihood.

The third and final segment, entitled "Consecrating the Hall," was to be a mandatory network special that would air at 10:00 p.m. Eastern on all four national networks and featured the dedication remarks by the Egyptian minister of culture and Wolfgang Jung. The balance of the show was divided into short scripted segments of interviews with key celebrities and their reactions to various aspects of the American Temple of Ra. Closing remarks were to be made by the WPBN anchors and then the fireworks show to celebrate the completed dedication at 11:00 p.m. Eastern. The affiliate stations would then be allowed to break away from network programming and go to their live local news.

Building up to the broadcast, the studio had been a hive of creative activity for weeks and the pace only increased as showtime approached. The segment "clock" for "The Rites of Karnak" was 175 minutes in length, and the WPBN network master clock was counting down to air across a system of slave clocks throughout the studio and electronic displays superimposed in the viewfinders of the TK-44s. Minding the time, the producers and directors communicated crisply with the on-air talent, the cameramen, soundmen, and cueing prompter, using the studio Interruptible Feedback Cueing Intercom. The IFB operated like a one-way party line carrying the instruction and chatter of the producer and director to the switching engineer operating the control console and the on-air teams located remotely from the Central Control Room. At sixty minutes to air the video control console was already showing ten live color images, the crews were in place and the IFB crackled to life with orders from the director to the on-air team scripting the presets and transitions he would use to create the magic of broadcast television.

"Camera ten, pull back from the building; include the WPBN tower in the frame, watch your depth of field. Good. Hold. OK, I know it's cold. We'll send out some hot cocoa!"

"Camera nine, frame the limo passenger door. Jimmy, flag the stop for the driver; the shot needs to capture the VIP when they exit. Hold that; good!"

"Camera eight, dolly left for VIP pickup on entrance; elevate to give me your best aerial shot; Hold."

"Camera seven, frame the orchestra from same elevation as Camera eight, Stop. Go back down. Stop and hold."

"Camera six, frame the VIP Speaker's Podium. Hold."

"Camera five, frame the entrance to the Hall of the Prince. Hold."

"Camera four, give me the long shot down the Hall. Hold."

"Cameras three, two, one, I'll direct when we're inside the segment."

"Who's writing the intro? We need hard copy to Rick and Suellen in ten minutes! And don't forget the TelePropmTer! Get it done, Samantha! Fifteen minutes to air, people, hustle it up!

"Camera nine, NINE! Where's the color guard! Holy shit! Where's the honor guard? Damn it, Rodney, the army guys are supposed to be in the opening shot, and I don't see 'em! GET THE FRIGGIN' HONOR GUARD IN THE SHOT NOW!" A panic-stricken young man with a headset and clipboard ran past the DHP security perimeter and grabbed Lieutenant Gonzales by the sleeve. "Hurry! Please hurry! All of you! I need you people on your marks right away!" Gonzales, the other three members of the Honor Guard and their DHP security escort were hustled past the official Redshirt identity checkpoint and to their assigned positions in front of the camera.

The four veteran members of the 141st Infantry Regiment Honor Guard were in place and at attention, flags flying, when the immaculate Rolls Royce Silver Cloud pulled to a gentle stop in the glare of the television lights.

"Tape 1: Cue Egyptian Masquerade; Sound! give me symphony in three, two, one. GO!"

Television screens across the WBPN Network faded to black and over the darkness began to hear the symphonic strains of "Love is Blue" and then the image of downtown Pittsburgh from a mile in the sky came to life in the screen. Skillfully synchronized with the music, the aerial mage zoomed slowly in on the Allegheny, past the glittering American Temple of Ra and then seamlessly into a live shot of the patriotic Honor Gard and then to an overview of the PSO, a close shot of Maestro Mauriat, and then a long shot of the costumed partygoers dancing between the conductor and the elegant and expansive speaker's podium.

"Good evening America! Suellen Schando with Rick Rogers, welcoming you to WPBN's extended coverage of the "Rites of Karnack," and Rick, the hottest ticket in the country tonight is happening in Pittsburgh right behind us."

"That's right, Suellen, it's called the "Egyptian Masquerade," and it's a chance to dance until the stars come out with their midnight unmasking. There are already many celebrities in the crowd behind us, but you'll have to wait along with us to see who they are—and they keep on arriving! Suellen, could you let the audience know who's coming in now?"

"Camera nine: pull back; pan left in three, two, one. GO!" The television image smoothly altered to show the ranking member of the First Pennsylvania, Division of Hometown Protection, greeting the costumed Jung with a sharp paramilitary-style salute as he exited the limousine. Always the gentleman, Jung helped Carol Dorance and her young granddaughter exit the passenger compartment and waited for Alfred Dorance to join them. As a group they waved to the crowd beyond the rope line. Dorance escorted his photogenic family out of the frame, leaving Jung and his DHP escort to inspect the Honor Guard.

Camera eight: push in on the army guys. Hold it there!

Camera eight; three, two, one. Go! The television image dissolved to an alternate location showing the audience a smiling Reichsführer Jung in full dress SS uniform, Red Swastika on his arm, and golden Death Head on his visor cap, aggressively "inspecting" the American Honor Guard. He then openly mocked the Veterans, who had captured him in combat over twenty years before, by flipping them a Nazi stiff arm salute. But the line held firm. Jung looked into each man's eyes, saw that they wouldn't break, and retreated to the cameras and the beaming blond news anchor. "Magnificent consume, Herr Jung! What a wonderful wit you have!" She gleamed, absently touching her IFB earphone, "Rick, I am here with Doctor Wolfgang Jung, the CEO of WPBN's parent company, Allegheny Innovations, and the host of tonight's celebration. Dr. Jung this is all so spectacular; could you please give the audience a hint at what they can expect over the next two hours?"

"Ah, Suellen, this is a fantastic evening and you are correct, there is much more to come!" He glowed. "I will make a surprise announcement with my remarks when we conclude the masquerade, and I promise a spectacular climax to our event!"

The camera pushed in on Suellen for commentary and the IFB crackled to life, "Rodney! Get the procession ready. Remember:

Honor Guard First, VIPs follow. We're going to entry sequence in thirty seconds."

Lieutenant Gonzales barked commands to move the 141st Regiment Honor Guard into position. The color unit consisted of four men dressed in dark olive US Army dress A uniforms with peaked garrison covers, two bearers carrying the American flag to the right and the pennant of the 141st Infantry Regiment to the left, and two riflemen armed with ceremonial M1903 Springfield Rifles; the unit was flanked by two men who appeared to be armed members of the Division of Hometown Protection.

The large doors opened on cue and following the script, Gonzales brought the unit into the large central rotunda and ordered their halt between the conductor and the speaker's podium. They stood at attention for the Pittsburgh Symphony Orchestra's rendition of "Das Lied der Deutschen" ("Song of the Germans"), the national anthem for Hitler's Germany followed by, "Bilady, laki hubbi wa fu'adi" ("My homeland, you have my love and my heart"), the national song of the United Arab Republic of Egypt, and finally the "Star Spangled Banner."

"We're in!" whispered Liberty Actual into his wrist microphone as he checked the time. "L four, sit rep."

The metallic whisper replied, "We have the mountain. Bandits neutralized. We're cleared for Phase Two."

"Copy that, L four, need status henhouse."

"Looks like only two roosters; no hens current; your status?"

"Liberty Actual status nominal; we're mobile; ETA objective in twenty. Stay sharp."

Once in the stairwell Parker and Mayer checked their side arms, their back-up weapons, and their chronographs to be certain of the time; less than two hours to zero. They were cutting it close.

They reached the bottom of the stairwell and held. "Liberty four; positon of roosters relative stairwell two. Do you copy?" whispered Actual.

"Copy, Actual; stairwell two is twenty meters to the rear of the checkpoint at service elevator doors, roosters discussing something now; looks like they're antsy. Over."

"So, my friend, how do we handle this?" asked Parker while he and Mayer took a moment to recover after rapidly descending thirty-three flights of stairs.

"Well, Captain, we could just sit here and wait," said Mayer, extracting a small handheld device from his uniform pocket, switching it on, and plugging in his earphone, "I've got a green light, and the audio is fine; I can hear the background noise in the reliquary and I can even hear the roosters at the checkpoint. In fact, hold on...one of 'em just said he needs to go to the bathroom pretty badly. His friend says they haven't been relieved in nearly eight hours. Their commander doesn't know what he's doing. The freight elevator is locked down and the service elevator has been restricted to VIP traffic from the parking garage. He's saying he HAS to go to the toilet."

"That's it; Carl, follow my lead," said Parker with a smile as he walked briskly out of the fire stair door. "Damn it, guys; we're sorry we're so late. We had to walk down all thirty-three floors; the commander's locked the elevator down. Anyone here yet?" Parker walked past the Redshirts to the checkpoint desk to take a look at the clipboard."

"Private, where's the toilet, I really need to go," said "Corporal" Mayer to the pair.

"The nearest toilet is thirty-three floors straight up; that's the big problem with this duty, sir," said the DHP private, indicating his profound discomfort.

"What's that?" asked Mayer pointing to the shallow reflecting pool inside the reliquary.

• • •

"Rabbi Mayer, I do believe you just took a whiz in the River Styx. Man, there's gotta be a rule about that in the Torah." The men laughed together for the first time. "Those kids really thought you were crazy, Carl! They hightailed it outta here like a couple of jackrabbits!"

joked Parker and they laughed even harder, both men checking the time as the laughter died away. Silence.

"How old are you, Bobby, if you don't mind my asking?" asked Mayer thoughtfully.

"I'll be seventy day after tomorrow, Carl, and you?"

"Just turned sixty-nine," said Mayer allowing their shared silence to blend with the dark mysteries contained in the reliquary.

"We're not getting out of here, are we?" asked Mayer.

"Carl, I didn't survive the European Theater and then build Parker Exploration by being a pessimist, but in this case, you might be right. It's a long way from here to daylight, and there's a godawful big bomb sitting less than twenty-five yards from where we're standing." The silence returned and grew thick.

"They're late." frowned Parker, checking his chronograph.

"You think Gonzales will be OK? We're changing the plan and he might like to know."

"Joe? No, he'll be fine. By now he's read the tea leaves just like we have. In fact, if anyone makes it out of here, I'd bet it'd be him. I've known the man nearly thirty years and he's always working on a backup plan." Parker smiled thinking about the distant past. "Of course you know his impoverished farmer bit is just for show. The man owns twenty percent of Parker Exploration, but the way he lives, you'd think he was barely scraping by. It's part of his public persona; he believes it gives him an edge most everywhere he goes, and I suppose in some ways it does." Parker smiled broadly with the cherished memory.

"He wouldn't want me telling you this, but I got my start from Joe. After VE, I mustered out with everyone else, came home to Pittsburgh, but nothing was the same. My wife just didn't want me anymore, my family didn't know how to react to any of it, so I started drinking. I lost everything in the divorce. I had about two dimes to rub together back then, and I used one of 'em to call Joe. He invited me to come out to Texas for a visit, so that's what I did. I worked for him on Pleasant Farms and lived with him and Paulina for nearly two years while I figured out what to do with my life. We helped each other get over the war a little, I think. He even converted me,"

Parker said with another smile, "baptized me right there in the stock pond; never had another drop after that. It was a good time for both of us, but I always think I got the better end of the deal. Anyway, when I decided on oil exploration, Joe loaned me the money to get started. Can you believe that? That poor old Mexican dirt farmer had the capital to start a pretty decent petroleum exploration company, and he was willing to bet it on some guy he knew for a few years in the army. Well, when we finally got the thing on its feet and I could afford to pay him back, he said he'd rather have a job than the money. We converted his capital investment to preferred stock and he became my first and only partner. Thanks to Joe, nearly every one of our core people are vets out of the hundred and forty-first; a lot of 'em volunteered for this mission."

"That's a great story," Mayer said with a smile, "and you're right. He'd hate it if I knew that deep down he's really an old softy and it probably would have completely ruined his breakfast if he'd had my head blown off that first morning out in the Permian." both men laughed again and then more silence.

"Bobby, would you have done anything differently?" asked Mayer. "The way you lived your life, I mean."

"No, Carl. Not really—you?"

"There was this girl in college. I always wished I'd had the courage to ask her out. But other than that, it's worked out pretty well for me too." The silence returned.

"No matter what, none of 'em gets out; can we agree on that, Captain?"

"Commander, you 'n' me both have a Colt nineteen eleven with seven in the box and one in the chamber and then there's Big Red; we have the firepower to get the job done, Carl. All we need is the grit to use it when the time comes."

After a moment, Mayer said, "Bobby, it's been an honor." He offered his hand.

"Shush! What's that sound?" asked Parker, "You hear that? There's something moving in there; sounds like it's coming from the tunnel."

Both men turned toward the open stainless steel security doors, shined their flashlights into the gloom and were startled by several very fast, very large animals that could have been apes running out of the reliquary into the cavern.

"What the hell?" began Mayer but he was cut off by the "ding" of the elevator annunciator. They looked back to see the oversized stainless steel doors part, exposing thirteen large middle-aged men, all of them dressed in red hooded cloaks. The Warlocks had arrived to prepare the reliquary for the Red Dragon Invocation.

• • •

The Pittsburgh Symphony Orchestra had surrendered the rotunda to their lesser brethren, the accomplished cover band known as the River City Rollers, which came highly recommended by Dede and Bunny, owing to the lineage of the pimply faced lead singer. They were doing an adequate job of belting out the top forty hits for the sweaty, enthusiastic crowd of quasi-famous masked dancers; "... And I saw her face, now I'm a believer, not a trace of doubt in my mind..." Jung, his honored guests, the Dorance family, President Sadat's ministerial proxy, Dedra Greyson, Easter Crawford, and their families, and local luminaries who made Pittsburgh run were observing the revelry from the slight elevation of the VIP rostrum. At precisely 9:59 the band's performance was brought to an elegant close by the WPBN floor director and the repositioned cameras were brought to focus on Rick and Suellen at the speaker's dais. The IFB came alive once more. "Listen up, people; good job so far; we are live via satellite to New York and eighty million people in ten seconds; good luck. Camera seven, give me Rick and Suellen in three, two, one. GO!

"Good Evening America! Welcome to Pittsburgh, Pennsylvania, and the long-anticipated 'Consecration of the Hall of the Prince.' Rick Rogers with Suellen Schando coming to you live from the world headquarters of Allegheny Innovations the home of 'America's Temple of Ra,' the inspired installation of the largest group of nonresident Egyptian antiquities in the world. This group of twelve magnificent seven-story high columns was given by the people of the United Arab Republic of Egypt to the people of the United States of America in the spirit of brotherhood and peace."

"That's right Rick and what a lovely gesture it is. We'll hear more about the gift and the people of Egypt in just a few minutes but to greet our viewers and introduce our keynote speaker form the Egyptian Ministry of Culture we'll hear first from the CEO of Allegheny Innovations and our host this evening Doctor Wolfgang Jung.

"Camera eight; Give me Jung in three, two, one. GO!"

Through bright lights, the camera pushed in tight on Jung, still attired in his Nazi SS dress uniform reading his Message to America from the teleprompter.

"Welcome to the Temple of Ra!" The crowd cheered and applauded. "This is a dream for all of us at Allegheny Innovations. For twenty years already I've been working to achieve this for you, for all of us!" More cheering. "We will consecrate this faculty for the good of the Amerike of the future; we shall make this sacrifice, you see, not for us do we do this but for the children!" Cheers and adoration from the crowd. Jung turned away from the camera and stooped low to pick up little Maria Vazquez. He held her up before all the crowd and eighty million television viewers. Cheers and applause from the crowd. "This is my goddaughter for the evening, Maria Carol Jean Vasquez, and her role tonight is very important. Maria will be the key to inviting the Prince of Amerike, the vitality of the heartland, you see, to live here forever." More cheers and applause. Jung turned her toward himself, looked her in the eye, pulled her cheek to his and then turned smiling to the camera, "So precious, couldn't you just eat her?"

WHUUMMMFFFF! There was a sudden tremendous boom, muffled yet clearly audible, followed immediately by a frightening deep rumbling screech from somewhere far below the rotunda, in the lowest bowels of the Allegheny. The TK-44 picked up the slight but perceptible tremor in the speaker's podium and in Wolfgang

Jung himself as the massive structural steel frame telegraphed the power of the explosion up and out into all parts of the seventy-story tower. The rotunda dome skewed and fractured slightly, causing small fragments of the magnificent 'Second Coming' fresco to fall like new year's confetti through the broadcast frame surrounding Jung; the lights flickered rapidly off, on, off, on, and then BBBBBRRRRRIINNGG! FLASH!FLASH! FLASH!...

Panic scarred Jung's face, the fire alarm klaxon blared and the strobe flashed throughout the building; someone in the crowd screamed FIRE! and the startled crowd launched itself into a dangerous stampede for the exits. Ever the professional, the WPBN engineer in master control switched the outgoing image to camera ten, the shot from the remote truck across the Monongahela River, and then he too ran through the white smoke and alarm strobes for the exit.

DING! DDING! DDDDING! The sixteen preprogrammed passenger elevator cars began arriving at the ground floor lobby and automatically locked their doors open so that riders from upper floors could join the rush to safety. Calmly, slowly, and effectively, the uniformed members of the TheissenCorr elevator team navigated against the crowd and assumed their positons inside the disabled cabins. The ordinance chief found his way to the fireman's control room, shut down the klaxon, released the fire alarm interlock, and freed Liberty Squad to move their cars to preestablished hoistway positons.

• • •

Gonzales slowly and cautiously crept out of the fire stair and into the seventieth floor corridor heading to Jung's executive suite. His hushed yet rapid progress was animated by the alarm strobe flashing into the smoky haze, which had crept into the air distribution system from the raging fire in the subbasement. He approached the frameless glass doors in the prone position, peered into the welcome center to see four uniformed DHP officers standing watch over what looked to be the bodies of the Dorance family: Alfred, Carol, and little Maria.

"Fear not." Gonzales snapped away from the voice behind, rolled sharply to the opposite side of the corridor, smoothly drew his 1911, trained it on the source, and saw yet another DHP officer holding out his open hand. The familiar bright countenance on the smiling man's face put Joe at ease. He holstered the weapon and took the hand up.

Looking toward the Dorance family, the Guardian spoke, "They are asleep and in the care of the Lord. When they wake, no memory of the passings this night shall remain. They are safe."

"Your mission waits even now." The luminous being pointed Joe toward the grand stairway leading up to the temple, "The Prince of Amerika has taken possession of the hall; the blood of an innocent has given him strong purchase. Only the Son of Man has the power to break his claim on this world and His time is not yet." The words spoken by this strange radiant man illuminated the mission in Joe's mind, chasing away all doubt and fear. He knew what he had to do and absently touched his sidearm as he started for the stair.

"The weapon will only hinder you." The Guardian smiled. Joe released the buckle and let the leather and its contents fall to the floor. He shed his uniform jacket, transferred his worn New Testament to the buttoned flap pocket of his khaki-colored uniform blouse, and checked the time once more. When he looked up he was alone again yet understood his objective was near.

When Joe entered the darkened Temple of Ra a plume of smoke was wafting into the starry night sky beyond the glass enclosure. Both the smoke and the stars were reflected in the polished black granite floor, causing him a momentary sense of vertigo. He was oriented by the clearance strobes of a helicopter approaching the roof at eye level and then the metallic voice of the pilot through the transceiver as he coordinated his approach with Jung. The objective was in sight, standing near a large panel of thick insulated glass at the far end of the Hall of the Prince.

With swift steps on soft soles, Joe used the Egyptian antiquities themselves to conceal his rapid advance until he was near enough to smell the sweat and fear of the Nazi war criminal only slightly beyond his reach.

"There's no helipad!" said the metallic voice to Jung. "You've got to get to the roof. I can hover the ship in to pick you up!"

Trapped, Jung seemed to panic for a moment and then visibly calmed himself. He drew his P38 from its leather and deftly placed two 9mm rounds through the glass panel, causing it to shatter and fall away, creating his path to salvation. The icy turbulence of the rotor wash swept powerfully into the opening, which caused Jung to pause at the threshold; it was something else entirely that persuaded him to step back into the temple and, with weapon in hand, face his nemesis hiding in dark shadows.

As lean and hard as the trench knife in his boot, Lieutenant Gonzales sprang to catch the enemy in his lethal embrace. It was a testament to rigorous preparation and soldierly devotion to the instrument of war that Jung experienced only slight discomfort when the precisely honed blade slid painlessly into his cervical spine between the C3 and C4 vertebrae causing instant paralysis. He was conscious, yet distantly so, as his head spun easily away from its quivering torso. Jung's final visual recognition was a lone star of argent surrounded by a garland of live oak above a shield of white, red, and deep blue. Below the shield was a scroll of heather blue with the silver inscription: "Remember the Alamo."

● ● ●

The ramshackle house at the ugly end of Rubicon Street was vacant that night and dark save for the muted television monitors animating the large second-floor bedroom, the one with the picture window facing Pittsburgh's Golden Triangle, less than a mile across the river. The view of the Allegheny was dramatic from that vantage point. The tower had gone dark less than an hour after the Type 91 warhead was detonated in the reliquary, liquefying its contents and causing extensive collateral damage to the Zero Point Generator vault directly above. The fires in the subbasement had finally caused the main electrical busses to disintegrate, cutting the power to everything but the hardened broadcast and life safety systems.

Within an hour the fires in the subbasement had spread to the parking garage that was packed for the gala and Pittsburgh Fire and Rescue had responded to the alarm. The PFR battalion chief was taken into custody for striking a federal law enforcement officer when he punched the fresh-faced commander of Pittsburgh's new Division of Hometown Protection unit for not allowing his men access to the federal reservation upon which the Allegheny was constructed; "national security", he had said. Frustrated and doing what they could to help whoever might be trying to escape the fires, Pittsburgh Fire and Rescue had used military surplus carbon arc search lights to dramatically illuminate the dying hulk. The blinding white beams gave the building shell and towering plume of white smoke a spectral presence when juxtaposed against other high-rises still fully illuminated and festively trimmed in Egyptian blue.

The four monitors in the war room, one each for WPBM and the Three Sisters in New York, were all showing the feed from camera ten though the fifteen-second delay caused by the satellite relay from the roof-mounted up-link to the networks. The interval created an eerie sense of déjà vu with the live event seen from the window appearing five seconds later on the WBPN feed and then ten seconds after that on the New York networks.

At precisely 11:00 Eastern, nearly ninety million Americans witnessed a series of sixteen massive orange-white flashes from deep inside the structure. They happened with military precision, less than a second apart and in sequence, from just below the American Temple of Ra and down. Like a zipper in a glass and polished granite body bag, the flashes exposed the grinning corpse of Project Kansas to the American people, yet only a handful would ever realize the significance of what they saw; fewer still the extreme cost of the show.

After the first explosion, during the brief moment before gravity took hold, the darkened alabaster double suns were launched laterally away from their foundations as the American Temple of Ra violently rotated, causing the colonnade of Egyptian antiquities to rack away from their moorings, crash into the glass enclosure, and disintegrate as they joined the mass of the building in its terminal seventy-story free fall, accelerating at thirty-two feet per second squared into the hellish pit that had once been the reliquary.

Less than a second after the fall of the tower, the signal compression buffer in the Fairview transmitter allowed the stunned national audience to see the same flashes in the distance and witness the 1,200-foot-tall WPBN tower collapse on itself. In five seconds the WPNB monitor went black, and ten seconds after that so did the New York feed from the Three Sisters.

• • •

Slightly more than day later, the team of senior DHP investigators probing the abandoned operations center found nothing to indicate the identity of the perpetrators. What the close cadre of veteran German National Socialists did find chilled them to the core. As if bearing silent witness to the detonation of the Allegheny, was a crude drawing of a large hairless head with a long nose and beady eyes that looked as if it were someone peering across the river from behind a covering wall and then the cryptic message: "Kilroy Was Here."

• • •

The Gulfstream II was well past the apex of the hop and descending as the flight crew began to slow the aircraft for its landing sequence. "Pardon me, General Washington," said the attractive Asian flight attendant, "the captain has asked that I advise you we'll be wheels down at Wintergarten in ten minutes. May I take your tray?" He smiled. Her hand had accidentally brushed his thigh as she cleared.

Only a moment later his impatience prompted the general to open his copy of the *Times* yet again. "What a cluster fuck," he said to himself and shook his head in disgust.

SAIGON INVADED, COMMUNISTS CAPTURE EMBASSY

And below the fold, even more strange news:

FREAK EARTHQUAKE TOPPLES PITTSBURGH TOWER; FLAWED DESIGN, JAP STEEL BLAMED

And finally the related insert:

ARCHITECT COMMITS SUICIDE

"The whole thing's gone to hell in a hand basket." He spat his words into the rarified air of the Gulfstream. Looking away from the news and then out across the frozen white wilderness, he checked his Breitling Chrono-Matic, did the math in his head and judged their positon to be somewhere north of the Arctic Circle. Wintergarten; yet another mystery.

He settled back once more to consider his circumstance; treated like a king aboard a showroom-new corporate jet, going god knows where to see god knows who about a significant promotion at the Pentagon. Admittedly, it was the anonymous seven-figure deposit into his numbered account that got his attention, but the mystery of the cryptic invitation and the woman who delivered it was what finally put him on the plane:

General William Washington
Your Progress Has Been Recognized
Please Present Yourself for Initiation
Ascended Master
Your Earliest Convenience
February 1968

16

DECISION THEORY

The precise nature of the realm of eternity is a great and terrible mystery for humans who may only fathom the depth of its reality upon suffering the pain of their own death. Therein lies the deep root of their most primal fear and the wellspring of their most profound curiosity.

The angels of the Lord know that the diaphanous plane, which protects the physical world of time, space, and substance from the divine radiance of Jehovah God, though impassable for mortals, is neither impenetrable nor inflexible. Since the time of Eden, human passions, moving synchronistically in a mirror play with the unseen forces of heaven, have washed over the veil creating a powerful aurora consisting of intense human emotion, which may occasionally penetrate the barrier and travel even unto the Holy of Holies piercing the tender heart of the Merciful Lord.

Fervent prayer from a righteous man may sometimes alter the veil, thickening or thinning, stretching, bending, and occasionally warping, so that it folds in upon itself as if it were a work of ineffable origami. These are the times and places of miracles and, occasionally, transference as the fold may be permanently creased causing a tiny spark of eternity to become embedded forever within the field of time.

The angels understand and are themselves products of the incompatible physics of time and eternity, for this is how they know and are able to serve the Lord. But like the angels, so also are Lucifer, the Prince of the Air, his generals, and his demonic legions, and it is with this knowledge and within this arena that a desperate combat rages for possession and dominion of the immortal soul of all mankind, temporal command of the mirror play, of the veil itself and the penetrating aurora with the power to wound even Almighty God.

• • •

As the cargo bay of the C-130 went weightless, an angel of the Lord appeared before David.

"Fear not," said the messenger, his radiance illuminating the cargo bay so intensely that David could see the top of the jungle canopy as it rapidly passed beneath his boots, beyond the deck plates of the C-130. "I am Gabriel, messenger of the most Holy Lord, sent to bring you a revelation of things that are now and things that are to come."

Overwhelmed, David released his harness, stood upright and then fell on his face before the angel.

"Arise, David," said Gabriel. "And be at peace, for the Lord your God has found favor with you among all men and this day will deliver you and your companions from your enemies and into His service."

As David stood, he saw that the others in the cargo bay were oblivious to the presence of the angel, that the roar of the turbo-props and JATOL rockets had fallen away, and that the silence that pervaded the craft was so complete he could hear the prayers for deliverance that Captain Magazzine and the others were silently offering to the Lord.

Gabriel took David's hand, and they began ascending beyond the aircraft fuselage to a high vantage point so that he might see the last of his Hmong disappearing into their concealed escape tunnel safely beyond the vision of the invading NVA and more remarkably, as it seemed to David, hundreds of lesser angelic beings were encircling their C-130, deflecting incoming small arms fire and providing additional lift to the heavily laden craft as it skimmed the treetops and began its climb out of the valley of death.

"And now the fields of your labor," said Gabriel as they touched lightly on the apex of the Washington Monument. From that vantage, David witnessed disciplined squadrons of angelic warriors and vile, horrific flocks of winged demons engaged in desperate aerial combat above the District of Columbia. The fighting was brutal, hand-to-hand, with cutting and striking weapons of unearthly origin and worse, even to every manner of twisting, biting, kicking, clawing, shrieking, and foul odor that the demonic horde could muster.

"This sacred precinct is not the prize," said Gabriel as David was allowed to see his friend, Al Vazquez, alone in his USDA office with many demons of various sizes, creeping closer and closer. Al looked terrified, pacing the floor in a panic with phone in hand, screaming into the receiver, but it was clear to David that that Al had no knowledge of the disembodied spirits in his office.

"We've got to do something! Gabriel, we've got to save him!" cried David. And then he saw many others and knew that the prize wasn't just Al's immortal soul, but the souls of all the people working in Washington and ultimately, the very soul of America herself.

They rose again into the stratosphere above Washington. David could see the blue black arc of Earth's suborbital horizon, but his attention was focused on a tiny speck of orange just off of the western coast of the last island in the Aleutian Arc.

"See now, David," said the archangel, "the Lord has prepared a place for you and has provided well for your labor."

On their approach David could clearly see that the speck was an active lava flow which had broken through the wall of a concealed tubular cave buried inside the massive granite foundation of a tiny island about two football fields long and one and a half fields wide.

On the island, David could see three soaring granite peaks, as high as skyscrapers, sheltering a small but verdant valley covered in deep green grass surrounding a clear, spring-fed, pool that nurtured dozens of fruit trees of different kinds. There was also such an abundance of fish and game as to make any outdoorsman envious.

Gabriel silently directed David's attention to rich mineral deposits located in the rocks near the valley and to a glittering outcrop

of what appeared to be either quartz or diamonds but more importantly, David saw signs of previous human habitation.

Slightly away from the crystal pool, up the leeside of the largest
mountain peak, were sixteen ancient stone structures of various sizes,
all circular in plan, rough masonry domes which reminded David
of human-sized beehives. But most significant, faintly etched in the
surface of a small standing stone, David saw an ancient Christian crucifix, the sign of Jesus Christ's sacrifice, and knew instantly that this
place was made by believers, and that it would one day be his home.

As he and Gabriel began to rise into the air once more, David
could see hundreds of angelic beings moving large floating sheets of
Arctic Drift ice into the white-orange radiance of the exposed lava
flow, which was also illuminating a lumbering C-130, circling low and
slow over the vast amber sea.

• • •

Rixon came to his senses sprawled on the deck of the C-130 with
Travis licking his face. "Captain, are you hit? Sir, are you with us?"
said Coats loudly over the roar of the turboprops.

Rixon sat up. "Sit rep, El Tee," he said weakly as he pulled himself back to the jump seat and buckled his harness.

"Sir: on course, just out of the valley, five minutes east southeast
of Omega, on course to rendezvous for in-flight refueling at 0945.
Looks like we made it away without serious damage to the aircraft
or any casualties. That is, sir, if you didn't get a hole poked in you
someplace I can't see," said Coats, inspecting his friend and superior
officer for signs of trauma.

Rixon looked aft, past the racks of secured cargo, to see nearly
thirty passengers sitting quietly, some of them sleeping, all of them
shielding themselves against the oppressive drone of the Allison
Turboprops.

"I'm OK, Tom. How about them?" asked Rixon

"Operators 'n' Uniforms are good, they've all seen way more
action than we just came through. The civvies though look pretty

peaked." There was a pause. "David, what the hell happened? One second you were strapped in, eyes closed, deep in prayer, and the next I saw you stand, come to attention for a second and fall to the deck like you were hit; like you were shot dead."

"We'll talk, Tom, but not now, not here," said Rixon. "There are people on the plane I don't know. Have you had a chance to interview them?"

Looking through the passenger manifest, he said, "Says in addition to a few regular people, we have a physicist, geologist, engineer, linguist, botanist, biologist, a poet, a novelist, and their families. These are the sorts of folks Hanoi loves to hate," said Rixon, looking through the list of people on the run from the Communists; thinking he might see a name he'd recognize.

"Tom, this name, Lam Uyen Lu—is this lady on board?" Coats checked his copy of the paperwork. "Affirmative, Captain, her and her little boy, Lam Uyen Chi; looks to be five maybe six years old."

"A Man with Purpose; that's the meaning of the boy's name; Chi," said Rixon scanning the passenger manifest.

"David, you know this woman? Sir, she's a hooch maid from Hue and the boy looks to be, well, sort of like an occupational hazard; US Army issue, if you get my drift."

"I can't really say I know the lady, El Tee, but if she's who I'm thinking of, she sort of saved my life once, so if it's all the same to you, let's make the ride as easy as we can on her and her son. We'll be on the ground in a day or so, and we'll sort everyone out then."

After reviewing the passenger list, David realized that the strangers on board the C-130 were refugees in the truest sense, running for their lives from the Communists. But Rixon also knew from his years of spying on the leadership in Hanoi that the worst was yet to come. The bloodbath everyone feared would be delayed for a year or two until it was logistically and politically possible for their relatively small numbers to effectively murder a million or more south Vietnamese.

Cash poor with their civil infrastructure in shambles and still in debt to the Financial Club of Paris and the secret American and

European banking coalition that had funded their bloody aggression against liberty, the Communists' first priority was to use their war-time allies in Washington and New York to persuade the American Congress to approve US War Reparations to the nascent Democratic Republic of Vietnam; a quid pro quo for normalized international relations and the return of American Prisoners of War, held hostage in flagrant violation of the Peace Accords. And even the hard-core Communists knew that for substantial amounts of American tax dollars to flow into Hanoi's treasury, a tolerant, benevolent image in the global press would be essential. And so the bloodbath would be saved for later in the game.

From his earliest observations of Ho to the secret deliberations of his successors in the Vietnamese Politburo, Rixon had been possessed of a sort of frightful awe at the passionless manner with which life-and-death decisions were made concerning the fate of the human beings under their control. To the Communist mind, Vietnam was simply a three-legged stool; the first leg was reunification with Hanoi as the capital, the second was full-scale Marxist revolution in the South with total wealth and land redistribution, and the third was the mass killing required to remove dissidents from the population for the purpose of creating a pure Communist generation with a single-minded focus on achieving the goals of the state. To delay the inevitable only slightly was simply expeditious; a sort of business decision, absolutely logical from their point of view but then there was also the paradox of immediate payback for the "Lackeys of US Imperialism," those deemed by the politburo to owe a "blood debt" to the people.

It was not publically known but when the American Embassy was captured during the fall of Saigon, the Communists came into possession of the CIA master list of thirty thousand Vietnamese who had worked for the agency on the highly classified counterinsurgency program called Project Phoenix, which had successfully eliminated thousands of Communist infiltrators from the south. In the short period since the fall of Saigon, the Communists had been unrestrained even by their own logic and were rapidly hunting down and murdering the people who were once America's most valuable human assets. Desperate and running for their lives the people on his aircraft were some of those assets. Rixon figured America owed them at least this one last chance and as expatriate representatives of his country, allowing these few to hitch a ride on the last flight out was the least they could do, even if their presence increased the risk for everyone.

Twenty hours into its flight to freedom the C-130 had missed two of its refueling rendezvous and was far off course, flying through a dangerous winter storm and running out of options. It was clear to the command staff that they had been betrayed by people at the agency, fellow Americans, who they believed could be trusted with their lives. The word was passed to the passengers that the flight crew would be forced to ditch the aircraft in the freezing, storm-swept open ocean.

In their final moments David had called together his most trusted companions and Christian friends to pray for their salvation: Tommy Coats and his wife, Wong Ah Kum; Donny and Scotty and their wives Donna and Scarlet. The tiny group of believers huddled close, heads together so that their prayers could be said over the drone of the turboprops and the horror of the turbulent winter storm. David began:

"Most Merciful Lord, Father, we are in mortal fear for our lives tonight and plead with you for our salvation so that we may continue to love one another and be of further service to You in Your world. We have faithfully read Your Eternal Word and know that Your Son, Jesus, rebuked the wind and rain and calmed the sea so that His disciples could continue to live and follow Him. And Lord, You have also told us through Your Prophet Jeremiah that You have a plan for our future, a plan for good and not for evil, a plan to give us a future and a hope. Almighty God it is our fervent prayer that we be allowed to lay claim to these miracles this night; that You will provide the means required to preserve our lives so that we may come into full possession of the future You have planned for all of us. We pray for these miracles urgently Father in the name of Your Son, Jesus Christ, our rock and our salvation. Amen"

Before another prayer could be offered violent atmospheric chop hit the ship in a wave and the powerful turbulence increased so rapidly that it seemed the airframe would be torn to pieces. In the chaos, the flight crew switched the lighting in the cargo bay from white to red and the passengers scrambled to strap themselves into their seats. The aircraft was descending rapidly and then pitched up violently. The cargo bay went dark, terrified screams spurred a panic, and then there was—nothing. Not a sound. Not a bump. The terrifying sense of uncontrolled oscillation and terminal atmospheric force was replaced with a pervading sense of stability and smooth control. There was another scream as the roar of the JATOL engines pierced every unprotected ear and the sense of directed forward motion was restored; they were moving again but this time they were going somewhere. Cheers went up from the civilians in the belief that their pilot had somehow saved them from certain death. And maybe he had.

Rixon and Coats crowded into the close corridor leading to the flight deck and looking past the flight engineer, Stanton Weathersby, witnessed a miraculous sight. Their aircraft was no longer in the storm or even over the ocean, but was being maneuvered by Chuck Magazzine into a large cavernous space. The landing lights were reflecting off what appeared to be a dense nest of very large sparkling rock formations set at crazy odd angles only yards beyond the wingspan of the C-130. There was also a sense of enormous scale, David's sensation was of a gigantic cavern, perhaps the size of the Houston Astrodome, and with a pervading darkness that consumed the brilliant white beams of the powerful quartz landing lights, limiting their useful range.

David and Tommy crouched low and held on as Magazzine found his best spot, brought the ship to a fixed hover, and then sat his baby on the deck and cut the JATOL. He and Commander Steve Barnes then proceeded calmly with their postflight checklist as if they had just landed at Hickam Field and were trying to get to an early dinner at Nick's Fish Market.

"Shock," thought David, "They're the only ones who really how close the shave was. Their training got them through, kept us all alive, and they're still doing their job. They'll process the event later."

"Commander Barnes," said Navigator Kenley Gardner, "sir, we're receiving a distress call on the five hundred kilohertz band; sir, it's OUR distress call and it's repeating." Gardner switched the radio output to the fight deck speakers and heard the Morse code MAYDAY: "-- -. -.- / ... .-. / ... — ... / .- .. -. / .- — . .-. .. -.-. .- / —... —... / ....- ..... .-.- ...-— / -. / .— —... ..... .-.-— — /, Any Ship SOS Southeast Asia Air seventy-seven forty-five point thirty north one seventy-five point zero zero east; Any Ship SOS Southeast Asia Air seventy-seven forty-five point thirty north one seventy-five point zero zero east..."

"Explanation, Ken? Is it something internal? asked Barnes. "You sure we aren't just toggled to the transmission side and monitoring our own outgoing transmission? Or maybe we got some damage?"

The navigator checked and finally powered off the transmitter; the 500 Hz band reception continued; "Any Ship SOS Southeast Asia Air seventy-seven forty-five point thirty north one seventy-five point zero zero east. Any Ship SOS Southeast Asia Air seventy-seven forty-five point thirty north one seventy-five point zero zero east..."

GAK! GAK! GGGGGGUUURRRRRGGGGGLLLLEEEEE! SPLOT! SPLOT! SPLOT! SWRONGEEE! SWRONGEEE!

It seemed the planet itself was dying. The deafening tectonic death rattle, a resonant mountain of extremely low frequency tremors pouring from the igneous rock formations that surrounded them, penetrated first their ship, then their bones and finally their viscera, inflaming the most primitive terror hidden in the center core of every human; the predator was on them! The fear spiked with the vibrations, and then all was quiet once more.

"What the...?" stammered Magazzine. Some of the children in the cargo bay were crying but most everyone else was stone silent.

"Don't know 'bout you but tha' skin just crawled off my back and's headin' for tha hills!" contributed Barnes.

"Any Ship SOS Southeast Asia Air seventy-seven forty-five point thirty north one seventy-five point zero zero east; Any Ship SOS Southeast Asia Air seventy-seven forty-five point thirty north one seventy-five point zero zero east...," cut the external feed, Ken, and switch the panel on, I wanna take a peek at the instruments," said Magazzine. They saw the ship's avionics were inoperable; the compass was spinning uselessly inside the gimbal.

"Sir, I know we're supposed to be radio silent but since we're on the ground now, should I try contacting Archangel? Maybe they could send in the cavalry, maybe get us outta here?" suggested the navigator.

"Hold that, Mr. Gardener," said Rixon. "The last people on earth I want to know about our status right now is Archangel..."

Coats gently cut him off. "And besides, Gardener, didn't anyone ever explain to you that we *are* the cavalry?"

"Captain, I suggest that me 'n' the scouts gear up and take a little stroll around our airplane, see if we still got all our parts 'n' pieces then maybe walk out a bit to place some flares at the perimeter so we can see if anything big 'n' bad's comin' ta get us."

"Lieutenant, this may not be accurate but we're reading an outside air temp of 112 degrees so you should make your trip a quick one; hyperthermia is a real danger in heat like this," said Barnes. Magazzine started wiggling his way of the pilot's seat, cutting Commander Barnes short.

"That sounds like a plan, Coats, and if ya' don't mind, I think I'll tag along. All due respect, but this here's the most advanced piece of aerospace hardware on the planet, and there's no way a grunt's ever gonna know want he's even looking at. If it's all the same to you, I mean, Lieutenant," he said with a smile.

"Captain, no joke, if this reading is accurate, you should keep the trip outside to around ten minutes just to be safe," said Barnes.

"Thanks Sparky, I'll take it under advisement. Coats, let's get a move on. I'm ready to stretch my legs!"

"Don't feel that hot to me," pronounced Lieutenant Coats as he stood at the threshold in the crew entry well sweating profusely. He shined his flashlight out into the darkness and checked his US Army issue chronograph, "It's 0300. Guess all the decent people in town are home tucked in 'n' sawin' logs like we outta be. Otherwise, I'm sure they'd be out here with a marchin' band bringin' us the key the city or some such; welcome wagon would sure be nice for a change," he chattered good-naturedly to ease the tension as he set the alarm for a ten-minute duration, locked the safety on his M16, and charged the chamber. "OK, troopers, let's go see if we can hunt us up a big 'ol cave monster!"

Captain Magazzine followed Coats and the scouts down the stairs, sealed the crew entry hatch, and jacked his headset into the external interphone port. "Stanton, you reading?" he said into the mic as he ran his hand over the aluminum skin and used his rubberized safety light to illuminate the nose wheel well, checking the tires and landing gear.

"Affirmative, Captain; you wanna run through the postflight external, or are you looking for something special?"

"Just the high points, Stan, mainly I wanna see after the JATOL pods and make sure the antenna is intact and operational. Shouldn't take more than a few minutes; I'll stay plugged in. By the way, Steve was right about the heat. Order me a cold Bud from the bar, will ya; we'll be back in a jiff."

Coats led Donny and Scotty out under the port wing past the turboprops to the tip, struck a red emergency flare and dropped it just outside the wingspan noticing the glass-smooth glossy surface. "Watch your footing, stay close, and keep your heads on the swivel, guys. We'll pace out fifty yards and spike another flare. Let's hustle it up. The commander's right about the heat."

With less than half the time expired, the squad climbed a small rise beyond the nose, laid down a flare and stood back to see that the aircraft was sitting in the middle of a natural cavern with at least seventy-five yards of clearance off each wing tip and tail. Forward of the Radome, there seemed to be no physical obstruction to the open ocean and then, off the edge of the cliff and an undetermined distance below, they spied a dark red river of molten rock and were nearly overcome by the tremendous heat and volcanic vapors rising beyond the cliff and flowing toward the ocean edge of the cavern.

"Dang! How in the world did the man get us in here?" wondered Coats aloud.

"Captain, you receiving?" said Coats into his transceiver, 'We've positioned flares fifty yards off the port, starboard, and aft of the aircraft. Sir, the space we're in is very large; our hand lanterns aren't powerful enough to hit the ceiling. Could you have Stan switch on the navigation and landing lights so we can get a better picture of our location?"

"Copy the lights, El Tee," the metallic voice replied. "Better start heading back, Tom. You're coming up on five minutes and Mrs. Coats is holding me at gunpoint; says she wants you back in one piece and I'd rather not disappoint her tonight."

"Affirmative, David, we'll be back in five."

A moment later the external lights of the C-130 came on and were instantly absorbed by the darkness, nothing reflected back off any perceptible surface. "The guys inside ain't gonna believe this. Scotty, pass me that flare gun, will ya?"

Coats inserted a silver 26mm distress load into the barrel, snapped it shut, and discharged it at a slight angle into the space above their aircraft. Coats estimated the red arch shot up six or seven hundred feet into the blackness, deployed its small parachute and was carried brilliantly down and away from the C-130 by air currents outside the flared perimeter. The red glow of the projectile reflected for a moment up and into the facets of the structure far above and then quickly faded to black.

GAK! GAK! SPLOT! SWRONG! SWRONG! AHH! AHH! AHEEEEEECCCCHHHHHEEEEEAARRRGG! GAK!

The massive wave of sound was unmistakable; a multitude of human beings screaming out in terror and pain and then being silenced. "What in God's name is this place?" asked Coats, trembling in fear and bathed in sweat.

"El Tee, head back NOW! THAT'S AN ORDER!" crackled the metallic voice in his hand.

• • •

The flight deck was crowded. Coats and Rixon were huddled with Magazzine, Barnes, Gardener, and Weathersby, sequestered and working on a plan. Wong Ah Kum, the scouts, and their wives and Travis were in the cargo bay working with Loadmaster Wesley Hewitt, doing what could be done for the men, women, and children who had hitched a ride with them out of harm's way.

"As far as I can tell, the ship's in perfect condition except for the paint; the leading edges and the belly are scoured clean down to the aluminum. We could fly it out of here tomorrow if we had the fuel and a runway," said Magazzine, debriefing the command staff.

"They say to save himself a dying man will grasp at straws and I guess that's just about what we were doing on the flight deck when we were sucked in here. I thought we were done for, and then I saw the drift ice. Talk about the right place at the right time! Well, we didn't have enough fuel to go around for a better approach but we were low enough and slow enough that we saw a chance to set down. Everyone was pretty sure it'd be a dead-stick landing but the thought was that since we still had ten percent fuel remaining for the JATOL, we might be able to get enough control to keep us from sliding into the water at the far end. Stan and Steve activated the system and we were just about to touch down when the side of the island blew out and sprayed red hot lava all over the ice and most of our runway was instantly gone.

"All four engines were dead by then and we were on terminal glide when the pressure wave hit us and I reflexively yanked back on the control column exposing the belly of the aircraft to the main force of the blast. That's probably what saved everybody on the flight deck from a windshield blowout.

"Then something even stranger happened," said Magazzine, uncharacteristically emotional, who looked to his flight crew for validation. "You're going to think I'm crazy but as I experienced it, the ship lost all forward momentum and was suspended in the explosive stream of hot volcanic gasses flowing out of a hole in the side of the island; I could actually see inside to what looked to me like the lake of fire it talks about in the Bible. Anyway, the airframe held together somehow and the aerodynamic properties of the ship brought it back to a proper flight attitude, and then something, maybe a vacuum created inside the mountain by the eruption, caused a significant reversal in airflow. The ship was stuck in what seemed like a small jet stream that drew us inside the hollow of the island. We are able to use the JATOL pods to slow our speed and set her down safely. I know none of it makes sense and if anybody's got a straitjacket I'll be happy to slip it on and go along peacefully to the rubber room. The only proof I have of anything is that we're alive and the ship we're sitting in is someplace where it could never be under normal circumstances."

"Affirmative on the engines, Captain, and you're not crazy," said Weathersby, "We lost power, just like you said, got trapped in some sort of volcanic vortex and were lucky that you decided to engage the JATOL when you did, 'cause without that we'd never have made it."

"I don't think you're crazy either, Chuck," said David, looking out at his people in the cargo bay. "In fact, you'll probably think I am after I tell you that there's a place for us here; a place for all of us to live for the long term if necessary; maybe for the rest of our lives if that's what it takes. I know this, Chuck, because I've been here before or at least my consciousness has. It happened in the valley, during the breakout from Omega, when I collapsed in the cargo bay. I saw the drift ice emergency strip, the volcanic eruption, the whole nine yards just like you described it.

"Our safe haven is away from here, out of this cavern, on the lee side of this island in a green valley sheltered by three tall mountain peaks. There are already stone houses there that we can live in and a freshwater stream with fish, and different sorts of fruit trees. There's wild game too but no natural predators; I guess we'll be the first. All we have to do is find our way out of this hole and everyone will be safe."

There was silence on the flight deck as the men considered the things that their leaders had revealed about their journey and destination, and then the cargo bay door opened; it was a very concerned Wong Ah Kum, "We need to get these people out; they've been inside the airplane for over thirty-six hours, and we're out of everything to eat and drink. Pretty soon we'll even be out of decent places to go to the bathroom!"

"Good Lord, would you look at that!" exclaimed Commander Barnes as a rainbow beam of refracted light pierced the forward windshield and illuminated the flight deck.

The sun had risen outside the cavern and its early morning rays had been captured by millions of crystal shards on the exterior surfaces of the phenomenal geological specimen that the squadron would later refer to as the Crystal Mountain. Scientists would one day ascribe the foreboding nighttime darkness and delightful daytime glow of the cavern to the heretofore undiscovered transducing capacity of the crystal armature in the mountain and its hypersensitivity to the full range of the known electromagnetic spectrum. Those charged with examining the phenomena would attribute it to the microscopic purity of the crystalline structure and extraordinary scale of its primary members, some of them as much as sixty meters in diameter and over one thousand meters in length. The potential for applications in science and commerce of just one of the larger members was unimaginable; the result of applying the entire mountain to a specific purpose was beyond mortal speculation.

Acting on Wong Ah Kum's urgent request, four two-man search teams were dispersed into the rainbow glow of the crystal cavern to find a suitable bivouac for their group outside the aircraft. Later that same day, Donny, Scotty, and Travis, true to their franchise, found a way to the surface and led everyone to the grassy slope and down to the stream and the cluster of small stone cottages.

They arrived in the late afternoon to find a welcoming campfire of dried peat moss bricks warming a stone crock filled with vegetable stew and thin leaves of flatbread crisping on the hot stones. The adults discovered that each stone house had its own small kitchen stocked with freshly harvested vegetables and fruits, crockery, and wooden utensils and a stone vase filled with beautiful freshly cut flowers. After their evening meal the children began to play "chase" with each other and Travis the war dog playfully ran after them through the cluster of small masonry dwellings. There were seven little ones in all, ranging in age from four to eleven, and their laughter and squeals of delight warmed and comforted the camp more than either the fire or the food.

Coats and Rixon were sitting apart from the group, enjoying their meal and watching the children play. "Did Donny and Scotty finally admit to making dinner for us?" asked Rixon.

"Nope never did. They claim it must have been a trickster local, someone watching us from the rocks, or an angel. They haven't made up their minds yet." He took another bite of the savory thick stew. "Whoever it was really laid out the welcome wagon for us. Funny. I sort of asked for that when we were hunting the cave monster last night. Anyway, the houses are all stocked with everything we'll need for a nice long vacation. We'll be fine 'till we find a way to get ourselves back to civilization." He took a deep drink of cool clear water and then another gigantic bite.

"How far along is she, Tom?" said David, noting Wong Ah Kum's advanced pregnancy. "She looks wonderful." She had Travis on her back playfully scratching her tummy when both men noticed the slight bulge in the animal's abdomen. "Travis is gonna be a mama too?" They both smiled at the thought of a litter of pups running around the camp with the children.

"We believe Ah Kum's in her sixth month, and thanks for asking, David," replied Coats. "You know after we lost our first, it hurt so bad that neither of us thought we'd ever be able to try again, but the Lord has a way of healing even those deep wounds and here we are," he said, smiling at his friend. "How about you and Karen? You gonna try to make it three when you get back?"

"We've been talking about it, Tom, but Karen hasn't made a decision yet. We appreciate having her parents with us permanently now but even with Grandma and Grandpa close, a nine-year-old and a seven-year-old will just wear you out," said Rixon, smiling to himself and thinking of home.

"Say, David, I know this is usually something you do and I don't want to try and take your place or nothin' but if you don't mind, I feel a tug in my heart to lead us all in prayer tonight," said Tom.

David smiled at his brother in Christ. "Pastor Tom, I believe it would be highly appropriate for you to lead us, especially tonight of all nights." David watched as Tommy gathered the group around the fire and then felt the need to slip away as they joined hands to give thanks to the Lord for their deliverance.

He ambled along the path back to the cavern and found his way back to the aircraft where he observed a band of luminous technicians working on different areas of the C-130. The crew chief greeted him at the entrance hatch. "Captain, we'll have your call ready in just a moment. The only difficulty we had was fabricating a DTMF tone generator to access the Bell System. After that it was a piece of cake," said the technician, beaming. "I hope you don't mind, but we've recalibrated your Zero Point Generator so we could use it to energize the crystal matrix of the mountain. The UHF transmitter in your aircraft worked beautifully to tune the frequency, which then connected easily to the geosynchronous Westar 1 communications satellite in orbit right above our position. We've even obtained the phone number for you from a nice lady at AT&T Directory Assistance. All you have to do now is dial," he said, holding out the headset and pointing to the jerry-rigged tone generator at the navigator's duty station.

Someone, clearly groggy, answered, "Hello," there was static and then silence. "Listen, you son of a bitch! You've been calling and hanging up all night, and I'm sick of it. Tell me who this is, or I'm hanging up and pulling the goddamned cord out of the wall!"

There was another pause and then through the static,"Qué pasa en Al?"

"Is this some kind of sick joke? WHO IS THIS?"

"Al, it's me, David," there was a long silence and then, "DDDDavid. Is this really you? Yyyyyou're OK?"

"Al, please listen, there isn't much time. You and your family are in danger. There are forces planning to kill you, Belinda, and Maria. Call my sister, Isabel, in Odessa. You have the number. She and her husband, Rod Peterson, will take you in at Pleasant Farms and they'll hide you until you decide what to do."

"David, where are you? How did you know we're in trouble?"

"Al, we survived the crash and are all safe someplace where no one will ever find us. We forgive you for your part in the plot but, Al, you've got to understand that there are dark spiritual forces after you as well. They want your soul, Al, and you must come to your senses and accept Christ or its all for nothing. In the end, they'll have you for all eternity and none of the money or houses or cars will matter. Please, Al. Promise me you'll do this tonight!"

"David, what do I do?"

"Get on your knees right now. Are you with me, Al? OK the scriptural basis for the prayer is second Corinthians six two: 'For God says, At just the right time, I heard you. On the day of salvation, I helped you. Indeed, the right time is now. Today is the day of salvation.' So Al, just like the scripture says, this is your time, please repeat after me: Dear God in heaven, I come to you in the name of Jesus. I acknowledge that I'm a sinner, and I'm sorry for my sins and the life that I've lived. I need your forgiveness. I believe that your only begotten, Son Jesus Christ, shed His precious blood on the cross at Cavalry and died for my sins, and I'm now willing to turn from my sin. You said in Your Holy Word that if we confess to the Lord our God and believe in our hearts that God raised Jesus from the dead, we shall be saved. Right now I confess Jesus as the Lord of my soul. In my heart, I believe that God raised Jesus from the dead and this very moment I accept

Jesus Christ as my own personal Savior and according to His Word, right now I am saved. Amen.

"Hold this prayer in your heart forever, Al, and get to Pleasant Farms. Isabel and Rod will help establish you and Belinda in the faith and hide you from your enemies. Do this for yourself, Al, do it for your family, and do it for me. Good-bye, old friend. I've always loved you like a brother and still do. Good-bye."

• • •

David spent the remaining hours of the dark night in the company of the crew chief, who revealed the divine wisdom regarding the physics of the Crystal Mountain. In the moments before dawn he emerged again from the cave to see the red-orange-purple glow of the approaching sun on the distant horizon, only just beginning to paint the tops of the triple crystal peaks that marked the limits of their safe haven. He had begun to retrace his steps to the stone village when he noticed that the slopes of the meadow from halfway up the peaks down to the shore were covered with brilliant yellow blossoms that began to glow in the early morning sun.

"Did everyone enjoy their supper?" said the friend who was closer than a brother. "It's one of my favorites. The herbs and vegetables grow only on the south face of the third mountain."

"So it was you?" said David smiling. "The scouts believed the stew and bread were left for us by a trickster who lives the rocks above, or maybe by an angel.

"Correct on both counts," he said with a laugh. "Those two are so special, alert to everything, and rock-solid faithful. Don't you agree?"

"Donny and Scotty have been with me since Rana Dat, so that's nearly ten years. I've lost track of the number of times they've save my life, even saved me from myself. Faithful doesn't begin to describe the core nature of these men," replied David.

"Tommy and Wong Ah Kum; what a fantastic couple they are! And what extraordinary parents they'll make." Both men smiled and they continued to lovingly discuss the members of the squad as they walked down the sleepy hillside, watching the sun rise farther into the eastern sky and then, the meadow woke up.

The heavy fragrance of the field of golden blossoms lured the bees to collect their nectar and spread their pollen; then the small rodents and creeping things became active and began to cross their path. They walked into a covey of quail looking for breakfast and were startled when it suddenly took wing.

Jays, magpies, robins, cardinals, and starlings were feeding in the fruit-laden bushes and trees. The urgency of their breakfast flights animated the morning sky but they made way for the red tail hawks that elegantly rode the high thermals around the Crystal Mountain, circled the three peaks, and then dove rapidly swooping to within feet of the men demonstrating their aerial skill and daring.

"Shush!" said David's friend as he pointed out a fawn and its mother sill coiled together in a deep slumber after spending the night under cover of the high grass. The two continued their walk stepping around an opossum carrying her babies home after a night of foraging when a small bluebird landed on David's shoulder, nuzzled his cheek, and began her morning song.

"Are we in heaven," asked David with a broad grin.

"Not even close," said his friend with a smile, gently brushing the little one away and stepping around a chattering ground squirrel while they moved on.

"I was wondering when you thought we should tell the others about the new mission. Being posted Sentry to the Gates of Hell sounds terribly frightening at first but after the chief explained the math behind the mountain and the phenomena of Zero Point Resonance. The specifics of the duty and the importance of our physical presence became clear. I'm honored and very excited to be part of it," said David, eager to know more.

The sweet air of the island and the swarm of industrious bees filled David's head with memories of the white hives at Pleasant Farms and his work in the garden with Papa Joe that hot summer before he began two-a-day workouts with the Panthers. They watched curiously as a strange red bird approached, languorously flapping and riding the gentle sea breeze up the hill toward them. When it came close, David saw that instead of a bird it was really a million tiny red and black butterflies flying in formation. As they watched, individuals began leaving the flock to join the bees in competition for the golden nectar.

BARK! BARK!

Travis had spotted David and made a path through the blossoms, bees, butterflies, critters, and even startled the deer as she ran toward her master.

David and his friend were both smiling as they knelt to hug Travis when she bounded into their arms. After a moment of play, Travis calmed and took her place at David's side, placing her wet nose and warm muzzle into the cup of his hand. The men walked on to the shore.

"I've spoken to Father about the mission, and He is very pleased with the squad," said the friend. Then, after a long moment, he asked, "David, do you love me?"

"I'm surprised you'd ask," said David more seriously. "Ever since I first called on you that Christmas Eve in the emergency room you've been with me every step of the way; you've been my deep well of strength, my cheerleader, my inspiration, my refuge, my most trusted adviser; through all of it, you've been my true companion. Of course I love you! How could I not?" David said, smiling through his tears, and the men hugged and wept together.

BARK! BARK! BARK!

Travis had run ahead to the beach and was barking at a small white boat being nudged to shore by a school of chattering, whistling bottlenose dolphins. David's friend waded out into the warm, clear aqua-blue water, frightening away a pair of curious sea otters and scattering a school of parrot fish. He took hold of the craft and pulled it to the beach.

Nearly blinded by the early morning sun glinting off the calm sea, David could see the oars and a day pack stored inside the craft. "There's a coral reef due east of here, just beyond the horizon. The temperature differential and crosscurrents cause some pretty treacherous surf where they collide with the reef. I want you to row east, right into the sunrise, and when you hit rough water just remember, hold true to course and you'll be fine."

"The squad will miss you, David, there's no denying that. You've been like their father all this time, and it'll be hard for them at first, but they're ready to stand on their own now. Don't worry. I'll explain everything to them over breakfast later this morning," he said with a reassuring smile and gentle touch on David's shoulder.

"I discussed this at length with Father. We considered other candidates, we weighed the options, and we're settled that the mission we're sending you on now is so very important to the future and so unique that only you can accomplish it."

BARK! BARK!

Travis had jumped inside the boat, took a position in the bow, and was beckoning her master. David climbed in, placed the oars in the gunwales, and checked the day pack to find a bottle of water, some fruit, cheese, and a round of flat bread. He stood in the stern of the little craft and accepted the warm respectful hand of his friend.

Working together they launched the boat away from the white sandy beach. "Good-bye David," said his friend. "I'll see you again soon and remember to always hold true to course!" He was smiling broadly, waving farewell from the waist-deep water.

David pulled vigorously on the oars and began to sweat as he used his back and legs to race the chattering, leaping dolphins far into the glass-smooth waters of the clear aqua bay. He was soon far enough away from the Island of the Crystal Mountain to see the iridescent Aurora of Tears; luminous sheets of florescent green, dancing dark blues, fast flowing rivers of purple, yellow, and red shimmering and swirling around the triple peaks and then rushing up to heaven.

Using his shadow to orient to the sunrise, he rowed farther out and over the blue water trough that separated the island's protected bay from the frigid blue violence of the Bering Sea. Ahead he heard the roar of the dangerous surf, and Travis urged him on as he pulled against the gunwales with all his might, cutting through the wall of water that threatened to swamp their boat and drown them both. Then, all at once, his tiny vessel was free, and he slipped quietly into a peaceful Pacific blue cove.

David turned to orient himself and looking past Travis to the far shore saw a beautiful woman with flaming red hair. She was sitting quietly on the beach watching two children at play, a boy and a girl, who were examining the small sea creatures hiding in the shallow tidal pools. David rowed on quietly and when he was close to shore Travis gave a BARK! of recognition and leapt from the boat into the water.

"DAVID!" called the redhead from the beach; on her feet in an instant, she was running to the water. With all his might he leapt over the freeboard and ran splashing through low tide to joyfully and tearfully embrace Karen, Randy, Marion, and Travis on the glistening white sand of Keyhole Cove.

Well done good and faithful servant. David Rixon was home.

BIBLIOGRAPHY

Alford, M. (2012). *Once Upon a Secret, My Affair with President John F. Kennedy and its Aftermath,* Random House, Inc., New York, NY 10019

Allen, G. (1976). *Non Dare Call It Conspiracy,* Buccaneer Books, Inc., P.O. Box 168, Cutchogue, New York 11935

Ayres, B. (2001). *Fugitive Days: A Memoir,* Beacon Press, 24 Farnsworth Street, Boston, MA 02210

Bain, S.K., (2012). *The Most Dangerous Book In The World – 9/11 As Mass Ritual,* Trine Day, LLC, PO Box 577, Walterville, OR 97489

Baldwin, C. and Baldwin, T., (2011). *Romans 13: The True Meaning of Submission,* Liberty Defense League, PO Box 1520, Kalispell, MT 59903

Bamford, J. (2001). *Body of Secrets: Anatomy of the Ultra-Secret National Security Agency,* Doubelday, 1745 Broadway, New York, NY 10019

Bernays, E. (1926). *Propaganda,* Ig Publishing, 392 Clinton Avenue, Brooklyn, NY 11238

Bloom, A. (1987). *The Closing of the American Mind, How Higher Education Has Failed Democracy and Impoverished The Souls of Today's Students,* Simon & Schuster, Inc. , 1230 Avenue of the Americas, New York, NY 10020

Boesak, A. and DeYoung, C. (2012), *Radical Reconciliation, Beyond Political Pietism and Christian Quietism,* Orbis Books, Box 302, Maryknoll, NY 10545

Bonneville, N. translated by di Luchetti, M. 1792. *Illuminati Manifesto of World Revolution,* BookSurge Publishing, www.amazon.com

Brezenski, Z. (1982). *Between Two Ages: America's Role in the Technetronic Era,* Praeger Publishers, Westport, CT 06881

Brezenski, Z. (1997). *The Grand Chessboard: American Primacy and its Geostrategic Imperatives,* Basic Books, 10 East 53 Street, New York, NY 10022

Butler, S. (1935). *War is a Racket,* Feral House, P.O. Box 39910, Los Angeles, CA 90039

Campbell, J. (1982). *Grammatical Man, Information, Language, and Life,* Simon & Schuster, Inc.,1230 Avenue of the Americas, New York, N.Y. 10020

Conboy, K. (1995). *Shadow War: The CIA's Secret War in Laos,* Paladin Press, Inc., 7077 Winchester Circle, Boulder, Colorado 80301

Coogan, P. (2012). *The Famine Plot: England's Role in Ireland's Greatest Tragedy,* Palgrave Macmillan, Dublin, Ireland, New York, NY

Crilly, T. (2007). *50 Mathematical Ideas You Really Need to Know,* Quercus Publiching Plc. 21 Bloomsbury Square, London WC1A 2NS

Crowley, A. (2007). *Gems From The Equinox, Instructions by Aleister Crowley for His Own Magical Order,* Collected Work published by Red Wheel/Weiser, LLC, 500 Third Street, San Francisco, California 94117

Crowley, A. (1926). *The Book of the Law, Liber Al Vel Legis,* Centennial Edition Published by Red Wheel/Weiser, LLC, 500 Third Street, San Francisco, California 94117

Dengler, D. (1979). *Escape from Laos,* Kensington Publishing Corp., 475 Park Avenue South, New York, NY 10016

Dohrn, B., Ayres, B., Jones, J., Sojourn, C. (1974), *Prairie Fire; The Politics of Revolutionary Anti-Imperialism, Political Statement of the Weather Underground,* Communications Co., PO Box 10614, Station C, San Francisco, CA 94110

Downs, F. (1978). *The Killing Zone, My Life in the Vietnam War,* W.W. Norton Company, New York, NY

Duncan, R. (2010). *Project: Soul Catcher,* Higher Order Thinkers, Boise Idaho

Ellsberg, D. (2003). *Secrets: A Memoir of Vietnam and the Pentagon Papers,* Penguin Group (USA), Inc., New York, NY 10014

Englehardt, T. (2014). *Shadow Government, Surveillance, Secret Wars, and a Global Security State in a Single Super Power World,* Haymarket Books, Chicago, Ill.

Gonzalez, S. (2010). *Psychological Warfare and the New World Order, The Secret War Against the American People*, Spookz Books, Oakland, CA

Greene, G. (1955). *The Quiet American*, Random House, Inc. New York, 1992; First Published, William Heinemann, LTD., London, 1955

Griffin, E.G. (1994). *The Creature form Jekyll Island, A Second Look at the Federal Reserve*, American Media, P.O. Box 4646. Westlake Village, California 91359

Grossman, D, (2009), *On Killing, The Psychological Cost of Learning to Kill in War and Society*, Back Bay Books/Little, Brown and Company, Hackett Book Group, 237 Park Avenue, New York, NY 10017

Grossman, D. (2012). *On Combat, The Psychology and Physiology of Deadly Conflict in War and in Peace*, Human Factor Research Group, Inc. Publications

Gunston, B. (1982). *Encyclopedia of World Air Power*, Aerospace Publishing, Ltd., 10 Barley Mow Passage, London W4, England

Harris, S. (2005). *The End of Faith: Religion, Terror and the Future of Reason*, W.W. Norton & Company, Inc., 500 Fifth Avenue, New York, NY 10110

Hall, J. (2009). *A New Breed: Satellite Terrorism in America*, Strategic Book Publisher, 845 Third Avenue, Suite 6016, New York, NY 10022

Harding, S. (2013). *The Last Battle; When US and German Soldiers Joined Forces in the Waning Hours of World War II in Europe*, Da Caop Press, 2300 Chestnut Street, Suite 200, Philadelphia, PA 19103

Hamilton-Merritt, J. (1993) *Tragic Mountains: the Hmong, the Americans, and the Secret Wars for Laos, 1942-1993*, Indiana University Press, 601 North Morton Street, Bloomington, IN 47404-3797

Henderson, B. (2010). *Hero Found: The Greatest POW Escape of the Vietnam War*, Harper Collins Publishers, 10 East 53rd Street, New York, N.Y. 10022

Hitchens, C. (2009). *God is Not Great: How Religion Poisons Everything*, 12 Books Publishing, 1290 Avenue of the Americas, New York, NY

Hoffman, M. (1989). *Secret Societies and Psychological Warfare*, Independent History and Research, Box 849, Coeur d'Alene, Idaho 83816

Hoffman, M. (1993). *They Were White and They Were Slaves: The Untold Story of the Enslavement of Whites in Early America*, Independent History and Research, Box 849, Coeur d'Alene, Idaho 83816

Holl, S. (2000), *Parallax*, Princeton Architectural Press, 37 East 7th Street, New York, N.Y. 10003

Hunter, J. (1991). *Culture Wars: The Struggle to Control the Family, Art, Education, Law and Politics in America*, Basic Books, Perseus Book Group, 250 west 57th Street, Suite 1500, New York, N.Y. 10107

Jacobs, J. (1992). *Systems of Survival, A Dialogue on the Moral Foundations of Commerce and Politics*, Random House, New York, N.Y.

Jaynes, J. (1976). *The Origins of Consciousness in the Breakdown of the Bicameral Mind*, Houghton Mifflin Company, 215 Park Avenue South, New York, N.Y. 10003

Jeremiah, D. (2006). *Angels; Who They Are and How They Help, What the Bible Reveals*, Multnomah Books, 12256 Oracle Blvd., Suite 200, Colorado Springs, CO 80921

Keith, J. (2003). *Mass Control: Engineering Human Consciousness*, Adventures Unlimited Press, One Adventure Place, Box 74, Kempton, IL 60946

Lewis, C.S. (1942). *The Screwtape Letters*, Harper Collins Publishers, 10 East53rd Street, New York, NY 10022

Lewis, C.S. (1947). *Miracles, A Preliminary Study*, Harper Collins Publishers, 10 East53rd Street, New York, NY 10022

Lewis, C.S. (1956). *Till We Have Faces, A Myth Retold*, Harcourt, Inc., 6277 Sea Harbor Drive, Orlando, Florida, 32887-6777

Liddick, D. (2004). *The Global Underworld: Transnational Crime and the United States (International and Comparative Criminology)*, Praeger Publishers, 88 Post Road West, Westport CT 06881

Loftus, J. (2010). *America's Nazi Secret*, TrineDay LLC, Walterville, OR 97489

Lombardi, N. (2013). *The Plain of Jars; A Novel*, Round Fire Books; John Hunt Publishing, LTD., Laurel House, Station Approach, Alresford, Hants, SO 24 9JH, UK

Lumpkin, J. (2011). *The Books of Enoch, The Angels, The Watchers and The Nephilim*, Fifth Estate Publishers, PO Box 116, Blountsville, AL

Manning, P. (1981). *Martin Bormann: Nazi in Exile*, Barricade Books/ Lyle Stewart Inc., New York, NY 10001

Marrs, J. (1989). *Crossfire, The Plot That Killed Kennedy*, Carroll & Gaff Publishers, Inc. 260 Fifth Avenue, New York, NY 10001

Marrs, J. (2008). *The Rise of the Fourth Reich, The Secret Societies That Threaten To Take Over America*, William Morrow, an imprint of HarperCollins Publishers, 10 East 53rd Street, New York, NY 10022

Marrs, J. (2013). *Our Occulted History, Do The Global Elite Conceal Ancient Aliens?*, William Morrow, an imprint of HarperCollins Publishers, 10 East 53rd Street, New York, NY 10022

Menninger, B. (1992). *Mortal Error: The Shot That Killed JFK*, St. Martin's Press, 175 Fifth Avenue, New York, NY 10010

McCoy, A. (2003). *The Politics of Heroin: CIA Complicity in the Global Drug Trade*, Harper Collins Publishers, Inc., 110 E. 53rd Street, New York, NY 10022

Melton, K. and Wallace, R. (2009). *The Official CIA Manual of Trickery and Deception*, HarperCollins Publishers, 195 Broadway, New York, NY 10007

Monteith, S. (2000). *Brotherhood of Darkness*, Hearthstone Publishing, Oklahoma City, OK 73101

Phillips, R. (2010), *Everyone's Guide to Demons and Spiritual Warfare*, Charisma House Book Group, 600 Rinehart Road, Lake Mary, Florida 32746

Quayle, S. (2011). *Angel Wars, Past, Present and Future*, End Time Thunder Publishers, 315 Edelweiss Dr., Bozeman, MT 50718

Quayle, S. (2014). *Xenogenesis; Changing Men into Monsters*, End Time Thunder Publishers, 315 Edelweiss Dr., Bozeman, MT 50718

Quigley, C. (1966). *Tragedy and Hope, A History of the World in Our Time*, The MacMillan Company, New York, NY

Rand, A. (1970). *The New Left: The Anti-Industrial Revolution*, The New American Library, Inc., 1301 Avenue of the Americas, New York, N.Y. 10019

Richards, L. (1998). *Every Good and Evil Angel in the Bible*, Thomas Nelson, Inc. Nashville, TN

Ronnau, C., (2006). *Blood Trails, The Combat Diary of a Foot Solder in Vietnam*, Ballantine Books, New York, NY

Rottman, G., (2007). *Mobile Strike Forces in Vietnam 1966-1970*, Osprey Publishing. Ltd., PB Box 140 Wellingborough, Northants, NNB 2FA UK

Rudd, M., (2010). *Underground: My Life with SDS and the Weathermen*, William Morrow Paperbacks, New York, NY

Scott, D., (2010). *American War Machine: Deep Politics, the CIA Global Drug Connection and the Road to Afghanistan*, Rowman & Littlefield Publishers, New York, Toronto, Plymouth, UK.

Skousen, W. Cleon (1981). *The 5000 Year Leap, The 28 Great Ideas That Changed The World*, National Center for Constitutional Studies, 3777 West Juniper Road, Malta, ID 83342

Steinman, R. (2009). *The Solders' Story, Vietnam In Their Own Words*, Fall River Press, An Imprint of Sterling Publishing, 387 Park Avenue South, New York, NY 10016

Taylor, D. (2005). *In Search of Sacred Places, Looking for Wisdom on Celtic Holy Islands*, Bog Walk Press, 1605 Lake Johanna Blvd., Saint Paul MN, 55112

Uki, G. (2003). *The Real Odessa: How Peron Brought the Nazi War Criminals to Argentina*, Granta UK.

USDOD (2011). *The Pentagon Papers: The Defense Departments Secret History of the Vietnam War*, Red and Black Publishers, Amazon Digital Services, Inc.

Valentine, D. (1990). *The Phoenix Program, America's Use of Terror in Vietnam*, William Morrow and Company, 10 East 53rd Street, New York, NY 10022

Webb, J. (1978). *Fields of Fire*, Bantam Books, New York, NY

Webb, J. (2004). *Born Fighting, How the Scots-Irish Shaped America*, Broadway Books, a division of Random House, New York, NY

West, D. (2013). *American Betrayal; The Secret Assault on Our Nations Character*, St. Martin's Press, New York, NY

Wiese, B. (2006). *23 Minutes in Hell*, Charisma House, 600 Rinehart Road, Lake Mary, FL 32746

Wiesel, E. (1958). *Night,* Hill and Wang, A Division of Farr, Straus and Giroux, 19 Union Square West, New York, NY, 10003

Wilson, S. et al (1995) *A Pictorial History of the 36th Division,* The 36th Division Association, Austin TX

Wolf, G. (2003). *Intruding Upon The Timeless, Meditations on Art, Faith, and Mystery,* Square Halo Books, P.O. Box 18954, Baltimore, MD 21206

Wolf, T. (1981). *From Bauhaus to Our House,* McGraw-Hill, New York, N.Y.

INTERNET SEARCHES BY SUBJECT

Black Swan Theory	https://en.wikipedia.org/wiki/Black_swan_theory
Boeing B-52D Stratoforterss	https://en.wikipedia.org/wiki/B-52_Stratofortress
Bormann, Martin	https://en.wikipedia.org/wiki/Martin_Bormann
Breitwinner Cave	http://www.cavelore.com/buchnerreport.htm
Bretton Woods System	http://en.wikipedia.org/wiki/Bretton_Woods_system
Central Intelligence Agency (CIA)	https://en.wikipedia.org/wiki/ Central_Intelligence_Agency
CIA Drug Running	http://www.ciadrugs.com/; http://www.huffingtonpost.com/2011/12/30/ron-paul-conspiracy-theory-cia-drug-traffickers_n_1176103.html
Club, Paris	https://en.wikipedia.org/wiki/Paris_Club
Combat Refusal	http://libcom.org/history/vietnam-collapse-armed-forces
Cochnchina	https://en.wikipedia.org/wiki/Cochinchina
Crystal Cave	http://en.wikipedia.org/wiki/Cave_of_the_Crystals
Dien Bien Phu, Battle of	https://en.wikipedia.org/wiki/Battle_of_Dien_Bien_Phu
Drift Ice	http://nsidc.org/cryosphere/seaice/processes/circulation.html
Drift Station	https://en.wikipedia.org/wiki/Drift_station
Egyptomania, Victorian	http://www.victorianweb.org/authors/wilde/hawes2.html http://en.wikipedia.org/wiki/Egyptomania
Ellsberg Paradox	https://en.wikipedia.org/wiki/Ellsberg_paradox

Enabling Act of 1933	https://en.wikipedia.org/wiki/Enabling_Act_of_1933
Federal Reserve System	https://en.wikipedia.org/wiki/Federal_Reserve_System
Fog of War	http://en.wikipedia.org/wiki/Fog_of_war
Fractional Reserve Fractional_Banking	https://en.wikipedia.org/wiki/reserve_banking
Gates of Hell	http://en.wikipedia.org/wiki/Gates_of_hell
Geothermal Energy	http://en.wikipedia.org/wiki/Geothermal_energy
Geothermal Gradient	https://en.wikipedia.org/wiki/Geothermal_gradient
Golden Dawn, Order	http://www.golden-dawn.com/eu/index.aspx http://en.wikipedia.org/wiki/Hermetic_Order_of_the_Golden_Dawn
Gold Smuggling, Macau	http://www.atimes.com/atimes/China_Business/JJ02Cb03.html
Guano Islands Act, 1856	http://en.wikipedia.org/wiki/Guano_Islands_Act
Gulf of Tonkin Incident	https://en.wikipedia.org/wiki/Gulf_of_Tonkin_incident
Gulfstream II	https://en.wikipedia.org/wiki/Grumman_Gulfstream_II
Hegelian Dialectic	https://en.wikipedia.org/wiki/Dialectic
Heidegger, Martin	https://en.wikipedia.org/wiki/Martin_Heidegger
Hitler, Thule Society	http://www.threeworldwars.com/world-war-2/adolf-hitler.htm
Hmong	http://en.wikipedia.org/wiki/Hmong_people http://www.hmongstudiesjournal.org/ http://www.wausauhmong.org/wahma_v1/index.php?q=content/hmong-history-life-laos

HMX Explosive	http://en.wikipedia.org/wiki/HMX
Ho's Stilt House	http://goseasia.about.com/od/hanoi/a/Ho-Chi-Minh-Stilt-House-Hanoi.htm
Holding Company	http://beginnersinvest.about.com/od/beginnerscorner/a/understanding-a-holding-company.htm
Hollow Earth	http://en.wikipedia.org/wiki/Hollow_Earth
	http://www.dailymail.co.uk/sciencetech/article-2441450/Er-Wang-Dong-cave-China-huge-weather-system.html
Holocaust, Mentality	http://www.spiegel.de/international/world/holocaust-as-career-the-khmer-rouge-the-nazis-and-the-banality-of-evil-a-667263.html
Holocaust, Rationale	http://watch.pair.com/asa2.html
Holocaust, Scale	http://www.dailymail.co.uk/news/article-2287071/Full-shocking-scale-Holocaust-revealed-researchers-Nazis-created-42-500-camps-ghettos-persecute-Jews-Europe.html
Hong Kong, History	https://en.wikipedia.org/wiki/History_of_Hong_Kong
Hotel Continental	http://travel.cnn.com/explorations/escape/heels-graham-greene-continental-saigon-726495
	http://www.nytimes.com/1988/01/30/world/ho-chi-minh-city-journal-a-haunt-of-old-saigon-gets-new-life.html
Human Testing	http://www.cnn.com/2012/03/01/health/human-test-subjects
IBM System/360	https://en.wikipedia.org/wiki/IBM_System/360
Imperial Bank of China	https://en.wikipedia.org/wiki/Imperial_Bank_of_China

JAG	http://en.wikipedia.org/wiki/Judge_Advocate_General's_Corps
Korean War	https://en.wikipedia.org/wiki/Korean_War
Lamb, Samuel	http://www.christianpost.com/news/death-of-pastor-samuel-lamb-leaves-hole-in-the-chinese-church-says-open-doors-usa-101621/
Lava Tube Cave	http://en.wikipedia.org/wiki/Lava_tube
Lockheed C-130 Talon	https://en.wikipedia.org/wiki/Lockheed_C-130_Hercules
AC-130 Specter	https://en.wikipedia.org/wiki/Lockheed_AC-130
Low Altitude Parachute Extraction System	http://en.wikipedia.org/wiki/Low_Altitude_Parachute_Extraction_System
Macau	http://en.wikipedia.org/wiki/Macau
MACV	https://en.wikipedia.org/wiki/Military_Assistance_Command,_Vietnam
Magic (cryptography)	http://en.wikipedia.org/wiki/Magic_(cryptography)
Martin M-130	http://en.wikipedia.org/wiki/Martin_M-130
Midway Atoll	http://en.wikipedia.org/wiki/Midway_Atoll
Midway, Battle of	http://www.pacificwar.org.au/Midway/MidwayIndex.html
	http://combinedfleet.com/battles/Battle_of_Midway
MIKE Force	http://en.wikipedia.org/wiki/MIKE_Force
MIKE Force History	http://www.mikeforcehistory.org/
Misdemeanor Murder	http://en.wikipedia.org/wiki/Misdemeanor_murder
MKUltra	http://en.wikipedia.org/wiki/Project_MKUltra

Montagnard People	http://en.wikipedia.org/wiki/Degar
Mound Builders	https://en.wikipedia.org/wiki/Mound_builder_(people)
Muller, Heinrich	https://en.wikipedia.org/wiki/Heinrich_M%C3%BCller_(Gestapo)
National Security Act of 1947	https://en.wikipedia.org/wiki/National_Security_Act_of_1947
National Security Action Memorandum	www.lbjlib.utexas.edu/johnson/archives.hom/NSAMs/nsamhom.asp
Nazi Flight Capital	http://archive.org/details/For_The_Record_305_The Bormann_Organization
Nazi Gold Deposits	http://www.german-way.com/gerpast.html
Nazi Occultism	https://en.wikipedia.org/wiki/Nazism_and_occultism
Nazi Party	https://en.wikipedia.org/wiki/Nazi_Party
Nazi Weltanschauung	http://www.theneworder.org/national-socialism/idea-movement/weltanschauung/
Nephilim	http://nephilimchronicles.wordpress.com/
	https://www.youtube.com/watch?v=1zz8_MxcnzY
	http://www.godinanutshell.com/
Normalcy Bias	https://en.wikipedia.org/wiki/Normalcy_bias
NSA, National Security Agency	http://www2.gwu.edu/~nsarchiv/NSAEBB/NSAEBB23/
Office of Policy Coordination	http://en.wikipedia.org/wiki/Office_of_Policy_Coordination
Office of Strategic Services (OSS)	https://en.wikipedia.org/wiki/Office_of_Strategic_Services
Operation Eagle Flight	http://archive.org/Details/For_The_Record_305_Borrmann

Operation Highjump   https://en.wikipedia.org/wiki/Operation_Highjump

Operation Northwoods   https://en.wikipedia.org/wiki/Operation_Northwoods

Operation Mockingbird   http://en.wikipedia.org/wiki/Operation_Mockingbird

Operation Paperclip   http://www.operationpaperclip.info/

Operation Starlight   https://en.wikipedia.org/wiki/Operation_Starlite

Opium Wars   https://en.wikipedia.org/wiki/Opium_Wars

OP-20-G   http://en.wikipedia.org/wiki/OP-20-G

Pentagon Papers   http://www.archives.gov/research/pentagon-papers/

Percy Foreman   http://en.wikipedia.org/wiki/Percy_Foreman

Phoenix Program   https://en.wikipedia.org/wiki/Phoenix_Program

Piezoelectricity   https://en.wikipedia.org/wiki/Piezoelectricity

Presidential Directive   https://en.wikipedia.org/wiki/National_Security_Council_Intelligence_ Directive

Psychic Driving   http://en.wikipedia.org/wiki/Psychic_driving

Purple, Japanese Cipher Machine   http://en.wikipedia.org/wiki/Purple_(cipher_machine)

Quantum Vacuum   https://en.wikipedia.org/wiki/Vacuum_state

Ratlines   https://en.wikipedia.org/wiki/Ratlines_(World_War_II)

Rules of Engagement   http://www.historynet.com/air-force-colonel-jacksel-jack-broughton-air-force-general-john-d-jack-lavelle-testing-the-rules-of-engagement-during-the-vietnam-war.htm

Santa Anna	https://en.wikipedia.org/wiki/Antonio_L%C3%B3pez_Santa_Anna
Sinners Prayer	http://www.salvationprayer.info/prayer.html
Scots-Irish	http://www.archives.com/experts/garstka-katharine/the-scots-irish-in-the-southern-united-states-an-overview.html
Secret War in Laos	https://en.wikipedia.org/wiki/Laotian_Civil_War
Sheep Dipped	http://www.urbandictionary.com/define.php?term=sheep%20dipped
Shelby Mustang	https://en.wikipedia.org/wiki/Shelby_Mustang
Signal Hill, Battle of	http://en.wikipedia.org/wiki/Battle_of_Signal_Hill_Vietnam
SIS/MI6	https://en.wikipedia.org/wiki/Secret_Intelligence_Service
Sin Sai, Hmong Legend	http://hmongstudies.org/Tapp2008.pdf
Slave Trade Act, 1794	https://en.wikipedia.org/wiki/Slave_Trade_Act_of_1794
Sovereign Immunity	http://en.wikipedia.org/wiki/Sovereign_immunity_in_the_United_States
Suitland, Maryland Intelligence Vaults	http://bostonreview.net/archives/BR10.3/loftus.html
Telstar	https://en.wikipedia.org/wiki/Telstar
Telex	https://en.wikipedia.org/wiki/Telex
Tet Offensive	http://en.wikipedia.org/wiki/Tet_Offensive
Thule Society	http://en.wikipedia.org/wiki/Thule_Society
Townsend, William C.	http://en.wikipedia.org/wiki/William_Cameron_Townsend
Trauma Based Mind Control	http://vigilantcitizen.com/hidden-knowledge/origins-and-techniques-of-monarch-mind-control/

Triad
http://en.wikipedia.org/wiki/Triad_ (underground_society)

UCMJ
http://en.wikipedia.org/wiki/Uniform_ Code_of_Military_Justice

Vatican Passport
http://www.theguardian.com/world/ 2011/may/25/nazis-escaped-on-red-cross-documents

Venn Diagram
https://en.wikipedia.org/wiki/Venn_ diagram

Walther P38
https://en.wikipedia.org/wiki/ Walther_P38

Waffen SS
https://en.wikipedia.org/wiki/Waffen-SS

White Light Laser
http://en.wikipedia.org/wiki/ Supercontinuum

White Slavery
http://www.electricscotland.com/history/other/white_slavery.htm

http://www.globalresearch.ca/the-irish-slave-trade-the-forgotten-white-slaves/31076

Zero Point Energy
https://en.wikipedia.org/wiki/Zero-point_energy

36th Infantry Division
https://en.wikipedia.org/wiki/36th_ Infantry_Division_(United_States)

500 kHz
http://en.wikipedia.org/wiki/500_kHz

END

About the Author

Steve A. Madison is an architect and an expert in the use of the Problem Seeking and Pattern Language methodologies for defining and solving complex problems.

In this ambitious work, Madison has used the professional disciplines of an architect to construct a modern mythology that examines the paradox of occulted federal America. The narrative posits a bureaucracy gone rogue and imagines: who writes its laws, plans its wars, decides how they'll be fought, who will win, where the profits go, and—most importantly—who owns the mechanisms used to subvert the constitution and subdue the people of the United States of America.

Madison lives, works, and plays in Texas with his wife, extended family, and a black Labrador named Ridley Scott.

Made in the USA
Coppell, TX
27 August 2020